Poison

EMILIA ROSE

Trigger Warnings

This book includes mention of sexual assault, sexual exploitation, slapping, name calling, degradation, death, and other potentially triggering topics. If you don't feel comfortable with the topics listed above, place the book down now.

To everyone who wishes they could bang three hot assholes on top of the principal's desk.

Chapter One

IMANI

"Are you coming over tonight?" my best friend, Allie, asked me over the phone.

We were supposed to study for our Biology test in a couple days because Mr. Barnes gave the worst exams on the entire planet. But I didn't want to head over to her house yet. I was tired, horny, and damn addicted to ... doing something that I shouldn't. If Als found out—hell, if *anyone* found out—I would be the laughing-stock of the senior class. And that was the *last* thing I wanted to be.

Staring out my bedroom window, I watched Mom drive off to her late shift at the hospital and locked my bedroom door in case Dad came home early. He always stayed at his company way past six p.m., so I didn't think I had to worry. I just ... nobody could find out *anything* about what I did.

"Hellllo?"

"I'll be there in two hours," I said, opening my laptop.

"Two hours?" Als asked. "What are you doing?"

"Nothing!" I said, heart racing in excitement. "Love you!"

And with that, I ended the call, slammed my phone down on the table, and signed into the Discord app on my computer under the name *Rosy*—definitely not my real name because I didn't want anyone to know the real me. If anyone at school found out that I was so desperate for a guy's attention that I had ... maybe cammed once or twice and had been chatting with some guys online for months, I would be done for.

It was just so fucking fun to watch a guy get all hot and bothered because of me.

I didn't get that kind of attention at school. Ever.

Scrolling through my *Friends* list, I clenched when I saw a green circle pop up next to Chris's name. I didn't think people called him Chris in real life, but that was who he was to me, just like I was Rosy to him.

Chris: You wanna chat?

After sucking in a sharp breath, I pulled my vibrator out of my desk drawer and adjusted my crop top, so I showed a little bit of cleavage. My chest was so small, but something was better than nothing. And Chris liked it, so I didn't mind.

Me: I can't talk all night, but YES <3

When an incoming call from Chris popped up onto the screen, I tilted the camera down just enough to where he would only be able to see everything south of my nose and clicked Accept, adrenaline coursing through my veins at the thought of watching him jerk off to me for the fourth night in a row this week.

Stretched out on his bed, Chris appeared on the screen with his taut abdomen flexed hard and tattoos crawling up the side of his rib cage. His face was hidden outside of the camera angle, just as mine was, and his cock was rock fucking hard.

I pressed my thighs together at the sight of him, warmth pooling between my legs. Chris leaned forward slightly, taking his dick in his hand and slowly stroking it already.

"Rosy, you look so sexy tonight," he purred, his husky voice drifting into my ears.

"I've been thinking about seeing you all day," I said, slipping a hand between my legs to rub my clit through my panties.

"You have your toy today?"

Biting down on my lower lip, I grabbed the toy from the desk and showed it to him, drawing my fingers up and down the vibrating shaft. Chris grunted softly, spit on his hand, and moved his camera closer to his thick and veiny cock.

"Suck on it. Get it wet, so it slides right into your tight little hole, Rosy."

After placing the tip on my lips, I pushed it into my mouth and sucked my cheeks in, bobbing my head back and forth and back and forth on the dildo and swirling my tongue around the shaft, wanting to make it wet with my spit so I didn't have to use lube later.

Chris stroked his cock faster, veins protruding from his bicep. "Just like that ..."

"I wish I were sucking your cock," I said, licking up the shaft and letting out a soft moan. "I haven't stopped imagining what it'd be like if you shoved yourself down my throat and pounded into my face."

It was big talk for someone who had never once given a man a blowjob in her entire life.

"Fuuuuck," Chris groaned.

Pushing the vibrator back into my mouth, I turned to the side and shoved it as far down my throat as it would go. And when the tip of it created a bulge in my throat, I wrapped my hand around my neck and face-fucked myself with it, my panties already soaked through. Spit rolled down my chin and dripped between my cleavage.

"You're so fucking sexy," Chris said, his free hand sprawled across his stomach, fingers curling against the hard muscle. "Pull down your panties, spread your legs, and move the camera down. I wanna see you play with yourself, baby."

Needing a release, I moved the camera down a couple inches, stood to strip off my already-ruined panties, and spread my legs far enough for him to be able to see everything. I placed the pink dildo right against my entrance and pushed it inside of me, turning it on the highest intensity.

"Slow it down, Rosy. You don't get to come yet," he said, plump lips curling into a smirk.

I wished that I could see his whole face, watch his eyes wander down my body. But this was all we were and all we could ever be—internet fuck buddies, if I could even call us *that*.

After turning the vibrator back down, I moved the camera closer to my pussy to show him how my walls tugged on the vibrator as I pulled it out, clenching hard around it, always aching to be filled up with something huge, like Chris's cock.

"I wanna bury myself inside you," Chris said, stroking harder and faster. "You look so tight. You think your pussy could handle my cock?"

Gently thrusting the vibrator in and out of me, I curled my toes. "I don't know," I said breathlessly. "You're so ... so big." Bigger than some of the guys I'd watched in porn. "You'd stretch me out. I don't know if I'd be able to take it."

"It would tear your tight little hole up, stretch that pussy apart," he groaned and stroked faster. "Fucking beg me to fuck you, Rosy. Beg me to fucking destroy it. Beg to fucking turn your vibrator up higher. And beg to come."

With my free hand, I rubbed my clit, aching to turn the vibrator up another setting. "Please, Chris. Please, let me do it. I want you inside of me so fucking bad," I pleaded, the pressure building in my core. "I need it now, please."

"Move your camera back, so I can see those lips, and then you can turn it up."

Once I pushed the camera back—careful not to show my entire face—I turned the vibrator up to a higher intensity and whimpered, the vibrating rabbit dildo sending waves of pleasure through my core. I gently tugged on my nipple through my crop top, another surge of ecstasy rushing through me.

"More," I whimpered. "More, please."

"Fuck, baby ... let me see those tits."

After yanking off my top so I sat completely naked inside my room —thank God for door locks—I spread my trembling legs wider and pulled on my nipple again. "Please, Chris. One more setting higher, and I'll ... I'll come for you."

Stroking his cock even faster, he flexed his tattooed abdomen hard. "Do it. I'm gonna fucking come with you."

I clicked the vibrator on a higher setting and screamed out his name as I came all over the vibrator, an unruly orgasm ripping through my body. Chris groaned again, coming all over his stomach, dick twitching as more cum pumped out.

Pulling my legs together, I turned the vibrator off and gently pulled it out of me, the vibrations too intense to continue—at least for now. I placed it on my desk, pulled my shirt back on, and took a deep breath.

"Oh my God ..." I whispered to myself, still feeling the pleasure rush through me.

Chris excused himself to get cleaned off as my phone buzzed beside me, Allie's name popping up on the screen. I leaned over slightly to read it.

Als: If you come over now, I'll buy you a pizza with pineapple, using my brother's card. ;) Plz. I'm lonely at home, and I hate Jace.

After smiling to myself, I turned my phone upside down and glanced up at the screen to see Chris back and sitting at what seemed to be a table, his eyes still out of the screen.

"You're cute when you smile," he said, a smirk on his lips. "Who are you talking to? A boyfriend?"

"If I had a boyfriend, I wouldn't be video-chatting with you," I said, brushing my fingers over my tight black curls. "And besides, I don't date. At least, not in this town."

"Oh, come on. With eyes like that—"

I sat up taller. "What do you mean, eyes like that? You haven't—"

He chuckled. "When you were reading that text, you must not have been paying attention to your camera. It's turned up, facing you. And, fuck, I didn't think I've been talking to you all these months, Imani."

The blood drained from my cheeks, my heart leaping in my chest. "What?" I asked, mouth dry. I quickly turned the camera off, a thousand different thoughts racing through my mind. *Oh my fucking God.* I was screwed—fucking screwed.

Everyone in this shitty town was going to know that I fucking cammed and had met ... whoever the fuck this was. Mom would ground me. Dad would scream. My life would be ruined—absolutely ruined.

"Who are you?" I asked through the microphone, nerves creeping up. "How do you know me?"

Chris leaned closer, still not showing his face. "I've seen you around Redwood Academy. Always thought you were a cutie," he said. "You were right, though. You don't date ... but I have a couple friends who might be interested. I'll see you tomorrow at school. Don't be late."

And with that, Chris ended the call.

Chapter Two

IMANI

After parking my car in the school lot the next morning, I stared at my phone and pushed out a breath, blowing away the thick curls in my face. My gaze lingered on the messages from Chris last night, my stomach tightening. When a little green bubble popped up next to his profile picture, I sucked in a breath.

Whoever Chris was ... he knew me, and he went to Redwood fucking Academy.

Tapping on his contact, I waited one, two, three minutes for him to type something to me, but nothing came through. He was probably on his phone, smirking down at his messages and at how worked up he had made me.

To stop my fingers from shaking, I held them still. I couldn't do this. I couldn't go to school today. *What if Chris has told everyone already? What if I am now the laughingstock of the entire school?* I didn't want to be *that* girl—even though that was exactly who I was.

So, I scrolled to Mom's contact and typed a message to her.

Me: Mom, I don't feel good.

She texted me back less than a minute later.

Mom: You didn't have a fever this morning, Imani. You're going in.

Cursing under my breath, I found Dad's messages and decided to text him instead.

Me: Dad, I don't feel good.

Dad: What your mother says goes. Don't get me in trouble.

After throwing a mini fit in the car, I blew out a breath, told myself that it wouldn't be *that* bad, and that if I didn't go in, Chris would tell *everyone* about our camming sessions. I opened the car door. During my entire walk from the parking lot to the school, I hugged my books to my chest and darted my gaze around like a crazy person.

While I walked down the halls, everyone stared at me—from Carter the quarterback, to Roger the nerd king of Redwood. Or ... maybe I was overreacting. It wasn't like they were staring intensely at me, just a couple side-glances.

I blew out a breath. That was what it was. Nothing more.

All I had to do was make it through the day and *not* draw attention to myself. Keep my head low. Stay out of drama. Talk to Allie like nothing was wrong. Like I wasn't being blackmailed by someone at Redwood.

"Morning, Imani," Mr. Freeman said, walking past me.

Halting in my tracks, I looked over my shoulder. My eyes widened, breath catching in the back of my throat. *What if it is one of the teachers?* Oh my Lord, Mom would kill me with a capital *K*. Chop me up into small pieces. Scream and lock my diced body in my bedroom for the rest of my life.

Pushing the thought from my mind, I hurried down the hall and decided not to go the short way through the main hallways, like I usually did to get to my locker. I needed to get through the day without having a heart attack at eighteen years old. It'd be nice to make it to nineteen. But the back hallways were where the bad boys of Redwood ruled—and by bad boys, I meant, the gang of boys named Poison, who scared the shit out of me.

After deciding that taking the long way was worth it, I slid into an empty back hallway and fast-walked down the corridor. I made it down the first two hallways quickly and without problem, but then I turned a corner—the last stretch of corridor until I hit my locker hallway—and stopped dead in my tracks.

Landon Caddell, the brawn behind Poison, slammed Akio against the lockers, Landon's fist square against his jaw. "Where's the fucking shit?" Landon asked through gritted teeth. "We gave you a fucking job."

João Rocha and Kai Koh watched blood seep out of Akio's nose. I stood completely still and held my breath, knowing that they hadn't seen me yet. Catching Poison dealing or doing anything was sure to earn anyone an ass-kicking. And I vowed to stay out of drama today.

Akio actually punched Landon back in the nose, his fist barely landing. Landon smashed Akio back into the lockers, the red metal denting. I winced and held back a shout, knowing that Akio would *die* in Landon's hands. Like all of Poison, Landon was a psychopath—and I meant that. He was pure fucking crazy.

Instead of walking away, like I should've, I found myself running toward the boys and pushing Landon away from Akio. "Stop it!" I shouted, my heart pounding as I blocked Landon from beating Akio to a pulp. I couldn't let someone like Poison kill a kid right in front of me without at least trying to stop it.

"You lucked the fuck out today," Landon said to Akio, spitting some blood on the ground. He nodded down the hallway. "Get the fuck out of here and don't come back without the damn shit."

Akio scrambled past me and down the hallway, disappearing around the corner. I swallowed hard and stared up at Landon with wide eyes, not sure if he was about to beat *me* up for interrupting their business.

Instead, João looked at Landon and let out a ... laugh—an empty one, of course.

Sucking in a breath, I watched their interaction and hiked my thumb back. "I'm going to ... go ..." I whispered, taking steady steps back and looking at Landon to make sure he wouldn't jump me if I turned around.

His gaze slowly traveled down my body and back up it, and he licked some blood off the corner of his lip, then smirked. Fucking smirked, like the psycho he was. My eyes widened slightly, and I shuffled back, nearly tripping over my own feet and stumbling into the lockers.

After cursing under my breath, I turned around and rushed down the hallway, needing to get out of there as soon as humanly possible because I did not want to be food for that wild, hungry, savage psycho of a man.

Chapter Three

IMANI

"He made me walk home in the pouring rain yesterday!" Allie said, shaking her head and angrily writing—well, more like ripping through the pages with her pen—in her notebook. She plastered it against the locker to write something. "I swear to God, I'm going to get him fucking back. He's the rudest, cruelest, annoyingest person in the world!"

I glanced over my shoulder to check for anyone. "You know, *annoyingest* isn't a word."

"Thanks for the vocab lesson, Imani," Allie said, playfully shoving my shoulder. "But you know what I mean. A day can't go by without him looking for a way to annoy me. And then you know what else?" She leaned in closer and lowered her voice. "He had the damn audacity to say, 'I thought you liked being wet.' Like, who does that?"

After letting out a sigh, I turned to her and grabbed her hands. "Your ex-boyfriend turned stepbrother, who you really shouldn't be obsessing over anymore, does that. Don't worry about him. It's not like you actually have feelings for him still, right?"

Allie stayed quiet.

"Right?"

"Yeah, yeah. You're right." She pulled a textbook out of her locker, refusing to maintain eye contact, and shuffled her feet. "Anyway, why're you so ... alert today? You haven't stopped looking over your shoulder."

"Um ..." I laughed nervously. "No reason."

She arched a brow and crossed her arms. "No reason, huh?"

"Nope! None."

I'm definitely not being blackmailed by a man who I masturbate with online.

Giving her my best, most innocent smile, I prayed that she would drop it because that would be a damn awkward conversation with her. We were best friends, and she told me everything, but ... she didn't know too much about *this* horny, desperate side of me. Some things were private, you know?

When my phone buzzed in my hand, I jumped up and placed a hand against my heart. Jesus Christ, if my death wasn't going to be from embarrassment, then I was surely going to have a damn heart attack before the day ended.

Chris: You're angsty today, Imani.

My face paled, heart pounding in my chest. I slammed my locker closed and held my books tighter to my chest, looking down both sides of the hallway for anyone looking a little suspicious because ...

He had seen me. He'd fucking seen me already. It hadn't even been twenty minutes since I'd stepped into Redwood.

I gulped and clicked off my phone, deciding to ignore him until I wasn't with Allie. I loved Allie with all my heart, but I didn't want her to find out. She didn't know how freaky I was, and I wanted to so badly keep it that way. She wouldn't tell anyone, but someone in Redwood might overhear us.

Before I slipped the phone into my pocket, it buzzed again.

Chris: You have some audacity not to text me back when I hold the key to ruining your perfect good-girl reputation.

My heart pounded, and I scrambled to text him back, my books falling onto the ground. I cursed yet again that this day was going far from how I'd hoped it would and crouched to pick up the books. Akio grabbed one for me and handed it over, a tissue stuffed up his nose to hold back the blood Landon had caused.

"What happened to you?" Allie asked with wide eyes, staring at his already-swelling eye.

Akio shrugged. "You know how it is."

"But you're like ... us? Who would want to mess with a nerd?"

I looked over my shoulder and gnawed on my cheek. "It's Poison," I whispered, hoping that they wouldn't hear me say their name. It wasn't against their Redwood rules to speak it, but ... that was how drama started. When I realized that the coast was clear, I turned back to him and shook my head. "What'd you do to them, Akio?"

"I didn't do anything," Akio said.

But Poison didn't mess with people over nothing. They had too much other business to deal with, other people to beat up and sell drugs to, than to deal with a nerd. Akio had to know *something* about the Poison boys to get them *that* angry.

My mind wandered to them, and my breath caught in my throat at the memory of the way each of those boys had looked at me earlier, like hungry freaking wolves ... and I hoped to God that they'd forget about me for the rest of eternity. I didn't want to be on their radar.

I couldn't.

Not now.

"Nothing happened. Don't worry." Akio shrugged again, lingering for longer than he should've. Then, he smiled, turned around toward History class, and called over his shoulder, "Thanks again, Imani. You saved me."

Allie raised a brow at me, gaze quickly flickering to Jace Harbor— her stepbrother—as he walked past us. She gritted her teeth, lip curling up in an ugly snarl, and slammed her locker door closed. "I'll see you in Mr. Barnes's class. I have to go deal with something."

Once she scurried after Jace—looking as if she was going to give him a couple pieces of her mind—I glanced back down at my phone and gripped it tightly in my hand, letting it vibrate.

Chris: Parking lot. 3 p.m.

Me: I'll be there.

Chapter Four

IMANI

During second period, I shifted in Mr. Barnes's Biology class, needing to pee so freaking badly, as he went on and on and on about the exam tomorrow. I pushed my reading glasses further up my nose, wrote furiously in my notebook, and squeezed my knees together.

Allie leaned closer to me. "Are you okay?"

"I have to pee," I whispered back, hoping Barnes wouldn't hear me. He loathed when people interrupted his lecture.

"Go," she urged me. "I'll give you my notes tonight."

Gnawing on the inside of my cheek, I placed my pen down, raised my hand, and asked Barnes to use the restroom.

He stopped his lecture, tilted his head down to look at me through his thick glasses, and sighed. "Go."

After giving him my best smile, I scurried out of the room and basically ran to the restroom, doing my business and slumping my shoulders forward. At least here, I didn't have to worry about seeing Chris in the hallways or in class. It was Imani time.

From under the stall, I watched the restroom door swing open, and two sets of legs hurried in, sloppy and wet sounds coming from the couple. They stumbled into the stall next to me, and I scrunched my nose.

Well, there goes that.

I flushed my toilet and quickly washed my hands, wanting to get out of there as soon as humanly possible. That was the first and last time I'd ever ask to use the restroom during class because I didn't want to listen to the starts of another *fucking during school* session.

Making it out of the restroom, I walked down the hall toward Barnes's classroom. When I passed that dreaded hallway that the bad boys of Redwood Academy ruled, someone shoved me against the lockers, slapped a hand over my mouth, and drew their nose up the side of my neck.

"Don't fucking say a word," he said into my ear, the voice from none other than my video-chatting hookup of a man, Chris.

I widened my eyes and nodded, my entire body tense and my breath catching in the back of my throat. Chris pressed himself into me from behind, face buried into the crook of my neck, and a strand of his dirty-blond hair was in my corner vision. He smelled like pine, his thick scent drifting through my nose.

"If I let go, you're not going to turn around."

When I nodded, he pulled his hand away from my mouth and placed it on the locker beside me. I sucked in a deep breath and glanced over at his bruised knuckles, aching to turn around to see who this man was. Walking around school today had been pure torture.

But I was terrified of who I'd find.

"What are you going to do?" I whispered, fear and ... excitement rushing through me.

I had never been this close to a guy before. Ever.

"I'm going to get used to your body before I introduce you to my friends."

"Your friends?" I whispered, chewing on my bottom lip. "You're really going to ..."

He growled against me, his hand wrapping around the front of my throat. "I told you not to say a fucking word." He trailed his other hand down the front of my body, between my breasts, and over my thin bralette, making my nipples hard. "Exactly how I imagined you'd feel."

I bit back a whimper, brows furrowing. "Chris ..."

With his free hand, he captured my nipple between his fingers and tugged on it until I couldn't hold back the whimper any longer. I moaned—fucking moaned—right in the middle of the empty hallway.

"You're a virgin, aren't you?" He said it like he could tell.

Instead of answering him, I pressed my lips together and found myself pushing back against him and loving the way he felt against my ass. In all of the videos, he had been so big, and somehow, he felt even bigger now. Heat gathered in my core.

He gently sucked on the skin below my ear and moved his hand lower and lower and lower until he cupped my pussy through my leggings. I whimpered again, and Chris covered my mouth with his large, callous hand.

"Scream as loud as you'd like. I should've known that a horny, dirty-mouthed virgin like you wouldn't be able to hold her moans back."

And then he shoved a hand into the front of my pants and drew a finger down my folds. I squeezed my eyes shut, knowing that I needed to get back to class, but I loved this too much to tell Chris that. He spread my folds with his fingers and brushed them against my clit. I yelped and tensed, breath catching.

Chris chuckled lowly. "Oh, baby ... I've barely touched you. What will happen when you have three sets of hands all over your body?"

I moaned into his hand and clenched, heat warming my core. Six hands, gliding across my body, touching every part of me, making me feel good. I couldn't imagine I'd last more than a couple moments like that.

Chris rubbed my clit faster and ground his bulge against my ass, his stubble brushing against my soft spot. I moaned again, unable to hold myself back, and pushed against him, too, needing more. I shuffled my shoes apart against the tiled floor, giving him better access.

"Please," I mumbled against his hand, my fingers turning white against the red lockers.

"You want more?"

I nodded.

He trailed his fingers down my pussy until they reached my entrance. Shoving two inside of me, he grunted against my neck. "Fuck. I've never felt anyone this tight before. My cock is going to feel so fucking good inside you."

I whimpered and clenched harder on him, pressure rising in my core. As he pumped his fingers into me, he hit my clit with the heel of his palm, driving me higher. Tightening around him even more, I curled my toes, and Chris pulled his hand away from my mouth. Before I could stop myself, I let out an ear-piercing scream.

Wave after wave of pleasure rushed through my body, my legs trembling. I bit my lip and slapped a hand over my mouth, moaning harder into it.

When he pulled his hand out of my pants, he wrapped his other hand around my throat, leaned in closer to me, and lifted his wet fingers to my mouth. "Lick yourself off my fingers, Imani."

I swallowed hard, gently taking the tips of his fingers between my lips, tasting the saltiness on my tongue. Before I could suck them in all the way, he pulled his fingers back and stuck them into his mouth, groaning into my ear. I clenched at the sound of him, still staring directly at the locker, like he'd told me to.

Once he finally pulled away, he grabbed the back of my neck, turned me toward Barnes's classroom, and stood behind me. "Walk down the hall, back to your class, and don't look back at me. Not once."

With a racing heart, I nodded and scurried away, down the hall, and didn't look back, no matter how much I wanted to.

Chapter Five

IMANI

"Come on," Allie said, grabbing my hand and squeezing tightly. "Please, please, please, don't leave me with Jace. Can you bring me home? My car broke down yesterday, and Jace didn't pick me up and—"

I glanced down at my phone to check the time, looked back out at the rain pouring outside the door, and frowned. Believe me, if I could drive Allie home tonight and hang with her, I definitely would, but Chris was on my every last nerve today, and I didn't want him telling *anyone*, not even her.

"I can't today, Als. I have … stuff to do with my parents."

Lie. I hated lying to her.

"Maybe if we get done quickly, I can come over, and we can study for Mr. Barnes's test tomorrow. You know it's going to be so freaking hard." The time on my phone read *2:59 p.m.*, and I stepped toward the door. "But don't wait up for me. I don't know how long it's going to take."

After giving her my best smile, I pushed the door open and stepped out into the pouring rain, balling my hands into tight fists and heading straight for the parking lot. This rain was going to make my hair so damn frizzy, and the hour I'd spent styling it this morning would be for nothing.

When I reached the lot, there were only a few cars that I recognized as the football players' who stayed after to practice on the field. I slowed down and glanced around, unsure about where I was meeting Chris or even if he meant this parking lot. All these cars were empty.

I pulled out my phone and opened his messages, rereading his last one over and over until someone put a bag—a fucking bag—over my head.

"Don't say a fucking word," the man said into my ear, a different voice than from earlier.

My entire body tensed, fear rushing through my veins. *What the fuck have I gotten into?*

Before I knew it, my hands were bound behind my back with rope, the knots tight and restricting, almost as if done professionally. I squirmed back and forth, wondering how nobody else was seeing this, and slammed my shoulder into whoever was handling me because it wasn't Chris.

"Let me go. I'm meeting with someone."

"You're meeting with us." He pushed me forward. When I almost stumbled over my feet on the pavement, he wrapped his hand around my upper arm to hold me steady and continued forward.

The world around me was dark, and while I could usually tell where I was, I had no freaking idea where he was bringing me.

"Can you let up?" I asked. "You're hurting me."

After grunting ever so softly, he released my arm, opened what sounded like a car door, and pushed me in. A moment later, the door closed, and I sucked in a breath. I felt like I was about to pee my damn pants. This was *not* what I'd thought would happen when I met with Chris.

I'd thought maybe he'd want something like a *slam, bam* kind of afternoon.

Not a *kidnap Imani* type.

"What do you want?" I asked. My heart pounded, sweat lining my lower back.

The car went silent again, and I swallowed hard, unable to think straight. Someone grabbed the top of the bag on my head and yanked it off. When they tore it off me completely, I kept my eyes closed, in pure fear of who I'd see staring back at me because it definitely wasn't *anyone* good. One moment passed, then two, and then I reluctantly opened my eyes. Staring back at me wasn't one, wasn't two, but it was all three of the most dangerous boys at Redwood.

Poison.

"I'm sorry for what I did earlier with Akio," I said, refusing to make eye contact with them.

If this was a damn punishment for getting in their business, I'd take whatever consequences they had because Chris was waiting for me somewhere out in the parking lot, and I didn't want—

"This isn't about Akio. This is about *Rosy*," Landon said.

I shifted my focus from Kai to João to Landon and sucked in a deep breath. Something about the way Landon looked at me, the way his eyes raked over my body like he had seen it a million times, and the way those full lips curled into that infamous crooked smile, I just knew.

"Oh my God, it's you." I shook my head and placed a hand over my mouth in disbelief.

Chris was Landon, Redwood's bad boy, and he now knew my darkest secrets.

They all stared at me with no emotion—no fucking emotion—for the longest time. And then they laughed.

My eyes widened, cheeks flushing. "What is wrong with you guys? Do you think that tying me up and putting a bag over my head is funny?! Because it's not! I could've died from suffocation, and you would have had a dead fucking body on your hands."

João curled his lips into a smirk. "Nothing we haven't dealt with before."

Somehow, my eyes widened even more. I didn't know why I was even fighting with them or why I was surprised. Poison was baaaad freaking news, and I couldn't be associated with them at all. But they now knew my secret, and I hated them for it.

"Imani," Landon teased, leaning forward from the passenger seat and tugging on one of my frizzy curls.

"Untie me," I said through gritted teeth, shoving my shoulder into him to push him away.

"A feisty one," João said.

When I didn't reply, he nodded to Kai, who leaned closer to untie the ropes around my wrists.

As soon as my hands were free, I rubbed my palms and gritted my teeth. "What do you want? I'll give you anything to keep this a secret. Please."

Landon chuckled. "Oh, we don't want your parents' dirty money, Imani. We want you."

Chapter Six

LANDON

An hour after our little chat with Imani, the guys and I went back to my place. While they walked right to the basement, I searched upstairs in the kitchen for a pair of scissors that João had asked for to cut the plants of cannabis downstairs, though I couldn't focus.

Mom lugged her purse into the house, heavy, dark bags under her eyes and a smile that didn't even make it past her lips. "You eat yet?" she asked, setting the bag down on the four-by-four kitchen table, on top of the mess of beer cans that Dad must've left earlier.

"Yeah."

I grabbed a pair of scissors from the counter and turned around to ask her about work today, but she was already out of the room and up the stairs, gone, like she always was. I glanced at the basement door. I practically fucking lived down there, which was fine with me, but if I didn't show my face up here once in a while, things got bad.

"You expect me to fucking believe that you were working?" Dad shouted at Mom upstairs, his hoarse voice booming through the walls. A door slammed open. "Don't ignore me, you bitch. You're five minutes late. Where were you?"

I grabbed my shit from the kitchen and lingered by the basement door, waiting. When all Mom did was yell back, I blew a breath through my nose and walked down the stairs, shutting the door behind me softly so Dad wouldn't barrel down the stairs, looking to pick a fight with me.

Walking down the creaky steps, I kicked my shoes off on the basement's cement floor. "What're you gonna do with these?" I asked, handing João the scissors.

He stood over the cannabis plants in the back room of the basement and clipped a couple that weren't ready yet.

"They're not even done."

"Jace Harbor texted me," João said, retrieving a plastic baggie.

"Harbor?" Kai asked, glancing up from his computer for a moment. "Allie's stepbrother?"

"What's he want?" I asked.

After following João out of the back room and locking the door, I walked to the stained brown couch and collapsed onto it, thinking back to all the nights I had lain on this couch and jerked myself off to Imani.

Imani fucking Abara.

The sexiest little nerd that Redwood would ever have the pleasure of knowing.

"Business."

"Jace isn't stupid. He's gonna know shit weed when he sees it," I said.

"Jace doesn't smoke weed," João said.

"Good," Kai chimed in.

João and I both side-eyed him. When he looked up and shrugged, I glanced back at João.

"What do you mean, he doesn't smoke it? Hasn't he been buying from us for months now? Where is it going?"

"I don't ask questions," João said, lighting up a cigarette and kicking a boot up onto the coffee table, knocking over an empty beer can in the process. "But he has a job for us to do. This could be what we need to finally take down these rich Redwood motherfuckers."

That garnered enough of Kai's attention, and he looked over. "Fucking finally. You think Jace has something to take all of Redwood down? I've been waiting for years now. The rich have shit on us one too many times."

"His daddy is one of the richest men in Redwood," João said. "All those rich bastards have dirt on them, but whatever Jace wants us to do sounds serious. It's not something we are going to want to miss out on. By the time we're through, this town will be burned to the mother-fucking ground."

My lips curled into a smirk. It was about time. All the rich did was treat us like garbage.

"The girl ... Imani, Rosy, whatever the fuck her name is, is the key."

"It's Imani," I said through gritted teeth.

João looked over his shoulder and gave me a half-smirk. "I'm just fucking with you. I've had my eye on her for a while."

"You have?" I asked tightly.

"Her family is one that all of Redwood adores. Mom is a neurosurgeon, Dad the CEO of an engineering company, and Imani's one of the top students in our graduating class. What better way of destroying Redwood than figuring out what their secret is and destroying them from the inside out? Redwood is only as good as its most adored family."

I looked over at Kai. "You don't have anything to say about this?"

Kai shrugged. "It'll work if they're actually doing something wrong."

"If they're not?"

João smirked. "If they're not, then we get to enjoy Imani. A win-win for all of us."

Lying back on the couch, I blew out a deep breath, my mind going back to the way Imani had felt in my hands earlier. Her pussy had been so fucking tight when I slipped my fingers inside of it. I knew that she had done nothing but talk herself up on every video chat we had, about how she'd take my cock down that throat of hers.

She was a virgin who had some dark secrets and fantasies. Over the course of the last year, she had told me every fucking one of them ... and more about herself than I had found out from the past twelve years we'd been in school together.

If she could hide something like this from the world, then her parents must've been hiding something, too.

"Come on," João said, tossing me the lighter. "She doesn't have you whipped already, does she? Cute little Rosy make you want to be a good guy now? I don't fucking believe it for a second, Landon."

But could I do something like this to her?

The short answer: yes, I could.

The long one: well ... that was a different story.

Chapter Seven

IMANI

Music thumped through Allie's house from downstairs, the thick stench of weed drifting under Allie's door. For some ungodly reason, Jace, her stepbrother who she definitely still had a thing for even though she swore she didn't, decided to throw a rager the Thursday night before our biggest Biology test.

I lay on my stomach and tapped through the PowerPoint on my Mac, chewing on my bottom lip, unable to concentrate. I hadn't been able to think straight all night, and it wasn't because of the party. Poison was on my mind and wouldn't fucking leave me alone.

Before they had kicked me out of João's car, they had made their point clear—they didn't want *any* of my parents' money. No matter how much money I offered, even up to five hundred thousand dollars, no matter how much I promised—I could give them a better place to stay in Redwood, a vacation that they so desperately needed to stop being pricks.

They would accept nothing but me.

"Jesus Christ, I'm going to kill him," Allie said under her breath about Jace, tugging on a strand of her frizzy brown hair.

"Why don't we stop for tonight? We've been at this for six hours now," I offered because I definitely wasn't retaining *any* of this information tonight. My fate with the outcome of this test had been sealed the moment Landon realized that Rosy wasn't my real name.

I'd fail the test tomorrow and get scolded by my parents.

But I'd rather be reprimanded than have my secrets revealed to all of Redwood.

When Allie frowned and pushed up the thick glasses on her nose, I closed my laptop and smiled at her.

"Or, if you want, you can come to my place to study."

"No, it's fine." She tossed her notebook on her desk. "I'll just fail."

I rolled my eyes. "Girl, stop. We all know that you're going to get over a hundred, especially with all the extra credit that Barnes gives." I pushed my laptop into my backpack. "And if you don't, you can always ask Barnes for more *extra credit*. You're hot enough to seduce him."

"Ew, gross." She wrinkled her nose. "He's, like, seventy."

"All I'm saying is that you don't even have to *work* for that A-plus, just shake a little ass," I said, moving my next-to-nothing ass for emphasis.

Lucky for Allie, she had a little more to shake for Barnes, if she really wanted to. Her ass was fat with a capital *F*, and I was definitely saying that out of jealousy.

But I loved her, anyway. I always would.

After I swung my backpack over my shoulder, we walked down the hallway and into the living room, dim lights illuminating a haze of smoke that sat heavily in the air. I glanced around the room like a crazy woman, looking for Poison. They always seemed to show up at parties like this, where there was enough weed to go around for years and where they could take advantage of the rich kids, maybe even steal some of their parents' shit.

"I can't wait to get out of this shitty town," Allie said.

"You can come back to my place for the night," I offered again, tugging on the straps of my backpack.

I wanted to get out of here as soon as humanly possible, but I knew Allie coming over probably wasn't the best idea if Landon tried to video-call me tonight. Who the fuck knew what was going through his mind now?

When we finally made it to the front door, one of the guys on the football team looked Allie up and down and made her cheeks flush a rosy red. She stared at Jamal for a moment longer than she should've, and I arched a brow.

"Well, I guess that's a no ... just be careful with Jamal. You know how guys like him act. He's like your stepbrother, and he will break your heart too, if you let him."

"Jace didn't break my heart," Allie said through clenched teeth. She opened the front door, and I sucked in a breath, my eyes widening. Landon and Kai walked up the steps, Landon passing a blunt to Kai. Kai took it and nudged him. As they hopped up the last stair and into the house, Landon looked me up and down and then ... continued walking.

Weird.

I held my breath the entire exchange, my body tense and my cheeks flaming hot. Hoping that Allie didn't see the look he had given me, I stared down at my feet and wiggled my toes in my sneakers, praying that if she did, she wouldn't say anything.

"And you're telling *me* to be careful," she said. "The Poison boys are no good. You should know that."

"I know," I reassured, stepping out the door and waving her off. "Don't worry about me."

But she should worry about me because Poison terrified everyone.

When I finally made it through the maze of cars to mine, I slumped my shoulders forward and let out a loud sigh, wishing I could exhale all my problems just as easily. I unlocked my car and threw my bag into the backseat.

"Not staying?" someone asked me from behind.

I jumped up, hand pressed over my heart, and turned around to see João leaning against his black Mercedes-Benz with tinted windows. With him being from the bad side of town, I couldn't fathom how he could afford a car like that, but I wasn't going to strike up a conversation to ask about it.

He inhaled smoke from a cigarette, grabbed it by his thumb and forefinger, and held it out for me. I wrinkled my nose and ignored it, opening the driver's door.

"No, I'm not." I sat in the car, about to slam the door, when he grabbed it and held it open, bicep flexing.

Tossing the cigarette onto the ground, he stomped it out with the heel of his boot. "Where are you going?" he asked with a Brazilian accent. I had only really heard that change in his voice when he was angry or annoyed at someone in Redwood's halls.

"That's none of your business." I slapped a hand over my mouth, my eyes wide.

The words had slipped out before I could stop them, my annoyance getting the best of me.

"I'm going home," I said quickly. "Home—that's all."

João stood there, expressionless, for a couple moments, and then he laughed lifelessly and shook his head. "Fucking Landon. That's why ..."

"Why what?" I asked, brows furrowed.

João released his death grip on the door, lips curling into a devilish smile. "Have fun tonight, Imani. It's your last night of freedom. We have plans for you tomorrow, plans that only we'll enjoy."

Chapter Eight

IMANI

Once I made it back home, I stared emptily at the steering wheel with my stomach in knots. All I could do was … imagine what these plans were that João had told me about earlier. I must've made six circles around the block, so lost in thought and panic and worry that I'd forgotten that I wanted to go home to relax.

"Get your ass in the house, Imani," Mom shouted from the front door, tired eyes narrowed at me.

From the look on her face, it seemed like she'd had a hard shift at the hospital. And when she had days like that, she came home and asked me a million and one questions to get her mind off it. It was sweet of her, but … all I wanted to do was get some much-needed sleep.

"It's freezing out here." She shuffled out of the house and crossed her arms, a silky red scarf wrapped around her hair, which meant that she and Dad were in for the night and that there was no way I could get out of a conversation.

No. Freaking. Way.

"Don't you have a test to study for tomorrow?"

After shutting off the car, I grabbed my backpack and walked up the sidewalk to the door. "Sorry, Mama." I kicked off my sneakers in the foyer, tightened my grip on my backpack, and hurried toward my bedroom. "I've had a long day, and I was just studying at Allie's. I need to finish up."

I was moments away from escaping her questions for the night until she cleared her throat. I stopped in my tracks and looked back at her, shifting from foot to foot uncomfortably.

She shut the front door and wrinkled her nose. "Why do you smell like weed? You didn't do any, did you? You know that stuff will ruin your life."

Before I could roll my eyes, I stopped myself. "Allie's stepbrother threw a party. We didn't go, but there was so much of it everywhere."

She eyed me for a moment, then nodded. "Good. You know better than to get involved with people like that. You're going places, sweetheart."

I gave her a tense smile. Definitely knew not to get involved with people like that, but ... it had kinda happened. It wasn't totally my fault. If I had known that Chris, my online fuck buddy, was really Landon—I gnawed on the inside of my cheek—hell, I probably wouldn't have done anything differently, except be way more careful about not showing my face.

That boy had a monster cock that I so desperately wanted inside of me.

The way it had felt against me earlier today ...

"Now, we gotta find you a nice boy!" Mom said with a genuine smile. "In fact ... we're having dinner with some people tomorrow night. They have a son your age. Do you know anybody named Akio?"

My eyes widened, nose wrinkling. Mom wanted to set me up with Akio?

"He's in a couple of my classes," I said, inching toward my bedroom.

"His father works as a cardiovascular surgeon at the hospital. We were chatting about a mutual patient the other day, and he told me that Akio is at the top of the class." She laughed. "And you know how I am, making sure he knew that my Imani was at the top. He seems like a nice boy, though. What do you think?"

What do I think? I thought that I didn't have time to date with Landon, João, and Kai up my ass about video-chatting naked, touching myself at the sight of Landon's sexy fucking body. I couldn't date Akio, especially now that I knew Poison had something against him.

"Are you trying to set me up with him?"

"Just dinner," she said.

She was definitely trying to set me up with him.

"Um ... he's not really my type," I said, hoping that she wouldn't push it. I didn't want her to find out that the boys she wanted me to stay away from—the pot-smoking, drug-dealing gang of assholes—were my type. That would not go over well.

After waving her hand dismissively, she ushered me to my bedroom. "Sleep on it. We'll go out with them tomorrow, and you can tell me what you think about him."

If that was the only way to keep her out of my business ...

"Sure," I called over my shoulder as I slipped down the long hallway to my bedroom.

Closing my door behind me, I dropped my backpack on the ground and rested my head against the doorframe, breathing in the scent of fresh pink roses that sat in a cream-colored flower pot on my bureau. I dimmed the lights on the chandelier above my bed, sat at my desk, and pressed the power button on my Mac monitor.

The screen turned on, a single black line flashing inside the password box. I quickly inputted my password and opened Discord, like I did every night, to wait for Landon. But tonight, I wasn't thinking about touching myself. Tonight, I was worried that if I didn't log on, Poison would do something to harm my reputation.

When the green circle popped up beside Landon's picture, I gnawed on the inside of my cheek, opened my desk drawer, and pulled out a bottle of Dad's Cheval Blanc 1947 wine. Was I supposed to have this hidden in my drawer? No, but I sure as hell needed it.

After popping off the cork, I put the bottle right to my lips and took a huge gulp of it, my nose wrinkling at its dry and bitter taste. God, I didn't know how anyone could like this shit. It tasted like beer that people who hated their lives drank.

Moving my comfy black swivel chair closer to the screen, I clicked on Landon's profile image and nervously rubbed my sweaty palms together. How had I not freaking noticed that he was really Landon? That smirk and those lips and—

"Obsessing over me already?" Landon said behind me.

I went to scream, but he slapped a hand over my mouth.

"Don't want your parents to hear us, do you?"

Once I successfully exited out of his profile, calmed the fuck down, and pulled his hand off me, I turned around with wide eyes. "What the fuck are you doing here?" I whisper-yelled at him, my cheeks flaming red at the thought of Landon catching me ogling his picture. "How did you get in? We have security."

Instead of answering me, Landon dragged his tongue across his full lower lip, and boy, did that do something to me. "Get on the bed."

"What?" I asked, throat dry and heat gathering in my core.

"Get on the bed, Imani."

"What are you going to do?"

"Nothing you don't want me to," Landon said. He grabbed me by the wrist and jerked me forward until my body was pressed against his taut, hard one. "I told you that I'm going to enjoy you first, and that's what I plan to do with you tonight."

Chapter Nine

IMANI

"Take off your clothes," Landon ordered, like he usually did over video.

But now, it was real.

I swallowed hard, looked to make sure my curtains were closed, and nervously fiddled with the bottom of my shirt. He tugged his shirt over his head, revealing his muscular chest and tattooed abdomen. My gaze traveled down his body to the two scars across his lower abdomen that seemed to be from a knife.

Heat gathering in my core, I pulled my shirt over my head and stood in my tiny bra before him.

Gaze flickering down to my tits, he smirked and looped his finger under my bra strap, tugging on it gently. "Cute."

"Cute?" I asked, cheeks flaming red.

It was cute—that was all. Not *hot* or *sexy*, like what guys like him called girls with bigger chests.

"Your nerves—it's cute," he clarified, drawing his finger down my stomach to my jeans. "These, too."

"You first," I whispered.

Landon chuckled and undid his jeans, button by button. I watched in anticipation, my mouth drying as he looped his thumbs under the waistband of his jeans and briefs, then pulled them down. My nipples hardened under my thin bralette, poking right fucking through it, my pussy clenching.

When his hard cock sprang out of his pants, I held back a gasp. Long, thick shaft that curved down slightly, a veiny and raging cock that I so desperately hoped fit inside of me. After ogling it for another moment, I pushed down my jeans and stood in my underwear.

He moved closer to me, his cock grazing against my stomach, and undid my bra, pulling down the straps and tossing it aside. I gazed down at his dick; all the things I'd sworn I'd do to him if he were with me going right out of the fucking window. I didn't know the first thing about giving a hand job or sucking his cock.

But instead of asking me for it, he sank a hand into my panties and touched my wet pussy, stepping closer to me and grabbing my chin with his free hand. "Last time I'm going to tell you. Get on the bed."

Sucking in a breath, I stumbled onto the bed and up to the headboard. He followed me up, grasping my hips and forcing me onto my back. After pulling off my panties, he looked up at me and let a wad of spit drip from his lips and onto my mound.

Hands gripping the backs of my thighs to hold them apart, Landon dipped his head and placed his hot mouth on my pussy. I sucked in a breath, my core clenching, and curled my toes. After I laced a hand into his hair and tugged softly, he flicked his tongue out against my clit and slowly started to move it around, his lips all over me.

Between him lapping at my clit, drawing his tongue up and down my folds, and trailing his hand up the side of my body to my nipple and flicking it around, the pressure built higher and higher in my core until I could barely handle it. He grunted against me, blue eyes closed, and continued to eat me out, not stopping once to breathe.

Someone knocked on my door, and I slapped a hand over my mouth to stop myself from moaning. My entire body tensed, and Landon looked up at me but still didn't stop. He moved his tongue faster, sucking my clit between his lips.

"About Akio tomorrow," Mom called through the door.

I paused, hoping that she'd go away.

"Sweetheart?"

"Yes, Mama?" I asked, tugging harder on Landon's hair and grinding my pussy against his face. I was fucking moments from coming all over him. He ate pussy so fucking well—better than I'd thought he would—like he actually loved doing it.

"I wanted to let you know that your father and I will be gone all day."

"Mmhmm ..." I gazed down at Landon, lowering my voice. "Please, more ..."

"Make sure you're ready at five p.m."

"Will ... d-d-do."

When I finally heard Mom walk down the hallway, I curled my toes and let out a loud moan, unable to stop myself as an orgasm ripped through my body. My legs trembled, my hips moving from side to side so I could displace all this pressure. Yet Landon held me steady and continued to lick my clit, building me higher again.

"Landon," I whispered. "You can stop now. I c-came."

"And you're gonna come again," Landon said, letting me rest one of my legs on his shoulder and burying his face deeper between my thighs. He pinched my nipple and tugged on it harshly, lips moving up and down my clit. He glanced up at me with those blue eyes, strands of dirty-blond hair on his forehead. "Have to break a virgin in slowly."

"Fuck," I murmured.

"Grind your pussy against my mouth," Landon said. "And make yourself come for me, like you do every night."

Holding his head steady, I ground my hips against his face leisurely at first, and then, unable to hold myself back, I moved my hips up and down faster and faster, the pressure so high that I felt like I was about to ... to come so fucking hard again.

Landon kept up with my pace, his tongue flicking out against my clit and his fingers sliding into my sopping cunt. Knowing that an orgasm was coming, I pushed on his head—the pressure too much— and shook my head from side to side, the silky sheets sliding around under my body.

"Oh fuck," I whispered, shoving his head back.

Yet every time I pushed on him, he pushed back and held me still.

"It's too ... too much."

I raised my hips into the air, my legs shaking so fucking bad, and grabbed his hair to hold my hands steady. Immense pleasure surged through my body, my arms and legs tingling in delight. Landon still didn't stop until I relaxed underneath him, my arms falling to my sides.

He moved up between my legs, the very tip of his cock against my entrance. I grabbed on to his shoulders and dug my claws into his muscle, waiting for him to finally be inside of me. He pushed the head of his bare cock into me, then pulled it out, refusing to give me all of him.

"Beg for it."

"Landon, please, don't make me. You know I want it."

Grasping my hips, he stilled with the head of his cock buried in my pussy. "Beg."

"Please," I whispered, feeling nothing but embarrassment.

Saying it aloud when he was in the room with me was so damn different. All my confidence was out the fucking window because I wasn't a nobody anymore. I was nothing but Imani Abara, nerdy girl from Redwood.

"Please what?"

"Please, give me your dick. I need it inside of me so freaking—"

Without letting me finish, he slammed himself inside of me. I shouted and slapped a hand over my mouth, moaning into it. He was so big that it both hurt and felt better than I could have ever even imagined that it would. My toes curled.

"Fuuuuck," he grunted in my ear. "Your pussy is squeezing my cock so tight."

I tightened even more around him, whimpering, "Please, more."

He pulled out slowly, then pushed himself back into me. "How does it feel to finally be full with cock instead of one of your toys?"

"Good," I moaned, moving my hips around. "Faster, Landon, please."

Landon moved in and out of me, picking up his pace until his balls were slapping against my bare pussy with every thrust. I curled my fingers into his chest and bit down on my lower lip to stop myself from screaming. He dipped his head, pressing his lips to mine and ramming himself even harder into me.

"I'm going to come again. Come with me," I pleaded against his lips. "Please."

Landon grunted against me, keeping up a rhythmic pace.

"Don't pull out either," I begged. "I'm on birth control."

"Oh fuck," Landon murmured, pumping faster and harder into me. "You can't fucking say something like that, Imani. You don't know what it does to a guy."

I wrapped my arms around him and dug my fingers into his back. "Please. Please, I'm about to come. Don't pull out. Please, don't pull—"

My back arched, my body trembling. Wave after wave of pleasure rushed through me as Landon buried himself as deep as he could and then tried to get even deeper, his cum spilling into my tight cunt.

Chapter Ten

LANDON

F*uck.*

I hadn't ever had sex that good.

Imani gathered a light-pink wool blanket in her hands and drew it over her body. Light from the glass chandelier above the bed glinted in her brown eyes, making them look glossy. But she wasn't crying; instead, she was smiling.

"I, uh, gotta get ready for bed."

Standing up, I tugged on my jeans. "Get ready."

She twisted a scarf in her hands, watching me from the bathroom door. "Can you go?"

"We need to talk."

"I have a test tomorrow. Can't this wait for the morning?"

After eyeing the scarf in her hands, she walked farther into her bathroom and looked back at me. "Fine, just don't ... steal anything, like my computer. I need it to study later. I have an exam tomorrow, and I—"

"Go, get ready."

When she shut the bathroom door, I walked around her bedroom and eyed all the ritzy things her rich parents had given her —pink-and-gray artwork that must've cost hundreds of dollars each, a walk-in closet filled with designer clothes that she rarely wore to school, a bottle of a hundred-thousand-dollar wine, a huge fucking computer.

I walked over to the screen with Discord still on full display. She had exited out of my profile picture the moment she heard me speak to her, leaving the screen on private messages between me and her and ... other people.

And not just any other people.

Other guys.

Sitting in her swivel chair, I scrolled down the list of names and clenched my jaw. Half the messages weren't even open, their names in bold, bright white letters. I balled my hands into fists and clicked on one, growling when someone named Carl J. asked if she wanted to chat.

Imani opened the bathroom door thirty minutes later, after I had scrolled through a bunch of her messages, some from over a year ago. It was fucking wrong—I knew that fucking shit—but it made me angry. She widened her eyes at me, adjusting her headwrap, and cheeks tinting against her brown skin.

"I thought you would've left by now."

I balled my hands into fists, pushed the chair out, and stalked closer to her. "You're done talking to other guys online."

She looked up at me with big brown eyes. "What?"

"You're fucking done talking to other people."

Rosy had been my fucking obsession for the past year, a woman I could chat and relax with for a few moments of my day. With her, I didn't have to be Landon, didn't have to keep up an image, didn't have to listen to my parents scream at each other.

It was only her.

But apparently, to her, it hadn't been only me.

Gaze flickering to her computer, she furrowed her brows and crossed her arms over her chest, narrowing her eyes at me and scowling like I had never seen before. "You went through my computer?"

Don't make the mistake of thinking I wanted a relationship with her. Relationships weren't my thing. When my parents had started fighting, I'd vowed to never date anyone fucking ever. I'd be with Poison for life. But ... that didn't mean she could talk to other fucking people.

"What is wrong with you?" she asked, keeping her voice low.

I wrapped my hand around the front of her throat and thrust her against the wall, desperately trying to keep my cool. Imani did something to me, and I could feel whatever that was inside me about to snap.

"I don't think you fucking understood when we had our little chat in the car earlier." I stepped closer to her and inhaled the fresh roses on her nightstand. It did nothing to calm me down. "There's no talking to other guys, no dating other guys, no fucking other guys—even virtually —or everyone in Redwood will find out your dirty little secrets. You're ours now—and only ours."

Chapter Eleven

IMANI

After what Landon had done last night, I let him go. I fucking let him go.

I should've done something, cursed him out, smacked him across the face, kneed him in the balls, but I didn't do any of that because I was so damn angry and in too much shock. He had gone through all my things and acted like he had done nothing wrong.

Once I undid my lock, I slammed my locker open and let it smack against the one beside me, the metal striking making my heart race. I might've not done anything about it last night, but I would today. All three of those boys would get a piece of my freaking mind.

"You never straighten your hair," Allie commented from my side, leaning against the lockers and smiling at me. "Why'd you torture yourself by getting up three hours earlier than usual? Trying to impress someone?"

"I didn't sleep last night," I said, wiping my eyes angrily. "I needed something to do."

"Why didn't you sleep?"

"I don't want to talk about it."

"Come on."

I wanted to flip out on her for pushing it, but it wasn't her fault that I hadn't gotten sleep. This was all Poison's doing, and they deserved my anger, not my best friend.

So, I wrapped my arms around her shoulders and pulled her into a much-needed hug. "I'm sorry. I'm cranky."

After patting my back, she pulled away. "It's okay."

"I'll tell you about last night." I turned on my heel and smirked at her. "But you tell me about Jace first."

"What?" she asked, brows furrowed. "Why do you want to know about—" Suddenly she stopped, gazed behind me, and cringed. "Yikes!"

Glancing over my shoulder, I saw Akio walking down the hallway toward us with his eye nearly swollen shut. My teeth clenched, fury racing through me again. I didn't care about Akio in the slightest, had barely talked to him for the twelve years we'd been in school together, but Landon had done this to him.

And that made me even angrier with that man.

Akio walked over to me with his hands stuffed into his pockets. "Hey, Imani."

I gave him a smile and stuffed a couple books into my locker, wondering why he was talking to me now. We hadn't spoken until yesterday. But instead of ignoring him and riling myself up even more about Landon, I said, "Hey."

Leaning against the red locker, he cleared his throat. "You coming tonight?"

After closing my locker, I pulled some books to my chest and looked over at him. "Yeah."

Allie arched a brow. "Where?"

"My mom is forcing me to go out to dinner with Akio." I gave him a half-smile. "No offense."

Akio sighed. "I don't want to go either. Our parents are trying to set us up."

Allie scrunched her nose at me, then smiled at Akio. "Oh, well, I'll leave you two lovebirds alone then. I'm going to be late. My class is all the way across campus." She winked at me behind Akio's back. "Have fun!"

When she disappeared down the hallway, Kai caught my eye. He stood at the end of the hallway, backpack slung over his shoulder and piercing brown eyes fixed on me. After a moment, he clenched his jaw and walked into the back hallway, where Poison always hung out. I balled my hands into fists and trailed after him.

"Where are you going?" Akio asked, following me like a lost puppy.

"To chat with Poison. I suggest you don't come, or Landon will kick your ass again," I said to him, tilting my head to the side, my voice coming out harsher than I'd meant it to. I didn't want to have to protect Akio again because this time, *I* would be the one smacking my hand across Landon's face.

Still, Akio followed me and grabbed my arm. "You're not really going to talk to them, are you?"

I stared down at his hand enclosed around my arm and pulled myself away, not liking the way he'd grabbed me so ... so harshly. Sure, I hadn't minded the way Landon touched me last night because I ... well, I ... I thought he was sexy. *That was all.* But that didn't mean anyone could pull me the way Akio had.

"Don't touch me," I said.

Akio pulled himself away. "Sorry, but you shouldn't get involved with people like that. They're bad news, Imani, and you're a good girl."

Good girl.

He knew nothing about me. I didn't do drugs and didn't hang out with gangbangers, but that didn't mean I was good, like everyone thought. I had business with Poison, and I was just getting angrier by the damn moment, talking to Akio.

"If they're bad news, then what did you do to get on their radar?"

Akio went dead silent and sucked in a breath. "I can't tell you."

"Okay. Then, if you want to get the shit kicked out of you today, be my guest and follow me."

"What's your problem today?" Akio asked, lips curling up in disgust. "You're on edge."

Instead of listening to him anymore, I stormed down the hall and left him. "I'm pissed off ..." *At the one and only group that seems to terrify everyone else in this school.*

All damn night, I had worked myself up, wondering how I could have let Landon leave after he snooped through my Discord and shoved me against the wall, scolding me for talking to other guys. But we were never exclusive, and besides, I hadn't messaged any of them back these past few months.

That didn't matter, though.

What mattered was that he'd looked through my things.

I took quick strides down the corridor to the hallway where Poison could always be found beating someone up or dealing drugs, found Landon leaning against a wall with a cigarette hanging out of his mouth, and marched right up to him.

Unable to stop, I slapped Landon right across the face so hard that my hand stung, and I grabbed him by the collar to pull him closer. "Don't you dare go through my computer, my phone, or my Discord again. You had no right to, no matter if I'm yours or not."

Adrenaline rushed through me. I shoved him away, turned on my heel, and stormed back down the hallway to the science wing. I had an exam today that I knew I was going to fail, but that didn't bother me as much as what Landon had done.

And I hoped that I'd knocked some damn sense into that boy.

Chapter Twelve

LANDON

With my face burning from the force of Imani's slap, I watched her storm down the hall and around the corner. I brushed my fingers against my cheek and clenched my jaw, chest tightening slightly at her anger and pain.

João and Kai, who had been silent up until now, burst out into a fit of laughter.

"What the fuck are you laughing at?" I growled and shoved João into the red lockers.

"The fuck did you do to her?" he asked.

Kai glanced back down the hall in her direction, cracking a small smile that I rarely saw anymore after his mom died. "I haven't ever seen her that angry before. She's usually a quiet little thing." Kai drew his tongue across his bottom lip, then turned in my direction. "What happened?"

I swung my backpack off my shoulder and pulled out a lighter. "Nothing."

"Bullshit."

After lighting up another cigarette, I blew out some smoke and stared out one of the open windows and into the parking lot down below. "What happened with Jace Harbor last night?"

"You'd know if you hadn't left when you saw Imani," João said.

"What's your problem?" I snapped.

"You want to get your dick wet too fucking badly."

"I've been talking to her for a year," I said, teeth gritted together.

"I don't want you to catch feelings for her," João said, taking the pack of cigarettes off my hands and snapping on the lighter. "She's to be used to destroy this town, nothing more, so don't get your feelings involved."

"They're not." I looked over at Kai. "You don't have shit to say about this?"

Kai shrugged. "She straightened her hair today," he said. And when we both looked back at him in question, he put a blunt to his lips, lit it, and leaned back against the cold red locker. "I like it better natural."

"Oh my fuck." João rubbed a hand across his face and collapsed on a windowsill next to me, shaking his head. "You're both fucking head over heels, and it hasn't even been a fucking day yet."

Principal Vaughn paused at the end of our hallway, stared directly at us, then kept walking, as if nothing was happening in his school. As strict as that man was, he knew best not to fuck with us. But there was something up with him; he had secrets that he obviously didn't want us looking into. But I was sure they'd come out someday.

Kai gently closed his eyes and slumped his shoulders forward. "You slept with her?"

I inhaled the smoke and watched a couple leaves fall off branches outside. "What's it to you?"

João glanced over. "She good in bed?"

"She was a virgin."

"I thought you said she cams," João said.

"She does, and she has a filthy fucking mouth, too, but she was a virgin."

"I figured she was," Kai said. "Nobody at Redwood has touched her."

"What do you do, stalk her?" João asked Kai.

Kai stayed quiet.

"She's going out to dinner with her parents and Akio tonight," I interrupted, directing the conversation elsewhere. "If we want to fuck with her, then tonight's the time. But if I see Akio with her, I'm going to fucking lose it."

Kai paused and glanced over at João, who looked pissed at the mere mention of Akio's name. "What are we going to do about him?" Kai asked João, setting the blunt on the windowsill. The bell rang, but none of us moved. "We have to do something, or Ana will—"

"I fucking know," João said through clenched teeth. "But if Akio loses his fucking job, we're out, and it's over." He rubbed a hand over his face and kicked himself off the windowsill. "I'll figure something out. Meet at my place at seven. We have Imani to play with tonight."

Chapter Thirteen

IMANI

I'd failed my fucking test because of Poison.

Grinding my teeth together, I glared out the car window and dug my nails into my palms. I hated them so fucking much that I couldn't put my hatred into words. All I wanted was to get through the rest of this year without Mom breathing down my neck, but that surely wasn't going to happen. When she saw that thirty-two percent on the test, she'd hound me for *every little thing*.

And I couldn't take it anymore.

"It's right around the corner," Mom said, pointing to the Stop sign.

Dad turned on his blinker and placed his hand on Mom's knee. "I know where it is, honey."

Unable to stop myself, I pulled out my phone and glared at the Discord app. Then, I tapped on it and glared at Landon's profile picture, which didn't have a green circle next to it for once, which meant that he wasn't online. I started typing out a long, angry message to him, giving him a piece of my mind.

But then I erased it all.

I didn't want to talk to him.

Yet I retyped the message. But I did want him to know not to fuck with me.

"What are you up to back there?" Dad said, glancing in the

rearview mirror. "All I hear are those buttons clicking about a million times a second."

After deciding not to send the message, I shoved my phone in my purse and forced a smile. "They're not buttons, Dad."

He smiled back at me and pulled to the side of the road. Balling my hands into fists, I stepped out of the car. Dad handed the keys to the valet and grabbed Mom's hand, pulling her toward the restaurant. A cold fall breeze whipped through the downtown streets, making my curls fly up in all directions.

Yeah, I know. Why waste three hours of my life straightening my hair, just to wash it again? Well, if I hadn't done something when I got home, I had been afraid that I'd call Landon on Discord to talk to him. And I didn't want to do that.

"How'd the test go?" Mom asked me when we stepped into the most upscale restaurant in all of Redwood.

It cost over a few hundred dollars per plate and was where most of the Redwood rich went to show off how much money they had. Honestly, it wasn't even that good, and I'd prefer some mac and cheese from the box any day.

Mom cleared her throat. "Don't tell me you failed it."

"No," I lied, giving her my best forced smile. "One hundred percent, like usual."

But in a couple days, when she checked my grades—yes, she was *that* kind of mom—she'd find out I'd lied to her.

"That's wonderful, sweetheart. All you have to do is keep studying. You'll stay at the top of your class come the spring, easy."

I pressed my lips together to suppress a grumble and followed her through the restaurant to Akio and his father. I didn't get why she wanted me at the top of the class. It was constant damn pressure and the reason I'd turned to video chatting in the first place—to relieve some stress. But now, I was fucked because of it.

After the overzealous greetings, I sat across from Akio and sank into the plush chair, hating that Mom had made me come tonight. I didn't like Akio and would *never* like Akio. All I could really think about were those three boys who had my damn life in their hands and could ruin not only *my* reputation, but my parents' reputation, too.

My parents had grown up on the bad side of Redwood and gone on to make a name for themselves.

Mom valued that more than anything and wanted our lives to be picture-perfect.

It was funny, what money did to people.

"How'd it go with Poison?" Akio whispered to me when our parents fell into easy conversation. He looked around when he said it because their mere name brought terror to the snooty, rich families of Redwood. It wasn't a secret that Poison wanted to use up every last one of them, sucking them dry in exchange for jobs.

I didn't doubt that they were going to use me, too.

But by the way Landon acted last night ...

Shaking my head, I pushed away the thought. If I thought Landon actually liked me, I was going freaking crazy. He just used me for my body. I was a girl he could get off to and talk to every night, even after we were done touching ourselves.

Maybe he does ...

"Uh, Imani?" Akio asked.

Once I blinked the thoughts away for good, I turned back to him and shrugged. "Good, I guess. I slapped Landon in the face for you. You're welcome." I glanced at Mom to make sure she wasn't secretly listening to us and leaned across the table. "Why are they after you? What did you do?"

For the second time today, Akio tensed. After sitting back, he stuck his fork into a piece of bread and plopped the entire thing into his mouth. His father sent him a scowl for his bad manners and turned back to Mom.

"Akio has an internship at the pharmacy," Akio's father boasted to Mom, as if it was a competition. "I'm so proud of that boy."

I arched a brow at Akio, who couldn't maintain eye contact with me. "The pharmacy? Do they give you access to all the drugs?"

Mom smacked my shoulder *playfully*, but she really meant it to tell me to shut the fuck up. "Oh, honey. Stop it. I'm sure he's working in the front room."

"Actually, right alongside the pharmacists," Akio's father said.

Akio sank lower in his seat, and I finally figured it out. Poison was using Akio to steal drugs for some reason. I mean, I knew they sold pot, but ... hard drugs? People thought it was right up their alley, but I had never heard of them selling anything else. They weren't called Poison because they sold drugs that could kill you, but because they were a drug that destroyed every part of this town.

"Interesting," I murmured, sipping my water and eyeing Mom's wine.

She would never let me have a sip of it, but I fucking needed one tonight. Poison wanted drugs for some ungodly reason, and as much as I despised him, I hoped to God that Landon wasn't using.

Chapter Fourteen

LANDON

After grabbing a couple things from the basement, I headed upstairs for a beer to take to João's place. I sure as fucking hell needed it after today. I could still feel the sting of Imani's slap and see the anger and hurt written all across her pretty face.

When I saw Mom and Dad sitting at the kitchen table, I cursed to myself and debated on leaving the house and getting alcohol on the go. One of the bars down in the slums would serve me something—they always did, didn't care that I had recently turned eighteen.

Mom's phone buzzed on the counter, and I balled my hands into fists, waiting in the doorway because I knew what was coming. It always came—*always*. I'd be concerned if Dad didn't make a comment because that would mean he had drunk himself into an early grave.

Dad lifted his can of beer to drink down the remaining contents. "Who was that?"

Once she glanced at the phone, she turned it over. "Work."

He snorted, voice gruff. "It's always work."

"It is," Mom snapped.

Dad looked at me but nodded to Mom. "You hear this? Your mother is a liar."

Mom shot up from the table and slammed her fists down. "Why don't you believe me?"

"Because you're a good-for-nothing whore." Dad seethed, then held out his hand. "If you don't have shit to hide, let me see it. Let me see your messages, your fucking profiles, everything in your fucking phone."

Tears welled up in Mom's eyes, and I ... I ... couldn't fucking handle it. She reminded me of Imani last night after I had done exactly this, exactly what Dad did every freaking time Mom received a message. A heap of guilt washed over me.

"Why can't I have any privacy?" Mom screamed, grabbing her phone.

I wanted to help her, like I usually did, but I couldn't move from the spot.

Last night, I had turned into Dad, the man I despised the most.

Before she could move, Dad grabbed her phone from her hand, tore it away from her, and shoved her back, sending her flying against the countertop.

She glared at him but didn't move to stop him, unlike Imani last night. "There is nothing there!"

Dad scrolled through the phone and shook his head. "What'd you do to his messages? Where are you hiding them?"

"I'm not talking to anyone!"

My heart ached, my throat closing up. All my life, I'd hated Dad, and now ... now, I was acting just like that motherfucker to someone that I wasn't even dating. But I couldn't even describe that feeling of seeing those other men on Imani's Discord. I'd felt like I was drowning, like I deserved this pain but refused to accept it.

I wanted her.

I wanted her so bad.

But she didn't want me.

Nobody did—at least not in a real relationship. Only to fuck.

"You're a fucking liar," Dad said to her, jaw clenched.

"She's not lying." I finally spoke up, nodding at Mom to leave the room while she could.

If she stayed any longer and continued to fight with him, it would get worse for all of us. It always did, every freaking night.

They were the reason I'd started talking to people online. I'd needed an escape.

"She's a whore."

"No, she's not."

"She sleeps with other men."

"She fucking doesn't," I snapped.

This wasn't about Mom anymore. I saw myself in Dad, talking shit about Imani. And I knew that Imani wasn't even fucking mine yet. She had every right to do what she wanted. I didn't want myself to ever become like this with her.

"If you believe those lies that whore tells you, you're going to let women walk all over you. They're nothing but worthless pieces of shit. They all do the same fuckin' thing. You're better off without one."

My phone buzzed in my back pocket. I pulled it from my jeans to see a message from João. Instead of reading it, I opened my Discord app and clicked on Imani's messages. I couldn't help myself. She'd changed her profile picture from one of her in sexy lingerie to one with her lips puckered, where you couldn't see anything other than her pouty little mouth.

A green circle appeared next to her picture, and she started typing almost immediately. I waited and waited and waited for her to write her message, watching intently.

Rosy: Why'd you do it?

Why? I didn't know why I had done it myself. When I had seen the first message last night, my throat had tightened, my mind going to one thing and one thing only, and I couldn't stop myself from proving myself right, proving my thoughts right, proving Dad right.

Rosy: ???

My finger hovered over the Reply button. I wanted to message her back.

Rosy: All you had to do was tell me that it made you uncomfortable.

It wasn't that easy. It couldn't be that easy. It was never that easy.

Rosy: If you're not going to respond to me, fine. Don't fucking message me back.

Dad smacked me across the face, and the only thing I could think of was Imani hitting me in the hallway. There had been so much hurt on her face and in the slap, but it was nothing like Dad's, who did it because he always had, because that was how he thought people deserved to be treated.

If Mom had let me, I would've killed that man by now.

"Look at me when I'm talking, boy," he said. "Don't think a woman could ever love someone as stupid and useless as you. Your mother can't even love me. Nobody will want a no-good son of a bitch like you."

Chapter Fifteen

IMANI

Landon was online.

Yet he didn't respond to me. I wanted to type more, to give him a piece of my mind, to curse him out, but more importantly, I wanted him to respond. We'd talked every freaking day for the past year almost, and today, he hadn't said a word to me.

From across the table, Mom glared heavily at me. I slipped my phone into my purse and gave her a tight smile, hoping she'd drop the intense stare. Only I could imagine the scolding she'd give me later about how phones weren't meant to be at the dinner table, especially when we were out with her coworkers.

My phone buzzed in my purse, and I ached to pull it back out to see if it was Landon. But Mom was still watching me like a hawk, never once pulling her gaze away as she chatted with Akio's dad. It was like I had to be perfect for her, and it was exhausting.

For the next fifteen minutes, my phone continued to buzz, seemingly only getting louder and louder. I goddamn hated not being able to look at his messages and see how he'd responded after what I did to him today.

To say I was proud that I'd gathered enough confidence to slap him was an understatement.

I had been radiating with pride all day until Mr. Barnes's test.

"That sounds wonderful!" Mom said to Akio's father, finally turning away.

Given a moment of freedom, I snuck my phone out of my purse and glanced down at the missed messages from a group chat that Landon had created. I sucked in a breath, looked up to see Mom in deep conversation, and tapped one open.

Landon: Outside.

My eyes widened slowly, and I looked out the window to see Landon, João, and Kai on the sidewalk outside the damn restaurant, as if they were waiting for me. They leaned against João's black Mercedes. They had to be insane. If Mom saw me leaving the restaurant and slipping into a car with the three most feared men in town ... she'd kill me herself. I couldn't get up and leave without being scolded.

I gulped and shook my head, trying to tell them to leave without drawing attention to myself.

Me: What the fuck are you doing here???

João: Do your parents know that Landon visited you last night?

I glanced at Mom to see her still talking, then at Dad, who had caught me typing on my phone but sent me a wink and let it slide, anyway. After forcing myself to stay calm even though my heart was racing, I sat up taller.

Me: What do you want?

João and Landon both started typing, and then Landon's name disappeared.

João: An answer.

Me: No! They don't know, and I'd like to keep it that way.

From inside the restaurant, I watched João smirk. He glanced over at the other two, then back at me, tapping his phone to show that he had sent me a message. But I was too damn scared to look down and see what it was. That man always had something up his sleeve.

João: Then, touch yourself for *all* of us.

Me: I'm having dinner with my family!

João: I don't care.

Me: How do you want me to do that?

João: Figure it out.

Clearing my throat, I smiled at Mom. "I need to use the restroom."

I sprang up from my seat, grabbed my purse, and hurried through the groups of snooty, rich families to the women's restroom, slamming and locking the door behind me.

I had to make this quick because someone was bound to try to get in soon.

João: We're waiting.

After repeating, "Fuck it," about a million times to myself, I hit the video call button in the group chat and waited until Landon answered. He didn't say anything to me, unlike what he usually did, and I didn't expect him to. He couldn't even answer me when I texted him before.

João grabbed the phone from Landon, walking down the sidewalk where everyone could see me if I started stripping here. He walked around his car and sat in the driver's seat, three doors slamming in the background.

"Don't be camera shy now, Imani. We all know what you do in front of Landon."

I swallowed hard, catching Landon in the background of the screen. I had never once seen his face on video, especially not while I was about to masturbate in front of him. It was ... weird, to say the least.

"Okay," I whispered, locking myself in a stall, too, and slipping my hand into my skirt.

My fingers moved against my clit almost naturally. Brows furrowing, I stared down at the camera, not daring to show them what exactly I was doing to myself. Landon parted his lips, finally relaxing.

"Let us see," Landon said.

"Landon, I—"

"Now."

Cursing, I pulled my skirt up enough for them to see me play with myself through my panties. The boys were all quiet, except João, who cursed under his breath. I continued to rub my clit in small circles, the pleasure rushing through my body, and let out a soft moan.

"We want to see your face, too." Kai finally spoke up.

"But—"

"Be a good girl, Imani," Landon said.

And I almost immediately turned the camera up, so they could see both my fingers stuffed deep into my panties and my face from the most terrible angle ever. Yet they all didn't seem to mind as they adjusted themselves outside of the camera angle.

"Are you ..." I started, cheeks flushing and voice quiet. "Are you guys ..."

"Fuck," João grunted, glancing over at Landon with a smirk. "No wonder you spent every fucking night online."

Loving the way they reacted to me, I pushed my panties down, so they could see my sopping pussy. Landon groaned and pushed his hand into his pants, like he usually did, his bicep flexing. I spread my legs a bit wider and rubbed my fingers across my clit, another wave of pleasure rushing through me.

"Oh my gosh," I whispered, toes curling. I slipped a finger into my pussy and whimpered, remembering how big Landon had felt inside of me last night. "It feels so good."

Someone wiggled the doorknob, and my breath caught in my throat. Yet I didn't stop because I couldn't. Not only was Poison blackmailing me, but I also so desperately wanted to come for them on video as they jerked off to me.

Masturbating in front of other people always gave me a rush.

After slipping another finger into my pussy, I curled my toes and smacked my bare palm against my clit. I threw my head back and moaned louder than I'd meant to, my arms and legs trembling. The lock popped on the door, and when it swung open, I pulled my hand out of my pussy and lifted the phone to my face.

"I have to go," I whispered, tapping the End Call button and hoping to God they wouldn't want anything more from me tonight. I blew out a breath and rested my head against the door, whispering to myself, "I'm sorry."

Chapter Sixteen

After I clicked the phone off, I stuffed it into my purse, sat on the toilet, and pressed my thighs together, the ache still lingering between them. Poison was going to totally flip out on me later, but ... I couldn't video-chat them while there were other people in the restroom with me.

Especially if it was Mom.

I shoved two fingers between my legs and rubbed my clit because the pressure was building already. Biting down on my lower lip, I furrowed my brows and looked under the stall, waiting to see Mom's heels. And in less than a moment, I'd hear her ask what was taking me so long.

Instead, the main door shut and locked again, and that was when I saw it.

Three pairs of men's shoes.

Breath hitching, I stared with wide eyes at the floor and tried to keep quiet.

They shuffled around the room until I heard João say, "Come out, Imani."

Once I gathered all my sanity, I pulled my panties up and opened the stall door to see the three *glorious* Poison boys standing in the women's restroom in the most upscale restaurant in town. And they didn't give a single fuck about it either.

"What are you guys doing here?" I whispered, heat rushing to my cheeks.

Landon didn't say anything as he stepped toward me and grasped my hips from behind like he owned me. When his stubble brushed against my neck, heat rushed to my core, and I cursed under my breath for my body reacting like this.

João trailed his fingers down my chest and groped my breasts, squeezing them softly. "We keep tabs on what's ours. I don't know if Landon made it clear, but we own you now, Imani. And tonight's the first night we *all* get you."

"H-here?" I asked, feeling my nipples harden under his hands.

"Her nipples are so hard; I can feel them through her bra," João said, lips curled into a devilish smirk, pinching and tugging on my nipples through my top.

I clenched, pushed my legs together, and tried hard to show him that this didn't affect me at all ... but I didn't want him to stop.

I just wanted to relax. Mom was too much.

João squeezed my tits again and placed his lips on my neck, sucking harshly on the skin. One hand slipped down my body and between my legs, resting right over my pussy. "Spread your legs for us."

My pussy clenched, my head feeling light and hazy. He rubbed his fingers over my clit, and my legs instinctively spread for him.

Landon chuckled in my ear, tugged on my hair with his free hand, and pulled it back harshly. "There you go," he said. "Now, pull down your panties again for us."

Heat rushed to my core, and I couldn't stop myself from kicking down the underwear, my pussy quivering already. I was going to hell for this—absolute hell. Mom would make sure of it if she caught me.

I had always tried to be a good girl, until Poison.

"All the way off," Landon said, pressing his huge bulge against my backside.

I spread my legs for them to watch as João's fingers slid into my pussy and started thrusting in and out. I relaxed back against Landon and moaned out loud, my pussy clenching on João's fingers.

"Take this thing off, too." Kai moved closer, looped one finger into my shirt near my cleavage, and tugged. "Your tits are too fucking nice to hide in this tiny little top," he said, pushing the top and bra straps off my shoulders and down my body until my small breasts bounced out of it.

"Fuck," Landon whispered, hand in his pants now, the sound of his zipper coming undone echoing throughout the room.

Kai grabbed my hand and placed it on his bulge, making me stroke him at the same pace João finger-fucked my tight hole. My breasts bounced with every thrust, and Kai dipped his head and took my nipple into his mouth, sucking on it.

He tugged on my other nipple to pull me closer to him, then moved his lips up my neck and to my lips, giving me a hot open-mouthed kiss. I clenched harder on João and moaned into the kiss.

"Please," I whispered. "More."

"Begging for it now?" João asked. He pulled his fingers out of me and stuck them right into my mouth, making me suck off my juices. "Kneel, Imani. Right on the dirty bathroom floor, like the little slut you are."

Landon growled at the nickname, shoving João back a couple inches.

But I couldn't help but get even wetter. I pulled his fingers out of my mouth with a slight pop and found myself kneeling in front of them, waiting for a cock. My stomach tightened. Never in my entire life had I given a blowjob, and never in my life had I seen three cocks at once.

I didn't know what to do, but I'd start with what I had seen in porn.

Maybe that would work. Either way, I was too horny to overthink it.

Landon pulled out his cock first, and then the others followed. I took it in my hand, gently placing my mouth on his head. My tongue swirled around it a couple times, and I opened my mouth wider to take more of him inside of me.

He laced one hand into my hair and grunted, "Fuck."

"More," I gargled on him, gagging when he hit the back of my throat. "More, please."

I wanted more. I wanted to forget about dinner. I wanted to feel fucking good.

Landon grabbed the sides of my head and started to face-fuck me, my throat making sloppy, wet gagging sounds. I grabbed both João's and Kai's cocks, stroking them hard. My pussy was pulsing, and I couldn't fucking wait for them to fill me up, like Landon had last night.

Was I a slut? Maybe, in my own little way. Did I enjoy it? Hell yes.

When Landon pulled out of me, João stepped forward, shoved himself into me, wrapped a hand around the front of my throat, and stroked his cock inside. My cheeks flushed, my eyes teary. I choked on him, needing to breathe, but he pushed himself farther down my throat and forced me to look up at him.

"Fuck," he murmured. "No way she was a virgin. No fucking way is virgin head this good."

When he finally pulled out of me, I doubled over, spit and drool rolling down my chin and dripping onto my tits. João wrapped his hand in my hair again and pulled me back to a kneeling position.

Before I could catch my breath, João thrust himself into my mouth once more and started to face-fuck me again. I stared up at him through teary eyes, grinding my legs together to try to ease the ache between them.

João hit the back of my throat hard—as if he wanted me to gag on him—and pulled himself back out, over and over and over again. His hand gently rubbed my cheek, then slapped it hard until it was red. My pussy tightened, and I moaned on him, almost choking on my spit.

When he pulled out of me, Kai pulled me up by the arm and pushed me over to the sink countertop. He hopped up onto the counter, pulled me on top of him, and sat me down on his cock, my back against his chest. Instead of immediately thrusting himself inside of me, he wrapped his arms around my thighs, spread my legs apart, and slowly set me down onto him.

He felt so big inside of me, his cock filling up my tight little hole. He spread my legs as wide as he could as Landon moved closer, took my chin gently in his hand, and pushed his cock into my pussy, too.

I moaned when they both started thrusting in and out of me almost at the same speed. The pressure rose in my core, and I furrowed my brows. God, this felt too fucking good to be just a quickie in the bathroom.

Someone wiggled the locked doorknob, and I tightened on Landon and Kai. Instead of stopping, they continued, harder and faster inside of me. Not giving a single fuck, João hopped up onto the counter too, kneeling near the sink. He grabbed the back of my head and forced himself into my mouth, so I was completely and utterly stuffed full with three huge cocks.

Pressure rose in my core as their hands roamed my body, slapping my tits, pinching my nipples, wrapping around my throat. So many sensations.

"Sweetheart!" Mom called from outside. "Are you okay in there?"

My eyes widened, yet João didn't pull out of me so I could answer. They kept fucking me until Landon came inside my pussy first, stilling and groaning loudly. When he pulled out, he wrapped his hands around my ankles and stretched my legs further apart, watching his cum drip from my pussy and down my ass.

"Imani?" Mom said again.

João grabbed a fistful of my hair, thrust himself all the way down my throat, and came as Kai pulled out and came all over my pussy lips. I choked on João's cum, and when he pulled out, I held a hand over my mouth to muffle my coughing and swallowed.

"Sweetheart?"

The knob jiggled again.

"I'll be out in a second, Mom!" I said, feeling the pressure rise in my core. "Don't worry. You can go sit back down."

There was some shuffling, the sound of her heels clicking away drifting into the room.

Landon pinched and tugged on my nipples, and Kai slapped a hand over my mouth, letting me moan into it. I came hard, my entire body shaking with pleasure. My eyes rolled back, my body relaxing against Kai's.

I pulled my legs together and curled them to my chest, the pleasure almost too much.

Fuck the Poison Boys. I hated them with everything I had ... yet I loved being fucked by them more.

Chapter Seventeen

IMANI

"Those boys didn't bother you, did they?" Mom asked over the phone, worry laced in her voice.

She had asked me the same question about fifteen times since she had seen me walk out of the restroom after Landon, João, and Kai did. I'd had to leave the freaking house because she was aggravating me so much.

If I blew up at her, she'd tighten her hold on me even more.

I already felt like I was suffocating.

So, instead, I tapped my fingers on the steering wheel of my car, parked in the center of the Redwood slums, and stared at the run-down house, which belonged to Landon. It had taken hours to figure out where that boy lived, but I needed to talk to him.

"No, they didn't." Lie.

"Are you sure? I have never seen them on our side of town before."

Light flooded out through one of the second-story windows, shouting drifting through the broken glass. I gnawed on the inside of my cheek. Maybe it wasn't a good idea to barge right in and demand answers that I had wondered about all day.

"Sweetheart?" Mom said.

"Yes, I'm sure, Mom."

"Weren't they those Poison boys who are always getting arrested?"

Biting my tongue, quite literally, until I drew blood, I held back my groan. This was my life, non-fucking-stop. And if those boys had made it any more obvious, I would've been grounded for the rest of my freaking high school career—maybe even longer.

"I'm not sure, Mom."

My answers were short because I wanted her to just drop it.

When a younger woman appeared near the window, I tensed and tightened my grip on the phone. Screw driving away. Sure, this woman might've been Landon's sister, but I thought that he was an only child. At least, that was what he'd told me on one of our many video calls.

But then, who the hell was she?

"I think—"

"Just pulled up to Allie's house!" I said to Mom, needing to shut the phone off ASAP. "We're going to be doing our nails and having a girls' night. She needs it. Her stepbrother is being annoying again. I'll let her know that you said hello."

Mom cleared her throat and sighed. "Okay, sweetie. Stay safe. I love you."

"I love you too, Mom. Good night."

With that, I hung up the phone and looked back up into the house. The woman disappeared from the window, and I found myself stepping out of the car without a plan and, for some damn reason, without a single clear thought in my head. I wanted to talk to Landon—and I might've wanted to check up on him too, see who he was hanging out with tonight.

On my way to their front door, my phone buzzed.

Allie: My mom is

Allie: SO FREAKING ANNOYING.

Allie: SHE LEFT ME WITH JACE FOR THE NEXT TWO WEEKS.

Allie: Can I stay over at your house? Please, I'll literally pay you.

Allie: Please, I can't be with Jace. He's the most annoying prick I've ever met.

While I wanted to answer her right away, I wanted *my* answers first. I stuffed my phone into my purse and knocked on Landon's front door, hands balled into tight fists and heart pounding. A girl like me should never even set foot on the bad side of town, never mind show up at someone's door, angry.

But I didn't care anymore. Poison had shown up unannounced at my dinner.

When nobody answered, I knocked again and tapped my shoe on the cracked pavement.

"Where the hell is he?" I muttered, debating on shouting his name so he could hear me through that open window.

João pulled up behind my car, almost immediately shutting off his car and rushing over to me. He grabbed my wrist and tried to pull me away. "What the fuck are you doing here, Imani? You can't just show up at Landon's place." He nervously looked behind me at the front door. "Come on."

Before we could get anywhere, the front door swung open, and a man swayed in its place with a can in his hand and the stench of beer coming off him in waves. "Who the fuck are you?"

João grabbed me forcefully and shoved me back. "Nobody, sir. She's lost."

"You know whose door you're knocking on, girl? A girl like you shouldn't be in these streets." He pushed open the torn screen door and stepped out of the house, stumbling and waving his can at me. "You show up to the wrong person's door, and bad fucking things happen."

João cursed under his breath, pushing me farther behind him. "She's leaving now."

After crushing the can in his fist, the man tossed it onto the lawn and pointed a finger at me. "You look like my son's age. Are you the whore my son's been hanging out with at all hours of the night? He doesn't even spend fucking time with us anymore. He's up all night on that phone of his, doing who knows fucking what."

The blood drained from my cheeks, my heart racing at how quickly he was approaching us.

I grabbed on to João's bicep and sucked in a sharp breath. "João ..." I whispered. "Is he going to hurt me?"

"Landon!" the man shouted. "Get your ass out here!"

A moment later, Landon stepped out of the front door. "What do you—" He stopped when he saw me, his eyes widening, and then he looked at his father and stepped between João and me and his dad.

João mumbled, "I'm out," and shook his head, heading to the back of his house.

"Your whore is here," Landon's father said.

Something in Landon snapped, jaw twitching. "She's not a whore."

For a second, Landon's father seemed as if he was going to snap, too. But then that woman caught his eye in the upstairs window, and he kicked the can of beer into the road and walked back into the house, mumbling something to himself.

As soon as he shut the door behind him, Landon grabbed me by the upper arm and hurried to the back, dragging me along with him. "Are you crazy, Imani? You can't come here and knock on my parents' front door! What the fuck are you doing here, anyway?"

When we approached a back door, I dug my feet into the dirt and ripped myself away from him. "I came here to see you. We need to talk. I need answers."

Landon clenched his jaw, nostrils flaring. A strong fall breeze blew his hair into his face. "What kind of answers are you willing to get killed for? A girl like you shouldn't be on the bad side of Redwood. Something might happen."

I rolled my eyes. "It's not like you really care about that, is it?"

"Of course I care!" he snapped.

Almost as quickly as the words had come out of his mouth, he smacked his full lips closed. The anger dropped from his face, cheeks paling. A couple moments of silence passed between us, the air thick with tension.

He kicked his filthy white shoes against the dirt. "I didn't mean it like that," he said, but he couldn't look me in the eye. "I just don't want to clean up your guts from my front lawn, if something happens."

"Gee, thanks."

Suddenly, he turned away from me and pulled out a cigarette. "Now, what do you want?"

I stood completely still, watching the way the fire from his lighter glimmered in his pale eyes, and felt a warmth in my chest. A warmth that I didn't like in the slightest because Landon wasn't someone any girl dated. He was someone to sleep with and then forget.

At least, that was how I had seen him for years at Redwood.

Until now.

"Wh—"

"I'm sorry," Landon said, taking the cigarette out of his mouth and staring at the lit end.

My eyes widened. Never in a million years did I think I'd hear an apology come out of this boy's mouth. All he ever did was slam his fists into things and faces, like hurting people was all he knew how to do.

"We were never exclusive online, Landon. You shouldn't have done what you did. It hurt me." I stared at his back, realizing that he wasn't about to turn around and face me. It was like he couldn't. "Still, even if we weren't exclusive, I haven't talked to anyone else in a couple months." I shook my head, hating that I was justifying my actions, and pushed back my shoulders to stand tall even though I was crumpling on the inside. "Why did you do it?"

He didn't say anything, so I stepped closer.

"Why, Landon? Tell me."

Still nothing.

"Give me something!" I shouted, the anger boiling inside of me. I didn't know why I needed an answer this badly, but I did. "Anything."

Instead of saying anything to me, he smashed the cigarette between his thumb and index finger and flicked it away, jaw clenched and breaths harsh. Then, he opened the back door and walked down the cement stairs to a basement, leaving me simmering in fury.

Chapter Eighteen

IMANI

Instead of going home or responding to Allie, like any good friend would, I followed Landon down the stairs and into the basement. I'd been so shitty to my best friend lately. I'd just been ticked off because of these assholes. But I would make it up to her and soon.

Mental note: book a spa day for us. We both needed it.

"Why is she still here?" João asked, glaring at me from a dirty couch beside Kai, who was inhaling smoke through a bong.

"I didn't ask her to stay," Landon said, storming right past them and into another room.

I went to follow after him, pissed off that he'd left me without acknowledging my question, but João snatched my wrist and pulled me back.

"You don't get to see the merchandise."

"The merchandise?"

Kai coughed and placed down the bong, red eyes hazy. "Cannabis. Weed. Whatever you want to call it."

"What, do you guys grow it?" I asked, brows furrowed.

João released my arm, letting me walk to the couch. "That's none of your business unless you're willing to buy. But a girl like you doesn't do shit like this."

"Why does everyone keep saying that?" I snapped. "Why is it

always, 'a girl like you'? None of you assholes know anything about me. Matter of fact, I smoked weed at a party once. Don't judge someone you don't freaking know."

Okay, maybe that was stretching it. I had inhaled some secondhand at one of Jace Harbor's parties, *thought* about smoking it, and was offered a puff on a guy's blunt. But … I never did it.

After I gave him a long scowl, Kai looked at me. "You want a hit?"

I swallowed hard, all the blood draining from my cheeks. "Not now."

João sat on the other end of the sofa. "You're full of shit, Imani. You haven't smoked."

"And you're a fucking asshole," I spat, crossing my arms and sitting closer to Kai than I'd expected to. Our thighs touched, goose bumps rising on my skin underneath my jeans. I didn't know why I was still here, but it wasn't like I could go home, so I sat back and closed my eyes. "So, you guys are expanding."

João cut his gaze to me. "I don't want to know what the fuck that's supposed to mean."

"You're using Akio for hard drugs now," I said, like I'd figured out something big.

I mean, maybe I could use this against them, too. Now, we both had something to hold over each other's heads. But everyone already thought they sold hard stuff, so that idea was out the window before it even came to fruition.

Kai tensed beside me. "Did Akio tell you that?"

"No. I figured it o—"

João shot up from his seat, grabbed my jaw, and crushed it in his hand. "Don't fucking get into our fucking business. Whatever we do isn't shit to you, you understand me? You snoop again, and I won't give a fuck what you are to us anymore. You'll suffer the same as Akio."

Eyes widening, I sucked in a breath and stared up into those big, devilish brown eyes.

"You got it?"

Though I couldn't seem to get any words out, I nodded.

He shoved me back until I slammed into the back of the couch. I pinched my lips together, suddenly in absolute fear and pressing my thighs together.

"Where the fuck is Jace Harbor?" João said, pacing around the room now, fury radiating off of him in thick, heated waves. "I've been messaging him for the past three fucking hours. If he wants a fucking job done, then he should answer his goddamn phone."

A phone on the table buzzed, and João stormed over. "That'd better be him."

Kai glanced at it. "It's your mom."

The anger faded from his face, his jaw unclenching. He grabbed the phone and clicked it on. "*Mamãe.*" There was a slight pause, and then he rubbed his forehead. "*Desculpa, não.*" He paused and asked, "Ana?"

While I listened some more, I couldn't make out a word he said the entire call, his accent getting thicker and thicker until his words sounded so jumbled that even the little bit of Spanish—*a sorta similar language, I think?*—Mom had forced me to take didn't help in the slightest.

Kai stared at him intently until the call ended, tapping his finger against the couch. When João deposited the phone into his jeans pocket, Kai cleared his throat. "How is she?"

João looked at me and clenched his jaw. "She's fine for now."

"Who?" I asked, curious.

"Nobody," João said at the same time Kai said, "Ana."

Sitting back, I smoothed out my jeans. "Who's she?"

After João gave Kai a death glare, João lit a cigarette. "My sister."

"What's wrong with her? You sounded worried."

"What did I fucking tell you about getting into my business?" João snapped.

"My mom is a doctor," I said. "Maybe I could help."

"You and your stuck-up mother could never help. We're from the bad side of fucking town, Imani. You seem like you've forgotten that. And the cold hard fucking truth is that *nobody* from your side of town gives a fuck about any of us. That won't change either—unless we do something about it."

Chapter Nineteen

IMANI

I poked Allie on the shoulder and slid out of sight of her, my lips curled into a smile at finally seeing her for the first time since Friday. Friday! That girl had left me alone to go on a date with God knew who, and I'd had to deal with Poison myself all ... damn ... weekend.

And to say that I was in a better mood than on Friday would be an understatement.

Allie glanced over her left shoulder and locked eyes with Jamal, who was leaning against his locker, tossing a football. Her cheeks flushed, and I stepped into her line of vision with my brow arched.

"God, I tap you on the shoulder, and suddenly, you're in love with Jamal, the football flirt"—I inched closer to her and lowered my voice —"just like your stepbrother, if I *have* to remind you. Please, don't tell me *he* was the guy you went on a date with on Saturday."

Allie playfully rolled her eyes, admitting it without speaking a word. "Nothing happened between us, I."

I arched my brow harder, held my books to my chest, and leaned against the locker next to Allie's, smirking. "Mmhmm, sure. That's what we're calling it nowadays ... *nothing*." I narrowed my eyes at her. "Come on. You went on a date with him to the *Overlook*. That's where everyone goes to hook up."

Scrunching her nose, she frowned and continued picking her books from her glossy red locker. "Maybe in the summer, but not in the fall or winter," she said, suddenly letting her gaze drift past me, as if she was thinking about something else.

And I knew exactly *who* that something was.

"Your stepbrother broke your heart," I said, trying hard to hit it home.

For some reason, she could never get over that SOB, no matter how much I'd tried to get her to see the truth about who he was. She was stuck in a fantasy that I didn't know she'd ever recover from, which was why I desperately begged her to go out with someone else. I just hadn't thought that someone would be *Jamal*.

Someone smacked a tattooed hand against Allie's locker door, slamming it shut. My eyes widened, cheeks flushing when I glanced up and saw João and Landon standing before us. They never came through this hallway, like *never*, never.

João towered over Allie, lips curled into a scowl. "Where's your brother?"

Landon moved closer to me, his finger curling around a strand of my hair and tugging on it right in front of everyone at Redwood Academy. I pushed his hand away and looked around at all the nosy students staring at us. It wasn't normal for Poison to confront two nerds in the main hallway.

"Can you not?" I whisper-yelled at him, turning my head back to Allie and João, feeling a bit perturbed that João was talking to her but barely liked saying anything to me. All I ever got from him were orders and a pissed off attitude.

"Are you still angry with me?" Landon asked, almost sounding ... vulnerable.

I glanced over at him and crossed my arms, not in anger, but because I didn't like all this attention Redwood was suddenly giving me. This was the main reason I couldn't have Landon or any of the Poison gang leak that I cammed naked.

"I'm annoyed with you, yes," I said, looking up at him for a moment, then away. "You couldn't even tell me why you did it. It wasn't even like you glossed through the people I had talked to in the past, but you went through all the messages."

Landon shuffled his dirty, beat-up shoes across the sparkling floor and stuffed his hands into his pockets. "I don't know what you want me to say."

Fully pissed now that everyone was listening, I leaned in closer and lowered my voice to a whisper. "You don't have to say anything. You made it completely clear that you don't trust me even though we're not even in a relationship!"

Landon stepped closer, placing one hand on the locker beside me. "It's not that I don't trust you."

"You literally went through my Discord and got angry without even asking me about it first. If that isn't you not trusting me, I don't know what is. And worst of all, I don't even know why I'm making a big deal out of this. I'm not stupid. You and your little gang are using me, anyway."

My stomach twisted into tight knots. I didn't care about Landon.

Not at all.

All he had been was someone to talk to. Every night. For almost a year now.

Yet, still, thinking that I felt nothing for him felt wrong. Because, if I didn't care about him, I wouldn't care that he went through my stuff. I wouldn't feel betrayed and hurt and untrusting of him now. But I didn't want a relationship with any of Redwood's bad boys.

Mom would have my head.

So, I turned away from him and back to Allie, who shrugged at João.

"I don't know. He's not my problem," she said.

João growled hoarsely under his breath and turned away without even looking in my direction. "If you see him, make sure he knows we're looking for him."

After João nodded at him, Landon gave me a weak smile that didn't make it to his eyes. Together, they both walked back down the corridor toward their self-proclaimed hall that they ruled, João pulling a pack of cigarettes out of his back jeans pocket and lighting it up.

"What was that about?" I asked Allie, feeling a tinge of jealousy nip at my insides.

Allie crossed her arms and smirked. "You would know if you weren't gawking at Landon."

I rolled my eyes and pretended like I didn't care anyway even though I did. João literally hated me with all his guts because I was one of those *rich girls* who got everything she wanted, but then he'd talked to Allie. Sure, it was about her brother, but ... ugh.

You know what? I don't care.

Glaring behind Allie while she gathered her books, I saw the crowd part for *the* Jace Harbor, football god of our school and the man I hated the most because he'd hurt my best friend. He stormed our way, and I nudged Allie.

"I guess I'll be going," I said, not wanting to be part of the fight between them that I could feel brewing. "Meet you in Bio."

Allie glared at me. "You are not leaving me." She seethed, hurrying to organize her locker to find all her books for class. "I am not spending a second alone with him."

"Imani," Jace said, taking a step closer to us and closing the distance, "I need to talk to Allie alone."

After giving Allie a pitiful smile, I hurried down the hall and bumped into Kai, who stood right at the edge of the hallway corner. He leaned against the locker with a laptop slung against his body and his tongue gliding across his front teeth, seemingly ... angry.

"What's wrong with you?" I asked.

Despite being part of Poison, Kai was usually the easiest to talk to. He didn't do drama and was actually more approachable than the other two boys.

He cleared his throat and looked up at me. "No Akio this morning?"

"I don't keep tabs on him."

"You've been talking to him more than usual."

"More than usual? What, have you been stalking me?"

He gave an empty laugh. "Keeping tabs on *you*."

"For your little group of annoying assholes?" I asked.

"No." Kai kicked himself off the lockers. "For myself."

Chapter Twenty

LANDON

Imani would barely look at me.

Not in the hallway this morning. Not in the cafeteria during lunch. Not in the one class I had with her. João would've told me to forget about her, that it was nothing, that she was now our property, and that she didn't need to like us. But I felt differently about her. I had for a while now.

She wouldn't even look at me now while we stood outside Redwood Academy, leaning against João's car and waiting for the other guys to finish business inside the school with Akio. Tonight, we had plans with Imani. João had told me to make sure she didn't leave school grounds, but—I glanced down at my phone and grimaced—I had a meeting in a couple minutes.

"Why can't I leave?" Imani asked, the wind blowing a thick strand of curls into her face. She angrily pushed it away and crossed her arms over her chest, glaring toward the football field, where the varsity team practiced. "I have homework to do."

I frowned at her, my chest tightening. I hadn't wanted to make her angry. Friday night, I'd really wanted to answer her and tell her everything, convince her that it wasn't her I didn't trust, but that I had learned this behavior from my shitty father, that I couldn't stop myself from thinking the worst.

But the closer I had gotten to telling her, the tighter my throat closed, the faster my heart raced, the more it'd felt like I was drowning in thoughts I knew weren't true.

We weren't even a fucking thing yet, and I was already ruining it.

Part of me believed what Dad had said the other night.

Nobody would want a no-good son of a bitch like me.

It was my worst fear, and I'd ruined the one fucking chance I had.

"We have business tonight," I said, wanting to come out with it.

"You, João, and Kai have business. Not me."

"*You* are our business."

After she rolled those big brown eyes of hers, she looked toward the school, where João and Kai exited through a side door—Kai hanging his head down, computer tight in his hands, and João walking toward us like he owned this entire school.

"Thank God," she said when she saw them, kicking herself off his car and taking a couple steps away from me, making me feel even shittier.

I couldn't man up and tell her how I really felt. I couldn't get anything past my lips, except a measly, "I'm sorry," which seemed to mean nothing to her. It hurt so bad—so fucking bad—that I couldn't even put it into words.

I tightened my hands into fists and slammed one into João's hood, denting it in and bloodying my knuckles.

Imani jumped back, placing her hand over her heart and staring at me with wide, frightened eyes. "What the hell is wrong with you?"

Finally here, João shoved me back. "Dude, what's your problem?"

Clenching my teeth, I pulled myself back and headed toward the street without them. "Take the money out of my cut this month to fix your shitty car."

"Where the fuck are you going?" João called after me.

I glanced over my shoulder to see Kai furrowing his brows, João gritting his teeth at me, and Imani looking—what seemed like—worried, but I knew better than that. She didn't give a fuck about me, and she never would. I was someone that she could get off with and nothing more.

My throat tightened.

Nothing ... *fucking* ... more.

"I have shit to do." I turned away. "I'll catch up."

"You can't just leave her alone with us," João said while Imani said, "Landon, you're not going to leave me alone with them."

But I didn't have time to turn around. I was already late to my first damn appointment because I'd had to wait for them, and I didn't want to miss the last half hour. It was the only fucking thing that might help me.

"Fucking asshole," João muttered. "Get in the car, Imani."

Instead of turning back like I wanted to, I forced myself to continue walking down the road, a fifteen-fucking-minute walk, until I came to her house. I didn't come here often, rarely ever anymore, but I didn't have any other choice.

Knocking twice on the grand white door, I waited in the cold with my hands stuffed in my pockets.

A couple moments later, the door swung open, and Misty stood with her hands on her hips, giving me that annoyed look. "You're late."

"I didn't want to even fucking come." I pulled a bag of weed out of my pocket and handed it to her. "Cut me some fucking slack—unless you want me to tell Aunt Linda about you turning to weed to deal with your family falling apart."

She ripped the bag from me, growled, and let me into her house. After she had gone off to college to make something of herself, she had come back to Redwood for some stupid reason, but now, she lived on the good side of town, and I hated her more for it. Between her eight-room mansion, art collection, and shitty attitude, it ticked me the fuck off.

Once she closed the front door, she led me to the living room and gestured toward the couch. "You only have a half hour. I have another appointment at three p.m." She sat in the chair opposite of the suede couch and pulled out a notebook. "Never thought you'd ask for therapy from me, but—"

"Don't fucking push it, Misty." I gritted my teeth. "And don't mention this to anyone."

For once, she dropped that annoyed expression from her face. "It's against my ethics."

I rolled my eyes. *Ethics?*

"Now, go on. I'm listening."

Taking a hesitant seat on the couch, I dug my fingers into the soft material and stared at her for the longest time.

This was a mistake. I shouldn't be here. I shouldn't have called her yesterday. I should've left school with João and Kai.

"It's hard," Misty said, voice softer than it usually was with me, "opening up to someone. I mean, for you especially. You've never been one to talk about your feelings. We don't have to talk about anything until you're ready to."

Just the thought of becoming like Dad sickened me to the point where I wanted to heave up lunch. But no matter how bad it was, I didn't know if I'd ever be ready to talk about this. I was screwed the fuck up. Nothing could fix me.

Chapter Twenty-One

JOÃO

"Where are you taking me?" Imani said from the backseat, staring into the rearview mirror at me.

Full lips pressed together, plucked eyebrows arched in an angry glare, and skin glowing under the setting sun, she was like the rest of the Redwood rich when in the presence of someone from the slums.

And it fucking disgusted me.

I tightened my hand around the steering wheel and stared through the windshield at the red light. Wherever the fuck Landon had gone, fuck, he'd better have needed it because I didn't want to deal with her. Soon, like all the girls at Redwood, she'd be nagging and complaining because the car didn't have heated seats or some shit.

"Are you both going to ignore me?"

Kai glanced over at me from the passenger seat.

"We're going to show you what Redwood is really like," I said.

"What's that supposed to mean?" she asked, pink tongue flicking against her white teeth.

"It means, you shut the fuck up until we tell you that you can talk," I snapped.

Landon must've loved getting his dick hard for her too much because I didn't know what kind of self-respecting person would ever want to deal with a girl like her, who had grown up on the other side of town. I couldn't stand any one of them, except Jace Harbor—*at times.* He knew what went on with wealthy families and didn't like it either.

Kai glanced over at me, tightness in his mouth that told me he didn't like this.

Well, fuck, neither did I.

But Kai had other reasons.

"Do you think this is a good idea?" Kai said, glancing into the rearview mirror at Imani, who flared her nostrils at us now and crossed her arms over her chest, inadvertently pressing her small breasts together. He shook his head. "I don't think she knows anything."

"I don't," Imani chirped from the backseat.

"She doesn't need to know anything," I growled.

Imani didn't need to know anything because she was valuable to influential people. She could be shaped, molded, changed from the good-girl star student to a dirty little slut who would do anything for us. Not only could we use that against her, but also against all these people in this town.

Nobody was safe from us. We would burn this town down.

"How's your sister?" Imani asked suddenly, breaking the silence and staring at me through the mirror with those intense brown eyes.

Unable to stop myself, I tightened my grip on the steering wheel. "I already told you, that's none of your business."

Before she could push it any longer, Kai's phone buzzed. He held it up to his ear and didn't say a word—very like Kai. I continued driving out of the wealthy and toward the ghetto. Kai looked over at me and nodded.

"Akio said he wants to meet," Kai said, pulling the phone away slightly.

Slamming my foot down on the brakes, I stopped the car with a *skrrt.*

Imani flew forward in her seat, the seat belt digging into her collarbone, and then smacked me on the back of the fucking head. "What the fuck was that? You could've killed us."

"We're going to see Akio."

Kai cleared his throat, phone still pressed to his ear. "Actually, he's only going to meet if it's with me and me alone."

I parked the car in the middle of the road and held out my hand. "Give me the phone."

"He's serious about thi—"

"Give me the fucking phone, Kai."

After blowing out a breath, Kai handed me the phone. I held it to my ear.

"You'd better have the damn shit, Akio. We're not fucking playing with you anymore. We needed it last week, so you either hand it over or I'll come take it from you."

"I have it, but I'm not meeting with you or Landon. Only Kai."

"You meet with all of us."

"No." Akio had finally found some confidence somewhere. "I figured out what you need the medication for, and by the way you're keeping it a secret, I'm sure you don't want Imani finding out about it —or anyone else in Redwood for that matter. Only Kai meets me, or you don't get it ever again, and I'll make sure your sister—"

Hand tightening around the phone, I said, "Fine. Kai will meet you in twenty minutes."

Then, I hung up and handed Kai the phone back, fury racing through my entire body. "Make sure that he gives it all to you. He's supposed to have more than a couple doses."

Once I pulled to the curb for him to get out, Kai looked into the backseat. "You going to be okay with Imani?"

"I'll be fine."

Kai raised his brows at me, as if he didn't believe that *I* would be able to keep calm with Imani sitting in the car with me. It wasn't like I was Landon, who couldn't seem to keep his dick in his pants with her.

"As fucking annoying as she is"—I glared in the rearview mirror at her and pulled a pack of cigarettes out of my pocket, needing one now —"Landon would torch my fucking car if I touched her."

Kai looked back at Imani, who was glaring at the back of my head. "Will you be—"

"I'll be fine." Imani turned away from me. "If he tries to kill me, I'll kick him in the balls."

Kai let out a short, quick laugh, got out of the car, and slammed the door. "I'll meet you at the place in half an hour," he said through the window. And with that, he disappeared down a back alleyway, heading toward our usual meeting spot with Akio.

After letting out a puff of smoke through my nose, I nodded to the passenger seat. "Get in the front seat," I said to Imani.

"If I get out of the car, you're going to leave me."

"I'm not going to leave you. Now, get in the fucking front seat."

Imani glared at me for a couple more moments, and then, instead of getting out of the car like any normal person, she climbed on top of the center console and crawled into the front seat, her ass in my face and her skirt tugging up a bit more than it should've.

Fuck.

I stared at her pussy through her silky black thong, my pants growing tight around the crotch. When she finally collapsed in the passenger seat, smoothed out her skirt, and clipped her seat belt, I gripped the steering wheel harder, my dick twitching in my jeans.

"Happy now?" she asked.

"I'll be happy once you finally shut the fuck up." I seethed through my teeth, but this time, that was a put-on. After seeing those silky little panties of hers, covering next to nothing, I wanted to hear those moans escape her lips, the same ones she'd let out in the restroom on Friday night.

But this time, I wanted them to be for me.

Chapter Twenty-Two

IMANI

After about five awkward minutes alone with João, I rested my head against the window and stared at the run-down houses in the Redwood slums. Though I hated João more than the other two Poison boys, I was happy that I was with him rather than at home.

Mom hadn't found out yet that I'd failed my Biology test, but Mr. Barnes was supposed to post the grades tonight. When I got home, I'd get a three-hour lecture about how I needed to study more because anything less than a hundred percent wasn't allowed in Mom's house.

João pulled up to the curb in front of a house without any lights on. I eyed the house that seemed a bit nicer than Landon's. At least there wasn't screaming or broken glass windows or beer cans on the front lawn—not that there really was much of a lawn.

"Is this your house?" I asked.

"What's it to you?"

I rolled my eyes and pressed my lips together, deciding not to snap at him right now. As much as I wanted to say I didn't mind coming to this part of town, that would be a big fat lie. I hated it here, even when Allie used to live a couple streets down.

"I'll be quick," he said.

"Okay. Bye."

João took the key out of the ignition and gestured toward the door. "Get out of the car."

"You said that you're going to be quick."

João glared over at me, nostrils flared. "I also said to get out of the fucking car."

After grumbling, I opened the door, shuffled out of the car, and waited on the cracked sidewalk for him. He locked his car and pushed by me, his shoulder bumping into mine. Definitely intentional.

"Come on. You're not staying out here alone."

Following him up the sidewalk, I stopped at the front door while João shoved his key into the lock. The one-story house looked small and out of place on a street filled with apartment houses and buildings, and it even had some tulips in a painted glass pot out front.

When I went to crouch down and admire them, João wrapped a large hand around my shoulder and forcefully yanked me toward the house. "I said to follow me in."

"What is your problem?" I asked, pushing him away and into the small, dark house.

Before I could say another word, he shoved me against the door, snapping it shut. His chest pressed against my back, and his hand tangled in my hair. He balled it into a fist and pulled it back toward him. My breath caught in the back of my throat, my pussy clenching as he pushed his bulge against my skirt.

"My problem's that my dick is hard because you decided to flash me in the car."

Placing a hand on my lower back, he forced me to arch, pulled up my skirt, and hooked one finger around my black silk thong. Instead of pulling it to the side to give him easy access, he pulled the material up and back and as tight as he could, making it slip a bit between my pussy lips. He reached around my waist to draw his finger down the slit in the middle.

"And you're going to fix that," he said.

"I'm not your slut," I said through clenched teeth, though my breaths were coming out choppier than before and my pussy was getting wetter by the damn second. My core clenched even harder somehow, the thought of him shoving his fat cock into my pussy making me ache.

The other night, he had only thrust himself into my mouth, and all this weekend ... I *might've* been thinking about how he'd feel inside of me. Maybe I *was* a bit of a slut, sleeping with three best friends who everyone at Redwood feared.

He rubbed his fingers faster against the slit. My juices soaked through the panties. I spread my legs a couple more inches apart, the pressure building in my core already, and bit my lip to hold back a moan. I didn't want him to know how much I liked this. He probably got off on making good girls like me bad for him.

When he pulled my underwear even tighter, the silky material disappeared completely between my pussy lips. João pinched them between his thumb and forefinger, squeezing them together. I whimpered, a wave of pleasure shooting through me.

"Fuck, your pussy lips are so fucking fat." He released his grip on them, undid his jeans from behind, and whipped out his hard cock, spitting on it and shoving it between my thighs. After pulling my panties to the side, he rubbed his cock against me.

I glanced down, watching the head of his glistening dick emerge between my lips.

My pussy clenched, the feeling of his dick sliding against my clit driving me wild.

He tightened his hand in my hair again and pushed against me. "Tell me you want it like the little slut you really are."

"Fuck you, João," I said between gritted teeth.

He stopped moving, the head of his cock right at my entrance, as if he were teasing me. I waited impatiently for him to ram himself into me or continue to rub against my clit, and when he did neither, I broke and ground my pussy against him, so desperate to get off.

"Please," I whimpered. "Please, give it to me."

João slid himself into my sloppy cunt, filling me. I dug my fingers into the wooden door and let out a moan as he started thrusting into me.

Then, he gripped my chin in his hand harshly. "I want you to hurt. I want to leave you a teary mess."

"Well, you're doing a damn bad job at that." I seethed at him, wanting him to hurt me more.

Nobody had been so rough with me before, and I kinda liked it. Okay, I *loved* all kinds of sex and masturbating in general, but this was so much different than what I'd done with Landon these past months. And I wanted more of it.

Landon was a bit rough, especially Friday night at the restaurant, but not *this* rough or this ruthless with me. João didn't care what he did, how much he hurt me, and who I was to him. He fucked me like he would fuck anyone.

João wrapped a large hand over my mouth and nose, hindering my breathing and pulling me closer to him to whisper into my ear, "Landon said that you were a fucking virgin, but you've had three cocks in your pussy this past week. Makes you another one of the slutty, rich girls walking around Redwood."

I tightened around João, the pressure rising in my core. All I wanted to do was twirl around and smack him in his face, give it to him good and knock some sense into him, like I had with Landon, but with João's cock buried deep in my pussy, I could do nothing.

"You fucking love being a slut, don't you?"

A toe-curling orgasm ripped through my body, and I moaned, coming all over his dick.

"You're going to take my cock and my cum down your throat again, like you did on Friday and like all good sluts do." He pulled out of me and shoved me to my knees, grabbed my chin, and pulled it open. "Tell me how you taste."

Before I could prepare myself, João stuffed himself down my throat, wrapping his hand around the base of his cock and his balls and forcing as much of himself into me as he could. When he hit the back of my throat, I gagged, my eyes becoming watery, and gargled on him, spit dripping out of my mouth.

Wave after wave of pleasure was still rushing through me, my head feeling light and hazy from the orgasm. Pushing himself as deep as he could go, he held the back of my head close to him and wrapped the other hand around the front of my neck, jerking himself off inside of me and grunting. When his cum shot down my throat, I widened my eyes, gagged, and tried to pull back, but he didn't move.

He made me take his cum.

All of it.

And when he finally pulled out of me, I placed my hands on the floor, coughing, licking up drool from my lips, and swallowing his cum, like the horny slut I had always wanted to be.

Chapter Twenty-Three

IMANI

The doorknob jiggled, and a woman's voice came from behind the door. "João!"

My eyes widened, and I shot up from the ground, wiping any sign of drool or cum off my face and pulling down my skirt. João cursed under his breath, redoing his jeans and pushing me behind him with concern on his face—an emotion that I never thought I would see.

"João!" a smaller voice said. "Mommy lost her key again!"

Oh God, this was bad.

I didn't want to be caught dead in João's house with him.

"Should I hide?" I whispered, gaze darting around the room like a madwoman. I looked at the couch, wondering if I could squeeze my body under it if I needed to or slip into one of the rooms off the hallway—if that even was a hallway.

João hadn't even turned the lights on yet.

"*Não*," João said, reaching for the doorknob. Then, a few moments later, he corrected himself, "No."

So, I stood awkwardly behind him and crossed my arms, knowing that this was about to get hella awkward. Who knew I'd be meeting João's family tonight out of all the fucking nights, right after he bent me over and took me like that? My cheeks were still flushed from it, I could tell.

When João opened the door, a girl—who seemed to be his sister—ran into the room and threw her hands around his neck. "João!" She started speaking quickly in Portuguese, a language that I wished I had taken instead of Spanish, like Mom had forced me to.

A young woman walked in after her, dark circles under her eyes and heels high enough to be stripper heels dangling from her fingers. She went in to give him a hug and a kiss on his cheek, but she looked over and saw me standing behind him instead.

"João, who is this?" she started, voice smooth but her accent even heavier than his.

With his sister in his arms, João turned around and looked at me, no emotion on his face whatsoever. It was as if what had happened moments ago hadn't happened at all—or at least, he hadn't felt anything from it. And while I knew that was probably the case, it still pissed me off a little.

"She's a friend."

She said something to João in Portuguese.

"It's for school."

The woman walked farther into the room and placed her shoes on a kitchen chair, raising her brows as if she didn't believe João. "I'm Luana," she said to me, giving me a smile that didn't reach her eyes. "I, uh ..." She glanced over at João.

João placed the girl down to her feet and ruffled her hair. "My mom doesn't speak much English," he started.

His mother said something to him again, brows drawn together, to which João responded with, "*Não.*"

The woman narrowed her eyes at him, and he sighed and turned back to me.

"She wants to know if you want anything to eat. She made feijoada earlier."

Cheeks flushing slightly, I smiled at her, then glanced at João. "What's that?"

João turned to his mother and spoke quickly, shaking his head and nodding to the door.

The little girl placed her hands on her hips and stared up at João, brown eyes pointed. "No, she didn't say that. She said that she doesn't know what that is."

His mother smacked João on the shoulder, grabbed my arm, and led me to the kitchen, pulling out a pot of black bean stew. "Feijoada." She pulled out a bowl and a ladle, pouring some stew into the bowl and handing it to me. "Eat. *Você é muito pequena.*"

After rubbing his hand over his face, João followed us into the kitchen and grabbed a bowl from his mom.

I dipped my spoon into the stew, leaned closer to João, and said, "Did she just call me small?"

João's sister grabbed a bowl and sat down at the table. "Yeah, she did."

My lips curled into a smile, and I stifled a laugh with how blunt she was. She looked so cute and so innocent. She grabbed a spoonful of stew while her mom disappeared into the back room.

"What's your name?"

"Imani," I said after chewing.

"Are you and João dating?"

João choked on his stew and shook his head, leaning against the counter. "No."

"Then, why is she here?"

"A school project, Ana."

"Yeah, but you don't even do any of your schoolwork ever."

This time, it was my turn to choke on the stew as a laugh bubbled up from my belly. This girl was hilarious, the complete opposite of João.

"So, you like her," Ana continued, pursing her small lips at João like she knew all his secrets. "It's the only logical explanation—unless she's your tutor, but I don't know who would *ever* want to tutor someone like you, you icky head."

Deciding that Ana and I were now best friends, I sat at the table across from her and leaned closer. "I think he's an icky head, too."

Ana giggled and smiled up at João. "Your girlfriend even thinks you're one."

João mumbled something in Portuguese to himself, running his dish under warm water in the sink, but then looked over his shoulder at me and Ana and actually ... gave us the smallest of smiles. I thought he thought I hadn't caught it, but I had.

After we finished, I grabbed my and Ana's bowls and cleaned them in the sink. João stood off to the side. He must have sent a message in the group chat we had because my phone buzzed in my skirt pocket. Yes, my skirt did have pockets.

Then, João turned to me. "Didn't think I'd see anyone like you washing dishes."

I cut my gaze to him. "That's because you keep thinking that I'm someone I'm not."

Not speaking further on it, he called something to his mom. Then, to me, he said, "We have to go."

Ana jumped up and looked at him. "Wait! Mommy and I made brigadeiros. You should have one before you leave." She opened the fridge and stood on her tippy-toes to reach a plate of twenty balls of what looked to be fudge or chocolate of some sort. "Take one."

Instead of taking one, João took two for himself. I grabbed one and thanked her, saying good-bye as João led me out of the house.

Before I could eat mine, he ushered me to the car. "We're late. The guys are waiting."

Chapter Twenty-Four

LANDON

Running my hands through my messy hair, I stepped into the abandoned warehouse on Kai's street.

Misty had stared at me for an entire half hour while I sat there, trying to find the words to say but feeling too ashamed to speak. If I said them out loud, then they were real. And if they were real, then I was my father.

She had told me that we could talk tomorrow, but I didn't even know if I'd be ready by then.

Kai leaned against a wall with his laptop in his hand, scrolling through it, while one of the Redwood teachers was sitting in the middle of the room, hands and ankles bound tightly to a chair and duct tape over his lips.

I glanced around, brows furrowed. "Where're Imani and João?"

"Don't know," Kai said, closing the laptop and shoving it into his backpack.

"How the fuck do you not know? Where'd they go?"

"I had to meet with Akio to get the stuff. They were supposed to come right here."

The back door opened, and João strode into the room with Imani following after him.

When her gaze met mine, she immediately hurried away from João and over to me, standing by my side and glaring up at me. "Don't you leave me with him again."

"What the fuck took you so long?"

"Where the fuck did you go off to?" João asked, refusing to answer my question.

Imani and João shared a look, and then João turned away and headed toward Mr. Harvey, a Redwood Academy technology teacher.

Finally catching sight of him, Imani widened her eyes and gasped. "What the hell is going on? Why is Mr. Harvey tied to a chair?!"

She went to rush toward him, but João caught her wrist and pulled her back. Kai pulled up a chair for Imani to sit, and João pushed her toward it.

"I told you that you're going to learn about what really goes on in Redwood tonight. So, sit down and shut up."

Clenching my jaw, I cut my gaze to João and adjusted the chair for Imani. "Sit."

Imani blew out a breath and sat down, crossing her arms yet still looking worried. "What's going on? I don't even understand what you're talking about. Mr. Harvey hasn't done anything to anyone." She looked at the graying teacher with a frown. "He's the nicest tech teacher at Redwood."

Kai stifled a laugh and looked at Harvey.

"Why are you laughing?" Imani asked, rubbing her hands on her thighs. "What'd he do?"

I walked over to Harvey and ripped the tape off his mouth. "Wanna tell her what you did?"

Harvey screamed out, snot dripping down his lip. "I didn't do anything."

Grabbing him by his thinning hair, I pulled his head back and hit him straight in the nose. Something I had been wanting to do for days now. Blood spurted out of his nose and stained his white dress shirt.

"Landon, what are you doing?!" Imani screamed and shot up from her chair.

João pushed her back down.

"What did you do?" I asked again, my knuckles soaked in his blood.

"Nothing."

I hurled my fist into the side of his face harder, knocking him over. His body and the chair smacked against the ground, a wheezing sound coming from the old man.

He grunted and shook his head, tears streaming down his face. "I didn't do anything!"

"Landon, stop," Imani said. "He didn't do—"

Kai placed his laptop in her lap. Imani looked down at it in confusion for a second, then stared at it with wide eyes, glancing up at Harvey.

"Did you really ... did you really do this?" she asked, voice barely above a whisper. She stood up, but this time, João didn't push her back down. "Mr. Harvey ..."

"Imani, don't listen to them," Harvey protested. "They're psychos. Look at them."

"That's me!" she said, turning the computer toward him.

On the screen was a recent video of Imani doing schoolwork on her computer in her bedroom, sitting in a tiny little tank top that anyone could see right through. The video was over an hour long, and Imani was doing more than just studying during some parts.

And there weren't only videos of her.

Harvey had hacked into computers of almost every one of his students and had some sort of footage of them—female *and* male students alike. Kai had found it this weekend, and all fucking day, I had been waiting to tear this man's face off for having this one of Imani.

I suspected that he wasn't the only person at Redwood who had done something similar. Harvey was buddy-buddy with the principal and even Redwood's most corrupt police chief. Pieces of shit, if you asked me.

"You see what happens behind the closed doors of Redwood's richest, Imani?" João asked, placing a hand on her shoulder and tugging her back. After snatching the computer from her hand, he nodded to me. "Give him what he deserves."

As soon as the words left his mouth, I snatched a fistful of the man's hair, pulled him up, and threw him back down across the room. He hit the wall hard, some chalky drywall falling down onto him.

Hurling fist after fist, kick after kick at his face, I made a bloody, swollen mess of him, all for her.

Imani screamed and cried, tucking her face away into Kai's shoulder. But I didn't stop. I would do anything for her, anything to keep her out of harm's way. Yet, in this town, nobody was safe from anything.

Chapter Twenty-Five

JOÃO

Harvey lay on the floor in a puddle of his own blood, twitching and bleeding through a gash in his head. Hyped up on anger, Landon stood over him with his jaw clenched and his breathing ragged. I leaned against the wall with my arms crossed.

"That's enough," I said.

It had been almost an hour of slamming Harvey against the concrete and bashing his head into the ground, making him pay for everything he had done to the students in his classes. And surprisingly, Miss Priss over there, who stood next to Kai, had stopped crying and started watching fifteen minutes ago, her full lips parted slightly.

I walked over to Harvey and pressed the tip of my shoe against his neck until he coughed up blood. "Next time you record people without their permission, we will kill you. You don't get another chance." I spit on the pathetic piece of shit and removed my foot, nodding to the door.

Imani stared at us with wide eyes. "You're just going to leave him like this?"

"You want us to clean him up after what he's done?" I asked, curling my lip at her in disgust.

After fucking everything that she had learned tonight, she wanted to help him. The fuck was wrong with her?

She furrowed her brows at me. "If you leave him here, aren't you going to get in trouble? Someone is going to find him and get you all arrested."

My lips curled into a smirk. Maybe I had fucked the good girl right out of her earlier.

"You care about us now?" I asked, chuckling slightly.

She narrowed her big brown eyes at me. "No. I don't care about you."

Landon looked uneasily between us, but I ignored him and decided to push Imani a bit further. She might've been the stuck-up rich girl from the ritzy side of Redwood, but her pussy was damn tight and fun to fuck.

"Lying to us now, too. Next, you'll be kicking the shit out of Harvey with Landon."

Imani balled her small hands into fists and hurled one at my chest. "Why do you have to be the most annoying piece of shit in this town? What is wrong with you? If you leave, someone is going to find Harvey and know that you do business here."

"We have someone who will clean up the mess," Kai said.

I cut my eyes to him, wishing he'd kept his mouth shut because I liked Imani worked up.

After shoving my hands into my pockets, I pulled out a pack of cigarettes and lit one up, walking through the door and into the back alleyway. Landon, Kai, and Imani walked out a couple moments later.

I leaned against my car and held out my hand to Kai. "Where's the shit from Akio?"

Kai pushed out a long breath, reached into his pocket, and handed me some medication. I stared at him, waiting for him to give me all of it, my hand outstretched.

Kai shrugged. "That's all he had."

"You're fucking with me."

"I wish," Kai said.

Glancing down at the medication in my hand, I clenched my jaw and pushed the medication back into my pocket. This wasn't close to enough. Ana needed pills nearly three times every day, or else she'd get sick again. This would barely last her a couple weeks.

"This is nothing," I said.

"It's something," Kai said.

I balled my hands into fists. "This isn't going to last her. She can't survive with this."

Imani furrowed her brows. "Who? Ana?"

Pressing my lips together, I growled, "Yes."

"Why does she need pills? She seemed fine and energetic when I was there."

Landon glanced between us again, face contorted in confusion and hands balled into fists by his sides. "When did you meet Ana? Is that where you guys went?"

I rubbed a hand over my face and groaned. *Fuck.*

Imani widened her eyes and stared at me, cheeks flushing. Swear to God, I bet she couldn't lie for her life. I could feel a fight brewing within Landon over her. But he was the one who had told us that we could share, so I was going to take my fair share of her.

"I had to get something back at home," I lied, knowing that he wouldn't believe me.

Landon looked over at Imani, who didn't look back. He tightened his fists even more and clenched his jaw. "Did he hurt you?"

Imani widened her eyes and turned back to him. "You're the one who left me with him! What does it matter what he did to me? You obviously didn't care if you could just go without bringing me with you. I had to deal with his annoying ass all night."

"He touched you, didn't he?" Landon said, jumping to conclusions again. He moved closer to me, nostrils flared and blood on his knuckles. "What the fuck did you do to her?"

Feeling pissed still because Akio hadn't given us enough medication, I wanted to pick a fight with someone. And it just so happened that Landon wanted one tonight, too.

So, I smirked and said, "Nothing that she didn't enjoy."

Landon shoved me back into the car and growled, jaw clenched hard. I shoved him back, and before I knew it, our fists and blood were soaring everywhere.

<h1 style="text-align:center">Chapter Twenty-Six</h1>

IMANI

For some reason, Landon and João started shoving and pushing and hitting each other. And honestly, I was done with watching people get the shit kicked out of themselves tonight, so I glanced at Kai, who nodded to his motorcycle behind João's car.

I snuck past Landon and João and slipped on the back of Kai's motorcycle with him, grabbing the helmet from him and putting it over my head. It would mess up my hair, but I wasn't about to wait for them to settle their differences, and I kinda wanted to ride on the back of a motorcycle for a while.

If Mom found out, she'd kill me.

He kicked the stand off the ground, started the engine, and looked over his shoulder at me. "Hold on tight."

After I wrapped my arms around his torso, he raced off into the night, leaving the two boys fighting with each other in some back alleyway that I didn't want to be in any longer. Against my forearms, I felt Kai's taut torso and all the muscle underneath. He usually wore oversize shirts, something that hid most of his body, but this ...

God, he was sexy as fuck.

Instead of taking the short way back to the school parking lot, Kai drove through Redwood and toward the Overlook, where we could see the ocean waves splashing against rocks. Nobody was here tonight, but

I had lost track of the time. It could've been bustling earlier with seniors snogging in the back of their cars.

Once Kai parked, he rested one forearm against the handlebar—if that was what they were even called on a motorcycle—and placed the other on my thigh, pulling me closer to him. My skirt rode up my legs, my silky panties flush against his backside.

"You're cold," he said, moving his fingers up my goose bump-covered thigh.

"It's, like, thirty degrees out here," I said, pulling the helmet off and inching even closer to him to see how he'd react.

Kai had always been quieter than the other two guys, and I wanted so desperately to see him more. He seemed like a guy with hundreds of secrets.

When I moved my legs closer to his, he stiffened and gently grasped my thigh without saying a word, rubbing his hand up and down one to keep it warm. Wanting more, something else—like for him to break—I kept one arm wrapped around his torso to hold myself steady, then wrapped my legs around his waist, the heat between my legs growing.

"Imani," Kai said softly, "don't."

"Why not?" I asked, slipping my arms under his oversize hoodie and clutching his muscular abdomen.

He felt so good underneath my fingers, so taut and sexy. I wanted to run my hands up and down his body, slip inside this shirt with him.

Kai glanced back at me with his jaw clenched, yet he didn't stop me.

"I'm horny," I murmured into his ear, not knowing how I was after what I had witnessed.

I moved my hands lower and inched closer to him, wanting him to turn around and fuck me on his bike. But instead, he leaned back slightly and let me run my hand across the front of his black cargo pants. I whimpered into his ear when I realized how hard he was.

"Kai ..."

He reached behind himself, slipped his hand underneath my skirt, and brushed his fingers against my silky panties. "Fuck ..." After a couple moments of teasing me, he pulled away. "I want to, Imani, but Landon's hung up over you so badly. I don't want to overstep."

"Landon isn't hung up over me. He left me with you and João today."

"That's what you think." Kai turned around on his bike enough to look at me. He grabbed my chin and curled his lip up slightly into the smallest of smiles. "You don't know how badly I want to give it to you. And I promise that I will, but not tonight."

Not wanting to push it because Kai was the only calm and collected member of Poison that I didn't mind spending time with, I smiled back at him. "You'd better keep your promises." I pulled the helmet back on and flipped down the visor. "Or I'll come hunt you down and tie you up for it."

Kai started up the engine again, heading for the school. "You wouldn't know how to tie someone up if your life depended on it."

"And you do?"

He chuckled, the sound getting lost in the fall breeze, but there was more than lightness to his laugh.

Chapter Twenty-Seven

LANDON

With a busted lip, I stormed up the stairs to my house to wash my face off in the kitchen sink. I didn't want to deal with Dad right now, but I needed to get this blood off me. Tonight had been fucking annoying as hell.

I'd left Imani with João, and he'd fucked her.

The one fucking guy who had wanted nothing to do with her a couple days ago brought her back to his house to put his dick inside of her. The mere thought made me angry. At least, I hadn't wanted him to fucking lie about it. If he was going to do it, he should've fucking told me. Maybe then I wouldn't have wanted to rip his head off.

Stepping into the house, I inhaled the thick scent of spilled beer and kicked the hundred and one empty beer bottles in the kitchen. I had stopped picking up after Dad once I figured out that he didn't give a single shit. If I picked up one, two more would be on the ground the next day.

"Why don't you stop fucking accusing me of cheating on you?!" Mom screamed at him in the living room. "I haven't done anything. You know that! You have my damn phone tracked. You see everything I do!"

I turned on the water and let it heat up underneath my fingers, sighing through my nose.

"You want to know why I don't trust you?" Dad shouted back, his words slurred. "Because you've done it before with your friends. You whore yourself around at work, flirt with all the customers. I bet you even fuck them in the bathroom because you're so desperate."

Running a towel underneath the water, I glanced over my shoulder to see Mom storming into the kitchen, her eye black and blue and bruises decorating her arms. I tensed up and turned the water off.

Fuck.

Dad was more than pissed off tonight.

"Has he been doing this to you all night?" I asked Mom, wiping some blood off her arm when I should've been cleaning myself up.

She yanked her arm out of mine and continued to grab her coat on the rack. "Don't get in this, Landon."

A couple moments later, Dad stumbled into the kitchen with bloodied knuckles and a sour grimace. "You're not going fucking anywhere. You're staying in with me tonight." He lunged toward her and grabbed a fistful of her hair, yanking her back. "You've slutted yourself out every night this week."

Mom pushed Dad back, making him let go of her hair. I tensed up, knowing that he was about to hit her again. He usually only slapped her around, not saying that was fine—I hated it so fucking much—but I never really witnessed him punching her.

Tonight was different for some reason. He was angrier than usual.

"I didn't do anything!" she screamed.

"Then, why the fuck did you come home with a bruise on your neck?"

I glanced down at Mom's neck to see a blotchy red hickey. My eyes widened slightly, breath catching in my throat at the sight. I stepped forward, pushing her hair to the side to see it better, my chest tightening by the moment.

"Mom," I whispered.

She didn't look me in the eye.

All this time, I had stood up for her against Dad, and she had really been with someone else; she had really cheated on him. In all honesty, Dad didn't treat her right, but she didn't have to lie to me about it, making me feel sorry for her.

"You see what a whore your mother is?" Dad said, grabbing her arm again. "I told you, son, women are only good for one fucking thing. You'll never find a good one. They're all like your mother."

Mom spit at Dad, right in his face, and pushed herself away.

When he hurled his fist down at Mom, I pushed her out of the way and took the brunt of his punch right in the eye. I flinched back and grabbed my face, feeling the pain shooting through my body. Dad stumbled back, then came back at me. I jumped up, pushed Mom into the other room, and dodged his punch.

He stumbled forward and bumped into the kitchen counter, knocking his head off a cabinet and falling onto the kitchen floor, a bump already forming on his forehead.

"What did you do to him?!" Mom screamed, crouching down by his side and taking his head in her hands. She pushed some thinning hair off his forehead and checked for a pulse. "What is wrong with you, Landon?"

My brows furrowed. "What are you talking about? He was—"

Mom stood up and smacked me hard on the cheek. "Don't you dare get in our business again. What happens between me and your father has nothing to do with you. Next time you do, I'm going to call the fucking police. You'd better thank fuck that he's still alive."

I stared at her in shock, not sure what to say or what to do. She had never hit me before.

She pointed to the door. "Now, go!"

"Mom—"

She smacked me again, even harder. "Don't talk back to me. I said, go."

Chapter Twenty-Eight

IMANI

When I pulled up the driveway, I knew that I was screwed. It was after midnight, Mom had probably seen my grade for that test on the school website, and ... I sorta smelled like those Poison boys, drenched in the thick scent of weed and smoke and sin.

Mom stood outside the front door with her plush pink robe, slippers, and headscarf on. With her arms crossed over her chest, she stared pointedly at me with her jaw clenched and her nostrils flared.

Fuck.

She was pissed.

I turned the car off and sat in the cold, hoping that she'd get too cold and walk back inside the house. I could sneak through the back door, run up to my room, and lock my door, saving myself a few moments of her scolding.

"Get your ass out of the car, Imani Abara!"

After bracing myself for the worst of the worst, I pulled the key out of the ignition, put on some perfume I kept in my car, and grabbed my backpack. I had never gotten below an A on any quiz or exam since the sixth grade. Last time I had gotten an A-minus, she had taken away my phone for two days.

Two days!

Once I walked up the stairs, she grabbed my arm and pulled me into the house. Dad sat in the living room in his chair with the remote in his lap and *Monday Night Football* reruns on the TV. He gave me one long, sorrowful look and sighed, muting the television.

"Where the hell were you?" Mom snapped after slamming the door.

"With Allie," I said.

"Oh, really? Because I saw Allie at the grocery store earlier and you weren't with her."

Dammit.

"So, I'm going to ask you one more time. Where were you?"

I sucked in a deep breath, not knowing what to say. Allie was always my only excuse. She would lie for me in a heartbeat, but if Mom had seen her out today ... then she knew I hadn't been with her and knew I had been off with someone else.

So, deciding to be her perfect little girl, I gave her a fake smile, which I knew she saw right through, and said, "I was studying with a couple of my other friends. We're working on a project for American History. I didn't want you to worry."

Mom flared her nostrils. "Do you think I'm that stupid?"

Unable to hold myself back, I threw my hands into the air. "Well, where do you think I went off to, then?"

That was the biggest mistake of my entire life. I should've kept my fucking mouth closed.

"Don't talk back to me, Imani. If you were out studying every night, then you wouldn't have failed your Biology test. Mr. Barnes posted the grades tonight, and you failed it, Imani. *Failed.* My daughter doesn't fail anything."

I pressed my lips together, so I didn't say something snarky back to her. My annoyed ass wanted to say something along the lines of, *Well, I guess I'm not your daughter then*, but I would get grounded for years.

"So, where were you?" Mom asked, tapping her foot.

"Why can't I have any privacy, Mom?" I asked. "I'm eighteen."

"And you're living under my roof."

"But—"

"Don't *but* me. I'm waiting for my answer."

She wanted the truth, but I wasn't going to tell her that I had been out with Redwood's most dangerous gang. Forget them killing me. She'd do it herself and make sure they watched. She could really be a psycho sometimes.

When I glanced over at Dad to see if he had anything to say, he blew out a heavy breath and grimaced. He never said anything when Mom went off on a one-sided screaming match with me. He always kept quiet, not wanting to get in on the drama. But I wished he would say something.

Instead of answering her, I crossed my arms and stood in front of her quietly, which made her even angrier. She stormed to the kitchen and came back with the bottle of wine that I had stolen from Dad the other night, shoving it in my face.

"And this! I found it in your bedroom. What, are you turning to alcohol now? You know what's next? You'll be doing drugs and getting into trouble and flunking out of high school. All the colleges you applied to will pull your application, and you'll end up being like the rest of Redwood's deadbeats."

My eyes widened, and I had the sudden urge to smack her across the face. She had never once made it seem like she was better than anyone on the bad side of Redwood. We donated to them all the time and volunteered together to help them out, but her calling them deadbeats ...

It did something to me.

"Don't you dare call them deadbeats." I seethed through my teeth. "If you don't remember, you and Dad grew up on the bad side of town! You know that it's so fucking difficult to get out of their situation. How dare you belittle them."

Her words had done more than offend me; they had enraged me.

"And look where we are. Everyone we grew up with is still living in the slums, Imani. The Abaras aren't deadbeats like them, and neither are you."

Maybe João and Landon and Kai were right. The Redwood rich were pieces of shit. I hadn't thought so before tonight, but seeing Mom like this ... it made me change my mind. Her true colors had come out.

"You're grounded until you can bring your grade back up to an A-plus."

My eyes widened. "Are you serious?!"

"You'd better get used to being in that room of yours without the alcohol because we're locking it up. All you're going to be doing here is studying for Biology. My daughter will be the top of her class, the valedictorian. Nobody, not even Allie or Akio, is going to pass you up."

<h1 style="text-align:center;">Chapter Twenty-Nine</h1>

LANDON

I shut Imani's bedroom window and walked into her dark room, trying to find the light switch. This place was so fucking big, and I had only been here a couple times. I didn't know where these rich people hid their switches because it wasn't on the fucking wall.

Jamming my shin into the corner of the bed, I stifled a grunt and continued through the room. All I wanted to do was scoop Imani into my arms and hug her. After Mom ... after she had done what she had ... I ... I ... I wanted to see Imani.

A couple moments later, Imani shoved the door open, stormed into the room, and slammed it behind her, turning the light on and locking the door. She clenched her jaw, her fiery brown eyes angry, and twirled around. When she saw me, the anger dropped from her face and was replaced with surprise.

Before she could say anything, I hurried over to her to wrap her in my arms. I didn't want to talk or fight with her. I needed her to fill a part of me that I couldn't, needed her to tell me that everything was going to be all right, needed to feel loved for a couple moments.

But I couldn't ask her.

Words and feelings weren't my thing.

So, I buried my face into her neck and pulled her as close as I could, breathing in her vanilla perfume. She froze for a moment. Then, when she wrapped her arms around my body to hug me, I couldn't stop a tear from racing down my cheek.

Imani might've been pissed at me, but ... she didn't smack me.

She didn't tell me not to get in her way.

She didn't hate me like my parents did.

"Landon," she said, voice soft. She pulled away enough to see my face, but before she could, I swiped the tear away. "What's wrong? Have you been crying?"

Parting my lips, I ached to tell her that I was fine, that I hadn't been crying, that I wasn't hurting on the inside. I didn't want to be broken anymore for her. I wanted us to work out so badly that it hurt. But I was broken, and I didn't even know if therapy could fix me.

So, I pressed my lips to hers and kissed her hard. I didn't want her to ask me any more questions that I couldn't answer. All I wanted was for her to make me feel something good, like she had always done before.

I walked with her toward the bed, pulling off her clothes and placing needy kisses down her neck. She ran her hands all over my body, pulling the bottom of my shirt and touching me how I imagined she had touched João earlier. After I pulled my shirt over my head and undid my jeans, I pushed her onto the bed and crawled up after her, lying between her parted legs, dipping my head to her stomach, and kissing below her navel.

Down her stomach and up the inside of her thighs, I placed open-mouthed kisses all over her body until I reached her pussy. I started to eat her out and interlocked my fingers with hers to keep her from pushing my head away whenever the pressure got to be too much for her. Her back arched, and she grasped my fingers tighter.

When she moaned out, I ground my hard dick against her bedsheets and flicked my tongue against her wet cunt.

"Landon, please," she said in a breathy whisper. "More ..."

I buried my face between her legs and flicked my tongue faster against her clit.

"I need you," she moaned softly. "Please."

I kissed back up her body, sucking on each of her nipples and grasping her small tits. She clenched when I brushed the head of my cock against her sopping pussy. Unable to hold back, I pressed my lips to hers in one lingering kiss, and then I rested my forehead against hers and slowly pushed myself inside of her.

She dug her fingers into my taut shoulders and moaned against my lips.

It felt good to be needed and even better to be wanted by her.

I brushed my thumb against her cheekbone and stared down into her big brown eyes. She wrapped her arms around my neck and pulled me toward her to kiss me again. As soon as our lips collided, I thrust harder into her pussy, pumping in and out and letting my tongue devour her mouth.

When I broke our kiss, I tugged her to my chest. She dug her fingers into my muscle, my heart pounding underneath her soft hands. I pounded into her harder, wanting to both get out all my anger and feel good. My hips hit hers roughly, my cock buried deep inside of her. She clenched hard around me, my cock twitching inside of her tight hole.

I stuffed my face back into the crook of her neck, placed my lips below her ear, and sucked on her skin. My body tensed, and I came inside of her, filling her with my cum. Imani whimpered, her legs trembling around my hips.

After wrapping my arms around her waist, I sat us both up on the bed and kept my cock inside of her, my cum slowly running down our thighs. My lips trembled as I stared at her, at the only person who hadn't fully pushed me away yet. And I hoped to God that she never would.

Chapter Thirty

IMANI

Early the next morning, Mom banged on my bedroom door. "Get up, Imani! It's time for school. You're going in early today to talk to Mr. Barnes about your grade and to see if you can redo your exam."

I rolled over onto my stomach and murmured into the pillow, staring at the moonlight shining through my window. The clock on my nightstand read four fifty a.m., and I cursed Mom for getting me up when she did. Honestly, I didn't know if I'd survive until the end of the school year.

And I wasn't being a dramatic bitch. She was too much all the time.

Landon set his hand on my hip from behind and curled his fingers into my skin. My eyes widened slightly at the feel of him behind me, of sleeping in his arms last night, of being with him intimately for the first time.

And when I said intimate, I didn't mean sex. Landon had *cried* to me last night.

Turning over in the bed, I stared into his light eyes and brushed my fingers across his cheekbone that was swelling slightly. Something had happened to him between the time I left João and him and the time he showed up in my room in tears. And I wanted to find out what it was.

114

"Morning," he said, voice groggy.

My breath caught in my throat, and I wanted to smile at him so bad. But I was still annoyed with him for leaving me with João, so I pushed some of his dirty-blond hair off his forehead and studied his face.

"Imani!" Mom shouted, banging on the door now.

I rolled my eyes and sat up in bed. "Sorry."

After a couple moments, Landon wiped his tired eyes, and then he stood up beside me and tugged on his clothes. The doorknob rattled again, shaking and trembling so hard that I thought the lock would pop right off. Mom had never once been this angry before, and it scared me.

"If you can't open the door, then I'm getting the key!" Mom shouted.

My eyes widened, betrayal running through my bones. I couldn't have any privacy. I couldn't get one bad grade on a test. I couldn't step out of line one fucking time, and I hated it so much. I had no freedom here, none.

I grabbed Landon's hand and pushed him into my walk-in closet, throwing his shoes and his backpack in after him. "Find somewhere to hide, please, Landon."

Just before I was about to close the door, Landon stopped me. "Imani, I—"

"Landon!" I scolded, my nerves getting the best of me. "Please. If she finds you here, she won't ever let me see you again. She'll home-school me, and she won't ever let me leave the house. Please, just ..." I glanced over my shoulder to see the doorknob jiggle again. "Please ..."

When my bedroom door opened, I slammed the closet door closed and hoped that he'd stay inside. If he didn't ... God, I was on the verge of tears already. I didn't want to never see him or Allie ever again. I couldn't lose the only people who kept me sane now.

Mom flicked on the main light. Brightness lit up the room, nearly blinding me.

I shielded my eyes away from her and groaned. "I'm up. I'm up."

"Why didn't you answer me?" Mom asked, hands on her hips and a pointed gaze on me. Her work badge hung from the waist of her skirt, her perfect picture glimmering under the light. "And why do you keep locking your door from me? Are you hiding something? You know we don't keep secrets in this house."

My chest tightened, and my stomach was in knots. "I'm sorry. I just got up. I'm not hiding anything. You know I don't keep secrets, Mama."

"And that bottle of your father's wine that I found in your room last night? That wasn't a secret?"

"I'm sorry," I whispered, tears filling my eyes. "It won't happen again. I've been stressed out lately. I ..."

"Stressed out?" Mom raised her voice at me. "You don't know stress, Imani. Your father and I provide everything for you. You have nothing to worry about. If you lived how we did, growing up, maybe you'd be more thankful."

A tear slipped down my cheek, and I quickly pushed it away. She hated when I cried. In her household, nobody cried. Everyone smiled. Everyone was always happy. Everyone did as she said.

Mom took one look at me, shook her head, and said, "Get ready. You leave in five minutes. I need to get to work, and when I get back, everything should be back to normal. You'll be studying every night this week from the moment you get home to the moment you go to sleep. And we'll see about you going to the football game with Allie on Friday."

With that, she walked out of the room and back down the hall.

"And you'd best be leaving your door unlocked from now on."

I stared at the empty doorway with tears flowing down my cheeks. So she or Landon wouldn't hear, I placed a hand over my mouth to suppress my sobs. I couldn't do this anymore. I couldn't. I didn't have any more energy to give. She had sucked it all out of me these past eighteen long years.

A couple moments later, I shut the door and wiped the tears from my eyes. Landon exited the closet and leaned against the door with a frown on his handsome face and his big arms crossed over his chest. He stared at me with such sorrow in his eyes, but I didn't want pity.

He and the rest of Poison thought I had an easy life because my parents had money.

But this wasn't easy.

Landon stepped closer to me, but I shoved my hands into his chest as the tears flowed down my cheeks.

"Don't touch me."

Yet I continued to push him back and back and back until he hit the wall, and even then, I continued to push him because I needed something. I didn't know what it was.

"You think I'm just some rich girl who has the perfect life."

Shove.

"Well, I don't."

Shove.

"I'm tired of this." I lowered my voice, the pain overtaking me, and buried my face into his chest and cried.

He wrapped his arms around me and pulled me closer to him, gently lacing his hand into my hair and stroking my head.

"I'm so tired, Landon."

Chapter Thirty-One

IMANI

"Good luck," Allie said, shoving her books into her backpack, then swinging it over her shoulder. She glanced over at Mr. Barnes, who sat behind his desk with his face stuffed in quizzes and exams less than a second after our class finished. "You're going to need it with him."

Allie was right. As much as I joked about Allie shaking a little ass for Barnes to raise her exam grade, he wasn't that kind of teacher. At least, that was what I thought. Who knew anymore? Last night, I had thought that Harvey was the best tech teacher to ever grace Redwood Academy, but I knew better now.

"Thanks," I said, gathering my books and giving her a small smile while she walked out the door. "I'll meet you at lunch."

When she and the rest of the class left, I inhaled sharply and walked up to Mr. Barnes's desk. "Hi, Mr. Barnes. Can I talk to you about, um ... something important?"

Barnes looked up at me, then placed his red pen down, nodding to give me the go-ahead. I had been thinking up something to say all morning to him, but I still hadn't found the right words. Never in my academic career had I asked a teacher to redo an exam this big. A quiz maybe.

"I know your policy is that students can't retake exams," I started,

118

feeling the nerves bubble up inside me. "Is there anything I can do to retake it, Mr. Barnes?" I asked, fiddling with the hem of my shirt and gnawing on my cheek.

As much as I freaking hated myself for sucking up to the teacher and vowing that I'd do anything—and I mean, *anything*—to get him to raise my grade, I had to do it to get Mom off my ass.

I didn't think I'd be able to handle staying home every single day until I died.

After inching a bit closer to him, I bit back my disgust. This was how so many girls *and guys* raised their grade and passed at Redwood; I'd just never thought that I'd be one of them. My goal for this year was to fly by without a grade lower than an A-plus.

Thanks to Poison, that goal had been ruined.

"Miss Abara, other teachers at Redwood might accept something like that, but I'm not like them," Mr. Barnes said, looking up at me from his desk. He cleared his throat and pulled off his glasses, intertwining his fingers. "It's usually against my policy to let anyone redo a test, and I don't do it often."

"Please," I pleaded. "I need to redo it. My mom is going to kill me."

Mr. Barnes arched a brow. "Kill you?"

"Just an exaggeration ..." Kinda. "But I really need to redo it."

A couple moments of silence passed, and I could tell that he was going to say no again, which I couldn't let happen. He wasn't like the rest of the teachers here, but ... but I needed to try something.

"I can—"

"You can redo it Thursday before school."

My eyes widened, heaviness falling off my shoulders. "Really?"

"Yes, Imani, really." Mr. Barnes stood. "You and Allie are both at the top of your class. I was shocked when I graded your exam. It was so unlike you. I'll give you one chance to redo the test, and whichever test you score higher on, I'll put that into the system."

Before I knew it, tears burst from my eyes and ran down my cheeks. I had the urge to hug him. He didn't know how much this meant to me; he didn't know that if I didn't retake this exam for a better grade, my whole life would be ruined.

After wiping some tears, I gave him my best smile. "Thank you."

When I walked out of Biology, completely elated, Akio kicked himself off the wall beside the classroom and caught up with me, his books by his side. "You asked Barnes to redo the exam we had last week?"

My brows knitted together. "Were you eavesdropping?"

"I, uh ... no?"

"Why're you asking me about it then?" I asked, stopping and turning to face him.

Akio paused, glanced around, then pulled me into an empty hallway. "Did you fail it because of Poison? I told you that if you get too in with them, they're going to ruin your life. Don't you want to get out of this hellhole and go off to college?"

"Of course I do," I snapped, anger rushing through me.

"If you keep hanging out with them, they'll drag you down."

Unable to stop myself, I shoved his shoulder. "Then, why do *you* keep hanging out with them? Why do you keep supplying them with drugs from your work? If anyone finds out about that, they'll do more than withdraw your acceptance from college!"

Akio ran a hand over his face, then looked over his shoulder. "It's not that simple."

"Yes, it is."

"It's not," he said sharply. "They have dirt on me and my family. If I don't do as they say, then everything my parents have worked so hard for will come crumbling down. And they'll blame me for it."

Crossing my arms, I raised a brow. "What kind of dirt?"

Akio cut his gaze to me. "As much as I like you, I would never tell you."

"Then, tell me what kind of medication you're giving João."

After cursing under his breath, he ripped out a piece of paper from his backpack and scribbled something on it. Before handing it to me, he swallowed hard. "Please, don't tell anyone. They'd have my fucking ass for it."

"I won't."

"Promise me."

"I promise, Akio."

I snatched the paper from him, but he didn't let go.

"I'm only telling you this because ..." He paused and frowned.

"Because I don't want anything to happen to you. João and Poison ... are dangerous—and not in the *I'll cut your throat* kind of way."

Narrowing my eyes at him, I put the paper into my bag. "I don't need you to tell me that." I thought about last night. "I already know how dangerous Poison is, and I don't plan on staying away."

Chapter Thirty-Two

IMANI

After the last bell rang, I walked out Redwood's front doors with Landon beside me. We hadn't really spoken about what had happened this morning, and I didn't know if he cared. He'd hugged me like he did, but I ... I didn't know what he thought of my mother.

With his hands stuffed into his pockets, he walked with me toward João's car.

João didn't look at him, his gaze landing on me instead. "Did Goody-Two shoes redo Barnes's test this morning?"

"You don't know shit about her, João," Landon said, pulling his phone out of his pocket. A text message popped up on his screen, and he tensed, then turned away from us. "I'll catch you guys later."

"Where are you going?" I asked, brows furrowed.

"We're supposed to be—" Kai started.

But Landon was already halfway down the sidewalk.

My heart hurt as I watched him go. All I had wanted was for him to stay a bit longer, so we could talk about what had happened at my house earlier. I needed someone to cry to, and I didn't want to cry to Allie. She didn't know about what had happened, only Landon did.

He had witnessed it.

"Forget him," João said, getting into his car.

After João pulled out of Redwood's parking lot, Kai leaned on his bike and crossed his arms, his oversized hoodie hiding all the muscle that I had felt yesterday. And I so wanted to slip my arms under his clothes again.

"What'd Akio have to say earlier?" Kai asked, a tinge of what sounded like jealousy in his voice.

"Akio?" I asked, my eyes widening slightly. *Did he see me talking to him this morning?*

"After your Biology class."

"You sound jealous."

"I'm looking out for you, Imani."

"In case Akio tries to sweep me off my feet?" I teased, clasping my hands behind my back and rocking on my heels.

Kai smirked, those brown eyes driving me wild.

I stepped closer to him, knowing that I only had a couple minutes before I had to leave. All I could imagine was climbing up onto his motorcycle again and rubbing my pussy against him from behind until I came on his seat and claimed it as mine with my cum. Gosh, I wanted him to fuck me on his bike so badly that it hurt.

"Take me on a ride," I said, gnawing on my bottom lip. "Bring me back to the Overlook."

Kai grabbed my wrist and yanked me closer, drawing his nose up the side of my neck. "You so desperately want me to give it to you alone, don't you?"

I whimpered and moved closer to him. My pussy clenched at the thought of spending the night alone with Kai. Sure, in the heat of the moment, he and the other two guys had fucked me in the restaurant bathroom. But little by little, I had learned a bit about the other two.

Landon was possessive but gentle.

João was a psychotic maniac.

And Kai ... I didn't quite know yet, but, damn, I wanted to find out.

"I want you to do anything you want with me," I whispered.

There was a moment of silence that passed between us, and then he growled into my ear.

"You don't know how badly I want to tie you up," Kai murmured against my skin. "Your arms bound behind your back." He grabbed my other wrist in his hand, tugging them together behind my back. "My belt around your neck." He wrapped his other hand around the front of my throat, tugging me closer to him so his knee slid between my thighs. "Your legs spread wide and bound with a spiral futomomo tie."

"A ... a what?" I whispered, heat growing between my legs.

"Something that'd give me complete control of you, sweetheart."

Unable to stop myself, I ground my pussy against his knee and whimpered. "Please, Kai ..." I inched closer to him, my pussy grinding further up his leg, closer to his bulge. "You're hard for me. Let me touch it. Let me make you feel good."

Hell, I needed it too.

After a tense moment, Kai pulled away with a small smirk on his lips. "No."

"Please, Kai," I whispered, rubbing my clit against his thigh.

Tightening his grip on my wrists, he glanced down to my lips and drew his tongue across his. The thought of him dragging it up my neck or between my thighs made me even tighter.

"If you keep rubbing yourself off on me, you're going to ruin my pants," he said.

My breath caught in my throat. "If you don't like it, then stop me."

God, I really was a horny bitch.

Instead of stopping me like he should've, he sat back and watched me grind myself against his leg and ruin his black cargo pants with my juices. The pressure rose in my core, the thought of him between my legs nearly making me tip over the edge.

"Tell me what else you'd do to me," I whispered, my nipples hardening underneath my shirt. A wind blew and made them even harder, and I ached so bad for him to squeeze them between his fingers.

Kai lowered his gaze to my chest, seeing the imprint of my nipples through my thin bralette. He moved his hand that was around my throat down my chest and lightly—so fucking lightly—brushed his thumb against my nipple. "I'd put nipple clamps on your tits." He brushed his fingers over my nipple again. "Clamp them so tight until you're crying out for me to take them off."

A wave of pleasure rushed through me. "Show me."

He chuckled and continued to gently graze his fingers against my nipples, barely touching me. "No."

"Kai ..."

"I'd stuff your mouth full with a ball gag, let you spit and drool all over yourself."

Behind my back, I balled my hands into tight fists.

"Are you going to come all over me already?" Kai asked. "I haven't even touched you yet."

One last time, I bucked my hips against him, stuffed my face into the crook of his shoulder, and cried out. Wave after wave of pleasure rushed through me, my legs trembling around him. God, this felt so fucking good.

When I finished, he released my hands. After kicking the kickstand of his bike, he started it up, looked over his shoulder at me, and said, "That mouth is going to get you in trouble one day, Imani." Then, he drove out of Redwood's parking lot and disappeared down the road.

Chapter Thirty-Three

LANDON

"My mom hit me last night," I said thirty minutes into my therapy session.

It was the first thing about my life I had said all day to Misty. Truth was that I hadn't wanted to be here yesterday, and I didn't want to be here today, but after listening to Imani's mother scream at her this morning and Imani telling me that she was so tired of it all, I had known that I had to come.

Not only did I have to come, but I had to talk.

I had to want to get better, so Imani had someone.

"She did?" Misty asked, eyes wide. After a couple moments of initial shock—it was her aunt too after all—she straightened out her shirt and looked back down at her notes. "How'd you feel when she did it?"

"Bad," I said, my voice barely above a whisper. "Really bad."

"What else?"

My chest tightened, the words so difficult to say. Saying them out loud would make them real, and if they were real, then I really was worthless to everyone around me, especially Imani.

Biting back my fear, I balled my hands into fists and swallowed hard. "Like I'm not good enough for anyone."

Misty went to say something else, but I cut her off again.

"Imani deserves so much more than me. I'm going nowhere in life. She has her whole life ahead of her, and I'm fucking it up slowly. She failed an exam, smacked me for looking through her phone, and I even heard her mother say that she started drinking."

This was my fault.

I shouldn't have fucked with Imani. I shouldn't have told the guys about her. I should've left her alone and never spoken to her again. If I had, then ... then things might've been different than they were now.

"If you think you're the cause of the problem, why haven't you left her alone?"

"Because I ... because ..."

The words wouldn't come out of my mouth; they were lodged in my throat.

"Because why, Landon?"

"Because I ... I love her," I whispered.

Saying it to Misty felt both relieving and ... something else, something worse.

"You say it as if it's a bad thing," Misty said. "Is she not worthy of your love?"

"It's not that."

"Then, what is it?"

"She's too good for me."

Misty placed her notes down on the table between us and leaned forward, giving me a small smile. "You don't give yourself enough credit for the things you endure at home and the goodness in your heart. And I'm not saying that as your therapist, Landon. I'm saying this as your cousin, who's watched you grow up."

Goodness in my heart? I fucking had none.

"Your parents abuse you, Landon. And still, earlier, you told me how bad you felt when you heard Imani's mom screaming at her. You told me how much it hurt you to see her in pain. Some people would relish in that pain, would love to see other people hurt. But you're not one of them."

My lips curled into a frown, and I gazed at the carpet.

For some fucked up reason, I didn't like compliments like this. I couldn't take them. I always thought people were lying when they gave me one because … I didn't believe the compliment myself. I didn't think I was good. I didn't think I was worthy.

"So, tell me, Landon, why is loving Imani so bad?"

"Because everyone I love always hurts me."

And I was afraid that Imani would, too. I was afraid that she'd realize I was nothing but dirt under her feet and kick me to the curb. I was afraid that she'd realize I wasn't going anywhere in life and that I was dragging her down with me. And I didn't fucking want that.

"What do you want?"

"I want her to love me back."

Misty sat back and smiled at me. "I think that's a good place to end for today."

* * *

After running out of there and away from my feelings as quickly as I could, I sat on the curb outside my house because Mom and Dad were at it again, and I ran through all the messages that Imani had ever written to me, thought about all the hours of video calls we had.

Most of this time hadn't been spent dirty talking. Most of this time had been … spent talking.

Incoming Video Call: Imani

I sat up straight and hovered my finger over the Accept Call button, then finally pressed it. Imani stood in her bathroom, tapping some cream on her face.

She looked down at the phone, brown eyes wide. "I didn't think you'd answer."

"What do you want?" I asked, cursing at myself for letting the words come out of my mouth like that. But I … I didn't want to remember what I had admitted only a few minutes ago. I couldn't have Imani know that I really loved her.

She scrunched her nose and walked into her bedroom, collapsing on her bed with some pillows. "My mom is coming home in ten minutes. I'll be studying all night. I wanted to talk to you."

My chest tightened. "To me?"

"Unless you're busy."

I hopped up from the curb and walked down the street, giving her a small smile. "I have time."

Chapter Thirty-Four

JOÃO

"Where's Mama?" Ana asked, sipping her box of Toddynho.

Ever since Mom had gotten her hooked on it, she refused to drink anything else, even chocolate milk. I didn't blame her, though; Toddynho was so much better than that shit.

She handed me the box and grabbed a handful of popcorn out of the pink bag in my lap. I sipped out of the straw and handed it back to her.

"Mom's working ..." At someone's house again.

After grabbing the remote and turning off the TV, Ana placed the popcorn on the couch beside us and sat in my lap, frowning. "Why's Mama always working? Even after I get home from school."

I rubbed my forehead. I hated when Ana asked questions.

She was far too young to really understand why she had to take pills every single day of her life—because she'd end up dead if she didn't—and why Mom worked endlessly for us.

"To give us a better life."

"But we have a good life," she said with a smile.

Life through a child's eyes must've been so fucking amazing. Redwood slums were far too shitty to be considered a good life.

Everyone looked down on us. Everyone hated us, arrested us, put us down whenever they got a chance and for whatever reason.

Ana would learn soon enough.

"Did you talk to your girlfriend today?" Ana asked, changing the subject.

"Ana, she's not my girlfriend."

"Mmhmm," she said, rolling her eyes and taking another sip of her drink. "She is. Mama even said that she thought so, too."

"When?"

"When you left with her."

I arched a brow at her and playfully dug my fingers into her sides to tickle her. "Take that back."

Ana broke out into a fit of giggles. "Never!"

Her laugh drifted through the air, so childish and gleeful that it made me smile. This was why Mom worked her ass off—to see Ana smile and laugh like this all the time.

"Jooooão! Stop it!"

Chuckling, I released her slowly when the front door opened. Mom walked into the room with dark bags under her eyes and her heels dangling from her fingers.

Ana ran over to her and wrapped her arms around her waist. "Mama! João was bullying me."

I rolled my eyes and shot Ana a playful smile. She returned it by sticking out her tongue.

"Go run the shower, Ana," Mom said, ushering her to the bathroom. "It's late."

"She's already showered," I said, standing and grabbing Mom's bag from her.

Mom gave me a weak smile. "Thank you."

After ushering Ana into her bedroom for the night, I set Mom's bag down on the kitchen table and handed her the food I had made for Ana a couple hours ago. Mom set it on the counter, rubbing a hand over her face and taking out some money from her purse, counting it.

"João," she said, shaking her head, "I can't do this anymore."

"I told you to quit," I said, keeping my voice low so Ana wouldn't hear. "You don't need to sell yourself out. I can take care of us, Mom."

"I will never have enough to support her, João." She collapsed at the kitchen table and shook her head, tears in her eyes. "The money isn't good enough. Ana will get so sick, and ... I'm so done with this life."

My chest tightened, and I sat beside her and pulled her close. "Mama, don't say that."

"It's true, João."

"Quit your job, then. I'll support us."

"With what?" Mom asked, staring up at me and shaking her head. "Where do you get your money? How do you get the pills for Ana? If it's legal, then fine. But if it's not, João, then you need to quit it right now."

I pressed my lips together. Selling pot and beating the Redwood rich to a pulp weren't technically legal, and Mom knew it. As long as I got my money from there, she would never quit her job. What she did might be illegal, but nobody would rat her house. All the people who *could* put her in jail were her clients. But, me? I could go to jail for much longer if someone caught me.

"João ..." She cupped my face in her hands, lips trembling. "I'm dealing with so much. You helping out around the house and with your sister is enough. It's all that is keeping me sane right now. I hope that you continue to watch out for her."

"You know I will."

"I just ..." She looked away from me. "I needed to hear you say it."

My chest tightened, pain shooting through my body. One day, she wouldn't have to sell her body out to anyone who would take it. This was another reason to loathe the Redwood rich.

After pressing her lips to my forehead, she headed to the hallway. "Good night, João."

When she left, I ran a hand through my hair and blew out a breath through my nose. Mom didn't make me angry by telling me that she couldn't do this anymore, and I wasn't even mad that I'd spend the rest of my life taking care of Ana.

What made me pissed was that my son-of-a-bitch father did nothing to help us.

Needing something quick to relax, I snatched my keys and texted Imani.

Me: I'm picking you up.

Chapter Thirty-Five

IMANI

Mom wanted me to keep my door open while I studied, so I sat in my room without any privacy at all and with her checking in on me every five minutes. My phone buzzed on the desk, and I quickly flipped it to read it before she came back.

João: I'm picking you up.

My heart raced, breath catching in my throat.

When I heard Mom's footsteps coming up the stairs, I shoved my phone in my desk and leaned over my books, yawning at the perfect time for her to catch it.

She leaned against the doorframe and crossed her arms. "Why don't you get some sleep?"

I looked over, pretending like I hadn't realized that she was there, and closed my textbook. God, it was about time. It was ten p.m., and I had been studying nonstop since three p.m. She had even brought dinner up to my room for me and wouldn't let me join her and Dad.

"Thanks, Mom," I said.

She gave me a tight smile. "I know you'll ace the test on Thursday."

Once she left my room and closed the door—thank fuck—I hurried into my closet to find a cute outfit instead of the frumpy pajamas that I wore. I needed to get the fuck out of here as soon as humanly possible.

This was the first time in six hours that I wasn't under constant surveillance, and I was going to take advantage of it. If Mom wanted to make my life hell, then I would live it however the fuck I wanted to when she wasn't looking.

After pulling on a plaid skirt and a small white crop top, I slipped on a pair of shoes, grabbed my phone, and made up the bed to make it seem like I was sleeping soundly. Mom's crazy ass would check up on me sometime tonight, and if I wasn't here …

My phone buzzed again.

João: I'm outside.

Peering out the window, I saw a car parked directly across the street with the lights on. I prayed that Mom wouldn't catch me, stepped onto my balcony, and climbed down until I dangled three feet from the ground, holding myself up by the arms.

"Fuck it," I whispered to myself.

I hit the ground with a thud, dusted myself off, and ran off the property to João's car. At lightning speed, I slid into the passenger seat and buckled my seat belt, not looking at him once. "Drive, please."

Seemed like we both needed this.

João didn't say anything to me as he drove out of the community and down some dark alleyway that led nowhere in the slums. I stared at the blank brick wall in front of us, my heart racing in my chest.

We sat there in silence for a few moments, and then I took off my seat belt and climbed into João's lap, needing a release. As soon as I straddled his waist, he wrapped his arms around my torso and crashed his lips down onto mine, his kiss hungry.

In the heat of the moment, I pulled his shirt over his head and dragged my hands over his muscular shoulders, the feel of his hands on my body making me clench. He pushed his seat back enough to give us room and dipped his hand between my legs and up my skirt.

He rubbed my clit through my panties and tugged on my hair with his other hand, pulling my head to the side to give him better access to my neck. Sucking my skin into his mouth, he slipped his hand into my underwear, then his fingers inside of my sopping pussy, moving them in quick come-hither motions.

"Fuck, you're so wet," he grunted against me.

I reached between us and stroked his cock through his jeans. I clenched around his fingers, whimpering at the feel of him. After I undid his jeans and pulled him out, he stuck his wet fingers into my mouth and lined himself up with my entrance, the head of his cock pressing against my core.

Unable to stop myself, I sucked his fingers, no matter how deep he pushed them. Instead of letting me lower myself onto him, João grabbed my hip in his other hand and pushed me down, filling me up quickly.

He thrust up into me hard and fast, dipping his head and taking one of my covered nipples between his teeth. I laced my hand into his hair and tugged him closer to me, the pressure building quickly in my cunt.

João kissed back up the column of my neck and grabbed my hair again, tugging on it roughly. When he sucked my bottom lip between his teeth, biting down so hard that he nearly drew blood, a toe-curling orgasm ripped through my entire body. My legs trembled around him, my mind feeling numb in a good way for once tonight.

A moment later, João stilled inside of me and pulled away, resting his head back against the seat, eyes rolling back into his head. His cum dripped down my thighs, and I whimpered at the feeling of being so full.

I could only imagine what it'd feel like if all three Poison boys came inside of me at once.

After crawling back into the passenger seat, I blew out a heavy breath and closed my eyes. João redid his pants and started the car.

"Where are you taking me?" I asked.

"To Landon's."

Chapter Thirty-Six

IMANI

When João and I walked into Landon's basement, Landon and Kai sat on his couch, passing a bong.

Landon glanced over his shoulder and tensed when he saw me, his eyes hazy. "What are you doing here? Shouldn't you be at home, studying?"

"I finished studying," I said.

Landon stood and glared at João. "Why'd you bring her here? She should be at home."

"She can be anywhere she fucking wants to be," João said, tossing his keys on the coffee table. "What, are you her mom now?"

Landon turned back to me. "Imani, you know that if she find—"

João pushed him back. "Why don't you shut the fuck up, Landon? I'm not in the mood to fuck with you right now. You've been pissy since the other day."

"Don't fucking push me," Landon said, shoving him back.

My heart raced as I glanced back and forth between the two.

"I don't get what your problem is. Are you really that fucking jealous that I slept with her?"

Landon's jaw twitched, and João gave an empty laugh.

"You want me to show you how I fucked her, huh? Is that what this is all about?" João asked, grabbing me by the waist and bending me over the couch forcefully. João stepped between my legs, pulled up my skirt, and unzipped his jeans, grinding his bulge against my underwear. "I'll fucking show you how I fucked her, Landon, so we can get this over with."

Emptying his jean pockets, João tossed a pack of cigarettes onto the couch, then picked up his phone. "Pull down your underwear, Imani. I'm going to fill you with my cum again for this asshole."

I glanced up at Landon, secretly loving that possessive yet lustful look in his eyes, and pulled down my underwear to my knees. João pulled out his cock, rubbed it against my entrance, and thrust himself into me like he had done earlier.

"I'll record it for you, too, so you can watch me fuck Imani over and over again. Let you fucking jerk off to it anytime you want since you're so obsessed with the idea of me fucking her behind your back."

My pussy tightened even more around him when I looked over my shoulder and saw that João had actually turned on his camera and started recording this. He grabbed a fistful of my hair, forcing me to look back at him as he burned this into his phone forever. Sliding his hand from my hair to around my jaw, he stuck two fingers into my mouth.

I stared back at him, delight rushing through my body, and sucked on his fingers like I had sucked on his cock the other night, milking all the cum out of it. João forced me to arch my back and pulled me closer to him, turning the camera around and recording him sucking on my neck, leaving a blotchy red hickey, then sticking his fingers farther into my mouth until I gagged on him.

"You like watching me fuck your girl, Landon?" João asked against my neck. "Because I fucking love being inside her tight little cunt, the way she whimpers on my fingers." He glanced up at him. "What, are you jealous?"

Landon's jaw twitched, and I tightened around João at the mere sight of it.

"Lie down on the couch," I said to João, desperately wanting Landon inside me, too. "I want to ride you."

João lay back on the couch and pulled me on top of him, setting me down on his cock, his phone still in hand. I reached for Landon, wanting him inside of me, too. Landon glanced once more between João and me, his shoulders tense but his cock hard in his jeans.

"Fuck me from behind, Landon," I demanded. "I want two cocks in my pussy."

Landon grunted, and then he undid his jeans and pulled out his cock, spitting on it and pressing his head against my entrance and against João's. João stilled and spread my legs wider to give Landon room; otherwise, my pussy would be too tight for both of them to fit.

When Landon thrust into me too, both of their cocks in my pussy, I placed my hands on João's chest and moaned, the slight pain turning to pleasure. They were both so fucking big, stretching me out farther than I should go.

With João under me on the couch and Landon behind me, I slipped my fingers under the waistband of Kai's jeans and tugged him closer to me. He slowly undid his belt and tugged it off of him, wrapping it around my neck like he had promised and buckling it on one of the tightest settings.

He curled the end in his hand and tugged it up, forcing me to look up into his dark brown eyes. "Open your mouth," he ordered.

My pussy tightened around João's and Landon's cock, and I opened my mouth for him. Kai undid his jeans and pulled out his huge cock, sticking his head into my mouth and waiting for me to take the rest of him.

When I went to suck more of him into my mouth, he tightened his grip on the belt to hold me in place, then grabbed the phone from João.

"I didn't say you could have it." He slid his tongue across his teeth. "Beg to suck on it, Imani. You've been nothing but desperate for it lately."

I wrapped my lips around the head of his cock, sucking lightly and looking at the phone. "Please, fuck my throat." I sucked a bit harder on the head of his cock, flicking my tongue out. "Please, Kai, please."

Kai pulled the belt forward, in turn pulling me forward and forcing his cock to slide into my mouth. My eyes widened and filled with water when he hit the back of my throat almost immediately. He was so fucking big, and with this belt snapped around my neck, I wasn't sure how he'd fit down my tight throat.

"More," Kai said.

Opening my mouth, I gargled and gagged on his cock, begging for him to give it to me, my throat making noises I had never heard before. Spit and drool rolled down my chin, the pressure rising in my core.

Tightening his grip on the belt even more, Kai slid himself all the way down my throat until my lips met the base of his cock. I stared up at him and the camera with teary eyes. Every time that João and Landon pounded into me, they sent Kai farther and farther down my throat.

Landon placed his hand on the back of my head, lightly grabbing a fistful of my curls and bobbing my head back and forth on Kai. My throat closed around him, and I had a sudden need to breathe. I placed my hand on his thigh to push him away slightly, but he held me in place.

"You can hold on for a little longer, Imani."

He took my hand off his thigh and placed it on my throat.

"Jerk me off inside your tight little throat, and I'll let you breathe."

Blinking back the tears, I wrapped my hand around my throat below the belt and stroked him up and down as quickly as I could. My pussy tightened even more around Landon and João, the pressure rising quickly. I didn't know how much longer I'd last.

"Please, come inside me," I gargled on Kai's cock, spit and drool dripping down my chin.

I felt like a dirty whore.

And I loved it.

"Take the phone, Landon," João ordered. "Record us filling up her cunt."

Landon pulled out of me and grabbed the phone from Kai. João wrapped his arms around my waist to hold me tighter to him and began pounding into me as quickly and as roughly as he could. He moved my body effortlessly up and down his cock, and then suddenly, he stopped, grunting into my ear.

"The second load you've gotten from me tonight, Imani," João said.

When he pulled out of me, I glanced over my shoulder to see Landon holding the phone to record but staring at me. He put a knee between mine on the couch and shoved his cock into me, grabbing me by Kai's belt and tugging my head back so he could see my face.

"Fuck, Imani …" Landon grunted, his thick cock shoving João's cum even deeper.

My pussy pulsed around him, the pressure rising high in my core.

Suddenly, Landon stilled and spilled his cum into my pussy too—two big, thick loads of cum sitting in my cunt. When Landon finally pulled out, Kai walked over and wrapped one arm under my right leg, pulling it into the air and onto his shoulder. I collapsed on João and stared back at Kai, my pussy tightening more and more.

The bottom of Kai's sweatshirt was lifted enough for me to see his abs underneath, and I couldn't help but cry out in ecstasy at the sight. I was being fucked by the three Poison boys, the most cutthroat gang in all of Redwood.

And I fucking loved every second of it.

With Landon still recording, Kai thrust deep in my pussy and stilled, then thrust in and out a couple more times, pushing all of their loads deeper into me. After he came and pulled out, I moved off João and leaned back, cum rushing out of my pussy.

João grabbed his phone back from Landon, keeping the camera on and pointed at me. I sat back on the couch with my legs spread, my knees near my chest, their cum dripping down my thighs and almost onto the couch.

My pussy pulsed over and over, pushing out more cum by the second. Wave after wave of pleasure rushed through me, my mind numb. João knelt down between my thighs, the camera near my pussy.

"Push our cum back into you," João ordered. "Show us how much of a cumslut you are."

Heat rushed through me, and I found myself catching the cum on my fingers and shoving it back into my pussy. There was so much of it that when I pushed my fingers as deep as they would go, more cum came out the sides, leaking and dripping down my thighs.

I scooped it up and pushed it back inside of me, more cum dripping out. Over and over, I pushed it back inside of me, my fingers moving faster and the pressure rising up in my core again.

"She loves it so fucking much that she's going to come again," João said.

The base of my palm smacked against my clit each time, and the pressure was almost too much to handle. Kai snatched the belt strap and tugged it down so my face was on the video, and I watched as I touched myself.

Landon walked behind me, tugging on my aching nipples and murmuring into my ear, "You love being a little slut on camera, don't you?" He tugged a bit harder, and pleasure surged through me. "Touching yourself. Turning on anyone and everyone watching. Making yourself"—he flicked his fingers against my nipples, and I screamed out—"come."

My pussy pulsed even harder and wilder than it had before, all of their cum being pushed out and rushing down my thighs until it stained the couch. I pulled my knees together and to my chest, my legs trembling harder than they ever had.

When I finally came down from my high, João still had the camera on. "Taste your cum-filled cunt, Imani. Show us how much you love when we fill you with our cum."

And so I pulled my wet fingers from my pussy and sucked them into my mouth, staring at the camera and loving every single moment of this. Landon was right. I loved the attention on me when on camera. I was a filthy little slut for them.

Chapter Thirty-Seven

LANDON

After I finally convinced Imani that staying at my place wasn't a good idea, I pushed her ass through her bedroom window and hopped in after her. She smoothed out her shirt and dusted off her knees, yawning.

"Thanks for coming home with me," she said. "You don't have to stay if you don't want to."

"I actually"—I blew out a deep breath—"wanted to talk to you."

She sat on the bed and patted the mattress next to her. "About what?"

"I ... I don't want ..." I ran a hand through my dirty-blond hair and sighed. "I don't want to fuck you up, Imani. Since I found out who you were, you've been drinking and sneaking out and doing shit that you never did before. If you stay with us anymore, we'll fuck you up. *I'll* fuck you up."

"Landon," Imani whispered, curling up in my lap and burying her head into my shoulder, "you've never been the problem. You and Allie are the only people that I've looked forward to talking to these past few months, and you're the only one who knows how bad my mom is. Allie hasn't even heard or seen her like that."

Suddenly, tears streamed down her face, and I didn't know what to say. For the longest time—before I found out that Imani was the girl I had been talking to online—I had thought she, along with the rest of the rich girls at Redwood, had it easy. I hadn't even thought that they had any real problems, not any problems like I did with my family.

"My mom puts so much pressure on me to succeed," she whimpered, body trembling in my hold. "I have to think about everything I do before I do it—to either make sure it is up to her standards or to make sure that she won't find out about it. It's constant, and I ..."

She hiccuped and slammed a hand over her mouth to muffle her sobs. Body trembling harder, cries becoming louder, she wrapped her arms around me and hugged me as tightly as she could, tighter than anyone had ever hugged me before.

And I hugged her back.

Not because I felt bad for her, but because I knew what it felt like to live my life and always feel like I wasn't ever good enough. This wasn't a thing that kids from the Redwood slums experienced. Even rich girls like Imani faced it, too.

"You don't have to be perfect for me," I said gently into her ear.

"I know," Imani whispered, voice trembling. "That's why I ..."

She paused, and I so desperately wanted to hear her say those three words to me that I had said aloud to Misty earlier. I wanted to hear that Imani loved me, too, because I had never heard those words spoken by anyone ever. Not Mom and definitely not Dad.

"That's why I appreciate you so much," she finished.

Disappointment washed over me, and those evil thoughts about not being good enough rushed through me—the seeds that Dad had planted years ago and watered daily. It fucking hurt. But while I slipped even lower into myself, I still held her tight because she hadn't let go yet.

After wiping her tears, Imani kissed me on the cheek. "Don't think you're the problem because you're not." She glanced at the time on her phone and stood. "Please, stay with me. I want you to."

I took her hand in mine. "Okay."

When Imani disappeared in the bathroom to prepare for bed, I lay back on the bed and blew out a breath. I'd never felt this way before, and it made me nervous. Nothing had felt this good before, and if it did ... it always came crumbling back down on me.

What if this was all a put-on? What if this was all an act to hurt me?

Imani's computer screen lit up with a notification from Discord. I glanced over at it, my heart leaping in my chest and all those horrid thoughts racing through my mind. Desperately trying not to make the same mistake as before, I paced around the room and stared at the ground. But from the corner of my eye, I saw another message pop up on her computer.

God, did I have the urge to go over and check who it was.

Even after our heart-to-heart, even after everything, I still didn't feel good enough. I still felt like any girl that I dated would cheat on me, would talk to other guys, would send them the same pictures that she sent me.

With Poison, I didn't care as much. As much as I hated the thought of Imani being alone with João, I trusted João and Kai. We'd all been shit on by Redwood and made a pact to stay together and take down this town, one corrupt man at a time.

But someone other than João and Kai ... scared me.

It was wrong. I knew it was.

I trusted Imani not to be like that. I forced myself to trust her.

Yet I still couldn't quite get it out of my system.

Those thoughts were torture themselves.

After pacing around the room for a couple more moments, I stopped at the window and glared out of it, my heart pounding in my chest so hard that I physically felt sick. My stomach twisted in knots, body heat rising.

What if those were messages from other guys she had met online?

The thoughts themselves were comfortable in a weird way. They were filled with anxiety, but I had thought them so many times that all those what-ifs were more comfortable than the thoughts I knew to be true—Imani wouldn't do that.

Still, no matter how much I wanted to puke up my dinner, I stayed glued to the spot.

Imani came out of the bathroom a couple moments later with her hair wrapped up and cream on the blemishes on her face. Brows drawn together, she hurried over to me. "What's wrong? What happened?"

"Nothing."

I couldn't tell her. I didn't want her to hate me for being so insecure.

"Why do you look like you're going to puke then?"

"I'm anxious."

She widened her eyes even more and moved closer. "About what? Landon, tell me. What's wrong? I've never seen you like this before. You're scaring me."

After a couple moments of silence, I finally came out with it. The pressure and anxiety were building up too fast and too heavily for me to hold it in. I would either come out and say it or burst into tears.

"Your messages," I whispered.

"Messages?" she asked, confusion written all over her face. "What messages?"

"On your computer."

Looking over her shoulder, she widened her eyes. "Did you look at them?"

"No!" I said quickly, so she wouldn't think I snooped on her again. "I just ... I don't want to lose you, and I ... I'm so fucking insecure about this, about us. I don't even know what we are, don't know if you want there to be an us. And ... And I'm sorry," I whispered.

"Sorry for what?"

"I'm sorry that I'm this way," I said again, tears welling up in my eyes. "I'm sorry that I can't stop thinking like this. There's something wrong with me. But I'm working on it—I promise I am. I'm trying to be better for you, Imani, but it's so hard."

Imani widened her eyes and pulled me to the bed and onto her lap, gently stroking my hair. "Landon, you don't have to be sorry, and there's nothing wrong with you." She kissed my forehead. "I don't understand why you ... why you don't trust me."

I tensed in her arms and wanted so desperately to disappear. Everything in my life, up until her and Poison, had fucked me over. I wanted to forget about it all and start over; I wanted to feel something else other than hurt and pain and anxiousness all the time.

"Please, talk to me, Landon."

I didn't want to tell her. I couldn't. I didn't want her to look at me any differently, and I ... I hated thinking about it. I'd rather bottle it all up and deal with it myself, on my own terms, by shoving my fist into another corrupt teacher's skull.

But I took a leap of faith because that was what Imani had done with me.

"My mom," I started, my voice barely above a whisper. "My parents ... they ... they ..."

"They what?" Imani asked, eyes growing even wider. Tears threatened to spill out of them.

"They abuse me."

The words stung on my tongue. They made me feel and seem so fucking weak. I had never said them aloud before, and besides Misty, nobody else knew about what Dad did to me, except João and Kai.

Imani was the only other person I had ever told.

"My mom cheats on my dad, and my dad always, always puts her down and looks through her phone. When he gets really bad, he hits me. And my mom is no better. She ... she hit me for the first time last night." Tears streamed down my cheeks. "I never feel good enough for anyone."

She stared at me, unblinking, for the longest time. And then when she finally did blink, tears spilled down her cheeks. She pushed them away quickly, but more ran down her face. "I'm so sorry. Oh God, Landon, I didn't know. If I had, I would've never ..." She stared down between us, bottom lip trembling, then gently grasped my face. "I would've never slapped you."

My body heaved back and forth, and I pressed my lips together so tightly, so no cries would come out. I hated feeling fucking weak like this. I wanted to take care of myself. I didn't want anyone to feel bad for me, especially Imani.

But I couldn't stop the tears, and I couldn't stop the cries tumbling past my lips. Imani held me tighter to her, resting my head above her heart, and I listened to the quiet and rapid thump. She pressed a hand to her mouth to suppress her cries and pulled me even closer somehow.

"I'm so sorry. You should never have to go through that."

"If you stay with me, Imani, I'm going to fuck you up."

"Don't say that," she scolded, forcing me to look into her big brown eyes. "You're the only person I care about anymore. I can't lose you."

Chapter Thirty-Eight

IMANI

Thursday morning, Mr. Barnes had to reschedule the makeup exam until lunch period. So, I waited outside his classroom, bounced on my toes, and prayed that I hadn't forgotten all the information that I'd memorized these past few days.

I could not fail this test.

If I had to, I'd sleep with the damn fucking principal to get him to change my grade.

Okay, I definitely wouldn't do that, but I was getting desperate.

When the lunch bell rang, students flooded out of the classroom.

I waited until everyone came out before I peeked my head in and gave Mr. Barnes a small smile. "Please say that you're still available for the retake."

Mr. Barnes stood up from his desk with an exam in his hand, placing it on the desk in front of him and knocking on the wood. "All ready. Apologies that I had to reschedule. Some kids TP'd my house."

"TP'd?"

"Threw rolls of toilet paper over it. I didn't know kids still did that."

"Me neither. Do you know who it was?"

"I suspect Poison, but who knows?"

Stifling a laugh, I slid onto the chair. Oh, if it was Poison, they

147

wouldn't throw toilet paper at his house. They'd do something more along the lines of setting fires at every one of his doors and windows and letting the poor man's house be engulfed in flames while he lay peacefully in bed.

"Good luck, Miss Abara."

After grabbing a pencil from my backpack, I flipped through the pages of the exam and took a deep breath. I could pass this with flying colors. I knew all the answers already. Once I aced it, I hoped that Mom would finally loosen her leash on me.

* * *

Thirty-five minutes later, I shoved my pencil into my backpack and handed Mr. Barnes the exam. I had checked it over at least three times, made sure all my answers were correct, and even written explanations as to how I'd gotten to that answer. I left no room for interpretation.

"I'll grade this during my free period and get it to you before the school day ends."

"Thank you so much," I said, hiking my backpack up on my shoulders. "This means more than you could even imagine."

Once I departed from class, I hurried to the cafeteria. Lunch ended in about ten minutes, which meant that I had exactly two minutes to eat and eight minutes to gossip with Allie about how much of a bitch my mom had been.

Allie didn't know everything, but she knew that I thought Mom was annoying.

When I reached the cafeteria, I eyed Poison's table. They sat alone —Landon smoking a cigarette inside the building, João with his feet up on the table, and Kai probably doing something illegal on his laptop.

Instead of sitting with them, like I kind of wanted to, I collapsed on the stool in front of Allie and sighed.

She shut her Biology textbook and pushed her glasses up her nose. "How'd it go?"

My lips curled into a smirk. "I aced it."

She grinned. "I knew you'd do good. Now, you get to come with me to the football game tomorrow."

I rolled my eyes. "If my mom lets me."

"She will." Allie nudged me from across the table. "As long as you're coming with me and *not* those three boys who are so damn infatuated with you that they can't ever look away." She glanced behind me. "Yuck, gross."

Unable to stop myself, I glanced over my shoulder to see Poison whispering with each other now and looking over at us. I turned away, knowing that I'd see them after school, and leaned forward. "They are not obsessed with me."

Allie snorted. "Yeah, okay. Keep telling yourself that."

"They're not!"

"Okay, I know that I hate them, *buuuuut* ... have you"—she leaned forward again and wiggled her eyebrows in my direction—"ya know, done it yet with them? I need the freaking deets, woman! I feel like I haven't talked to you in so long."

My lips curled into a small smile. "Maybe ..."

Allie smacked her palms onto the table, making some people, including Jace, look over at her from the popular table. She moved her hand in a come-here motion. "Give it to me now. Was it one-on-one? Two-on-one? What about you all together?"

I gnawed on my bottom lip. "A bit of everything."

"Girl." Allie placed a hand over her heart and closed her eyes. "You're telling me that you got gang-banged by three hot guys and didn't tell me?! God, you're living every girl's literal wet dream, I'm telling you."

"I don't know about that," I said.

My life was far from a fantasy, but maybe the guys were making it a bit better.

Chapter Thirty-Nine

IMANI

I leaned against João's car alongside Landon with my head on his shoulder. It was Thursday afternoon. Mr. Barnes had graded my exam already as a ninety-eight percent, and Mom had finally let me have the night to myself. Even if she hadn't, I would have snuck out anyway, so it didn't *really* matter.

But if she caught me, I wouldn't hear the end of it.

"What are you doing tonight?" I asked Landon.

Part of me wanted to reach out and intertwine my fingers with his. I never had a boyfriend before, and I didn't know if that was what he wanted to be to me. But I liked Landon a whole lot more than just wanting him to be my fuck buddy.

Even after the other night, when Landon and I had told each other everything, he didn't seem to want to get closer—physically at least and definitely not in public. Maybe that would make the whole relationship thing real for him, and he wasn't ready quite yet. I didn't know.

Kai and João walked out of the side door of Redwood, looking awfully suspicious as they approached us.

"What's up?" Kai asked. "We hanging out tonight?"

"Uh ..." Landon stuffed his hands into his pockets and pulled out his phone. "No."

Glancing over his shoulder, I tensed. Three text messages from a girl named Misty.

Misty: Are you coming over today?
Misty: Landon, are you going to answer me?
Misty: You're thirty minutes late.

Jealousy rushing through me, I stepped away from Landon and pressed my lips together. The first thought that popped into my head was that Landon was seeing another girl. It was so fucked up, but he had put the thought into my head.

This had happened to Allie, my best friend, before—when her last boyfriend had told her not to worry about anything and then he ran off with the captain of the cheer team. Sometimes, the people who worried about someone cheating on them the most were the ones doing it behind their back.

Instead of accusing him immediately, I crossed my arms to keep my hands from shaking. "Who's Misty?"

Landon widened his eyes and thrust his phone back into his pocket. "Nobody."

I parted my lips, glancing between Kai and João, who stood around us, looking as confused as I was.

"Do you guys know who Misty is?" I asked them, furrowing my brows and feeling nothing but hurt rush through me.

Both Kai and João shook their heads, so I turned back to Landon. "Who is she?"

Landon turned his body from me, arms crossing over his chest and his shoulders sinking in on himself. "She's nobody, Imani," he whispered, shaking his head like he had done the other night when he didn't want to talk to me. "Nobody you need to worry about."

"But you ..." I took a deep breath to keep my voice from trembling, but it didn't work.

"Is this why you've been bailing on us all week?" João asked, narrowing his eyes.

Kai mumbled something, then pulled out a pack of cigarettes, sticking one in the corner of his mouth. I stared at Landon's tense back and wanted him to say something, anything that would get me to believe him. I didn't understand what was so bad about it. If he wasn't seeing someone else, then why couldn't he tell us?

"Who is she?" I asked again, desperate. "Landon—"

"She's nobody!" Landon snapped, walking away in the same direction he did after school every night this week. "Can you guys stop it? I don't want to talk about it, Imani. Not here and especially not now."

Before he could get far, I stepped forward. "Are you cheating on me?" I asked, the words coming out louder and more heartbreaking than I had wanted them to.

We weren't even a couple or a thing—honestly, I couldn't tell you what we were.

But this felt like betrayal.

Landon stopped in his tracks, tensed even harder, and looked over his shoulder, shaking his head. "I wouldn't do that to you," he said, his voice barely above a whisper. "You know that I wouldn't, Imani. I lo ..." He paused and apparently decided to change what he was about to say. "I wouldn't."

A wave of hurt washed over me, my stomach twisting into tight knots. I shouldn't assume; that was what Landon had done the other day, and it put him into a world full of hurt. But seeing another girl's name pop up on his phone, and he wouldn't tell me how he knew her ... that was a little suspicious.

I had told him who those guys on Discord were.

And I had also told him that I didn't talk to any of them anymore.

Here Landon was, disappearing every day after school without an explanation and with a girl asking him when he was coming over. He was late to seeing her by, apparently, half a fucking hour.

"Then, who is she?" I whispered, aching for answers.

There was so much hurt in his eyes, so much pain. He glanced over at Kai and João, brows furrowing in agony. Then, he turned toward me and frowned. "I'll tell you later."

"After you fuck her?" I asked, the words slipping right out of my mouth.

As soon as they did, I slapped a hand over my mouth and glanced down at the gravel. It was wrong, so wrong, but I couldn't help it. What if he was? He had been way too adamant about my messages. What if that was his way of trying to ... trying to hide something himself?

"Imani," Landon said tensely. "I'm not going to fuck her."

"Go," I snapped, pressing my trembling lips together. "Fucking go."

"Imani …"

"You're already late, Landon."

"Imani, come on," Landon said, stepping forward and grasping my arm. "She's my cousin."

"Your cousin?" I asked.

Maybe I was ticked off this week or so damn tired and moody because I had to study for hours on end to retake a test that these damn boys had made me fail the first time, but I didn't quite believe him.

I needed some time to myself, needed to calm down, and definitely needed some sleep.

Right now, I knew I wouldn't be able to think straight. I knew I'd get more and more annoyed the longer he stayed here, and I didn't want to hurt him by saying something rude if he was telling the truth. His parents had already done so much shit to him; I didn't want to be another source of pain.

"Go, Landon," I whispered, tugging myself away. "We can talk later."

Turning away from him, I pulled João's car door open and slid into the passenger seat without his permission, staring at Landon's departing figure through the tinted windows and biting my lip to hold back a whimper.

That man meant more to me than I had thought he did.

If Misty really wasn't his cousin, I didn't know what I'd do.

Chapter Forty

JOÃO

I wasn't in the mood to fuck, but Imani had slid into my passenger seat after Landon pissed her off. Hell, he fucking pissed me off too. He had been sneaking around this past week and skipping out on shit we had to do, all to see some chick named Mindy or Misty or some shit.

"Where are we going?" Imani asked once I started the car.

"Why don't you shut your mouth and you'll see? You're the one who got into my car," I said to her, wanting her to get angry. She was hot when she pursed those thick lips together and glared at me.

Maybe I *was* horny.

Imani glared through the windshield. "Why do you always have to be a dick?"

"Why do you always want to ride one?"

She cut her gaze to me and curled her lip up in disgust. After rolling her eyes, she stared back out the window and shook her head, the frown reappearing on her face. "Do you think Misty is actually Landon's cousin?"

Gripping the steering wheel a bit harder, I drove toward my house. Ana would be home soon, if she wasn't already. For some fucking reason, her day care always fucking got out early, and the bus dropped her off before I even got home some days.

"Landon has a lot of cousins," I said, strumming my fingers against the wheel. "But I've never met a Misty before, never even heard of her either. It could be on his mom's side. He never really talks about them."

Imani stared out the window. "Do you think he'd cheat?"

"Are you two a couple now?" I asked, kind of feeling pissed off at the thought.

Staying quiet, Imani shrugged. "I don't know. Landon isn't really good with relationships."

"If you want someone who's good with relationships, you've met the wrong gang."

Once I pulled up to the house, I slammed my door closed, leaving Imani in the car, and walked toward the front door. Ana had a key, but if she was home, the door would be unlocked. As many times as I told her to lock the door, she never did. When I went to turn the knob, it wouldn't budge.

"You are literally the most annoying turd that I have ever come across." Imani stepped out of the car and crossed her arms at me.

Behind her, a bus pulled up to the curb, and Ana hopped out, her pigtails bouncing in the wind like they always did.

"João!" she shouted, hurrying over to me.

After wrapping her arms around my leg, she glanced up at Imani. "And João's girlfriend!"

Once Ana finished hugging Imani, I grimaced at Imani and shoved my key into the door. I didn't like the way she and Mom thought that Imani was my girlfriend or how much Ana liked Imani. I didn't plan on keeping Imani around that long, anyway.

I hoped Landon's thing with her would pass quickly because no girl got in the middle of Poison, especially a rich one like Imani. She wouldn't last a couple months, watching the shit that we did. I was surprised that she had stayed after we kicked the shit out of Harvey.

Ana wrapped her hand around Imani's and led her into the house, switching on the light and grabbing a couple boxes of Toddynho for her and Imani. I turned on the TV and switched it to Ana's favorite channel, the words all in Portuguese. Imani wouldn't understand any of it, but she was going to sit down and endure it all like I did almost every afternoon.

Ana sat on the opposite side of the couch as me, wiggling her eyebrows at me as she left the only room in the middle for Imani. Imani sat down on the small couch between Ana and me, our thighs touching.

"What are we watching?" Imani asked, sipping her carton.

"You won't understand it," I said.

Ana turned her body toward me, narrowing her little eyes and tossing her pigtail over her shoulder. "It's in Portuguese, but I'll teach you it. Don't worry about João. He's a meanie and a bad boyfriend."

Imani stifled a laugh and turned toward her. "He is a bad boyfriend."

God, they were annoying.

And so, for the next hour, I listened to Ana teach Imani every damn word of her favorite show. I'd bet Imani retained none of it. The words were probably too throaty and nasally for her to understand anything.

The front door opened, and Mom came home early. Ana ran over to her, smiling from ear to ear and asking her what we would have for dinner. My smile faltered as Mom looked even more tired today than she had yesterday. Every fucking day, she looked more and more drained, less and less happy anymore.

"I'll cook for you, Mama," I said. "Why don't you rest?"

When Mom saw Imani behind me, she shook her head. "No, João. I'll do it."

Imani must've picked up a couple new words because she stood up beside me and shook her head, giving my mom a soft smile. "It's okay. We can do it."

After Mom nodded, she took Ana in the back room to prepare her for dinner.

Imani followed after me to the kitchen, clapping her hands together and giving me a smile. "What are we cooking?"

I grabbed a couple things from the cupboard. "You aren't cooking anything."

"*Ensin-ah* ... meh?" Imani said, scrunching her nose. "Is that how you say it?"

"Are you asking me to teach you?"

"No," Imani said, eyes wide. "I'm telling you to teach me." She stood on her toes beside me. "Teach me how to make your favorite

Brazilian dish and then maybe teach me some Portuguese. Ana was just flying through the words during her show."

My lips curled into a smile, and an unknown lightness was in my stomach. Imani actually wanted me to teach her Portuguese and how to make my favorite dish that Mom made? I almost didn't believe it.

So, I handed her some ingredients and a bowl, watching her crack an egg against the counter. When she put it into the dish, I leaned against the counter.

"What'd you and Landon talk about the other night? He seemed different this morning."

Imani tensed and stirred the ingredients. "We talked about my mom."

"About how she gives you everything?"

"No," Imani said, voice harsh. "About how controlling she is. She grounded me the other night, forced me to study for ten hours straight, and refused to give me any privacy anymore." Imani's lips trembled. "You think I have a perfect life, João—I know that you think that. But I don't. I want to be normal sometimes, too."

Brows furrowing slightly, I stared at her for a long time, trying to peel apart her lie, searching her face for any kind of deceit, but it wasn't there. Imani was telling me the truth about her family as much as I didn't want to admit it.

After a couple moments, she placed the spoon down and turned toward me, frowning. And then, to my surprise, Imani wrapped her arms around my torso and rested her chin on my sternum. "I don't know what you're going through with your sister, but ... I hope things work out. I hope she gets better."

My entire body tensed. Why was she doing this? Why did she care?

"If there is anything that I can do to help, I will help you."

"No, you won't," I said, the words coming out as a mere whisper. "I don't believe it."

"You don't have to believe me, João." She pulled away from me and returned to stirring, her back turned toward me. "You think you're the only one who has problems. You think nobody else is nice enough to actually help you, but that's because you don't ask for help. You assume we're all bad people."

"I don't assume," I said, my throat closing up. "I know."

"How?"

"My dad." Those two words tumbled out of my mouth before I could stop them.

I expected Imani to turn on her heel, snarl at me, and ask what on earth a scumbag like him could do to someone like me, but she continued stirring.

"He works with Jace Harbor's father. He has all the fucking money in the world, just like your parents." I stepped next to her at the counter, but I didn't look in her direction. "But the rich don't give a fuck about anyone, even their own children."

Imani glanced over and pushed some hair off my forehead. "I know that all too well."

I dug my fingers against the counter until they turned white. "When he lived with us, my father did drugs for as long as I could remember. One night, he had a party, had a bunch of his shitty fucking friends over to get high, got my mom drunk enough that she couldn't stand straight. Used needles all over the floor from his friends. My sister …"

Pain shot through me at the memory. I should've fucking been there to stop it.

"Ana wasn't even fucking two yet."

Imani widened her eyes. "What happened?"

"She crawled on a bunch of used needles. One of those sons of bitches gave her HIV."

Chapter Forty-One

IMANI

"No," I whispered.

I smacked a hand over my mouth to hide my sob. This couldn't be. Ana couldn't have HIV. She couldn't live day after day, feeding herself pills for the rest of her goddamn life. *I ... who ... fuck.*

João stood beside me, jaw twitching and fingers pressed so hard against the countertop that they turned white. I didn't know what to say to him. That had to be one of the most fucked up things I had ever heard.

How could a father let that happen? How could someone live with themselves after letting their daughter crawl all over bloodied needles? Ana's life was and would forever be in danger, especially if she didn't get medication.

No wonder João hated his father and all the Redwood rich.

Instead of telling him that it was okay—because this wasn't in the slightest—I placed a hand on his back, slid it around his torso, and ended up hugging him from the side, holding on as tight as I could.

"I'm sorry, João," I whispered into his shoulder. "I'm so sorry this happened to her."

João stayed quiet for a while longer, the only sounds coming from Ana in the tub with her mother. Pulling away from me, João turned his back. "Don't cry, Imani. There's nothing you can do about it. It happened, and I'm the only fucking person who can help her now."

"João"—I placed my hand on his back again, refusing to let him move away from me—"you don't have to do this alone. I want to help you. If you had trusted me from the beginning—"

"What would you have done, Imani?" João snapped, turning toward me and seething. "Spread gossip about her all over Redwood? Made her the laughingstock of the fucking town? Huh? You can't do shit for her."

My lips trembled. "I don't know what I can do, but ... I want to try."

I needed to do something, figure out who had given her the illness, find his father, retrieve some medicine so João didn't have to worry about finding it for her anymore. He looked like he was driving himself insane because of this.

"I'll get you something," I said even though I knew that he didn't believe me. "I promise."

"Don't make empty promises."

"All I want to do is help."

"I shouldn't have even told you," João said, shaking his head.

"Then, why did you?"

"Because I ..." He paused and swiped a hand across his face, the wicked and rageful glare dropping. "I'm tired of doing this alone."

Stepping closer to him again, I pushed some hair out of his face. "You have Poison, and you have me now. You're not doing this alone. If you let me, I'll help you without spreading rumors, without telling everyone, and without leaving like your father."

João stared at me for a couple moments. "How do I know I can trust you?"

"Because I'm not going to leave you upset tonight," I said, letting my fingers drift down the side of his face. "Let me stay here tonight with you. Let me show you that I don't care about how fancy the house is that I stay in, how expensive the food is, or how perfect you think my life is."

João stared at me for a couple moments, lips twitching. "You wouldn't."

"Watch me." I pulled out my phone and dialed Mom's number,

stepping toward the front door. "Mom"—I lowered my voice and walked out onto João's sidewalk in the middle of the Redwood slums —"please, can I stay over at Allie's house tonight? I've been in the house, studying all week, for hours on end. I think it'd be nice to recharge."

Funny thing was that I'd rather spend the night here, in the shitty side of town with a man that I hated, than go back home and face the devil herself. If that didn't say how terrible my life was, I didn't know what could.

"It's a school night, Imani," Mom scolded through the phone. "No."

My stomach tightened, and I had the urge to smash my phone to pieces and throw up my lunch. I fucking hated her so much. She could never let me do anything that I wanted *or* anything that I needed.

"Please," I whispered.

Desperate.

That was what I was.

And for once, it wasn't for one of the Poison boys.

"Imani," Mom said, voice sharper, "if you can tell me which question on the exam that you got wrong this time around and give me the correct answer, I'll let you stay the night over at her house."

"So, that's what this is about?" I snapped. "You won't let me stay because I got a ninety-eight percent and not a perfect one hundred, huh?" My stomach twisted, and my throat closed up. Hot tears threatened to spill down my cheeks. "God, I can never do anything right for you, can I?"

"That's not what I—"

"Yes, it is!" I sobbed, stepping onto the pothole-covered street. Ugly, fat tears streamed down my cheeks. "It always is. I'm never good enough for you. I try so hard, so freaking hard, Mom, and I can never please you."

I could barely get out any comprehensible words anymore. My nose was running, my tears were racing into my mouth, and my body was heaving. I squatted down in the middle of the most fucked up road I had ever been on and hugged my knees to my chest, needing something.

"I'm not good enough."

The words really set in.

"I will never be good enough."

"Imani, baby, you know that—"

"No, Mom, I don't know," I whispered, the pain almost too much to bear. "I don't know what you want of me anymore. I'm trying my hardest, and you still hate me for it." I knew the words coming out of my mouth would get me my ass kicked later, but ... I couldn't stop them.

"I don't hate you, Imani," Mom said, voice steady. After a moment of silence, she sighed. "You can stay at Allie's for tonight. Please, text me tomorrow before you head to the football game. I want to make sure you're okay."

I stayed quiet. For the second time tonight, I didn't know what to say.

"Okay?" Mom repeated.

"Okay," I whispered.

I didn't even know if she could hear me, but I didn't want her to know that I couldn't stop crying, that the tears wouldn't stop falling down my cheeks like a fucking river, that my chest was tight, and that my heart was telling me that she didn't love me.

My own mother didn't love me.

"Have fun, sweetheart."

"Okay," I whispered.

I felt so empty as my body heaved back and forth. Why did I feel so alone?

"Good night," Mom said.

"Good night."

And with that, I shut off the phone, slapped a hand over my mouth, and posted my other arm on the concrete road, fingers digging into the asphalt. Pain shot through my body. No matter how hard I tried, I couldn't stop it.

It kept coming.

It suffocated me.

João approached me from behind, his feet padding against the road. I tensed and quickly wiped away my tears, not wanting him to see how much of a mess I was. For some godforsaken reason, he hated me and maybe even thought I was being dramatic. I wanted to be strong for him tonight.

As much as he probably wanted to see me hurt, I didn't want to give him that satisfaction. He didn't fucking deserve it with all the shit he had put me through and all of the fucking pain I felt every day.

Yet, instead of barking at me that I had it all so I shouldn't be a crying mess, João stopped behind me and said, "Get up, Imani." His words were harsh, almost cutting right through the thin layer of sanity that I had left.

When I stood, I crossed my arms over my chest and turned around to glare at him, hot tears still welled up in my eyes. I didn't know if I wanted to stay anymore or if I should leave and vow to never see João again.

He was—

"Come here," João said quietly, as if the words were foreign on his tongue.

I stared at him for a couple moments with my eyes widening, and then ... I hurried toward him and wrapped my arms around his waist, my face buried in his chest. He wrapped his arms around me and held me tight.

Chapter Forty-Two

LANDON

Leaning against Imani's car, I pulled out a pack of cigarettes and stuck one into my mouth. Seeing her get out of the car with João this morning pissed me the fuck off, and I hadn't been able to think clearly all fucking day.

Fredrick even kicked me out of last fucking period. I had been waiting for classes to end for the past forty minutes, so I could talk to Imani and try to make up for hiding Misty from her for the past week.

Imani hadn't answered any of my calls or texts last night, and I needed to talk to her so badly. Last night, while Mom and Dad were having another fucking screaming match upstairs, I had made the hard decision of telling Imani about Misty.

I didn't want Imani to think I was cheating on her because ... that feeling sucked more than I wanted her to know. I just didn't want her or any of the other guys to look down on me for getting help through therapy.

Kai hadn't needed anything after his father died, and João thought that only rich kids had therapists. Technically, in Redwood, it was true. Nobody in the slums could afford that kind of shit, especially when all of the therapists catered to the rich. No matter how fucking accepting they acted, they didn't care about all the poor kids because we couldn't give them any money.

At least Misty liked being paid in weed.

The bell rang, and a couple moments later, people started to spill out of the doors. I lit the cigarette, nerves shooting through my body, and paced in front of Imani's car.

What if she doesn't believe me? What if she doesn't want anything to do with me? What if—

After taking a deep breath, I tossed my cigarette to the ground and stomped it out with the heel of my boot. Misty had told me to stop thinking in what-ifs but ... fuck, it was so hard. It was comfortable. That was all that I had fucking known for the past eighteen years.

Imani walked out of the front doors, her hair in two puffs on top of her head and her gaze on her phone. I frowned and rubbed my sweaty hands together, my heart pounding. Fuck, I hated feeling like this. I fucking hated it.

I couldn't wait until tonight. João had some fucking asshole we needed to deal with later, and I really needed to get this tension out somehow. And smashing someone's face in was definitely the only way that I liked to do it, too.

"What are you doing here, Landon?" Imani asked, approaching me and crossing her arms. Under the gray clouds sitting overhead, Imani's eyes looked darker than usual, so closed off and distant.

I grabbed her hand, and she let me.

"I want you to meet Misty." The words came out of my mouth so quietly that I didn't know if she heard them.

But her eyes widened, and she got all quiet. "Who is she?"

"You'll see."

I grabbed her hand and walked with her down the street toward Misty's house. Since it was Friday, we weren't supposed to be meeting today, but she told me that she'd be around until six tonight, and I needed to pay her anyway.

"Is she really your cousin?" Imani asked, tensing. "João said that he hadn't heard of her."

"Yes, she's my cousin."

"Are you sure?"

After glancing over at her, I stopped on the sidewalk and took her chin in one of my hands. "Yes, Imani, I'm sure she's my cousin. I wouldn't be able to see her if she wasn't. She's ... she ..." My throat seemed to close up when I tried to tell Imani who she really was and what she did for me.

All I felt was ashamed to say that I was so fucked up that I needed therapy.

"She's who?" Imani asked.

A couple moments passed, and I grabbed her hand tightly again and continued walking toward Misty's house, passing all the fucking mansions and sports cars parked in the driveways of people who had shit I had never had and never would have.

"You walk all this way every day after school?" Imani asked, breathing heavier. "Jesus Christ, she must be good at whatever the hell it is she does for you." After a couple moments, Imani stopped and hiked her thumb back in the direction of Redwood. "You know, I could have driven us."

"We're close," I said.

Imani sighed softly and continued beside me, inching closer every moment. "I'm sorry that I didn't call you back last night. I wanted to give myself space. I don't want to hurt you unintentionally, and that's all I seemed to be doing yesterday."

I tightened my grip on her hand and squeezed, not knowing what to say. I didn't do apologies well. Hell, I didn't do anything with relationships well. What was I even supposed to say back to her?

When I spotted Misty's house, I made a beeline for it, cutting through people's yards and driveways, stepping over their plants. All I cared about was making sure Imani believed that I was trying so hard to get better for her.

Banging my fist against the door, I waited with Imani, my heart racing. Once Misty answered the door, there wasn't any turning back. Imani would know the secret I had been keeping from her to protect myself.

Fuck.

Maybe I should leave.

Misty opened the door. "Hey, Landon." She looked over at Imani and smiled.

"Imani, this is Misty ..." I said slowly, my throat drying. "Misty, Imani."

Misty held out a hand for Imani to shake, and Imani grabbed it hesitantly.

"How do you know each other?" Imani asked her.

"I'm Landon's cousin and his therapist now, too," Misty said.

Imani stared up at me with wide eyes. "Your therapist?" she whispered, eyes glossing over. She parted her lips to say something, but no words came out for the longest time. And then she finally frowned. "Landon, I'm so sorry that I … I didn't believe you."

Handing Misty a bag of weed, I ushered Imani back down Misty's walkway. We weren't supposed to stay, anyway. I just wanted Imani to know that Misty wasn't anyone she needed to worry about.

"It's okay," I said.

"No, it's not. I accused you."

"It's fine, Imani."

She grabbed my hand again. "Why're you seeing her?"

"So …" I paused. "So I can be better for you."

In the middle of Redwood's richest neighborhoods, Imani stopped, turned toward me, and kissed me right on the mouth, her smaller arms wrapping around my shoulders and pulling me closer. My heart thrashed against my rib cage.

It was stupid, but I had never kissed a girl I liked this much in public, like … this.

"You don't have to do that," she said when she pulled away.

I rested my head against hers and pulled her closer. "Yes, I do. For you and for me. I don't want to lose you."

Chapter Forty-Three

IMANI

Walking down the bleachers with Allie during halftime, I looked into the parking lot and on the street for the guys. I hadn't seen them since school ended, except Landon. Poison rarely showed up to football games, probably thought that only rich kids like Allie and I went to them, but I kinda wished that they had tonight. I had been hanging out with them about every night this week, and not seeing them tonight felt off.

After last night with João and even earlier today with Landon, I was starting to … maybe … miss seeing their annoying asses constantly. They were bad people and even worse influences, but they were all a bit misunderstood. At least, João and Landon were. I hadn't gotten a chance to crack Kai yet.

"If my mom asks, I was with you last night," I said, grabbing a hot dog from the concession stand and bouncing on my toes to keep warm.

When some raindrops hit my face, I pulled my hood up over my hair and stared out onto the football field during halftime. The cheerleaders shouted at the stands, dressed in the smallest and tightest outfits the higher-ups at Redwood could find for them.

Allie wiped some rain off her glasses and grabbed her soda. "Do I want to know?"

I grinned at her and hooked my arm around hers, walking back up to our seats in the stands. "Hmm ..." I said, tapping my chin, then resting my forehead against her shoulder. "Probably not. You'd yell at me, like Mom did."

"Your mom yelled at you?" Allie asked. "For what?"

After unwrapping the tinfoil around the hot dog, I scrunched my nose. God, Redwood had all the money in the world, yet they still couldn't buy hot dogs that didn't smell like ass. Go figure.

"Trying to ignore me, so you don't have to answer?" Allie teased.

Once I collapsed on the bleachers with the most annoying brats behind me, I took a bite of the hot dog and sighed. "You know how I redid that test for Barnes? I got a ninety-eight percent—*ninety-fucking-eight*—and she had to scold me for missing one question. I'm so done with it." I tightened my hand around the hot dog. "I try so hard, Allie, just to get screamed at."

Allie frowned at me and pulled me closer. "Don't listen to her. You're in, like, the top five of our class. Who cares if you get first or not? We've both already applied to colleges, our fate is sealed, so ... it shouldn't matter at this point."

"I know," I whispered. "I can't deal with the constant pressure. If I fuck up, she makes sure I know that I did, and she punishes me for it."

After grimacing, Allie stole one of the fries from my plate. "Yeah, but at least she cares, right? She could be like any of the other parents in Redwood and not give a fuck about their children anymore."

And while I knew that she was trying to cheer me up and look at the positive side of things, it didn't make me feel any better. Mom didn't really care about me. If she did, she would understand that I couldn't be perfect all the time. Nobody could.

"Speaking of people who don't give a shit ..." I started, clearing my throat and thinking back to my conversations with João last night, after he told me that Ana had contracted HIV from some careless rich pricks. "Do you know any of Jace's father's friends?"

She glanced over her shoulder with her brows furrowed. A cold fall wind drifted through the stands, her hair blowing against her glasses. After pushing it away, she frowned and leaned closer to me to shout because the crowd started cheering.

"Harlan's friends? Not really. Why?"

I thought back to João last night, my heart aching. The look in his eyes—damn it, I'd never thought I'd see such despair from someone like him. Though I knew that I would never ever be able to find out who it was or who had done that to poor Ana, I wanted to at least see if I could help.

Maybe then, João would start really trusting me.

If I could help him in any way I could, I so would.

"I was talking to a couple of the guys ..." I started, gnawing on the inside of my cheek. "And one of them mentioned something about Harlan's friends doing drugs, like hard drugs. Does Harlan do that kind of stuff?"

"Not that I know of." Allie scrunched her nose. "At least, I hope that he doesn't. I don't want my mom to get into that kind of stuff. He's completely taken her away from me, and I hate it so much."

"Me neither," I said and grabbed her hand. "If you find out any information, please, tell me. I can't really answer any questions about it, but ... but I need you to trust me on this. If you find out who does it, please, I—"

"You're not trying to get Poison business, are you?" Allie asked.

"No," I assured. "Just, please, trust me."

After a couple moments, Allie wrapped her arms around my shoulders and pulled me closer to her. "Sure, I'll do that for you, but I don't want you getting into any trouble with them. Promise me that you won't."

"I promise, Allie."

"Imani!" Akio shouted from across the stands.

He stood at the very bottom and waved at me, looking so out of place here. Akio never—and I meant, *never*—went to football games. He had told me that his dad didn't let him, but I knew that he just didn't like attending them. None of his friends went, anyway.

Allie glanced down at him and scrunched his nose. "Is that Akio?"

"No, it's Jace Harbor."

She playfully shoved me. "Hey, it's not my fault this rain is making my glasses foggy."

After shooting her a grin, I glanced back down at Akio to see him pushing past people to walk up the bleachers, and then he slid into our bleacher with us. "Do you have room for one more?" he asked.

"Decided that you finally want to watch Redwood kick everyone else's asses on the field?" Allie asked him.

"Actually ..."

Akio glanced at me, and I scrunched my nose. Why'd he look over at me like that?

"I want to talk to you after the game is over."

"It's only halftime," I said awkwardly, thinking back to the other day when Kai had told me to stay away from Akio because he didn't like it, because he was jealous of him. Still, this felt kinda ... weird. "It'll be at least an hour before the game ends."

"I have time," Akio said, shoving his hands into his pockets. "It's important."

Chapter Forty-Four

KAI

"You should be here," I whispered to Dad.

Rain poured down around me, drenching my bike parked on the side of the road. I shifted from foot to foot, coating my boots in a layer of thick mud, and fell to my knees in the middle of the cemetery. My fingers brushed against his gravestone.

"It's not fair."

I squeezed my eyes closed, the rain hiding the fucking tears that threatened to spill down my cheeks. Dad would hate that I wanted to cry for him. When he had been alive, I'd wished that I could spend more time with him, but … he had his other family, too. I used to hate his kid, but … she was just like me now.

Broken.

My phone buzzed in my soaked jeans pocket.

João: You coming?

After drawing my fingers against the words etched in Dad's gravestone, I pulled out a flask of bourbon—his favorite drink—took a sip, and poured the rest over the grass above his casket. Then, I stood up and forced myself to walk back to my bike.

I didn't come here as often as I should, and I made sure not to come when his other kid came to see him. She didn't know about me, and I wanted to keep it that way. That was how Dad had wanted it.

When I hopped onto my bike, I secured my helmet and pulled out my phone again.

Me: I'm busy tonight.

Truth was that I needed to take a break. I needed something other than watching Landon smash someone's head into a concrete wall. I wanted to relax tonight even if it was only for a couple moments.

So, I glanced one last time back at the gravestone, started the engine, and drove to Redwood. Imani was at the football game tonight, which should be ending in the next few minutes, if it hadn't already. I wanted to see her.

After parking on the side of the road and watching all the students spill out of the bleachers and stumble back toward the parking lot—half of them drunk off their asses and the police not doing shit about it—I spotted Allie Hall walking by herself out of the stadium.

I placed my helmet on the bike and shielded my face from the rain, jogging up to her. "Where's Imani?"

She paused and readjusted her glasses, pointing over her shoulder. "Under the bleachers to try to stay away from the rain. She's talking to Akio now. She should still be there."

"Thanks," I said, slipping into the stadium with my hands balled into fists.

Within a couple moments, I spotted Akio talking tensely with Imani. I would've been fine with it, but I had told Akio to stay the fuck away from her earlier this week.

And that fucker obviously didn't like to listen.

So, I stormed up to them and shoved Akio back. "What the fuck are you doing?"

Akio stumbled back into the metal bleacher, and Imani stared up at me with wide eyes.

"What are you doing, Kai?"

"Putting Akio back in his fucking place," I said through gritted teeth.

Fuck, I had so much rage inside me tonight because of the memories of Dad that *I* wanted to hurt someone. Forget wanting to rest. Akio thought he could go around touching what didn't belong to him.

"I don't see Landon anywhere, ready to kick my ass," Akio said, regaining his composure. "I think I'm good to talk to whoever the hell I want to talk to, Kai. You're not going to do—"

I pulled the gun out of the waistband of my jeans, shoved him against the steel beam that held up the bleachers, and pressed the muzzle against his abdomen. Out of sight of all the teachers and police roaming around, I made sure to slam it into his rib cage so fucking hard that he knew not to fuck with me.

My day had already been shit.

"I told you not to fucking talk to Imani," I said through gritted teeth, my face inches from his. "Next time, you'd better listen to me, or I'll put a bullet straight through your fucking skull. Do you understand me?"

Akio pressed himself as close to the steel beam as he could get and nodded. "Yes."

But I stepped closer to him, so Imani wouldn't see me with a gun in my hand, threatening to kill one of the top students at Redwood because he had talked to her. I rarely did shit like this, but Akio kept talking to what was ours.

When I finally let him run off like the scared boy he was, I hid the gun from Imani, turned around, and tucked it into my waistband.

"What are you doing?" Imani whispered, staring at me with wide eyes, then glancing down at my waistband of my jeans, where I had hidden my gun. She shifted from foot to foot and gnawed on the inside of her cheek. "With a ... with a gun?"

"What are you doing, talking to Akio?" I asked through gritted teeth.

I usually never got this pissed, not at Imani, and the truth was that I wasn't really. I just couldn't stop thinking about how the rich in Redwood got away with so much shit, like killing my father and making it look like an accident.

"You threatened him with a gun." She moved closer to me and glanced down at my waistband again. "Do you always have a gun on you? Even when we're in school?"

"You're not going to like my answer," I said. "You should get back home. It's late."

She sucked in a breath, glanced down at our feet, and inched her thighs closer. After a moment, she pressed them together and grabbed my hand, placing it right over her pussy through her leggings. "If you slip your hand into my panties, you'd know that your answer has done nothing but made my pussy sopping wet for you."

Fuck.

My jeans tightened around my crotch, my dick hardening.

I had wanted to wait, had been desperate to wait to take her. But tonight, all my emotions, wants, and needs had been thrust to the forefront. I wanted Imani, and tonight, I would have her.

My hand cupped her mound, and she pressed her thighs even closer together. I had been inside her pussy before, and I knew how tight she could get, but fuck ... I had wanted to spend the night alone with her for so long, so fucking long.

"Touch me," she taunted. "Let me show you how wet your possessiveness made me."

Before she could slip my hand into her leggings—under the damn Redwood football bleachers—I snatched it away and nodded to my bike. "Come on. I'm not going to fuck you here."

I had a better place with a whole bunch of toys I could use on her.

A place where she'd beg to come again and again.

Chapter Forty-Five

IMANI

"Where are Landon and João?" I asked, sliding onto Kai's bike behind him.

"Out."

"Is it a good idea that they're alone?"

They might have been getting along better since the other day, but I didn't quite like the fact that they had both been ready to cut, stab, and kill each other. Having them together *and alone* didn't seem like the smartest idea that Poison had had.

"Probably not," Kai said, shoving the helmet over my head and sliding onto the bike in front of me. He started it up and looked over his shoulder. "Hold on tight, Imani. It's slippery outside."

Fine by me.

I inched closer to him, pressing my breasts against the back of his chest and looking over his shoulder as he zoomed by all the drunk Redwood students who had decided to head over to Carter the quarterback's house for a celebration party tonight.

Raindrops smacked against the helmet visor, a breeze giving me goosebumps. Kai drove away from the high school and toward the slums, approaching the Overlook first. His bike kicked up rainwater behind him, splashing me slightly, but I didn't care.

All I could seem to think about was how fucking sexy Kai had looked, holding that gun earlier. Don't get me wrong; I didn't like guns in the slightest, *but* seeing Kai—the least aggressive person out of all of Poison—pull one out and hold it to Akio's stomach, *for me* ... that did something to me.

Something bad.

I wrapped my arms around Kai's abdomen and pulled the visor of the helmet up. "Pull over," I said, spotting the Overlook down the road. There was no way in hell that I'd be able to wait much longer for wherever he was taking me.

And seeing as he pulled over beside the Overlook, he couldn't either.

Waves crashed against the rocks below. Rain poured down against us, my clothes sticking to my body.

He turned the bike off and looked over his shoulder. "We shouldn't stay out here for long, Imani. It's pouring."

After tearing off the helmet, I set it on the ground beside the bike and moved closer to him. I hooked one leg over his from behind. My pussy ground against the gun in his waistband, and I couldn't help but grow warmer.

I didn't care if it was raining. I didn't care that my clothes were soaked all the way through. And I certainly didn't care that I was shamelessly grinding myself against him in public. Nobody would come out in this weather, anyway.

Instead of telling me no like he had last time, Kai placed his hand on my thigh and rubbed the sticky, wet leggings back and forth, his hand getting closer to my core every single time. I wrapped my arms around his waist and groped his bulge through his jeans, stroking.

Kai glanced over his shoulder at me, brown eyes dark under the moonlight, placed his hand on the side of my face, and pulled me closer to him to kiss me. Ecstasy rushed through my body, my nipples hardening under my shirt.

"Fuck," I breathed into our kiss, stroking him harder.

Unlike he had the other night, Kai lifted me up and set me on his lap. I ground my pussy back and forth against his hardness, the rain plastering our clothes to our bodies. With one hand around the back of my neck, he slipped his other hand into my leggings and touched my aching cunt.

"Oh my gosh," I whispered into his mouth.

Waves crashed onto the rocks below us, the harsh sounds and the way Kai's fingers moved around my clit driving me higher. I grabbed the bottom of his sweatshirt and pulled it over his head, letting the rain drench his white V-neck until every one of his muscles was plastered against it.

Kai grunted. "I want to fuck you so badly."

I undid his belt buckle and slid down his jeans zipper, stroking his cock back and forth. The pressure rose in my core, my toes curling. My hair stuck to my face, and lightning struck through the dark sky.

"Fuck me," I pleaded. "Please, Kai ... I can't handle it any longer."

Setting my legs on either side of his seat, I desperately ground my pussy against his hardness. I pressed my mouth back against his, sucking on his lower lip like I would his cock—desperate. So fucking desperate.

After unzipping my jacket and tearing it off me, Kai moved his hands up my torso and groped my small breasts, his mouth dropping to one of my nipples that was plastered against my wet shirt. He bit down slightly and tugged, a wave of pleasure shooting through my body.

I gripped his shoulders and continued to grind myself against him as he teased my breasts, tongue flicking out against them and gaze focused on my eyes. After wrapping one arm around my waist, he trailed his lips back up my chest to my lips. He lifted me into the air, stepped off the bike, then set me back down on the seat sideways.

Kai pulled the gun out of his jeans and tossed it onto the asphalt beside us, and then he grabbed the waistband of my leggings and underwear and pulled them off me. Right in goddamn public, but fuck it.

Nobody would show up.

Not at this time and especially not in the pouring rain.

He grabbed my hips and pulled them all the way to the edge of the seat, kneeling between them and pressing his warm mouth to my cunt. He rested my thighs on his shoulders, his tongue moving in quick, tortuous circles around me, lapping at my juices.

Grunting again, Kai held my legs steady as they quickly began shaking around him, his biceps flexing against my thighs. Pressure rose in my core. My body tensed up. I sucked in a sharp breath. Then, I came all over him, my moans getting lost in the sound of the downpour.

"Please," I begged, my pussy pulsing.

Kai stood up in front of me and shoved his pants and underwear to his knees. If he hadn't had a hold on my waist to keep me on the bike, I would've dropped to my knees and sucked him off until he came all over my face.

After resting his forehead against mine, Kai lined his cock up with my entrance. When he kissed me hard, he shoved himself into me, sliding every inch of his huge cock into my tight hole. I dug my fingers into his back and moaned into our kiss, my pussy wrapping around him as tight as it could.

"Fuck, Imani," Kai murmured against me, thrusting in and out. He sucked my bottom lip between his teeth and pulled back on it. "You're the sexiest fucking woman I have ever met, and your cunt ..."

I tightened even harder.

"Your cunt is tight as fuck."

"You feel so good inside me," I whispered into his ear, holding on to him as tightly as I could, my eyes closed from the rain.

Every time he pumped into me, the pressure rose in my core.

Down the road, headlights pierced through the dark sky.

I clenched on Kai and glanced over my shoulder. "Kai, we should stop."

"We should," Kai mumbled against me, thrusting even faster into me, biting and sucking on my neck, breathing ragged. "But I want to feel your walls pulse around me when I come deep in your pussy."

The car drove closer to us, and I felt myself about to tip over the edge again at the mere thought of being caught with one of the Poison boys' dick inside of my pussy. Redwood's good girl turned oh-so bad.

Kai thrust one last time, deep inside of me, and stilled. I exploded around him, my pussy pulsing over and over on his cock, milking out as much of his cum as it could get, as the car pulled up behind us.

Chapter Forty-Six

IMANI

Red and blue lights flashed on top of the patrol car. I pushed Kai away from me and pulled up my underwear and pants. Fuck, this wasn't good in the freaking slightest. If the police caught me with Poison, Mom would find out within a couple hours. She had connections.

And if I thought she had been bad before when I failed the test … oh boy, she'd literally murder me. I wouldn't see sunlight for weeks and would be put right into homeschool for the rest of the year, and who knew … maybe for my college education too.

The police car parked right behind Kai's motorcycle, the sirens on now. Kai pulled up his jeans and quickly buckled his belt, handing me his helmet and telling me to hop onto the bike. My heart raced in my chest, but I slid onto the back and let him get on after me.

"What are you doing?!" I shouted. "We can't run from the police."

Kai started the bike. "We either run or your mom finds out about this." He paused and looked over his shoulder at me. "João and Landon told me how strict your mom is, and I don't want to never see you again."

My chest grew warm, a fuzzy feeling growing inside me. I curled my arms around his taut abdomen and inched closer to him. Who the fuck knew that I'd run from the police with the Poison boys in my final year at Redwood?

The headlights glared even harder in our direction, making the hairs on the back of my neck stand up. We were fucked. I didn't think we'd be able to outrun the police, especially with all Redwood's grumpy, underpaid cops looking to put someone away on a Friday night.

Shoving open the door, someone stepped out of the car.

I looked over my shoulder and tightened my grasp on Kai. "Kai, they're com—"

Over the loud hum of Kai's motorcycle and the rain, the man chuckled, so menacingly and loud, voice filled with laughter instead of the usual anger that the Redwood cops had against the world. I tensed and squinted my eyes at him, the sound so eerily familiar.

"How'd I know that you two would be here?" the man said, moving closer.

"Fuck," Kai said under his breath, suddenly cutting the engine. "What the hell are you doing here?"

The man stepped closer, and my heart dropped. Fucking João stood behind us with his lips curled into a small smirk and his arms crossed over his chest. The rain poured down around us, waves crashing against the rocks.

I looked into the passenger seat to see Landon sitting in the warm car, looking into the backseat, where there was a police officer tied the fuck up and gagged. My eyes nearly bugged out of my head, and I jumped off the bike and stormed toward João.

"What are you doing?!" I shouted.

"What are *you* doing?" João asked, arching a brow. "Couldn't wait until you got home?"

After rolling my eyes, I hurried toward the passenger seat and knocked on the window. Landon glanced at me, then at Kai, and rolled down the window. The police officer in the backseat shouted through his gag, rope binding his ankles and wrists.

"What?" Landon asked.

"What are you doing, Landon?" I asked, eyes wide and chest tight. João might've been bound for jail, but I did not want Landon heading there anytime soon. "You stole a police car?! You can go to jail for this! What is wrong with you?"

Landon flicked his tongue against his teeth and looked back at Kai. "We're working."

"Working?!" I asked. "How is this working?!"

The man squirmed around in the backseat, kicking Landon's seat. Landon growled and threw his hand back, hitting the guy right in the head and sending his head flying back so hard that the guy passed the fuck out.

My eyes widened.

Landon turned back toward me. "You were saying?"

"Landon, what have you gotten into? Why are you doing this?"

There had to be a reason—there fucking had to be. Poison always had a reason for something, like beating Harvey the tech teacher to a literal pulp earlier this week. I knew they were bad boys who sold weed, but stealing a police car?!

"Bring her back with you, Kai," João said, grabbing my arm to pull me away from the car and shoving me toward Kai's bike.

Landon seethed at him but rolled the window up, and when João got into the car, Landon said something that I couldn't quite make out.

Grumbling to myself, I slid on the back of Kai's bike and pulled the helmet back over my frizzy, matted hair. It was going to be a bitch redoing it tonight because I sure as hell couldn't go to sleep like this.

Kai sat back on his bike and pulled my arms around his torso. After starting the bike, he zipped out of the Overlook and down the beachy streets, taking the roads back to the same abandoned warehouse where João and Landon had fought the other night. He parked in the back, where his bike would be hidden, while João pulled up behind us, blocking us in.

As he tore open the warehouse door, Landon grabbed the unconscious man out of the backseat and dragged him on the pavement—the man's face literally sliding against sharp rocks and broken glass—into the warehouse.

"How the fuck did you tie him up?" Kai said once Landon finally dropped the officer in the center of the warehouse, where he had beaten up Harvey a couple nights ago.

I wondered if they had been back recently; there looked to be fresh blood on the ground.

"Well, you could've done it," Landon growled. "But you decided that you wanted to be inside Imani instead."

Kai sucked in a breath, glancing from João to Landon to me, then knelt by the officer's side, undoing the jumbled ties. He laid the man on his stomach, pulled his arms and legs behind his back, and tied them together, fingers moving effortlessly, like he had done this many, many times before.

And something about it was so … sexy.

He had promised to tie me up, but I hadn't thought he would be *that* good at something like this.

Once Kai finally pulled back, he pulled together the extra rope that he didn't need to use and handed it to me, moving close until our shoulders touched and his lips were nearly against my ear. "Hide it in your room, Imani. We'll be sure to use it one day."

With that, he nodded to the boys, who were both glaring at him. "Officer Rak is all yours."

Chapter Forty-Seven

LANDON

"**W**hat else do you know about Harbor?" I asked after slamming my fist into Officer Rak's face. He lay on his stomach with his wrists bound to his ankles behind his back, his body contorted in such a way that he could barely move. "Harlan Harbor."

Jace had wanted us to get him information about his family, and we were meeting with him tomorrow. We had been so caught up with Imani that we hadn't had much of a chance yet to get the shit he needed.

Imani stood across from us with her lips curled into an ugly scowl. When I had first started kicking the living shithead to a pulp, she was disgusted with me. Now, it was with him. He had admitted to so fucking much tonight that my knuckles were swelling.

"That's all I know," Rak said. "I swear to—"

The toe of my boot collided with his nose, a crack echoing throughout the room.

"That's enough," João said, stomping out a cigarette beside Imani. "Jace hasn't paid us enough yet to kill the fucking man. Let up." João grabbed Imani harshly by the elbow and dragged her closer to us. "Your turn."

"My turn?" Imani asked with wide eyes. "I'm not touching him."

"Afraid to get your thousand-dollar sneakers a little dirty?" João asked her.

"No," she said between clenched teeth. "I don't want to hurt anyone."

"You're part of Poison now," João said, shoving her toward Rak, then walking around his limp body on the ground. "Do it."

I stood off to the side, loathing the way João had handled Imani but curious to see if he could break her. I didn't want her to be like me, but Imani had some grit to her, and I wanted to see how far she would go.

João was right.

She might've started off as a toy to us, but she was part of Poison now.

Even if she didn't end up in the gang, she was mine, too. And I had vowed to stay with the guys forever.

Staring down at the officer, Imani balled her hands into fists behind her back. Part of me knew that she wanted to hit him. Imani had so much anger inside her tiny body, especially with her mother constantly hounding her over and over and over again.

"Officer Rak over here has been talking shit about Allie and Jace Harbor," João said, pulling Rak's bloody face off the cement and smacking him on the cheek. "Haven't you?"

Imani glanced between João and me, brows furrowing in an angry stare. "About what?"

"Calling their relationship incest," João said.

I cut my eyes to João and bit back a growl. He had said no such fucking thing about Jace and Allie, and I highly doubted that he even kept up with the latest gossip at school about them. He was a grown fucking man after all.

But something snapped in Imani.

Imani barreled toward Rak with her nostrils flared. "You know nothing about their relationship, so fuck"—Imani smashed the heel of her foot against Rak's jaw, cracking it right out of place—"off."

My eyes widened. Kai's eyes widened. Rak's eyes widened.

João stood back and smirked at her, gaze flicking to me for a moment. He raised his eyebrows, as if he was proud of himself for corrupting Imani like this, making her just like us. Then, he stepped closer to her.

"He deserves more than that, Imani. He was going to hurt Allie with that information."

Balling her hands into tight fists, Imani kicked him in the face again, one of his teeth flying out onto the pavement beside him. "Everyone in this town is a piece of literal garbage. You have nothing better to do than fuck with people, including you, João."

I didn't know what exactly it was that turned me on so much, but seeing Imani fight ... fuck, it made me hard. She wasn't *great* at it. I could teach her how to be better, where to hit to make the victim feel worse. But she looked damn sexy when she was angry like this.

After one last smash of her sneaker against Rak's throat, she stomped away toward an empty corner and crossed her arms over her chest. "I swear that I fucking hate this town," she muttered underneath her breath before commenting about how she needed to call Allie and tell her.

Who knew all we had to do to see Imani the bad girl was to talk about the people she cared about the most? Maybe she'd get that angry over someone talking shit about me or the guys one day and do something much, much worse.

Chapter Forty-Eight

KAI

João nodded at me from across the warehouse. "You have fun with her?"

Landon had left about ten minutes ago after Imani asked him to come over to her house while João and I finished up with Officer Rak.

I wiped my hands on my pants and tore off my soaked-through shirt. "That's none of your business."

"Come on. I'm not Landon."

Not wanting to deal with the conversation with him right now, I tossed him his car keys. "Leave. I'll take care of Officer Rak. See you tomorrow at Jace's. Bright and fucking early, João. Don't fucking forget."

After rolling his eyes, João stormed out the back room. "Whatever, dude."

Once João drove down the road, I locked all the doors, shut off the main light, and flicked on the one that hovered directly over Officer Rak. I grabbed a knife from a back room and stalked over to him, my heart pounding.

Rak wasn't just a bad guy.

Rak was one of the officers who had written off my father's death as an accident.

It wasn't a fucking accident, and Rak had known it when he got to the scene.

Kicking the toe of my boot against him, I turned him over and onto his back. I wanted him to see my fucking face when I did this. He didn't have anywhere to turn and nobody to hide behind anymore. Redwood Police were more corrupt than I had thought ...

Rak widened his eyes and stared up at me, blood dripping down his face from where Landon had repeatedly punched him earlier. I crouched by his side and drew the knife up the column of his throat, not hard enough to draw blood.

Yet.

I pulled the gag out of his mouth. "Do you remember me?"

Rak spit up some phlegm and blood, snot running from his nose. "No."

Anger rushed through me, and I punched him hard in the face, relishing in the sound of Rak's head snapping against the concrete. He deserved that *and more*. He deserved every fucking punch and every fucking kick he had received tonight.

"Oh, come on, Rak. I know you're not stupid."

Spitting up some more blood, Rak stared at me and shook his head. "I don't—"

I hit him again, this time harder.

For a moment, his eyes fluttered closed. "I swear, I don't know."

Unable to stop myself, I grabbed a fistful of his hair and placed the knife right against his artery, pressing in only enough for a single drop of blood to roll down his neck.

Chest heaving up and down, he shook his head. "I ... I ..." He stopped and widened his eyes. "You're that kid from the car accident."

My heart thrashed against my rib cage, and the memories flooded back into me, haunting me down to my very core. I fucking hated them, but they never went away. Every time I closed my damn eyes, I saw Dad's dead ones staring back at me.

"You wrote my father's death off as an accident," I said through gritted teeth. "You knew that the other man had caused that accident, yet you let that man go. You let him off the hook for killing my father! Killing him!" The knife shook in my hand. "How much did he pay you?"

"It *was* an accident!"

I pressed the knife hard again, and another drop of blood rolled down.

"How. Fucking. Much?"

"Half a million."

"Half a million fucking dollars for someone's life," I repeated quietly, the anger rising quicker and quicker with every second that passed.

How could someone take a life for money and go about his job like it was nothing, like he had done no wrong?

But shit cops like him killed people for a lot less.

A lot fucking less.

Pulling his phone out of my back pocket—the one I had taken from the cruiser earlier—I pulled up his banking app and used his fingerprint to access his bank account.

"What are you doing?" he said, spitting up some more blood, unable to move. "I need that money! I have a wife and a daughter."

"And I had a father once, too." I transferred his entire savings into the overseas bank account that Poison had opened years ago for shit like this. "Your wife is having an affair with a businessman, far wealthier than you would have ever been, anyway. She'll be fine."

"Don't lie about her," he screamed at me through his bloody teeth.

And because I wanted his last moment on this earth to be one of despair and shock and betrayal, I sank the knife deep in his throat and slit it, making sure to cut the artery all the way through until the life drained from his eyes and his body fell completely limp.

Like Harvey hadn't been in school all week either, this officer wouldn't show up to his job for the rest of his pathetic life. Nobody— and I meant, nobody—fucked with the people that I cared about. I would do anything to protect them from the bad, corrupt people in Redwood.

Anything.

I picked up the body, dumped it into the back of the plate-less car that we kept here for emergencies, and slammed the trunk. Nobody would find Officer Rak again. Once I was finished with him, all traces of him would be wiped out from this world.

One less asshole would walk through Redwood's streets.

Chapter Forty-Nine

IMANI

When I pulled into the driveway with Landon in my passenger seat, the front light turned on. I cursed under my breath, knowing Mom had been waiting for me to come home. She couldn't berate me last night, so she had to now.

"I'll let you in through the back door in, like, twenty minutes, okay?" I told Landon.

"All right."

I narrowed my eyes at him. "Promise me you won't go anywhere."

"I promise, Imani."

After arching my brow, I grabbed my backpack and things from the backseat and ran through the rain and to the house, taking a deep breath before I stepped through the door.

"How was the game?" Mom asked as soon as I stepped into the house, my hair frizzy beyond belief and matted to my forehead.

I hated getting my hair wet in the rain, but I would one thousand percent do it again for Kai.

Mom arched a brow. "And why are you soaking wet?"

"Redwood won," I said, keeping my response short and sweet.

These past few days had taught me one thing. I didn't want to talk to Mom because talking led to an argument and an argument led to me being grounded or me crying or me feeling like shit because of her. So, I put up a wall.

She closed the door behind me and pulled together her comfy housecoat. "And you're wet because?"

"Because it's raining."

Mom pressed her lips together in a tight line. "I made you dinner."

"I already ate with Allie." I slid off my shoes and started toward the stairs, hoping that she wouldn't continue to talk to me. All I wanted to do was dry off and sink into my mattress with Landon beside me, my head in the crook of his arm and his soft breathing in my ear.

"How's Allie doing?"

I balled my hands into fists behind my back and gave Mom a pleasant smile. "Good."

What was with all the questions?

Before she could get any words out, I hopped onto the steps, then turned around. "Hey, Mom ... do you deal with many patients with HIV or AIDS?" I asked, my heart racing. I knew that she'd ask me why I wanted to know, but I couldn't help myself. "You probably don't, but ..."

"It's not my area of expertise, Imani. Why?"

"If a child has it, what are her chances of survival?"

Mom furrowed her brows. "Don't tell me that you have—"

"No," I clarified, annoyed that she would assume that. "I don't. We're learning about it in class, and I was wondering about how it affects children." I gnawed on the inside of my cheek, knowing that she probably didn't know anything about it, anyway. "Never mind. Anyway, I'm tired. I'll see you in the morning. Good night."

Taking the stairs two at a time, I made it to the second flood with lightning speed and continued down the hallway toward my bedroom. I had to make it to the back door without Mom noticing in less than fifteen minutes now. I had to be quick.

Opening my bedroom door, I flicked on the light and jumped in surprise when I saw Landon lying on my bed and the window ajar. "How the hell did you get up here so quickly?" I asked, placing a hand against my heart.

"You leave your windows unlocked."

I shut the door behind me, and despite Mom's orders not to lock it,

I did. "I told you that I was going to unlock the back for you, so you didn't have to climb up the side of the—"

Landon grabbed my hand and pulled me down onto the bed with him, placing his hot mouth on mine and kissing me softly. "I'm here now. You don't have to worry about it, but you should be locking your windows."

After playfully shoving him, I smiled into our kiss and peeled off my wet shirt and bra, grabbing the pajamas that I had left on the bed from the other night. Low-key, I was surprised Mom hadn't scolded me for leaving my clothes all over the room. She had to have been in here last night; I didn't doubt it.

"I thought you were going to shower and do your hair again," Landon said.

Collapsing beside him, I rested my head on his shoulder. "I'm too lazy now, but I'll regret it in the morning."

Once I pulled out my phone, I texted Allie because I needed her to know that people knew about her and her stepbrother getting back together already. I'd kinda, sorta had a feeling about it, but I didn't want her getting hurt. Redwood was cruel to everyone, no matter how popular or rich one might be.

When Allie didn't respond, I sighed and placed the phone in my lap. It buzzed, and a Discord message popped up on the screen from the group chat between me and Poison. I leaned closer to Landon and tapped on the video that João had sent.

In the video, João grabbed a fistful of my hair and forced me to look back into the camera as he fucked me senseless. Heat gathered in my core at the video he had taunted us with, and Landon tensed beside me, his jeans growing tight.

When I sucked João's fingers into my mouth in the video, I clenched and rubbed my thighs together. Landon grabbed my waist, lifted me into the air, and sat me between his legs, glancing over his shoulder to watch. He slipped his arm around my waist and dipped his fingers between my thighs.

"You love being on camera, don't you?" he murmured against me.

"You like watching me fuck your girl, Landon?" João asked in the video. "Because I fucking love being inside her tight little cunt, the way she whimpers on my fingers."

And while Landon might've hated it at the time, now that he was watching the sex tape we had made, he rubbed my cunt and pressed his hardness against my backside.

On the phone, I pushed João down onto the couch and climbed on top of him, reaching out for Landon to fill me up from behind.

"Answer me, Imani," Landon murmured against my ear, rubbing faster circles around my clit and making me whimper softly.

I spread my legs as far as I could get them, needing him to touch me more, to touch me all over my body, every place he could get.

"Fuck me from behind, Landon. I want two cocks in my pussy," I said in the video.

Landon spit on his fingers and placed them back on my cunt, rubbing harder and faster. The pressure rose in my core, and I reached behind me with my free hand, stroking Landon's cock up and down, touching every inch of it through his jeans.

"Fuck it," Landon said to me, undoing his jeans and pulling my pajamas to the side. He pulled me on top of him, his dick sliding into my wet pussy with ease, and sucked on the skin below my ear. "Keep watching your little sex tape as I fuck you."

My cunt tightened around him, and I put the video full screen, watching Landon thrust his huge cock into my pussy with João. They stretched my pussy out farther than it had ever been. Kai wrapped his belt around my throat and lifted it slightly, shoving his cock into my mouth. The camera was facing me, and I looked like a dirty, desperate slut with two men in my cunt and another filling my mouth, my lips coated in spit and drool.

I pulled my gaze away from the video for a moment and closed my eyes. Landon thrust up into me hard and fast, keeping up with the steady rhythm that Kai had kept while fucking my throat. It was like Landon and I were watching porn together, except this was ours.

Just like those night cam sessions were ours, too.

"You can hold on for a little longer, Imani."

Landon wrapped his arms around the backs of my knees and spread my legs even farther apart, thrusting as deep inside of me as he could get.

"Jerk me off inside your tight little throat, and I'll let you breathe."

Below me, Landon grunted into my ear.

In the video, I blinked back tears, wrapped my hand around my throat, and stroked Kai up and down as quickly as I could. My pussy tightened even more around Landon, and I threw the phone down, the pressure inside me about to tip me over the edge.

"Please, come inside me," I begged Landon.

Landon grabbed the phone and handed it back to me. "You're going to finish watching us fill you up."

On video, João pounded himself into me, then suddenly stiffened. When he pulled out, his cock was covered with my cum. Landon came in me next, spilling into my pussy, too—two thick loads deep in me. Then, Kai shoved himself into my pussy and came—all three loads dripping down my thighs.

My toes curled, my legs shaking in Landon's hold. I slapped a hand over my mouth and cried out, chest heaving up and down quickly. My pussy pulsed over and over on Landon's cock, the pleasure rushing out of me. Landon grunted in my ear and stilled inside of me, his hand moving against my clit like fucking magic.

Once I finished, Landon pulled out of me, laid me on the bed beside him, and curled up behind me, his warm breath in my ear and his nose gliding up the side of my neck.

"Imani, I ..." he whispered, sighing softly. "I ..." He paused again, then kissed me on the cheek. "Good night."

Chapter Fifty

"You got the shit?" I asked Kai once we pulled into Jace Harbor's ritzy community.

Landon sat in the passenger seat, flicking a cigarette out the window angrily because I had torn him away from his little girlfriend this morning. I had told him last night not to stay too late at her house, but that asshole couldn't stay away from her.

I tightened my hand around the steering wheel and parked in Jace's driveway, spotting his car in the open garage. Good, that fucker was home. We needed to have a little chat with him because these cops were up to something, and I had a bad fucking feeling that it was connected to whatever Jace needed help with.

"Yeah, I got it," Kai said.

"Good."

After stepping out of the car, I walked up to the front door and didn't wait for Kai or Landon. Their slow asses would catch up. I rang the doorbell as the guys stepped behind me, Landon tapping his shoe on the ground and driving me fucking nuts.

Jace Harbor stood inside the house, rolling his eyes when he saw us through the front window. He stormed over to the door and ripped it open, breathing heavily through his mouth.

God, what was with him and Landon today? Couldn't be without their girls for a fucking minute.

Whipped.

"You know not to show up at my fucking house," Jace said through gritted teeth, opening the door and letting me, Landon, and Kai saunter into the foyer of the mansion, an enormous chandelier hanging above us.

I patted him on the shoulder. "Oh, don't worry about it, Harbor. We love coming to pay you a visit in your daddy's mansion. It's always a pleasure." I walked around the foyer and glanced down the wide halls. "Is Allie home?"

Jace clenched his jaw. "Don't push it."

"Is lover boy jealous?" Landon asked, cracking a smirk. "Heard Allie's been going out with Jamal. Your best friend and your stepsister." He shook his head. "Must be hard, especially since you still love her, huh?"

He was one to fucking talk about jealousy. Hell, so was I though.

As much as I hated Imani and gave Landon shit for it, I wanted her to myself.

Kai swung his backpack over his shoulder, tugged out a manila folder labeled *Harbor*, and handed it to Jace. Jace swallowed and flicked open the folder, blowing out a breath through his nose. Inside the folder were papers about his father, about his money, about Jace Harbor himself. He had wanted us to get him information about his own family, and we had gotten it, especially out of that shit cop last night.

"You know that I can't fucking use this." Jace slammed it back against Kai's chest. "I asked you to find me something useful, not shit that won't hold up in any fucking court."

Landon leaned against the wall, posting a foot on it and crossing his tattooed arms over his chest. "If you want more than this, you have to pay more, Harbor."

"You're asking us to break into the police chief's house in a guarded neighborhood, steal a stack of papers from a locked safe, and not get caught by Nicole's father or Nicole," I said, leaning back on the leather couch and hanging an unlit cigarette out of my mouth. That was what he had wanted about a couple weeks ago.

And while it might've been worthwhile, especially to put another rich Redwood bitch away, we needed more money. I was fine with stealing a cop car, but the police chief didn't fuck around.

"Can you fucking do it or not?" Jace asked through gritted teeth.

"Of course we can do it." Kai walked around the living room, staring at all the expensive shit that Jace owned. "But it's going to cost you."

"How much?" Jace asked.

I lit my cigarette and puffed on it. "Two mil."

Jace's eyes widened slightly. "Are you fucking kidding me?"

"How much is it worth to you, Harbor?" I said, standing up and sauntering over to him.

We had our own shit to worry about too, and we couldn't be risking our lives just to get fucking caught. I slung an arm around Jace's shoulders and nodded out the window to Allie, who was being dropped off by Jamal in front of the house.

"How much is *she* worth to you? You *are* doing this to keep her safe, aren't you?"

Two million was nothing to Jace and his father.

Jace balled his hands into fists. "Two mil."

"We also need entrance into Nicole's neighborhood," Kai said, referring to the police chief's daughter who went to school with us. "They watch the gates and the perimeter like fucking hawks. And we don't fuck with anyone in the police chief's neighborhood after what happened last time."

Jace cursed under his breath.

"Don't worry about Nicole and getting onto their property," he said. "I'll get you into the neighborhood, but you need to fucking deliver shit that's better than what's in that folder."

"Money in cash by next Friday. You'll hand it over after the game, back of the parking lot by the dumpster. Make it look like we're giving you weed. Don't be suspicious about it, Harbor. The chief of police and the principal are watching your every move."

When Allie, Imani's best friend, opened the front door, I slid a baggie of weed into Jace's hand, and Jace stuffed it in his pocket, staring at her with a blank and cold expression, unlike a couple moments ago, when he was freaking the fuck out about her not being here.

Kai nodded in Allie's direction, as if to say, *What's up?*

"Catch you later," Jace said to us.

Allie crossed her arms over her chest, watching us like a hawk.

Landon smiled at her and leaned close. "Tell Imani I said hi," he said and shut the door behind us.

Two fucking million dollars could help Ana so much, and I hoped to God that Jace pulled through.

Chapter Fifty-One

IMANI

"Landon?" I whispered, turning over on the mattress and opening my eyes.

Beside me, the bed was empty. Landon's scent and even all his clothes from last night were gone completely from my bedroom. I sat up to lean against the headboard, yawning and scanning the room for any trace of him that he might've left behind.

The window was cracked slightly, a cold wind rolling into the room. My nipples poked through my shirt. After pulling the blankets around my shoulders, I dragged myself out of the bed and moved toward the bathroom to start the shower.

I frowned at the empty bed again, wishing that Landon had at least let me know he was leaving this morning. I wanted to be able to wake up next to him again. It made me feel so good, seeing his sleepy face next to me in the morning.

"Wake up, sweetheart!" Mom said, knocking on the door and turning the knob. When she realized that the door was locked, she banged a bit harder, her voice tense. "Sweetheart! Open up! We have brunch today."

Quickly hurrying toward the door so Mom wouldn't ground me for locking it, I yanked it open and gave her a soft smile—at least, the best one I could muster because all I wanted to do was seethe in her direction.

"Morning," she said, glancing behind me and around the room, as if she was *looking* to scold me for doing something wrong. When she found nothing—thank goodness that Landon had cleaned up all his stuff—she turned back to me. "I thought I told you not to lock your door."

"Habit," I lied.

After giving me a once-over, Mom surprisingly nodded. "Okay, well, get ready. Akio and his father are coming over for brunch."

"Akio? Why is he coming over?"

Mom gave me a tense smile, then scrunched her nose. "Oh, dear, you need to shower and redo your hair. I thought you were going to take a shower last night, when you got home. They'll be over in less than an hour and—"

Deciding that I wouldn't get any kind of answer from her, I stepped toward the bathroom. "Okay, I need to go shower if you want me to be ready in time. I'll be quick, I promise."

Once I finally convinced Mom to leave, I shut my bedroom door— and didn't lock it—and blew out a long breath, eyeing the window. Part of me wanted to jump out of it, run to Landon's house, and never turn back. Being with him and living in his basement would be far better than this.

"Fuck." I dragged a hand over my face and headed toward the bath- room, stepping into the shower and reluctantly wiping away all traces of Landon last night.

If it were anyone else coming over, I would've left, but it was Akio.

I wanted to apologize to him about how Kai had acted last night after the game ...

And maybe get some information out of him about the people he gave medication to at the pharmacy. He had to know something or someone in this town who had HIV, and I knew people weren't supposed to give out information to randos.

It was unethical.

But it was also unethical to drop used fucking needles all over the place and let a baby crawl all over them. I had promised João that I would get him some information for him to trust me, and this had to be it. I had to at least try.

Because whoever had ruined Ana's life needed his life to be fucking ruined, too.

* * *

Two hours later, I sat across from Akio at the dining room table. Akio's father and Mom were in a heated conversation *again* about who would be at the top of our class once we graduated. Akio stared emptily at the table in front of him, emotion evaporated from his face.

The look on his face mirrored what I felt inside.

I kicked him under the table. When he glanced up at me, I nodded to the other room and excused myself from the end of brunch. Mom gave me the stink eye, but I politely told her that Akio and I were going to talk in the other room.

She probably thought that Akio and I would be flirting or something because she immediately plastered a smile on her face and ushered us to the other room, shutting the double doors behind us.

Akio stuffed his hands into his pockets and walked around the living room, sighing. "Thanks for that."

"Don't worry about it," I said. "I couldn't last another second in there."

"Me neither."

I awkwardly scratched the back of my head. "About last night ... I'm sorry about Kai."

"It's fine," Akio said, staring out the window at the orange and brown leaves on the trees.

"I also ... kinda wanted to ask you about the pharmacy."

Akio finally turned to me and arched a dark brow. "Is this about João?"

I chewed on the inside of my cheek. "Maybe ..."

"You want information about why he needs that medication from me?"

"No," I said quickly. "I know why he needs it. I just want to know who else gets it too."

Akio tensed. "You know that I can't give you that kind of information, Imani."

"Please, Akio," I begged, grabbing his hand. "It's important to me."

To my surprise, Akio pulled his hand out of mine and looked toward the doors, lowering his voice. "I'll tell you, if you promise to hang out with me this week, maybe study for Barnes's class with me?"

"Why do you want me to hang out with you?"

Akio glanced down at his feet, jaw twitching. "Because, Imani, nobody else understands what it's like to have parents like ours. The other rich kids become like their parents, and the kids who live in the slums hate us. I don't ..." He swallowed hard and shook his head. "I don't have anyone else to talk to about this shit."

And it was the first time that I really understood what he was saying and why he constantly bothered me at school. Akio didn't have any friends, especially ones like me, who understood the struggle of having a mom like—I cut my eyes to the door—her.

Instead of making Akio feel worse about his situation—I knew that horrible feeling way too well—I gave him a small smile and nodded. "In exchange for names, I'll hang out with you. We can go get ice cream with Allie or something."

Akio pushed his glasses up his nose and curled his lip up. "Really?"

"Yes, really."

The Poison boys would be angry with me for even talking to Akio —never mind hanging out with him—but they didn't run my life. They were only a part of it. And I didn't want anyone to live like this. I had everything I could ever ask for, but still, I felt so alone.

Chapter Fifty-Two

JOÃO

"You're going to stir the pot?" I asked Ana.

She pushed a chair across the kitchen floor and toward the stove, hopped up onto it next to me, and snatched the spoon from my hand, stirring the chocolate inside the pot around and around and around.

I watched her intently, making sure she didn't burn herself on the gas flames coming from the burner, and crossed my arms over chest.

Ana noticed me staring and shoved me back with her free hand. "I know how to make them, João. Let me do it by myself, or I'm going to tell your girlfriend that you're a loser. Oh, wait, she already knows."

"Actually, she thinks you're a stinker," I said, poking Ana in the side.

She doubled over and giggled, continuing to stir the pot of chocolate. I smiled in response, cherishing every moment that I had with her because I didn't know when or if I'd have enough medicine to keep her alive forever. Hell, I didn't even know if I would have enough medicine for the next year.

Someone knocked on the front door, and Ana looked out the window, brown eyes growing wide. "Your girlfriend is here!" she cheered, jumping off the chair and running to the door with the chocolate-covered spoon in her hand.

Before she could dirty the house with it, I snatched it from her hand and placed it back in the pot, twirling the chocolate around so the brigadeiros would come out like they should and not like the time Kai had helped Ana make them.

Damn, I didn't hear the end of that from Ana. We couldn't even form them into balls of chocolate; they had flattened every time.

"João!" Ana shouted, walking back into the kitchen with Imani's hand in hers. "Your girlfriend is here!"

I glanced over my shoulder at Imani and smirked. "You liked that video so much last night that you needed to pay me a visit?"

Imani glared at me and covered Ana's ears. "Can you not?!"

Ana ran back over to me and climbed back onto the chair, grabbing the spoon from me and stirring again.

I stepped back toward Imani. "What are you doing here, then? You don't usually show up at my house for no reason at all."

"I wanted to see you and Ana."

I tensed and unintentionally turned my stare into a glare. "No, you didn't," I snapped before I could stop myself.

But all my life, I had been conditioned to think that all the rich assholes in this town only came around when they wanted or needed something.

They never came around just because.

"Actually, I didn't come for you," Imani said, playfully shoving my shoulder. "I only came to see Ana because Ana isn't mean to me. Right, Ana?"

Ana sassily looked over her shoulder and smirked. "Yeah, that's right."

Imani walked closer to her. "Ooh, you're making brigadeiros? Yummy!"

When she turned her back toward me, I let myself smile at Imani, and—for a split second—I had the urge to wrap my arms around them both and pull them closer. But I stopped myself because I never did shit like that, and I never felt this way for anyone.

I vowed that I never ever would.

The front door opened again, and Mom hurried into the room with her heels in her hand and tears in her eyes. When she saw us, she quickly looked away and rushed down the hallway, muttering about needing a moment.

My stomach twisted into knots. I glanced over at Imani, who furrowed her brows at me pitifully and gestured toward the hallway that Mom had disappeared down a couple moments ago.

"Go. I'll watch Ana." She turned back toward Ana. "We're gonna make the best brigadeiros ever, right, Ana?"

Ana grinned up at her.

After grimacing at Imani, I hurried down the hall toward Mom's room. I knocked twice, but she told me to go away, so I opened the door, stepped into the room, and shut it behind me. Mom sat at the edge of her bed with her back turned to me and her head in her hands.

"What happened?" I asked tensely.

She sat up straight and shook her head, wiping away more tears. "Nothing, João."

I stepped closer to her and balled my hands into fists behind my back. "What happened?"

"Nothing."

When she pulled her hair into an elastic, I saw her neck covered in bruises, her skin with blotchy red hickeys, and her swollen lower lip. Rage rushed through me, and I stopped myself from putting a damn hole through the drywall.

"Who the fuck did that to you? I'll kill the motherfucker."

Mom stood and faced me, shaking her head. "Please, drop it," she said, voice so quiet that I could barely hear it. "This was what I signed up for. I knew what I had to do when your father left. It's the only way …"

"You didn't sign up to get raped."

More tears slipped down Mom's cheeks. "João …"

"That's what's happening, Mom," I snapped quietly so Ana wouldn't hear. Our house was too small. I moved closer to her, my mouth drying. I didn't understand why she did this day in and day out. It hurt to see her like this, after I had begged her to stop it.

After a couple moments of silence, she finally dropped her head. "I need a couple minutes alone." She glanced over at her nightstand. "Please, João. Give me a couple moments."

Knowing that she wouldn't tell me—no matter how hard I tried—I walked out of the room and pushed away the hot tears that threatened to fall. If she wasn't careful, Mom would drive herself into the ground.

When I finally emerged from the hallway, Ana was putting the plate of chocolate into the refrigerator to cool. She ran in front of me toward the front door and grabbed her jacket. "Come on, João! Imani said that she'll make a leaf pile with us."

"I'll be out in a second," Imani said to her.

When Ana disappeared through the front door, Imani turned to me. "How is she?"

"Good," I said quickly, grabbing my coat.

Before I could follow Ana outside, Imani grabbed my hand and stuffed a piece of paper into it. "Here."

"What's this?" I asked Imani.

She wrapped her hand around mine and smiled up at me. "A list of names who could've given Ana HIV. At least, if he's still in Redwood."

I curled my hand around the piece of paper and shoved it into my pocket. "Where did you find this? Was it Akio? That fucker told me that he didn't have access to that fucking information."

"That's none of your business," Imani said, glancing out the front window at Ana, who was playing in the fall leaves.

With her coat bundled up to her chin and her brown hair blowing into her face, she looked toward us and waved.

"Be happy that you have it, João. And use it wisely."

<h1 style="text-align:center">Chapter Fifty-Three</h1>

IMANI

Forty-five minutes later, João and I each sat on a swing at the park while Ana climbed up ladders and slid down slides, giggling with the other kids and having a good time. I pumped my legs back and forth slowly, gliding in the air, while João sat there.

"I heard what happened," I said to João, not making eye contact with him.

João looked over at me briefly, trying to keep a blank face. But then he frowned, and I caught his bottom lip trembling. He quickly glanced away and back at Ana, who didn't have a clue about what her mother did for a living or how it was tearing João apart.

She stood on the tallest part of the playground and waved to us. "João! Imani!"

I waved back enthusiastically while João gave her a curt nod.

"You don't have to talk to me about it," I said, slowing down on the swing. "But I wanted to let you know that I'll be here to listen to you whenever you need it. I'm definitely part of Poison now, so you'd better get used to it."

"You're *not* part of Poison."

"Actually, I am," I said with a smirk, knowing that this was annoying him.

João rolled his eyes, but I didn't miss the small smile on his face. "You're not part of Poison until you kill someone."

A laugh escaped my lips. "Kill someone? You're kidding me."

I didn't believe for a moment that João, Landon, and Kai had killed anyone. Maybe João and Landon together—I hoped not—but Kai? Come on; he was the nicest one of all of Poison.

Besides, I'd never even heard rumors about Poison killing people. They beat people up, stole shit from the rich, and sold drugs to their victims. Not murdered people in cold blood. And I definitely would never do something like that.

"Whatever."

"João! Why is your name written on the inside of the slide?" Ana said once she emerged from the tunnel slide. She ran over to us, cheeks flushed red and nostrils flared, trying to get as much air into her little body as possible. "Can I carve my name into it too?"

"No, Ana," João said. "That's another João."

Ana arched a brow and pressed her lips together. "There isn't even another João in this *town*."

"Go play," João ordered.

When Ana ran back to the slide, I glanced at João. "You definitely carved your name into that slide, didn't you?"

"That used to be my favorite place to hide," he said, actually smirking a bit.

"This is the ritzy Redwood playground. What were you doing here?"

"I told you that my dad was loaded. We used to come here all the time."

"Right ..." I said, kicking some wood chips at him. "He must've not taught you any manners if you carved your name into the plastic."

"He didn't have any fucking manners. Looks like I became him, huh?"

"You'd be him if you didn't care about anyone or anything," I said, softly. "But you do."

"I don't give a fuck about you," João said without looking at me.

I rolled my eyes, but I felt hurt on the inside. "I'm talking about Ana and your mom. Not me." But, damn, did I want to be talking about myself too.

We fell into an awkward silence, and the sounds of Ana giggling drifted through my ears. Wind whipped some hair into my face, and I pushed it away, pissed off at this wind already today. Why the hell was it so cold in this town, anyway?

"I'm afraid for my mom," he finally said, leaning against the swing with his arms crossed, not making eye contact with me once. "Since Ana's diagnosis, she's taken it so bad. She overworks herself and sells her body and ..."

He shook his head and turned his back to me, so I couldn't see the tears in his eyes, but I knew they were there; I had seen them after he talked with his mom too.

"And I haven't seen her smile, like really fucking smile. It's been so fucking long, and I'm terrified that something's going to happen to her."

"I'm sorry," I whispered, moving closer to him and taking his hands in mine.

"I don't need your pity," João spit back, trying weakly to pull his hands away from me.

But I refused to let him. All I did was hold them tighter.

"You'll fix this," I said.

He might not believe that anything good could come from this, but I would do anything to make his and Ana's lives better. Anything.

Chapter Fifty-Four

LANDON

After paying Jace a visit, Kai and I went back to his house to come up with a plan. If Jace Harbor could come through with two million dollars, we would need to risk our lives to get information for him. A month ago, I would have been fine with it because I really didn't have anything at Redwood to look forward to, but now ...

I had Imani.

"You think Jace will actually come through?" I asked Kai.

"Yes." Kai tapped a couple keys on his computer, the many screens lighting up the room. "But we have bigger problems than that." He pulled up some information on the cop we had tortured last night and then Harvey, the tech teacher, and furrowed his brow.

Grabbing my coat, which really did nothing to warm me with all the fucking holes in it, I pulled it over my body. "What is it?" I asked, knowing that Kai had something against the police since his father had died.

I didn't know if it had to do with that or something ... worse.

"I don't know yet," Kai said, typing faster on his keyboard, lost in his own world. "But I'm going to find out."

* * *

Because I had nowhere else to fucking go, I headed back home. I wanted to ignore Mom and Dad as much as possible, so I decided to disappear into the basement, but blood was smeared on the back door.

I froze in my tracks and stared with wide eyes.

Fuck.

What the fuck happened?

Hurrying toward the door, I thrust the kitchen door open. Chairs were knocked over, glass plates had been shattered to pieces, and more blood was everywhere. I stepped over the glass and rushed through the room, following the sound of Dad shouting in the living room.

"You're a crazy fucking bitch," Dad slurred.

When I reached the living room, I saw Mom standing in front of a man I had never seen before, and Dad was … holding a gun.

A fucking gun.

I didn't know where the fuck he had gotten it from. I had found his last one and thrown it the fuck out because I was terrified this would happen, that he would get drunk off his ass and threaten me or Mom. Mom might've loved the man in some fucked up way, but he would kill her, whether it was an accident or not.

"Landon!" Mom scolded when she spotted me. "Leave now."

Dad turned toward me, waving his gun everywhere. The man behind Mom grasped his leg, where blood gushed from.

I tensed and furrowed my brows, my heart racing. "What's happening? What did you do?"

"Shot the fucking bastard that your mother slept with."

He took another threatening step toward Mom and grabbed her by her hair, forcing her to her knees. Tears streamed down her face, her eyes red and puffy.

"Why do you have a gun?" I whispered.

Terrified.

I was terrified that he'd shoot me too, that I wouldn't get to see Imani ever again.

"For shit like this." He stuck the gun against her temple.

I waved my raised hands at him. "Please, let her go, Dad. She's your wife."

"You sticking up for her, boy?" Dad asked, waving his gun at me too.

"No, I'm not sticking up for her." I raised my hands up higher to show him that I wasn't a threat. "I just want you to put the gun down. You're going to kill someone with it."

"Maybe I fucking should," he said, slurring his words and holding the gun to Mom's throat. "This whore deserves it." He tightened his grip on her hair harder and smacked her in the side of the face with the barrel. "Don't you?"

Mom grabbed the hand holding her hair and sobbed, tears pouring down her cheeks. "Please, let go of me. I haven't done shit to you! Leave, Landon. You're just making him angrier. I had it under fucking control."

My heart pounded inside my chest. I wished I hadn't come home. It seemed like I only made things fucking worse around here. I couldn't even fucking come back to the house without getting smacked or threatened.

A car pulled up outside, the engine shutting off. I decided to ignore it and stepped closer to Dad. As much as Mom thought that I was making it worse, I couldn't leave her with him while he was out of his mind and had a gun to her head. She was fucking crazy if she thought I'd do that.

Dad looked out the front window and toward the street. "Your little slutty friend came in time for the show." He chuckled menacingly. "You want me to show you what I'm going to do to your mother? Your friend will be the perfect fucking example."

Chest tightening, I sucked in a breath and looked over my shoulder. Imani stood outside the house, about to knock on the basement door with a huge smile plastered on her face. Dad threw Mom to the ground and barreled toward the door with the gun.

And I knew I had to do anything to keep Imani safe.

Chapter Fifty-Five

IMANI

Not wanting to go back home, I had driven down a couple streets to Landon's house. All day, I had been wanting to see him again. He had left this morning without saying goodbye or waking me, and I kinda, sorta missed him.

After taking a deep breath, I knocked on the basement door. I didn't know if Landon was even home, but staying all day with João had been kinda weird. He had other stuff to do, and I had barely talked to Kai since our little *thing* last night.

A moment later, the house door flew open. Landon stumbled out before his drunk-off-his-ass father staggered out after him. Landon stood in front of me, pushing me back and telling me to run as fast and as far as I could.

"Get the fuck away from her, you son of a bitch," Landon's dad slurred.

Confusion shot through me. I furrowed my brows and glanced around Landon toward his father. My eyes widened, my feet suddenly heavy. He held a gun in his hand, waving it around at Landon. *My Landon.*

I grasped Landon's hand and pulled him back, heart pounding. "Landon ..."

"Go, Imani," Landon said through gritted teeth, voice tense. "Now."

"Not without you," I said to him, tugging him harder.

He stepped back a couple paces and pulled his hand away from mine. "Please," he whispered over his shoulder, making sure to keep distance between me and his father. "I can't lose you, Imani. You have to go."

Instead of running away, I stood behind him and kept my gaze on Landon's father, who was approaching us quickly. Landon couldn't lose me, but I couldn't lose him either. It was so damn stubborn of me to stay, but I wouldn't leave and let his father kill Landon.

I loved Landon.

"Don't defend the slut," Landon's dad said. "You know she's whoring herself out to those boys you hang around with. She's like your mother. They all are, boy. Let me fucking finish her too."

"Stop it," Landon said through gritted teeth. "Your problem is with Mom, not Imani."

"I've always known your mother was a whore, even when I married her. You can't see that your friend is one too. So, let me show you." He stepped closer to us, and Landon pushed me farther into the yard, toward the barbed wire fence.

Landon balled his hands into fists. "Leave her alone. She's not a whore."

"Is that what you think?"

Instead of continuing to back away, Landon stepped forward toward his father and met him eye to eye. Landon's mother stood at the door with another man, scowling at her husband—or maybe she was looking at Landon like that.

"I told you to leave, Landon," his mother scolded, looking absolutely disgusted with everyone and everything right now. "You didn't listen to me. You're going to get everything that you deserve."

My heart broke into a thousand pieces. How could ... how could someone say that to their child? How could a mother want their own child to hurt physically? But ... part of me knew why. People in this town were selfish pieces of shit, like my mom.

I had known Landon didn't have a good home life, but this ...

His father stepped closer to Landon, not backing down, waving his gun. "You're a worthless piece of shit. I thought I raised you fuckin' better than this." He smacked the gun against Landon's chest. "You can let your whore walk all over you if you want."

The vein in Landon's neck twitched, like it did right before he was about to snap at someone in that abandoned warehouse or in the school hallways. "Call her a whore one more time."

"She's a fucking who—"

Before he could finish his sentence, Landon punched him square in the jaw, as if he didn't have a gun in his hand and could shoot him at any moment. My eyes widened, and adrenaline rushed through me.

His father stumbled back, and Landon moved faster toward him, punching and kicking and letting out all his damn aggression on his father. Smashing in his face. Kicking out his teeth. Kneeing the asshole in the balls.

"Landon," I said nervously.

Landon might've had the upper hand, but he didn't have the gun.

"Stop hurting your father!" Landon's mother shouted, hurrying toward them and trying to wedge herself between them.

His father took one hand and shoved her back, then tightened his grip on the gun, a sea of *fuck you* and *asshole* tumbling out of his mouth.

"Landon!" I shouted, hoping he could hear me. "Stop it! Please!"

I wanted to rush into the chaos and pull him away, run down the street with him and never turn back. But everything was happening so quickly that I barely had time to react when the gun went off and rang out through the night.

My entire body seemed to shut down, and I found myself collapsing to my knees. Landon and Landon's mother both stopped struggling with his father. Landon's mother grasped her arm, and Landon clutched his stomach, stumbling back on the grass and smacking his head against the earth.

Unable to stop myself, I crawled over to him and pulled him into my lap, tears flowing down my cheeks. "No. No. No. No. No. No. No." I pressed my hand to his side, where blood gushed out, and held him tight to me. "Someone, help him!"

Landon's father dropped the gun and widened his eyes at his wife and son, as if he couldn't comprehend what he had just done. I held him even closer. Landon looked up at me one last time and pushed some hair out of my face with a trembling hand.

"I love you," he whispered. "I never told you, but I love you so much, Imani."

Chapter Fifty-Six

IMANI

My shaky hands were soaked in a thick layer of Landon's blood. I cried out for someone to help me, but neither Landon's mother nor his father moved. They both looked too shocked to even help, and that other man did nothing but slam the front door closed and rush to his car.

Tears streamed down my face, blurring my vision. But I wouldn't let Landon die right here and right now, not in my arms. I loved him more than I had thought, and the thought of losing him ... fuck, I couldn't let that happen.

So, I ran over to open the back door of my car, then used all the strength I had in my small body to lift Landon's unconscious one from the ground. Struggling, I stumbled a couple feet, nearly dropping him on the street, but pushed him into the car.

After rushing behind the wheel, I started the car, pressed the gas to the floor, and sped to the hospital. I fumbled to grab my phone in the passenger seat, glancing back at Landon and the amount of blood he kept losing every moment.

Nine-one-one.

The phone rang for what seemed like forever.

"Nine-one-one. What's your emergency?"

"I'm coming to the hospital," I said, voice trembling. "Someone's been shot. Please, please, be ready to take him in. He's bleeding out in my backseat." I glanced into the backseat to see more blood pouring out of Landon. "Oh my gosh, there's so much blood."

"Please, calm down, miss," the operator said over the phone.

"I can't lose him," I sobbed.

Ahead, the traffic light turned red. Cursing into the phone, I swerved onto the sidewalk to bypass some cars that had stopped and took a hard right turn at the corner when I knew nobody was coming. It was reckless, but I didn't have much time.

Cars blasted their horns at me. I shoved my foot on the gas and sped down the road toward the hospital, the operator still talking in my ear. But honestly, I couldn't even focus at the moment. My mind was everywhere but on the phone.

When I saw the signs for the hospital, I drove even faster and ignored the speed limit. Maybe I'd end up going to jail for this, but as long as Landon lived ... that was all I cared about now. Landon didn't deserve any of this.

Sliding into the emergency vehicle entrance, I parked the car and ran into the hospital. An ugly sob escaped my lips.

"Help him, please! Find someone to help him!" I shouted. "Please, help me."

A couple nurses ran over, and I pointed toward my car parked outside.

"My boyfriend ... he's been shot. Someone help him!"

A small group of people ran outside to take Landon out of my car. They rushed him into the hospital, and I hurried with them down the halls. I wouldn't be let into the room, but I had to try. Once they realized that he was part of the slums, they wouldn't do anything to help him.

Even doctors and nurses at Redwood loathed people in the slums.

They wouldn't do as much for him as they would for someone like me.

Mom spotted me from down the hall. "Why are you here, Imani?" Mom asked, hurrying toward me. "And why is there blood all over your hands? Are you hurt? Did something happen with Allie and Jace?" She grasped my face. "Talk to me, honey."

"Landon," I cried, pulling myself out of her arms. "He can't die. I can't let him die!"

Before I could slip into the room with them, Mom grabbed me. "That boy they brought in from the slums? Why are you here with him?"

"Because I love him, Mom!" I shouted at her. "I love Landon. I love someone from the fucking slums, and he's dying right now. If you ever cared about me in the slightest, you'd put your ignorance to the side and help him!"

She reached for me. "Imani ..."

I ripped myself out of her grip, hugged my hands around my body, and fell to my knees, my legs giving out. "Don't touch me. Find someone to help him, please. A good doctor too, not just someone that you assign to everyone in the slums."

Mom pressed her trembling lips together and stared at me with teary eyes, and then she turned away from me. And, fuck, I still felt so abandoned by her. Every day of my life, no matter what, she never—

"Get Dr. Erwick to the ER now," Mom said to the nurses at the front desk. "And every emergency nurse that we have. We're not letting that boy die on us."

Chapter Fifty-Seven

KAI

After hours of trying to figure out what was up with this town, I sat back in my chair in the middle of the surveillance room and turned on the video of Imani from the other night on the biggest monitor.

With my belt around Imani's throat, she wrapped her full lips around my cock, and her throat tightened on me.

I pressed a hand against the front of my pants and blew out a breath. I couldn't wait to finally tie her up here in my bedroom and force her to watch the spit dribble down her chin from a ball gag in her mouth.

My phone buzzed, but I ignored it. It was probably João complaining about some shit.

Turning back to the video, I watched João and Landon stretch Imani out as she stared up at the camera—*up at me.*

"You can hold on for a little longer, Imani," I said in the video, mouthing the words now and unzipping my pants. "Jerk me off inside your tight little throat, and I'll let you breathe."

My phone buzzed again, then again.

I tried hard to ignore it, stroking my cock and desperate to come *again* while thinking about Imani. The ropes were upstairs, lying on my bed; I had even bought a vibrator to clip onto Imani's panties and make her ache and whimper while she was tied up.

When my phone buzzed one last time, I growled and opened up Discord. Imani had sent about fifteen messages in the group chat, one after another after another after another. I scrolled through them and tensed at the last few.

Imani: Get to the hospital now.
Imani: Landon's been shot.
Imani: Please come now. I'm here alone.

João hadn't answered yet; he must be with Ana. I zipped my pants, shut off the video, and headed toward my bike, sliding onto it in the drizzle and speeding toward João's house, banging on the door twice.

The second time, João opened the door with elastic bands in his hair, which I was sure Ana had forced him into wearing. I peeked into the room to see Ana sitting on the couch with some brigadeiros in front of her and a princess cartoon on the TV.

She jumped up from the couch and ran over, wrapping her arms around my waist. "Kai!"

"What are you doing here?" João asked.

"Have you checked Discord lately?" I pulled my phone out, knowing that this wasn't news for Ana, and showed it to him. "We have to go to the hospital now."

João tensed, jaw twitching. "My mom is sleeping."

"Then, bring Ana."

"Yeah! Bring me!" She grabbed João's hand. "Where are we going?"

"Go get your shoes," João said, then turned toward me. "I'll meet you there."

* * *

When I walked through the hospital doors, Imani shot up from her seat and threw her arms around my shoulders.

"They shot him, Kai. Why would they do that to their own son? They didn't even seem remorseful for it either."

Her body was trembling, her legs shaking so hard that I thought they'd give out. I pulled her toward the nearest set of chairs and into my lap, gently rubbing her back. She clutched on to me tightly and pulled me closer.

"Imani!" Ana shouted when she and João walked into the waiting room. Ana ran over to us and climbed into Imani's lap, frowning at her teary-eyed face. "What's wrong, Imani?"

"Nothing," Imani said through her sobs. "Nothing is wrong."

"João!" Ana said, motioning for him to come sit down.

But João crossed his arms and paced around the room, not even sparing Imani a glance. I stared at him, then at her, seeing the hurt on her face.

I placed my hand on her knee and squeezed tightly. "Don't worry about him. João hates hospitals."

Ana jumped off Imani and stomped over to João, tugging hard on his hand, but he didn't budge, and then he told her to go sit down. He continued to pace around the room and ran a hand through his hair.

"The last time João was in one was when they found out about Ana."

Imani pressed her lips together. "I hate his dad and both of Landon's parents."

I pulled Imani closer. "You would've liked mine if they were both still alive," I whispered mostly to myself, then to her. I wasn't even sure she could hear me because she started sobbing harder and harder again, body visibly shaking back and forth.

"Tell me that we'll fix this," Imani whispered.

"We'll fix this—and the rest of this shitty town too."

Chapter Fifty-Eight

IMANI

"We need to talk, Imani," Mom said, sitting beside me in the waiting room. She intertwined her fingers together, fidgeting more than she ever had with me before, and gave Kai a tense smile that didn't reach her eyes. "Can I have a minute alone with my daughter?" After Kai left, she turned back toward me. "We need to talk about that boy."

I pushed tears off my cheeks. "His name is Landon."

"Landon," Mom repeated. "He's part of that Poison gang, isn't he?"

Anxiety rushed through my body. I tightened my hands into fists, not wanting to listen to her lecture me right now. "If you want to ground me for loving someone, then ground me, Mom. Don't fucking sugarcoat it. But as hard as you try, you're not going to stop me from seeing him or being with him or loving him."

"Sweetie ..." Mom glanced around at the doctors and nurses at the front desk, and then she sighed. "All I wanted to say was that you could've gotten hurt. That could be you in that emergency room, with a bullet through your organs."

"But it isn't."

"No, but it could've been," she said, tears welling in her eyes. "If that happened to you, I would never ever forgive myself. Your father

223

and I tried for years to get pregnant with you; we struggled with so many fertility issues ... I wanted us to have a perfect life. I can't lose you, Imani. That's why I push you so hard. I want you to have a life like your father's and mine. I don't want you mixed up with guns and drugs."

I crossed my arms over my chest and bit back my tears. Logically, I knew that Mom was right. I didn't want to be mixed up with the wrong people and didn't want to fear something like this happening once or twice every week. But ... I wouldn't leave Landon.

"I love him," I whispered, tightening my grip around myself. "He didn't ask to be born into his family. He deserves to live and to have a life too; it's not only the rich who deserve to be happy and healthy, Mom. Everyone matters despite his or her upbringing. You should know that better than anyone."

Mom stayed silent and stared down at her lap, a pained expression on her picture-perfect face. "Tell me about him."

My eyes widened. "What?"

"Tell me about ... Landon."

Breath caught in my throat, I stared at her and couldn't fathom what she was asking me. She never *ever* asked me to talk about anyone other than the top five students in Redwood's senior class. But I wouldn't pass up the chance to show her that Landon—despite him being part of Poison—was a good guy.

"His parents physically abuse him, mainly his father, but today, I saw his mother do it too," I sobbed. Pain shot through me, and I couldn't stop myself from curling into a ball and leaning on her for support. "Why would someone do that? How could he live like that, Mom?"

Mom wrapped her arm around my body and pulled me closer to her, gently stroking my back. She stayed quiet, not saying anything as her body tensed. "I'm sorry if that's how you've felt. Your father told me that I was being too much again. And I ... I don't want you to feel like I don't care about you."

Tears streamed down my face, but I didn't say anything. I wasn't going to say it was okay because it wasn't. She had abused me for so long—not like Landon's parents, but it still freaking hurt me.

A couple moments later, Mom patted me on the shoulder. "Allie and Jace Harbor are here."

I glanced up to see Allie and Jace standing at the front desk waiting room, Jace's hands awkwardly stuck in his pockets as he looked at his stepsister. After eyeing them for a couple moments, I hopped up and hurried over to them, wrapping my arms around Allie's torso.

"What are you doing here?" I asked her, snot running from my nose.

"Your mom called me and said that you were here," Allie said, pulling me toward the seats where Kai and Ana sat. João was still pacing around the room, looking extremely uncomfortable. "What happened?"

"Landon got shot," I whispered, the words barely able to come out of my mouth.

"Can't we call the police or something?" Allie asked, rubbing my shoulder.

"No," Kai said quickly.

"If we did call the police, they wouldn't go to jail," Jace said, balling his hands into fists. "The police chief is a corrupt bastard. He wouldn't give a shit about someone from the slums. All he cares about is himself and his fucking image."

"Well, won't someone call them?" I asked.

It might've been the Redwood slums, but not everyone was scummy there. That was where Jamal lived, Jace's best friend, along with so many of the nicest kids at Redwood. The rich were never ever as nice as people from the bad side of town, who didn't have anything.

Kai looked at João.

João gave him a look back. "We should go get the shit."

"Just in case."

They didn't have to say anything for me to know they were talking about the drugs they grew in Landon's basement. If the cops came, they would probably search every inch of that house for any evidence of wrongdoing.

"I'll meet you there," João said, grabbing Ana's hand. "Once I bring her home."

I stood. "I'm coming with you."

"You're not coming with us, Imani," João said.

"Yes, I am."

"No, you're not."

"They shot Landon!" I shouted at him, drawing the entire waiting room's attention. I stepped closer to him, grabbed him by the front of his shirt, and pulled him closer to me, seething at him so he'd know that I was serious. "I'm coming whether you like it or not."

I would go to their house and make them pay for what they had done to Landon.

Chapter Fifty-Nine

JOÃO

"I want to come with you! Mommy is sleeping," Ana whined as I dropped off at home.

I stood beside my car with the engine running and the back door wide open. "Ana, please, don't make me fight with you. It's serious. Landon is hurt, and we need to make sure that everything is okay at his house."

Ana stared at Imani, who sat in the front seat, staring with both anger and hurt through the windshield. Rain gently dropped onto the windows, and I impatiently tapped my foot on the ground.

"Ana, now. Don't make me ask again."

After grumbling to herself, she unbuckled her seat belt, stood up in the car, and wrapped her arms around Imani from behind. "João will make it okay." She kissed Imani's forehead and giggled. "He always does, no matter what."

Smiling softly for the first time tonight, Imani placed her hand on top of one of Ana's and thanked her. When Imani pulled away, Ana jumped out of the car and stomped past me to the front door. She walked into the house and angrily stared at me through the window.

"Lock the door, Ana," I shouted at her.

She gave me another angry glare and stomped back through the house toward the door. Once she was settled in, I hurried back to the car and slid into the driver's seat. Imani balled her hands into her fists by her sides, becoming angrier by the second.

"How could they do that to him?" She seethed.

"That's who they are."

"They're pieces of shit!"

"Listen, Imani," I said between my teeth. "Don't tell Landon that we brought you here."

If he found out we had brought her back to his house *after* his father shot him, then he would actually try to kill me. I shouldn't bring her there, but I knew that if I didn't take her, she would drive up to his house on her own and by herself.

So, I let Imani be and continued to his house. When we reached the house, Kai's bike was out front. He must've been in the basement, trying to get things cleaned up. But Landon's pathetic mother and father were shoving suitcases in the backseat of their beat-up, run-down car, their fucking clothes falling out of them and a nervous expression on their faces.

After I parked, I stormed out of the car, grabbed the suitcase from the drunk asshole's hands, and dumped all his and his wife's clothes all over the bloodied ground, stomping them into their son's blood and into the mud forming from the rain.

"What the fuck are you doing?!" his father slurred.

His mother rushed into the car. "Get the fuck inside, Dave! Those boys are dangerous."

I stepped closer. "You're lucky I'm not pissing on your raggedy-ass clothes."

"You kids are nothing but assholes!"

"We're the assholes?" Imani shouted, storming toward him with nothing but fury on her face. She rushed past me, but I grabbed her waist and held her back. "You're nothing but pieces of shit! You shot your own son!"

Imani twisted and turned, desperate to escape my hold and run at them. While part of me thought it was the sexiest fucking thing, I refused to let Imani become part of this. Landon's father still had that gun for all we knew. If he shot Imani ...

His father laughed emptily. "He deserved it."

Kai hurried up from the basement and rushed toward us, eyeing Landon's father.

"You fucking deserve it!" Imani screamed. "Both of you deserve to be in the ground!"

"Stay away from us or—"

Kai pulled out his gun and shoved it against the bottom of Landon's father's chin. "You threaten her, and I'll blow your fucking brains out. If you're going to leave, get the fuck out of here now. I'm losing my fucking patience with you."

Landon's father tensed, then scurried to his car, slipping into the driver's seat and starting the engine.

As they drove down the road, Imani scrambled in my arms. "You're just going to let them go after what they did to Landon?! I thought you guys *killed people*!"

She threw my stupid words back at me from earlier. I restrained Imani until she calmed down and glanced over at Kai, who put his gun back into his waistband.

"We don't need to check out the house if they're gone. Nobody is coming here."

Kai gave me a nod, then turned back toward his motorcycle, his entire body tense and his gaze focused on the road that they had disappeared down. While Kai might not have wanted to kill in front of Imani yet, I knew that he had wanted to murder Landon's mother and father in cold blood right fucking here. And I didn't blame him. We might not get along all the time, but Landon was a third of Poison and had done so much shit with us.

We were in this together until we died.

Chapter Sixty

LANDON

Everything fucking hurt.

I grunted softly, opened my eyes, and clutched my waist, where the pain seemed to radiate from. Light flooded in from the windows. The curtain and door of the hospital room were both closed. After glancing around for Imani and not finding her, I pushed myself to a seated position and rested my head against the headboard, eyeing the bandages on my stomach.

While I didn't believe in any sort of god, I thanked the world that my parents weren't here. And I prayed that they wouldn't show up here either. I didn't want to see either of them ever again, and I really didn't want Imani to get messed up in their shit.

But, fuck, I didn't know where I would go. I couldn't go back home with them. And how was I going to pay for any of this? As soon as I had turned eighteen, Mom had taken me off their insurance, not that it would cover hospital bills like this, anyway.

The monitor beeped steadily beside me, the annoying sound not stopping once. I ripped the IV, or whatever the fuck kind of cord it was, off me, and the noise stopped. Someone hurried down the hallway toward my room and opened the door, and the nurse blew out a relieved breath.

"Please, keep this in," she said to me, hooking me back up to the stupid monitor. "You haven't been discharged yet."

"Is there anyone waiting here for me?" I asked.

She glanced up at me once she finished. "A couple of boys and a girl, who refused to go home, even after visiting hours were over. I'll let them know you're awake, but only if you feel up to seeing them."

"I'll tell them," Imani's mother said, standing at the door and crossing her arms, giving me the most pointed look, which she had probably given Imani plenty of times before. "Go back to the front desk, Aanya."

Aanya scurried out of the room and left me with Imani's mother. I swallowed hard and stared back at her, knowing that this was my only chance to really make an impression on her, whether it be a good or bad one. By the look in her eye, I already knew that she didn't like me.

"My daughter cares about you," she said.

I pressed my lips together. "I care about her."

She took a threatening step closer to me. "She begged me to find a doctor to save your life."

My lips curled into a small smile, and I looked at my lap. Not because I was threatened by her, but because I couldn't fathom how much Imani cared about me. Nobody cared about me like she did, not even my own damn mother and father. They had shot me and ... didn't even come to see if I was okay, not that I wanted them to.

"If you hurt my daughter, I will personally make sure that you and your little crew don't live to see another day outside of Redwood's prison. Do you understand me?" she asked, pressing her full lips together and glaring at me.

"I won't hurt her," I whispered, aching to tell her that *she* was the only person who hurt Imani. She wouldn't believe me or wouldn't let me see her daughter if I did. As much as it pained me, I bit back the snarky reply and gave her the best forced smile that I could.

After eyeing me for a couple more moments, she turned on her heel, opened the door, and plastered a fake smile on her face. "Imani!" she called down the hallway, her heels clacking against the ground, probably headed toward the waiting room.

There were some murmurs in the hallway, and then three sets of footsteps hurried toward my room. When Imani appeared at the door,

I found myself sitting up even further and smiling at her, again thanking someone who didn't exist that she was okay.

I wouldn't put it past my parents to try to hurt her too.

Kai and João followed her into the room.

João leaned against the wall and stared out the window. "Surprised you didn't die."

"Fuck you," I said back to him.

João curled his lips up slightly. "Glad you're all right."

Imani moved closer to me, eyeing the bandages. "Does it hurt?"

"Yeah," I said, brushing my fingers over my ribs and wincing. "I just ... don't ever get in the middle of something like that, Imani. If it had been you, my father would have shot you and not my mom and me."

Imani frowned at me and sat on the chair beside me.

"Don't worry about them," Kai said. "They've skipped town. You have the house to yourself. Nothing is fucked with down in the basement. And we'll take care of your parents. Don't *fucking* worry about that. I put a tracker on their car—for whenever you're better."

"Can I have a second with Imani?" I asked, glancing from João to Kai.

After they disappeared into the hallway, Imani shut the door and hurried over to my bedside with tears in her eyes. She pulled up the chair beside me, but I wasn't having it. I ignored the stabbing pain in my side, picked her up, and placed her on the bed beside me.

"But won't it ... hurt?"

"We need to talk," I whispered, pushing some of her black hair out of her face. "I ..."

"I love you, too."

My lips parted in surprise as Imani stared at me with wide eyes.

"You what?" I asked so quietly that I almost didn't hear myself. "You love me?"

"I love you." She pushed her lips against mine. "I love you so much."

Chapter Sixty-One

JOÃO

"That's him," Kai said, nodding to an old man walking his German shepherd down the street, filled with mansions and millionaires.

He hobbled along, barely able to bend over to pick up the dog's shit without cracking his spine.

"He's a bit too old to be friends with João's dad, don't you think?" Landon asked.

"My dad wasn't friends with him," I said.

I tightened my hand around the steering wheel and clenched my jaw. This was fucking useless. Since Landon couldn't do much shit today, we had skipped school to drive around Redwood to find one of my asshole father's friends who must've given Ana HIV.

We had almost gone through the entire list of names that Imani had given me, and nothing.

Fucking nothing.

"Where'd you even get this list of names?" Landon asked, snatching it from me.

Kai arched a brow into the rearview mirror, as if he wanted to know where I had gotten it too. We had beaten the shit out of Akio for months for any information and for more medication, but he wouldn't slip up.

"Imani," I said.

"Where'd Imani find it?" Landon asked.

"Fucking Akio gave it to her." Kai cursed under his breath, the jealousy heavy in his voice. "He had to have."

"You sound jealous," I said, grabbing the list back from Landon and crossing off Rickie Taffle, the fucking dog walker for millionaires who looked like he was about to drop dead from old age at any second.

Swear to fucking God, these rich assholes didn't care who they overworked.

They'd all get what was coming to them.

"Like you haven't been?" Kai spit back.

He was always one to keep quiet and to himself unless something really bothered him, which my little comment did. That meant he liked her too, and that pissed me the fuck off even more than the thought of Landon having Imani to himself.

"Imani told you that she loves you, huh?" I asked Landon, tightening my hand even more around the steering wheel until my knuckles turned white and my heart hammered against my tight chest.

Landon didn't have to say two fucking words for me to know that something had happened between them in that hospital room. He'd had the biggest, stupidest grin on his face when Imani let us back into the room.

I fucking hated it because I didn't want them to be exclusive. *I* wanted to be with Imani.

Sure, she was sometimes an annoying rich girl from the good side of town, who I should've loathed. But when she had stood up to her mother the other day at the hospital, fuck ... I hadn't known how much I loved that fire in her until then.

She didn't brush off Landon like the other ritzy girls would. She fucking fought for him.

But if they were exclusive ... fuck that.

"Yeah," Landon said, "she did."

"What's that mean for us?" I asked, lighting a blunt because a cigarette wasn't fucking strong enough. Part of me wanted to not care that they were together, to forget everything that had happened this weekend. "Huh? You going to run off with her into the sunset now?"

"Why are you always pissed the fuck off?" Landon asked, turning toward me and wincing from the bandages holding his stomach together.

"I'm not pissed." Fucking lie.

Landon muttered something under his breath and looked out the windshield, pulling an orange bottle of pain pills from his pocket and swallowing two. "If it makes you feel any better, no, I'm not going to run off with Imani into the sunset or whatever shit you just said. I'm staying in Redwood with you two pieces of shit, and we're going to clean this fucking place up."

Not wanting to think about how Imani fit into this anymore—because I was pissed off at the thought of Landon not liking the fact that Imani was ours and not only his—I glanced down at the list of names. We had gone through all of them on the list, except for two.

"People like my parents and your father, João, are done for," Landon continued. "We're going to fucking take them all down, and nobody is going to stop us. I don't give a fuck what we have to do."

"And Imani?" Kai suddenly said from the backseat. "How does she fit into this?"

Staring emptily out the window, Landon shook his head. "I don't fucking know."

"She's either with us or she's not, L. You choose."

Landon balled his fists and glared through the windshield, tension written all over his face. "We're fucking Poison. We made a pact to stay together, no matter what. A girl isn't going to come between us."

"He's not fucking talking about Imani pulling you away from us," I snapped. "He wants to know if he can fuck her on his little bike again."

Fuck, I wanted to know too.

Because there was no way in hell that I would willingly give Imani up.

Not now. Not after I'd seen how much Ana adored her. Not after she had given me this list of names of who could've poisoned Ana.

I shook my head and cringed at my fucking thoughts about Imani. It wasn't like that between us. She didn't fucking like me, and I didn't like her. But I couldn't give her up after knowing she gave damn good head.

Chapter Sixty-Two

IMANI

Yawning, I opened my lunch box and stared past Allie at the cafeteria table that Poison had claimed. Today, it was completely empty. My lips curled into a frown. I'd expected Landon to take a couple days off, but that didn't mean they all had to —unless they were off doing a job.

And if they were at a job, then that meant they were probably getting into some trouble.

"So, how's Landon?" Allie asked.

I pulled my gaze away from their table and sighed. "As good as you can be after your father shoots you in the stomach."

I curled my lip in disgust and balled my hands into fists under the table. If João had let me land one punch on his father's ugly face, I would've.

It wasn't fair. João didn't witness what I did. I wanted to kill his father for what he did.

"Are you guys ... a thing?" Allie asked me, biting her sandwich.

After pulling out some chips, I tore open the bag. What would I even call us? Were we boyfriend-girlfriend? That was what I would label us as, but then how would I explain my relationship with the other guys? Were Landon and I exclusive or ... not? Because, honestly, I didn't know if I could stop thinking about João and Kai.

Part of me was falling for them too, much slower than Landon, but I had known Landon for nearly a year now. I couldn't see myself not having a relationship with the others even if it was just sexual.

"Kinda," I said, gnawing on the inside of my cheek but then yawning again.

I mean, if we weren't a thing, then he wouldn't have wanted me to stay with him every night that he was at the hospital this past weekend, right? Mom had asked me to come home multiple times over the past few days, but I had straight-up refused. Landon didn't have his own family anymore, and I wouldn't let mine get in the middle of it.

"What about the other guys?" she asked. "How are they doing?"

"João is just as fucked up as Landon, but Kai ..." I sucked in a breath and pressed my thighs together, thinking about him taking me on the back of his bike the other day. "I haven't really had time to figure him out. He tends to stay on the quieter side."

"He always has," Allie said, taking another bite of her sandwich and talking on and on about Jace Harbor, her stepbrother, who I never really liked after what he had done to her two years ago.

That man had broken her heart, and now, it seemed like she was falling back in love with him.

But like me, there was no convincing her that the guy she liked wasn't good for her.

She had already known he wasn't, and she slept with him anyway.

After lunch, Allie headed to sixth period, and I found my legs taking me right into the restroom because, well, I was horny from lying beside Landon all weekend and not being able to touch him myself. The doctor had given him strict orders not to move too much while he was in the beginning stages of healing.

And me bouncing on his dick wouldn't cut it.

I walked into the restroom, checked every stall to make sure it was empty, then locked myself in one, immediately thrusting a hand down my pants and grasping on to the metal red stall wall, the pressure rising in my core.

When my phone buzzed in my purse, I pulled it out to see a text in the group chat.

João: Having fun at school alone?

My heart leaped in my chest, and I decided to test the waters because I didn't want to send them a slutty video of me if Landon wasn't comfortable with this anymore. I mean, he never really was one hundred percent, but we were never *this* exclusive.

After taking a deep breath, I pulled the front of my shirt down a couple inches and took a selfie that showed my lips and the smallest bit of cleavage. Only to see how they'd all react to it because if Landon wasn't okay, I would really have to reevaluate my horny life right now.

Once I gathered enough courage, I hit the Send button and waited, the heat gathering hotter in my core. I shifted from foot to foot, pressed my thighs together, and even started rubbing myself off again, desperate to relieve the pressure.

Landon: I haven't been able to touch you all weekend, and you send only *this*?

I rubbed my clit in smaller, faster circles.

Me: Do you want more?

My pussy pulsed, my legs shaking slightly.

João: Hell yes, we do.

Landon: I didn't get shot for you to be a tease.

After putting in my earbuds and pushing my panties to my ankles, I leaned my phone against my backpack on the ground and started a video call with the guys, knowing that they were together. Landon answered on the first ring.

They stayed quiet as I drew my fingers up my bare thighs and slowly pulled up my skirt for them to see my aching pussy. I spread my legs a couple inches wider and squatted down, so they could get a better view of me touching myself.

João grunted in the background, the sound making me clench even harder.

"Fucking rub that pussy, baby," he said. "Just like that."

I rubbed my clit harder, loving the attention and confidence I had on camera, and pressed my lips together to suppress a moan. The pressure built higher in my core, my legs trembling harder now.

"Stick two fingers into your cunt," Landon said.

Instead of listening to Landon, I rummaged through my backpack and grabbed the rose quartz *paperweight* from my backpack that *definitely wasn't* shaped like a dildo and *definitely wasn't* really one either.

That was what I had told Allie when she accidentally found it last month and asked me what it was.

If I told her I really was so horny that I brought a dildo to school, she'd definitely judge. Hell, I judged myself for it, but it helped in times like this.

After shifting the camera down slightly, I slowly thrust it into my pussy, letting them watch how much it stretched me out. When I slid all the way down onto it, I placed my hand back on my clit and rubbed myself off, the pressure rising in my core once more.

Through my earbuds, I could hear all three of them cursing and grunting, muttering incoherent things to themselves about me. But I continued, loving this feeling. I bounced up and down on the dildo, letting it nearly pop out of me before sliding it right back in.

And when I was about to come, someone walked into the restroom.

I desperately wanted to stop, but I couldn't.

I fucking couldn't.

I pressed my lips together, rubbed myself off faster, and slapped a hand over my mouth when wave after wave of pleasure rushed through me. My legs trembled as my pussy pulsed over and over on the dildo. I bit my lip so hard that I drew blood, all to stop myself from moaning out loud.

A moment passed, then two, and I pulled the cum-coated dildo out of my pussy and moved the camera closer to me, so they could see how ruined my cunt was for them. Deciding that I wanted to have some fun, I put the camera finally on my face and sucked the dildo into my mouth, knowing that they would fucking love this.

Moving it back and forth, I cleaned it with my tongue and stared at the camera with watering eyes. When the sink turned on, I pressed my thighs together again, getting even hornier at the sounds they were making through my earbuds.

The student left, leaving me alone in the restroom again, and I finally let loose, allowing myself to gag, spit, swallow on the dildo, making throaty sounds that nobody should be making in Redwood Academy.

And when all three of the Poison boys came, I pulled it out of my mouth, smiled at the camera, and said, "You boys are missing out on today's lessons. Too bad for you." And then I shut off the phone.

Chapter Sixty-Three

After school, I sat across from Akio at Beestra, a fast-food place where all the Redwood students hung out on the weekends. I stared at my Bio textbook and grabbed a fry from the center of the table, furrowing my brows at the words on the page.

"I don't know why Barnes decides to give us tests every other week," I said.

"Because he has nothing better to do."

"We don't even cover this much material in class," I grumbled to myself, angrily biting the fry and staring at the chapters. "Does he expect us to teach ourselves, understand the material, *and* ace the test?"

Akio glanced up from his textbook. "We do, don't we?"

My lips curled into a snarl. "Yeah, but still, he's annoying."

A couple of the football players strolled in to grab a milkshake after practice, the notorious Jace Harbor following them but looking highly unamused by them flirting with random girls. He typed aimlessly on his phone and barely looked up at the woman who was *definitely* flirting with him at the counter.

I eyed him for a couple moments and scrunched up my nose. That was ... different.

Once he grabbed his milkshake, he turned around and made eye contact with me. While I would usually look away, I made sure he knew that I was watching him because I didn't trust that man as blindly as Allie might've. He nodded to me, as if to say, *What's up?* and followed the guys out of Beestra.

Snapping my book closed, I glanced up at Akio. "All right, enough studying. Let's talk."

Akio glanced up at me and readjusted his glasses. "About what?"

"Are your parents as annoying as mine are?" I asked him, dipping another fry in ketchup and kicking my legs back and forth under the table. "My mom literally scolds me if I don't do the smallest things right. I just ... ugh ..."

I had been holding this in for so damn long. Now that Akio had admitted that his parents weren't the *best*, I kinda, sorta had someone to vent to about them, someone who understood what it was like, being one of the *rich kids* who really didn't have it all, at least family-wise.

Akio ran a hand across his face. "He isn't *that* annoying, but he pushes me to get together with you. He wants me to be with you so badly, and it's so annoying," Akio admitted. "All he does is talk about you when I'm at home. How I have to be just like you, how we'd work well together. It's nonstop, Imani."

"Well ..." I smiled, thinking back to the Poison boys. "I'm off the market."

Akio playfully kicked me under the table. "Well, I don't like you, anyway."

"Who do you like?"

He shrugged and looked away, chewing a fry. "Nobody."

"Who?"

"Nobody."

I leaned across the table. "Oh, come on! You wanted to hang out and be friends. This is what friends do. They tell each other who they like, so their friend can go out, stalk their crush, and secretly make it happen!"

Akio stared at me with wide eyes and blinked a few times. "Exactly why I can't tell you."

"So, you're going to live the rest of your life alone?" I asked.

"God, you're so dramatic."

Tossing some of my curls over my shoulder, I smiled. "Thank you. I try."

After Akio rolled his eyes, he glanced behind me at a group of girls who walked into the building and right toward the cashier. I glanced over my shoulder to see Nicole, head of the cheerleading team, dressed in the tightest pair of leggings and a cute white crop top.

"Ugh, she's so—" I started, but when I turned back around and saw Akio staring at her, my jaw nearly dropped. "You like her?!"

Akio looked back at me. "Can you not scream that?"

I lowered my voice and leaned farther across the table. "Nicole?" I whisper-yelled at him. "The head bitch of the cheer team and the police chief's daughter?" I fake gagged. "Gross. She sleeps with, like, the entire school."

"And you sleep with the three most dangerous guys in Redwood."

"All right, you got me," I said with a smile and raised my glass of water. "Cheers to being a slut ... but she's the rudest damn person that I've met, and she has the unhealthiest obsession with Jace, Allie's ... stepbrother."

"So?" Akio said. "I think she's hot."

But I could tell that there was more. Akio didn't think she was just hot; he actually liked her for some reason. Maybe he liked bad girls like her, ones who would be nothing but rude to him and who only passed every class because she flirted hard with the teachers and principal.

"It doesn't matter," Akio said, finally tearing his gaze away from her. "She would never like me anyway. And if, miraculously, she did, my father would never approve of her. He'd take one look at her and judge her, the way that he judges everyone."

And while Akio was talking about Nicole, I understood the way he felt. Being part of a rich family meant that we had to be perfect, could never screw up, and could only be with people that our parents approved of. It wasn't our lives; it was theirs.

But that would change.

"Every decision that you make doesn't have to be for him," I said, giving him a smile. "Sometimes, the best ones are the decisions you make for yourself because being the perfect son in his eyes will never be achievable. I've tried, so don't worry about what he thinks. You do you."

Chapter Sixty-Four

IMANI

After my study session with Akio, I drove to Landon's house and knocked on the basement door.

João opened it and arched his brow. "Look who it is. Redwood's little tease must've decided that touching herself on camera wasn't enough."

"Very funny," I said without even trying to laugh, and then I walked down the stairs.

Landon sat on the couch with his shirt off and his fingers running over the bandages. "Fuck, it hurts," he mumbled to himself. Then, he looked up at me, his eyes immediately lighting up and making my stomach do flips.

Kai sat across from him in a chair with one leg propped up on the coffee table. I dropped my backpack next to it and sat beside Landon, my pussy clenching at the thought of earlier in Redwood's restroom, my nipples hardening against my bralette.

From across the table, Kai glanced down at them poking through my shirt and stood up before I could even say anything to any of the guys. He walked over to me, captured my nipples between his fingers, and tugged on them.

"Landon might not be able to move, but that doesn't mean we can't fuck you."

Heat swarmed in my core, and I inhaled sharply at the sudden dominance in his voice. I had known that he had a darker side, but I didn't think I would get to see it anytime soon. I'd thought that he'd at least wait until we were alone.

"Kai, I—"

He tugged on my nipples harder until I dropped from the couch to my knees. I stared up at him, my chest rising and falling quickly, and drew my hand up his thigh to the front of his pants, where his cock was throbbing.

My pussy clenched, and I whimpered softly at the pain shooting from my nipples.

When I went to open my mouth, Kai released my nipples, snapped it shut, and crouched by my side, domineeringly stroking his thumb across my cheek. "You're going to suck Landon off while we fuck you."

Again, I was at a loss for words. I swallowed hard and stared up at him with big eyes, my heart pounding in my chest. Hazily, I nodded and crawled toward Landon, placing my hands on his knees and glancing from him to his hard cock inside those tight gray sweatpants. Wetness pooled between my thighs.

After pulling down his sweatpants and letting his cock spring out, I rested my forearms on either side of the couch beside him and leaned over enough for my skirt to ride up my ass.

Behind me, João smacked his hand across one of my asscheeks, then grabbed it. "Arch your back and stick out your ass, Imani."

Kai looped his fingers around the hem of my underwear, kissed me above it on my hip, and pulled it down to my knees. "Take her," he said to João. "Her cunt is sopping fucking wet. She's probably been thinking about this all day."

At the sound of Kai finally taking control, I moaned and sucked Landon into my mouth, gently running my tongue across his head to get it nice and wet for me before he fucked my throat dry.

As João positioned himself behind me, Kai disappeared somewhere in the room. When Kai unzipped my backpack, João thrust himself into me, and I clenched around him, taking more of Landon inside my mouth.

João filled my tight cunt, and Kai walked around to my side. With Landon's cock in my mouth, I glanced back with watery eyes and watched Kai let a wad of spit drip from his mouth onto the rose quartz dildo that I had used earlier in the restroom.

My eyes widened slightly as his other hand fondled my ass, a couple fingers slipping into me. I tightened around João, and he groaned and thrust into me harder and faster.

"Fuck, she loves that."

Landon pulled the hair out of my face and held it back, moving my head up and down his length, telling me that I could take more of it, that I could get his huge monster cock farther down my throat. I swallowed on it, taking a deep breath, and forced him deeper.

Kai moved the wet dildo to my ass and slowly thrust it inside of me. For a moment, I winced, and then it easily slid right in. When Kai started moving it in and out, he grasped my hard nipple in his other and tugged harshly on it. The pressure rose in my core, my pussy clenching harder and harder on João.

I moaned on Landon's cock and reached down to grab Kai's through his pants. With help, I undid his zipper and pulled him out, spitting on my hand and stroking it quickly.

He grunted into my ear, "Just like that. Keep stroking that cock, baby."

With pleasure rushing through me, I closed my eyes and bobbed my head up and down Landon's cock, using my other hand to gently massage his balls the way I knew he loved. Landon groaned and tugged on my hair harder, keeping my head down on his cock.

After blinking my eyes open, I stared up at him through watery eyes and stuck my tongue out to lick his balls. Landon pushed his hips up to get another inch inside of me. As João continued to fuck my pussy from behind, he wrapped one of his hands around the front of my throat and stroked Landon's cock.

Landon threw his head back, his cum shooting out deep into my throat. When he finally let me go, I pulled my head back and gasped for air, his cum dripping out of my mouth and rolling down my chin.

João wrapped his hands around my mouth, snapping my jaw closed like a muzzle, and shoved his cock as deep into my pussy as he could get it, stilling and releasing his load inside of me. When he pulled out, Kai placed my hand over his on the dildo.

"Keep fucking your tight little ass with this," he said, gently pushing me back onto my knees. He stood up in front of me, captured my nipples between his fingers again, and pulled on them until they were red and aching. He shoved his cock into my mouth and face-fucked me harder than he ever had, making sloppy, wet noises come out of my throat.

Strings of thick spit and Landon's cum strung from my lips to the base of his cock. He continued to fuck my throat, harder and harder, pinching and tugging and rolling my nipples until I screamed out on him and came harder than I ever had before.

After he came inside me, he pulled out of my throat and left me an aching mess in the middle of Landon's basement.

Chapter Sixty-Five

LANDON

"So ..." Imani said, sitting up on the couch with her cheeks flushed and her bra straps hanging off her shoulders. She pulled them up and grabbed a beer from the table, opening it up. "What does this mean for ... us?"

Surprisingly, João's big mouth stayed quiet. He and Kai looked over at me curiously. Earlier, when they had asked me that question, I hadn't answered it. Honestly, I didn't know what to say or how to say it.

I loved Imani so much, but I ... I knew the way she felt about João and Kai too.

"What the fuck do you mean?" João said, sitting on the other couch and rolling a blunt.

After narrowing her eyes at him, she scrunched her nose. "You know what I mean."

Imani might not have felt this way in the beginning, but she now looked at them the way she looked at me too. There was something more between them than meaningless sex—even if João would never admit to it. He didn't want to get hurt, especially by a *rich girl*.

"If you think I'm in love with you because we've fucked a couple times ..." João started, flicking on his lighter and taking a hit. He pulled the blunt away from his mouth and coughed. "Then you can fuck off, princess."

Reeling in anger, Imani hurled a pillow at him, knocking him right in the head. "What is your problem? Every single day, you're always furious at the world. News flash, idiot: everyone has a shitty life, just like you."

João leaned forward. "You think my life is shitty?"

"You've been a dick to everyone lately," I said to him.

"I'm always a dick."

"You're only a dick when you like someone," I said, wanting to get on his nerves.

"Dude, shut the fuck up," João said. "You always gotta say some shit, don't you?"

Imani leaned forward with a smirk on her face. "Who do you like, João?" she teased.

Every single one of us knew that he liked Imani too. It was obvious as fuck, and I was stalling because I still didn't know what the hell to say to Imani.

How did I feel about her being with someone else? One of these guys? Both of them?

Part of me hated the idea of Imani being with anyone other than me.

The other part of me knew that I would never leave these guys. Since we had formed Poison, we had vowed to never stop until we cleaned up this town. And while things might change in the future, I couldn't see any of us leaving Poison. We were far too deep in this shit.

"Obviously not an annoying bitch like you," João said.

Used to his remarks, Imani rolled her eyes. "Well, I doubt any other bitch could put up with your ass anyway, so it looks like you're going to be lonely forever."

"She's got a point." Kai chuckled and sat back on the couch beside Imani, scrolling through his phone. "Shit," he said, shooting up from his seat. "I have somewhere to be. If you don't show up for school this week, L, make sure you're ready to go Friday night."

Imani furrowed her brows. "What happens Friday night?"

Ignoring her because I didn't want her to find out about us doing a job for Jace Harbor, I nodded to him. "I'll be there."

He shrugged on his coat. "See you later, Imani."

Imani followed Kai with her gaze until he walked out of the basement door, and then she pressed her thighs together and nervously rubbed her hands against them. "Anyway, what's going on Friday night? I want to come."

"No," I said.

"You'd fuck it up," João said.

Balling her hands into fists, Imani seethed. "I'm going to smack you one day, I swear."

I picked up the bong from the ground and grabbed my lighter, the pain from my wound shooting up my side. After wincing, I placed my mouth on it and inhaled deeply, letting the smoke fill my lungs.

Imani moved closer to me when I exhaled and put her legs over mine. "Can I try?"

"No," I said.

"Come on. It's been a long week already with you in the hospital."

"No," I said again, placing the bong on the ground, opposite of her.

She pressed her lips together and crossed her arms. "But—"

"No."

"Here," João said, handing her the blunt.

I knew what that fucker was doing too. When he had talked about Imani and me earlier, I had recognized that look in his eyes because that was how *I* felt about Imani, and I knew that was how Kai felt about Imani when she spoke to Akio.

Jealousy.

João wanted Imani to himself—or at least for her to like him too—as much as he wanted her to believe that he didn't give a fuck about her.

"What the fuck are you doing?" I asked him.

João smirked. "Making her part of Poison one slow step at a time."

"You'd better not fucking give that to her," I said between clenched teeth.

"What are you going to do?" João taunted me, waving the blunt at Imani for her to take. He tilted his head as if to test me and banked on me not being able to take a hit. "Hit me? I'd knock you back on your ass with a wound like that."

"It's fine," Imani said, waving it off. "I don't want it."

"Don't let this asshole influence you," João said.

Imani snatched the blunt from his hand and watched the satisfied smirk he placed on his face, and then she hurried to the bathroom and flushed it down the toilet. "That's for being a dick to me." Then, she smacked him across the face. "And that's because I felt like it. Stop being an asshole."

And with that, she sat on the couch next to me and rested her head on my shoulder. "Now, can you please tell me what's happening on Friday?"

But as much as she begged me, I would never tell her. She might want to be a part of Poison, but she would be in way too much danger if she was.

Chapter Sixty-Six

KAI

Imani sat at her lunch table with Allie and Jamal, glancing over at us and gnawing on the inside of her cheek. I eyed her, unable to think about anything other than her tied up in Landon's basement with her hard little nipples pinched between my fingers until they turned red.

Allie muttered something to Imani, and she tore her gaze away from us, cheeks flushing.

I readjusted myself in my black cargo pants, my dick rock fucking hard at the thought of finally having Imani to myself one of these nights. She'd be tied to my bedposts, her legs bound with rope, and tears in those big brown eyes of hers.

"Landon's bad news," Jamal's loud mouth said to Imani, drawing Landon's attention.

Landon growled beside me, picking at his soggy fries that the lunch ladies cooked here.

"If you're going to go for any of them, try Kai. He's chill," Jamal said. "Allie and I grew up with him on Pierce Road."

My lips curled into a small smile, and I glanced from Imani to Allie, remembering how often I'd play with her out on her rusty, old swing set. That was before everything had changed for fucking good and Dad died.

"Don't get fucking pride from that," João said to me. "It's Jamal who's talking."

Imani glanced over at us and gave us an amused smile. "*Or* I can try all three."

Jace Harbor walked into the cafeteria, and João stood.

"I'll be back."

João and Jace stood off to the side, talking tensely with each other about the deal we had with Jace. If Jace pulled through and somehow pulled two million dollars out of his ass by Friday, then we would be robbing the police chief's house for documents.

Usually, I'd be fine with it.

But I didn't want Imani to get involved, even a little. Yet that seemed like far too much to ask for. Allie wasn't only Jace Harbor's stepsister, but also Imani's best friend. If Jace fucking screwed up and Allie found out about it, she might spill to Imani. And then we'd have a problem.

A couple moments later, Principal Vaughn walked out of the cafeteria and down the hall with his hands clasped together. I tossed my lunch in the trash, told Landon that I'd meet up with him a bit later, and followed Vaughn in the halls.

Last week, I had found out that he and that policeman that I had killed were connected. And it wasn't sitting well with me how they knew each other or even why. I wanted to get to the bottom of it before something serious happened.

That was how it always was in Redwood.

This time, I wanted to be ahead.

When he walked out the front doors, I slipped out quietly behind him, so he wouldn't hear the door reopen and close. He pulled out his phone and placed his other hand on his hip, pushing back his suit jacket.

"Friday," he muttered into the phone. "I'll see you then."

I leaned against the brick wall and pulled a pack of cigarettes out of my pocket, listening to the lunch bell ring, signaling the beginning of sixth period. He hummed to himself and shut off the phone, turning back around and staring at me with wide eyes.

"What are you doing here, Kai?"

"What's up, Vaughn?" I asked, lighting up the cigarette. "Who was on the phone?"

"It's Principal Vaughn to you, and that's none of your business. You should be in class."

He went to snatch the cigarette out of my hand, but I pulled it away before he could grab it, then shoved the tip against his jacket, staining his precious suit.

"Be fucking careful, Vaughn. There's always someone watching."

And while he would've given anyone else detention for that, he was scared of Poison.

As he should be.

When he stormed through the front doors again, I sat on the stairs and lit another cigarette to think. I didn't know what the fuck he was up to, but the way his face had paled when he saw me standing behind him ... it had to be something bad.

The door opened behind me, and I waved the cigarette in the air.

"I'm not going back to class, Vaughn. Don't even try."

After a couple quiet moments passed, I looked behind me. Allie stepped out into the cold, tugging her jacket around her body. It was thin and from Walmart, the same one she'd had when she still lived on Pierce Road, a couple houses down from Mom and me.

She had Jace's father's money now. She could be wearing something thicker.

I didn't understand why she didn't use him up and suck him dry. She knew how hard it was to live in the fucking slums. She didn't have to live with ripped clothes anymore, but for some reason, she did.

"What're you doing, skipping class?" I asked.

She ignored me and sat on the steps. "I need to talk to you about Jace."

"We don't talk about jobs or clients." I flicked the cigarette on the step in front of me and stomped it out. "You know that, Allie. I can't give up shit about him, or he won't pay."

Snow drifted down around us, her breath coming out as a white fog—looking like *she* was smoking a cigarette. "I don't need information on him. I need you to cut off communication with him, stop giving him drugs. It's going to ruin his chances of getting into the NFL, if he gets addicted."

I paused for a moment and furrowed my brows. "I thought you hated him after what he did to you. Why do you care about what happens to him because of his own senseless decisions?"

She pressed her lips together and glanced down at the slush by her feet, watching it melt as she stepped on it. "I don't know," she whispered, hugging her arms around her body, probably to stay warm. "Just, please, don't give him any more shit."

The front door opened again, and João walked out of the building, zipping up his coat. Face paling, Allie shot up to her feet.

"What's going on here?" João asked.

"Nothing," she said quickly.

"If he pays up, he gets what he wants, Allie," I said. "We can't do anything for you."

After staring between me and João, she excused herself to go back into the building.

João furrowed his brows at me, then at the door. "You didn't tell her shit, did you? Because it looks like Jace Harbor is going to be paying up. We have to hope he doesn't chicken out at the last minute."

Chapter Sixty-Seven

JOÃO

"These people need to fucking die," I said, staring out at our classmates who flooded out of the football stadium and into the streets, not caring who they walked in front of on Friday night. "One of these fucking days, I'm going to plow right through them. There're too many."

The students cheered and laughed together, celebrating a Redwood win.

Like winning by one point in overtime should be celebrated.

When the red light turned green in front of me and people continued to walk right across the crosswalk without a care in the world, I laid on the horn and cursed out of the window. "Fucking move, before I make you."

We were late to meet Jace in the back parking lot to grab the money. Kai had gotten there about ten minutes ago and was still waiting for him to come out of the locker room, but I wanted to be there when he did because I needed to make sure he wasn't going to back out.

He needed to get us entrance into the police chief's house.

As the crowd finally died out and the light turned yellow, I sped around the corner, my wheels screeching against the asphalt. I pulled into the back parking lot next to Jace's car and cursed when I saw him talking to Kai already.

"You got it?" I asked, stepping out of the car with Landon.

Jace swallowed hard and looked around nervously, as if he didn't want to do this.

Landon arched his brow. "Anxious tonight? You almost lost the damn game for us."

"You want the money or not?" Jace asked through clenched teeth, opening his trunk.

Landon, Kai, and I walked around to the back.

When I saw the duffel bags, I unzipped one and nodded, a smirk crossing my lips. "Didn't think you'd be able to get this much in time," I said to Jace, then nodded to Landon. "Take it."

Landon gathered the bags and put them in my trunk.

"Text the details to Kai," I said to Jace, shutting the trunk. I shouldn't be surprised that he was going through with this because his father was almost as big of a dick as mine was, but still ... I had expected a rich boy to act differently when it came down to it.

"When will it be done?"

"We'll count the money tonight. If it's all there, we can do it tomorrow at the earliest. And the girls stay out of this." Then, I climbed into my car and nodded to Kai. "Meet us back at Landon's." I slammed my door and sped out of the parking lot, looping around the school one more time to see if Imani had finally left the game yet.

Kids filled the main student parking lot, hanging out of their cars, crowding the sidewalks, making plans on where to party tonight because after every Redwood win, there *had* to be a party somewhere.

I scanned the parking lot for Imani, and when I didn't find her, I continued down the road toward the field one last time. Imani walked down the sidewalk with Allie and Akio, sinking deep into her winter coat.

Slowing down, I parked on the opposite side of the road and glanced into my rearview mirror to watch her walk back to her car. I didn't fucking care if she got back to her car all right, but there were too many rowdy kids tonight, already drunk off their asses.

Landon didn't say anything about me stopping and stared into the rearview mirror too. "What the fuck is Akio doing with her?"

"I don't know, but when Kai finds out, he's going to kick his ass. Kai hates Akio."

"For good reasons, but especially for what Akio's family did to his parents."

I shook my head. "Another piece-of-shit family. Who fucking knew Redwood was shit?"

Suddenly, Jace sped around the corner to the student parking lot in his car, and he parked and got out when he saw Nicole. I threw the car in reverse and backed up enough to get a better view of the action. Between him and Nicole and Allie who was about to walk over, something was bound to happen.

And I hoped to fuck Imani wasn't about to be in the middle of a Redwood fight.

She'd be able to kick anyone's ass, but still.

Nicole moved closer to him, biting her lip and looking actually ridiculous. I rolled down my window, hoping to hear something but couldn't over the loud murmurs of the crowd. Jace swung an arm around her waist and pulled her closer, flirting to get us access into her father's house for tomorrow night.

But shit ...

I knew how much he cared about Allie now.

Jace snatched Nicole's jaw, making psycho Nicole giggle. When she stepped away, Allie stopped mid-stride and froze along with Imani and Akio. They all stared at the scene with wide eyes, Imani scrunching her nose.

"Fuck," Landon said, undoing his seat belt. "Shit is about to go down."

"Stay here," I said, clutching the steering wheel and waiting. "Nothing will happen."

When Nicole disappeared, Allie started screaming at Jace. Imani wrapped her arms around Allie's waist and dragged her flailing body to the car, then said something inaudible to Jace. After Imani gave him the finger, she screeched out of the parking lot. I started the car and followed behind her, making sure she got home without trouble.

I wouldn't put it past Nicole to try to start something with her and Allie.

"You wouldn't do this shit for just anyone," Landon said. "Just admit that you like her."

I kept my gaze focused on the windshield and tightened my hand around the wheel because if I looked over at him, I knew I'd punch his face in for saying what he just had. Truth was that I really fucking liked Imani, but I ... I didn't want her to hurt me.

Between my father and finding medication for Ana and comforting Mom every night, I didn't have time for a relationship. What Imani and I had now was enough. It had to be.

Chapter Sixty-Eight

IMANI

"No! I can't do this again!" Allie mumbled in her sleep, her head turning from side to side and a pained expression on her face.

I hadn't been able to sleep all night. Allie had been having nightmares for the past six hours, forcing me awake.

Mom gently knocked on my bedroom door, actually learning manners for once. I walked over to it and opened the door, careful not to wake Allie.

Mom handed me a glass of tea. "How is she taking it?"

I glanced over my shoulder. "Bad."

Last night at the football game, Allie had found Jace accepting an invitation to fuck Nicole at her house. Allie was devastated and admitted to being in love with Jace in front of everyone. And Jace Harbor had done nothing but make my best friend look like an idiot.

"Thanks for the tea," I said, turning back to the bedroom.

"Imani," Mom said before I shut the door so Dad wouldn't wake, "can we talk later?"

After glancing at her for a moment, I silently sighed to myself and nodded. Even though I hated talking to her, she was becoming more bearable by the day. But I was nervous that this was all some big sort of facade, that she'd one day flip another switch and start scolding me for everything that I did.

I didn't think that I'd be able to take it if she did.

Once I shut the door, I logged in to my computer to get some homework done. But the more Allie tossed and turned, the more I tried to piece things together. When Allie had admitted to Jace that she loved him, Jace had looked so happy to hear those words yet so devastated for what he had done.

Even the other day at Beestra, Jace Harbor had barely even looked at any of the girls who flirted with him. It almost made me think that ... he actually loved her back. But that wouldn't make any sense that he would get back together with Nicole.

Unless ...

I clenched my teeth and opened Discord to the group chat I had with Poison.

Unless *they* had something to do with it.

They had said they had something to do last night after the game. They showed up with about five minutes left in overtime and left shortly after the game was over, disappearing completely on me and driving toward the back school parking lot.

If they had done something to Jace, which would in turn hurt Allie, I would kick their ass for real this time. I didn't care who they were or what they meant to me. Nobody hurt Allie. Nobody made Allie a crying mess like she had been last night. She was my best fucking friend.

"Stop it!" Allie shouted.

Having had enough of watching her in agony, I climbed on top of her flailing body and shook her. "Allie, wake up!" I shouted. She thrust her hands up at me, but I pinned them to her pillow beside her head. "Allie!"

A couple moments later, she opened her eyes. Her body was trembling underneath mine, tears pouring down her cheeks. She sobbed loudly and curled herself into a ball underneath me, clutching her knees to her chest. Hiccups escaped her mouth.

"I'm so dumb. I'm so fucking dumb and stupid!" She threw her head in her hands. "I tried everything to get him to love me again, fucking everything. Sleeping with him, making him jealous in hopes that ... he'd show me he fucking cared."

My heart ached for my best friend. I wrapped my arms around her and rested my head on her shoulder, holding her tight to me. "Stop it, Allie. He's not worth your tears."

"Nothing worked. He'll never love me like I love him. I'm not good enough for him. He just keeps me around to fuck. That's all I am to him, a stupid fucking fuck buddy he can use to get off. He's never cared about me."

I stroked her hair and pushed some tears from her face, wanting to take away all her pain. "He's a rich, spoiled brat. You deserve so much more. You don't want someone like him who doesn't care about your feelings."

"But I love him so much that it hurts. I will never stop loving him. I've tried so many times, Imani. He's fucking sewn himself into my heart, and he keeps stabbing me with the needle." She wiped the tears from her cheeks and shook her head. "And I'm the stupid girl who keeps letting him."

"You're not stupid. He is." I pulled her closer to me and stared out the window, watching small flakes of snow fall from the white sky. "My mom made breakfast for us. I know how you love her French toast. Wanna go get some with me?"

Allie sniffled. "Did she really?"

"Yes."

"And you're okay with being down there with her?"

"For you?" I said with a smile, tugging on her hand and pulling her up. "Yes."

So, I dragged Allie downstairs to the dining room and sat next to Mom at the table.

Allie sat across from us and grabbed some French toast, tears still sliding down her cheeks. "Thank you so much, Mrs. Abara."

"Oh, honey, stop crying," she said with a smile. "He's not worth your tears. He'll figure out what he did wrong and come crawling back to you, just watch."

"And when he does, I'll be right there to kick his ass," I said.

Mom arched a brow at me. "I hope those boys aren't teaching you this."

I awkwardly scratched the back of my neck and stuffed my face with French toast. Maybe they were, but one thing was certain. If those boys really had had something to do with this, then I would be the one to kick *their* asses.

Chapter Sixty-Nine

IMANI

After Allie *convinced* me that she was okay—I knew that she wasn't but that she needed to clear her head—I texted Mom that I'd be hanging out with Akio today and drove to Landon's house. João's car and Kai's bike were parked out front.

I slid up behind the black Mercedes with tinted windows and pulled the key out of the ignition, rushing up to the back door to the basement and banging my fist against it. "Open up! I know you guys are in there."

A couple moments later, Kai opened the door with his hair a mess and his eyes tired, as if he had just woken up. He wiped them and stepped out of the way for me to walk down the stairs. I marched down to the basement to see Landon and João sitting up on the couch, yawning.

"What the fuck, Imani?" João said. "It's nine in the morning on a Saturday."

"Yeah, it is, and I've been up since last night." I crossed my arms and narrowed my eyes at each one of them.

"So, you decided to bother us?" João asked.

"What are you guys doing with Jace Harbor?" I asked, anger rushing through my veins at the thought of them being involved with the way that Jace had acted toward Allie yesterday. If they'd had any-fucking-thing to do with it, I swore to God that they wouldn't get any pussy for days.

Weeks maybe.

They might be the guys I was fucking, but Allie was my best friend.

"Nothing," João said.

I glanced over at Kai, who refused to look at me, then at Landon, who looked away after we made eye contact. Something was up with them, and I needed to find out what it was because I refused to let Allie get in the middle of this.

"What happened?" I asked, making my voice sterner so they'd take me seriously.

But they were Poison. They faced people far more dangerous than me. They wouldn't admit to anything even if I pulled a gun on them and tortured them for days. Their lips were sealed the fuck shut.

And I loathed that.

Another moment passed, and I decided to take a different approach.

I sat beside Landon, curled up into his lap, and pushed some hair out of his face. "Can you please tell me what happened? Allie's hurt."

"Allie?" Kai asked, sitting up and suddenly interested. "What happened to her?"

"Jace Harbor happened," I said, confused at his sudden reaction to my best friend.

Kai clenched his jaw and cursed Jace under his breath. Jealousy bubbled inside of me, the more I studied him.

What the hell was that? Why is he acting like this about Allie? He is supposed to get pissed off when someone hurts *me*.

Angry, I turned back to Landon. "Please, Landon. I'm not going to tell anyone."

The look in Landon's eyes told me that he desperately wanted to tell me everything that was going on. But instead, he placed his callous hand on my thigh, squeezed lightly, and tore his gaze away. "I can't. It's too dangerous."

"Please," I pleaded, batting my lashes.

"No."

Pissed off now, I scrambled off him, stood back up, and placed my hands on my hips. "I don't understand you guys. First, you want me to be part of Poison; you get me deep in your shit and make me watch you kick the life out of two people, and now, you won't tell me why you're working with Jace."

"We're not working with Jace," João said.

"You're a terrible liar, João," I said, nostrils flaring.

"We're not."

"Then, you wouldn't mind if I—"

For the first time today, my gaze fell on the two duffel bags in the corner of the room, which were both unzipped and had bricks of hundred-dollar bills spilling out of them. My eyes widened, and I rushed over to them, picking up the cash.

There must've been over a million dollars here.

"What did you do?" I asked, glancing over my shoulder. "How do you have this much cash?"

João stalked over to us, grabbed my upper arm, and yanked me up. "Stay out of our fucking business, Imani." He snatched the cash from me and threw it back into the duffel bag. "You don't need to know what we do for our money."

"This is Jace's money," I said.

The other kids at Redwood might've been rich, but not as rich as Jace Harbor's father. They didn't have money coming out of the ass like he did. He probably had so much cash that he wouldn't even notice a million or more stolen by his son.

"Go back home," João said. "And stay there. We'll be too busy tonight to deal with you."

"To deal with me?" I asked, brow arched.

"To deal with your dramatic fucking ass," João said.

I yanked myself out of his grip and shoved him back hard. "Fuck you. I hate you."

Then, I stomped back up the stairs and to the basement door without saying good-bye to either of the others. I slammed the door closed and pulled out my phone. I wasn't going to sit out and stay away like they wanted me to do. I would figure out what they were doing with Jace tonight.

"Hey," I said over the phone. "Wanna hang out tonight? I'm going spying."

"What about Allie?"

"God, Akio, you asked me to hang out with you more. Allie can't come, anyway."

He let out a long sigh over the phone. "Fine."

"Good. I'll pick you up at six. Make sure you're ready."

<h1 style="text-align:center">Chapter Seventy</h1>

KAI

"You're fucking shoving your elbow into my bandage," Landon said between clenched teeth at João.

We sat in the back of Jace Harbor's father's car, more so in the trunk, so we could sneak into the police chief's neighborhood.

I tightened my hand around the black ski mask and glanced to the front of the car when Jace stopped.

"Jace Harbor ..."

The guard at the neighborhood gates flashed his light into the car to look into the backseat. I ducked my head and hoped that he wouldn't search the trunk, but from what I had researched, this security guard barely got off his ass, so we should be good.

"Who are you here to see?"

"Who I come to see here every time, Jack," Jace said. "Nicole."

From the way he had said her name, I could tell that he really didn't want to be here. After what had happened with Allie last night, I heard that he had nearly drunk himself into an early grave. If it wasn't for his friend Jamal helping him out, I doubted he would've even woken up.

No matter how much Jace Harbor wanted Allie to think that he didn't love her still, he did.

He fucking did.

Just like I liked Imani.

I glanced up behind the very last row of seats to see the security guard scanning Jace's license. He opened the gates for Jace, and Jace rolled up my window as soon as he could. I pulled out my laptop and tapped through a couple screens, hacking into the cameras posted on every street corner in this neighborhood and shutting them down.

Then, I texted Jace.

Me: Cameras are down.

Jace pulled over to the curb near some large shrubs and popped the trunk. João hopped out first and slid into the passenger seat, and then I jumped out and helped Landon out of the trunk, opening the backseat and handing him his ski mask.

When we all sat in the car, João lit a cigarette and took two puffs. "Last chance to turn back, Harbor."

Jace tightened his grip on the steering wheel and continued to drive. I glanced into the rearview mirror to see a car about a half-mile down the road that had been following behind us now for the past two miles. Nobody else had noticed it yet, except me.

And if it was anyone other than Imani, I would've told Jace to take a couple circles around the neighborhood to lose them. But even after we had warned Imani to stay away from this business because it was risky, she couldn't.

I'd punish her for it later.

Jace pulled into Nicole's driveway.

"Huh?" João asked. "Still in?"

"We're going through with it." Jace yanked the key out of the ignition. "Get me what I need."

After Jace hopped out of the car and walked to the front door, I pulled the ski mask over my face and secured my laptop in the trunk. Based on what I had read about the police chief's security system, once Jace disabled it, we would have ten minutes, max, unless Jace put it off completely.

But I doubted he knew how to do that.

"Hey, Jacey," Nicole said, pulling the door open in a silky robe. "I was just freshening up."

Jace stepped into the house. "You look good."

Yet again, the words didn't match his tone.

When the door closed, João glanced into the backseat. "You think he'll actually be able to disable the security system? He's not as tech savvy as you."

"He'll do it." I quietly opened the back door and stepped out of the car. "Come on. We won't have much time once he does."

I grabbed all the essentials I needed for sneaking into the police chief's office, which was most likely locked, even in a secure house like his. I walked with Landon and João to the front door. Jace stood in the kitchen, downing a glass of wine faster than I had seen anyone drink.

He poured two more glasses, then fumbled with the security system in the hallway. When he pulled away, he glanced out the front door at us and curtly nodded, as if to give us the go-ahead, and then he walked back into the living room with a glass of wine for him and a glass of wine for Nicole.

João opened the front door, the house staying quiet, and snuck in with Landon right behind him. I glanced over my shoulder and back at the street, spotting Imani and Akio driving slowly by Nicole's house and looking at me.

Her brown eyes widened slightly when she saw me staring back. I balled my hands into fists, wondering why the fuck he was with her, and vowed to myself that the first thing I'd do when I saw her pretty face again was bound every part of her body until she became immobile and punish her for following us and getting involved.

Chapter Seventy-One

IMANI

*F*uck.

Kai had spotted me.

I had tried so hard to hide from them, stayed behind car after car on the way over to Nicole's place, and had even driven about a half-mile behind them when there weren't any cars between us.

I swallowed hard and focused on the road in front of me, my stomach in tight knots.

These past few days, they had been so serious about me staying away from this particular job, so much so that I desperately wanted to know what they were up to. If only I could've hidden myself better because now, they were going to explode on me.

And not in the good kind of way.

I didn't care that he was about to chew my ass out for snooping, but ... I didn't want Landon to find out, too, and be disappointed in me. I just wanted to help them out. They'd taken me this far into Redwood's bullshit, and they might've played a hand in Jace hurting Allie.

It wasn't cool to me that, suddenly, I couldn't come.

"Are you okay?" Akio asked, furrowing his brows and staring at me in confusion. "You look like you've seen a ghost."

"Not a ghost," I said, taking another drive by Nicole's house. "But maybe my death …"

If they had already seen me, what did it matter if we staked out the place for the next few minutes, right? Nobody was going to find out that we might've been stalking the Poison boys to get some information on Jace and his shitty life choices.

"Fuck it," I mumbled to myself, parking the car across the street and cutting all the lights. I pulled out a pair of binoculars that I had in my car when I used to stalk Jace Harbor after he hurt Allie the first time. I had never trusted that bastard and needed to know why he would break it off after confessing his love to her.

And this bitch Nicole was always the damn problem.

"Why do you have binoculars in your—"

"Bird-watching, Akio," I snapped, zooming in so I could see more clearly. "AKA none of your business." I nodded to the glove compartment. "There is another pair in there for you, if you want to snoop. I know you like her, so you might as well see how big of a bitch she is."

I knew that I really shouldn't be rude to him about who he liked, but I still couldn't really understand his fascination with *her*. Out of all the girls in Redwood who would love to be with someone like him, who had both brains and cash, he liked her.

"Why do you care that I like her so much?" Akio asked, putting the binoculars to his face.

"Because friends don't let friends make bad decisions," I said.

"You let Allie fall for Jace again."

Cutting my eyes to him, I gave him the finger behind his back. "That's different."

Back to spying, I leaned closer to the passenger window. But no matter the angle I got, I really couldn't see into the house. We were both too far away and not in a good place to look into any of the first-floor windows. And if we were, most were covered with thick curtains.

After pulling the key from the ignition, I nodded to Akio. "Come on."

"Come on?" he asked.

I snuck out of the car and shut the door quietly behind me, sprinting across the street and slipping between Nicole's house and her hedges. Akio stared at me with wide eyes from the passenger door, then cursed out loud and ran after me.

"What are we doing?" he asked. "We can't stalk someone. It's against the law!"

"Yeah, yeah, yeah," I said, waving him off. "There is a better place to see into her house around the back."

"How do you know this?!" Akio asked, hurrying after me. "It's Poison, isn't it?"

Stopping on my heel, I whirled around and poked a finger into his chest. "No, it's not Poison. I've done this, far before I ever met them, so stop thinking that I'm such a good girl, and let's have fun, snooping on Jace Harbor and the girl you like ... and Poison."

After Akio finally got over the initial shock and relaxed, he followed me around the back. We pressed our bodies flat against the house and inched closer to the back door that led to the pool. They had curtains to cover the glass, but I doubted the police chief let Nicole close them.

He loved seeing what he earned by ripping off all of Redwood, especially the poor.

"Are you sure this is okay?" he asked.

"No, but we're doing it anyway." I glanced over my shoulder at him. "You ready?"

"Uh ..." He scratched the back of his head. "Sure?"

I crouched and glanced in through the back glass door window to see Nicole on her knees in front of Jace Harbor, who looked incredibly uncomfortable. He gave her a forced smile and tensed when she moved her hands up his thighs.

Pulling back suddenly, I hit my head hard into Akio's and winced. "Jeez, Akio," I said, rubbing the spot. "You have a hard-ass head. Now, do you see who Nicole really is? Look how uncomfortable she's making him and she—" I glanced back into the room. "Wait."

That didn't make any sense. Jace looked ... uncomfortable?

Usually, a dick like him loved being sucked off by the cheer squad. Yet all I could see was the anguish and pain on his face. He swallowed hard and stared up at the ceiling, and I swore that I saw tears in his eyes.

He didn't want to be here. He didn't want to do this.

Though I didn't have much time to figure out why he was here because a couple moments later, while Nicole was distracted, the

Poison boys snuck through a back hallway. I cursed to myself and shoved Akio back, pushing him around the house and making a beeline for my car.

"Go, Akio! They're going to see us if you don't get your ass in gear."

The front door opened, and I slipped into my car, my heart pounding inside my chest. Before they could make their grand exit, I thrust my key into the ignition, waited for Akio to shut his door, and slammed my foot on the gas pedal to speed the fuck out of there.

Yet when I looked into the rearview mirror, Kai pulled off his ski mask, made sure that I knew he was watching me, and slipped into Jace's car. And all I knew was that I was really screwed tonight. He had definitely seen me.

Chapter Seventy-Two

JOÃO

"Not going to fucking lie," Landon said, holding up the manila folder we had stolen from the police chief's home office and clutching his stomach. "Whatever is in here has to be big if Jace paid us two million dollars for it. I'm kinda afraid to open it."

I snatched the folder from his hand. "Don't be a baby."

"You sure you don't want to wait until Jace—"

"No."

Deciding that Jace Harbor was probably getting fucked right now because he was taking too fucking long with Nicole, I flipped the flap open and sifted through the paperwork and evidence that the chief must've hidden from the detectives during the investigation into Jace's mom's death years ago.

It was no accident.

Who would've thought that the corrupt police would be in on it?

"This shit is bad," I said, reaching for a letter from the police chief himself and swallowing.

After handing the shit back to Kai and Landon, I stared through the windshield with both anger and literal fear rushing through my veins. Everyone in Redwood knew that the police were shit, but seeing everything that they'd done over the years sickened me.

"Fuck," Kai whispered.

"This is worth way more than two million," Landon said.

And he was right.

This single folder had the dirt on nearly every rich resident of Redwood, every cop, every official. It was like the chief had been hoarding this for blackmail. That fucking asshole probably was. How else would he have gone from living in the Redwood slums, like the rest of us, to having this kind of house in a gated neighborhood?

Fifteen more minutes passed before Jace Harbor walked out the front door with his head hanging low and guilt written all over his face. He ripped open the driver's door and collapsed into the car, his hand tight around the steering wheel.

"Damn, what was she doing with you in there the entire time?" Landon asked when he slid into the car with a makeup wipe in one hand and his dignity in the other. "Prettying you up, Harbor?"

Without saying a word, Jace backed out of the driveway and parked by some shrubs. He opened his mirror and wiped off all the fucking makeup Nicole had put on his face. When he got it all off, he threw the sheet into the garbage on the side of the door.

"Did you get my shit or not?" he asked through clenched teeth.

I handed him the folder. "This was what we found. There's a lot of shit in there that could put a lot of people in this town away. That prick is probably blackmailing the rich to get money from them. That's how he got enough cash to move into a guarded neighborhood."

Jace opened the file and blew out a breath through his nose, flipping through it until he reached the name Harlan Harbor. There were a couple of documents on him, like copies of messages to Rick Santos and a copy of a check written to the police chief himself for over a hundred million.

"Is this enough?" Jace asked us.

Would it be enough, for what? To put him away?

"How would we know?" I asked.

"You guys have been to fucking jail."

"So have you," Landon said.

I went to grab the folder back from him, but he pulled it away.

"This is worth more than two million dollars," he said to us. "I take what I need about my father. You promise to do whatever the fuck I need you to do for me. Understand?"

After glancing into the backseat at Kai and Landon, I nodded. "Deal. Anything you need, you got it." As long as we got what we needed to destroy everyone here, then I was fucking fine with doing whatever he needed from us.

Once he stuffed his father's shit into the glove compartment, he handed me the documents and drove to Landon's house. Kai and Landon climbed out of the backseat, Landon hobbling across the street to the curb with his hand pressed harder against his abdomen.

I was surprised he hadn't taken any more pain pills tonight.

"I told you there would be consequences if you hurt Allie," Kai said, looking at Jace through the passenger window. "The job you asked for is done. Watch your fucking back, Harbor."

Jace swallowed hard and nodded. I rolled up the window, wanting to have a second alone with Jace.

"Plan it strategically," I said to him. "Whatever information you took out of that folder, make sure it won't get *you* sent to jail. You're eighteen now. You won't be sent to juvie this time, if you can't convict him."

Jace rubbed a hand over his face. He had to be strategic about this, but he also couldn't wait that much longer. The police chief wasn't stupid. He'd figure out what was going on within a couple days. And Jace's father would find two million missing from his savings.

Once Jace said that he'd be fine, I climbed out of the car and walked across the street to Landon and Kai, watching Jace Harbor drive off. If he wasn't careful, this could land all of us in prison. And he was a wreck right now.

<h1 style="text-align:center">Chapter Seventy-Three</h1>

KAI

Imani's car was parked right outside Landon's house. As Jace Harbor drove off and out of the Redwood slums, I glanced into the windows at the empty car and clenched my jaw at the mere thought of Imani being out with Akio tonight.

Not only had she come to a job with us, but she brought him too.

After I had told him to stay away from her.

Instead of saying anything to the guys, I followed them into the back toward the basement door.

Landon glanced around the backyard, brows furrowed. "Where the hell is she? She doesn't have a key."

When Landon opened the basement, we could see Imani's figure sitting on the couch.

"Did you guys find what you needed to find?" Imani asked, sitting on Landon's basement couch in the dark with her arms crossed over her chest. "Did you do what you needed to do?"

"Why are you sitting in the dark?" Landon asked, flicking on a light switch.

"Probably couldn't find the light," João said, pointing it out to her as if she were a toddler.

Imani stood and stomped over to him, nostrils flaring. "Actually, I wanted the element of surprise." She poked him in the chest. "But you wouldn't understand that because you guys don't care who sees or hears you."

"It would've been more of a surprise if your car wasn't out front," João said, brushing past her and farther into the room.

Everyone was on edge tonight, even him.

Fuming with anger, Imani shoved him back and stomped back to her place on the couch, hands balled into tiny fists by her sides. It would almost be cute if she hadn't snuck into Nicole's neighborhood with us and now needed to be punished.

"So, did you?"

"None of your business," João said, sitting beside her.

When neither João nor Landon said a word about Imani being there with us tonight—because they didn't know—she turned toward me.

She furrowed her brows slightly, as if to silently ask, *You haven't told them that I was a bad, bad girl?*

And when I raised my brows at her, she turned away and sucked in a sharp breath.

"What's got you so flustered?" Landon asked, sitting on the opposite couch and clutching his stomach. He pulled out an orange bottle of pills and took two, and then he washed it down by lighting a blunt and relaxing against the cushion. "Fuck."

Knowing that she was in the wrong, she pressed her lips together. "None of your business. And you shouldn't be taking pills and smoking at the same time. They don't mix well together."

"Says the girl who wanted a hit," João said.

"Have I told you how much I hate you?" She seethed, nostrils flaring.

"Why don't you get the fuck out of here?" João snapped back to her. "We're not finished for the night. We still have shit to do. And if you're going to sit here, complain, and try to get up into our business, you're going to really piss me off."

Imani pressed her lips together, suddenly quieting down. "What'd you do with Jace?"

"What the fuck did I just say?" João said.

"All I heard from you was whining. Blah, blah, blah, blah, blah." She grabbed her keys and stood. "You all either want me here so you can fuck me or you don't want me here at all, and I'm getting so fucking annoyed with it. I don't understand why you can't be honest with me."

"Because your dramatic ass wouldn't be able to handle it," João said.

And we all knew that was a lie, though neither Landon nor I tried to refute it because Imani needed to stay out of this. She might've gone through a couple rounds of kicking people's asses with us, but she didn't—and shouldn't—know about this heavy shit.

She shouldn't know that we'd done things far worse than kick someone's face in.

That we'd killed.

"It's late." I crossed my arms and watched a flustered Imani. "I'll take you home."

"No," Imani said, shaking her head and glancing nervously at me. "It's fine. I can—"

"I'm taking you home," I said with finality, not giving her room to argue.

Landon passed a blunt to João, who took it and threw the file down onto the couch. "You're not going to stay, Kai. This is some heavy shit, and we need to figure out what the fuck we're going to do about it."

"Yeah, Kai," Imani said, inching toward the door. "Why don't you stay? Nobody wants me here anyway."

I narrowed my eyes at her, silently asking if this was really how she wanted to play this little game. I had the power to ruin her night by telling Landon and João that she had followed us to a job and snooped around the house while we worked. She didn't want that.

"You keep digging yourself a bigger hole," I said.

Her face paled.

"My bike. Now."

After quickly gathering all her belongings, she scurried up the basement steps and slipped out the door. I told the guys that I'd be back soon, though I didn't know how long I'd take to punish Imani for what she'd done, and I left without answering any of their questions.

Imani stood by my bike, shifting uncomfortably from foot to foot. "I really should be—"

"Get on." I handed her my helmet and slapped the seat. "We're going for a ride."

Chapter Seventy-Four

IMANI

"This isn't my house," I squeaked, staring at an abandoned house in the slums.

Kai parked in the back and slipped off the bike, and then he tugged off my helmet and placed it on his seat. He grabbed my hand tightly and pulled me toward a back door, where there were cameras aimed at the porch. "No, it's mine."

"Wh-why are we here?" I whispered, my voice so small, an ache growing in my core.

I knew why we were here.

This was my punishment.

Kai was finally going to have his way with me, and I couldn't fucking wait. But still, I couldn't believe that he hadn't even mentioned to the guys that I had been following them tonight. Maybe he wanted me to himself. And if that was the reason ... God, I couldn't wait.

My pussy was already wet and clenching at the thought.

"You know what we're doing here," he said, unlocking and opening the door for me. When I went to step into the house, he grasped the back of my neck suddenly and pulled me closer to him, his brown eyes so domineering. "Don't you?"

"Yes," I whispered.

"Why?"

"Because I followed you."

He released his hold on me and let me walk into the room. Instead of letting me settle in and look around, he led me right to the back bedroom and shut the door.

"You don't have to worry about being quiet. I live alone, and these walls are soundproof."

My eyes widened, and I pressed my thighs together, standing awkwardly in the corner of the bleak gray room. He strolled over to a dresser and pulled out three thick black ropes, tossing them onto the bed, along with a ball gag and a vibrator that looked new.

As he unraveled the rope, he watched me intently. "Take off your clothes."

I sucked in a sharp breath and pulled off my top and bottoms, standing in nothing but some small panties and a bralette, my nipples begging to be touched and tugged on like he had done the other night.

When the rope was completely unraveled, Kai snapped it between his fists and raised his brows with an even sterner gaze. "You're aching to be punished, aren't you?" he asked, looking down at my thighs pressed tightly together. "Take off your underwear and don't make me say it again."

My heart pounded in my chest at the sight of the rope, but I unfastened my bra and pushed my soaked panties to my ankles, standing completely naked in front of him and bouncing on my toes.

"Knees," he ordered.

And for some ungodly reason, I found myself kneeling in front of him.

He stepped closer to me and cocked a finger, beckoning me forward. I crawled toward him until I knelt at his feet and stared up at him, my face inches from the bulge in his black cargo pants. All I wanted to do was run my hands all over him as I sucked him off.

"Beg me to punish you."

Heat gathered between my legs, and I batted my lashes at him. "Please, punish me."

"More."

"Please, Kai," I pleaded. "Tie me up and punish me for sneaking out tonight."

"Make it believable," he ordered, grasping my chin. "Show me how much you want it."

Unable to stop myself, I placed my mouth right over his bulge and sucked on it through his clothes. "Please, fuck me," I begged, pulling back for the slightest moment. I moved forward and sucked on it some more. "Stuff my mouth full. Tie me up. Hurt me."

Kai wrapped his hand around the front of my throat and lifted me until I stumbled to my feet, and then he twirled me around and bent me over the bed, tugging my arms behind my back.

"Good girl."

He looped the rope around my arms, pulling them as far back as they could go without hurting me and restraining them so I could barely move them.

"Kai," I whimpered, sticking my ass out and desperately wanting him inside me. "Please."

He posted one knee on the bed next to me and pulled me further onto the bed, so I sat back on it. After forcing me to bend my leg until my foot met the back of my thigh, he tied up my leg in an intricate design, then did so with the other leg, making me immobile.

"You're going to learn what happens when you're a bad girl, Imani."

Leaving me on the bed, naked and restrained, he walked back to his dresser and pulled out what looked to be some sort of separation bar, hooking each side around my knees to separate and spread my legs. With it on, I couldn't pull my thighs together even a couple inches.

My legs were spread out for him to do whatever he wanted with me.

"Almost done," he said, strapping the ball gag around my mouth.

I sucked the ball in my mouth, feeling more like a little slut by the second, and whined for him to finally touch me. He took the wand vibrator in his hand and crawled onto the bed with me, turning it on the lowest setting and grasping my chin with his free hand.

"How do you feel?"

"Good," I said, my word gargled from the ball gag.

"What was that?" he asked, stroking his thumb against my jaw.

"Good," I tried to say again, but a wad of spit rolled down my chin and onto my chest.

He placed the vibrating head against my stomach softly. "Hmm?"

I whimpered, my core aching at the feel of him moving the vibrator lower and lower until he reached my mound. When he touched the head against my clit, I tried to pull my thighs together—the pressure was almost too much to handle already—but the bondage separator stopped me.

"I bet you're feeling really good, aren't you?"

Nodding like a wild woman, I stared at him as more saliva rolled down my chin.

He turned the vibrator up another notch and laid it against the bed, right against my clit. "You don't get to move even an inch unless I tell you that you can," he said, stroking his thumb against my jaw again. "Be a good girl for me, Imani."

Before he stepped back, he turned the wand up to its highest setting. I yelped, the intensity too high, and nearly collapsed forward on the bed. My legs trembled, and wave after wave of pleasure rushed through me as I came on the vibrator.

Kai pulled his black sweatshirt over his head, showing me his taut and muscular body. And, God, I almost came again at the sight of it. But I held myself together and stared at him, more drool running down my chin and my nipples aching.

"Please," I gargled again.

Kai watched me with an amused expression on his face.

The vibrator moved continuously against my clit, sending me over the edge again. My body trembled, but I didn't move from the spot. Ecstasy surged through me, my core never once resting from the vibrations.

"Kai," I whined.

Spit rolled down my neck to my chest, making my nipples glisten.

Kai pulled up a damn chair and leaned back in it, his legs outstretched and his hand on his bulge. His muscles rippled under the moonlight flooding in through the window. He ran his gaze down my body to my quivering pussy.

"Come."

It was a word. One single word.

And it made me tumble over the edge yet again, my moans muffled from the ball gag in my mouth. The pressure was so intense, the vibrations continuing over and over and over. Once that orgasm was finally over, I was on the brink of a fourth tonight.

"Come."

Again, I cried out and came.

"Again," Kai said.

My legs trembled, and I came.

Kai shoved off his pants and grabbed his huge cock through his briefs. "Come for me another time, Imani."

A sixth time. A fucking sixth time.

"Please," I tried saying, the pressure almost to the point where it hurt me.

"We're not stopping until you learn."

"I've learned. I've learned!" I gargled on the gag.

"Did you say that you're still going to be a bad girl?" Kai asked, a smirk on his lips.

I shook my head from side to side. "No."

"Come again, Imani."

I screamed out, my body shaking now. I still couldn't move my arms or my legs. And I felt hopeless. Kai was going to make me come over and over and over again until I couldn't stand tomorrow.

"And again."

Unable to stop myself, I doubled over as the pleasure shot through my body. I stared up at Kai through teary eyes and watched him stroke his fat cock, and I came again, the sight far too sexy. He smirked at me and stood up with his hard dick between his legs.

"Good girl," he said, putting the vibrator on another setting.

It stopped completely, and I thanked fuck that he was giving me a chance to rest. But as I relaxed against the bed, the vibrator turned back on at full intensity for a moment. Then, it stopped and turned back on. Over and over.

Kai pulled the ball gag from my mouth, and I coughed up some spit.

"Coming for me without me having to order you," he said, gently stroking my cheek with his large, callous hand. He knelt on the bed and wrapped his hand around the ropes around my arms to seize complete control of my upper body.

Instead of untying me, he gently pushed my upper body down, so I bent at the hip. With the vibrator still going on and off in a terrorizing rhythm, he pushed his cock into my mouth. I gagged on it when he hit the back of my throat and stared up at him through watery eyes.

"Kai," I gargled on his fat cock, spit, drool, and saliva pouring down my chin.

When he moved his dick a couple more inches down my throat, I sucked on him and came hard on the vibrator, my entire body trembling. Kai pulled out of me, then thrust himself into me again, beginning to pound my tight little throat with his huge cock.

"Are you learning?" he asked me, thrusting harder and faster.

The pressure rose in my core again, and I whimpered out, furiously bobbing my head on his dick and sucking him off. My clit felt so swollen and sensitive. And as much as I wanted to be a full-on brat with him sometimes, there was no way in hell I'd disobey *him* anymore.

Not one damn chance.

When he pulled out of me, I gasped for air.

"I won't do it again! Please, I promise. I won't do it again, Kai," I said, my eyes filled with water from the lack of air and my pussy aching so badly. "I promise. I'll do whatever you ask. Please."

Kai stopped the vibrator for good this time and pulled it away from my clit. Then, he pinched my pussy lips between his fingers, watching me intently. "How does this feel?" he asked me, squeezing tighter.

"I want you," I whispered.

"How does it feel?" he repeated.

"Good. It feels so good."

Kai spit on his fingers and rubbed them against my clit. "Look at how swollen and sensitive your clit is. And your tight little cunt is sopping wet, ready for me to slip right into it." He stuck his fingers into his mouth and sucked off my juices.

After he undid the bondage separator and pulled it off me, he gently set me back on the mattress, my entire body still restrained. He moved closer to me, holding my thighs apart, and let another wad of spit drip from his lips to the head of his cock. Once it was glistening, he pressed it against my entrance.

My body jerked up, feeling every single inch of him slide into my pussy. I wrapped around him and moaned out his name. Because my pussy was so sensitive, I could feel every fucking inch of him sliding in and out of me.

"More! Please, more! You feel so good."

Kai continued to pump in and out of me, his cock filling my pussy each time. And when he pressed his lips to mine, I cried out into his mouth, coming, but this time ... damn, it felt good again. Kai moaned against me—fucking moaned—and stilled.

I clenched around him, and then he pulled out of me and stared up at the ceiling.

Best punishment ever.

Chapter Seventy-Five

After undoing my restraints, Kai placed the rope back into one of his drawers, handed me a glass of water, and lay beside me, his hands all over my body again, but this time, they weren't rough and demanding.

This time, he was soft and gentle and—dare I say—loving.

"Drink that, then lie down with me," he said.

I took a big gulp to wet my dry throat and placed the cup on the side table, lying back in the bed and in his arms. Gently, he rubbed my arms where the ropes had been, massaging the skin as if he hadn't been punishing me moments ago, his curly hair covering his forehead and his dark eyes drifting across my face.

"What are you doing?" I whispered.

This was strange. After I fucked João, he acted like it hadn't happened. And Landon didn't really cuddle like this. Never once had a guy done this to me, and I was kinda, sorta weirded out and really into it at the same time.

"Making sure you're okay," he said, pushing some hair off my face with his finger.

"Really?" I asked, my heart pounding and butterflies filling my stomach.

I didn't know what it was, but Kai always made me feel a certain kind of way. He might not be as open about his feelings like Landon, but he cared. So much.

"Yes, really, Imani," Kai said. "I'm not going to walk out on you like João does."

"I just ..." I smiled, my cheeks flushing. "I really like this."

He moved closer to me and pulled me toward his chest, drawing his fingers down my lips and smiling so softly. "Before you, I've never been this close to someone, especially not this intimate."

I inhaled his soothing scent and relaxed in his arms. "Really?"

"But when Landon mentioned that you were a freak, I couldn't stop myself from wanting to tie you to my bedposts and make those pretty brown eyes of yours teary," he murmured against my skin.

My lips curled into a smile, and I playfully shoved him away. "Ugh, way to ruin the moment," I teased, the tension in the air finally simmering down. Around us, the world sounded so quiet, but my mind was so loud that it was deafening. So, I finally said, "Why didn't you tell Landon that I was there?"

"Because ..." Kai chuckled, the soothing sound drifting through my ears. "I wanted you to myself for tonight."

After a few more quiet moments of relaxation, I sat up and glanced around his bedroom. "I want to explore your place. I've seen Landon's basement and João's house. Now, it's your turn. I want to see how the quiet, nerdy third of Poison lives every day after school."

Tugging on his oversize shirt, I padded through his small house. While Kai didn't live in the best neighborhood, he had fixed up his basement with as much technology as he could get. One room was completely covered in computer and TV monitors, which each ran the latest news, articles about Redwood, and code that looked too complicated to figure out.

I walked around the room in amazement, drawing my fingers across the desk he must've sat in to devise all his plans. Landon might've been the brawn behind Poison, and João might've been their fearless businessman leader, but Kai was the brains.

"Do you code?" I asked, sitting down in his chair and staring at the lit-up keyboard.

"A bit," he said from the corner of the room, intently watching me.

"This is so cool," I whispered. "I didn't expect that you'd have something like this."

But, honestly, I should've. Kai always had a laptop, phone, or tablet nearly everywhere that he went. I should've expected that his home was filled with the latest technology, aimed to bring Redwood to its knees.

Twirling around in the swivel chair, I caught sight of a closed door. Unlike the rest of the finished cellar, this door had an intricate lock on it that I doubted anyone but Kai would be able to get into, even with the highest lock-picking skills.

"What's in here?" I asked, jumping up and skipping to the door.

Kai stuffed his hands into his pockets, tensed, and hurried to pull me away. "Nothing."

"Oh, come on," I said, playfully shoving him. "What is it?"

"You won't like it if I show you, so it's better if you don't see it."

"You just tied me to the bed and showed me your dark side. I think that I can take it," I said, arching my brow. "But if it's a shrine to João, I swear I'm leaving this place and never looking back."

"It's no shrine," he said, unlocking the door and grasping the door handle. He inhaled sharply. "Before I open the door, you should know that my father was in the military. Most of the shit in here wasn't bought by me."

Then, he swung the door open and stepped back behind me.

I widened my eyes and stared into the room without even taking a step in. I parted my lips and pressed them back together, my throat suddenly drying up and my heart racing. "What is this?"

"I told you that you wouldn't like it."

Daring myself to move closer, I stepped into the room and stared around at the guns, ammo, and weapons lining every wall. I didn't know what to say or how to say it or even what I felt. This was nothing like I'd expected or even thought Kai would have.

Sure, I had seen him use his gun before.

But ... I hadn't thought he had this many.

"You know how to use all these?" I whispered.

He scratched the back of his head. "Maybe."

"What do you ... what do you use these for?" I whispered.

Kai grimaced and glanced around at the room, flooded with weapons. "Imani ..."

"João wasn't lying," I whispered more to myself than to him, wrapping my arms around my body and suddenly feeling so nervous about the boys I had been hanging out with. "You guys really do kill people, don't you?"

Chapter Seventy-Six

IMANI

"Are you okay?" Kai asked, staring at me from the door.

I turned my back toward the room full of guns and weapons that could kill people in an instant. Even though Kai hadn't answered my question about if Poison really did end lives, I could tell that I was right by the mere look on his face.

Poison killed people.

They really fucking killed people.

"Yes," I lied. "I'm fine."

Straightening my back and smoothing out his shirt that covered my body, I shifted from foot to foot. I'd thought that it was all some joke. I'd thought that ... that it was a rumor that they had spread to keep people in line, so nobody would fuck with them.

Stupid me hadn't thought it was true.

"Imani," Kai said, touching my elbow.

But I walked past him and into the bedroom to gather my clothes and belongings. "I need to go home. My mom is going to be looking for me. And if she finds me hanging out with you, then she won't let me see anyone ever again."

The only damn time I could use Mom as an excuse and enjoy it.

Kai followed me into the room. "You're not angry, are you?"

"No."

"You're angry," he concluded, shaking his head. "I knew I shouldn't have shown you."

"I'm not angry," I snapped.

Maybe I was a bit angry, but I also just needed some time.

When I had gotten involved with Poison, I had known exactly what I was getting myself into. I knew that they were bad news, I knew they did shit that I never wanted to know, and I knew that I would be putting myself in danger.

But Kai ...

He seemed like the least dangerous and violent. Seeing his little secret hideout with all those guns and watching the way he had pulled one on Akio the other night... It wasn't a bluff. He would've really shot Akio dead if he didn't leave me alone.

I had been wrong about Kai this entire time.

Kai was the most dangerous third of Poison.

Especially because, most of the time, I couldn't figure out what he was thinking.

"Can you please take me back to Landon's to get my car?" I asked, gathering all my courage to glance up at him. I wasn't nervous that he'd hurt me because after spending the night with him, I knew he wouldn't. Instead, I was nervous because I didn't know what he was capable of.

How many people had Poison killed over the years? How many people had disappeared from Redwood because of them? How dirty were their hands? What was the worst that they had done to someone? And what the hell were they doing with Jace Harbor?

After sighing through his nose, he grabbed my hand very softly and pulled me toward his bedroom door. Suddenly, he stopped, dropped it, and picked up a coat from the ground, holding it out for me to put my arms into.

"It's cold outside," he said. "You shouldn't only be wearing my thin T-shirt."

I stared at him for a couple moments, then sighed and shrugged into the oversize jacket, warmth spreading throughout my body. Kai twirled me around and grasped the zipper, zipping the jacket up slowly, his gaze following it.

Being this close to him, no matter what I had found out, made me suck in a breath.

When he zipped it all the way to the top, he kept moving his gaze further and further up my body—from my neck to my lips to my eyes. His brown eyes sparkled in the moonlight that flooded in through the window.

"Don't hate me," he whispered.

All I wanted to do was scream at him that I didn't hate him. He looked so vulnerable right now. But I couldn't get myself to say a single damn word. My lips were glued shut, and my heart was pounding inside my chest so hard that I thought I would have a damn heart attack.

With his finger, he pushed a curl off my forehead. "I need you."

My breath caught in my throat. "What?" I whispered.

Landon and João had never and would never admit something like that so freely. Hearing Kai say that took me by the utmost surprise. I stared at him through wide eyes, wondering if I had even heard him clearly.

"Don't hate me," he said again, grasping my chin. "Because I need you."

"You need me?"

"More than you think I do," he said.

I grabbed his hand on my chin and frowned. "When was the last time you killed?"

Kai grimaced and clenched his jaw. "Don't do this."

"When?" I asked.

Instead of responding to me, Kai glanced down at his feet, dropped his hand from my chin, and grabbed his keys. "I don't want to get you involved in all our shit. We haven't even brought you into half the fucked up shit we deal with, Imani. You want to go home, so let's go."

Staring at his departing figure down the hallway, I clenched my jaw and followed him out into the cold, sliding on the back of his bike. I didn't understand why none of these boys wanted me involved in any of their shit anymore.

In the beginning, it had been fine.

Suddenly, it wasn't.

I wrapped my arms around Kai from behind as he whizzed down

Redwood's streets toward Landon's place. His muscles were flexed more than they usually were, and he stayed quiet the entire time.

Thoughts raced through my mind, and my stomach was in knots.

When he parked out front, I stayed on the back of his bike and hugged him closer to me. "I need you too, Kai," I said, then slid off the bike and walked back to my car. When I slid into the driver's seat and shut the door, I watched him speed off into the night. "I fucking need you too."

Chapter Seventy-Seven

KAI

Imani hadn't talked to me since Saturday night.

I parked my bike in Redwood's parking lot, tossed my backpack over my shoulder, and walked toward the building with a lit cigarette in my mouth. Usually, I didn't smoke as much as João and Landon, but, shit, I'd needed it lately.

After Imani had submitted to me—tied down by my ropes—and spent the night with me, I couldn't get her out of my fucking head. She might've known how much Landon needed her or how much João did —even though he was a bitch about it.

But she hadn't known that I needed her too.

Now, she wouldn't talk to me.

Before stepping into the building, I stomped out the cigarette. I pulled up the hood to my sweatshirt and walked into the corridor, listening to people gossip about Allie and Jace and last Friday night. My chest tightened, and I had the urge to punch someone's face fucking in.

It wasn't even my drama, but people couldn't mind their own business.

And I was already pissed.

I made a beeline for the next hallway over, found Akio digging through his locker for books, and stormed over to him. I hadn't made myself clear last time, but this time, I would make fucking sure that I did.

Akio might've come off as innocent, but his parents were pieces of shit for what they had done.

Absolute shit.

When I approached, Akio shut his locker and held his books to his chest, eyes wide. I clenched my jaw and glared at him, balling my hands into fists behind my back so I didn't hurl one into his face.

"I told you to stay the fuck away from Imani," I said between clenched teeth.

"I-I did."

I wrapped one hand around his collar and shoved him against the locker. "Don't fucking lie to me. You were at Nicole's house on Saturday night, spying on us, weren't you?"

His face paled. "How do you know that? Did she tell you?"

"No, Imani didn't tell me anything. I saw you with her."

"Look," he said, shaking his head. "Nothing happened. We were hanging out. I ... I don't even like Imani like that. She's not my type, and I ... I just wanted a friend. It's not my fault that you guys wouldn't hang out with her this weekend."

"We were doing a fucking job," I said.

"What do you want me to say, Kai?" he asked.

"I want you to tell her what your parents did to mine, and then we'll see if she still wants to be your fucking friend," I said, so much anger and rage boiling up inside me, more than usual, all because of Imani.

Nobody had ever made me this cranky, ruthless, and jealous.

My phone buzzed, and I released Akio to pull it out of my pocket. There was a picture of Allie Harbor with a stack of *Playboy* and *Mayfair* magazines and porn DVDs that must have fallen out of her locker, desperately trying to pick them up. It looked like it had been taken moments ago, and it was already circulating social media.

"You're fucking lucky that I have other shit to deal with," I said to Akio.

When the first bell rang, I stepped backward and gave him one last warning look, my hands aching to close around his throat. People rushed down the hallways, scrambling to get to their first period while gossiping about Allie and Jace.

Another picture popped up on social media of Allie standing in front of a thick-as-fuck ten-inch dildo, suction-cupped to her locker. I growled underneath my breath, wanting to go back home already to delete all this shit from social media. Allie didn't deserve this.

Allie was Imani's best friend, but I'd try to take the pictures down even if she wasn't.

As the second bell rang, I rounded the corner to find Allie standing in an empty hallway with Carter—Redwood's quarterback and an absolute piece of shit. He stood over her with a sinister smirk that he and his brothers all had.

"Your date with Jamal go good?" Carter asked, leaning against the locker and crossing his muscular arms over his chest. "You finally let him hit it after those soggy Saturday night fries?"

"Fuck you, Carter," Allie said through clenched teeth, scrambling to get her books for the day without the DVDs and magazines falling out of it.

Carter pulled the dildo out of her locker. "You buy this because Jamal wasn't big enough for you, baby?" He stepped closer to her and rested his hand on her shoulder, leaning in. "You wouldn't have to worry about that with me. I'd fill your tight little ass up until you screamed."

I stormed down the hall and watched Allie punch him square in the jaw. He stumbled back and smirked.

"Feisty," he said. "Just how I like them. You'd fucking learn to be a good little"—he placed a single finger on her thigh, beneath her skirt—"whor—"

Pulling the gun from my waistband, I stuck it against the back of his neck. "You fucking move your finger a fucking millimeter up her thigh, and you'll get a bullet in your skull."

Carter chuckled and put his hands into the air. "You got me." He walked past us and down the hall, turning around to face Allie one last time. "You want to get your world rocked, Allie? You know where to find me after school."

Fuming, I shoved the gun back into my waistband and scowled at his departing figure. "You're welcome."

"Thanks," she said, retrieving the books out of her locker. "What do you want?"

"To talk," I said, leaning against the locker. "About Jace."

She arched her brow. "What about him?"

"He's hurt you for the past two years," I started. "Don't you think it's time for a little payback?"

"I don't have money to pay you to get Jace back for me," she said.

"Free of charge, Allie," I said, sprawling a hand across my chest. "I'm doing this out of the goodness of my heart."

And because I wanted to hurt someone. It had been this way since Imani had left me Saturday night.

"You and the rest of Poison don't have any goodness in your hearts."

"True, but I owed your dad a favor before he died. We'd be even after this."

"Why'd you owe my dad a favor?" she asked, crossing her arms.

"That's none of your business," I said, stuffing a hand into my pants pocket. "You want my help or not? I have some ways to torture Jace that you'd be interested in—rumors, embarrassing pictures, money you can donate to whatever kind of charity that you want, and some other stuff that can't be discussed on school grounds."

She slapped her hand against my chest. "How about you take all the porno magazines, DVDs, and the dildo out of my locker, and we'll call it even?" she asked.

A giant ten-inch dildo to fuck Jace Harbor to hell? I wouldn't pass that up.

I arched my brow, a smirk crossing my face. "Deal."

Chapter Seventy-Eight

IMANI

It wasn't my fault, okay?

After Landon's father had shot him and split, then Kai had shown me how many guns he had in that little room of his, I kinda ... maybe ... got a bit nervous. It really hadn't set in until this weekend that I really was in deep with the Poison boys.

Deeper than I'd ever thought I'd be.

I strolled into the cafeteria, steering clear of Poison's table, and headed toward the self-designated *nerd* table, where Allie and I always sat.

All weekend, I had been on stakeout and surveillance, trying to figure out what the hell Jace Harbor was up to with my best friend. Little did I know about this shit stirring at Redwood. People had been gossiping about Allie and her stepbrother and making fun of her at her locker this morning.

Allie had told me that Kai had helped her out before first period.

Part of me hoped that he wasn't doing it to get on my good side. And the other part of me wished he were because I was slowly getting jealous of how nice he was to Allie and how worried he was about her. Something was up with him, and I wanted to find out what it was.

But not while I was trying to figure other things out.

After perching my ass at the empty table, Allie walked into the room with her head held low. I watched her and Kai share a look—which made me ball my hands into fists under the table—and then she glanced over at Jace.

"Do you want to eat in the library?" I asked her, clenching my jaw at Poison. "People are pissing me the fuck off with those pictures of you. I don't want you to feel like we have to sit here."

Before Allie could respond, Jamal sat next to me and gave Allie a half-smile. "Don't listen to them, Allie. They're just immature fucking brats. I'll find out who stuffed all that shit in there."

I gave him a side-eye at how close he was to me and scooted an inch to my left. "Yeah, don't listen to them. They mean nothing anyway. They're not going anywhere in life, and they will stay in Redwood for the rest of their lives, especially Nicole."

"Fuck that bitch," Jamal and I said at the same time.

I gave Jamal another stink eye, then continued to eat my sandwich. Allie sank in her seat, shoulders slumping forward as she tried to make herself small again. Everyone was staring at us, literally everyone—from Nicole to the cheer team to Poison to the teachers.

Suddenly, Jace fucking Harbor sat next to Allie. "I saved a seat for you."

Almost instinctively, Allie pushed his hand away and stared at me. This bitch ...

Narrowing my eyes, I gave her the hardest death glare I could muster. She'd better not have made up with him this weekend, especially after what he did to her on Friday. Did she not remember how heartbroken she was?!

After the whispers finally died down, I cleared my throat. "So, Allie, where were you this morning? And what happened between you and Mr. Barnes? He couldn't make eye contact with you all class."

She shifted uncomfortably in her seat and glanced at Jace. "We, um, woke up late."

I narrowed my eyes even harder and snatched her wrist. "Okay, we need to talk," I said, dragging Allie away from the table and the boys. When we were far enough away, I slapped her chest. "What the hell?" I whisper-yelled. "I thought you weren't getting back together with Jace. What happened to 'I hate him with all my heart. He's a dickhead. He deserves to die'?"

This ho couldn't make up her damn mind.

She needed to keep me updated on these things, so I could do my little surveillance with the right intention. If I had known she had gotten back together with him yesterday, I would've staked out their house to try to catch anything fishy, *not* actively trying to figure out the best course of action on how to teach Jace a lesson.

Glancing back over at the table, I noticed Jace smiling at Allie.

I wanted to hurl.

"He had a reason," Allie admitted, "for doing everything that he did to me."

I scrunched my nose. "Come on. Are you seriously going to believe him? He's a player, and everyone knows it."

Allie grabbed my hand and squeezed it hard. "I can't tell you what it is, but I can promise you that I'm not being stupid ..." This ho was being stupid again, but I loved her anyway. "Jace has been through so much that he's been hiding from me. I ... I still love him. I always will."

"Just know that if he fucking hurts you again, I will get Poison on his ass to kill him," I threatened, glancing over at Poison even though I was pissed at them—sorta. "You know that they would too. They hate rich, bratty kids like him."

She held out her pinkie finger and let me curl mine around hers. "Deal. If Jace breaks my heart again, you can get Poison on his ass," she said, giggling. "Make them do anything that they want to do to him. Kai has some ideas."

Kai.

There it was again.

Had they been plotting together at his house or something? I fucking hoped not.

Because as scared as I was to be with them now, I wasn't about to walk away.

All three of the Poison boys were mine.

Chapter Seventy-Nine

"Cousin to cousin," Misty said, leaning back in her chair and clicking her pen, "that's some fucked up shit. I mean, I figured that your father would do some shit like that, but your mom being in on it too?"

I ran a hand across my face, leaned against her couch, and blew some blond hair out of my face. "I haven't fucking seen them since they packed up and left after Dad shot me. And I swear that if they come back, I'll kill him myself with my own two hands."

Misty frowned and sighed. "You haven't even gotten a call?"

"Nothing."

"What are you going to do about your mom?" she asked.

My gaze dropped from her to my lap. What would I do about Mom if I ever saw her again? Truth was that I didn't even know how I'd react when I saw her for the first time after she ran out with Dad.

She had never been this ... disgusting toward me.

All I had ever wanted to do was protect her from Dad when he drank a bit too much and became violent. I had always done everything I could, and every fucking time, she never once appreciated it.

"I don't know," I whispered. "What can I do?"

Sucking in a breath, Misty readjusted herself. "I can't give you much advice. It's too muddled with my family. All I can say is that I would never allow her to control you like that again. You might not be able to see it, but your mom isn't a good woman, Landon, and you keep protecting her. You deserve something more."

"Imani," I said, her name sounding like fucking heaven on my lips.

And I didn't even believe in that shit.

"Don't let your parents ruin what you have with Imani," Misty said, actually smiling at me for once. She leaned forward and placed a hand on my knee. "I can tell how happy she makes you. She is the best thing to happen to you in a long time. Don't lose that."

"I don't plan to."

A deafening silence fell over us, and I felt those butterflies fluttering in my stomach at the thought of having Imani forever. Never once had I felt so strongly about someone. And I swore that I'd kill anyone else who got in the way of us.

I would never lose her.

I refused.

"She told me that she loves me," I said, voice barely above a whisper. "She loves me."

Still, even after almost a week, I couldn't believe it. It seemed so surreal, like this was all some sort of joke or dream or something because shit like this didn't happen to people like me. The dirty kids in the slums never found love. We only found people to survive together with.

Warmth spread around my chest, and I grinned like a fucking doofus. Imani loved me.

"She told you that?" Misty asked, smiling even wider.

"When I was in the hospital," I said, knowing that it was a moment I would never forget. I had ingrained it in my memories for forever and refused to let it go. "Sometimes, I think back to it and still don't believe that she could love someone like me."

"We need to work on that confidence, Landon." Misty shook her head and chuckled. "Looks like we're at the end of our session today. Am I going to see you tomorrow, or do you want to push our sessions back to every couple days, once a week even?"

"Do you think I'm ready for that?" I asked, actually nervous.

Now that I had Imani, I didn't want to fuck this up. I didn't want to fall back into the same fucking self-destructive pattern that I had been in, always on high fucking alert around her and her phone. I couldn't.

"You've improved quite a bit since we started."

"You think so?" I asked.

"I asked you how the phone situation was going earlier, and it was a second thought, Landon," she said. "I think we could push it back to every couple days, but only if you're comfortable with that."

"Okay, every few days then." I stood, then headed to the front door. "And, Misty, thank you for everything. I don't know what I would've done without you because I definitely wouldn't be here today."

Not in a place where Imani could love me.

"Anytime." Misty smiled and glanced out the door. "And get those boys out of here."

"What bo—" I glanced out the door to see João's car parked in Misty's driveway.

João and Kai were in the front seats with their gazes fixed on me, as if they were either angry or fucking furious.

They had been that way since this weekend because of Imani.

I hadn't figured out what had happened. Neither of those assholes liked to talk.

"Fuck, I'll handle it," I said. "See ya later."

Stepping out into the cold, I shoved my hands into my pockets and walked toward João's car, knowing that this bitch wasn't going to let me walk past him and pretend like I hadn't even seen him. He'd run me the fuck over if I tried that.

I pulled open the back door and slid into the car. "What the fuck are you doing here?"

"Where were you?" João asked, hand tightening around the steering wheel.

"None of your fucking business."

"Is this the chick you've been hanging out with after school?" João asked. "The chick you've been cheating on Imani with?"

"I'm not fucking cheating on Imani," I said between clenched teeth. "She's my cousin."

Kai stayed quiet from the front seat.

"Your fucking cousin, huh?" João asked.

"Yes, my cousin."

"Does Imani know that?" Kai finally asked.

"Yes, she fucking does," I said, balling my hands into fists. "Don't get fucking angry with me because you both pissed her off this weekend. I don't know what the fuck you did to make her angry, but that shit isn't my problem."

"Bullshit," João said. "She hasn't talked to you today either."

"For someone who doesn't like her, you fucking care a lot about what she does," I said.

João shut off the car. "If you won't tell me what the fuck you and your *cousin* are up to, then I'll fucking ask her. And it won't be pretty, Landon. This was your fucking—"

"She's my fucking therapist!" I shouted, pissed the fuck off at them.

Both João and Kai became quiet.

I loathed that they'd had to find out this way. "Maybe you two could use it too. I'm fucking tired of hearing you complain, João. We're all fucked up in the head. Now, fucking drop it."

Chapter Eighty

JOÃO

After five hours of stalking a couple more people on that damn list that Imani had given me, I dropped off Landon and Kai at Landon's house and tightened my hand around the steering wheel, glaring at Landon through the windshield.

"Get the fuck out of my car," I said between gritted teeth.

Therapy.

He was one fucking asshole for suggesting that.

"You wonder why Imani doesn't like you," Landon said, one hand on the roof of my car, the other flicking on a lighter to light the cigarette hanging out of his mouth. "It's because you're a moody piece of shit."

Before he could continue, I shifted the gear into reverse and hit the gas, giving him the finger through the windshield. Who the fuck did Landon think he was, telling me that I needed therapy?

The only kind of therapy I needed was one where I put a bullet through the head of everyone who pissed me the fuck off, everyone who fucked over the people living in the Redwood slums. I didn't fucking need to talk or shit.

And who the fuck said I wanted Imani to like me? Not me.

Not me at all.

I drove back through the Redwood slums to see Mom and Ana for the night. For fucking once, she had the day off and away from those fucking assholes who raped her every night, and I wanted to at least spend a couple hours with her and my sister.

Just a few.

But when I pulled up at home, Mom's car wasn't parked in the driveway. I tensed and leaped out of the car, hurrying to the front door. Ana immediately pulled the door open with wide and watery eyes and jumped into my arms.

"João! Where were you? I've been home alone all day."

"All day?" I picked her up and kicked the door closed with my heel. "Where's Mom?"

"I don't know," she said, wiping away her tears with the backs of her hands. "She never came home. You said that she was going to be here when I got off the bus today and that she didn't have to work tonight. You lied."

Fuck.

Where is she?

"I didn't lie, Ana." I gently rubbed her back and walked throughout the house, checking in each of the rooms to make sure Mom wasn't passed out somewhere. She should've been here. "She told me that she'd be home tonight."

"Then, where is she?" Ana asked again, tears filling with eyes. "Why doesn't Mama love us anymore? She never comes home and doesn't spend any time with us when she does. She always gets so mad at me too."

Ana didn't understand, and there wasn't much of a way I could explain what Mom did. She thought that Mom disappeared every night because Mom didn't love us, but that wasn't true. But how could I tell my sister that Mom sold her body to provide for us?

Tears poured down Ana's cheeks, her body heaving back and forth. I placed her on the ground and crouched down to her level, taking her tiny face in my hands and wiping away her tears with my thumbs.

"Ana, you might not understand," I started. "But Mom does this for us."

"No, she doesn't!" she said, shaking her head. "She doesn't love us."

"She loves us," I whispered, my chest tightening. "She does."

Ana's cries and hiccups slowly turned to sniffles. She wiped her forearm across her runny nose and frowned at me. "Where is Mom then? What is she doing? I want her to be with us, João." She pushed some hair out of my face. "Don't you want her too?"

"I do," I whispered, my voice even lower than before.

But I didn't know where the fuck she could be. She worked all over Redwood, and even outside of it whenever she was desperate for work and money. Where would she have gone? She loved spending time with Ana, no matter what. Why would she ditch Ana for her job?

Unless she … never came home last night.

My stomach tightened, and I gulped. I hadn't seen her this morning when I brought Ana to school. She might've had a bad night go really fucking terrible, could've been stuck somewhere with someone she didn't want to be with.

"João!" Ana yelled, becoming fussier. "Where is she?"

She had been here alone all day. She must've been angry and frustrated.

"Ana, let me think, please. I—"

"But … I …" Ana burst out in tears again and threw her small arms around my neck, clutching on to me tightly.

After cursing under my breath, I pulled my phone from my pocket. I couldn't take care of Ana and find Mom alone. I needed someone to help, and Kai and Landon had just spent the past five fucking hours hunting down those assholes on Imani's list for me.

So, I clicked on her contact and dialed her number.

"What do you want, João?" Imani said on the other line, pissed off.

"I need you to come over," I whispered. "For Ana."

But really, it was for me.

I couldn't keep doing this alone.

Chapter Eighty-One

As soon as I parked my car in front of João's house, he snapped open the front door and ran a hand through his messy hair. I quickly undid my seat belt, my heart thrashing against my rib cage, and hurried out of the car.

"What's going on?" I asked.

João pulled me into the house, shut the door behind me, and pulled on his coat. "I need you to watch Ana. I have to go out."

Furrowing my brows, I glared at him. "That's why you wanted me to come over?"

"I'm going to find my mom," João said.

I smacked my lips together and stared up at him through wide eyes. "Your mom? What happened? Is everything okay?" I asked, fear suddenly striking me in the chest. While I knew what she did for a living, I also knew that she *always* came home.

Always.

"She was supposed to be here when Ana got off the bus. Ana's been alone all day."

"No," I whispered, wrapping my arms around myself.

Sometimes, when sex workers went missing, they weren't found.

Or they were found dead.

If João walked out that door and found her dead, what would he do? How would he raise Ana alone? Would he even be able to keep Ana? What if the court ruled against it and she was thrust into the system?

"Ana's in the bathroom." João turned toward the door. "Watch her."

"Wait," I said, grasping his wrist and pulling him back into a hug.

His entire body tensed, but I held him tightly to me anyway, resting my head on his chest and hoping that he'd calm down a little bit. After a couple moments, João rested his arms around my shoulders and pulled me even closer.

"What's this for?" he whispered.

"Because you need it."

And because I knew that once I pulled away, that man would rush out that door without thinking anything through. I didn't want him to run into something so blindly. He had said it himself that Redwood was dangerous, that even some of the richest people here had secrets.

Now that they had shown me the true side of Redwood, I knew it to be true.

João needed to be smart about this because she probably wasn't with someone in the slums. If she was selling her body, it was to some rich, old guy who didn't give a fuck about her and who could dispose of her like she was nothing.

"Please, be safe," I whispered to him. "Call Landon or Kai to go with you."

"I don't have time for them to catch up," João said, pulling away and stepping away from me, snatching the front door knob. "I have to find my mom as soon as I can. She's in danger—I can just feel it."

"João!" Ana shouted, running into the room from the back. "Where are you going?"

João took one last glance at her and gave her a small smile that didn't reach his eyes, and then he looked back up at me. "Please, watch her. I'll pay you or get you whatever the hell you want. I need to go."

Before I could get out another word, João slipped through the door and jogged to his car. He slid into the passenger seat, the car roaring to life, then sped down the street and disappeared into the cold winter night.

I stared out the front door with my stomach in knots.

João wouldn't be cautious or careful. João was about to tear up every rich person's house in Redwood to find his mother. He was going to willingly put himself in danger, not in a sane state of mind.

"Imani," Ana said, tugging on my shirt. "Where'd João go? Why is he leaving me too?"

Picking up Ana, I walked to the kitchen and searched through the cupboards for the ingredients to make her favorite snack—brigadeiros. But the cupboards were relatively empty, and I couldn't find condensed milk and cocoa powder anywhere.

So, I walked with her to the door, placed her on her feet, and pulled a small jacket over her shoulders. "We're going to the store to get some ingredients to make brigadeiros. You know what we need, right?"

A huge grin graced her face. "Really? I'm so excited."

"João will be back soon, but let's try to make them before he gets back because he's in a bad mood."

Ana giggled and grabbed my hand. "He's always in a bad mood."

"Girl, tell me about it," I said, stepping out the front door.

I opened my car door as Ana grabbed her car seat and shoved it into the backseat. I strapped her into the car and told her I had to make a quick call. Then, I gently shut the door and pulled out my phone, hoping that he'd answer the phone.

"Imani," Landon said.

Staring at Ana, I paced back and forth on the sidewalk. "Landon, you and Kai have to go find João. He left me with Ana and is going to look for his mom. She didn't come home today, and he stormed out, not thinking straight. Please, go find him. Make sure he doesn't do anything—"

"Slow down," Landon said. "I can barely hear you."

"Please, Landon," I whispered after taking a deep breath. "Go find João."

<h1 style="text-align:center">Chapter Eighty-Two</h1>

JOÃO

I sped around Redwood's gated communities, checking to see if Mom's car was parked in any of the driveways and fucking driving myself insane. Though it seemed everywhere I went, I couldn't find any damn trance of her.

Nothing. Nothing. Nothing. Nothing. Nothing.

Where the fuck is she?

After taking another loop around the most prestigious part of town, I slammed on my brakes at a red light and punched the steering wheel. She worked here. She fucking worked in this shitty town. She couldn't have gone far.

She had to be close.

Pulling out my phone, I checked it to see if she had left me any missed calls or texts. But she hadn't messaged me since last night, a couple moments after she left for work. One single text from her that I would fucking cherish forever.

Mom: Sorry for getting angry with you the other night. I love you, João.

Someone slammed on their horn behind me, and I threw my hand out the window and gave him a hard middle finger. The light in front of me was green, yet I couldn't find myself able to step on the gas.

Driving around like this wouldn't get me *anywhere*.

I had to be smart about where she could've gone.

Then, suddenly, it hit me. I clicked on her contact. She had shared her location with me.

Again, the man slammed on his horn. Angrily, I parked my fucking car and stormed out of it, pulling my gun from my waistband and ready to shut this fucking man up. Why the fuck couldn't he go around me?

When he saw the gun in my hand, he threw the car in reverse, hit a hard U-turn, and sped down the road, deciding to go in the other direction, like he fucking should've. Stupid rich assholes who thought they owned the fucking world.

After tucking my gun back into my waistband, I stormed to the car and found Mom's last known location on Main Street, down in the ritzy part of town. Just as I started the car, Landon jogged up to my car and yanked the door open, sliding into the passenger seat.

"Whose fucking ass are we going to beat?" Landon asked, shaking off some snow and staring at the windshield. He glanced over at me and popped some pain pills into his mouth. "Imani called us."

"Us?" I asked.

Kai pulled up on his bike beside me and looked in through the open window.

I tightened my hand around the steering wheel and nodded toward downtown, where all the fucking rich snobs would be tonight. "Main Street," I said to Kai and then shoved my foot on the accelerator and speeding right through a stop light.

Fuck the red lights. I would save Mom tonight.

After speeding to Main Street, I parked my car at the end and shoved my keys into my pocket. One side of the road were restaurants that cost over a hundred dollars a plate, the other side the raging ocean. Waves pounded against the fence of rocks as I stormed down the sidewalk, hurrying to glance into every restaurant to see if she was with anyone tonight.

She never came down here unless it was work.

Unless someone paid her to be their arm candy.

Kai ran his bike up and down Main Street twice, disappearing into the parking garages a couple times and racing back toward me. He paused on the other side of the road and shook his head. "Your mother's car isn't here."

"Fuck!" I shouted, pacing in front of the rocks and glaring out into the dark, raging sea, where yachts would be parked in the summer season. Now, it was cold and empty, like my fucking heart. "She was here. Her phone is here somewhere. It has to be. Her location is on."

All I could think about was what I would tell Ana.

If Mom was dead, how the fuck could I tell her that? She wouldn't understand that Mom could never come back to see her, to smile at her, to be there, even when times were rough. Ana deserved to have a family. And Mom didn't fucking deserve death.

"I told her so many times to quit," I said, running a hand through my hair. "I fucking told her. I knew some shit was going to happen. I ... I'm going to fucking kill whoever did this shit to her. Someone had to have taken her. They must've."

"I'll drive around again," Kai said, speeding away.

Landon grasped my shoulder and kept me walking next to him on the sidewalk. "We're going to find her. Come on. Don't lose it, João. She's here somewhere."

"And if she's fucking dead?" I snapped, yanking myself away from him and storming down the sidewalk, glaring into all the restaurant windows to see if she was in there again. If I didn't find her this time around, then I would be storming in each one soon.

Just as we reached the end of Main Street, Kai sped around the corner and slammed on his brakes to stop in front of us. "Around the corner. Williams's restaurant. Something shady is going on in the back. There is more security crawling around than usual. I—"

Before he could finish his sentence, I sprinted down the street to Alex Williams's restaurant. That man was a known fucking drug distributer, a user himself, and one of Dad's old friends. Why the fuck would Mom be there?

I ran to the end of the street, rounded the corner, and found the security all walking back in through the back door. Rushing up to the door, I went to bang my fist against the metal but saw Mom instead.

Dumped by the dumpster.

In nothing but white lingerie that was covered in blood.

Bruises in her arms and needles littered around her.

"No!" I shouted, shaking my head from side to side and doubling over her body. I pressed my shaky fingers to her wrist to find a weak pulse and clenched my jaw. "Fucking no!"

I needed to get her out of here.

She needed a hospital now.

Scooping her into my arms, I ran toward my car and passed Landon and Kai on the way. "Make sure Williams doesn't leave," I said. "And someone make sure that Imani and Ana are okay. I need to bring Mom to the hospital."

She wasn't going to die on me. Not tonight.

Chapter Eighty-Three

JOÃO

If I called the ambulance, then I would be waiting for fucking hours.

They didn't come as quickly as when someone from the rich side of town called.

So, I dumped Mom's body in the back of my car and stepped on the fucking accelerator to head toward the hospital. While glancing back at Mom every now and then, I whizzed by cars and vowed to get there before Mom died in my backseat.

She couldn't fucking die. She couldn't. She fucking couldn't.

My chest tightened, my breathing heavy.

What would I tell Ana if Mom died? How could I explain that to her? That Mom had sold her body to the rich to support us and one of those fucking idiots had force-fed her drugs and made her overdose again?

Once I sped into the hospital, I slammed my foot on the brakes and parked the car right out front. Imani's mother walked toward her car and glanced over at me. I wanted to curse that fucking bitch out, but Mom was more important than a rich chick like her. So, I scooped Mom up into my arms and kicked the door closed.

"Stay with me, Mom," I said desperately, clutching her tightly. "Please."

"Can I help you?" Imani's mother said, suddenly at my side.

"Get out of my fucking way and leave me alone," I said, cutting my eyes toward her and continuing through the automatic emergency entrance doors. A wave of cold air hit me at once, and I hurried up to the front desk. "I need help. Please."

The woman stared at me and clicked her pen. "With what?"

"My mother overdosed."

She rolled her eyes. "Another slum's overdose tonight."

"What's wrong with you?" Imani's mother asked the woman, stepping up to the desk, glaring at her, and calling the emergency room physicians and nurses to come help. "I'll deal with you later."

A couple people flooded out of a back room and took Mom from me, checking her vitals and determining that she wasn't breathing anymore. When they hurried her into a back room and shut the door, telling me that they would do everything in their power to save her, I tried to shove myself through the doors to see her.

"Let me see her," I said through gritted teeth, pushing past a couple women.

Someone seized my arms and pulled me back, shoving me against the wall. A security guard snapped his hand around my throat to hold me in place and started mumbling something about hating dealing with the slums every night.

When I shoved him back and he came back toward me twice as hard, Imani's mother stepped in his way and placed her hands on his chest, shoving him back. "Don't touch him. Go sit back down at your post. I'll handle this."

"Dr. Abara, he's dangerous."

"So are you with that gun on your hip," she said, pointing to his post behind the counter. "Now, sit your ass down and let me handle João."

Since when does she know my fucking name?

The security guard took one last long look at me, then turned and moped all the way back behind the counter to his lousy, shitty little seat to resume his boring fucking shift for tonight. Imani's mother turned back toward me.

"Are you okay?" she asked.

"What the fuck do you care?"

"He choked you."

"I barely felt it. Are you done?"

"I'm just trying to help you."

Snapping, I directed all my anger toward her. "How have you ever helped anyone like me?! If it wasn't for Imani, you wouldn't have looked twice at me outside. You would've walked right by, rolled your eyes like that fucking lady at the desk, and said that this was what happened every fucking night. You don't give a fuck about people like me."

Imani's mother stared at me with wide eyes, her body suddenly shrinking in on itself, as if she were scared of me. And she fucking should be. I could fuck her entire life up with the gun I had in *my* waistband.

"You're right," she said, gulping.

"Of course I'm fucking right. That's all you rich bitches ever do."

Imani's mother pushed back her shoulders. "And I'm sorry."

"That's—" I stopped mid-sentence and grimaced at her. "What?"

"I'm sorry, João," Imani's mother said, brushing her fingers against my forearm. "I'm sorry that it took my daughter *liking* someone like you for me to care. I'm sorry that I haven't always treated people like you equally."

Growling, I yanked myself away from her. "Don't fucking touch me. It's because of people like you that my mother is dying."

"João," Imani's mother said, her voice quiet. "What happened to her?"

I glared at her and wanted to give her a taste of what Redwood was really fucking like. I wasn't ashamed of what my mother did—most of Redwood already fucking knew anyway. It was a sad fucking reality that we lived in.

"My mother sells her body to support us," I started, my chest tightening at the thought. "She sells her body, and people got her addicted to fucking drugs again. If she fucking dies, then I have to raise my little sister all by myself. No high school kid should have to fucking do that, and no kid should have to grow up without her mother."

While her eyes quivered, she stood tall. "Who was her last client?"

"Williams."

She readjusted her coat. "I'll take care of him."

"No," I growled, turning back toward the doors and storming toward my car. "I will."

Chapter Eighty-Four

IMANI

Ana lay on the couch, sleeping, with a plate of brigadeiros on her lap and chocolate all over her mouth. I turned off the TV and grabbed the half-eaten plate from her, then set it on the table. Picking up my phone, I cursed under my breath.

No new messages.

Three entire hours of nothing.

Something wasn't right. My stomach tightened. I hoped João's mom was okay.

I opened our Discord chat and typed to the guys.

Me: Is everything okay?

Me: Where are you guys?

I paced around the house, picking up all the dirty clothes and putting them into the hamper, deciding to clean up a bit to help keep myself calm. But my stomach was in knots, and I kept tugging on my hair. I just ... I wanted to make sure they were okay.

As annoyed with them as I was, I hated being left in the dark like this.

João wasn't okay right now, and if something happened to his mother, he would go off the fucking rails and burn this town to the ground. I tapped through the channels on Discord and stared at my messages. Kai was the only person out of the three who was online at the moment, and still, he didn't message me back. Maybe that was because I had been a bitch to him lately.

Me: Please, let me know what's going on.

Me: I'm nervous.

Suddenly, someone knocked on the front door. Ana stirred on the couch, turning onto her side and smearing chocolate on the torn black sofa. I hurried over to the door before they could knock again and wake her.

Looking out the window, I saw Kai standing outside with his hands stuffed into the pockets of his oversized black cargo pants. I pulled open the door and wrapped him into a long hug, thanking whoever it was watching us that he was okay.

Unlike João, he didn't hesitate to wrap his arms around me. I closed my eyes and breathed in his scent, remembering the way I'd felt in his arms the other night after we slept together. He had held me so tightly to him, his body shaping against mine.

"You're here," I whispered, glancing up at him. "Is everything okay?"

Kai glanced into the room. "Is Ana around?"

After hiking my thumb back to the couch, I stepped to the side to let him into the room. He shook the snow off his gray sweatshirt and stepped into the house, glancing at Ana sleeping soundly in the living room. Instead of answering my questions, he walked over to her and scooped her into his arms.

"Kai," she said sleepily, smiling up at him with her eyes closed.

"Go back to sleep, Ana. I'm taking you to your bedroom."

"Okay," she whispered, her small and quiet snores filling the living room again.

He disappeared down the hallway and into a back bedroom for a couple moments. I waited impatiently in the living room, gathering the clothes and throwing them into the washer they had in the kitchen, pressing the on button and watching it fill with water.

God, I was so nervous.

If Kai didn't want to talk in front of Ana, then that meant something bad had happened.

Something really bad.

"You're doing their laundry," Kai said, leaning against the kitchen counter, one shoulder against the wall. He moved closer to me and looked down. "And you cleaned up?"

I rubbed my hands together. "I didn't know what else to do. I couldn't just sit around."

Kai gently grasped my jaw. "You're a good girl, Imani Abara."

My breath caught in my throat as I stared up into his dark, hooded eyes. All those fears of being with three men who killed people ruthlessly suddenly started to dissipate. They might have been rough with others, but to me ... they were soft and vulnerable guys who needed a bit of love.

"What's happening?" I asked him. "Is everything okay?"

Suddenly, Kai's small smile dropped. "No."

My chest tightened. "Then, what's going on? Is João hurt?"

"A long time ago, João's mother used to be addicted to drugs. It was all his father's doing. He hung out with the wrong people and made his wife slowly addicted. She was passed out drunk and high when Ana crawled over those needles."

Mouth drying, I stared up at him through watery eyes. "Why are you telling me this?"

"Because she cleaned herself up," Kai said. "She hadn't touched drugs since that night, but she worked tonight at the Williams's restaurant in North Redwood. He's known to deal and use drugs regularly and do some other things with sex workers." Kai stopped and clenched his jaw. "I know João's mother would never use again willingly, especially not when she has Ana to care for. But we found her behind William's restaurant tonight."

A sob escaped my mouth, and I slapped my hand over it, so Ana wouldn't hear.

No.

It couldn't be. It ... she ... Mr. Williams?

Kai wrapped his arms around me and pulled me closer to his chest, so I could cry against him. I buried my face against his oversize gray sweatshirt and held on to him tightly. "Is she dead?"

"João took her to the hospital."

"And Williams?" I asked, sniffling. "What'll happen to him?"

Kai tensed and pressed his lips together. "I don't think you want to know, Imani." He scooped me up into his arms and walked toward the couch to lay me down onto it, and then he took a seat beside me and cupped my face. "Why don't you get some sleep? It's almost two a.m."

"What will happen to Williams?" I asked again.

"João will kill him," Kai said as if it were nothing.

Something inside me snapped, and I nodded. "Good."

"Good?" Kai asked, eyes widening and brows shooting up. "I thought you hated that."

I swept my fingers across his cheek. "I'm sorry about the other night. I overreacted and was scared because I had never seen so many weapons in one place. But I don't blame you for wanting to protect the people you love. And anyone who drugs and dumps a woman deserves to die."

Chapter Eighty-Five

JOÃO

Fuck Imani's mother's *good intentions*.

She'd probably slap Alex Williams on the fucking wrist and tell him to fuck with another person from the Redwood slums. But that fucking shit didn't fly with me. Tonight, Alex Williams was going to fucking learn the consequences of raping, drugging, and dumping an innocent woman.

I pulled back up to Main Street and parked my car in the back, where Landon sat on the curb, smoking a cigarette. I blew out a deep breath, clenched my jaw, and checked my gun to make sure it was loaded.

Landon stood and stomped out his cigarette. "You ready?"

"To kill this fucker?" I asked, clutching the gun in my hand. "You fucking bet your ass."

Stepping up to the back door, I gripped the handle and glanced back at Landon, who pulled a gun from his waistband. Landon never used a gun unless we were dealing with real fucking shit like this.

"Kai's with Ana and Imani?" I asked.

"Yeah, he left an hour ago."

After vowing that I'd get back to Ana, especially if they couldn't revive Mom, I kicked the door open and drew my gun at the fuckers in the back, playing poker. Cigars smoke lingered heavily in the air, and I glared from each asshole to the next until my gaze landed on Alex.

"Everyone, out," I growled.

"Stay," Alex said, standing to meet my gaze. "Who are you?"

"The man who's going to kill you tonight." I cocked my gun to the rest of the fucking assholes here. "So, if you don't want to die alongside him, get the fuck out and keep your mouths fucking shut. Or you're next."

Alex chuckled darkly, then called for security. One walked in through the main door, and I shot the guard in the neck without thinking twice about it. I wasn't fucking around tonight, and this man was making me angrier by the second.

As if they fucking realized that I was serious, Alex's buddies flooded out of the room through the back door, slid into their Porsches, and sped off Main Street, back to their shitty mansions. I would fucking deal with them later if they had taken part in this.

Putting out his cigar, Alex pulled his wallet out of his suit jacket. "Look, kid. I don't want trouble. How much you want?"

"How much do I fucking want?" I growled at him, storming forward and sticking the gun to his temple. "I don't want any of your fucking money, Alex. I told you that I'm not here for money, for power, or for my five fucking minutes of Redwood fame. I'm here to kill you."

Overcome with fury, I slammed my left fist into his nose and shoved him backward. He stumbled back into the wall and grasped his nose, which gushed with blood. I would kill him, but first, I would torture this fucker, the same way he had tortured Mom.

"Luana Rocha," I said. "You fucking drugged her."

"Luana Rocha?" he said, shaking his head. "I've never heard of her before."

I threw my gun onto the table and hit him square in the jaw this time, sending him to the ground. Blood covered my knuckles, but I wasn't finished with him. I knelt by his side and slammed my fist into him again. And again. And again.

"The sex worker you hired last night," I said between gritted teeth.

"Oh, the whore," he said, spitting up blood. "What do you want with her?"

Grabbing him by the collar in one hand, I pounded my right fist into his head, hitting him hard enough each time that his head banged against the tiled floor. Blood pooled underneath him, but I continued.

"She's my fucking mother." Another punch. "And you drugged her." Punch. "Raped her." Punch. "Dumped her like she was less than nothing." Punch. "And you don't give a fuck about her. You didn't even know her fucking name."

He opened his mouth to talk back to me, and I punched in his teeth. His two front teeth cracked and fell into his mouth, down his throat. I snapped his sorry mouth closed and forced him to swallow his own two teeth and start choking on them.

Fucker deserved it.

"Give me a fucking knife, Landon."

Landon pulled a knife from his pocket and set it in my hand. I cut Alex Williams's shirt down the middle and stuck the knife against his chest, carving the words *Whore Lover* into his pasty-ass skin.

Mom was a whore, but not in a bad sense.

She did what she had to.

People in the slums didn't care what their neighbors had to do to survive, but those words meant something to the rich. Those words were shameful to these rich fuckers for some fucking reason, and I wanted everyone to know what kind of man this guy was when they found his body.

He struggled underneath me, but I pushed the knife deeper each time until he stayed still. And when I carved the final letter into his thin chest, I sank my knife into his muscle until it hit his sternum, and then I released the handle and clasped my hands around his neck.

"What's her name?" I asked him.

"Fuck you," he said, spitting up blood.

I sank my thumbs deeper into his throat. "What's her fucking name?"

He gargled a mouthful of blood.

"Tell me her fucking name, and I'll let go."

"Luana Rocha," he repeated without a problem this time.

Keeping my promise, I pulled my hands away from his throat and stood up. With shaky hands, he grasped the knife in his chest and pulled it out while spitting and coughing up blood. I grabbed the gun from the table and aimed it at his head.

He knew her name. He knew what he had done wrong.

This bitch deserved to die.

Without a second thought, I put two bullets straight through his skull and watched him bleed to death.

Chapter Eighty-Six

IMANI

My phone buzzed on the coffee table, lighting up the dark room. I picked my head up off Kai's chest and glanced over at the screen, my stomach twisting and turning at the mere thought of what kind of news Landon and João could have for us.

Except it wasn't either of them.

Mom: Where are you?

I rolled my eyes and ignored it, resting my head back on Kai's chest and curling into his body. After our little chat, we hadn't talked much. Kai was never really a talker anyway. So, we sat on the sofa in the dark, and I tried hard to relax a bit.

João and Landon had it handled, and at least João's mom was at the hospital now.

Mom: Imani! Please, answer me. I'm worried. It's really late.

"You should answer her," Kai said, chest rumbling slightly.

Once I let out a long sigh, I pulled myself away from Kai and sat up, snatching my phone from the table. Before I responded to her, I checked the Discord group chat again—hoping that João or Landon had said something. When I came up empty-handed, I opened Mom's messages.

Me: I'm babysitting.

Mom: Where? Why didn't you tell me?

Clenching my jaw, I glared at the messages. Mom might've been acting like she was trying, but this ... fuck, I hated having to deal with this shit all the time. I was her daughter, and I lived under her roof, but I was an adult. I had a life too.

Me: I'm babysitting my friend's little sister.

Mom: João's?

My eyes widened. *How the hell does she know?*

Though I didn't want to fight with her right now because I had other stuff to deal with, like worrying endlessly about João and Landon burning Redwood to the ground, I bit my tongue and responded to her.

Me: Yes.

I thought she'd come back with a snarky reply and tell me that I needed to get out of this neighborhood as soon as possible or that people around the slums were no good. But instead, she called me and actually expected me to pick up the damn phone.

After everything she had put me through.

My phone buzzed in my hand.

Over. And over. And over. And over.

I sent it to voice mail.

Mom: Please answer.

Mom: It's important.

Mom: João's mom is in the hospital, and the doctors stabilized her.

Three little bubbles appeared next to her contact image. I clicked on her image and called her. She should be at home now. Her shift had ended over an hour ago. *What is she doing at the hospital, updating me about João's mom?* She hated him.

"Mom?" I asked when she picked up. "What's going on?"

"João's mother is in the hospital. She's recovering, but João ran out and hasn't come back for almost an hour now. Nobody knows how to contact him, and nobody here has even tried. Those girls at the front desk are—"

"Didn't you get off an hour ago?" I asked, confused.

"Yes, but I saw João with his mother."

"So, you stayed?" I whispered in disbelief.

Why would she do that? She hated every single one of the Poison boys and didn't care what happened to them, never mind their parents, especially one who sold her body for money. It didn't make any sense.

"Yes, I stayed. I wanted to make sure that she got proper care."

I pulled my phone away from my ear and stared at the contact to make sure that I was still talking to Mom. Maybe I had called the wrong number by accident, or maybe this was some fucked up dream of some sort. Because Mom ... she didn't care, did she?

"Imani?" Mom said through the phone.

After confirming that this was definitely Mom's number, I pressed the phone against my ear again. "Yeah, I'm here. I just ..." I rubbed a hand over my face and sat crisscrossed beside Kai, furrowing my brows. "Why? Why'd you stay? You don't care about people like him."

A moment passed, and the line remained quiet.

"I care about you, Imani," she whispered. "And I know you might not believe me, but after your friend was shot by his own parents, I haven't been able to stop thinking about how your father and I grew up in the slums. Stuff like that happened all the time, and nobody talked about it. Nobody cared. That's why I wanted to become a doctor. It wasn't for the money." She let out a sorrowful sigh. "Somewhere along the way, I lost sight of that."

I didn't know what to say, so I didn't say anything to her. What could I say? It had taken Landon getting shot and almost dying *and me caring for him* for her to realize that she'd been a bitch for the past eighteen years of my life.

Maybe part of me didn't believe her still. She had screwed me up.

"You don't have to believe me, Imani," she said. "But I'm not as bad of a person as you might think. I've tried to do some good over the years to people who were in bad situations. I've tried to help them out the best I could."

"Like who?" I snapped, still in shock and in disbelief.

Mom was trying, but was she really? Or did she just want me to believe that?

"I can't tell you, Imani. It will put you in danger."

I balled my hand into a tight fist. Of course she couldn't tell me. She hadn't saved anyone. She was lying yet again, and I fucking hated it. I hated how she thought being nice to a couple of my friends would make up for years of hurting me mentally.

It didn't make anything better.

"I'll be at the hospital in a little bit," I said through the phone, then shut it off without saying good-bye. I stared at the screen and frowned, tears welling up in my eyes. I didn't even know why I wanted to cry right now, but I did.

I fucking wanted to so badly.

It wasn't fair.

After quickly texting João, shoving my phone into my pocket, and refusing to let any tears fall, I stood and grabbed Kai's hand. "Come on, Kai. We have to head to the hospital. João's mother is stable, but he isn't there yet."

"Are you okay?" Kai asked, following me to Ana's room.

"I'm fine," I whispered. "I just don't know why I keep expecting Mom to be different."

Once Kai picked up Ana from her bedroom, he placed her in the car seat in the back of my car. I slid into the driver's seat and glanced into the rearview mirror at Ana, who swayed in her seat and grabbed a bunch of Kai's wavy hair.

"Where are we going?" she mumbled, half-asleep.

"Go to sleep, Ana," Kai said, smiling softly at her. "I'll wake you up when we get there."

"Okay," she said, resting her head against the back of the seat and snoring already.

My lips curled into a small smile, and I started the car, ready and anxious to get to the hospital already. Kai slid into the passenger seat and clicked on his seat belt, looking over at me as I headed toward the hospital.

"What're you smiling for?" Kai asked me.

"No reason," I said.

But really, butterflies fluttered in my stomach at the thought and sight of Kai being so good with kids. Don't get me wrong; João was good with Ana, too, because she was his sister, but Kai was almost innately good for someone who didn't have any siblings.

"What is it?" Kai asked.

"You're just"—my smile turned into a full-on grin—"cute."

"Cute?" Kai asked when I pulled into the parking lot, a small smile stretching across his lips. He glanced over at me and lifted Ana from her car seat, who didn't wake up this time, then followed me through the emergency exit doors.

When we entered, I spotted Mom behind the front desk with a couple nurses. She smiled at me, and I grimaced and sat beside Kai, who cradled Ana in his strong arms. I leaned closer to him. "When do you think João will—"

Before I could even finish my sentence, João stormed through the hospital emergency doors with Landon following behind him. He had changed into a pair of black sweatpants and a long-sleeved shirt. I could only imagine what his other clothes looked like right now, covered with the Redwood rich blood.

"João," I said, standing up and hurrying over to him. "Your mom is stable."

Pissed off, João pushed past me and walked right back into the back hallway, as if he already knew where to go. He disappeared into a room and slammed the door behind him, the sound echoing through the quiet hospital.

* * *

An hour later, João finally came out of the hospital room and walked right out the emergency exit doors. I yawned and followed him out the doors to find him sitting on one of the benches outside.

"Are you okay?" I asked him, leaning against a pole and wrapping my arms around my body to stay warm.

Snow drifted down around us, piling up on the streets and sticking to my hair.

João glared up at me. "I don't want to fucking talk about it."

"Okay," I said, swaying back and forth on my heels.

Usually, I would push him to talk, but tonight, something felt different. He had witnessed his mother almost die in the fucking back of a rich man's restaurant. He had every right to keep his mouth shut for now. I didn't know how that man processed shit, but it definitely wasn't by talking it out.

So, I decided to change the subject.

"So, do you remember when you asked me to watch Ana, you said that you'd do anything for me?" I asked, rocking back on my heels again and clasping my hands behind my back. "Well ... I know what I want from you."

João leaned back, rubbed a hand over his face, and groaned. "Can't this wait?"

"No."

After clenching his jaw, he stared up at me with those dark brown eyes. "What is it?"

"A date."

João chuckled and pulled out a pack of cigarettes from his back pocket. "You're fucking with me, right?" he asked, sticking a cigarette between the corner of his lips and lighting it. "Out of everything you could possibly want, you want me to bring you on a date."

"Yes, I do."

The lightness in his eyes suddenly disappeared, his gaze hardening. He pulled the cigarette out of his mouth and shook his head, blowing out a puff of smoke. "I'm not fucking bringing you out on a date."

"You have to."

"I don't have to do shit, Imani."

"I watched Ana for you."

Instead of coming at me twice as hard with an insult, João tossed his barely smoked cigarette onto the ground, stomped it out, and stood, studying me. "Don't get any fucking ideas. I'm only going to do it for Ana, not because I like you."

"I don't like you either, dickhead," I said, but maybe I did a little. "I just want to go out."

"Why can't you ask Landon?" João snapped.

"Because I want to go out with you."

João stared at me for a few long moments again until he finally turned on his heel and walked past me toward the hospital doors. "Be ready. Tuesday night. Eight p.m. And don't fucking expect it to be a nice date. I don't do that shit."

Chapter Eighty-Seven

LANDON

"Just like that," I murmured, grasping Imani's waist and watching her above me.

She placed her hands on my bare chest and bucked her hips back and forth on my dick, her pussy tightening harder and harder with every damn moment that passed. I reached up and tugged on her nipples poking out through her white tank top.

After Kai had brought Ana home and João decided to stay at the hospital tonight, Imani and I went back to her place. Her mother had gone home an hour before us, so sneaking into her house had been easy.

Not that I would've really cared if Imani's mom had found me.

"More," she whispered. "Give me more."

Seizing her hips, I held them steady and pounded up into her. With her brows furrowed, she parted her lips and let out a quiet moan, her legs quivering around me. She slipped a hand between her legs to rub her clit.

"I'm going to come," she whispered, her other fingers digging into my chest. "Landon."

I gripped her tighter, my dick fucking swelling inside her, and slammed up into her one last time, coming deep in her pussy. She slapped a hand over her mouth and moaned loudly into it, her pussy pulsing over and over on my dick to suck out all the cum.

When she finished, she rolled over onto the bed beside me and curled into my side. After a few moments, she calmed her heavy breathing, the room overcome with silence. She lay in my arms with her head tucked into the crook of my arm.

"Did João kill him?" she whispered, staring up at the ceiling and tensing.

I inhaled deeply, not wanting to involve Imani in any more of our shit, and gently rubbed her shoulder. As far as I knew, she didn't like it when we even kicked the shit out of other people. She really wouldn't like to know what João had done to that man.

But as much as I wanted to hide this from her, I couldn't anymore.

João might've not agreed, but Imani was as much a part of Poison as all of us were. She had been with us for weeks, had witnessed so much shit that we forced her into and that she happened upon by herself. She deserved to know the truth about the monsters we were.

"Yes," I said.

Imani relaxed on top of me. "Good."

"Good?" I asked, taken aback. "I thought you hated shit like that."

"I do, but sometimes, people deserve it." She glanced over at me, then rolled on top and rested her palms against my bare chest. "João was protecting his family and doing what anyone should do for the people they love."

I drew my fingers down the side of her face, where her skin met the hem of her silk hair wrap. My chest tightened at the sight of her face glowing in the moonlight. "You know, as much of an asshole as he is, he would do anything for you too."

She rolled her eyes playfully. "Yeah, right."

After chuckling—because maybe she was right; João *was* a bitch to everyone but his family—I wrapped my arms around her small waist and held her tightly to me. João might or might not do anything for her, but I would.

Gently brushing her fingers across my bandages around my ribs, Imani suddenly frowned and stared at it, her voice quiet. "João and Kai promised me not to tell you, so don't get mad at them. But after I saw what your father did to you, I forced them to bring me back to your place while you were recovering."

My entire body tensed. "You what?"

What was she doing, putting herself in danger like that? She knew to stay away from them, and so did those fucking assholes. Why the fuck would they bring her back to my place after my own fucking father shot me?

"Please," Imani whispered, finally glancing back up at me with big eyes. "Promise me that you won't get mad at them. I forced them to bring me, or I would've gone by myself. I know it was stupid, but I had so much pent-up anger. All I wanted to do was"—she paused and lowered her voice even more—"kill them."

"Imani," I whispered, shock running through my body, paralyzing me to the spot.

She tightened her tiny fists on my chest and stared up at me through watery eyes. "I wanted to kill them for what they did to you. I hate them so much. I can't even begin to imagine what I would've done if he had actually killed you."

And while this whole thing might've started because we were getting each other off through a video chat, this woman had really done something to me these past few months. She became the only fucking person that I wanted to protect from the bad things at Redwood. She had become a woman I loved.

"I really wanted to kill them." A tear slid down her cheek. "And I still do." She curled her fingers into my chest and stared down at me. "I know you guys do that stuff all the time, but I ... does that make me a bad person? Am I a bad person for wanting to kill the people who almost killed you?"

Pulling her tighter to my chest, I shook my head. "That doesn't make you a bad person."

"But I want to end their lives," Imani whispered. "Your own parents."

"You're protecting someone that you"—I sucked in another breath, my chest tightening—"love, Imani. You said it yourself; you want to do what anyone would do to protect the people they love. That doesn't make you a bad person, especially to me."

Chapter Eighty-Eight

KAI

Landon had skipped school after second period, complaining that his ribs hurt too damn much. João had spent the day at the hospital with his mom and grabbed Ana off the bus since his mother wouldn't be home. So, that meant I had Imani to myself.

She walked down the hallway alone after school, dressed in a cute plaid skirt. I followed after her quietly. When she turned down a secluded hallway, I smacked my hand over her mouth from behind and pulled her behind some lockers, burying my nose into her hair.

"Be quiet, Imani," I murmured to her. "I'm going to play with you."

Before anyone could see us, I pulled her into a dark classroom and locked the door behind us, then let my hand fall from her mouth. She gasped softly, her ass rubbing against the front of my pants as I continued to pull her.

"Kai," she whispered. "We're at school."

"You've masturbated for us at school over video, Imani. You've done worse."

When I finally found the teacher's swivel chair up in the front of the room, I sat back and pulled Imani down onto my lap. She inhaled sharply, her nipples pressing through the thin fabric of her shirt. I tugged her scarf off her shoulders and pulled her arms behind her back to tie her up with it.

"Kai," she said, glancing over her shoulder at the locked door. "Someone might see."

After I finished restraining her arms, I grasped her chin in one hand and her nipple in the other, tugging roughly. "Nobody is going to see me fuck you, and if they do, I'll take care of them for you."

She pressed her thighs together and stared at me with wide eyes, her pupils dilated.

I sank a hand under her skirt and touched her soaked panties. "You love the thought of that, don't you?"

When I brushed my fingers against her clit, she moaned. "Yes."

"Spread your legs for me."

She spread her legs like a good girl and rubbed her swollen clit back and forth against my cargo pants, whimpering softly. My dick swelled inside my pants, and I wanted to bury it inside of her right fucking now.

"You're so sexy," I murmured to her, undoing my pants and pulling out my cock. "Come up here"—I patted my thigh—"and ride me."

Instead of climbing up onto me like I had asked her, she scooted her ass off me and knelt between my legs, her warm mouth wrapping around the head of my hard dick. She dipped her head and stared up at me, taking more and more of me into her.

With her hands tied behind her back, she bobbed her head up and down on me until spit and slobber ran down her chin. She choked on my cock but slid her mouth down until her lips touched the base and her tongue glided against my balls.

I gripped them in my hand, wanting her to take more of me into that tight mouth of hers. She opened her mouth a bit wider and forced her head down further on my cock, gagging on it and taking my balls inside her too.

When I hit the back of her throat, I grunted and grabbed two fistfuls of her hair, thrusting my hips up to face-fuck my little slut's throat. Imani stared up at me through watery eyes, her slobber dripping onto the ground and creating a puddle underneath us.

Gargling on my dick, Imani pulled back and gasped for air. "More. I want more."

She took my dick back into her mouth and bobbed her head harder and faster than I had been throat-fucking her, ignoring her gagging and forcing me to hit the back of her throat each time.

I wrapped my hand around her neck to feel myself buried deep inside her, my dick getting even fucking harder at the sight of Imani taking all of me inside her, even my balls, her warm mouth stuffed full and her cheeks flushed.

"Oh fuck, baby," I grunted, thrusting my hips up to meet hers each time. "If you keep doing that, you're going to make me fucking come."

Wanting her to feel good too, I reached underneath her, pulled up her shirt, and pinched her nipples hard between my fingers and tugged. She slid her mouth down on my cock until there wasn't any more to take and stared up at me, moaning loudly on my dick.

Her tiny body shook in pleasure, the way it always did when she orgasmed. And, fuck, I couldn't stop myself from exploding into her tight mouth, filling her throat with my cum. She widened her eyes, choking on it, and came even harder, body trembling on the ground.

When she finally pulled back for air, a wad of my cum and her spit dripped out of her mouth and onto her tits. She breathed heavily, chest heaving up and down. I pulled down her white shirt and rubbed the spit and cum into it, so it became almost see-through around her nipples.

Fuck, she was so sexy.

After I untied her, I placed the scarf around her shoulders, reluctantly covering her small breasts.

To my surprise, Imani stood up and pressed her thighs together again, whimpering. "God, I'm so horny."

She pulled out her phone, pushed the scarf to the side, and snapped a selfie of her cum-covered tits, sending it to the group chat.

Imani: You guys missed out today. ;) @landon @joão

I watched her and chuckled, drawing my tongue across my lower lip.

Imani tossed her backpack over her shoulder and nodded to the door. "We should get to the hospital."

"I'll meet you and the guys at the hospital a bit later," I said to Imani, pulling her hair behind her shoulders and kissing her neck from behind her. "I have something that I need to take care of today."

Imani frowned but nodded. "Sure."

After she disappeared through the side doors of Redwood Academy, I headed toward my locker and grabbed the porno magazines and purple dildo that someone had stuffed in Allie Hall's locker. I had told her that I would take care of it for her, and I knew exactly what I was going to do with it.

I headed out in the cold toward the football field and spotted Jace Harbor on the field.

I never liked him.

He was too arrogant and too cocky for a good girl, especially for Allie Hall. Jace had shit that happened to him and paid us well for the jobs that we did for him, but ever since he had hurt Allie two years ago, I fucking loathed the man.

So, after someone had stuffed that giant purple dildo and porno magazines in Allie's locker, I had confiscated them from her and decided to get him back. She didn't want me to hurt him for some reason, but I wanted payback even if it was only a bit.

Pulling up my hood, I stuffed my hands into my sweatshirt pockets and glanced over at the football team practicing out in the light snow. They ran up and down the field, throwing and catching the ball.

When I knew nobody would see me, I slipped into the football locker room and locked the door behind me. After finding Jace's locker, I easily undid the lock and stuffed the magazines and purple dildo inside it, well enough for it to tumble out when he opened it up.

It wasn't the biggest payback, but it was what Allie would allow me to do.

Once I shut and locked Jace's locker back up, I walked out through the side exit and toward my bike. Snow drifted down around me, a thick layer already piled up on the seat. I cursed and slid my hand across the leather to push it off.

Dressed in a skintight cheerleading outfit that the sleazy principal must've made girls like her wear, Nicole stormed up to me as I finished and crossed her arms, glaring at me with a pointed look that she must've thought would scare me. "What'd you do?"

I threw one leg over my bike and grabbed my helmet. "You have to be clearer, Nicole. Poison does a lot of shit."

She fumbled a bit, and for a moment, I thought she'd throw a tantrum like a little girl. "You know what I'm talking about. I don't know when you did it, but you got into my house just over the weekend. You had to have."

"What are you talking about?" I asked, confused as fuck.

Why couldn't she have a normal conversation?

"You got into my father's files somehow. You're the only person I know who could do something like that." She poked a hard, manicured finger into my chest. "I'm not stupid. You're the brains behind Poison, and my father's files are gone. He knows about it."

Not wanting to give off that we surely had snuck into her house, I shook my head. "What files? I don't know what you're talking about."

"The files my father keeps in his office."

"About?" I asked, furrowing my brows.

She paused, and it almost looked like she wanted me to know anything about who stole the files for some reason. "You know what they're about."

"If you're looking for someone to blame"—I pulled my helmet over my head and started the bike—"it's not going to be me. When you have fucking evidence that I stole them, then fucking come to me. I didn't do anything."

Before she had a chance to respond, I sped out of the parking lot and off toward the hospital. We had shit to do, and I didn't want Nicole to start any rumors about me. I hated her police chief father, and that fucker would do anything to get all of us sent to jail.

Chapter Eighty-Nine

"On your next exam, you will be asked about the differences between mitosis and meiosis, so I suggest that all of you go home and study this weekend. This will be one of the hardest exams of the semester," Mr. Barnes, my Bio teacher, said.

I wrote down a couple notes in my planner and glanced over at Allie, who stared at him with wide, scared eyes, as if she wouldn't get a hundred percent on his tests like she always did. My lips curled into a small smile, and I turned back to the front.

"Did you see Carter's face?" Jenny whispered behind us to her friend.

"Someone fucked him up bad," another student whispered.

All people had talked about today was how badly Carter, Redwood's most idiotic quarterback, had gotten beat up the other night. I didn't care much for drama, but I ate this up like it was damn chocolate because I hated Carter.

Everyone did.

He deserved to get fucked.

I leaned closer to Allie. "Have *you* seen him yet? I heard he looks like shit."

Allie swallowed hard and shook her head. "No, I'm too nervous to see."

"Why?" I asked, grinning now. "He's a dick."

"Because I think that Jace did—"

Mr. Barnes cleared his throat and narrowed his eyes at Allie. "Do you have a question?"

Jenny and the other student pressed their lips together and looked at Allie, as if she were the only one who had been talking during the lecture and not them too. Ugh, bitches like them annoyed the shit out of me.

Allie shook her head and took one for the entire Biology class. "No, sir."

After Mr. Barnes grimaced and looked away, she slumped down in her seat and rested her head against my shoulder. I took down the rest of the notes in class, knowing that I needed to ace this exam or else Mom would really kill me this time.

"Class is dismissed," Mr. Barnes said once he finished talking. "Allie, stay behind. We need to chat."

All the blood drained from Allie's face.

When everyone started packing up their materials, I glanced over at her. "What's that all about?" I asked, pulling off my reading glasses and placing them into my case.

"I don't know," Allie said, gathering her belongings and walking up to Mr. Barnes's desk. "I'll meet you in the hall."

After taking one last look at her, I walked out of the classroom and stood by the door. Students rushed around me to get to their next period class, loud chatter echoing through the hallways.

Suddenly, all the chatter stopped.

I glanced up from my phone to see Carter walking down the hallways with both his eyes nearly swollen shut and his lip busted in three different places. My eyes widened as he passed me, yet I couldn't even look away.

This was the best damn thing I had seen in a while.

Just as he disappeared around the corner, a young and handsome man with piercing blue eyes walked over and tried to shove his keys into a classroom diagonal from us. I had never seen the man before, but he was damn attractive.

"Who's that?" Allie asked, walking out from Mr. Barnes's class.

"A new teacher, I guess," I said, squinting at the door. "Computer science, it looks like."

"Doesn't Mrs. Goldman teach computer science?" Allie asked.

Deciding not to gawk, I looped my arm around hers and began walking down Redwood's halls. "Mrs. Goldman got caught hacking into some of her students' parents' computers and accounts," I said, shaking my head. "She had been taking money from them. I think she stole almost a half-billion dollars."

Allie's eyes widened. "What?! When did this happen?"

"Last week. You've been too preoccupied with your stepbrother's cock to listen to the gossip, it seems."

But the only reason I knew about it was because Kai had told me what happened at the hospital last night. I might've been too preoccupied with them to keep up with the drama too, but she didn't need to know that.

Allie cut her eyes to me, and I laughed.

"What? It's true, isn't it? You guys have been sleeping together for weeks now." I playfully narrowed my eyes at her. "I don't approve of the man after what he did to you, but you can't keep something *that good* from me. I picked it up."

I still hated the guy, but whenever Allie was with him, she was happier.

It kinda pissed me off because he was a dick, but I couldn't do anything about it.

Since our lockers were near each other's, she stopped at mine and leaned against it. "So ... you talk to the Poison boys lately?" she asked, arching a brow at me. "If you want gossip about me and Jace, you gotta give me some juicy details about your life."

I bit my lip and glanced down the hall toward Landon, who leaned against his locker and talked to Kai. Allie glanced their way. My boys were bad news, but I couldn't stay away from them. They were all mine.

"So, they're kinda, um, blackmailing me," I whispered, rubbing the front of my neck.

God, I'd waited so damn long to talk to her about this, and I couldn't wait any longer.

"What?!" she shouted, causing a couple people to look over, including Landon and Kai.

I placed my hand over her mouth. "Don't yell about it!" When I knew she wouldn't say anything else, I removed my hand and tucked some curly black hair behind my ear. "Long story short, they found out about ... my freaky side and—"

She snorted. "Your freaky side?"

I grinned at her. "Okay, don't judge me, Ms. I Love Having Public Sex with My Stepbrother After He Fucked Me Over." I gestured up and down my body. "A girl has needs, and ya girl is a freak."

"Who's a freak?" Jamal said, walking up to us and leaning beside Allie.

"Allie is, but you'd never find that out," I said, glancing behind them both to see Carter sauntering down the hallway again.

This time, he walked toward us and stared at Allie with a clenched jaw.

Allie turned her head and glanced at him, her eyes wide.

"He looks like he got ran over by a fucking train," I said.

As he walked by us, he mouthed the words, *This is your fault, bitch*, to Allie.

I balled my hands into fists by my sides and glared at him for merely mouthing those words to my best fucking friend. It was like he wanted to threaten her or something, and that wasn't cool with me. I glanced over at Landon and Kai, then nodded to Carter.

And almost as if they understood me, those boys followed Carter down the hall and into another secluded hallway to take care of him for me.

Chapter Ninety

JOÃO

"You're fucking sure that he knows?" I asked Kai, staring at him through my rearview mirror.

Landon sat beside me, clutching his side and grunting about the wound by his ribs that seemed to be getting worse by the fucking day.

"Yeah," Kai said. "Nicole's father knows his files have been taken."

Jace Harbor pulled up his driveway and parked his car beside me. Allie sat in his passenger seat, eyes wide.

Kai glanced over at her, then back at me. "It's fine that she's here. She's not going to ask any questions."

After stepping out of the car, Jace nodded to me. We got out of the car and walked to the front door, not wanting to say this aloud anywhere out here. I didn't know who the fuck was listening in on us.

Jace opened Allie's door and grabbed her hand, leading her inside the house. He held the door open and locked it behind us. "What do you want?" he asked me.

Allie rocked back on her heels, standing behind Jace and staring between the three of us. She crossed her arms and glanced at Kai. "Before you leave, I need to talk to you," she said to him, then disappeared into the living room.

"You have a problem," I said to Jace.

"*Me*?" Jace asked.

"Nicole's father found out about the missing evidence," Landon said, crossing his arms over his chest. "He doesn't know who did it, but he knows that it was sometime between Friday night and Tuesday morning."

Jace tensed and glanced into the living room, where Allie sat on the couch on her phone.

"Since it wasn't only your mother's case that was stolen, he can't pinpoint who it was. It could literally be anyone. Nicole has so many people over at her house all the time. The cheerleaders, football players, even some nobodies that she likes sleeping with," I said. "But he knows that it's gone, and Nicole tried to blame Kai yesterday."

"You don't want Allie hurt. You'd better have a plan to come out with it all," Kai said to him, following his gaze into the living room. "Soon."

Jace ran a hand over his face and groaned internally. "I need more time. I'm not ready. I don't have everything I need or the people I need to get this information out. Once I release it, all of Redwood is going to rally behind my father's back, and you fucking know it."

I smirked and pulled a pack of cigarettes out of my back pocket, lighting one up in Mr. Moneybags's living room. "Not if all of Redwood's richest burn with him," I said. "We have the information to blackmail and destroy some of the most prestigious families here. They can't defend anyone else when their reputations are on the line."

"You want to blackmail all of Redwood?" Jace asked.

I blew out a puff of smoke. "Redwood billionaires have treated the poor like we're trash for the past hundred years. I know you would never understand that, as your daddy has given you everything, but it's fucking time we push back. Fuck the billionaires. I want to watch them desperately grasp on to their hope as we crush them under our fucking boots."

Jace rubbed his forehead and cursed.

"Are you in?" I asked.

It would happen with or without him anyway.

Jace ran his tongue against his teeth. "Once you take care of Carter for me, I'm in."

"Take care of Carter," Landon said, glancing at Kai. "We got that covered."

"Looks like you got yourself a deal, Harbor," I said, heading toward the door. "You'd better pull through for us."

After Kai talked to Allie in the living room, I drove them back to Landon's place, made up some excuse that I needed to watch Ana tonight so I couldn't hang, and sped back home in time to find Vera, one of the nerds from school who lived across from me, standing at my front door.

I hurriedly got out of my car and nodded to her. "You're going to do it?"

She pressed her lips together. "Sure."

Once I kicked my shoes off at the front door, I let her into the house, passed Ana's room to tell her that someone was babysitting her tonight, took a quick shower, and tried to pick out something that I could wear on this fucking date.

What the fuck did people even wear? Dating and girls were too fucking hard.

Deciding to open the box of clothes that I swore I would never wear again—they were clothes Dad had gotten me when we used to live with him—I picked out something decent and ran a hand through my wet hair.

My phone buzzed, and Imani's name popped up.

Imani: Where are you?

Fuck it. I had to go.

I grabbed my coat and keys, and walked back into the living room to see Vera at the kitchen table with an angry Ana. Ana only liked to be watched by Kai, Landon, or Imani. Vera was going to have hell tonight.

When Ana saw me, she jumped up. "João! Why do you look so good?"

"They're just clothes, Ana," I said, hurrying to the door.

"Nice clothes."

"Just clothes," I repeated.

"But you never wear a suit."

"I'm not wearing a suit," I said between gritted teeth.

Ana furrowed her little brows at me and marched back to the

kitchen table to angrily eat her dinner. She was moody this week for some reason, even after Imani and Kai had watched her the other night.

"How long do you need me to babysit?" Vera asked, arms crossed over her chest while she stared at me. "You'd better be paying me too. I'm not babysitting for free again. Ana is a sweetheart, but I could be doing schoolwork."

"You'll be paid." I tossed my jacket over my shoulder. "I'll be home when I get home."

After stepping out into the cold, I slid into my car, started it, and stared at my reflection in the rearview mirror, my heart pounding inside my chest harder than it ever had before tonight. I had never been on a date before, especially not with someone like Imani.

And I was ... nervous, okay? I was fucking nervous.

I didn't give a shit about what we did. I didn't even have anything planned.

But, shit, I was going on a date with Imani.

I didn't want to fuck it up.

Chapter Ninety-One

JOÃO

I pulled into Imani's driveway behind her mother's car and stared at the front door, my stomach tightening in knots. With one hand wrapped tightly around the steering wheel, I took my phone from my pocket and pulled Imani's contact up on Discord.

A green bubble appeared beside her name, signaling that she was online.

After typing out, **I'm outside**, I erased it and shoved my phone back into my pocket. I huffed to myself and slammed my driver's door open, shuffling out of the car and to her front door, shielding myself from the snow with my suit jacket.

That was the reason I had dressed up. Not because I wanted to impress Imani.

Knocking twice on the door, I stuffed my hands into my pockets and pressed my lips together. Whatever this feeling was spreading throughout my body, zipping up and down my arms and legs, I didn't fucking like it at all.

The door opened, and Imani's mother stood on the other side.

"João," she said, crossing her arms over her chest. "What're you doing here?"

"Picking up Imani. Can you get her?"

She shuffled back a few steps to let me into the room, but I didn't move from the doorway. I didn't like this bitch at all, not only because she was a snotty asshole like the rest of the rich, but also because of how she treated Imani.

I remembered how utterly heartbroken Imani had been the other day, tears pouring down her cheeks in the middle of the street. It didn't fucking sit well with me, especially how quickly her mother had changed her ways.

This bitch wasn't trustworthy.

"Your mother is doing better," she said.

Clenching my jaw, I glared at her. "I fucking know. I've been at the hospital as much as I could since."

"If you want—"

"I *want* you to call your daughter down," I said between gritted teeth.

Keeping an eye on me, Imani's mother walked to the foot of the stairs. "Imani!"

After some rustling upstairs, Imani ran down the stairs in a pair of fitted jeans and a bright yellow crop top, her curly hair sitting naturally around her shoulders. I clenched my jaw at how utterly awkward this was.

"João," Imani whispered, staring at me with wide eyes. Her gaze slowly drifted down my body—from my tie to my leather belt to the dress shoes on my feet. Glancing back up at my face, Imani curled her lips into a small smile. "Why'd you dress up? I thought we were—"

"You want to go out or not?" I growled.

I didn't like the way she was looking at me. Nobody looked at me like that ever.

It was ... fucking weird.

"Yes!" she said quickly, tucking some thick, curly black hair behind her ear. "I do."

"Go get dressed in something nice," I said, pulling out a pack of cigarettes out of my suit pocket because standing here in Imani's fancy fucking mansion and having her look at me like this before I took her out on a date ... it stressed me the fuck out.

"Okay, give me five minutes." Imani quickly jogged to the stairs, turned around right before she ran up them, and said, "And, João, you look really good in that suit."

A warmth spread throughout my body—something I hadn't really ever felt. I pulled out a cigarette and lit it up outside the house, pacing back and forth on the walkway and glancing up at the second floor.

The light in one of the rooms turned on, and Imani tugged her shirt over her head through the window. She walked into another room and disappeared from my line of vision. I rubbed a hand over my face and pulled the cigarette from my mouth, unable to believe that Imani had talked me into taking her on a date.

I don't date.

I don't care.

I …

Imani hurried out the front door in a silky pink dress that hugged her petite body and complemented her dark skin. I slowly blew the smoke out of my mouth and stared at her, unable to pull my gaze away.

Fuck.

"You ready?" she asked after a couple moments.

After shaking myself awake from the damn trance, I tossed my cigarette onto the pavement and stomped on it with the tip of my dress shoe, and then I nodded toward my car. I slipped into the driver's seat and stared right ahead at me.

If I looked over at her, I … fuck, I'd want her now.

Instead of ruining everything, I drove toward downtown.

"Where are we going?" Imani asked me as I parallel parked on the busy downtown streets where restaurants usually cost more than even the ones in the city a couple hours away. She glanced around with her brows furrowed. "Are you sure you want to go down here? It's expensive."

"Get out of the car," I said, shoving my door open and stepping out into the snow.

Imani shuffled out onto the sidewalk, and I quickly snatched up her hand in my larger one. My heart pounded inside my chest. This was what people did on dates, right? They held hands and shit?

Tensing briefly, Imani glanced down at our hands and intertwined her fingers with mine.

"It's expensive down here, João."

"Just your taste, right?" I asked.

Imani stopped in the middle of the cold-ass street and stared up at me through wide eyes. "I'm fine if we just go to the movies or literally eat McDonald's fries in your car. We don't have to go to some restaurant like this."

Staring down into her big brown eyes, I wondered *how* someone who had millions of dollars to her family name could grow up to want fries and ketchup on a date. Most girls like her wanted more than something that simple.

After sucking in a breath, I grasped her hand tighter. "I want to bring you out. Come on."

Once I pulled her to Harleen Steakhouse, I nodded to Blaise Harleen—Redwood's skateboarding punk—who leaned against the hostess station, flirting with one of the girls from Redwood Academy.

When he saw me, he pushed himself off the counter and nodded to me. "Finally made it."

Blaise might've been from a rich family whose family owned this place, but he didn't act picture-perfect and stuck-up like the rest of them. He hung by himself and only really came around when he needed some weed, but he wasn't a dick. Plus, he owed me a favor.

"Thanks for getting us in."

"Two for João Rocha," Blaise said to the hostess, knocking on the counter and grabbing his coat to head out. "We're even now, João."

And with that, the hostess grabbed two menus and headed toward the seating area. Imani glanced back at me and followed her through the crowded restaurant, and I hesitantly followed her, knowing that this was the beginning of a long night.

<h1 style="text-align:center">Chapter Ninety-Two</h1>

IMANI

We sat in silence.

In actual silence.

For the entire date.

I had always thought that Kai was the quiet one, but besides shit-talking, I didn't think João actually had much to talk about. If he wanted, he could've gone on and on about Landon or Kai or someone in Redwood that he hated, but he didn't bring any of that up tonight.

And it seemed like he was kinda, sorta nervous.

João Rocha, Poison's leader and the baddest boy at Redwood Academy, was nervous.

My lips curled into a smile at the mere thought. I cut into the last of my steak, pulling the meat apart from the fat, and shoved it into my mouth, moaning softly at the taste. Lately, Allie and I had been having nothing but milkshakes and fries. This was a change.

I stared at him and smiled.

"What?" he asked.

"Nothing."

"Don't piss me off, Imani. What the hell do you want?"

I shrugged and took a bite of food. "You know you're supposed to talk on dates."

"I didn't want to go out. You forced me."

"If you didn't want to go out, then why are we at a fancy restaurant?"

João clenched his jaw and growled, not responding to me.

"I didn't know how awkward you really were, João," I teased, grinning across the table at the gang member dressed in a suit with his dark brown hair tousled and his eyes filled with so many secrets.

"I'm never bringing you on a date again," he said between gritted teeth.

"Too bad I already have another one planned," I said back to him. "My treat next time."

João cut his eyes up to mine and placed his fork and knife parallel on his plate to signal that he was finished with his food.

Impressed, I raised my brows and leaned forward. "You do know that means that you're finished with your food."

"I've done this before," João said.

"You've brought other girls on fancy dates like this?" I asked with a tinge of jealousy.

João's jaw twitched. "My father was a rich asshole."

"So, that's a no?" I asked, kicking my legs back and forth underneath the table and grinning like a madwoman, my jealousy suddenly fading away. "Am I the first person you've been on a date with?"

Instead of answering me, João grabbed a random waiter and handed him his card. "Pay for our bill. Be fucking quick. I want to get the fuck out of here." When the waiter shuffled away, João grabbed his drink and took a sip.

Maybe I *was* the first person he'd been on a date with.

That would explain why he was so awkward about it.

A couple moments later, the waiter came back with a check to sign. João scribbled his signature on the page and stuffed his hands into his pockets, nodding to the exit. I followed after him, curling my arm around his and grasping his large bicep.

"Thank you," I said.

João tensed, as if he had never heard a *rich girl* thank him for anything, and then he pulled his hand out of his pocket. I dropped my hand from his bicep to his hand, and before I could take his in mine, he grasped mine tightly.

This was what normal people did on dates.

But ... this was a big deal for João to grab my hand *twice*.

When we got back to his car, he opened the door for me, then slipped into the other side, starting the car and blasting the heat. Like at the restaurant, João didn't say much to me on the ride back to my place.

I didn't know if he liked the date or not, but I hoped he did.

Especially if it was his first.

After a couple moments, he pulled up to my house.

"Do you want to come in?" I asked. "My parents are having dinner with Akio's family tonight. They probably won't be back until late."

I didn't know why I was so nervous. I'd done worse than sneak a boy into my house while my parents weren't home. Hell, I had kicked someone's face in a couple weeks ago and snuck Landon into my room countless times.

But my stomach was in tight knots.

"We can, uh ... have sex ... watch a movie."

My core warmed, and I clenched, my lacy panties soaked between my thighs. I'd had sex with João before, alone and not just with the guys. But João hadn't really been his *don't fuck with me because I'll kill you* self tonight.

Something felt different.

João stared down at me, the moonlight reflecting off his knowing brown eyes. He knew exactly why I was inviting him into the house, why I wanted him to come up to my room, and why I suggested we watch a movie.

And while I didn't want to be an easy score, he looked too damn good in that suit.

I wanted him.

So badly.

"Come on," João said, getting out of the car and walking up the sidewalk.

Quickly, I pulled off my heels and ran up the pathway after him with bare feet on the snow. I pulled my key from my purse and shoved it into the doorknob while João stood behind me, his shadow towering over mine against the door.

He was close. So close.

With his body heat radiating off him, he felt like he was mere centimeters from me, his fingers close to my waist, his head dipping by my neck. I inhaled deeply and hurriedly tried to unlock the damn door.

It might've been twenty degrees Fahrenheit outside, but my body was on fire.

"Open the door, Imani," João said, finally seizing my waist from behind, his rough fingers digging into my hips and his nose against my ear. He pressed his body against mine from behind, his suit pants against my ass. "It's fucking cold out here."

But he wasn't shivering either.

Desperately, I twisted the key and shoved open the door. I got merely one step into the house before João slipped in after me, shut the front door, and slammed me against it, my back against the door and his body against mine.

He wrapped his large hand around the front of my throat to pin me against the door, growling into my ear. His touch was so rough, his voice so low and ruthless. I wanted him to be inside me so badly. It was all I could think about the past few hours.

Suddenly, he unclenched his jaw and softened his eyes and stared at me how he had when I came down the stairs in a silky pink dress. He had never looked at me like this before tonight, and I loved it.

Loosening his hard grip on my throat, João Rocha gently took my face in his hands and kissed me. Not ruthlessly, but lovingly.

Chapter Ninety-Three

IMANI

Stumbling up the stairs, we pulled each other's clothes off, littering them all over my parents' house. When we both stood naked in my bedroom, he shut the door, lifted me into the air, and sat down with me on his lap on the bed.

"Sit on my face," João mumbled into our kiss. "Fuck, I've been waiting to taste you all night."

He lay back on the bed and easily seized my waist, pulling me onto him. With my knees posted on either side of his head, I clutched the headboard and stared down at João, who spread my legs wider to sit my cunt right on his mouth.

Grasping my ass with his hands to hold me in place, João flicked his tongue over and over across my clit. I moaned softly and dug my fingers harder into the headboard, pleasure shooting through my entire body.

After grunting, he kneaded and massaged my flesh with his rough fingers. He moved one hand underneath me to finger my pussy. When he slipped his fingers inside me, I moaned louder and clenched around him.

"I want you to come on my face," João murmured against my aching clit, his tongue flicking over the sensitive bud. "I want to feel your pussy quivering on me." He added another finger and curled them right over my G-spot. "Your tight little hole pulsing around my fingers."

"Oh God," I whispered, my body tensing.

The pressure built in my core, driving me higher and higher. I grasped the headboard harder and threw my head back, moments away from coming anywhere he asked me to. Gently, I bucked my hips back and forth across his mouth, his slight stubble tickling my inner thighs.

"Just like that, baby," he murmured to me. "Don't stop until you're dripping all over me."

When he curled his fingers against my G-spot one last time, I screamed out, my legs trembling. The orgasm was so intense that I immediately jumped up to move his mouth away from my clit, the pressure feeling unbearably good.

João wrapped his strong arms around my thighs and forced me to stay down on him, his tongue continuing to move in quick, tortuous circles around my clit. Pleasure rushed through my body from my core, my pussy pulsing all over his fingers and dripping onto his lips.

"João," I whispered, finally lifting myself off him when I finished coming.

He tossed me onto the bed beside him and crawled between my legs, his elbows posted right above my shoulders on the bed and his nose drawing up the column of my neck. He gently kissed my soft spot and positioned himself at my entrance.

"Fuck, Imani," he mumbled to me, biting down on my shoulder.

After a couple moments, he pushed himself inside me. Unlike the last time we'd had sex together, he wasn't rough. Instead, he was gentle and slow, letting me feel every inch of his cock slide into my tight hole.

When he was snug inside me, he moved his lips further up my neck until he reached my jaw. I placed my hands on either side of his face and pulled his lips onto mine, kissing him softly on the mouth.

He pushed into me, his hips bucking back and forth in a steady rhythm and his mouth moving more hungrily against mine. Resting his forehead against mine, he grunted against my lips, making me clench on him from the mere sound.

"More," I murmured against him. "Please."

João pumped into me faster, pulling out all eight inches and pushing himself back into me. My walls wrapped around each groove of his dick, clutching on to him, desperate for him to stay inside me.

Grunting and growling into my ear, João crashed his lips back down onto mine and continued to drive into me. I wrapped my arms around his back and dug my fingers into the muscle, moaning into the kiss as my pussy exploded around his thick cock.

I cried out, sucking on his bottom lip and shaking underneath him.

João pumped into me a couple more times. "I'm going to come inside you."

My pussy tightened around him even more, the thought of him spilling himself into my tight hole driving me even higher with pleasure. I sank into the bedsheets and panted. "Please, God, please."

After a couple more thrusts, João suddenly tensed and stilled inside me. He grunted louder than he ever had, his eyes rolling to the back of his head. I stared up at him, pleasure rushing out of my body.

When he finished, he pulled out of me and collapsed onto the bed beside me, his chest rising and falling rapidly. He rested a hand across his taut abs and stared up at the ceiling without saying a word.

I glanced over at him and hesitantly inched closer to him, wanting to cuddle. Nervously—because I doubted that he liked to cuddle—I placed my hand on his chest and laid my head on his shoulder. "Is this okay?" I whispered.

Instead of verbally answering me, he nodded.

"Are *you* okay?"

"I'm fine," João said, pressing his lips together.

After I sat up to stare down at him, about to ask what was bothering him, he pulled me back down onto his chest, holding one hand against my head gently and stroking his fingers through my hair.

"Please. Don't push it," he said, chest tight.

"Okay," I whispered, curling closer to him. "But I'm always here if you need anything. I've told you that from the beginning."

"I know." He blew out a breath, relaxing slightly underneath me. "I know, Imani."

Chapter Ninety-Four

KAI

Wiping Carter's blood from my hands, I walked with Landon from the warehouse where we had taken care of Carter tonight to João's place. We didn't kill Carter, but we had taught him a lesson in not fucking with Allie or Jace anymore.

Though I doubted that he'd actually listen.

"Where the fuck is João?" Landon asked, nodding to the empty driveway.

I furrowed my brows and shrugged. "Hospital?"

"Then, why's the light on in the living room?"

Pulling up my hood to stop the windchill from freezing off my ears, I followed Landon across the yard to the front door. Landon glanced in the windows and pounded the side of his fist against the door.

Vera Rodriguez answered the door, her hair pulled into a high ponytail and dark bags under her eyes. Dressed in fluffy, long pajama pants and a Redwood Academy sweatshirt, Vera tilted her head and yawned. "What do you want?"

"Where's João?"

"I was going to ask you guys that. He left me here with Ana, like, six hours ago." She glanced over her shoulder at Ana, who was passed out on the couch with chocolate all over her lips and cartoons blasting on the TV. "I need to go."

"He didn't say where he was going?" Landon asked.

"No," Vera said. "Can you watch her? I have a test tomorrow and need to study."

"Yeah, we have to study too," Landon said.

Vera rolled her eyes and padded back into the house. "Since when do you study?"

"We don't," I said, cutting into the conversation and stepping into the house. "We need to find João, though. Was he doing anything when he left?"

"I don't know. He was dressed in a nice suit."

"A suit?" Landon and I asked at the same time.

"He almost looked like he was going on a date," Vera said.

Landon and I looked at each other, and he arched a brow. I shrugged my shoulders, not really believing that *João* would dress in a suit or go out on a date with anyone. He didn't care about impressing anyone, especially not Imani.

"You think he's out with Imani?" Landon asked.

"I don't know," I said, pulling out a wad of cash from my wallet and handing it to Vera. "Get back home and study. We'll watch Ana."

Vera thanked me, pulled on her coat, and hurried out the door while slinging her backpack over her shoulders. She ran across the street through the snowstorm, shielding her face from the harsh wind, and stepped into her house.

I shut the door and slumped down on a seat at the kitchen table.

Landon sat on the couch, phone on the coffee table, head resting against the back of the sofa, and eyes closed. "Why wouldn't either of them tell us they were going out together tonight?"

"He probably didn't want us to get pissed off."

"Get pissed off?" Landon asked, glancing over at me. "You get pissed about Imani being with someone else?"

Though Imani might've had a thing with Landon and they might've been a couple and exchanged *I love you*s, that didn't mean that I didn't feel something for her too. I had spent a couple nights with her alone, and nothing had ever felt better.

Even if they were my best friends, I could still be jealous.

"Does it matter?" I asked, pulling my computer out of my backpack and opening it up on the kitchen table. After typing in my password, I opened the screens that I had been looking through before we visited Jace earlier.

After Nicole had accused me of stealing her father's files, I had dived back into them and found shit that didn't quite make sense. Like why Principal Vaughn of Redwood Academy had constant communication and a signed agreement with Nicole's police chief father.

The shit in the contract was highly vague, but still ...

I couldn't piece it together. What were they doing behind closed doors?

Landon's phone buzzed, and I found myself looking at the Discord app on my computer to see if it was Imani texting the group chat. But both Imani and João were offline, and nobody had said anything in the chat.

Shifting through the police chief's documents, I pulled up one about my father's death and Akio's family. I stared at it for a couple moments and gritted my teeth, fingernails cutting into my palms until they nearly split open.

If Imani knew about this, she would drop Akio faster than—

Another buzz.

I glanced over at Landon, who sat in the same spot with his hand over his bullet wound.

"Fuck, I wish I'd brought those pills. This shit's a bitch." He winced and sat up to grab his phone, frowning at the screen.

"Is that Imani?" I asked, glancing down at our Discord group chat again.

Neither she nor João had been answering our texts tonight. Usually, João wanted to work on week nights, especially when we were so close to exposing Redwood for all it was. We had even taken care of Carter by ourselves.

João never missed a chance to kick the shit out of someone like him.

He must've had something going on tonight. Or someone.

Landon inhaled sharply and drew a hand over his face, grunting. "No."

"Who is it?"

He shrugged his shoulders. "Unknown number."

"They've been calling you all night."

"If it was important, they would leave a message."

After eyeing him for a couple moments, I turned back to the documents on my laptop. My stomach tightened, my heart pounding inside my chest. No matter how much I looked at these documents we had stolen and scanned, I couldn't figure it out.

And I could almost *always* figure shit like this out.

But something didn't feel right. This *was* Redwood for crying out loud.

Nothing was ever right here.

Chapter Ninety-Five

"It's six in the morning!" I shouted at the Poison boys, who had dragged me into school bright and goddamn early in the morning. "Why did you bring me here this early? And why the hell are we heading toward the principal's office? Did you guys get in trouble or something?"

After Friday night, I hadn't talked to *any* of the guys until this morning. I didn't know what I had done to piss them off, but even Landon and Kai hadn't said a word to me when João showed up at my house earlier with them.

"Did you guys have fun Friday night?" Landon asked, walking down the hallway.

I glanced over at João, who continued walking with his jaw clenched. "You told them?"

"I didn't tell them shit," he said.

While I couldn't really tell if he was annoyed or not, Landon stopped in the middle of the hallway right before we passed a meeting room. The windows were covered with blinds, the door closed, and people were crowded into the room.

Kai peeked into the small crack between the blinds, letting him see into the room. "Just as I expected—a meeting with the most influential

367

men in Redwood. But what the hell are they doing here, talking to the principal?"

Inching closer to him, I glanced into the room to see the police chief, the principal, some cops, and other men dressed in fancy suits who worked down in the city. It was such an odd group of people to be crowded in a school room this early in the morning.

"Is this why we're here?" I whispered.

"No," Kai said, backing up into me.

Almost immediately, his hand came around my waist to steady me, and then he pulled it away quickly, as if he didn't want to touch me. But maybe that was my mind fucking with me.

I would've told them that João and I were going out, but I thought it was going to be, like, a quick stop at a fast-food joint or something. I hadn't thought it would be this huge deal that João—and now, Landon and Kai—made it out to be.

"Then, why are we here?" I asked.

"João didn't tell you after all the time you spent together?" Landon asked.

Rolling my eyes, I followed them farther down the hallway. "Oh my God. You guys are so dramatic. All that happened was a date because I forced him to. He owed me a favor, and I wanted him to have a fun night."

Landon grabbed my hand for the first time today. "I bet it was really fun."

"It was, dickhead," João said, stopping at the principal's office door and pulling a key out of his pocket. He thrust the key into the door, turned the knob, and opened the door. "Now, fucking drop it. We need information."

My eyes widened slightly as I watched Kai and João walk into the room as if it were the most normal thing ever. I glanced back down the hallway at the meeting room and clutched my stomach.

"We're breaking into the principal's office?!" I whisper-yelled.

"If we don't get caught from that big mouth of yours," João snapped, holding the door open and narrowing his dark eyes at me. Unlike Friday night, those eyes were back to being hard and unreadable. "Shut it and get in here."

Landon pulled me into the room, locked the door behind us, then closed the window blinds. I stood at the door with wide eyes and crossed my arms, nervous that the principal would walk in here at any second.

They still hadn't really told me why we were here—or why *I* was here.

If Vaughn walked into the room and caught us snooping in his drawers, he would either give us detention or suspend us. And I didn't even want to *think* about how Mom would react to that kind of news.

All my college acceptances would be revoked, and I'd have to live in this shithole town for the rest of my life. I glanced over my shoulder at the locked door and gnawed on the inside of my cheek. I refused to let that happen.

"Can I leave?" I asked.

Kai sat at Principal Vaughn's desk, João behind him with one hand posted on the desk while the other was on the back of Kai's seat.

João glanced up at me and laughed lifelessly. "I thought you wanted to be part of Poison? You don't get to pick and choose what jobs you do."

"But—"

"You're not leaving."

"João, I don't want to get in trouble. The principal is literally in the next room with half of Redwood's police force. If they find us here, then we're all screwed!" I shook my head back and forth, arms outstretched for emphasis. "Do you guys not care?!"

"Come here," João said, nodding toward the desk he stood at. When I didn't move, he lowered his voice. "Now."

"Why did you bring me here?" I asked, glaring at him and refusing to back down now.

"You want to know why we brought you here?" João asked, tapping the desk. "Come here, and we'll show you."

Knowing that they wouldn't leave until I followed orders—they were fucking sadists like that—I hurried to the desk in front of João and glared at him even harder. "Can you please tell me, so we can get out of here?!"

Before I knew it, João picked me up right off the ground and sat me on Principal Vaughn's desk, his hand slipping up my skirt. I sucked in a sharp breath, gasping lightly, and stared up at him, warmth spreading through my core.

"*This* is why we brought you here, Imani," João said, moving his fingers around my clit. "These two dickheads wouldn't stop giving me shit for taking you out Friday night and not telling them. So, you're here to make it up to them."

"Make it up to them?" I whispered, heart pounding in my chest.

I glanced over at Kai, who pulled a flash drive from the computer, stuffed it into his pocket, and looked over at me, sharp jaw clenched. Landon stood by the door, watching me intensely as João fingered me.

"Here?" I asked, my mouth drying.

João shoved my skirt up my thighs, hooked his fingers around my underwear, and pulled them down my thighs, stuffing them into Principal Vaughn's desk. "A gift for our lovely principal to make up for your pussy drooling all over his desk."

"We're doing this now?" I asked. "Right now?"

"Right now, Imani." Moving his fingers between my legs again, he slipped them into me. "Try to be quiet. Don't want anyone to hear you."

Chapter Ninety-Six

IMANI

João pumped his fingers in and out, his cold and callous gaze focused on me, lips turned up in one of his signature asshole smirks. I bit my lip to muffle a moan and pressed my thighs together, a rush of heat warming my pussy.

With his fingers still massaging my G-spot, he pulled his phone from his back pocket, flipped on his camera, and handed it to me. "Record yourself getting finger-fucked, Imani. We're not stopping until your pussy is drooling all over us today."

I grabbed the phone in a shaky hand and held the camera toward my flipped-up skirt. João's fingers pumped in and out of me, the base of his palm pounding against my clit over and over again, sending me higher.

My legs shook gently, and I whimpered, desperate to hold the camera still.

While I hated the thought of fucking in the principal's office, I couldn't help but tighten around him. I loved being on camera, getting to show myself off as I came all over a dildo or on my own two fingers. And that damn video we had taken last time ...

I watched it almost every night.

As he glanced up at Landon and Kai, João's smirk widened. "Take her sopping little hole, Landon."

After he pulled his fingers from my pussy, he stuck them into my mouth and forced me to suck off my juices. I wrapped my lips around his fingers, taking them all the way down to the knuckles and sucking.

Once he pulled them out of me, he took his phone from me to record himself.

Landon stalked closer to me, hooking his strong arms around the backs of my thighs and pulling them to the edge of the desk. I placed my palms on the wood behind me to hold myself upright as Landon spread my legs apart and back, so he'd be able to sink his dick inside me as deep as it could go.

João stepped beside Landon, tilting the camera toward my pussy as Landon ground the bulge in his jeans against it and ruined his pants with my juices.

"Fuck, look at her cunt from that angle," João said, adjusting himself with his free hand.

I dug my nails into Principal Vaughn's important papers. "Please," I begged. "More."

"She's so fucking flexible," Landon said, unzipping his jeans and glancing up at me. "You don't know how good it's going to feel to get this deep inside of you with your legs pulled back like this, Imani. I'm going to ruin your fucking pussy, down to your cervix."

Heat rushed through my body, and I clenched.

"Fuck, dude," João said, clenching his jaw. "Look at that desperate hole clenching and waiting to be filled."

"Please," I pleaded.

Landon pulled his huge cock out of his jeans and took the base in his hand. I stared down at it, my pussy pulsing at the mere sight and the thought of it being buried deep inside me. Landon wasn't lying. He had ruined me with his dick many times before, and from this angle, he'd destroy my tight cunt. I wouldn't be surprised if he really could reach my cervix.

"If you keep clenching like that, Imani"—Landon rested his dick on my stomach until it reached my belly button, his balls rubbing against my entrance—"you're going to milk out all my cum as soon as I push myself into you."

After sucking in a breath, I rested one of my hands against the head of his cock and squeezed. Landon's cock was so big that he'd reach so damn deep inside me, beating my pussy until it was trembling around him.

"Please, put it inside me," I said, placing my feet on the desk and lifting my hips off the table, desperate to maneuver myself in such a way that he slipped inside me now. "Please, I can't wait anymore. I need it."

Landon took his dick in his hand again and positioned himself at my entrance. Slowly, he shoved himself inside of me, filling me completely inch by inch. I threw my head back and moaned softly, so nobody in the other room would hear us.

Kai moved behind me and grasped my waist, his hands roaming up my body to my tiny breasts. Like he had during the night we spent together, he grasped my nipples through my thin bralette and tugged up on them.

With one hand, he reached down to my clit and rubbed it in small, torturous circles as Landon pumped into me. He buried his nose into the crook of my neck and gently sucked on my soft spot. "All your holes are going to be filled with our cum when we're finished with you."

Pleasure rushed to my pussy, and I let out another soft moan.

"You don't know how badly I want to see your sexy body covered in rope again, your arms and legs restrained so we could use you in any way that we want." He chuckled. "But we're going to do that anyway."

Before I could respond, Kai pulled me back, so I lay against the desk with my head hanging off the edge, and he unzipped his black cargo pants. Once he let them drop to his knees, he moved closer to me, his dick raging inside his gray briefs.

I didn't know how the hell Poison did it, but they made me into a cock-loving slut.

Desperate for it, I lifted my head slightly and placed my mouth on his dick and balls through his briefs, sucking gently on them until they were soaked with my saliva and his dick was throbbing against my lips.

Reaching behind me, I hooked my fingers around the waistband and tugged them down, letting his cock smack me in the face. If anyone walked in on us right now, I knew that we'd immediately be expelled from this school.

And somehow, now, I couldn't find a single fuck to give.

It was like I *needed* their cocks. It wasn't just a want or desire.

"Fuck my throat," I said, wrapping my lips around his head. "Please."

To my surprise, Kai didn't slam himself deep into me. He pushed himself into me slowly, moving his finger down the column of my throat to trace the head of his dick sliding into it. When he reached the bottom, he grunted.

"Get this on camera," Kai said, his thumb on one side of his dick and his middle and pointer finger on the other side, grasping his length through my neck. "Look at the bulge in her throat. She can take it so deep."

João moved around the table toward us. Kai stayed deep in my throat, and I swallowed hard, desperate to breathe but unable to. I placed my hands on his thighs to push him away, coughing up spit and drool all over my face.

"Move your hands, Imani," Kai ordered in the low, dominant tone he had used the other night with me alone. "You can take my dick for a bit longer. You asked me to fuck your mouth. This is what your throat is for. Taking dick."

And so I dropped my hands and tightened around Landon, feeling him pump harder in and out of me. I moaned on Kai's cock as he leaned over me, placing one hand on the desk and beginning to pound into my throat.

Pleasure rushed through my body, pushing me higher and higher.

"Fuck," João groaned. "Turn her around."

Both Kai and Landon pulled out of me. I lay back on the desk with my chest rising and falling quickly as I tried to gasp for air. Landon lay down beside me on Principal Vaughn's desk, picked me up, and set me on his lap in a cowgirl position.

Spit, drool, and saliva covered my face. I wanted to push it away, but I didn't have any time before Landon slammed his cock back into my tight pussy and Kai pulled my head back down to take his cock back in my mouth.

With his camera still recording, João scrambled through my purse and found my most expensive lipstick. He walked around me, lifted my skirt, and pulled the cap off the stick. I glanced back at him as Kai fucked my mouth, my eyes watery.

In bright pink lipstick, João wrote something on my ass, then tossed it on the desk beside us. He positioned himself against my back-side and slipped himself inside me, filling up my last empty hole.

My pussy tightened around Landon, the pressure rising in my core. Kai grasped my jaw and glanced over at the words written across my ass, smirking and grunting. He thrust his dick all the way down my throat and stilled, his cum shooting into my throat and filling my mouth.

"Don't fucking swallow that, Imani," João instructed.

When Kai pulled out of my mouth, João pulled back on my arms with one of his hands and leaned over me, positioning the camera so it was focused on both of us. "Let that cum spill out of your mouth on camera for us."

I stared into the camera and let Kai's cum drip off my lips and down my chin. João smirked, wrapped his free hand around my chin, rubbed the cum all over my face, and shoved all four of his fingers into my mouth, pounding into me from behind.

The pressure rose in my core, and I gargled on him.

"You want to know what you are, Imani?" he asked into my ear. "Poison's slut."

My pussy tightened on Landon, and I whimpered.

"Taking our cocks and all of our cum, letting us use you wherever and whenever we want, following our orders like any good slut would." João turned my head toward the camera. "Look at you."

With spit and cum smeared across my face, João's fingers in my mouth, and what looked to be *Poison's Slut* written across my ass in bright pink lipstick, I was desperate for them. A desperate little ...

Landon pounded up into me, tipping me over the edge.

I cried out on João's fingers as an earth-shattering orgasm ripped through my entire body. My legs trembled around Landon. Wave after wave of pleasure rushed through me, my pussy pulsing over and over.

João and Landon stilled a couple moments later, spilling their cum into my holes. When they pulled out of me, I collapsed against Landon's chest and clung on to him, my breathing unsteady and ragged.

João smacked my ass and flipped my skirt back down. "You're going to walk around all day with that lipstick smeared on your ass, so if your skirt flips up in the wind while you're crossing campus, everyone will fucking know that you belong to us, Imani."

Chapter Ninety-Seven

After our little sexcapades in the principal's office, I walked down the hallway without the guys or Imani. I wasn't angry with her, but I was kinda pissed that she hadn't told me that she went on a date with João.

We hadn't gone out together officially yet, and João was nothing but an ass to her.

"Hey!" Imani called from behind me, the spit cleaned from her face. "Wait up, Landon."

A couple of kids looked over at her, but I didn't turn around because, well, I might've been a bit angry and annoyed with her. She had gone out with *him* first and not me. She had asked him out on a date after she told *me* that she loved me.

What the fuck was that?

Before I could get another step, she wrapped her small hand around mine and stared up at me through big brown eyes, her brows furrowed. "What's going on? Are you really annoyed with me, like João said you were?"

I stopped in the middle of the hallway and glanced down at her fingers intertwined with mine, and then I clenched my jaw. For a mere moment, I had the urge to pull my hand away from hers and storm down the hallway.

But I was working on myself for her.

"People are staring, Imani. You want to hold hands?" I asked instead, drawing my tongue across my teeth. I didn't give a fuck about people staring. Most people at Redwood already knew that Imani and Poison had a thing.

Though I didn't think Imani wanted people to know that we were a couple. Or a quad or whatever the hell it was when she had a different relationship with all damn three of us. That'd probably be fucking weird for a girl like her.

It was a bit for me.

"I don't have a problem with it," Imani said. "But you have one with me obviously."

"I don't have a problem with you."

"Come on, Landon," Imani said. "Don't do that to me. You're closing yourself off again."

Once I let out a slow breath, I rubbed my hand over my face and frowned. She was right, but I didn't want to argue with her. These feelings shouldn't be getting in the way because I was the one who had told Poison about her.

I had fucked this up.

"I don't have a problem with you," I said truthfully. "I'm just ... fuck, it's so stupid."

"Are you jealous?" she asked.

"Of João?" I asked with a laugh. "Why would I be jealous of him?"

"Because I went out with him and not you," Imani said, voice quiet. "That's why, isn't it?"

Stopping in the middle of the hallway, I frowned down at her. "Yeah, I'm jealous, okay?"

She stood on her toes to stare at me. "I might've gone out with João, but you're the only man I've told that I love before." She softened her lips into a smile. "You don't have to worry about me losing feelings for you, Landon. You're the only guy who gets me, really freaking gets me."

I shuffled my feet.

When I didn't answer, she grasped my face. "Okay?"

"Okay," I repeated.

After staring at me for a couple moments, she nodded. "Good. So, what'd you do this weekend?" she asked, inching closer to me with every step and suddenly becoming quiet, her cheeks rounding the way she always did when she was embarrassed—not that much embarrassed her nowadays. "I missed you."

Warmth spread throughout my chest. "You missed me?"

"You don't have to scream it!" she whisper-yelled, stepping toward her locker and rocking back on her heels, gaze focused on the ground. She took a peek up at me and smiled a bit harder. "But, yes, I missed you."

"I missed you too."

"You know, boyfriends and girlfriends are supposed to tell each other the fun things they've done." Imani grinned and took another peek up at me when she said the words *boyfriends and girlfriends*. "So, did you do anything fun? I just sat at home and hung with Allie because *someone* wasn't answering his phone."

"We brought João's mom home from the hospital," I said.

Imani smacked me on the chest. "You what?! Why wasn't I invited?"

My lips curled into a smirk. "Ana was asking for you."

"That did not answer my question!"

"Why don't you tell me how the date was first?"

"Are you asking because you're jealous or because you actually want to know?"

"I want to know what I have to compete with."

"Ugh, boys ..." She rolled her eyes, then turned to me with the wickedest grin. "As long as you promise not to tell anyone. The dinner was the most awkward dinner I have ever been to. Oh my God, I don't think he's ever dated anyone. We sat in silence the entire time."

"There's no way that he's been on a date before," I said, grinning, not because I didn't like the guy, but because he was so cold and callous and never let anyone inside. He didn't give a fuck about many people, but he cared a ton about the people he did. "He's too cold."

"Yeah, but after"—she softened her smirk into a smile—"he was really sweet."

"Sweet?" I asked. "João was sweet?"

She giggled like a madwoman. "Yeah, I thought the same. Part of me couldn't believe it."

I leaned against the locker beside hers. Dark, coiled hair in her face, full lips covered in a swipe of lip gloss, and a fucking smile that could kill me, she pulled out giant Biology textbooks from her locker.

"Come here," I said, admiring her.

I grabbed her fingers and pulled her closer until her chest was pressed against mine and she was staring up at me through those bright brown eyes. Then, in front of all of Redwood Academy, I kissed the one woman who had changed my life for good.

Chapter Ninety-Eight

JOÃO

After school, Kai skipped out on Poison's business and hurried home, telling us that he wanted to look into the shit he had found on Principal Vaughn's computer earlier. Landon, Imani, and I went back to my place.

While Imani wanted to see Ana, I needed to watch Mom. Since they had discharged her from the hospital, she hadn't gone back to work, *and* I fucking refused to let her. But if I left her alone for too long, I feared that she'd try because, now, we had hospital bills piling up.

She had worked her ass off these past few years to keep us alive and without growing amounts of debt. And that had landed her raped, beaten, and almost fucking dead outside some rich guy's restaurant.

Not fucking happening again.

"Imani! Landon!" Ana called, jumping into their arms as soon as we walked through the door. She wrapped one arm around each of them, grinning from ear to ear. "Wanna make brigadeiros with me? I made them on Friday with Vera from across the street, but she makes them bad."

"Landon's not going to make them any better," I said to Ana, kicking off my shoes.

"Come on, Ana," Landon said, walking to the kitchen. "We're

going to make some kick-ass brigadeiros. Better than João could ever make them."

Ana burst out into a fit of giggles. "Landon said a bad word!"

Imani scolded him briefly with her eyes, then followed Ana into the kitchen, glancing back at me with worry in her gaze, as if to ask if I would be okay, handling Mom myself. She didn't fucking understand that I had been dealing with this shit for far longer than she'd been around us.

Sucking in a deep breath, I walked through the hallway and toward Mom's bedroom. The door was closed, which it usually never was when she and Ana were home alone. Instead of knocking—because I knew that she should be in bed—I walked into the room.

Mom sat up against the headboard with a bottle of pills in her hand.

My entire body tensed. I cleared my throat. "Mama?"

She glanced up at me with wide and guilty eyes. "They're for the pain, João," Mom said, struggling to open the orange pill bottle. "My body aches so badly."

I stared down at her on the bed and clenched my jaw, promising myself that I wouldn't let it get bad. Last time she had even touched a prescription drug was before Ana became infected. She vowed to never fucking do any drugs again.

And that fucker had messed her up.

With a shaky hand, she handed me the bottle. "Please, help me."

Pushing away the hot tears welling in my eyes, I swallowed hard, grabbed the pill bottle, and undid the cap. Mom immediately reached for them, but I pulled it away from her and took two capsules from the container before quickly locking it back up.

When I handed Mom the pills, she took them and frowned at me, tears pooling in her eyes. "You don't trust me with them," she whispered in Portuguese.

While her tears threatened to spill, that damn look on her face was what got me.

How could I let Mom near pills and drugs again after what happened last time? How could I watch the one woman in my life who I loved more than anything, besides Ana, slip back into that fucking shit? How could I not fucking do something about it?

"João," she whispered, tears pouring down her cheeks now. "Why don't you trust me?"

"Mama," I said, voice cracking.

I didn't want her to think that I didn't trust her with them. She was the one person I looked up to in fucking life. She had done so much for us to survive after Dad left us with nothing. I didn't want to disappoint her, but I already had.

Instead of taking the pills, she placed them on the nightstand and sank further down in her bed, pulling the blankets over her body and turning her head away from me. "If you don't trust me with them, then I won't take them."

"You have to for the pain," I said reluctantly.

As much as I fucking didn't like it, Imani's mother had told me it was essential. I might've hated that fucking bitch, but I didn't want to see Mom in any more pain. She had been drugged, beaten, raped, and left for dead less than a damn week ago.

Grabbing the pills from the nightstand, I handed them to her. "Take them."

She stared at them, then at me for a long time. Then, finally, she grabbed the pills from me and swallowed them with a huge gulp of water. And as if the drugs had hit her system immediately, her entire body trembled with delight, and she finally relaxed in her bed, closed her eyes, and smiled softly.

"Thank you, João."

With tears welling in my eyes—because I could feel that something was wrong—I turned toward the door and let a couple fall down my cheeks. "You're welcome," I whispered, grabbing the door handle and pulling it open. "I love you, Mama."

"I love you too," she hummed. "Can you shut the light off?"

After turning off the light and shutting the door, I stepped out into the hallway and leaned my forehead against the wood, my hands balled into tight fists by my sides. I cursed to myself over and over, loathing this feeling inside of me.

I shouldn't have given her the pills. I shouldn't have fed into her addiction.

But I couldn't see her in pain.

"João?" Imani asked, peeking into the hallway from the living room.

Body tensing, I refused to turn around and look back at her. I didn't want her to see how fucked up this made me, how fucking sick all of the Redwood rich had forced me to become. I was supposed to be the fearless fucking leader of Poison.

Not a bitch who cried for his mom.

Imani hurried down the hall, her footsteps quick.

"Don't touch me," I said between gritted teeth, hoping she'd walk away and forget it.

Before I knew it, her arms were around my torso, and her ear was pressed against my back. Her body felt so warm behind me, her breathing surprisingly even and steady. And while I might've wanted to push her away and tell her to get out, I let her hug me.

Because she always knew exactly what I needed.

A couple moments passed, and I finally unraveled my hands, still holding the pill bottle in one, and turned around. Unable to stop myself, I wrapped her into a hug and held back the sob that threatened to escape my throat.

The truth was fucking ugly.

I didn't trust Mom with the pills.

Chapter Ninety-Nine

KAI

Nothing.

I had searched all night and found nothing.

I swiped my hand across my face and glanced at the time on my phone, the screen glaring at me in the dark, windowless computer room—7:12 a.m. After grunting, I wiped my tired eyes again and turned back to the computer.

On any normal day, I'd be at school by now, swapping weed for money in the student parking lot—or occasionally the teacher's lot too. I even had a fucking meetup planned for this morning, but I was so fucking close to figuring this shit out. I'd stayed up all night.

Clicking through the contents and files that I had downloaded on a flash drive from Principal Vaughn's computer, I opened another document that only had a couple words on it. There wasn't even any high school academy shit on his computer.

Just documents with unfinished thoughts—some blank, some with only a couple words on each, some with entire paragraphs of shit. And I was fucking tired of reading aimlessly about purple clouds and bulls and the types of chairs Vaughn wanted for his home kitchen.

What kind of shit was that?

Pissed, I scrolled further through the files and decided not to look at any more fucking documents. I didn't have time for that shit anymore. I needed to figure it out as soon as fucking possible because we needed Redwood to fall.

After finding a zipped folder, I clicked on it and typed in Vaughn's password that he used for everything. *What a great way to secure important documents, dickhead.* He had no sense for being the principal of a prestigious academy.

Once I was into the folder, I found a series of about a hundred videos. Maybe more.

I clicked on the first one as a message popped up on the Discord group chat between Imani and Poison.

Imani: Where are you guys???

Imani: Please, get to school. It's an emergency.

While both João and Landon were online, neither one of them messaged her back. So, I paused the video at the one second mark and typed out a message, telling her that I'd be there as quickly as I could.

I'd watch this video, then head to class for the day. I hadn't been able to find anything last night, no matter how long I stayed awake. Part of me was starting to believe that there wasn't anything to find.

But I knew that wasn't true.

Principal Vaughn and the police force were hiding something. And I needed to find it out.

Imani: Please be quick.

My heart raced for a moment. Imani might've needed us sometimes to do her dirty work, like deal with Carter when he was messing with Allie, but she had never been this urgent in her texts, which must've meant drama was unfolding at Redwood Academy.

After shutting off my phone, I clicked the space key on my keyboard to start the video. The black screen turned to a recording of the empty boys' football locker room. I sat up in my seat and moved closer to the table, brows furrowed.

What the hell is this? Why is there a recording of the boys' locker room? Hell, why is there a camera inside of it? I hadn't seen it the other day when I snuck in and stuffed that dildo inside of Jace Harbor's locker.

Suddenly, Allie Hall and Jace Harbor walked into the locker room, locking lips and tearing each other's clothes off. I stopped the video before I saw either of them naked and quickly skipped to the next video on the camera roll.

Once I watched it for a couple moments, I skipped to the next, then the next, then the next. Then, I sat back in my seat and shook my head, unable to fathom what I had watched for nearly ten minutes.

No fucking way.

My stomach dropped, and I turned off the videos. Adrenaline rushed through my entire system, my blood running ice cold. Redwood's fucking principal was more of a fucking creep than I'd thought.

And today he would get what was coming to him. Today we'd put an end to this all.

This was what we needed to bring Redwood to its knees. This was how we'd destroy the prestigious town from the inside out, expose the rich for who they really were—coldhearted, perverted criminals.

Chapter One Hundred

IMANI

Racing through the school, I ripped flyers of Jace and Allie at a pharmacy—kissing and picking out a box of Plan B—off the hallway walls and lockers. They were posted everywhere in the school corridors, on every locker, on every bulletin board, on every classroom door.

My heart pounded in my chest, and I hoped to catch Allie before she walked into Redwood. Nobody was answering their damn phone this morning, except Kai, and I really needed their help with removing all this shit.

When I reached a window, I peeked outside to see Jace Harbor's Maserati pull into its designated spot in the student parking lot. After cursing to myself, I hurried out the front door and through the snowstorm toward his car.

Snow got caught in my thick black hair as I sprinted toward the lot. Allie slid out of the passenger seat, and I grabbed her hands.

"You should go home," I said to her, glancing back at the school and all the passersby who looked over at us. "Don't step foot in the hallways, Allie. I mean it."

She furrowed her brows. "What're you talking about?"

The first bell rang, and she stepped beside me to walk toward school.

I moved in front of her again. "Allie, please, just leave."

"What's wrong?" she asked, continuing to the building. "I can't miss class."

Jace and Poison walked behind us, talking about something I *doubted* I wanted to take part in after they ruined me in Principal Vaughn's office yesterday morning.

"I'll skip with you," I said desperately, earning a look from Landon.

Allie stopped dead in her tracks and stared at me with wide eyes. "What is it?" she asked, brows furrowed. "You never skip class. What don't you want me to see in there?"

I frowned, tears piling up in my eyes, and glanced over her shoulder at Jace. I parted my lips to say something, then pressed them back together three times in a row. When I finally got something out, I shook my head. "There are pictures ..."

Before I could stop her, Allie was storming up the stairs to Redwood's entrance and shoving the door open to see this for herself. The colored flyers of Jace and Allie were scattered around the halls, accompanied by the words *whore, slut,* and *incest.*

Allie plucked the flyers off the lockers as quickly as she could, her cheeks flushed as people stared and whispered in her direction. I followed her, tearing down the flyers and telling people to fuck off, until we reached her locker. People were crowded around it and staring at something.

She pushed her way through the crowd and collapsed when she saw the pictures of Jace and her in the locker room. My jaw dropped. They weren't just any pictures either. They were of Jace eating her out, of him fucking her, of his fingers in her mouth, her brows furrowed in a lustful stare.

"Oh my God," she whispered, body heaving on Redwood's dirty hallway floor.

Not wanting anyone else to see them, I shoved my way through the crowd and ripped the flyers off her locker. "I'm sorry, Allie. I didn't see these ones. I would've taken them down. I'm so sorry." I continued to rip them all off until there weren't any more naked pictures of her in Redwood's locker room.

"You think this is fucking funny?" Jace shouted through the halls.

For the first time ever, all the chatting stopped, and Redwood's halls were completely silent. Students shuffled to the side of the hall-ways and stared wide-eyed at Jace, who looked like he was on the verge of losing control.

I wrapped my arms around my best friend's body and pulled her into my lap, stroking her hair. "I'm going to bring you home," I whispered to her and wiped tears from her cheeks. "Don't cry. People are mean, Allie. People are so mean. I'm so sorry."

"Who the fuck did this?" Jace shouted.

When nobody answered, Jace stormed through the halls toward us. "Allie is my stepsister. We're not related by blood, and all of you fucking know that already." Jace grabbed Allie's hand and tugged her to her feet. "You can continue to talk shit about us, but I love Allie, and nothing you do is going to change my mind about it. Grow the fuck up and stop being childish about a relationship you know nothing about."

Everyone stayed quiet and glanced between them, then started whispering again.

"If you want to call Allie a fucking whore or slut or mention anything about incest, say it to my fucking face," Jace said, glaring from person to person. "Because you have to deal with *me* now. Nobody insults Allie ever fucking again."

The second bell rang through the halls, yet nobody moved.

"Do you understand me?"

Nobody spoke a word.

"Do you. Fucking. Understand me?"

A flurry of yeses echoed through the hallway, and then everyone scurried to their classes.

Jace wrapped an arm around Allie's waist and pushed the tears off her cheek. "Allie, I'm so sorry. If I had known there was someone fucking watching us, I would've never done that. Fuck school. Let's go home."

"I can't miss another day," she whispered.

I scoffed. "If I can miss a day, you can too." I grabbed her hand. "Come on."

"Jace Harbor." Principal Vaughn stepped out of his office with arms crossed over his chest and hairy gray brows furrowed in a furious stare at us. "My office. Now."

Jace cursed and turned toward me. "Take Allie home."

"Jace," Allie whispered, shaking her head. "Don't go."

"My office now, Harbor," Vaughn said.

Allie pulled herself out of my hold and walked to Jace's side. "I'm coming too."

"You have class," Principal Vaughn said to her.

"Allie, go," Jace said to her.

She crossed her arms over her chest. "No. If you expel him, you're going to have to expel me, too, for what I did with him." Allie looped her arm around Jace's. "You can't put the entire blame on him. He doesn't deserve it."

Jace removed her arm from his. "Go home, Allie. This isn't your fight."

Though he looked surprised at first, Principal Vaughn cleared his throat. "If that's what you want, then I'd like to see both of you in my office." He held the door open and pointed into the room, glaring between them.

"She doesn't want that, sir," Jace said through clenched teeth. "She's going home. Now."

"No, I'm not. You're not going down alone."

"My office now."

Adrenaline rushed through my system. Allie didn't deserve to go down for this. This wasn't fair, and I wouldn't let her go down without a fight. She was my best friend, and someone wanted to fuck around with her.

I stepped forward. "If you expel them, you're going to have to expel me too. I fucked Poison in your office before school yesterday!"

Principal Vaughn, Allie, and Jace all looked over at me with wide eyes. I swallowed hard, ignored the gazes from other students, and uncomfortably crossed my arms over my chest. I gave Allie my best supportive smile and nudged her.

"That's enough. I don't want to hear about anyone else's sexcapades. All three of you. Inside my office before I call security." Principal Vaughn walked into his office and sat at his desk.

I wrapped my arms around Allie's and walked with her into the room. Before I could shut the door behind us, João stuck the tip of his shoe between the door and the doorframe and shoved the door open, stepping into the room with Landon and now with Kai, who looked pissed the fuck off.

They walked into the room and locked the door behind them.

"You're not expelling anyone," João said to the principal, sliding his ass onto the desk and lighting a cigarette right in Vaughn's face. "If you do, we'll release your file to the community."

Vaughn went to snatch the cigarette from João's hand, but he pulled it away.

"Don't you want to know *which* file? There are tons of them out there on you. And all the damn money in the world won't save your ass this time."

I stared at him in confusion for a moment, then remembered that Kai had stolen files off Vaughn's computer yesterday morning and had been sifting through them all last night. He must've found something.

Principal Vaughn flared his nostrils. "I don't know what you're talking about."

"The cameras that you installed *yourself* in the locker rooms two years ago."

All the blood drained from Vaughn's face. Allie tensed and looked at Jace nervously.

"H-how do you know about that?" Vaughn asked. "It's erased."

Landon walked around the desk and clasped his hands on Vaughn's shoulders, clamping down tightly. "Once it's out in the world, you can't erase anything. You can hide it behind money, but money won't buy our silence about it."

Kai grabbed the flyers from my hands and uncrumpled them, showing him the pictures of Allie and Jace from the locker room. "Do those look like they were taken by a phone or a video recorder, Jace?"

Jace's eyes widened as it all started to come together. "You have cameras in the football locker room?" he asked through clenched teeth, standing up. "What the fuck do you do? Jerk off to naked and underage high school kids?"

"You have no proof," Vaughn said.

"Kai, can you pull up the camera recordings from last night?" João asked.

Kai shoved Vaughn out of the way to get onto his computer, hacked into the camera footage with ease, and played a recording of none other than Vaughn hanging up those pictures of them late last night at school.

Overcome with rage, Jace swung his fist at Vaughn and hit him across the face.

Vaughn's head swung back, blood spurting out of his nose. "I'm going to get you arrested for that. You're going to be—"

João held up a finger and waggled it. "No, you're not. You're going to remove those cameras and not say a word to anyone for the rest of the year. You won't expel Jace or Allie or especially Imani. *You're going to be our bitch.*"

"Why?" Allie asked suddenly with tears in her eyes. "Why would you do that to me, to us? Why would you put those DVDs and dildo in my locker and post pictures around campus of us?"

Vaughn wiped the blood from his nose with his sleeve and looked away from Allie. Landon slapped him hard across the cheek, and I ached to hit him harder than that. He fucking deserved it.

"She asked you a question," Landon said.

"Because ..." Vaughn answered.

"Say it," João said.

"Because I fucking love watching innocent schoolgirls like you squirm."

Jace hit him right across the face again, giving him a black eye. "You fucking disgust me," he said, spitting in his face. He snatched Allie's hand and led her to the door, nodding toward me. "Imani, come on. I'm taking you home. Poison will deal with this."

I scurried to my feet, feeling so disgusted, and glanced back at Poison.

My stomach turned. I had never seen Kai look so dangerous before. He looked like he was going to fucking snap someone's neck—or worse ... torture and kill the man. And I knew that Poison really would.

Tomorrow, Principal Vaughn wouldn't show up for school.

Tomorrow, Principal Vaughn would be dead.

Chapter One Hundred One

JOÃO

"I don't think you want to do that, Harbor," Principal Vaughn said to Jace.

I slid onto Vaughn's desk, where we had fucked Imani yesterday morning, and leaned back, watching his every fucking move because part of me wanted to end this motherfucker right now. He was the most annoying prick at Redwood Academy, and there were a lot of senseless assholes here.

Jace stopped. "And why's that?" he asked through clenched teeth.

Allie scooted closer to Imani, and Vaughn glanced at her like the perverted fucking man he was. Principal Vaughn jerked himself out of Landon's grasp and straightened out his suit.

"How was your father's vacation?" he asked Jace, rocking back on his heels and clasping his hands behind his back. "He was gone for longer than expected, wasn't he?"

Jace tensed. "What do you care?"

Vaughn grinned with his yellow fucking teeth. "He called me this morning and asked what happened when he was gone. I mentioned that there were some interesting things that I found while he was out."

"He's bluffing," Allie said, stepping forward. "He hasn't told Harlan anything yet because Harlan hasn't paid him. Has he?"

I let out a cold laugh. That man didn't do shit without money.

Vaughn cleared his throat and scowled. "That doesn't mean that I won't tell him." Vaughn took a threatening step toward Jace. "If you leave school today, I will tell your father everything that has been going on with you, so I can watch Redwood's notorious Jace Harbor fall into oblivion and lose out on all his chances of making it big, and then I get to get off to the videos of his girlfriend."

Little nerdy Allie lunged forward to hit Vaughn herself. But before she could make impact, Kai caught her wrist to hold her back, and Jace shoved Vaughn hard against the wall.

"You won't fucking do a thing." Jace seethed through clenched teeth, brown eyes wide in fury. "I will fucking kill you for even thinking about touching her."

When Allie stopped struggling, Kai let her go. She wrapped her arms around Jace and tugged him off our deadbeat principal. "Jace, please, stop."

Jace stepped away from Principal Vaughn, and I jumped off the desk, crossing my arms and glancing at Imani to make sure she wouldn't jump into the middle of this and hit Vaughn herself. I had never seen her so furious.

Vaughn straightened out his clothes again and smiled. "Your father is looking into you right now, Harbor," he said. "I won't tell him anything I know if you all keep your mouth shut, or I can tell him that you've been fucking your sister on school grounds and getting into fights in the locker rooms."

"You don't have proof," Kai said. "You can't show him proof without him knowing how fucking perverted you are."

"That's where you're wrong," Vaughn said. "Mr. Harbor doesn't need any evidence. He has money, and he has me as a witness. All he needs to do is slide some money into some people's hands, and everything will be taken care of."

Jace tensed and pressed his lips together.

"So, Jace, what's it going to be?" Vaughn said, arching a brow. "Are you going to keep this quiet? Or do you want me to tell your father everything, so he can toss you in jail and I can keep your sister for myself?"

Jace growled at him, grabbed Allie's hand, and tugged her toward the door. "Don't say anything to my father," he said and walked out into the hallway toward Allie's second period class. "We're staying here for now. It's the only place that's safe. As soon as school ends, meet me by my car. We'll go home once I know my dad is gone. Don't leave with anyone."

Allie furrowed her brows. "We're just going to let him continue to video innocent people?"

Jace pressed his lips together, flared his nostrils, and looked down. "My dad is far more of a threat than Vaughn. Let me take care of him, and we can take Vaughn down along with the rest of Redwood's most corrupt." He brushed some hair out of her face in the hallway. "Okay?"

"Let's go," I said to Poison, following Jace and Allie out of the room.

Vaughn grinned like he had won this little battle between us all, but that asshole didn't know what was coming to him. He had pissed off the most ruthless gang in Redwood, who had done far worse than all those rich fuckers.

Chapter One Hundred Two

IMANI

After glancing down the hallway, where Jace and Allie chatted tensely and she was crying hard tears, I turned back to the guys and crossed my arms, jaw clenching. "How do you plan on taking care of Principal Vaughn?"

"Imani," Landon said, jaw twitching. "Don't."

João slapped him across the shoulder and stepped closer to me. "Oh, come on, Landon. Imani wants to be a big girl. She's part of Poison now, and she knows exactly what we plan on doing to him." He moved even closer, inches from me, and stared down intensely at me. "We're going to kill him. Would you like to watch?"

Landon shoved João away from me and against the lockers hard, causing some students skipping class to glance over at us. "What the fuck is wrong with you?" Landon asked João, glaring down at one of his best friends.

I placed a hand on his shoulder to calm him down and pull him away. "It's okay."

João straightened out his jacket. "So, you coming or not?"

Once I arched a brow at João, I crossed my arms. "No, I'm not coming to watch."

But part of me wanted to see *that* man squirm. Still, I couldn't help but feel the nerves zip up and down my body. I knew that they would torture our principal, but how would they kill him? Would it be clean? Bloody?

I still didn't love the thought of killing someone. Honestly, I hated it. But I knew that Principal Vaughn fucking deserved it after what he did to my best friend. He had probably watched that video of Allie and Jace a thousand times and touched himself to it.

It was disgusting.

Shivering, I turned away and walked toward Allie. "I don't want any part in it."

"Hey," João said before I could even get a few feet away. "Be at Landon's tonight."

I glanced over my shoulder at the three bad boys who seemed to run my life lately and shook my head. "Sorry, can't. My mom is making me go to dinner with Akio. And, unfortunately, I can't get out of it this time."

Truthfully, I could probably get out of it. But I didn't want to be around when they made plans on how they'd kill Redwood's most corrupt principal. I wanted no part in it and didn't want to aid in murder. It would ruin my life if anyone found out that I was involved.

Kai's jaw twitched, and then he suddenly turned away from us and stormed down the hallway in the opposite direction. João and Landon glanced back at him, and then João pulled a pack of cigarettes out of his pocket, stuffing one into his mouth and lighting it up.

"Next time you see that fucker, why don't you ask him what his parents did to Kai's?" João said, blowing smoke from his nostrils and filling Redwood's hallways with haze. "Unless you want to keep being a bitch to Kai like that."

I stopped in my tracks. "How am I being a bitch?"

"He fucking told you that he doesn't like Akio."

"My mom is making me go," I said through gritted teeth.

And Akio wasn't his parents. Didn't they understand that? They all had fucked up parents, too, but that didn't mean they were going to turn out just like them. As annoying as he was, Akio only wanted to be friends with me. Hell, he liked Nicole, bitchy head cheerleader, not me. Anyway, I had to hang out with him since he had given me the list of people who had HIV and AIDs in Redwood.

If anyone found out, Akio could get fired *and* have his college admissions all revoked.

Still, I couldn't help but feel bad about it.

João was right. Kai had told me multiple times to stay away from Akio, that he didn't like me hanging around him, that he would kill him if we got too close to each other. And I didn't doubt that he would with all those weapons at his house.

And that look on his face before he stormed away.

I frowned, took a deep breath, and walked away from Landon and João to comfort Allie.

After pulling her away from Jace, I decided that we might not be going home now, but we weren't going to class. I looped my arm around hers and hurried through the empty hallways to the library, where there was a small reading corner that nobody ever used.

I sank down in one of the bean bag chairs next to Allie and pulled her water bottle from her backpack, making sure she drank some. She sat next to me with her arms wrapped around her body and tears streaming down her face, quietly sobbing.

Wrapping my arms around her body, I pulled her closer to me and rested her head on my shoulder, stroking her hair gently. She cried into my shoulder, and I let her because that was what good friends did.

Good friends also took care of the men who tried to take advantage of them.

And I got Poison on Principal Vaughn.

After almost an hour of trembling against me, Allie pulled away from me and wiped the tears from her cheeks. I didn't want to bring up Principal Vaughn or the Redwood Academy student body, so I changed the conversation to get her to smile.

"So ... Jace's dick ..." I said, whistling and trying to lighten the conversation.

Allie glanced up through watery eyes and curled her lips into a smile, a very small giggle escaping her throat. "Stop it."

I held my hands up. "All I'm saying is that Landon is bigger."

She let out another giggle and straightened her back a bit. "No, he's not."

Holding my hands about two feet apart from each other, I smirked. "This big."

She burst out into a fit of laughter. "Landon is not carrying a two-foot-long dick in his pants. If he was, you would be wrecked and not be able to walk for weeks."

"That's what *you* think."

After a couple moments, she moved closer to me and smiled a bit wider. "Did you really have sex with them in the principal's office, or were you just lying to get me out of being suspended along with Jace?"

"Oh, it happened." I grinned. "And I made sure we ruined *all* his important documents."

Scrunching her nose, Allie fake gagged. "Ew, gross."

"Bitch, I saw those pictures. You do worse shit with your step-brother. Don't judge."

Allie broke out into another fit of giggles, earning a hard glare from the librarian. I ignored her and smiled at my best friend, glad she was feeling somewhat better. I knew that I could never make up for what had happened, but I was hoping Poison could.

Chapter One Hundred Three

KAI

At five p.m., the sun had set upon Redwood. I pulled into the dark cemetery with my gun in my waistband and anger rushing through me. I had been so pissed off today that I didn't even sit with Poison at lunch. I hadn't wanted to see Imani.

Pulling up to the curb, I shut my bike off and pulled out my buzzing phone.

Imani: Can we talk?

Imani: Please?

I stared down at her messages and the small green bubble next to her profile picture, which meant that she was online and waiting for me to respond. But right now, I didn't have anything to say to her.

She knew I didn't like Akio.

She knew I'd told her to stay away.

She knew something had happened between his parents and mine.

Yet she continued to see him and sit at dinners with him and his parents. She could've easily told her mother that she didn't want to go. Her mother had been more lenient with Imani than usual these past few weeks; Imani could've gotten out of that dinner if she wanted, and she knew it.

Instead of responding to her, I clicked off my screen, slid the phone into the back pocket of my black cargo pants, and pulled my hood over my head, so fall-wintery weather in New England wouldn't freeze my fucking ears off.

After parking my bike, I walked to Dad's grave and stuffed my hands into my pockets. Despite the coldness, someone had laid his favorite flowers in front of his gravestone, the petals withering in the wind.

I stared down at the stone and frowned, a wave of sorrow and rage rushing through me.

My thoughts drifted to Allie, and I clenched my fists at what had happened today with Principal Vaughn. She hadn't fucking deserved to have pictures posted all around Redwood of her with Jace, and she really hadn't deserved to have Vaughn jerking off to her.

It was fucking disgusting.

And tonight, Poison and I would come up with something to make this right. I wanted him to pay. To hurt. To fucking die in my hands. Nobody deserved to have an old piece of shit do that to them, just because.

Who knew what else he and the police force were doing?

The thought made me furious.

Pulling a small flask of bourbon from my pocket, I poured the alcohol all over the frozen grass above his casket and watched it sink into the dirt. It used to be his favorite drink. It was the least that I could do for him now that he was gone.

Once I walked to the other side of the cemetery, I sat down by Mom's gravestone and rested my head against it, pulling a pack of cigarettes and a lighter from my pocket. After lighting it up, I took a puff of it and stared emptily out into the trees that surrounded this place.

A couple moments passed, and I took out my phone. Three new messages from Imani lit up my screen from Discord, but I scrolled past them and clicked on my photos app, scrolling through the endless pictures I had taken with Mom before she died.

My hand tightened around the phone, tears welling up in my eyes.

"You fucking deserved more than this," I whispered.

In all the pictures before Dad died, she'd had the biggest, most contagious grin. I smiled softly at the screen and took another puff of my cigarette, blowing smoke from my nose and wishing she could still be here with me.

When I reached the end of the album, I let my phone slip from my hand and onto the frozen ground between my legs. I finished my cigarette and stood up to head to Landon's house for the night. We had shit to plan for Principal Vaughn.

"One day, I'll make them pay for everything they did." I took one last look at her gravestone and scooped up my phone. "I promise you, Mom, they won't get away with it."

<h1 style="text-align:center">Chapter One Hundred Four</h1>

LANDON

Someone banged on my basement door. I stood up from the couch, where Poison and I were plotting on how to fuck over Principal Vaughn, and jogged up the steps to answer the door. Outside, Jace Harbor stood with Allie.

"What?" I asked.

With bruises all over his body, Jace pulled out a wad of cash and slapped about five hundred-dollar bills into my hand. "Watch Allie."

I glanced over at Allie and lit a cigarette. "Looks like you need a smoke, Jace."

Jace started toward his car. "Don't let anyone fucking touch her. I'll be back."

Allie's eyes widened, and she followed Jace back to his Maserati. "You're leaving me with them?" she asked, grasping his wrist and tugging him back.

Jace snatched his hand out of her grip and turned toward her.

"Please," Allie whispered. "Don't go back."

"Get in the fucking house," Jace said to her, pointing at me.

She grasped his hand. "Please, let me at least clean you up."

After a couple moments, Jace pulled away from her again and slid into his car. "Later. I'll be back for you."

I watched him throw the car in reverse and back out of the gravel driveway, and then I flicked my cigarette onto the ground and stomped it out with the heel of my boot. "You coming?" I asked her, wondering if Imani would show up tonight, too, at some point.

Allie walked into the house and down the steps. I closed the door behind us and followed her. Kai and João looked over at her when she walked into the room, Kai raising his brows at me. We didn't have time to fuck around tonight.

"Jace," I said as a lousy answer.

Kai nodded to another couch across from us for Allie to sit on and handed her a cold beer. Allie sat on the couch awkwardly, crossing her arms over her chest, and glanced around the room.

João looked over at Allie, then at the unopened can in her hand. "Loosen up, buttercup. Take a swig." He took the can from her, opened it up, and handed it back.

To my surprise, Allie took a sip.

"Feel better?" João asked.

"No." She blew out a harsh breath, then grabbed some napkins from the table, placing them on the back of her head to stop blood. "I'm not."

I sat on the couch next to her and tossed the cash Jace had given me onto the table. It was rude to ask what happened—hell, I'd hated when people asked where I got some of my bruises from when Dad was still around—so I shrugged my shoulders. "Don't worry about Jace. He'll be all right. He always is."

"You don't know what he's going through."

"His dad hits him. Everyone here knows it. He brought you here because he doesn't want you getting hurt. Daddy is probably off drinking or some shit." João waved his hand dismissively. "It's not a secret to us. He's handled worse shit than that. Am I right?" João said.

She stayed quiet and took a huge fucking gulp of the beer, staring aimlessly at the paint chipping off the wall.

"So, how's Imani?" João asked, lighting up another cigarette and blowing the smoke out of his nose.

She arched a brow at me and narrowed her eyes. "Why are you guys blackmailing her?"

I looked over and chuckled. "Wouldn't you love to know? What we do with Imani is none of your business."

"Yes, it is. She's my best friend, and I don't want you guys ruining her life like you ruined Jace's. I'm sick of you butting into everyone's business. Stop bothering good people and bringing them down."

While João and I looked over at her, Kai flicked his cigarette into the ashtray and slumped down on the couch. "She's had a hard night," he said, waving us off. Well, mainly João. "Let it slide."

Allie glared at Kai and crossed her arms over her chest. "I want to go home. I need to make sure that Jace is okay. He can't stay with Harlan tonight. You know what he'll do to him."

"You're staying here tonight. I can't let you go back over there. Jace would try to kill me." Kai placed a hand on her shoulder and turned toward her. "And, plus, it's the only way you're safe."

"Why does he trust you guys?" she asked.

"Jace?" Kai asked, brows furrowed. "Because we do good work for him."

"And why did my dad trust you?"

All the emotion on Kai's face evaporated. He sat back up very uncomfortably and shifted in his seat. "What makes you think your dad trusted me?" he asked. Not trusted Poison, but him—Kai.

Something had gone on between Allie's father and Kai, and I didn't think that Kai wanted her to know about it yet. If he did, he would've told her every secret that he had about him. He wasn't ready for her to know.

"A couple weeks ago, you said he did a favor for you," she said to him. "What was it?"

Kai tore his gaze away from her and grabbed her beer. "You keep asking me questions that you know I can't answer about our business." He was suddenly cold and distant even. "Ask me something I can answer."

"No." She crossed her arms and lay back on the couch. "I want you to answer this for me. He was my father. I want to know what kind of business he was in before he was killed."

"Keep dreamin'," João said from the other side of the couch. "If you want to know what happens when we do business with someone, why don't you offer up a job, and we'll show you how it works?"

She narrowed her eyes at him and then tore her gaze away and stayed silent, bleeding all over my couch. But I didn't give a fuck anymore. This was all my parents' shit, and they wouldn't be back for it.

Chapter One Hundred Five

IMANI

Later that night, I reluctantly sat at the dinner table in my home, jaw clenched as Akio's mother said something to Mom. While I sat at the dinner table with Akio and his parents, I couldn't focus on the conversation in the slightest. My thoughts raced not only with *how* Redwood's gang would kill Principal Vaughn, but also on why Kai hadn't answered my texts from earlier.

Mom gave a fake laugh to whatever had been said and smiled over at me tensely, elbowing me. Mom was another one of the snotty rich from Redwood, but today, she looked uneasy, being in the presence of someone like herself. Maybe after being exposed to what had happened with Landon at the hospital, then João's mom, she had some sympathy now.

But I wasn't holding my breath.

People like her could act.

Not wanting to listen to Akio's mother go on and on and on like everything was perfect in her life, I cleared my throat. "What'd you do to the Koh family?" I blurted out because I didn't want to be here.

All that happened at these dinner parties was talking about people who were either richer than them or the poor, who could barely afford to eat. And they fucking thought that it was cool or something. All of it was annoying and disgusting.

Everyone at the dinner table sucked in a collective breath, an awkward silence falling heavily upon the room. I pursed my lips and stared between Akio's mother and father, who were suddenly pale.

"So?" I asked, eyebrow arched. "What happened?"

Akio's mother, who I rarely saw, smiled too widely at me and continued eating her steak. "Nothing, sweetie." She glanced over at Akio and narrowed her eyes ever so slightly, as if she was secretly accusing him of something. "Why do you think something happened?"

"Because Kai Koh's parents are both dead."

"Why do you think we had something to do with it?"

Oh, this bitch wants to test me today...

"Imani," Mom said, giving me the stink eye she always did before a scolding. "Stop it."

Pissed off, I pushed out of my chair and shot up. Leaning over the table with my hands posted on it, I towered over Akio's mother and narrowed my eyes. "People like you won't get away with everything. Whatever you did to them, you will pay for it one day."

"Are you threatening me?" Akio's mother asked, voice tense.

Deciding that she wouldn't intimidate me, I held her intense stare. "Yes."

She gave a shrill laugh. I didn't want to be here and attend *another* dinner with this bitch, so I walked out of the room and into the kitchen while Mom called for me to come back in and sit down. But I was eighteen. I would take her scolding later. I didn't care.

"Akio, why don't you take care of your *friend*?" Akio's mother said from the other room.

I expected her to follow with the words, *Before I have to.*

But she didn't.

A moment later, Akio hurried into the other room with me. "What are you doing?! You can't say stuff like—"

"Come on," I said, grabbing my keys from my purse and walking toward the back door to leave this house until Akio's family was gone for tonight because I didn't want to deal with their shit.

To my surprise, Akio shrugged on his coat and followed after me quickly, as if he didn't want to be at dinner with them either. I kinda felt bad for the kid. He had to live with those assholes every single day of his life.

So, I drove around Redwood in silence with Akio in my passenger seat, not really having anything to say to him because I knew he wouldn't tell me what his parents had done to Kai's parents. They had to have done something because that look on Akio's face earlier at dinner ...

It seemed like Akio *feared* his parents, especially his mother.

After taking a spin downtown, I found myself driving around Main Street and glancing out into the dark ocean. Restaurants and shops were filled with the Redwood rich, drinking and laughing as if their lives were perfect, as if they didn't care that the poor got raped and left for dead in their alleyways.

Across the street, near the restaurant where João's mother had been raped, a lone woman walked on the side of the road and chatted with a big, burly man.

When it registered in my brain that it was João's mom, I slammed on the brakes. The car behind me laid on its horn, and I turned on my blinker and pulled to the side of the road, glaring at the car as he sped past.

"What the hell are you doing?" Akio asked, grabbing his seat belt.

"João's mother," I said, undoing mine to get out of the car.

She shouldn't be around here, especially after what had happened. João wasn't home, watching Ana, which meant that his mom should be at home, watching her. Ana shouldn't be left home alone in a neighborhood like that. She was so young.

An uneasy feeling bubbled in the pit of my stomach. I sprinted down the sidewalk to see if I could catch her outside to ask her why she had come back after what happened, to see if Ana was with her. I didn't know much Portuguese yet, but I could at least try to say a couple words to her.

"Imani!" Akio called, but I continued.

When I turned the corner, the woman was gone.

"Where'd that woman go?" I asked the burly man standing outside.

He stared at me for a couple moments. "You're Poison's friend, aren't you?" he asked.

I swallowed hard and stared up at him, not liking the way he looked at me. Poison had a lot of enemies, even in this part of town, apparently. So, I had to lie to whoever they had pissed off lately.

I shook my head. "No."

"Yeah, you are." He stepped closer, his burly frame towering over me. "And João murdered my boss last week. It looks like it's time to return the fucking favor."

Before I could react, the man pulled out a gun from his pocket. A gunshot rang out through the air. I ducked and shielded my head. And when I didn't feel any pain, I glanced up to see the man had dropped his gun and was clutching his bloody hand.

My eyes widened, and I picked up the gun in a shaky hand, so he couldn't hurt me with it. I turned around, expecting to see Kai or João or even Landon behind me, but Akio stood there, looking like a deer in fucking headlights with a gun in his hand.

Unable to believe what was happening, I sprinted toward him and shoved him back into my car before any of that man's friends could come out and shoot at us. My heart pounded against my chest, my thoughts racing.

Akio stared through the windshield, tears in his eyes. "I-I'm sorry. He ... he was going to kill you. He had a gun. I didn't think ..." Akio continued stumbling over his words, never really completing a full, coherent sentence.

Still in shock, I sped to the Overlook and parked my car. After glancing in my rearview mirror about a hundred times to make sure nobody had followed us, I turned toward Akio and stared at him with wide eyes, taking his gun out of his shaky hand and shoving both his and now my gun into the glove box.

"What the hell was that?!" I asked, swallowing hard. I had so many fucking questions running through my mind that I didn't even know if I wanted to find out the answers. "Where did you get a gun?! Where did you learn how to shoot it like that?!"

Chapter One Hundred Six

IMANI

While I should've gone right home for the night or told Poison what had happened, I found myself driving toward João's house to see if I had imagined the entire thing. João's mother couldn't—*wouldn't*—leave Ana at the house alone.

Not willingly.

If Ana was here, then we would pick her up, drop her off at Landon's, and go out to find João's mother. She shouldn't be hanging out on Main Street with those rich bastards who had nearly killed her a week or so ago.

"We need to get out of here," Akio said, glancing into the rearview mirror. He adjusted his glasses and breathed heavily, his chest moving up and down, nervously rubbing his hands together. "We can't stay in this car. We have to ditch it. They'll be coming."

"We don't have time!" I said, cutting a corner a bit too sharply.

The right tires must've come off the ground a couple inches, and Akio grabbed hold of any handle he could find, shrieking and still in shock. My heart pounded against my chest, but I pushed my foot to the floor, making the car accelerate.

God, I was learning a lot of bad habits from Poison.

And I meant, *a lot.*

When I finally pulled up to João's house, I parked, literally dragged Akio from the car, and marched up to the front door, banging on it with the side of my fist.

Akio stood beside me with wide eyes and muttered, "No," over and over again.

"Stop it, Akio," I said, adrenaline rushing through me.

I had almost died tonight, but I could think of nothing but making sure she was safe.

"You're giving me anxiety," I said, banging on the door again and searching for a key that they might have left under the doormat or in the bushes, under a rock, something. I needed to get in. The lights were on in Ana's room, and the gas stove was on with a pot on top of it.

Ana might've been trying to make brigadeiros by herself. Maybe.

If she wasn't careful ...

"Imani, we should go," Akio said, arms wrapped around his body. He rocked back and forth on his heels and shook his head, gnawing on the inside of his cheek. "We should go, get out of here. You're not saf—"

Before he could finish his sentence, the door swung open. João's mom stood inside with a cheap plush robe on and tired eyes. I furrowed my brows, knowing that I had seen her down on Main Street tonight.

Being the rude bitch I had been lately, I stepped into her house, uninvited, and pulled Akio into the room behind me. I barely knew Portuguese, but I knew some, so I desperately tried to ask her where she was.

She furrowed my brows and pointed to the hallway.

"Não," I said, shaking my head, then followed with the Portuguese word for *tonight*.

At least, that was what I hoped I was saying. Who the hell knew anymore? I could barely think straight. My heart pounded hard against my chest, and I argued back and forth with her for a couple moments.

After becoming thoroughly annoyed at my lack of knowledge of her native language, I shook my head and stormed to the back room to see Ana sleeping soundly in her bed. I blew out a deep breath and held my hand over my heart.

She had on some bright green Princess Tiana pajamas and hugged a stuffed dog to her chest, snoring softly. I quietly closed her door, so she couldn't hear me talking—or arguing—with her mother, and I walked back out to the kitchen.

"Did you go out tonight?" I finally asked in plain English. "Did you leave Ana alone?"

"Não. Não."

"I saw you on Main Street."

"Não."

Every single question I asked her, she answered with no. But I was sure that I had seen her, almost surer than I was that her son was maybe, actually starting to open up to me. Yet this was João's family I was thinking about ...

His mother had always been nice to me, but the more questions I asked her, the angrier and more annoyed she was becoming with me, her brows furrowing in a pissed stare and her nostrils flaring the way João's did when he was pissed.

"You've been here the entire night?" I asked. "With Ana?"

"With Ana," she repeated.

Deciding that I wouldn't get anywhere with her, I walked back, noticed an orange bottle of pills on the kitchen table from her hospital visit, and said good night to her, not trusting a word she had said to me tonight.

I needed to tell João, but I couldn't bring Akio over to Landon's house, especially if Kai was going to be there tonight. And I refused to bring Akio back to his house because I didn't want to face his parents. They had probably left dinner a while ago.

Instead of dropping Akio off in his gated community, I turned onto my street and parked in the driveway, hoping that Mom wouldn't kill me for leaving and that she would bring Akio home for me. She was friendly with them, right? Had probably smoothed everything over by now.

Glancing up at the front door, I frowned at the front porch light that wasn't on. Usually, Mom stood like a hawk outside when I was supposed to be coming home. She was always perched and waiting to chew me out or scold me for something.

After deciding not to worry about it, I hurried in through the front door and tugged a still-shocked Akio in behind me. "Mom!"

No answer.

Once I locked the door behind me, I let go of Akio and turned on the foyer lights. "MOM!"

Nothing.

I turned the corner to step into the living room and froze, letting out a piercing scream. My knees gave out, and I collapsed onto the hardwood floor. In a puddle of blood, Mom and Dad lay on the couch, beaten, bruised, and bleeding.

"Akio!" I screamed, tears streaming down my face. "Akio! What did your parents do?"

Akio scrambled to the living room, caught sight of my parents, then ran through the house toward the bathroom. A couple moments later, he reemerged with a bunch of medical tools to stop the bleeding and heal their wounds.

Neither of us were doctors, but we had to do something.

We had to heal them. They couldn't die.

Once we secured the bandages around their wounds and sat them up, Akio gave them some oral medication to ease the pain and knock them out for a little bit, and then he stood back and ran a hand through his hair.

"They sent them a warning," Akio said. "To keep their daughter from getting in their business."

Chapter One Hundred Seven

KAI

"There are cameras around the back. We're going to need to—"

Someone banged on the basement door, three times and hard as hell. Allie stirred on the couch beside me, turning onto her side and shaking her head back and forth. She had just fucking fallen asleep, finally giving us time to make plans about Vaughn.

"Open up!" Imani screamed from outside, banging harder on the door.

Landon hopped up from the couch and jogged up the stairs to grab the door. Imani hurried in, wrapping her arms around his waist and crying ugly fucking tears into it. I hadn't heard from her all night, had been ignoring her because I didn't want to talk to her. She had been with Akio tonight.

"Why do you have blood on your hands?" Landon asked when he pulled away.

Allie mumbled in her sleep about her parents and her new stepfather, who might've killed Jace by now. Neither she nor any of us with Poison had heard from him since he had left earlier tonight.

Imani hurried down the steps with Akio by her side, hands trembling, then looked at Allie. "They ... they beat my parents up. I found them almost dead. I ... I didn't know what to do. I bandaged them as much as I could, but I ... I don't know if I did it right."

João stood with a cigarette hanging out of his mouth. "Slow the fuck down. What happened?"

After glancing over her shoulder at Akio, she turned back to us and shook her head. "Over dinner, I asked Akio's parents what they did to Kai's. They were being assholes, so I left with Akio. We went down to Main Street, and ... and I swore that I saw your mother talking to someone. I went to confront him to make sure she was okay, and he tried to kill me. Then—"

"Who the fuck tried to kill you?" I asked, standing up and tucking my gun into the waistband of my cargo pants.

Tears ran down her cheeks, but she quickly pushed them away. "Some guy on Main Street. The same place João found his mother. Akio ..." She looked over her shoulder at that fucking guy, who looked pale as fuck. "Akio saved me."

My lip twitched, and I snarled. Fucking Akio.

His family never had any good intentions.

Imani sat beside Landon, wiping the blood from her hands with a wet towel.

Snatching the back of Akio's jacket, I pulled him back toward the door, up the stairs, and through the basement door while Imani cried downstairs. After slamming the door behind me, I threw him up against the side of the house.

"If I find out that you touched a hair on her fucking head, I will kill you."

Akio trembled. "I didn't. I swear."

With fury rushing through me, I pushed him off the house and toward the street. "Walk home."

Turning around, Akio stopped. "You have to protect her from my parents. You know how violent they can be to anyone who disrespects them. Imani ... she told my mom off during dinner. My mom will want me to kill her for it, and if I don't do it, they will. Please, keep her safe."

"Get the fuck out of here," I said through gritted teeth. "You're not welcome."

"Please, Kai. I can't protect her," he whispered. "They'll kill me if I don't."

Jaw clenching, I stared emptily at him, not having a single ounce of pity for him or his family. What they had done to mine fucking tore me apart, ripped me to fucking pieces, and they would *never* do that to Imani. I would make sure of it.

"Leave."

After shaking his head, Akio walked down the street and disappeared from view. A couple moments later, the door reopened behind me, and Imani walked out.

"Where did he go?" Imani asked, wiping her tears with the backs of her hands.

"Why'd you bring him here?" I asked through gritted teeth.

"He saved me, Kai."

"The next time you bring Akio here, I'll put a bullet straight through his head."

"Can you stop being an asshole right now?" she screamed at me, probably waking all the neighbors. "I almost died, for fuck's sake!"

I clenched my jaw and stayed quiet because she was right. And I loathed him even more. I didn't want to owe him shit for saving Imani. I didn't want her liking him more or spending time with him. I hated that fucker.

"And what about Allie?" she asked, crossing her arms over her chest. "Huh? You get angry with me for hanging out with Akio, but I see the way that you look at her and talk about her, Kai. What is so special about her?"

"Don't go there, Imani."

Not only wasn't I ready to say the words out loud, but she and Allie weren't ready to hear them. It wasn't the right time to tell them about Dad, not even fucking close. And I didn't have the courage to even say those words out loud.

"No." She shoved me hard in the chest, pushing me back. "This isn't fair." She pushed me back again, closer toward my bike. "You can't get jealous, then look at Allie like that. It's not fair! I want to be the only one you look at." Another push. "Me, Kai, me!"

"You're the only fucking woman I look at like that."

She shoved me again.

When I stumbled back into my bike, I snatched her chin. "Stop it."

As soon as the words left my mouth, Imani stilled and stared up at me the way she had when I brought her back to my place and tied her sexy ass up with rope, brown eyes wide and full lips parted slightly.

Completely submissive.

Chapter One Hundred Eight

IMANI

Callous, cold, and commanding.

Kai only used that voice during sex.

And my body must've remembered it, had learned to obey, had become weak from the mere sound of his voice because I stopped fighting him verbally and physically. My body froze, and I stared up into those dark eyes.

Before I knew it, Kai had spun me around and shoved me against the side of Landon's house, pushing my feet apart and stepping between them, his hand clasped around the column of my throat.

"You're mine," he growled into my ear, his teeth grazing against my soft spot.

He sank his hand into the front of my skirt, his palm cupping my cunt. "This is mine."

I whimpered, aching for him to stroke his fingers against my clit. All I wanted was to push away the thought of tonight, of almost fucking dying—because I had never been closer—of Mom and Dad getting beaten up by Akio's parents and left in a puddle of their own blood. I needed something to help me forget for a moment, with someone I knew would always protect me.

"Say it, Imani," he said into my ear. "Before I have to fuck those two words out of you."

Breath catching in my throat, I whimpered, "I'm yours."

"Not his."

"Not his," I repeated. "Never his."

"Hands on the wall, above your head."

Submissively, I placed my palms on the wall above my head. He crossed them over one another, grasped my hips roughly, and pulled them back, forcing me to stick out my ass and arch my back hard for him.

"What's mine?" Kai asked, undoing his pants. He positioned the head of his dick at my entrance. He pressed himself against it slightly, teasing me with it until all I could do was whine. "Tell me, Imani. What part of you belongs to me?"

"Will you give it to me?" I asked breathily, craving him inside me.

He slid his hand around my throat once more and grasped my chin hard, moving closer to me, his breath hot in my ear and the tips of his fingers sinking into my mouth. "I'm not going to give it to you until I think your submissive little cunt is ready for it. And you're not ready until you can answer me without talking back."

With his free hand, he cupped the front of my pussy again, his fingers stroking my clit, rubbing it in small, tortuous circles, making my little cunt salivate all over the head of his cock. I balled my hands into fists and arched my back harder, pressing my breasts against the side of the house to get some kind of friction.

My nipples rubbed against the wall, and I whimpered out on his fingers, "Please."

"What's mine?" he repeated.

"Kai ..." I whined.

Instead of scolding me in that sexy dom voice like I expected, Kai smacked my wet clit with his palm. "What's mine?"

I tilted my head to the side, my lips brushing against his, and moaned, a wave of pleasure shooting through my entire body. God, I wanted him to touch me there again, to tease and taunt my pussy until it was a sopping mess.

"More," I said.

Kai smacked my clit again, making another wave of pleasure shoot through me.

"God, yes," I moaned.

Kai's cock twitched against my pussy, and I knew that he would break soon, that my moans were doing more than just turning him on. He wanted—needed—me as much as I needed him right now.

He wanted to show me that I was his, not Akio's.

Losing control, he smacked my clit over and over again, sending pleasure surging through my body. I balled my hands into fists, the pressure rising high in my core, and let the head of his cock slide into me.

With every smack, my pussy pulsed over and over on his cock, squeezing it.

Kai grunted into my ear, then pulled his hand from my pussy, wrapping them both around my chin and mouth like a muzzle, stilling so he didn't slide any further into me. "You're bratty tonight, Imani."

He shoved himself all the way into me, harder than anyone had before, forcing me flush against the wall and pulling me toward him with his hands. "You're not in control," he whispered harshly into my ear, pulling out of me. After pausing for a moment, he thrust himself back into my tight hole. "I am."

I whimpered into his hands and moaned softly, my pussy clenching around him. Kai used my body for his pleasure, pumping and stroking in and out of me. I tightened harder and harder on his cock, so close to coming.

"What's mine?" he asked for a final time. "All you have to do is say it, and I'll let you come. I'll let your pussy explode all over my cock. And if you want to keep being bratty, then I'm going to shove you to the ground and shoot my cum down your throat instead of your pussy, where I know you're aching for it."

He pulled all the way out of me and pressed the head of his cock against my pussy, teasing it. I clenched and dug my fingers into the wall, moments from exploding, moments from the pleasure surging through every single bit of my body.

"I'm yours," I said. "Every part of me, Kai, you fucking own it—"

Before I could finish my sentence, he slammed himself inside me. I screamed out in pleasure and exploded all over his cock, coating it in my cum and trembling in pleasure. Kai pumped into me one time, then stilled deep in my pussy, unloading all his cum into me.

After he pulled out, he sank his fingers into my cunt to push his dripping cum deeper, showing me that my pussy didn't belong to me. It belonged to every one of the Poison boys. I was theirs, whether I liked it or not.

I took a deep breath, chest rising and falling, and slumped my back against the wall. Once I pulled down the bottom of my skirt, I looked over at Kai, who was suddenly distant again.

"Listen," I said, pushing some hair from his face. "I'm sorry about whatever Akio's family did to yours. I know that you don't want to tell me about it, know that you'd rather keep it all to yourself, but Akio saved me tonight."

Kai clenched jaw and tore his gaze away from me. "He might've saved you, but he didn't kill the fucking bastard, did he?" Kai asked. He threw a leg over his bike and started the engine. "Only I will do that for you."

And with that, he kicked up the kickstand and sped down the road toward Main Street.

Chapter One Hundred Nine

LANDON

"Are you sure you saw my mom?" João asked twenty minutes later.

Imani crawled up onto the couch with me and rested her head on my chest, frowning. "I'm ninety-nine percent sure that she was there. I was so nervous that Ana wasn't with her, so I went to your house. By the time I got there, they were already home. I don't know how she got back so quickly, but ..."

"But?" João asked, sticking a cigarette into his mouth and lighting it up, the way he did when he was nervous. João always brushed it off as something he did to look cool, but he had started smoking after a doctor diagnosed Ana with HIV.

"But I'm sure, João. I saw her."

Shrugging on his coat, João grabbed his keys and walked up the stairs and out the basement door, leaving me with Allie and Imani for the night.

Allie slept on one couch in my basement, and Imani lay on my lap on the other.

With her eyes closed, she shifted back and forth, then looked up at me and frowned. "Do you really sleep on this every night?"

"Yeah."

"How?" she asked, curling into my lap. "I need to get you a mattress or something."

I stayed quiet, not wanting Imani to spend her money on me. She had college that she'd have to pay for soon, and if she was going to go to a big college far away from here, then she'd need it, especially if Akio's parents and hers weren't on good terms.

Who knew what Akio's parents do to Imani's?

"Are you going away for college?" I asked her, my chest tightening and my fingers curling a bit harder into her. After all the shit we'd been through and all the time we spent together, I didn't want to lose her.

I couldn't.

"Maybe," Imani said quietly. "Can we not talk about that right now?"

"I want to prepare."

"Prepare for what?" she asked me, gazing up with big, wide brown eyes.

My chest tightened even more, and I felt like I couldn't breathe for a moment. Ever since Mom and Dad had left me, I had been doing better. But tonight, the thought of losing Imani, of even hearing that someone had tried to kill her, it was breaking my heart.

Everyone who was supposed to love me had always walked away.

If Imani went off to college—which she would because she was the smartest, most incredible fucking human being that I'd ever met—then she might find someone better for her than me. There were so many other fucking guys out there who could give her more than I could in this run-down basement.

"Prepare for what, Landon?" Imani asked, hardening her stare. "What're you worried about? Talk to me."

"I don't want to lose you," I whispered, pushing some curls off her forehead.

"Landon," Imani said, smiling, "you're never going to lose me. Not to anyone."

"You don't know that," I said, my insecurities talking. "You might find someone—"

Before I could finish my sentence, Imani grasped the sides of my face and pressed her lips to mine, kissing me deeply. "Stop it," she said breathily against my mouth. "You're mine. I'm not letting you go, no matter what. And if I go to a college in another state, then I'll bring you and all of Poison with me. We can plot the fall of Redwood from afar."

"You promise?" I asked.

"Pinkie," she said, holding out her pinkie.

I wrapped mine around hers, and she squeezed.

"Landon Caddell, I promise to bring you on all my college adventures, so you can slam your fist into any frat boy's face who tries to hit on me."

Lips curling into a smile, I pulled her back down toward me and kissed her softly.

My phone buzzed on the table, but I ignored it. People kept fucking calling from different numbers and not leaving a voice message. I wasn't going to pick that shit up, especially if it wasn't important. I was spending time with Imani now.

"How are your parents?" I asked because while I hated her mother, I didn't want to see her dead. There were tons of fuckups in Redwood, but Imani wasn't one of them. She deserved to have someone in her life who cared about her more than anyone in the entire world, someone who could give her everything.

"They'll live, hopefully." A moment passed, and she looked at Allie on the other couch. "Have you come up with any plans about Principal Vaughn?"

"Some, but we haven't talked much about it yet. Allie has been here almost all night," I said, glancing over at Allie, who was twisting and turning on the couch. "When Jace brought her here, he was bleeding and bruised all over."

Suddenly, Imani sat up with wide eyes. "What? How?"

"His father kicked his ass for something."

"Harlan did that to him? Did he touch Allie?!"

"She was bleeding a bit."

"What?!" she whisper-yelled, smacking me on the chest. "Why didn't you tell me?"

After hopping up, she hurried over to Allie's couch and glanced at her. When she found the gash on the back of her head, she hurried to the bathroom, grabbed a clean rag, and wet it down, cleaning her up.

My lips curled into a small smile, my chest tightening at the sight of

Imani caring so much for her friend. She had such a big fucking heart, something I had never really experienced before now, before her.

Nobody in Redwood cared as much as she did despite growing up in a rich family.

Once she cleaned her wound and bandaged her up, she brushed some hair from her best friend's face and frowned.

"Can you do me a tiny favor before you kill Principal Vaughn?" she asked me. "Cut off his small dick and tell him it was compliments of Imani Abara. He deserves it."

Chapter One Hundred Ten

JOÃO

"**M**ama!" I shouted as soon as I walked through the front door.

The light in her room was on, which meant that she was awake. I shut and locked the door behind me, shutting off the front light. Then, I kicked off my shoes and turned up the heat in this damn house because it was fucking cold outside.

When Imani had told me that she spotted Mom on Main Street, I believed her. I didn't know why; I had trusted Mom for years to do the right thing, but ... I couldn't stop thinking about Mom going back down to where she had gotten raped.

"João, it's almost two in the morning." Mom wiped her tired eyes and padded out into the kitchen. "I'm tired."

I glossed over her once, looking for any fresh needle marks on her arms, any sign that she had gone down there to get high. The thought killed me on the inside because not only would that mean Mom was on drugs again, but it would also mean that Ana would lose her.

Like I had when I was a child.

"Did you leave tonight?" I asked her.

Mom froze for a moment, then regained her composure. "Did that girl tell you that?"

Something about Mom calling Imani *that girl* pissed me off. Mom knew her fucking name and had met her multiple times. Imani had even come over to watch Ana with me a couple times, had joked around with Ana that we were dating.

"You know what her name is, Mama," I said through gritted teeth, balling my hands into fists and seeing red. "Don't try to turn this around on her when you're acting suspicious about where you've been all night."

"I'm not acting suspicious. I'm tired and in pain."

"So, you didn't go out?"

"No."

"You didn't fucking leave this house?"

"No, João. Drop it."

"You're fucking lying!" I shouted.

"You're going to wake Ana."

"Then, let me wake her up. Tell me where you were."

"You might be an adult, João, but I'm your mother. I don't have to answer to you about where I've been. I don't ask you what you're doing when you're out during all hours of the night, do I? Drop it and drop Imani, too, while you're at it."

All I wanted was to punch a fucking hole straight through our wall. She was lying. I could tell by the guilty look in her eyes. She could tell me that she had been here all night, but she hadn't been. She had left.

I glanced around the kitchen, looking for something. "What's this?" I asked, holding up the pills on the table.

"They're the pills the hospital gave me for the pain," she said, looking me right in the eye. After crossing her arms over her plush robe, she marched back through the hallway. "I'm going back to sleep."

I almost believed her. She was almost *that* convincing.

But Imani wouldn't lie to me about this.

I searched every kitchen cabinet, our shared bathroom, the living room, and even Mom's and Ana's rooms while Mom slept. There had to be something that I was missing. Mom wouldn't go to Main Street to fuck around. She must've been looking for something.

After finding nothing, I collapsed at the kitchen table and rubbed a hand over my face, the bottle of pills that Mom had gotten from the hospital in front of me. I snatched it in my fist and wanted to hurl it at the other side of the room.

But it was full.

Last time I had checked it, the bottle had been half-empty.

"João," Ana mumbled, padding into the dark kitchen in her green Princess Tiana pajamas. She climbed up into my lap and wrapped her small arms around my shoulders. "I'm tired. I want to go to bed."

"I thought that you were sleeping."

"I heard you and Mama fighting."

Grimacing, I wrapped my arms around her and stood up to bring her back to her bedroom. I rubbed her back and hoped that she would forget about this all because I didn't want to explain why we had been fighting.

But if I found out that Mom had left Ana here to head down to Main Street, we were going to have some problems. I loved Mom, but I loved Ana more. I had been doing all this shit because I needed Ana to survive. I would fucking die for her.

After placing her in bed, I pulled the blankets over her small body and smiled at her. "Don't worry about Mom and me. We were just talking. I'll make sure that we're quiet from now on, so you can sleep."

"Yeah ..." Ana yawned and turned onto her side, tucking one hand underneath her pillow and closing her eyes. "But Mama lied to you."

My chest tightened. "What?"

"Mama lied to you, João. Mama and I did leave tonight."

"What are you talking about?" I asked her.

"We went down to see the ocean, and then she visited some man at a restaurant. She told me not to tell you. He gave her some medicine to make her feel better."

Chapter One Hundred Eleven

JOÃO

F*uck.*

I pulled Ana's blankets off her small body and gathered her in my arms, holding her close to my chest.

She rested her head against my shoulder and whined softly, rubbing her eyes. "What are you doing?"

"We're going for a ride."

"But, João!" Ana whined, drool rolling down her lips and onto my shoulder. She clung on to me, her fingers digging into my chest and back and her breath unsteady in my ear. "I want to sleep in my bed. Mommy is here."

"You can sleep at Landon's house," I said, grabbing a bag and stuffing her clothes and some toys into it.

She shifted on my hip and wrapped her arms around my shoulders, whining into my ear about Mom.

But I refused to leave her here for another moment.

Mom had fucking brought her to buy drugs. Mom had fucking put her own daughter in danger.

I didn't want Ana to see Mom high or buying fucking drugs.

That was shit—absolutely shit.

With Ana on one hip, I desperately tried to gather a shit-ton of her stuff without Mom noticing. But, fuck, single parents must've had it

430

hard as shit. I kept tripping over things in the dark, Ana was weighing me down and making me shift my weight every few moments, and I couldn't find shit.

I hated that I needed to do this, but I didn't trust Mom with Ana anymore. She had lied to me about leaving the house. She had lied to me about buying drugs. She had lied to me about *doing* drugs again. And to her, it could be pain relief, but this was how she slipped back into something worse.

Who knew if she'd end up becoming a druggie again? Fuck no.

Ana wouldn't walk around here with needles all over the place again.

"João, I wanna go back to bed."

"Imani is over at Landon's house tonight," I said.

"Really?" she said, smiling hazily at me.

"Yes, really."

After throwing her bag over my shoulder, I hurried out of Ana's bedroom and to the kitchen. Once I snatched the pills from the table, I fastened a winter coat onto Ana, stuffed her feet into some winter boots, and stormed out the front door. I grabbed Ana's car seat out of Mom's car, slid it into mine, and strapped her into the car.

The light turned on in the kitchen, and Mom hurried out. "What are you doing, João?"

I shut Ana's door and hoped that she'd fall asleep quickly.

"You lied to me, Mama!" I shouted at her, probably waking all the neighbors. "You told me that you didn't leave this house and didn't go down to Main Street to get more pills, and you fucking did! Ana told me."

Mom screamed at me, violently trying to yank on my car door handle and waking up Ana. Ana sat in the backseat, kicking and screaming back, tears streaming down her face.

Mom reached for my keys to try to take them from me. "You can't take my child from me!"

"You can't bring Ana to buy drugs!"

Suddenly, Mom stopped reaching for the keys, stopped trying to get Ana out of the car, and stopped screaming. She stood in front of me, completely still, and hung her head low, mumbling something incoherent underneath her breath.

"You can't put her in danger like that again," I said, lowering my voice enough so Ana wouldn't hear. "You almost got her killed once, Mama. I'm not letting it happen again. If you're going out to get pills or to get high, you can't bring Ana with you, and you certainly can't leave her by herself at home."

"What do you expect me to do?" Mom asked, tears welling up in her eyes.

I stared at her, unsure about what to say. What *could* I say to her? I had never been addicted to hard drugs or pills. I understood how it affected people, but I never had a fucking daughter either.

But, fuck, I couldn't understand how she could do that to Ana.

After everything.

"Don't do drugs," I said, plain and simple.

"The pills are for the pain."

"No," I said harshly. "The pills the hospital gave you are for the pain. The pills you bought out on the street are because you're fucking addicted to them again. And if you're fucking addicted, then you're going to lose your daughter. You're going to lose everything," I whispered. "Even me."

My chest tightened, my heart fucking aching. I never wanted to live without her, especially after Dad left. But I couldn't trust her to do the right thing and to choose her family over drugs.

"João," she whispered, shaking her head. "I'm sorry. I'm so sorry."

All I could do was stare at her wavering eyes and see the pain inside them. I gulped and walked toward the driver's door, then slid into the car. Mom tried to get into the car, to grab Ana, but I couldn't let her.

Before she could, I shut and locked my doors. Ana screamed in the backseat, kicking my seat and throwing a fit, crying for Mom to come get her. I threw the car in reverse and backed down the street since Mom stood angrily in front of the car.

And then I did a U-turn and drove toward Landon's house, glancing into the rearview mirror with tears in my eyes, my chest tight and my lips pulled in a frown. This wasn't how I had pictured my night going or how Mom would turn out.

"João!" Ana cried. "I want Mama!"

"Not right now," I said, hand tight around the steering wheel.

It broke my fucking heart to hear Ana beg for me to turn around, to see her sobbing. She already didn't have a father; she deserved to have a mother, someone she could look up to and to teach her about life.

But Mom wanted to get high.

To calm Ana down, I drove past Landon's and took a couple spins around Redwood until she fell asleep in the backseat. Then, I pulled up to the desolate turnaround at the Overlook and stared out my windshield at the ocean.

I slammed my fist into the steering wheel.

Once.

Twice.

Then, hot tears streamed down my fucking cheeks.

Chapter One Hundred Twelve

KAI

I knocked out one of his front teeth, smashing my heel right into his mouth until blood filled it and poured down his chin.

The man who had tried to kill Imani hadn't been hard to find.

How could he be when he stood on Main Street with his hand wrapped in bandages where Akio had shot him, bragging about how he had almost killed Poison's girl? All I had to do was pull up in the back, stick a gun in his buddies' faces, and tell them to get lost.

Then, I had tied that asshole up, making sure to bind the rope so tightly that he lost feeling in his bloody hand, and brought him to the back of the warehouse where Poison and I did our business. It would be easier to clean up the blood when I was finished.

With his wrists and ankles bound behind his back, I dropped to my knees and hurled my fist at the man's face over and over, taking all my anger with Akio and his family out on the man, putting him through pure torture for nearly killing Imani earlier tonight.

"Please." He spit out blood. "Stop."

"You pulled a gun on my girl."

A knee to the nose. Another fist to the jaw. Bones cracked. Blood splattered.

I didn't fucking stop until his body twitched. Then, I stood up and kicked my foot into the side of his bloodied face, smashing in his jaw, and then I kicked his throat, snapping the artery in his neck through one of the many open wounds I had given him.

When he stopped moving, I stood, spit on the man, and pulled out my phone. After capturing a picture of the corpse on his own phone, I sent it through all the contacts that this man had. This wasn't just revenge; this made a fucking statement. If people touched—or even thought about touching—Imani, then they would have to face Poison.

And Poison didn't fuck around when it came to the people they cared about.

What I hated most about this whole damn thing was that I now owed Akio. That wimpy fucking bitch with mob parents who ran this town had protected our Imani from a man who could've killed them both in a moment's notice.

All I had wanted to do for so long was put a bullet straight through his head and kill him, take away something that his parents loved like they had taken someone who I loved in what cops had claimed was a car accident. Every fucking cop there had known whose fault it really was.

Not my father's, like they had reported.

Dad wouldn't get into a wreck that badly; he didn't drink and drive, like the report had said.

Now that Akio had saved Imani, how could I fucking kill him? He had saved the one person that every member of Poison kinda, sorta had a thing for.

Once I stuffed the guy in a black bag, I took care of the trash and cleaned the blood and any trace of whoever the fuck this guy was from the warehouse. I wiped the blood from my bare chest and pulled my sweatshirt over my head, grabbed my keys, and texted Imani.

Me: Don't get yourself in trouble again.

Imani started texting, then stopped, the three typing dots disappearing on our personal Discord chat. I glided my tongue across my teeth and decided to show her what Akio should've done if he had wanted to protect her—and what would happen to him if she kept bringing him around me.

I sent the picture of the corpse to Imani.

Imani: KAI!

Imani: CAN YOU NOT SEND THAT TO ME?!
Me: This is for you.
Imani: I DON'T WANT TO BE PART OF THIS!

Part of me regretted sending the picture—because I knew that she probably was having an anxiety attack now. She had probably never seen a dead body like this, but Imani needed to fucking know what happened to people who tried to fuck with a member of Poison.

Me: Don't get yourself in trouble again.
Me: Or next time, I'll make you kill the man yourself.

Suddenly, those typing bubbles disappeared again, and she didn't respond. I slid my phone into my back pocket and slipped out the back door. A fierce wind hit me as soon as I closed the door.

I pulled up my hood and climbed on my bike to head toward Landon's to let Imani know that I was serious about this shit and to finally get a chance to plan how we'd kill Redwood's infamous principal next.

Chapter One Hundred Thirteen

Kai sat on the couch opposite of me and Landon.

I stared at him and swallowed hard, my stomach in tight knots. I couldn't stop thinking about the picture he had sent privately to me earlier tonight. That image of a man he had beaten to death was burned into my memory forever.

And I didn't know what to think. Kai was more violent than I'd thought, a monster almost.

After smoking out of a bong, Kai rested it on his knee and leaned back with his heavy gaze still focused on me. I shifted on the couch and sank down against Landon, pulling my eyes away from Kai and hoping that he wouldn't show me that picture again.

Or keep his promise that if I got in trouble again, I would have to kill a man like that.

Still, I couldn't help but look over at him one more time. There was a splatter of blood on his neck, which he must've forgotten to wash off or something. Maybe he had wanted me to see it, wanted to taunt me with it.

Whatever the reason, it was working.

Once I decided to *forget* about it, I looked up at Landon and closed my eyes. Just as I was about to fall asleep in Landon's arms, someone banged on the basement door. Landon moved me off him and hurried up the stairs.

With Ana in his arms, João stood outside the basement door. I ran up the stairs after Landon and stood behind him, staring at João's bloodshot eyes, and frowned. Less than two hours ago, João had left to go home.

Now, he was back, and ... I was nervous that something bad had happened.

"Unlock your fucking house, Landon. I'm bringing Ana up to your parents' old room." João pulled Ana tight to his chest to keep her sleeping little frame warm. "You've cleaned it out, right? There's no shit lying around, is there?"

Landon pulled a key out of his pocket and opened the back door, turning on the light switch and holding the door open. "It should be all good. I'm going to bring Allie up with her, so she's not lying up there alone all night."

After Landon disappeared into the basement to pick up a sleeping Allie, I followed João into Landon's house and up the stairs to a small bedroom that looked like it hadn't been touched in weeks. And I was fucking thankful that Landon's parents hadn't been back.

When João placed Ana down, she shifted around and reached her small arms into the air, grabbing João by the neck. "Kissies," she murmured, pulling him down to meet her.

He kissed her on the cheek and told her good night.

I stared at the exchange from the doorway, my heart clenching.

João might be the unsympathetic gangbanger, but he loved his family. Hard.

Once Landon made it upstairs with Allie, he placed her in bed beside Ana. As they talked tensely in the hallway about something, I pulled the blankets over my best friend's and Ana's bodies to keep them warm and frowned.

They both deserved so much more.

Redwood had failed them.

Turning off the light, I shut the door behind me and stepped out into the hallway, where João stood by himself. I chewed on the inside of my lip and stared at him for a couple moments, knowing that he wanted to talk.

If he didn't, then he would've gone down to the basement with Landon.

"Are you okay?" I whispered, brushing some hair out of his face.

Very unlike João, he avoided eye contact with me and stared at the ground. "Move out of the way, Imani. I want to smoke and forget about this whole night. Why don't you go to bed with Ana and Allie?"

He tried to move past me, but I stepped into his way. "Talk to me."

Like I thought he would, João tried to push past me to get down the steps to the basement. I moved in his way again and crossed my arms, refusing to let him by. We pushed and shoved, back and forth, for a couple moments. Then, suddenly, his arms came around me.

And he hugged me.

Tightly.

We stood quietly in the middle of the dark hallway, João's body tensing more with every passing moment. I rubbed his back gently and laced one hand into his dark hair, wanting him to know that he didn't have to be all big and bad with me.

"What's wrong?"

"My mom," he said, clutching on to me, his fingers digging into my shoulders so tightly. It was as if he thought that if he let go of me, I would slip away from him. He buried his nose in my hair and tensed. "She was out on Main Street tonight, buying pills. You were right."

My stomach dropped.

Even though I had seen her, all night, I had wished it weren't true. I wished that I had been delusional and imagined the entire thing. I didn't want this to be real. I didn't want João's mom to get messed up with drugs, especially if she was the primary caretaker for Ana.

"And ..." João tensed even harder, his body trembling. Then, his voice broke. "She brought Ana with her." He cried into my shoulder, body visibly shaking now, chest heaving heavily. "She fucking brought Ana."

I pulled him closer to me and rubbed his back, tears welling up in my eyes. "I'm sorry."

"Don't say anything," João said, steadying himself slightly. "I don't want your pity. I want ..."

"What?" I whispered when he didn't finish his sentence. "What do you want?"

João's body jerked again. "I want someone to love us."

My chest tightened, pain shooting through my body. I rocked us back and forth slightly, knowing that he didn't want my sympathy or pity. But that wasn't what I wanted to give him. I wanted to show him that people *did* care.

"You have Poison," I whispered, "who'd do anything for you and Ana."

"What about ..." João suddenly snapped his mouth closed. "Forget it."

"What about what?"

He stiffened even more and peeled himself away from me. "Nothing."

Then, that man turned his back toward me, walked down the stairs, and disappeared into the darkness, leaving me alone with his sister and my best friend, thinking that wasn't the answer João had been looking for.

It was almost as if João had wanted *me* to tell him that I loved them too.

Chapter One Hundred Fourteen

LANDON

The next day, João convinced Vera Rodriguez to watch Ana, and Kai brought Allie home. When they came back, Imani decided to stay upstairs on the first floor of my parents' house to do some homework for school while we plotted on how to kill Vaughn for fucking good.

It was the first time we were able to talk about anything in detail before all shit had broken loose last night. We talked for hours about how we wanted to do this shit and which would be the best way to destroy half of Redwood while we were at it.

Someone banged on the basement door, and I lifted my head. "It's open, Imani."

The bang came again.

"Poison! Open the door, for fuck's sake."

I sighed and leaped up from the couch, taking the stairs two at a time as Kai and João followed me to get some fresh air. When I opened the door, Allie and Jamal Simmons—Jace's best friend—stood outside of it with tears racing down her cheeks.

The house door opened, and Imani pushed her way between us to see Allie. "Oh my gosh, what happened to you?" she asked, pulling open the screen door and pulling Allie into the house.

Allie sobbed in her arms. "I—Jace ... he-he's gone. I haven't heard from him in over twenty-four hours. When Kai dropped me off this morning, he was gone. I'm so afraid that he's dead."

Imani looked back at us. "Have you heard from him?"

Before any of them could answer, a black SUV with tinted windows skirted around the bend and screeched up to the side of the road. Kai grabbed Imani's waist and pulled her to the ground, as if someone was about to pull up and start shooting.

The driver's door swung open, and Jace shot out of the car toward Allie. "Thank fucking God you're okay."

Allie ran her hands against his cheeks and shook her head in disbelief as blood coated her fingers. Jace *looked* like he had gone to hell and come back. There were so many bruises up and down every exposed place of his body.

"The fuck happened to you?" João asked, nodding toward the inside of the basement.

Jamal wrapped one arm around Jace's torso to hold him up, and Jace flinched.

"Sorry, dude," Jamal said, helping him inside.

Imani wrapped Allie up in her arms and ushered her inside the house and to the basement. After Jamal rested Jace on the couch, Allie sat next to him and gently grasped his knee.

"What happened to you?" she asked, searching the room.

João grabbed a cheap bottle of vodka from the dirty white refrigerator and held it out for Jace. Jace went to grab it, but Allie tore the bottle out of his hand and glared at João.

"What's your damn problem? This is not a time to get drunk. He needs to be healed. Now."

"We could go see my mom, but she's, uh—" Jamal glanced down at his watch and frowned. "She's probably at work right about now. Her night shift starts in, like, five minutes. She leaves at ten thirty p.m."

"My mom should be home," Imani said, eyeing Kai, João, and me. She gnawed on the inside of her lip and shook her head, as if saying screw it. "If we leave now, she'll probably still be awake too, but she has a surgery scheduled for early tomorrow morning, so we need to hurry."

"Imani, are you sure?" Allie asked, eyeing the boys.

I guessed that she, too, knew Imani's mother definitely didn't like us.

Imani nodded. "Let's go."

Before Jace could follow Imani to her car, Allie grabbed his hand. "Jace, I need to tell you something first about ... about your father," she whispered.

Jace froze and tightened his grip on her hand. "Don't tell me that fucker touched you."

"He-he-he burned those papers and all the evidence in that file you told me to protect."

Tears streamed down her face, and I froze. All that shit we had done to get those papers, and they were gone.

"I'm so sorry! I-I tried to stop him. I really did."

Jace slumped his shoulders forward and blew out a deep breath. "Don't fucking scare me like that. I thought he hit you," Jace said, wrapping his arms around her shoulders and pulling her closer to him. He gently stroked her hair. "Don't worry about it, Allie. Everything in that file was a copy. The real ones are somewhere where nobody will ever find them."

"You have them?" she asked, looking up at him. "You really do?"

He gave her the smallest of smiles. "I do, but don't say anything to my dad. We're going to let him think that he hasn't been caught and won't be caught. Then ... we'll watch him burn."

"Just like the rest of Redwood," João said. "Just like the fucking rest of those fuckers."

Chapter One Hundred Fifteen

IMANI

"Listen …" I crossed my arms and glared at the boys as we stood in front of my house.

Jamal had left to watch his brother and sisters while his mom was at work, so it was me, them, Jace, and Allie. I eyed each one of them, knowing that I was risking my damn freedom by showing up with them all this late at night.

"Don't say anything to my parents. They don't like you guys, so don't be fucking jerks."

Landon wrapped his arm around my shoulders. "We wouldn't do that."

I elbowed him in the ribs. "I mean it this time."

"Why don't you ever invite us over?" João asked, glancing into the house through the window.

He was testing me today, really testing me. My parents had gotten beaten up by the mob the other night, my best friend had gotten kicked around by her stepfather, and now, Jace had nearly died doing God knew what. I didn't have time for his remarks right now.

I cut my eyes to him and curled my upper lip up. "I'm not in the mood. Don't push it, João." I looked back toward the other two, daring them to say something to me, but they both kept their mouths shut.

I pushed the front door open. "MOM!"

"In the office," Mom shouted back. "What do you need?"

"I need you. Now."

"Not the first time we've heard that," Landon said.

I rolled my eyes and continued into the house, locking the door behind us.

Mom appeared in the foyer and sucked in a deep breath, hurrying over to Jace. "Oh my goodness, what happened to you?" she asked, taking him to the other room and sitting him on our white couch. It was bound to get stained, but Mom was rich enough to have ten identical couches like this here within the hour, if she cared.

She had already swapped out the couch that Akio's parents had left her bleeding out on. It was like that little *scene* had never even happened. If it wasn't for her bruises, I would've thought I'd daydreamed the entire thing.

We hadn't spoken about it at all.

Everyone glanced around at each other, not knowing what to say. Jace grimaced at Allie and shook his head.

"I got into a fight with someone on the football team," Jace lied. "And got my ass kicked."

Mom blew a breath out her nose. "Looks like it."

After Mom ushered us all farther into the house, Allie glanced over at me, eyeing the bruises all over Mom's face. "What happened to your mom?" she whispered.

I winced. "You don't want to know."

And it wasn't like I would tell her that Akio's family was part of the damn Redwood mob. She already had too much shit on her plate between Jace and his father.

Mom glanced up and noticed the Poison boys for the first time tonight. She gave them a hard and long look, then pressed her lips together and nodded to the other room. "I'm going to grab some supplies. Allie and Imani, please, help me."

Once I told the boys not to touch anything, I followed Mom and Allie to the bathroom. Mom rummaged through some stuff in the closet, pulling out the same medical supplies that I used to kinda, sorta heal her the other day.

"If they're going to be over here, please watch them," she said to me. "And, sweetie"—she looked at Allie—"make sure they don't steal anything. Those boys are bad news. I told her not to see them." She continued as if I weren't here. "Why is she bringing them into the house? Can you try to talk some sense into her?"

Allie glanced back at me, and I glared at the back of Mom's head, really not wanting to fight with her tonight. We'd been through so much shit these past few days. I didn't have patience for her anymore.

"They're just, um ... *friends*," Allie said, shrugging.

"Mmhmm," Mom said, giving me the side-eye.

She still didn't trust me with them.

She gathered some supplies from our bathroom closet and handed them to Allie. "I'm telling you, those boys had better not distract you, Imani. You're set to be top ten in your graduating class, and you know how hard it is to get to the top at Redwood with everyone having the best tutors around."

After we walked back into the living room, Mom started to clean Jace up.

"Allie!" Dad shouted as he walked into the room, looking twice as badly bruised as Mom did. Despite Mom's hesitation with four of Redwood's *finest* boys in our living room, Dad didn't seem to mind. He squeezed Allie's shoulder. "You think about that internship yet?"

My dad was a biochemical engineer who had been suggesting Allie apply for an internship at his work for months now. With everything going on, applying to colleges, and dealing with Jace drama during the summer, Allie had been brushing it off.

"Internship?" Jace asked.

"Don't move, honey," Mom said to him, stitching up his head.

"We're working on finding someone for a bioengineering internship. I know you're going to school for biology next year. Why don't you give this a try? A new position just opened." Dad smiled at Allie. "So? What do you say? You going to apply?"

"Um ..." She glanced over at Jace.

"Do it," Jace said.

"Didn't I just tell this boy not to move?" Mom said, eyeing Poison again.

Allie nodded. "Sure. I'll do it."

Dad clapped his hands. "Great! I'll set up an interview with the hiring manager."

When Mom was finished, she pulled out an orange bottle of medication and handed it to Jace. "I'm not supposed to do this, Jace, but you're going to need this." She leaned closer to us and grimaced. "Don't say this to *anyone*. I'm doing this because you're Allie's stepbrother, and that's all."

So, Mom did have access to some kinds of medication.

Maybe she could get Ana hers, whenever she needed it.

After Jace thanked her and my parents left the room, Allie grabbed his hand. "Jace," she whispered, "I need to make sure that my mom is okay. I haven't seen her in twenty-four hours, so ... I need to go back to the house. I'll meet you at Poison's place in an hour."

When Allie went to stand, Jace grabbed her hand. "I'm coming with you. You're not going there alone."

"But, Jace ..." She shook her head. "He's going to kill you."

"Don't worry about that," Jace said with certainty

João placed a hand on each of their shoulders and stepped between them. "Wherever you're going, make sure you show up to the football game this week. You're going to want to be there. Shit is going to go down."

Chapter One Hundred Sixteen

LANDON

Once Imani's mom finally calmed down, Jace and Allie left. I wrapped my arm around Imani's waist and pulled her closer to me, glancing at João and Kai, who lingered by the door and eyed Imani. João pulled out his keys and lit a cigarette on the walkway.

"You're not staying?" I asked.

"I need to check on Ana." He clenched his jaw. "I promised her that I'd bring her home to see Mom today, but I'm not leaving them alone together." He headed toward the car. "I don't trust her."

"Be safe," Imani said to João. "And tell Ana I said hi."

With his back already turned toward her, João stiffened. "I will."

Imani stared at their departing figures for a few moments, then shut the front door behind them. She glanced over my shoulder at the empty living room, then at me, her cheeks rounded and her lips pulled into a soft smile. "My parents are in bed." She tugged me toward the stairs. "Come on. Let's go upstairs."

"You know I've never been in your house without having to sneak around," I said, looking around at all the shit they had in here. Her living room alone must've been worth a million fucking dollars with all the original artwork and sculptures.

But to Imani, it was nothing.

"Imani," her mother warned, glancing out from a room on the main floor and giving her those intense, glaring eyes. After a moment's pause, she sighed and slumped her shoulders forward, dragging a hand across her face. "Be careful, okay?"

Imani gave her a small smile, then pulled me up the stairs toward her bedroom. My phone buzzed in my back pocket. I pulled it out to see an unknown number. Again. This must've been, like, the twelfth call from that number in the past forty-eight hours.

"Why don't you answer it?" Imani asked, walking into her room.

"Because it's my parents," I said, shutting off my phone and lying back on her bed.

I ran a hand over my face and grunted, hating the thought of them *still* trying to fuck up my life. It was like as soon as I was better, as soon as I started healing from their bullshit, they wanted to tear me down.

Why the fuck were some people like that?

"Well, fuck them then," Imani said, shutting the door and crawling onto the bed with me. She cuddled close, one leg draped over mine and her pussy warm against my thigh. After twisting and turning for a couple moments, she whimpered, "I'm so horny."

I wrapped my arm around her and cupped her ass.

She ground herself back and forth on my thigh, then crawled up to the headboard. "I want to watch our sex tape," Imani murmured into my ear, biting down softly on the skin below it. "The one in Vaughn's office."

After pulling her between my legs, with my chest against her back, I wrapped my arm around her small waist and rubbed her swollen clit through her soaked panties. "What if we made one?" I whispered into her ear. "Me and you on camera like we used to do, but instead of watching each other, you get to sit on my cock and ride me all night long while I tug on these"—I pulled my hand away from her pussy, captured both her nipples between my fingers, and tugged—"perky little tits of yours."

"Will you really?" she asked breathlessly.

She pulled out her phone and set it on the nightstand beside us, clicking the red record button once. I leaned back on the bed, cocking my finger toward her. She crawled between my legs, curling her fingers around the waistband of my jeans.

After unzipping my pants, she pulled out my cock and sucked the head into her warm mouth. With her lips wrapped around the shaft, she inched her knees forward and arched her back. I grasped a fistful of her hair, pushing her head down further until she took all of me and gargled on my cock.

"Fuck," I grunted, smacking and grabbing a handful of her ass. "You're sexy as fuck."

Bobbing her head, she took all of me into her mouth, over and over, until she slobbered all over me.

"Come up here," I said, drawing her up to me again and facing the camera.

I parted my legs, and she rested hers on either side of mine, her thighs spread wide for the camera, and then I slipped my hand inside her panties to touch her. My fingers moved around inside her underwear, rubbing and smacking her clit, my knuckles pressing against the thin and silky fabric.

As she parted her lips and moaned, I slid four fingers into her mouth to gag her with them. Her eyes rolled back, her mouth salivating on my fingers, spit and drool covering them already. I reached them to the back of her throat until she gagged, my other fingers moving quickly around her clit.

She mumbled on my fingers, legs trembling, and glanced over at me through watery eyes. "More," she said, voice muffled. "Give me more."

After positioning us toward the camera, I moved my fingers faster against her clit, ground myself against her from behind, and forced my hand farther into her sloppy little mouth. She whined on me again and spread her legs wide, pussy pulsing over and over, her hole tightening again and again for the camera.

Unable to hold back anymore, I pulled my hand out of her mouth and my other from her panties, laid her down on the bed, and climbed between her trembling legs. After resting my forehead against hers, I shoved myself into her pussy.

She pressed her lips against mine and moaned into our kiss, her walls tightening around my dick. I pumped in and out of her quickly, my knees on the bed right underneath the tops of her thighs.

Digging her nails into my shoulders, she scratched down my back, probably leaving deep red marks, which only made me want to fuck her harder. I wrapped one arm around her shoulders and posted the other on the headboard, pounding into her as fast and as hard as I could.

"I'm going to come again, Landon," she murmured, fastening her legs around my waist.

She buried her face into the crook of my neck and moaned loudly against my skin, pussy milking the damn cum out of my balls. After a couple moments, her breathy little moans softened, and she pulled me down toward her, so I lay between her legs.

"You're fucking amazing," she whispered. "Don't you dare answer your phone for those douchebags and let them think you're anything less ever again."

Chapter One Hundred Seventeen

JOÃO

"Why did we leave Mama?" Ana asked, holding my hand the next evening. From my car, we walked up the lawn to the front door, her body wrapped up tightly in a winter coat. She padded over the frozen dirt lawn and stopped me at the front door. "Did she do something bad?"

"Mama needed some time to relax," I said to her, lying straight through my fucking teeth. I knew that I should've told her what was really going on with Mom—she deserved to know—but I couldn't get myself to say it. Not only because of her, but because of myself too.

When I opened the door, the thick scent of brigadeiros hit me. And I knew it was Mom's way of getting Ana on her side, to show her that she wasn't the monster I had supposedly made her out to be, even though all I wanted was for Mom to be healthy for us again.

"Mama!" Ana shouted, grinning and running over toward her.

Mom glanced over her shoulder from the stove, smiled widely, and crouched to her level, scooping Ana up into her arms and twirling her around. "Ana! I missed you so much." She turned toward the stove with Ana. "I'm making your favorite."

"I missed you too, Mama." Ana ran her fingers through Mom's thick hair and frowned. "Did you get some rest? João said that you needed some for the past couple days. I hope that you relaxed."

While I placed my coat on the back of a chair, Mom glanced over at me. Black bags lay underneath her eyes, her lips pulled into a tight and taut smile, one that didn't reach her eyes. I didn't know if it was because she felt guilty, if she didn't want to see me but didn't want Ana to know, or if she had stayed up all night, getting high.

And I didn't want to ask either.

After Mom and Ana made their brigadeiros and sat on the couch to watch cartoons together, I looked in the medicine cabinet and clenched my jaw. Ana didn't have much medication left. And it wasn't like we had fucking insurance.

I ran a hand over my face and blew out a breath, trying to figure out what the fuck I was going to do between the bills piling up on the kitchen table that Mom hadn't been able to pay since she had gotten discharged from the hospital, to the hospital bill itself, to this medication that probably wouldn't last another week.

Once Poison had split that two mil from Jace three ways and we took care of a couple things for the *business*, I was left with five hundred grand. And in the northeast, that kind of money went quickly with how expensive shit was around here, like hospital bills, the house, fucking groceries.

Ana's medication wasn't cheap either.

I'd rather still get it for free.

Maybe after the football game, when everyone started panicking, pharmacies would be under less intense security. Now, they had fucking cops posted at nearly all of them, especially the ones that carried this kind of shit.

We'd have to go then.

I stood in the kitchen, watching the stupid cartoons on the TV in the living room. Ana kicked her legs back and forth and smiled at the TV as Mom moved from the couch to me.

She stood by my side and gave me a small smile. Almost too sweetly.

"I'm trying, João," she whispered, anxiously rubbing her hands back and forth. "But I ..."

There was a long pause, and I had the urge to leave right then and there. I knew something shitty was about to come out of her mouth, but I wanted to believe that she had just stayed up all night, worrying about us.

I wanted to believe that she was still the woman I had looked up to for so long.

"What is it?" I asked quietly.

She pulled her pupil-dilated gaze away. "I need those pills. Just one. For the pain."

My entire body froze. I swallowed hard. My heart pounded against my rib cage, and my stomach dropped. Fuck, I knew that I should've left. I knew I should've fucking left while we were on *some* kind of decent relationship.

I didn't want to fight with her.

"No," I said sternly.

"They're my pills from the hospital. All I need is one." She moved closer to me, and I noticed the thin layer of sweat on the back of her neck, her dark hair stuck to the tan skin. She grabbed my forearm. "Please."

"Drop it, Mama." I looked over at Ana, who sat on the couch with a plate of cooled brigadeiros on her lap, rocking her head from side to side while she ate and watched cartoons. "I came here, so you could spend time with Ana, not for you to pester me about pills."

She rubbed her muscles. "Please, João. My body aches."

Blinking back tears, I pressed my lips together and stared at Ana. Between her aching muscles and sweating and dilated pupils, Mom was going through withdrawal. I didn't want her to be in pain, but I couldn't give her any pills.

I remembered what had happened last time. I remembered that Dad had made a monster.

"João," Mom pleaded.

"No," I shouted, then turned to Ana. "Come on, Ana. We're going."

Ana glanced over at us with wide eyes and brows furrowed. "But ... but I want to stay."

Mom stepped in front of Ana, like she was going to fight me if I took her away again. But it was either I took Ana away or the state did, and if those monsters dragged her away, Mom would *never* fucking see her daughter again.

Deciding that I wasn't going to deal with this shit, I pushed past Mom and grabbed Ana along with the plate of goodies. I placed her on my hip and started toward the front door to get the fuck out of here.

Mom tried to block my path every single step of the way. When I reached the door, I had had enough of it. I wanted her to stop, to see this for what it was, to fucking change so she could love us the way Ana needed her to.

I shoved past her and stormed through the door. "Once you choose your daughter over getting fucking high, then we can fucking talk."

But I knew that Mom would never be able to do that, not a second time, not now when she was addicted. All those endorphins had probably rushed through her system as soon as she tasted the pills, reminding her of how numb she had felt to the pain around her.

Once I strapped Ana into my car, I drove.

Not wanting to deal with my emotions while Ana sat in the backseat, crying, I called Vera Rodriguez, who had watched Ana last time, and told her that I was dropping Ana off. Vera's parents were never home that much, so she didn't mind.

Or at least, I didn't care.

"João! Please, bring me back to Mama!" Ana cried when I parked in front of Vera's house.

Vera stomped out of her front door in a plush robe and a glare so intense that it could've probably killed me if I gave a fuck. I stepped out of the car and gathered all of Ana's belongings and handed them to her.

"I'll pay you triple what I paid you last time."

"You didn't pay me shit last time," Vera whisper-yelled at me. "And the time before that, Kai paid me."

"Well, I'll pay you triple what Kai paid you. I need you to watch her. Poison and I have shit we need to take care of, and my mom ..." I started, unable to finish my sentence. "My mom can't watch her right now. Don't bring her home and don't answer your door, no matter how hard my mom bangs on it."

Vera suddenly stared up at me through wide eyes. "What happened?"

"Nothing," I snapped. "Watch her."

"I can't do it myself. I have someone ov—"

Blaise Harleen appeared at the door, his button-up shirt undone. "You coming back, V?"

I arched my brow and scrunched my nose. "You're dating him?"

"No, we're not dating."

Deciding to forget about it, I shook it off. "You have a kid you're watching tonight," I called to Blaise. "Don't be a dick to her, or I'll kill you. She's my sister." I turned back to Vera. "This will be the last time. I promise."

After a couple moments, she sighed and nodded to Ana. "Come on, Ana."

I picked Ana out of the backseat and kissed her cheek. "Please, be good for her. I have some things to take care of. I'll take you back over to Mama's as soon as things get better. She's sick."

"Mama's sick?" Ana asked, eyes wide.

"Yes," I whispered. "Sick. Now, will you be good?"

After wiping her cheeks with the backs of her hands, she nodded. "Okay."

Once I kissed her once more, I hurried back to my car and pulled out of the driveway, driving around the block and parking under some flickering streetlights. I pulled out my phone, everything suddenly hitting me hard, and stared at Imani's contact, wanting so badly to see her right now.

And so, I pushed away all those thoughts that said I didn't need anything from anyone, and I called her because I wanted something from Imani, and it was more than what I had been giving her. It was more than sex.

For the first time, I realized that I wanted her to love me.

Chapter One Hundred Eighteen

IMANI

"**W**hat the hell is he doing here?" João asked, sliding into the backseat behind Landon.

I pulled off the curb in the middle of nowhere—because he hadn't wanted me to meet him at his house, where he had brought Ana earlier—and merged back onto the main road. "Did you want to spend another date night with me, João? How cute."

João rolled his eyes and pulled a pack of cigarettes out of his pocket, lighting one up and puffing on it. "I don't fucking like you that much." He glared out the window, jaw twitching, as if he wanted to say more but refused. "Get it out of your head."

Ignoring him, I continued to drive aimlessly through Redwood.

"How's Ana?" I asked, glancing in the rearview mirror at João. "Is she safe?"

"She's with Vera," João said.

"Vera?"

"Vera Rodriguez. Nerd. Hangs out with Maddie Weber," João said, turning on his phone, sliding it into his pocket, then glancing up at me through the mirror. "Don't all you nerds know each other?"

I narrowed my eyes. "Just because we're smart doesn't mean we hang out. And besides, I'm not a nerd." I looked over at Landon. "Am I?"

"You're kinda a nerd," Landon said. "You and Allie love Biology."

"Yeah, but I also like you guys. What does that say about me?"

"That you're both nerdy and a fucking idiot for wanting to hang out with a bunch of thugs," João said.

I rolled my eyes.

"Where are we going?" he asked, pulling the cigarette out of his mouth.

I turned onto Pierce Road. "To pick up Kai. I thought we could spend tonight together."

João nearly snorted in the backseat and shook his head, as if he couldn't believe me.

I stopped in front of Kai's house and parked the car, turning to face João. "Why do you always have a problem with me?"

Jaw twitching again, João stared at me for a couple moments, his gaze flickering to my lips for the briefest moment. I almost didn't think I had seen it. But I had. I pressed my thighs together and turned back toward the steering wheel.

So, that was why he had wanted me to come over. He wanted sex.

Instead of entertaining him anymore, I picked up my phone and texted Kai.

Me: Get off your computer.

Me: Come hang with us.

A couple moments later, Kai emerged from his back door and walked into the driveway, holding up his hand to block his eyes from the headlights. He walked to the opposite side of the car and slid into the backseat beside João.

"What are you doing here?" Kai asked.

"We're getting ice cream," I said. It seemed like all that had happened lately was drama, and I wanted one drama-free night with the Poison boys before this town turned to hell. They were planning on fucking with Principal Vaughn tonight. "I wanted to hang out with you guys."

"It's, like, twenty degrees outside," Kai said. "You want ice cream."

"I want you guys not to violently kill people, but that's too hard to obtain," I said, cutting my gaze to him. That image he had sent me the other day was still burned in my memory. "So, ice cream it is."

Once I pulled into the ice cream parlor parking lot, all three boys decided that it was *too cold* to get out. So, I marched up to the counter myself and ordered four cones for us. After I did, I slipped back into the car and handed each of them a cone. Then, I took my ice cream in one hand and turned the car on with the other.

"Ana is going to need more medication soon," João said, lips pulled into a tight line as he stared out the backseat window. We weren't going anywhere specific, just driving through great ol' Redwood because there was nothing better to do in this shitty town. "We'll go this weekend."

I licked the strawberry ice cream, so it wouldn't drip all over my leather seat and headed toward the Overlook. I didn't want any part in stealing from a pharmacy or beating up poor Akio, so I changed the subject. "Did you have time to go through the list of people that—Akio —" I started, but then caught myself because I didn't want him to know where I had gotten it from. "That I gave you?"

"*He* got it for *you*?" Kai asked, teeth gritted.

I suppressed an eye roll, though I so desperately wanted to give him one. I got it, okay? He hated Akio for what Akio's parents had done to his parents and now for what they had done to me too, but Akio wasn't to blame. It even seemed like Akio feared his own parents.

"So?" I asked João. "Did you?"

"Fuck no," João groaned. "We've been so fucking busy lately."

"Have any of you heard from Allie either?" I asked, gnawing on the inside of my cheek.

A bunch of mumbles rang out through the car. I tightened my hand on the steering wheel as we came to a stoplight and glanced over my messages with her. I wanted to see how she was doing after what had happened, but she hasn't responded to me.

Which was unusual.

"She hasn't answered my messages."

I glanced into the rearview mirror to see Kai tense, and then I gritted my teeth. What the fucking hell was his thing with her? He had told me not to worry about her, and then he got tense and nervous when I mentioned that she hadn't responded to me.

"Do you know where she is, Kai?" I asked blankly, tired of this feeling.

"No," Kai said, licking his ice cream. "I don't keep tabs on her like I do with you."

"But you do keep up with her whereabouts."

Everyone in the car got quiet, including João and his loud mouth. I decided to drop it because we were having a good time and continued driving to the Overlook, trying to lighten the heavy conversation with some music or bad dad jokes that Dad always cracked.

"Shit," Landon said, melted ice cream running down his fingers. "Did we get napkins?"

"There should be some in the glove compartment."

Landon opened the compartment. "What the hell is this?"

I glanced over at him and saw the two guns—one from that man who had tried to kill me and another from Akio—sitting in the glove box because I hadn't remembered to remove them. My eyes widened slightly, and I pulled to the side of the road at the Overlook, pulling out the napkins and slamming the glove box shut.

"Don't worry about it!" I said, cheeks flaming.

Landon looked over his shoulder at Kai. "Did you give her a fucking gun?"

"They're not mine," Kai said, licking the chocolate off his fingers.

"Don't you fucking look at me either," João said to Landon, biting the ice cream like any sane psychopath would. "I wouldn't give her shit. She doesn't even know how to use it. She'd probably shoot herself by accident."

"Where'd you get the guns from?" Landon asked.

I chewed on the inside of my cheek. "Nobody. They're mine."

João and Kai burst out into a fit of laughter in the backseat while Landon waited impatiently for me to answer him. It might've been his idea to get me involved with Poison, but he never really liked the thought of me becoming like any of them.

"Those are *your* guns?" João asked, chuckling softly.

"Yeah, they are." I raised my eyebrows in the rearview mirror. "They are mine now."

"You don't even know how to use the thing," Kai asked. "Do you?"

"Whose are they?" Landon asked again.

After blowing out a soft sigh, I glanced over at him and reopened the glove box. "The man who tried to kill me. And this one"—I picked up the other gun that felt like it was still heavily loaded—"is Akio's. He was in too much shock after he shot the guy to even hold the gun straight."

"I'll teach you how to shoot it," Kai said to me. "Head back to my place."

"Where are you going to teach me? Don't I need to go to a shooting range or something?" I asked, taking the last bite of the cone and wiping my fingers with a napkin. "It's too cold to practice outside."

"You just ate ice cream," João said. "What do you care about the cold?"

"Do *you* have dry skin?" I asked him before answering the question myself. "No, you don't, so shut your mouth. I'm not practicing anything outside." And truthfully, I would rather not learn how to shoot a gun at all.

João was right. I would probably end up accidentally shooting myself.

"I have a range inside," Kai said.

"You what?!" I asked, my eyes bugging out of my head.

I'd seen the weapons, but a range too? Wasn't that the tiniest bit excessive? Hell, I was just looking for a reason or an excuse, some way to get out of this. But I didn't have any good excuse for not wanting to practice or for still having the guns in my car.

Honestly, part of me believed that I had intentionally left them there.

Maybe ... I wanted to be able to protect myself from anyone who might try to kill me.

No matter what the guys said, I was part of Poison now. I would have a target on my back for even the smallest of things. It didn't matter who my parents were or how much money I had. Poison had enemies.

Enemies who wanted to kill me.

Chapter One Hundred Nineteen

IMANI

Kai was a sadist.

That was the only conclusion I had thought up with all this evidence. First, he was the quiet type, the type nobody would suspect had tons upon tons of loaded guns and sharp weapons in his house. Now, I'd found out that he had a fucking shooting range that he had been hiding all this time.

Not only that, but he also had some targets that he took off the walls where all the bullet holes were right in the damn center. A perfect fucking shot. It was ... terrifying, to say the absolute least. But something about him was ...

I glanced over at him as he loaded one of the guns from my car and gnawed on the inside of my lips. Something about him was irresistible. On the outside, he was quiet and caring. But deep down, something sinister lurked.

"Take the gun and aim at the target," he said, walking over to me.

Landon and João stood on the other side of the room, big arms crossed over their chest, both watching me intensely. This was what I had wanted for such a long time, and I was finally getting it, so why the hell was I so ... nervous?

João gave me that look that told me he didn't think I would be able to do it. So, to spite him, I grabbed the gun from Kai's hand and held it in my hand the way that I had the other night.

After swallowing hard, I stepped toward the target and aimed the gun, tilting my head down slightly to line up the sight with the middle circle—whatever it was called. My finger hovered over the trigger, but my hand started to shake.

I had never shot a gun before. Hell, I'd barely hurt anyone before.

How could I shoot someone even if I needed to protect myself? How could I potentially end someone's life? Once I did, they would never take another breath, never live another moment, never make another memory.

"Some people don't deserve to make another memory," Kai said.

And I realized that I had been talking out loud, expressing all my fears to the three baddest and most cutthroat thugs in all of Redwood, baring my soul like I had been begging them to do for so long.

"If you don't know how to protect yourself, then *you* won't be making any more memories," Kai said, stepping closer to me and eyeing the gun. "Now, aim and shoot, Imani. Don't think about it."

My heart raced. "I ..." I swallowed hard again. "I don't think I can."

Instead of rolling his eyes like João did—which I returned with a glare—Kai moved closer to *help* me. He placed one hand on my hip to steady me. I inhaled sharply, the feel of his fingers stretched across the front of my stomach making me tingle in places it really shouldn't while I held a weapon that could kill.

"Relax," he murmured into my ear.

After I blew out an unsteady breath, Kai grasped my other hip and stepped closer to me, the front of his pants rubbing against the back of mine, his bulge right between my jean-covered asscheeks, his warm breath fanning my neck.

"I said to relax," he whispered, voice gruff.

"I can't," I admitted, swallowing and tightening my grasp on the gun. "Not with you behind me like this."

From my hip to my waist, around my breast and down my arm, one hand traveled up the side of my body slowly. I stared at the target and took another breath, heart pounding inside my chest quickly. He moved my arm up slightly to aim the gun more accurately, then placed his pointer finger over mine.

"Are you ready?" he asked me, fingers strumming against my hips.

"No," I whispered.

"Three."

"Kai, I don't know if—"

"Two."

"But I can't—"

"One."

Before I could finish my sentence, he pulled our fingers back on the trigger. I squeezed my eyes closed. The bullet shot one way, and I flew back against Kai in the other direction, my back against his taut chest and his arms wrapped tightly around me so I wouldn't fall to the ground.

"Damn, Imani," João said. "It has a recoil, but not that bad."

Kai ushered me to my feet, his body flush against mine again. He lifted my arm to shoot it at the target again, his nose buried against the crook of my neck. "You're going to do it again, and again, and again until it's second nature to you."

"But, Kai, I—"

He pulled my index finger back and helped me shoot the gun. I inhaled sharply, regaining my balance quicker this time, though I still stumbled back a couple inches. Like he had done the first time, Kai lifted my arm again and positioned my hips steady.

"Again, Imani," he whispered into my ear, his voice low and sultry.

I grasped the gun in both my hands and aimed it at the target. Kai's hand slipped from my arm to around my waist, his fingers digging into the front of my hips. I took a steady breath, aimed it straighter, and pulled the trigger.

My breath caught in my throat as the bullet whizzed through the air and pierced the target. Kai slipped his fingers further south, right where my hips met my thighs, and pulled himself closer until I could feel the tightness of his pants against mine.

"This turns you on," I whispered, glancing over at the other guys.

"The last time I had you here alone, you were tied to my bed and coming all over my sheets." Kai drew his nose up the side of my neck and wrapped one hand around the front of my throat. "Seeing you like this makes me want to do it again."

I inhaled sharply and pressed my thighs together. "You should."

He looked up briefly at João and Landon. "Next time when I get you alone."

"Why not with them?" I asked, aiming the gun at the target.

"Because, Imani," he said, gently biting down on my neck, "the only name I want to hear you moaning on a ball gag is mine."

Chapter One Hundred Twenty

KAI

After Imani left, I reopened the weapons room and flicked on the light, pulling out a couple duffel bags and bins that could hold whatever kind of weapon the boys wanted to use on Vaughn tonight.

"Take your pick, then throw it into the bag," I said, walking down the aisle of guns and weaponry, sorting through the long and sharp swords and machetes.

"We're cutting off his dick, compliments of Imani," Landon said, glancing over my shoulder. "Make sure to take one of those machetes to do it. We can feed it to him when we're finished with him."

Once we gathered all the shit, we piled into João's car to finally get back at Principal Vaughn. After we dropped our stuff at the abandoned warehouse where we did all our dirty work, I grabbed some rope and tape from the bag and walked back to the car, where João had the window cracked. A cloud of smoke drifted out of the car as João flicked a cigarette out of it.

I slipped into the backseat, my fingers trailing over the coarse rope the way they had before I tied up Imani in my bedroom. Fuck, I couldn't wait until I got her alone again. All I had been imagining was gagging her with my cock, forcing her legs apart, and rubbing her pussy until she was a crying, slobbering, sopping mess for me, her tiny moans escaping her tight little throat.

João pulled into the Redwood rich neighborhood and turned on to a secured street.

Principal Vaughn hadn't always lived in this ritzy neighborhood. Before he and the police chief had paid us to burn down the old, shitty high school for the poor kids and force blame on the rich kids, he had lived in the ghetto with us.

But along with the police chief, Vaughn knew how to fucking exploit everyone.

"Thank fuck that security in this neighborhood is shit," João said, driving right past the sleeping guard and into the gated community that housed more pieces of Redwood rich trash. He cut the lights and pulled up to a grand house that had all its lights on.

Just as we were about to slip out of the car, someone opened the front door. A cheerleader—one of Nicole's friends—walked out the door, adjusting her top and fixing her wild, messy hair.

We stopped and watched her collapse in her car, head dropping against the steering wheel for a moment. Then, she took a deep breath, wiped something off her cheeks, and backed out of his driveway.

After she drove down the road, we waited for fifteen more minutes. I stared into Vaughn's house and tried to piece together why one of the cheerleaders would be here this late at night with him.

He might've had money, but she already had a Lamborghini.

Whatever the reason that she had been here ... it wasn't for the money.

"It's now or never," João said, leaning his forearm onto the steering wheel and glancing through the windshield at the Vaughn's house. "Let's kill this fucking bastard. I'm fucking finished with all his shit that he puts us through."

After moving out of the car, Landon and I snuck around the back of the house while João straight-up walked through the front door like he didn't give a fuck about Vaughn catching him. If we wanted to capture him, we would have to be a little less obvious about it though.

Landon wiggled the back door that led from the house to the hot tub, which was running, and opened it with ease, the door swinging open without even the slightest creak. We walked into the house slowly and met João in the foyer.

"That bitch is upstairs," João whispered, nodding to the stairs, then to the hallway to our left. "But his bedroom is that way. If he's stooped so low to fuck a couple chicks from Redwood, then we should give him a nice, lovely surprise. Don't you think, boys?"

I grasped the rope in my hand, glanced up the steps, then followed João and Landon down the hallway and toward the master bedroom. Lying on the bed was a bottle of lube, a package of Viagra, and two condoms filled with cum.

João raised his brows in disgust and tossed me the Viagra. "We'll use that on him later."

Someone padded down the hallway. I slipped into a dark corner of the room while Landon moved behind the door. And João ... he lay right on the bed next to the condoms with a smirk on his face.

João leaned against the headboard with his legs crossed at the ankles. When Vaughn walked into the room, João smiled at him.

"What the hell are you doing—"

Before he could finish his sentence, Landon stepped out behind his door and wrapped his arms around Vaughn's neck in a rear naked choke. Vaughn threw his body in every direction, desperate to escape, but Landon locked the choke on tighter until Vaughn stilled.

Once Landon tossed his unconscious body onto the bed, I grabbed the rope and tied his ass up, making his arms and legs immovable so he wouldn't be able to escape. Some people might've thought that they could escape with the use of their money.

But not Vaughn. Not now. Not after what he had done to Allie.

"He's good?" João asked from the other side of the room, snooping through Vaughn's dresser. He looked over his shoulder at Vaughn, then nodded to Landon. "Bring him to the car. We're heading out."

After departing, I glanced around to make sure nobody watched from a distance, then shut and locked the front door. Tonight was Vaughn's last night on this earth, and we planned to give him a helluva good time. A time that all of Redwood would remember forever.

Chapter One Hundred Twenty-One

KAI

After we reached the abandoned warehouse, I grabbed Principal Vaughn by his thinning, graying hair and dragged him into the building. He had woken up sometime on the ride over here with his mouth duct-taped shut and his appendages tied behind his back.

João flicked on the lights and propped the door open for us. I threw Vaughn into the room and sat him in a metal chair. Landon grabbed a knife from our bag of weapons and slid it across the T-shirt Vaughn had on.

Once he was stripped naked, I set up a camera in front of him and pulled on a black ski mask with the others, so our entire bodies were covered in clothing and so nobody would even be able to figure out who killed the man videoing underage girls and boys at Redwood.

"Vaughn likes to play with his students," João said, tossing me my gun from the bag and grabbing a full water bottle from the fridge we had here. He walked over to Vaughn and pulled back his head by his hair. "Why don't we have a bit of fun with him?"

Vaughn screamed through the duct tape, furiously shaking his head.

João ripped the tape off his mouth and stuck the barrel of his gun between his lips. Vaughn's eyes widened, his body trembling and tears streaming down his face. He continued to shake his head, mumbling something on the gun.

"Shut the fuck up and sit still," João said, holding the bottle up to his face, pressing his gun even farther into his mouth until it hit the back of his throat. "If this falls, we fuck you up. You understand me, bitch?"

After Vaughn nodded, João placed the water bottle on his head as a target and slowly pulled the gun out of his mouth.

João walked back over to us and nodded. "Go ahead. Show that fucker what it feels like to be treated like trash."

When I aimed the gun at the water bottle, Vaughn shook with so much fear that it fell off his head and onto the ground beside him. Knowing that he had done something wrong, he widened his eyes, and he shook his head and started apologizing profusely.

João stormed up to him and shoved the gun into his waistband, then pulled out a knife from his pocket. João cut his right ear off, not giving a fuck about the blood spurting everywhere, and placed the bottle back on his head.

"Next time you fucking drop that shit, it's your other ear."

Vaughn pissed himself, covering himself in pee and blood and tears. After João walked back behind the camera, I aimed the gun again and pulled the trigger, shooting a hole straight through the bottle. It broke, and all the water dumped over his head, covering him.

Landon handed João a couple trophies. "Found these at his house. They gotta mean something to him. Why don't we do these next?"

João put a trophy on his head and shot it off, breaking it right in half. Vaughn screamed every time we shot another trophy, another bottle, anything off his stupid fucking head, like he thought he deserved better.

After we exhausted all the trophies and bottles from the fridge, Landon walked over to the bag of weapons and grabbed a knife. "We're going to chop your fucking head off," Landon said.

Vaughn wailed, snot dripping from his nose and down onto his lips, tears flowing from his eyes. He shook his head from side to side, letting out ugly fucking cries, like so many girls would do when they found out what he had done to them. "Please, no! I'm sorry! I'm sorry!"

"Turn on the video," Landon said.

I held my phone up to Vaughn's face and turned on one of the many videos he had on his computer of the girls' and boys' locker rooms. Vaughn slowly stopped wailing and sniffled, watching the videos like he was addicted.

And as we expected ...

"That fucker's hard," João said, shaking his head. He turned toward our recording camera and pointed to Vaughn. "Redwood Academy, your principal is fucking hard to the hundreds of recordings of Redwood students naked in the locker rooms. Is this who you think is fit to lead your school? Is this who we're giving thousands of dollars to every year? Is this someone you think deserves to live?"

Landon walked over to Vaughn and sliced the knife right across the head of Vaughn's hard dick. Blood spurted everywhere. Vaughn's sad and severed dick dropped to the ground as he screamed out in pain.

Instead of ending it there, Landon picked the fucking thing up and stuffed it into his mouth. "You can thank Imani Abara for that, asshole," Landon whispered so it couldn't be heard over the camera we had recording. He looked over his shoulder at me and nodded to the duct tape. "Hand me the tape. I want this fucker to eat his own dick."

After tossing him the duct tape, Landon forced his mouth closed. With his mouth stuffed full, Vaughn stared up at us with tears in his eyes. His cheeks were flushed, and if he didn't swallow his dick soon, then he'd kill himself with it.

A moment passed, and Vaughn swallowed, a bulge traveling down his throat.

"That's not the only punishment that the Redwood will receive for their sins," João continued at the camera. "Over the course of the next few months, all the lies, all the secrets, all the scandals that have run this town will be exposed. Nobody is safe from the truth." João put his hand over the camera and placed his mouth right next to the microphone. "Welcome to the end, Redwood."

Once I turned off the camera, João pulled off his ski mask and threw it down, then rolled up his sleeves. After slamming his fist straight into the side of his face over and over, João spit at Vaughn.

"Cut off his fucking head," João said, glancing in the bag of weapons. "And make it fucking brutal." After a couple moments, he threw the bag to the ground. "Don't use any of this shit. We have a chain saw in the back room."

He disappeared into the back room for a couple moments, then reappeared with a saw and handed it to me. I grabbed it from him, walked behind Vaughn, and hit the power button. I had never killed someone this way, but the Redwood rich deserved it.

We weren't fucking around anymore. This proved that Poison meant business, that we would burn this town to the fucking ground. With a final cut, the last few arteries and skin snapped apart, and Vaughn's head fell to the ground at our feet.

Chapter One Hundred Twenty-Two

IMANI

Surprisingly, when I had gotten home from Kai's last night, Mom hadn't said two words to me.

She had stayed up to see if I got home all right, but after a, "Good night," she went right to bed. I hadn't pushed it because I didn't want to argue.

But the next day, I needed answers to my burning questions. I sat at the kitchen island on my computer and glanced at Mom, who made her coffee with her hair pulled into a bonnet this late in the morning, which was unusual.

Her eyes were still black, the bruises on her lip still prominent.

"Can we talk about Akio's family?" I asked her.

"No."

"Yes, we need to," I said. "Are they the mob?"

"Don't worry about them," she said quickly, blowing on her hot coffee and refusing to look up at me. Instead, she took a seat across from me and swallowed hard. "We took care of them for you."

"Took care, as in killed?"

"No! Imani, who do you think we are?"

"I don't know, Mom. Who are you? Why do you have connections to the Redwood mob? A couple days ago, I didn't even think there was a mob in this town!" I shook my head, still unable to believe it. "And how the hell are you involved in it?"

After a couple moments, she looked around, as if someone were listening, and leaned closer to me. "They helped fund your father's engineering business when he first started," she admitted. "We owe them everything. Even after we paid the debt, they won't stop coming. They demand more money, more money, more money. It never stops."

"So, you invite them over more often?" I asked, brows drawn together.

"We have to, Imani." Mom's voice was firm. "We don't have a choice. Just *never* do something like that again. You cannot do anything to them or talk back to them. And be careful around Akio. He seems like a nice boy, but all of them do until they show you their true colors."

I guessed that I wouldn't tell Mom that Akio had shot a man for me ...

We fell into an awkward silence because I didn't know what to say to her, and then I went back to what I had been researching on my MacBook. I wanted to talk to her, to be able to have a good relationship with her again, but ... God, I didn't know if that was even possible.

But it couldn't hurt to try, right?

"Do you think you could help me?" I asked Mom.

"With what, sweetheart?"

"Something for the"—I paused—"for the boys."

"For the Poison boys?" she asked me with her jaw clenched, yet it wasn't as taut as it had been every other time that I hung out with them or talked about those three boys who must've killed our principal by now.

I hoped that they had gotten rid of his body, so nobody could trace his death back to them.

"Yes, it's for them."

Mom stared intensely at me, but I didn't back down like I would've done before I met them. I stared back at her with the same amount of intensity, so she knew that I was serious about this. Each of those boys meant something to me.

After a couple moments, Mom finally sighed and pulled out the seat beside me, sitting and glancing over my shoulder at my MacBook screen. She furrowed her brows. "Why are you looking for insurance?"

I gnawed on the inside of my cheek, chest tightening. "I don't think they're on insurance. I mean, I assume that they're not."

Landon's family was fucked. Kai didn't have a family. And João's mother had unpaid hospital bills that were way more expensive than the bill I had gotten a couple years ago when I broke my wrist.

Granted, it wasn't the same thing, but ... her bills were in the tens of thousands of dollars.

Insurance would've covered some of that, wouldn't it have?

"They have so many bills, especially João with his mother and Ana ..." I sucked in a sharp breath, unsure if I should tell her about Ana's sickness. But I needed to tell her something to get her to help me. "His sister is sick. Really sick."

"I know," Mom said.

"You know?" I asked, brows furrowing.

"I wasn't going to let my daughter run off with those three all night without figuring out who they and their families were. I know more than you think about those three boys," she said. "And still, I let you run off with them."

"Because you know that they'd protect me," I said. "You've seen them do it."

Mom stayed quiet. "What do they mean to you?"

I gnawed on the inside of my cheek, knowing that if I told her I had a thing for *all* of them, she wouldn't understand. I didn't even know how she'd react. Her daughter was a slut for Poison. I couldn't stop myself.

"I don't understand this," I whispered, glancing nervously back at the screen. I had been researching hundreds of insurances that they could get on. "They have their own problems that they're taking care of. They don't have time to look through all this stuff, and the window where they can get insurance is closing at the beginning of December, isn't it?"

Mom parted her lips and pressed them back together, glancing from the screen to me. Suddenly, she pulled me into a hug and held me to her so tightly, tighter than she ever had. I hesitantly rubbed her back, unsure why she was now hugging me.

"You're so much better than me," she whispered when she pulled away. "Don't ever lose this about yourself."

"Do you know how I can sign them up? What kind of documents do they need?" I asked.

"I don't like them. I don't trust them. But ..." She gently grasped my chin and gave me a soft smile. "You're serious about helping them, aren't you?"

"Yes."

She grabbed a sticky note from her desk and scribbled a couple things on it, then handed it to me. "Tell them to gather these documents. I will bring you all to the mall this weekend and help them sign up at one of those stations advertising health care."

My eyes widened, surprised. "Really?"

"Yes."

I smiled and hugged her back. "Thank you."

After a couple moments, my phone buzzed on the table, and Allie's name popped up.

Allie: Football game starts in forty minutes. I know that we have so much shit going on, but I thought we could go to ... you know, relax for a bit? If you wanna go, can you pick me up?

Mom glanced at my message and gently nudged my back. "Go pick Allie up. Have fun. We'll talk more when you get home."

Chapter One Hundred Twenty-Three

IMANI

"Go Redwood!" Allie screamed beside me, grinning as Jace walked along the sidelines next to his coach and gave advice to the players. He was far too fucked up from his father to do anything other than watch tonight.

It was the first time I had seen her smile like that in a long time. So much shit had happened these past few days, and now that the principal was gone, we didn't have to worry about a thing. Poison would burn his body, and everything would return to normal.

"You're lucky," Akio said beside me, leaning in closer.

I hadn't invited him, but I wasn't going to shoo him away after he saved me.

"My mom hasn't said a word about you since the dinner. I expected her to"—he glanced over my shoulder at Allie cheering for our team—"to want me to kill you."

"My mom said to drop it," I said to him, making sure Allie didn't hear. I didn't want her to worry about me the way that I worried about her. She had been taking this whole Jace thing really badly lately. I nudged him. "But you know that I won't."

"It would be smart if you did," he said.

"Your mom nearly killed my parents! Have *you* killed anyone?" I whisper-yelled at him.

"No!" he said. "I would never do that. You know I wouldn't."

"Touchdown!" Allie shouted beside me, jumping up and down.

I gave Akio a look that said we'd talk about this later, and he excused himself to get some drinks and hot dogs for us at the stand down below. I turned back to the football game and jumped excitedly with Allie. She loved these games.

Carter, Redwood's most annoying quarterback, walked arrogantly back to the sidelines, tearing off his helmet after his first touchdown of the game. He threw Jace a smirk and grabbed his water bottle, saying a few words to Jace.

To me, it looked like Jace ignored it. But Allie stood next to me, gritting her teeth at him, like she wanted to tear that man-whore into two pieces. I didn't judge her for it either. Carter was the most annoying guy in all of Redwood, and there were *tons* of annoying assholes here.

"Let's go, Redwood!" Nicole, head cheerleader, shouted. "Woohoo!"

I inched closer to Allie to stay warm and glanced down at my phone. I had messaged Poison about five times since this morning, expecting a response, but nobody had gotten back to me yet. I'd even checked the police reports this morning and listened in on their calls to see if Poison had gotten picked up.

Nothing.

"Ugh," Allie said, crossing her arms and staring down at the field. "Why isn't Jace icing his eye? Your mom told him to the other night before we left."

A running back from the opposite team ran forty yards to the five-yard line before one of our defensive members tackled him. Jace sighed and glanced up at us. When he did, Allie gave him the stink eye and pointed to her face, as if to tell him to ice that swollen eye right this second.

After giving her his best smile, Jace grabbed an ice packet, waved it in the air, and placed it on his face like she wanted him to. Then, he turned back to the game and slowly watched the time run down before our rival team was about to score.

A buzzer rang throughout the stadium, the bright white lights on the scoreboard reading 14 to 6. The teams retreated to their sides of the field, packing up to head to the locker room for halftime, when the lights in the stadium turned off.

Every single one of them. Even the scoreboard.

Phones started buzzing uncontrollably and lighting up across the stands. I glanced down at mine, hoping it was the Poison boys, and watched a prerecorded multimedia message pop up onto the screen of Principal Vaughn sitting naked in the abandoned warehouse where Poison did their work.

Someone came over the intercom, using a voice enhancer to hide their true identity. But I knew who it was. The only people who would stir up any really bad trouble in Redwood—Poison. My three boys.

The video started with Vaughn trembling in fear as someone shot a bottle of water off his head, then a couple trophies. Then, one of the masked guys came on the screen and showed Vaughn a recording of the girls' and boys' locker rooms.

The entire stadium erupted into whispers.

"Redwood Academy, your principal is jerking off to the hundreds of recordings of Redwood students naked in the locker rooms. Is this who you think is fit to lead your school? Is this who we're giving thousands of dollars to every year? Is this someone you think deserves to live?"

Then, Landon—it had to be Landon—walked into the frame with a knife and cut Vaughn's dick clean off his body and stuffed it into his mouth. I watched him put duct tape over his lips, and then Vaughn swallowed his own cock.

I gagged and had the urge to throw up my lunch.

"That's not the only punishment that the Redwood rich will receive for their sins," João said over the speakers. I could tell it was him by the simple way he talked even though his voice was changed. "Over the course of the next few months, all the lies, all the secrets, all the scandals that have run this town will be exposed. Nobody is safe from the truth."

That's when the visual recording stopped, and the lights turned back on. Suddenly, from somewhere in the bleachers, a ball was hurled through the air and toward the field. The ball bounced once, then twice, and then I realized that it wasn't a ball at all, but Principal Vaughn's head.

Screams erupted through the crowd.

"Welcome to the end, Redwood," João said.

Chapter One Hundred Twenty-Four

IMANI

The cheerleaders screamed around us, and the football players rushed off the field through a back entrance. Vaughn's head lay feet from Jace, blood splattered across the white field lines. Allie grabbed my hand and pulled me toward the exit with the herd of students rushing down the bleachers.

Everything turned to pure chaos within mere moments, the crowd erupting into screams and shouts. Red and blue police lights turned on around the field. When Poison had told me they would kill the principal, I had not expected *this*.

What were they thinking?!

People started rushing down the bleachers and knocking people out of the way.

"Jace!" Allie screamed, but with the people around us, we couldn't see shit. Once we finally made it down to the solid ground, Allie stopped. "JACE!"

More and more people pushed to get the fuck out of here.

I glanced around nervously, knowing that we had to move or these animals would trample us. So, I grabbed Allie and pushed her to the exit along with the group. "We have to go. Jace will get out of here safely."

Everything happened so quickly. Students shoved us until we

reached the sidewalks. Allie stood beside me, standing on her tiptoes to try to see above the crowd. She was so worried about Jace, and I was so fucking worried about the three dumbasses who had recorded themselves torturing our principal.

If someone linked this back to them ... I might lose them forever.

Forever, forever.

What if they went to jail? To prison? What if I never got to see them again?

Cops stood around us, trying to calm people down and make sure they were safe, trying to be *nice*. But everyone knew that cops in Redwood were never nice; they were always corrupt. Now, they were scared that they'd be next to be exposed and killed by Poison.

"Come on, Imani. We need to go," Allie said.

But suddenly, it all hit me at once. Poison had done more than kill Principal Vaughn. I'd expected it to be a quiet death, something that I wouldn't have to witness. But Vaughn's head was sitting on the football field, and they'd had fun in that video.

They'd loved torturing him.

"Imani," Allie said again, but she sounded so distant.

Tears burst from my eyes. I couldn't stop them, no matter how hard I tried. I didn't know why I was crying, but ... I hadn't expected this. My heart was aching. My mind buzzing with so many fears of losing them and fears that they had enjoyed that a little too much.

I went to wipe my tears away, but I couldn't even pull my arms up enough to reach my cheeks with my trembling hands. I glanced at Allie and mouthed her name, but no words came out. Pain shot through me. I should've expected this and nothing less.

Allie wrapped her arms around me like I had done to her countless times and stroked my back. "Imani, we have to go. We don't know what else they have planned."

She ushered me forward, but I knew that if Poison had anything else planned, then they wouldn't have let me come to the game.

Would they have?

Maybe João was trying to scare me away again. Maybe he wanted to test me to see how I'd react. But how the hell was I supposed to react when I just saw our principal's head fly across the bleachers and onto the field?

I shook my head, still unmoving. "They-they killed someone!"

Allie swallowed hard and continued to push me forward with the other students and parents, so we wouldn't be trampled by the growing crowd. "That's what they do," Allie said, careful not to speak their name out loud and in public.

While everyone had to have known that this was their doing, I didn't want to incriminate them.

I wrapped my arms around her as we kept up with the students. "I knew they were bad news, but ... I-I-I didn't think that they'd do anything like this. They took a life and put it on display like it was ... *nothing.*"

We made it farther onto the sidewalks, where everyone was dispersing onto the streets and speeding out of the parking lots.

"How many times do you think they've done that before? Like that violently? Once? Twice? Hundreds of times? Did you see how much fun they were having?"

After scanning the crowd, she turned back to me. "I don't know, Imani," she answered.

I shook my head and turned back to the stadium, anger shooting through me. "I'm going to scream at them for this! How do you just kill someone and throw their fucking head onto the field during a football game?! You have to be fucking insane."

They were nuts! Psycho! Fucking crazy!

Allie grabbed me by the wrist and dug her heels into the ground to *try* to stop me from barreling back to find them. They had to be here somewhere. I knew they were watching.

"If you go back in there, the cops will question you and pressure you to give up any information you have on them. You don't want to get them sent to jail, do you?" she asked me.

"They chopped someone's head off and showed the entire school, Allie. Doesn't that scare you?!" I asked, continuing back to the gated entrance to the football field.

A couple cops looked over at us, giving us *that look* all cops gave when they thought that they had something stuffed in the bag, thought that they could coerce an innocent person into lying or spilling more than the truth to prove their own beliefs.

"They won't even be inside," she argued. "They're probably watching from a distance."

Knowing she was right, I stopped. "Watching from a distance ..." I whispered.

When I turned back around, João's black car drove by us, almost as if on cue. Though the windows were tinted, I didn't miss the small smirk I saw from the driver's window from João when they drove under a streetlight.

As the car drove down the street, I went to chase after it like a madwoman.

Allie captured my wrist again and dragged me down the street toward the bad side of Redwood. "There is no point in chasing them. They're already gone."

Allie scanned the field again for any sign of Jace and frowned. I hurried down the sidewalk and inched closer to her. It had to be below freezing out here at the moment—my curls had fucking icicles hanging off them.

We had to get to my car, but the students were getting rowdy in the student parking lot. It would be dangerous—too dangerous. Suddenly, a car pulled up to the sidewalk a few feet ahead, and whoever was driving rolled down the passenger window.

"Get in," Nicole, head cheerleader, said to us. "You'll freeze out there."

Allie's eyes widened slightly.

What was she doing here, and why was she offering us help? I'd expected her to be the one to add to the drama, not help out two students caught in the middle of it.

"We're not going anywhere with you," Allie said, hurrying down the sidewalk.

Nicole sped up enough to catch up. "Get in, Allie. Jace is looking for you."

After we glanced at the student section one last time, listening to the hollering and car alarms going off, Allie opened Nicole's car door, and I hoped that I didn't regret this.

"This doesn't make us friends," Allie said.

"Fine by me," Nicole said, driving off once we were both in the car. "Poison's place it is."

Chapter One Hundred Twenty-Five

JOÃO

An hour after the game, I stood with Jace, Landon, and Kai in Landon's basement, waiting for the girls to show up because fiery Imani was bound to run in here with that mouth of hers, shouting about how we shouldn't have done that.

On cue, the basement door swung open, and a furious Imani barreled down the stairs. "What the hell was that?!" she screamed at me.

I leaned against the wall with a cigarette between my lips.

"Are you guys dumb?!" She shoved me, her hands against my chest. "You are the stupidest fucking people I've met!"

I grasped her hands and shoved them off. "Don't push me."

Because her hands felt too good on me.

Imani continued to scream at all three of us now. "What's wrong with you guys?! You can be thrown in jail. You can't just send out a video to everyone around! Then throw a head into a football game?! Are you serious?!"

"Relax, Imani," I said, knowing that she wouldn't be able to handle this.

She always acted tough, but she would never do shit like this.

"Nobody is going to jail," Landon continued, taking the pack of cigarettes from me and lighting one up. He puffed on it once and blew out a puff of smoke, slumping down on the couch and sighing. "Nothing will happen."

"You don't know that!" Imani continued.

Kai placed a hand on her shoulder and glanced at Allie for the quickest second, probably to make sure she was okay. Jace moved closer to Allie and brought her to the couch beside Landon, smoking.

"We've done this before," Kai said, trying to soothe Imani, though he usually wasn't one with many words. But with Imani, he had changed, and I didn't like it. "We know how to clean shit up and hide the evidence. Don't make a big deal out of it."

Imani widened her eyes, shook her head, and backed away. "All three of you are insane." She looked at Allie and Nicole. "Why aren't you both freaking out more?! We just saw our principal's head in the middle of the football field."

Instead of freaking out like I'd thought she would, Allie blew out a long breath and shrugged her shoulders. She looked tired, and I didn't blame her. Her principal had jerked off to her and her stepbrother fucking in the boys' locker room.

"You guys can't just—"

"Calm the fuck down!" I shouted, tired of hearing Imani's mouth run, fury laced in my words. I put out my cigarette. "You know what we did when you got involved with us. I gave you a chance to leave. You didn't. So, sit down and keep your mouth shut before someone hears you screaming at us for what happened."

Imani marched right up to me and smacked me right across the face, leaving a big fat red handprint on my cheek. I clenched my jaw and narrowed my eyes at her as she muttered something under her breath.

"You want to say that a little louder?" I asked her, annoyed as fuck now because we had done exactly what she wanted—we had cut off his dick and killed the man. "Because you're one more mistake away from me teaching you a fucking lesson on how to behave, Imani."

Imani turned on her heel, walked to the other side of the room, and sat against the wall. "Fuck you, João. I hate you."

When the room went quiet, Nicole turned to Jace. "Well ..." She cleared her throat and adjusted herself in the seat beside Allie.

Allie sat up taller and narrowed her eyes at Nicole.

"My dad is going to blame you for letting those files leak," Nicole said to Jace. "I know he will. He knows that you were the only person in my house the weekend all the files got stolen."

Allie looked up at Jace and frowned. "Is that true?"

Jace tensed. "Allie, you know that I went—"

Allie shook her head and looked back at Nicole. "He'll blame Jace?"

Nicole nodded, brows furrowed. "I know he will. He hates him."

Landon waved his hand dismissively. "Don't worry about the police chief. We're taking care of him next. He's the only person standing in the way of Redwood's fall. All the other police officers don't know shit about all the blackmail your father has been doing throughout the years."

Nicole teetered back and forth on the sofa, toying with the ends of her skirt. "And me?"

I rolled my eyes and shifted my glare from Nicole to Imani, addressing Nicole. "Piss us off, and you'll find out like this."

Imani glared back at me, her lips curled up in disgust. I clenched my jaw and balled my fists, knowing that if she didn't stop fucking staring at me like that, I would shove her back up those basement stairs and lock us both out in the cold to teach her a fucking lesson.

I hated the way she glared at me. I hated the way she made me feel. I had made it this far in life without feeling this way about a woman. I didn't need this shit now. I didn't need to feel this way about her.

But, fuck, I wanted to.

"We need to talk about what we're going to do about your father, Jace," Kai said, tapping his fingers on a side table. "Once Nicole's father is gone, it will be easy to put him in jail. Is that what you want? Or do you want him tortured and dead?"

Allie tensed beside Jace and looked up at him, waiting for his answer. He swallowed hard and looked away from her.

"Those are two different ball games," I said, finally pulling my gaze away from Imani—because the more I looked at her, the more guilt I felt for letting her go to the game tonight to see that. I sat across from Allie and Jace. "Your father has increased his security, which I'm sure you saw. It's difficult to get him alone. If you want him dead—"

"We'll talk about this later," Jace said, ending the discussion. "When the girls are gone."

We fell into silence again until Imani stood up and marched to the basement steps. "I'm not sitting here any longer. I'm going upstairs."

And before I could stop myself, I walked up the stairs behind her, taking two stairs at a time, and slammed the basement door closed behind us, grabbing her by the back of the neck and pulling her back to me. "You're not going anywhere."

Chapter One Hundred Twenty-Six

IMANI

With his hand wrapped tightly around the back of my neck, João shoved me toward Landon's parents' old bedroom on the second floor of his house. After pushing me into the room, he slammed the door closed and locked it behind us.

Warmth spread throughout my body. João wanted *to try* to teach me a lesson.

But it wouldn't work. Not this time. I couldn't get over the fact that, tonight, he'd let me watch our principal's head fly onto the football field during halftime and almost get trampled in the Redwood herd, nor could I believe that they were stupid enough to *record* themselves killing Vaughn.

Instead of bending me over the bed, like I'd thought he would, João shoved me down to my knees. Then, he grasped my jaw in one hand and undid the button on his jeans with the other. I stared up at him through wide eyes, not once glancing at his cock as he pulled it out.

"I fucking hate you," I said between gritted teeth.

"Why don't you shut the fuck up and use that fucking mouth to swallow my cock?" he said, pulling my mouth open and shoving himself into me. In his first thrust, he hit the back of my throat and made me gag.

I placed my hands on his knees, fingernails sinking into his knee, and stared up at him through watery eyes. He was trying to break me down, to submit to him and apologize, but I wasn't having any of it. He was going to have to try a lot harder than this.

While he ruthlessly fucked my throat, I opened my mouth wider to challenge him because I knew that it would make him even angrier. One hand wrapped around the front of my throat to feel himself thrusting inside me, and he placed his other hand on the back of my head, bobbing me.

Spit and drool rolled down my lips and chin. I dug my fingers even deeper into his leg muscle, refusing to give in to him now, refusing to back down. I fucking hated João, but I wasn't going to give him the satisfaction that he'd won, that he could overpower me.

So my spit and drool wouldn't ruin my top, I unbuttoned it and pulled it and my bra off my shoulders. As my throat gagged and squeaked for João every time he entered me, João smirked, then finally pulled out of me.

My entire chest and chin were covered in spit. I wiped my mouth with the back of my hand, then grabbed his cock to pull him back toward me. "If this is your way of trying to get me to give in to you, to stop being angry, you're not going to win."

When I captured the head of his cock between my lips and sucked again, he chuckled menacingly at me. "This is my way of showing you that you're a monster too, Imani. You claim to hate me so much, but you can't stop gagging on my dick. I've ruined you."

My eyes widened, and I pulled him out of me. "Wh-what?"

He pulled me up to my feet and bent me over the bed, one hand grasping my hair to hold my head against the mattress and the other pushing down my pants. He positioned himself at my entrance, the head of his cock teasing my sopping and aching pussy. In one thrust, he shoved himself all the way into me.

I moaned into the mattress, my legs trembling in total pleasure. While thrusting into me, he leaned over, so his upper body was against mine and his mouth was against my ear.

"I thought I was going to have to teach you a lesson, but you've taught yourself one." He pulled me up and toward a rusty mirror in the corner of the room. "You'll never hate me more than you love my cock being buried inside you."

While his cock pumped in and out of me, I stared into the mirror and clenched around him. The pressure rose in my core, and an undeniable warmth shot throughout my body. He dipped his head to my ear, his dark gaze on me, then ran his hands all over my body.

"These hands that are running all over your body have killed more people than you would ever believe," he growled into my ear. "They have been covered with blood of the Redwood rich for years now, and you're afraid of someone's head flying across the football field?"

And it was at that moment that I realized ... I didn't fear Poison. I feared that I liked this too much. I feared that Mom was right all those weeks ago; they'd turned me into being part of them. I feared that I loved the thought of these hands having killed bastards and assholes. I feared that I loved João, too, because I knew he'd break my heart.

Along with the rest of Poison, João might've killed and hurt people to no end. But my being with him right here and right now, with his hands wrapped around my neck, his teeth grazing against my throat, his cock buried deep inside me ... he had every chance to hurt me.

But he didn't, and he never had.

With his hand around my chin, he forced me to watch himself pump in and out of me through the rusty mirror. "Watch."

After shoving his fingers into my mouth and wetting them with my saliva, he rubbed them over my face, smearing the red *R* that Allie had drawn on my cheek before the football game and the eyeliner that I'd spent an hour on this morning.

"I don't care what you think of me," he snarled, "because I know what your pussy feels like whenever I'm fucking it. I know that your tight holes don't drip for anyone like they do for me. I know that when I shove my dick into you, you'll come all over me because you love the way I make you feel."

I gritted my teeth and clenched around him, unable to deny his words. Everything he had said was nothing but the truth—the truth that fucking stung because João was a monster who I couldn't stop thinking about, who I couldn't stop gravitating toward.

Pressure rose in my core. I squeezed my eyes shut, my toes curling against the cheap rug underneath my feet and my legs beginning to tremble uncontrollably. I grasped on to his forearms, desperately trying to still my body.

When I went to place my hands on the mirror, to grip something and steady myself, João pulled me out of reach of it. So all I was touching was him, all I could feel was him, all I could do was be in his control.

"Keep struggling, Imani," João growled, "because I fucking love it."

My entire body shook, my pussy aching. I threw my head back and let out another moan.

Moments ... I was fucking moments from releasing around him.

"The monster you're so terrified of is going to blow his fucking load into your tight cunt."

A body-trembling orgasm shot through me. My knees gave out, but João held me up and continued to pump into me until he grunted deeply into my ear, the sound shoving me over the edge again.

But that didn't stop the immense annoyance that I had for him or the fear I had of losing him.

Chapter One Hundred Twenty-Seven

JOÃO

"Will you stop fucking flipping out now?" I growled down at Imani.

With her curly hair in all different directions and her eyes wide, she lay on Landon's parents' bed in a daze. "I just ..." she whispered, peeling her gaze away from mine and pulling on her clothes. "I don't want any of you to go to jail for this."

"We won't go to jail."

She tugged on her jeans and buttoned them. "You don't know that."

I clenched my hands into tight fists by the door, annoyance rushing through me. I'd thought fucking her would relax us both, would show her that this was all fucking for her, but I guessed that hadn't been enough.

"We won't," I said.

"But what if you do, João?" she snapped, staring at me with just as much annoyance.

"We won't!" I said, raising my voice louder than expected.

"But—"

"Why does it matter so much to you?" I pushed. "Why do you care about us going to jail?"

When she parted her lips, my chest tightened. I couldn't help the thoughts racing through my head. This was the same way I'd felt the other night with her when I collapsed into her arms, pulled her tight, and admitted to her that I wanted someone to love Ana and me.

Truth was that I wanted *her* to be the one to love us. To love me.

She stayed quiet for a long time. All I wanted was for her to say something, to tell me that she didn't want me in jail because she loved me. I had been waiting for that for so long, yet still, she didn't say anything.

"Say it," I whispered.

"Because I ..."

The moments passed so agonizingly slowly. I could hear each unsteady breath exiting my mouth, could feel my throat closing as she shifted her gaze, those dark brown eyes trembling for a moment.

"Because I ..." She tucked some hair behind her ear, swallowed, and softened her stare. "I care about you guys."

My heart dropped, and the words I had wanted her so desperately to say seemed so lost and distant now. I hadn't wanted to hear that she cared about us. If she hadn't, she wouldn't have given a fuck about Ana or my family or any of the shit we did.

I wanted to hear that she loved me.

Me.

"I don't want you guys to leave me. You're the ones who've made me stronger, the ones who showed me the real side of Redwood." She frowned and stared at the scuffed wooden floorboards. "You can't go to jail for this, and you know that someone will try to blame you."

She continued talking, continued to speak shit that I couldn't focus on at the moment. Anger rushed through me. She had already told Landon that she loved him. If she felt that way about me too, she would've said it. Which meant that ...

I ran a hand through my hair and stormed to the door. "Fuck this."

Imani widened her eyes. "What the hell are you doing?"

"Fucking leaving."

"Why?!" Imani asked, hurrying after me. "I tell you why I don't want you to—"

"I don't want to hear it anymore, Imani," I said through gritted teeth, hastily pulling on my clothes so I could head back downstairs to the basement.

Maybe I'd take a drive instead and pick Ana up from Vera's house, deal with Mom's shit by myself. I'd been doing it by myself for this long. I could do it for the rest of my fucking life alone too.

"Can you stop and listen to me?!" She hurried over to me and grabbed my forearm, pulling me back. "Please, João."

I yanked myself away from her and opened the door.

"Why are you so hard-headed?!" she shouted, voice trembling, making me stop dead in my tracks, entire body tense.

I didn't know what the fuck this woman did to me, and I couldn't fucking make it stop.

"Why can't you just listen for once?! I don't know what you want me to say to you. I answer your question, and you flip out on me."

"I didn't like your answer."

"Well, what do you want me to say then?"

"That you love me!" I shouted before I could stop myself.

As soon as the words left my mouth, we both froze. It was fucking out in the world, and I couldn't take it back. Not after she had heard me. Not when she was staring at me with those huge brown eyes that filtered through so many emotions. I didn't know what to say.

I swallowed hard and glanced at the ground between us. "That you fucking love me," I whispered to myself, knowing that I had fucking screwed up by admitting some shit like that to her because, fuck, I didn't even know what we were anymore.

She and Landon were together. Were we fuck buddies on the side?

Neither of us made a move to leave the room or to ... to say much of anything to each other. But I didn't like that look making its way onto that flawless fucking face of hers. I fucking loathed the pity, the hurt.

"João," Imani whispered, lips parted in surprise. "I—"

"Forget I said anything," I said between gritted teeth and stormed out of the room, not giving Imani even a moment to speak. I didn't want to hear an excuse or any shit like that. I *couldn't* hear it.

As much as I hated to admit it, she had been so good with Ana.

And I was too invested in her to hear a rejection.

"João!" she shouted again.

But I was already on the ground floor and heading toward my car.

Fuck walking back downstairs and shit-talking with the guys for the rest of the night. I needed time alone. I needed to go pick up Ana.

I shoved the back door open and hurried to my car, then slid into the driver's seat and started it. A couple moments later, Imani appeared at the back door, hurrying out into the snow and the cold, her curls blowing everywhere.

She opened her mouth and yelled something at me, but I put the car into drive and sped down the road. She followed a few houses, then finally slowed to a jog. I stared into the rearview mirror, knowing that I should stop and go back.

But I fucking couldn't get myself to do it. So, I kept driving.

Chapter One Hundred Twenty-Eight

IMANI

I stared at João's taillights as they disappeared down the cold and snowy street. My chest was tight, and thoughts were rushing through my head so quickly. After wrapping my arms around myself, I bit my lip to hold back a whimper.

This night had been all over the place. First, Poison had thrown our principal's head onto the football field during a football game. Then, João had nearly fucked me senseless and admitted that he wanted me to love him too. Now, he was driving away, and I couldn't even follow him. My car was still at the school.

After kicking some snow with my heel, I walked back to Landon's basement to find him alone with Kai. Allie, Jace, and Nicole must've left while João was buried inside me and pinning me to Landon's parents' bed.

Kai twirled my keys around his pointer finger and paused beside me at the foot of the stairs. "I'm going to get your car at the school. Stay here until I get back, but then you should leave the slums for the night. It won't be safe."

Once he left, I continued into the room to see Landon on the phone.

"Yeah, she's okay," Landon said, holding my phone up to his ear. He glanced over at me when I walked into the room, his eyebrows drawn together in worry. "She's staying with me tonight, Mrs. Abara. She'll be back in the morning."

My eyes widened, and I hurried over. Mom's voice rang out through the phone so loudly that I was surprised Landon didn't go deaf. I snatched the phone from him, not wanting her to scream at him for this.

"What does she want?" I whispered to him, holding my hand over it.

"She had called about ten times, looking for you. I thought I'd answer it."

After taking a deep breath and preparing myself, I placed the phone to my ear. "Mom?"

"Imani," she said with a relieved sigh. "Thank God you're okay. I heard what happened at the football game and wanted to make sure that you got back all right. You're with the boys?"

"Uh, yes ..."

"Good," she said.

I pulled my ear away from the phone to make sure that this was really Mom's number, then furrowed my brows at the screen. It was really her number, but what the hell was Mom on? One moment, she hated these guys, and the next, she was grateful that I was with them.

"You're okay with that?"

"Yes."

"Why?" I asked.

She had to know that they were the guys who had done that shit. If she was calling, she must've seen the video of the three boys who oddly resembled Poison. Shouldn't she be freaking out, like I had been?

"Because"—she took a deep breath—"you were right. They'll protect you."

"You do know that they—"

"I know. You should come home."

"I'm staying with Landon for tonight. I ..." I glanced up toward the basement door, where Kai walked back into the room with my keys in his hand—he must've already brought my car back that... quickly? Hell, I wasn't going to ask how he did it—and handed them to me. After saying a couple words to Landon, he disappeared back up the stairs and out of the basement. "I need to stay with him tonight. I know that you don't agree, but I really ne—"

"Bring him home too."

My eyes widened. "You want me to bring Landon back to our house?"

"It's safer than sleeping in the slums tonight. The rich will suspect that Poison is behind this, and they'll easily find Landon's house. It's in the middle of the slums and where they do their business, isn't it?"

I parted my lips and furrowed my brows, wanting to ask her how she knew this too. But maybe it was common information. God, I wished that I knew, but at least ... at least, we could be safe tonight. Hopefully, João and Kai would be too.

"Okay," I said. "We'll be back there soon."

After I hung up the phone, I shoved it into my pocket and nodded to Landon. "My mom wants us both to come back to my house for the night," I said, nervously gnawing on the inside of my cheek. "Could you message Kai and João to tell them to stay safe for me? They're welcome to come over too. João doesn't really want to talk to me now. He probably won't even open my messages."

"João's going to listen to you before he gives a fuck about what I say," Landon said.

"No, he won't," I said, my jaw tight. He couldn't even let me finish what I was going to tell him earlier in the bedroom. "Can you, please?"

Landon sighed, then nodded to the door. "I'll text them on the way over."

* * *

Once we made it back home, Mom pulled the door open and wrapped her arms around me, sighing softly. I pulled myself out of her grip and walked upstairs with Landon, surprisingly without much backlash from her.

Landon shut my bedroom door, then lay back on the bed. I crawled up the bed beside him, forgoing my skin care routine, and curled my body into his, tears welling up in my eyes from everything that had happened tonight.

"I knew that you shouldn't have come, Imani," Landon said, gently massaging my hip, guilt heavy in his eyes. "I fucking fought with João all morning to tell you to stay home, but he wanted you there. He wanted to show you what the fuck happened to people who fucked with Poison, who hurt one of their own."

But that wasn't true because Vaughn hadn't hurt any members of Poison. All João had wanted was for me to watch what he could do.

"Which one of you did Vaughn hurt?" I asked through gritted teeth and through the tears.

"You."

I parted my lips but then pressed them back together, my heart fucking aching. And for some reason, all I could do was cry even harder.

João had known that Vaughn had hurt my best friend, which in turn hurt me.

And he had wanted to show me was what Poison would do for me, what he would do for me.

"Don't cry, Imani," Landon whispered, taking me into his arms and pulling me to his chest. "I'll make sure you don't ever see any shit like that again."

Landon might've thought that these tears were for Principal Vaughn, but he wasn't even close. These tears streaming down my face, the emptiness and hurt I held in my heart, the pain spreading through every part of my body were for João.

Chapter One Hundred Twenty-Nine

JOÃO

Fuck, I felt so fucking stupid.

I tightened my hand around the steering wheel and pulled up to Vera's house. After getting out of the car and slamming the door, I stormed up to the house door and banged on it hard enough to wake the neighbors. But I didn't give a shit right now. I was fucking pissed at myself for doing that shit.

"Vera!" I shouted. "Open up."

All I wanted to do was go home and erase Imani from my fucking head. I tried to do that every night, tried to shake away these feelings of her, but I fucking couldn't. I didn't want to see her again this weekend. Maybe not this week either.

I shouldn't have ever let that slip out of my mouth.

"VERA!"

A couple moments later, Blaise Harleen—who was apparently Vera's boyfriend now—opened the front door. "Fuck, dude. Why are you calling my girl's name like that? It's almost two in the fucking morning. What's wrong with you?"

"I'm picking up my sister," I said, pushing past him into the house. "Fucking watch it."

Blaise shut the door behind me and called for Vera, who walked out one of the few bedrooms with Ana sleeping in her arms. She padded into the living room and handed her to me. I pulled out a wad of cash and shoved it into her hand.

"This is the last time this week that I'm watching her," Vera warned. "I have shit to do."

"Like this fucker?" I asked, nodding to Blaise.

Vera rolled her eyes, placed both her hands on my back, and pushed me toward the door. "Yes, that fucker. Now, please. It's two in the morning. Next time, get Imani to watch her or something. She's good for me, but I've been so busy lately."

After clenching my jaw at the mere sound of her name, I walked with Ana to the car and strapped her into her car seat, then drove to my house. When we made it there, the living room light was on. With Ana in my arms once more, I opened the front door to a quiet house.

Ana shifted in my arms, mumbling something incoherent in her sleep. I stepped into the house and turned on the kitchen light, glancing over at Mom passed out on the couch with the TV still on, which never happened.

After depositing Ana into her bed and pulling the blankets over her small body, I took a deep breath to prepare myself and walked back into the living room, where the kitchen light dimly illuminated Mom's body. In her hands, she had the remote and another orange pill bottle.

I balled my hands into tight fists and refrained from slamming them into the drywall.

Mom had chosen fucking drugs over her own children. Tonight, she had gone out and fucking bought some more somewhere in Redwood. She had decided that it was more important to get high than to get clean for Ana.

Like I had done with the other pills, I took these ones and flushed them down the toilet, then walked to the driveway, grabbed a baseball bat, and smashed it into the pill bottle over and over and over until it became nothing but plastic pieces.

One fucking day, I would find out who the fuck was giving these to her and kill him. I didn't give a fuck about what Imani would think of me. I protected my family, no matter what. I didn't even fucking care if the police found out about it.

Once I finished, I hurled the baseball bat into the front yard and stormed back into the house. Instead of heading to my bedroom, I slipped into Ana's room and lay down beside her. I told myself that I was lying with her because if I didn't, then I feared Mom would take her away from me in the middle of the night. But that was only part of the reason.

So many thoughts raced through my head. I was angry, annoyed, and pissed at Imani, at Mom, at everything happening in this fucking town. I hated it here, more than anything ever. Everyone here deserved to fucking burn.

"What's wrong, João?" Ana whispered, voice groggy.

I blinked to see Ana staring at me with big eyes, like she was wide awake now.

"Go to sleep," I said, closing my eyes again.

She pushed some hair off my forehead and snuggled closer to me. "But you're sad. You always listen to me when I'm sad. Is everything okay?"

"Everything is fine, Ana."

"Even with Imani?"

I clenched my jaw and opened my eyes, staring at Ana, who was inches from my face. She had her brows furrowed and a deep frown on her face. She took her two pointer fingers and placed them on the corner of my lips, pulling them up and forcing me to smile even though I fucking wanted to kill something right now.

"Even with Imani," I said.

"You're lying." Ana sat crisscrossed on the bed in front of me. "What happened?"

"Nothing."

"Then, why are you sad?"

"Nothing. I ..."

I just wanted to talk to someone.

But Ana wasn't supposed to be in on any of this drama. Just like Mom's problems shouldn't become her own, Imani's and my relationship wasn't her problem either. And I fucking hated how I had brought it home.

I didn't know what to do anymore. I fucking wanted Imani more than anyone ever, except I kept pushing her away. I couldn't stop it either because I didn't want to be attached. The only other woman that

I loved had chosen drugs over her own family. If Imani told me she loved me too and then left, I would fucking fall to pieces.

I refused to do that to Ana.

So, I plastered a fake smile on my face and pretended. "Nothing's wrong. I'm happy, Ana."

I'm as happy as I could fucking be.

Chapter One Hundred Thirty

LANDON

The next morning, I woke up before Imani and rolled over to admire how the morning sun glistened off her brown face, making it glow. I brushed my fingers across her cheek, her skin so soft, and placed a kiss on her forehead.

My phone buzzed on the nightstand. I reached over and saw Kai's name on the screen in Poison's Discord chat without Imani. We planned shit in there that I didn't want Imani to know *anything* about, especially after last night.

Kai: Good you left your house with Imani last night. Your upstairs windows are broken. Security cameras that I put up in front and back of your house show some guy from the police force did it last night.

Eyes widening slightly, I tensed and glanced down at Imani. She would freak the fuck out when she found out about this. She shifted in my arms and smiled against my chest, mumbling something incoherent.

I texted the group back.

Me: You two good?

João: Those fuckers didn't bother Mom and Ana last night. Good here.

Kai: Fine.

Kai: I'm going to get as much info about the guy who broke the windows and send it to you when I do. We'll destroy his fucking life. Then, I'm heading to your place to get the weed and shit from there. Anything you want?

Me: Nah, I'm good.

I didn't have anything that I wanted saved. Mom and Dad had never saved anything from my childhood, no pictures, no memories. So, I didn't give a fuck what happened to that house. We would find another place to put all our shit, in case the Redwood rich wanted to make another move on it.

After depositing my phone back on the nightstand, I glanced into my wallet to make sure that I still had my picture of Imani. It was the only one that I had, and I might have stolen it from this house one day that I snuck into her room.

Her mom had had it sitting in one of their picture frames, and I couldn't fucking help it.

Mrs. Abara opened the door slightly and peeked inside the room while I quickly shoved it back into my wallet to hide it from her. "You awake?"

Part of me was pissed that she watched over Imani like a hawk all the time, but I wanted to take this time to talk to her. We never really had a civil conversation with each other, and if I really wanted this to continue with Imani, then I needed to at least talk to her, right?

Imani might've thought differently though. Maybe I should've too.

I slid out of the bed and pulled on my shirt from last night, then walked to the hallway, where Mrs. Abara stood uncomfortably.

She pressed her lips together and glanced back into the room at a sleeping Imani. "She's still sleeping?"

"Yes," I said after biting back a snarky reply.

After another couple awkward moments, she nodded. "Come with me to the kitchen. We'll make breakfast for her. She loves waffles with strawberries with a large glass of chocolate milk on Sunday mornings."

She walked down the hallway toward the stairs, and I stared in surprise at her. When I had stepped out of the room, I really hadn't thought that I was going to be asked to make waffles and breakfast for Imani with Mrs. Abara—one woman who loathed Poison. But ... she had let me stay over last night in her daughter's room.

So, I followed her down the stairs to the quiet kitchen. Snores from Mr. Abara drifted down the stairway and into the room, but Mrs. Abara quickly shut the door to drown them out.

Opening the fridge, she pulled out some fresh fruit and milk. "Do you know how to cook?"

"Uh ..." I scratched the back of my head. "Not really."

"Your parents never taught you?"

Clenching my jaw slightly, I grabbed the food from her and set it on the counter. "No. My mom and dad never really were around to teach me any shit. They're gone for good now. At least ... I hope they are."

With her back turned toward me, Mrs. Abara tensed for a moment. "Mr. Abara's parents were never there either. I can't say that I relate to you at all, but he's told me stories about it. I've had to teach him a lot of things." She nodded to the knife. "Why don't you wash and cut the fruit? If you're going to date my daughter, then you have to learn how to cook."

Once I washed the strawberries, I spread them out on the cutting board and went to work on cutting them. I never really cooked, usually just picked shit up from the store or school. Mom and Dad had never really taught me how to do any of this.

What great parents they were ...

My phone buzzed in my pocket; it was the buzz of my vibration notification that I'd set for any unknown or hidden number. Which meant that ... they were trying to call me yet again. I didn't pick up the phone for them, and they didn't leave a message.

But I knew that it was them every time.

What were they calling for? I didn't know, and I didn't care.

"You know, Imani might not seem like it, but she's high mainte-nance," Mrs. Abara said. "She's gotta get her nails and toes done every week, her hair styled for the biggest events at school. Oh, and you're going to have a ball with her at senior prom. She'll drive you nuts over looking perfect, but you have to please her. Do you understand?"

"If you're trying to deter me from her"—I slid the knife through the end of a strawberry to cut off the stem—"it's not going to work. I ... I love her."

"I'm not trying to deter you from her. I'm informing you."

"Why? Why are you acting this way to me?" I asked. "I thought you hated me."

"Because Imani is right. I know that you and your little gang are able to protect her in ways that I'm not cut out for." She paused, as if she was contemplating on saying more. "And I fear that, one day, I won't be able to protect my daughter at all. Akio's parents are killers," she whispered. "They'll take advantage of the town being in chaos the way it is now, and one day ... Imani's father and I will be next on their hit list."

Chapter One Hundred Thirty-One

IMANI

When I woke up this morning, Landon wasn't lying in my bed. I padded out of my bedroom with my pajamas buttoned to my neck, so Mom wouldn't think anything fishy had gone down in my bedroom last night.

The thick, buttery scent of waffles drifted up the stairs. After looking for Landon in all the bedrooms on the second floor, I walked down the stairs. When I reached the bottom floor, I stopped and stared wide-eyed at Landon, who sat at the kitchen island across from Mom, who was ... laughing?!

I quickly walked over to them, unsure if Mom laughing was a good or bad thing, and slid next to Landon, brows drawn together in confusion. She sipped her coffee and smiled over at me as Landon laid his large hand on my knee.

"You guys are ..."

"Oh, Landon was just telling me about the first time you met." Mom laughed.

Like a fucking psycho, I turned my head ninety degrees to the right and glared at Landon, giving him my best *I'm going to kill you* smile. "You were telling my mom how we met?" I asked through gritted teeth.

"When you slapped me in the hallway," Landon clarified.

After releasing my balled fists, I took a deep breath and turned back to the counter. I swore, if that boy ever told Mom that he and I used to cam naked with each other, I would literally cut off his balls like he had with Principal Vaughn's dick, then feed them to him.

Mom continued to laugh silently while finishing a huge plate of waffles with strawberries, chocolate fudge, and whipped cream. I eyed her carefully, totally confused. Mom was laughing with Landon. What kind of sorcery was that?

"You didn't spike her coffee, did you?" I whispered, leaning closer to him.

Landon squeezed my knee. "No, but if you want me to, then I—"

"No, I'm good. She just hasn't laughed like this in so long, especially with *you*."

After placing the plate in front of Landon and me, Mom took another sip of coffee. "Are the others going to meet us at the mall?"

"The mall?" Landon asked. "Why are we going there?"

"I, um ... kinda asked my mom to help me sign you guys up for health insurance. I hope that's okay. I want to make sure that you guys are covered, especially if you're going to do shit like you did last night with"—I glanced at Mom and lowered my voice—"Vaughn."

"Your principal deserved to die that way after what he did to Allie," Mom interjected with her back turned toward me as she made a plate of waffles for herself. "If he had done that to you, I would've wanted them to do much worse than what they did. Redwood has done far worse."

Parting my lips, I stared at her in surprise. Who was this new woman acting as my mother?! Maybe this was the real her, coming out after all these years. She knew that she wasn't going to change me and couldn't protect me anymore.

"Health insurance?" Landon asked me, eyes widening and a small smile stretching across his face, as if he couldn't believe someone could love him so fucking much that they wanted to make sure he was good in that area of his life. "You really asked your mom to help us do something like that?"

"Yes, so ... can you ask them to come? Also, don't mention that I will be there today, okay?" I asked Landon, inching closer to him and gnawing on the inside of my cheek. Nerves bubbled in my stomach. "If you do, then João won't come."

"What happened?" Landon asked, stuffing waffles into his mouth.

I swallowed hard, thoughts of last night clouding my mind. It had all happened so fast. João had brought me upstairs and into a bedroom, fucked me senseless, then wanted me to admit that not only did I care about him, but that I ... loved him too.

How would Landon react to something like that? He was the only boy who I'd ever told I loved, and he had some minor anxieties about me finding someone else. If I told him that I might've loved João too ...

Fuck, I didn't even know if I did.

I mean, that boy did something to me. He was the quickest to get me angry. It was a constant battle with him, trying to get him to see things from my point of view, but ... he was the Poison member who had forced me to grow outside the Redwood rich bubble Mom had put over me.

I ...

My stomach tightened. I had feelings for him, but it was so much different than how I felt about Landon. When João and I were in the same room, we were like a fucking fire with each other. I could feel the tension in my body from merely thinking about him.

What did that mean? That I loved him? If I did, what would happen with Landon and me?

"Thank you, Mrs. Abara," Landon said once we were finished. He cleaned the dish off in the sink, then stored it in the dishwasher. He glanced over at me and gave me a small, boyish smile. "Nobody has ever made me waffles before."

While my thoughts might've been of João, I couldn't stop the warmth that burst through my chest at how happy Landon looked at this moment. He might've never had parents who cared, and Mom wasn't the *best* parent in the world, but at least she was warming up to Landon.

"Well, get used to it," I said, jumping off my seat and walking over to the sink.

Landon took my plate from me and washed it under the water, glancing over at me with those piercing blue eyes that would've given me shivers if I didn't know how emotional he was, especially with me.

"I hope you don't think he's staying over all the time," Mom said, glancing over her shoulder at me while she cleared the kitchen island. She placed the dishes on the counter beside Landon, looked at him, then cracked a smile. "I'm kidding. I'm kidding. You're welcome to come over, but no guns or weapons in my house."

"No guns or weapons in your house," Landon said.

"Yeah, Landon uses his fists as weapons," I said, wondering what the hell was going on with Mom.

Since last night, she'd been acting a bit more ... understanding of the Poison boys, especially Landon.

I wondered what had happened, what had changed her mind and attitude toward him.

My stomach tightened. Maybe I didn't want to know. It couldn't be good, could it?

Chapter One Hundred Thirty-Two

JOÃO

"Come on, Ana," I said, taking her hand and tugging her into the mall.

She clutched my fingers with her smaller ones, her hair in high pigtails and her body dressed in a pink ballerina dress that she had begged me to wear, her grin so wide. "This is the mall?!" she asked, glancing at everyone walking around. "It is so big!"

"So many stores here too," I said. "Do you wanna shop afterward?"

"Yeah! Do you think they have a princess store?"

"Maybe."

Giggling to herself, she bounced up and down beside me. I pulled my phone out of my pocket to see where the hell Landon wanted us to meet him. He had texted me this morning and said it was urgent and gave us a location but not much else.

I was glad that he hadn't made plans with Imani after spending the night at her house. Part of me hadn't wanted to come and definitely didn't want to face him because all I would see in his eyes was Imani. But Poison was together to the fucking end.

"Landon is over here!" Ana said, pointing and pulling me along.

"Christ, Ana," I said, stuffing my phone into my jeans and hurrying after her. "Slow down."

Ana slowed her pace, gaze falling on the Dairy Queen that we passed. "Can we get ice cream after too?"

Mid-head nod, I glanced up at Landon and Kai ... *and Imani* standing across the food court. I froze and scowled, any lightness inside of me disappearing when I saw her face. I didn't know what the fuck was wrong with me. I had been the fucking one to admit to her my feelings last night. I just ... didn't want to face her today.

"Ana, we're leaving," I said, about to turn around.

But Ana escaped my grasp and ran over to Imani, her sneakers slapping hard against the tiled ground and lighting up with pink flashing lights. "Imani!" she shouted, jumping into Imani's arms and grinning.

Imani picked her up and smiled, glancing over at me. I rolled my eyes and walked over to the guys, not once looking over at her. But, fuck, I wanted to watch her and Ana. She cared about Ana, and Ana fucking loved her too.

"Come here, Ana," I said sternly.

Ana shook her head and clutched on to Imani's shoulders tighter. "Imani!"

Imani stared at me, her gaze burning into my fucking body.

Ana cuddled closer to her and laid her head on Imani's shoulder. "Guess what, Imani. João was sad last night because of you."

The guys and Imani turned toward me, and I clenched my jaw and glared at Ana. After I had convinced her that nothing was wrong so she could go to sleep, she had still told Imani about last night. And, fuck, I didn't want Imani to know about any of that shit.

"Are you guys coming?" someone said from behind me.

I glanced over my shoulder to see Imani's mother standing behind me. "Fuck, this day keeps getting fucking worse," I said underneath my breath.

Landon was going to fucking get it later for forcing me to come to this shit.

"What are we doing here?" Kai asked, hands stuffed into his cargo pants.

"We're going to get you guys on health insurance," Imani said. "You know, so you don't go into piles of debt, dealing with medical bills." She looked over at me. "And so you can have a good start when you finally get out of this shithole of a town."

Health insurance?

We were here to get health insurance?

"Come on," Imani's mother said. "I've made appointments for all of you."

* * *

Forty minutes later, I had filled out a plethora of forms for Ana and me to get on our own health insurance because we didn't have any right now. This town didn't support drug addicts or previous drug addicts who had gotten clean, like it should've. And Mom couldn't afford it for us either.

Ana sat in Landon's lap as he filled out some papers with the health insurance worker. I stood off to the side with my arms crossed over my chest and nothing but annoyance on my mind because Imani wouldn't stop glancing over at me.

She hopped up from the chair beside Landon and walked over. "We need to talk."

"No, we don't."

Instead of walking back to her seat, she stood next to me and crossed her arms, mirroring my pose. Then, she rocked back on her heels, lips curling into an uncomfortable smile. "So, you were sad because of me?"

"Don't be a fucking bitch," I said through gritted teeth.

She smacked me across the face. "Don't call me a bitch."

"You fucking are," I growled, rubbing my cheek.

"Just because I didn't tell you that I loved you?" she asked, the words so damn sharp and sour. "Are you really that butthurt over it, João? Because if you are, you should've let me at least respond to you last night before running out of Landon's and driving away like a maniac!"

"I needed to get Ana."

"That's always going to be your excuse."

"It's not a fucking excuse." I seethed. "My mom fucking brought Ana where she got raped, all to buy some fucking drugs. I'm not going to let that fucking happen again, Imani. If I need to leave to get her, then I'll do as I fucking please."

She poked a finger hard into my chest. "That doesn't give you the right to call me a bitch. And still ... you could've waited two fucking minutes for me to tell you that I—" She paused and glanced behind me.

"That you what?" I asked and followed her gaze, my eyes landing on Landon and Ana together.

Jealousy shot through me. I wanted Imani. *I* fucking wanted her, but all she wanted was Landon. I ripped myself away from her and stormed off, not wanting to see any more of this.

"Of fucking course."

"João, come on," she said, hurrying after me. "How do you expect me to love you when all you are is rude to me?! God, you're so frustrating." She ran her hands through her hair, frustration all over her face. "Don't be stupid! If I didn't love you, I wouldn't be doing any of this shit!"

For a split moment, my heart stopped.

A black fucking cloud of unknown bullshit suddenly loomed over me.

"I'm not being fucking stupid," I growled.

I was fucking scared.

Scared because ... what if Imani did really love me? What if she wasn't saying this out of pity for how shitty all of our lives had turned out? What if she was saying this and had really asked her mom to bring us here because ... she loved me?

What if Imani loved me, and one day, I lost her?

Chapter One Hundred Thirty-Three

IMANI

The words seemed to tumble out of my mouth before I could stop them. I stared at João, who seemed not to even have heard what I said to him. All he had gotten from my confession was that I thought that he was stupid.

"Did you hear what I said, João?" I whispered.

Until this moment, I hadn't known that I needed to hear him say it back. I hadn't thought that I would ever tell João that I loved him. He had always been so pissy with me, always showed me his dark side and wanted me to break. He rarely showed me this side of him.

He was so fragile.

We stared at each other for a few long moments. My heart pounded hard inside my chest. I wanted him to tell me that he loved me too. I didn't want to be a fool, standing in the middle of the mall with my mom and trying to get him on insurance for nothing.

After a heated moment, João turned away from me and headed toward the guys. "Come on, Ana," he called.

Not letting him get away that easily, I jogged over to him, grabbed his wrist, and pulled him back to face me. We stood inches from each other, the tension between us making me anxious more than ever.

"Say it back," I whispered, my voice trembling.

João clenched his jaw, gaze flickering from my eyes to my lips, then back. He shoved my hand off his wrist and watched me carefully, his gaze making me unusually nervous around him. "You didn't say shit to me, Imani."

"Yes, I did."

"No," he clarified. "You skirted around those three words."

Hatred rushed through me. All João ever wanted was to make himself feel good. He had heard what I said to him. He knew how I felt about him. He was now content enough and didn't give a fuck about saying it back.

I shoved him back. "Why are you so aggravating? Why can't you admit it to me too?"

Something shifted in João's brown eyes, and for a moment, I thought he would finally tell me that he loved me too, that he cared about me as much as I cared about him and his family. But instead, he swallowed hard.

"Ana! We're leaving."

Once I balled my hands into tight fists, I gritted my teeth. "You're an asshole."

João stared at me with so much emotion in his eyes. It was like he wanted to tell me so many different things, admit so much to me, but he would never be open enough to do any of that shit.

Ana walked over to us, her sneakers lighting up, and hung her head low. "I want to stay. You said that we can get ice cream and walk around to the stores."

Deciding to piss off João, I crouched down to Ana's level and held out my hand for her to take. "Come on, Ana. I'll take you shopping and to get ice cream. I know the cutest little store for a princess like you."

She giggled and grabbed my hand, then waved João off. "We're going girl shopping. See you later."

"I'm taking you shopping, Ana," João said through gritted teeth.

But Ana was already pulling me down the mall and pointing into the different stores that she wanted to go into and shop. I gave her my full attention, spending the next few hours helping her try on clothes and accessories and buying her whatever she wanted.

I expected João to leave, but he and the others stayed in the food court. When we finished shopping, I held about twenty bags of clothes for her and for me in my hands while Ana walked down the corridor with a wide grin and new sunglasses that sparkled.

"Look at this fashionista!" I said, dropping the bags on the table and spinning Ana.

If the Poison boys thought that *I* was dramatic, they obviously hadn't met this side of Ana. With an ice cream in one hand, she strutted back and forth down the aisles, her free hand on her hip, striking poses left and right in her new sunglasses.

"She'll have to do a fashion show for you guys later," I said, smiling at how happy and excited that Ana looked. "She found so many cute princess clothes."

I looked over at the guys and caught João staring at me with softer eyes than the ones he had been giving me a few hours ago. He quickly looked away and clenched his jaw, taking Ana's bags from the table.

"I have to go," he said, calling Ana back over to the table. "Ana, you're going with Landon and Kai. I have to—"

"Yay!" Ana said, bouncing over to us and jumping into Kai's arms. "Can we make brigadeiros?"

"No, we have to clean up Landon's house," Kai said. "Maybe after."

My brows furrowed. "What happened at Landon's?"

All the guys suddenly became tense. I looked from each of them until my gaze landed on Landon, who awkwardly scratched his head.

"Someone broke in last night and smashed some windows. We didn't want you to worry."

"Someone broke in?" I asked, eyes wide.

"Yes."

"Landon," I whispered, heart racing. "Please don't tell me that you'll be staying there tonight. I can ask my mom if you can stay with us or something. You shouldn't be sleeping in the slums with broken windows, especially not when it's this cold outside."

Landon took my face in his hands and kissed me. "I'll be fine, Imani."

"Promise me?" I asked, worried.

"Yes," he said. "Now, I have to go."

After I said good-bye to Ana, Landon, and Kai, they disappeared through the mall doors.

I stood awkwardly next to João and cleared my throat, taking a peek over at him. "Have you finally calmed down now?"

"I have shit to do, Imani," João said. "I can't stand here and talk."

"Fine." I crossed my arms. "I have shit to do too."

Yet he didn't move, nor did I.

Truthfully, I didn't want him to leave. I didn't think I would be able to bear it, but I was so nervous because I didn't want him to hurt me. João rarely loved anyone. All he did was hurt people who got too close to him.

"Then, go," he said, nodding to the doors.

"You first."

Still, neither of us took a step.

And then, almost as if we both knew what the other was thinking, we stepped closer to each other. My hands found his face, as his found my waist. Unable to stop myself, I pulled him closer to me and kissed him hard on the mouth.

Chapter One Hundred Thirty-Four

LANDON

"They fucking destroyed this place."

I stood in front of my parents' house and looked from window to window. All of them had been smashed through, glass littered around the cement sidewalks. I didn't know if I wanted to step into the house.

"I took a look around this morning," Kai said, holding Ana on his hip. "It's not *that* bad."

After shoving my key into the front door, the door creaked open. I didn't even have to turn the key. The lock must've been broken from whichever police officer had raided the place late last night.

Inside, drawers were pulled open. Papers littered the floor. Shelves were knocked over. I headed right toward the basement because they might've raided my house and found nothing, but that was because we didn't keep any important shit up here.

"The basement is clear," Kai said, walking in behind me and setting Ana on the ground. "I swept it this morning for bugs, cameras, anything they might have placed there. They tried to get into our room in the back, but the alarm on the lock must've scared them off."

I pulled out a broom from the closet and tossed it to Kai. "You find out who it was?"

Kai walked to one of the many broken windows in my house,

521

beginning to sweep. "Not yet. They were pretty covered up but had one of those tattoos that all the Redwood cops have. I'm trying to find a match to anyone inside the police database."

My lips curled into a smile as I grabbed a garbage bag from the kitchen. "You hacked into the Redwood Police database?"

Once he threw me a smirk, he swept the glass into a pile. "Of course I did. And you can stay at my place. This place is kinda fucked right now. If they raid you again, it'll be easier to get in," Kai said. "I have a couple spare rooms for you to crash."

"I'll stay there for a little while," I said.

"But we gotta do all our business here and at the warehouse," he continued, sweeping the glass into the garbage bag. "I don't want anyone finding where I live. We got all the money and guns stashed there."

If they found Kai's place, we'd be fucked. We never did business there and had only brought Imani there a couple times. Nobody else had really stepped foot inside his house, and we all wanted to keep it that way.

His lips curled into a small smirk as he swept some glass off the wooden floor. "I'm sure Imani would love to come over and help you get set up. The other day at lunch, she was talking about rearranging her room, and fuck, was she so excited."

Jealousy, or maybe it was possessiveness, burned inside me. He looked so happy, thinking about her.

I glanced over at Ana, who sat on the living room couch on his phone, watching a video on YouTube. She giggled, her small nose scrunching up, then looked over at us. "How do you spell brigadeiro?"

"Why do you want to spell that?" I asked.

"Because I want to watch videos of people making them."

"Why?"

"Because I want to make them for João. He's been sad lately."

"What do you think João and Imani were talking about today?" Kai asked me, a rigidness suddenly in his voice.

It was as if he didn't know what to think of João and Imani's conversation at the mall either. After Imani had told me they were in a fight last night, it had bothered me all night.

"João usually gets pissy, but not like that."

"I know," Ana announced, grinning as Kai changed the YouTube video to a How to Make Brigadeiros by Yourself video. "João likes Imani!"

I picked up the papers from the floor and clenched my jaw.

"We know that," Kai said, emptying another batch of glass into the trash. "What's he pissy about today though? It has to be something big, if he won't stop acting like a bitch, especially to her while Ana is around."

"Maybe she doesn't like him back," I joked.

But it was far from it because I knew that Imani liked him back. I had seen the way she looked at João, even when he was being an asshole to her. Hell, he'd even brought her out on a date that *she* wanted to go on with him.

"He loves her!" Ana said, looking at the glass on the floor and picking up a piece.

Kai quickly took it out of her hand, body suddenly stiffening, and clenched his jaw as he deposited the glass into the trash. He didn't look up at me, didn't even take a glance.

João loved Imani?

João didn't love many things, except his family.

He never dated, said that no girl could ever keep his interest and that all the girls from Redwood Academy were the same and boring as hell. He rarely hung out with anyone other than Ana and us. He fucking hated the goddamn world.

But sometime in the last few months, that had changed. Imani had changed it.

Kai turned his back toward me and continued cleaning.

"You like her too?" I asked, noticing the way he had suddenly become tense.

He paused for a long time. "You know how it is," Kai finally said.

Jealousy built up inside of me, and I couldn't help but curse myself out because of it. Imani was something fucking special, something amazing, and not just to me anymore. I balled my hands into fists and drew my tongue across my front teeth.

I had been so caught up with Imani possibly talking to someone else on the internet that I didn't realize my best fucking friends, the guys I had made a pact to destroy Redwood with, the gang we had vowed to never leave, had fallen for her too.

While I might've hated the fact that she liked the other guys too, Kai had been fucking happier than I had ever seen him after his parents died, and João had never even been on a formal date, never mind let any girl meet his family.

In some fucked up kind of way, we were a dysfunctional kind of family. But it was a family that I didn't despise. It was a fucking family who cared about me. Nothing like Mom and Dad. And I refused to let anyone or anything take that away from me even if that person was myself.

Nobody was going to come between us. Nobody was going to split us apart.

Poison forever.

Chapter One Hundred Thirty-Five

KAI

Akio: Can we talk?
Akio: It's important.

I stared at my phone, still in disbelief that Akio had texted me while I helped Landon clean his house with Ana, and placed my bike helmet on my motorcycle. There hadn't been a chance in the world that I would willingly meet with him, but the next message was what had gotten my ass up and out of that house quicker than anything.

Akio: It's about Imani and my parents.
Akio: Please.

Sighing, I shoved my phone into my pants pocket and walked into the empty warehouse where Poison did business. I had told Akio to meet me here, not only because I didn't want to be seen with that fucker in public, but also because I wanted to show him where I would kill him if he ever *touched* Imani.

I unlocked the warehouse back door and stepped into the large and empty room, turning on one of the lights and finding a seat on the concrete floor while I waited for Akio to show the fuck up. Part of me couldn't believe that he had the fucking audacity to message me.

Like a fucking idiot, twenty minutes later, Akio knocked on the warehouse door. I rolled my eyes and walked over to the door, snatching the handle and pulling it open. He stood at the door and immediately broke eye contact with me, his right eye black and swollen.

"I can't believe that you're fucking here," I said through gritted teeth.

"Me neither."

"Get in before someone sees you."

Akio warily walked into the warehouse and stomped his snowy shoes off at the door. With his hands shoved into his pockets, he walked around the empty warehouse and stopped where there was still a small puddle of Principal Vaughn's blood.

"This is where it went down, huh?" Akio asked, mostly to himself. "Where you killed him."

Careful not to say anything aloud, in case he had a fucking wire on him, I pressed my lips together and walked over to him, searching him for any wires or cameras that he might have on him. I didn't trust him or his parents.

After I searched and found nothing, I stepped back and nodded. "It's where I'll kill you one day if I find out that you've touched Imani. One wrong move, one fucking finger on her body, and I'll make sure your death is far worse than Vaughn's."

Face paling, Akio nodded and swallowed hard. "I know."

"Let's get one thing straight." I stepped toward him, arms crossed over my chest, and clenched my jaw. "I'm only here this one time because you saved Imani the other day. If it wasn't for you, she'd be dead."

"She would be."

I clenched my jaw. "What do you want?"

Akio paced back and forth in front of me and rubbed his palms together. "You shouldn't have recorded killing Principal Vaughn. People know that you guys did it. They know, and they're going to target you."

"They would've known anyway," I said. "Nobody has the balls to do shit like that."

"You don't understand," Akio said, pushing up his glasses. "People are going to target you. And by you, I mean that they won't target *you*, but the people you all care about. Who does that leave?"

"Imani."

"Yes, Imani, and I—"

"Who is targeting her?" I asked.

He clenched his jaw and gave me one look. That one look told me everything. It wasn't just anyone who was targeting Imani, but his mother and father, the bosses of the Redwood mob, which must've been why he had that nasty bruise.

"Your parents gave you that," I said, nodding to his eye. "Didn't they?"

After a couple moments, Akio sighed. "Listen ... you can't tell anyone that I told you. They were talking about getting rid of her and her family, if things get much worse. They know you have shit on them, and they don't want to risk anything with the Feds."

Anger rushing through me, I grabbed him by the collar. "If you find out that they plan on killing her, you tell me. I don't care how the fuck you do it. You make sure that I'm the first fucking person to find out. Do you understand me? You get me anything you can on them."

Akio nodded. "They don't have any plans that I know of yet, but I will let you know. I don't want Imani to get in the middle of this. All she's trying to do is get out of Redwood. If she can get through the rest of this year alive, then she'll be safe."

"Why are you fucking doing this?" I asked.

"Because I don't want Imani to get hurt."

"Why?"

"Because I care about her."

"Do you like her?"

"As a friend," Akio said. "Nothing more, Kai. I swear. I like someone else."

"Who?" I pressed because if he withheld any information on his parents wanting to hurt Imani, then I would hurt the person who he cared about the most. Living in Redwood wasn't all fun and games. It was blackmail like this.

And I didn't give a fuck about playing along.

As long as Imani was safe.

Akio shook his head. "Nobody. You don't even know—"

"Who?" I asked, hand behind my back and clutching my gun to let him know that I was serious.

Akio might carry a gun, but he didn't use it and wasn't comfortable using it the way that I was. If he was, he would've killed that guard who had tried to kill Imani.

"Nicole," Akio said, shielding his face from me. "Okay? I like Nicole."

I let my gun go and scrunched my nose. "The cheerleader?"

"Yes, the cheerleader."

My lips curled into a smile, and I laughed. I couldn't stop myself. Akio and Nicole, huh? That was not what I had expected in the slightest. Nicole would never *ever* like someone like Akio. All she did was flirt with the football team and cry to her police chief daddy.

"If you withhold any information about your parents, I'll torture Nicole in front of you." I glanced down at the blood by his feet, then back up at him. "And you know that I'm not fucking around. Get me information, Akio."

Chapter One Hundred Thirty-Six

IMANI

Monday morning, I stepped out of my car and into the chilly winter air. Mom had hounded me this morning and made me swear that I would be safe today. She almost didn't want to send me because of what had happened with Principal Vaughn.

But I'd convinced her, mostly because I didn't want to miss another day.

Akio pulled up in his designated spot and stepped out of his car, his right eye swollen shut. He glanced over at me, giving me a half-smile, and didn't waste any time in hurrying to his classroom. I wanted to follow after him, but he had class in a different building than me.

If I found out that Kai had done something to him, I swore I would flip.

Redwood Academy had been getting on my nerves lately, almost too much.

Nostrils flared, I stormed down the hallways toward Allie's locker. I had tried everything—*everything*—to understand João yesterday, but after our kiss, he had walked away from me without saying two words, and all sense and reason had flown out the damn window. What was his fucking problem?

It didn't matter whether I told him I loved him or not. He always reacted the same way. Pissed off and annoyed. And it was making *me* pissed off and annoyed with him. I hadn't gotten a full hour of sleep because I couldn't for the life of me understand him.

Poison stood in the hallway with each other, earlier than they usually got to school, and watched me carefully. But I didn't give them any of my attention. I just needed to see my best friend right now.

My coiled black hair bounced in a ponytail. Even my hair had been annoying me today, so much so that I decided to throw it into a ponytail, and I *never* did shit like that. I snatched Allie's hand and tugged her past the three Poison boys without saying good morning to them.

"He's so annoying, so fucking annoying," I said between gritted teeth to Allie when she asked why João was scowling at me like that. I didn't have any other words for her besides that because I wasn't even going to say his name today.

"Well, good morning to you too," Allie said, pushing her glasses up her nose.

I stopped by my locker and fumbled with the lock. "Sorry, not sorry. He's been annoying all weekend, and I'm done with it."

Allie leaned against the lockers and arched a brow. "Done with him? I'm surprised you haven't jumped back into bed with them already."

After giving her the deadliest glare that I could muster, I pulled some books from my locker. "Says the girl who's sleeping with her stepbrother after he broke her heart." I glanced back over at Allie and curled my lips into a smile, a giggle escaping my mouth. "I need to get more damn sleep." I wrapped my arms around her waist and rested my head on her shoulder. "Thanks for dealing with me when I'm cranky."

She patted my back and giggled. "Thanks for dealing with me when I make dumbass decisions, like the stepbrother thing."

"Anytime." I pulled the remaining books from my locker and shut it. We started down the hall toward our Biology class with my arm looped around hers. "Looks like Redwood is off to a *wonderful* start after what happened on Saturday night."

Students from AP Biology waited outside Mr. Barnes's classroom, gossiping with each other. Surprisingly, school went on like it always did, even after Principal Vaughn's death. The only thing that was different was that he wasn't in these halls, creepily staring down every girl's shirt.

"Just be careful, Maddie," someone said to our right.

The shy girl in our Bio class, Maddie Weber, crossed her arms over her chest and nodded at her brother, Oliver. Oliver hiked a large duffel bag—probably filled with his hockey gear—over his shoulder.

Alec, another guy on the hockey team, slapped Oliver on the shoulder. "Come on, dude. Let her be. You think *she* has secrets worth knowing?" Alec threw Maddie a smirk behind Oliver's back that suggested a bit more but persuaded Oliver to leave.

When he was gone, Maddie inched closer to the wall and shuffled from foot to foot. She glanced over at us with her cheeks tinted red. "Did you see that?" she asked, eyes wide in fear.

Allie and I burst out laughing at the same time.

"Girl, we don't care." I cocked my thumb at Allie. "She's sleeping with her stepbrother, and I'm about to forgive the three most fucked up guys in the entire school. Your secret is safe with us."

Maddie moved closer and lowered her voice. "Are you talking about Poison?"

Allie's lips curled into a smile, and she nodded. "Yep."

Maddie widened her eyes even more. "Rumor has it that they are the ones who killed the principal last Saturday. Is that true?" she asked. Allie and I looked at each other as Maddie grinned. "Because I want to thank them. That man was nothing but a creep. Every time I was around him, I thought he was staring down my shirt. He ..." She shivered. "He always got way too close to me, and nobody would believe me."

Deciding that Maddie wasn't going to be a tattletale, Allie leaned closer to me. "Exhibit A for why you shouldn't hate Poison for what they did," she whispered.

I playfully pushed her. "So, you're on Poison's side now?"

"No, I ... agree with them. You shouldn't be annoyed with them for that, especially the dick-eating part."

"Oh." I laughed. "Allie, baby, that was my idea. I told Landon to cut off his dick for what he did to you. I'm not annoyed about that as much anymore. I just ..." João flashed into my mind. "João and I aren't getting along."

"João doesn't get along with anyone," Allie said. "But I guess Kai and you are good, right?"

"Kai?" I asked, brows furrowed.

Why'd she bring him up? Was it because he was always looking at us? Always staring at Allie? Always ... bringing her name up too? It kinda, sorta pissed me off even more. It wasn't Allie's fault, but Kai wouldn't tell me why he was so interested in Allie yet.

"Kai," she said, nodding behind me.

Leaning against the wall at the end of the hallway, Kai watched us closely, as if he was waiting for the hallway to clear or to get me alone for the first time since the other night.

Mr. Barnes walked down the hall and unlocked his classroom for us. Everyone piled into the room before Allie, Maddie, and me. Just as the second bell rang and as I was about to step into the room, Kai caught my wrist and whisked me away.

Chapter One Hundred Thirty-Seven

IMANI

"Where are we going?" I asked with wide eyes. "I have class!"

Kai pulled me down the hallway toward the door without saying a word.

"What the hell did you do to Akio?!" I whisper-yelled at him.

I was supposed to be in my science period. The hallways were eerily quiet now, only a couple kids walking to the restroom or lingering in empty doorways. He pulled me out into a stairway that led to the student parking lot.

"Fuck, Vera," someone grunted from a couple floors above us. "I have been fucking *dreaming* about coming in your pussy again. You felt so good last time. I'm not waiting any longer to fill you again."

"There are cameras, Blaise!" a female said back.

"Fuck the cameras."

My eyes widened, and I glanced up the staircase, unable to see anything. But it seemed like some people were having a hell of a good time up there, about to start fucking senselessly in the middle of Redwood Academy.

But who was I to talk? Kai Koh was forcing me to skip class, all so ... what? He could fuck me on his motorcycle in the middle of the school parking lot? Maybe he planned to bring me back to his place this time.

After he guided me out the door and toward the parking lot, I glanced back at our high school. Skipping class was wrong. I had a nearly perfect track record with my attendance—besides those few times I had stayed in the restroom too long, masturbating for Poison on the phone and stuff.

"Nobody is watching for students skipping class," Kai said, stopping at his bike. "Especially not today. Everyone's too worried about being the next person who gets exposed to the entire town."

"But—"

"Put on the helmet"—he slid onto the bike and looked back at me —"and get on."

Once I slipped on the helmet, I slid onto the bike behind Kai and wrapped my arms around his oversize sweatshirt-covered abdomen. I pulled up the visor. "Can you at least tell me where we're going?"

"Somewhere for you to learn how to shoot your gun," Kai said, driving toward his home.

* * *

"Kai, I shouldn't be learning how to shoot a gun during class!" I said.

With his hand on the small of my back, he guided me down the stairs of his home.

When we reached his weapons storage area, I turned around. "We really—"

He wrapped his rough, large hand around my chin, pulled me toward him, and kissed me hard on the mouth. My breath caught in my throat, my body tensing for a few moments, before I finally relaxed and moved my lips against his, deepening the kiss.

When he finally pulled away, my head was in a complete daze. I stared at him, trying to catch my breath. But he had that sinful look in his eyes, the same look he had given me the other night when he took me to his shooting range and told me that I'd be his again.

"What was that?" he asked, voice filled with overwhelming dominance.

I let out a small squeak.

He pulled me closer again and slipped his hand from my chin to my throat, his mouth against my ear. "You do as I say, Imani. Do you understand me? You might have João and Landon wrapped around your finger, but"—he wrapped his finger around one of my curls and gently tugged on it—"you're wrapped around mine, and you know it. You *fucking* love it."

"You didn't bring me here to shoot guns, did you?" I asked, voice barely above a whisper.

Heat gathered in my core. I already knew the answer.

Instead of responding, he picked me up, tossed me over his shoulder, and walked with me to his bedroom, where there was a short rope hanging from the ceiling. After pulling off my clothes, he took both of my wrists and bound them above my head. My tiptoes barely scraped against the ground.

"I bought a new toy for you," he murmured into my ear from behind. "Open your mouth."

Unable to move, I opened my mouth. He took what looked like to be a ball gag out from behind him and placed the ball into my mouth. But the moment it entered me, I realized that it wasn't a ball gag at all. It was a dildo that he had slipped inside my mouth, and he strapped it around my neck like a ball gag.

Spit rolled down my chin. Kai stepped back, as if admiring his naked masterpiece for a few moments, then exited the room. I struggled against the ropes, tiptoes grazing against the ground and nipples hardening from the sudden chill.

When he reentered the room minutes later, spit and slobber covered my chest and tits. Kai walked over to me, his hooded gaze drifting from my eyes to my mouth, and then he captured my nipples between his fingers and tugged.

I moaned on the dildo, more spit dripping from my mouth, my brows knotting together.

"Do you like that?" he asked, tugging harder.

My pussy pulsed, and I whimpered again, feeling the pressure build up inside me.

He slid his hands down my thighs, curled his fingers around my legs, then pulled them up into the air, resting them on his shoulders so

I was suspended in the air. When his mouth connected with my cunt, I threw my head back and moaned again.

While licking my clit, he glanced up at me, at the spit and drool covering my body and the dildo inside of me. I grasped the ropes and tugged on them, my fingers digging into my palm.

"More," I murmured, the sound muffled.

The pressure rose in my core, every breath becoming raspier.

God, I loved this. I fucking loved this.

I loved what all the guys gave me in the bedroom and appreciated how they were so different, but letting Kai take me alone was something else entirely. I drifted off to a whole different world of submissiveness.

"Please," I whimpered on the toy. "More, please!"

He held my trembling legs harder against his shoulders and groaned on my clit. I screamed out on the toy, strings of spit dripping from my mouth when I couldn't keep it closed. Wave after wave of pleasure rushed over me.

When I came down from my orgasm, Kai gently set down my legs, then grabbed a thick black rope from another room. From the top of my thighs to my ankles, he tied my legs together.

I pointed my toes to try to touch the ground, but he grasped my hips from behind instead and pulled my ass into the air, squeezing and grabbing it all over. Then, he pulled me closer and positioned himself behind me.

Kai thrust into me from behind, using my body like it was made for his pleasure. With my hands tied up, my legs bound together, and my mouth stuffed full, I had no control over the situation. He was using me as he wanted.

And I fucking loved it.

He continued to pound into my tight hole until I was choking on the dildo and crying out over and over again. Pleasure rushed through me, my pussy pulsing over and over on his cock. When Kai finally came deep inside me, he stuffed himself as deep as he could go and grunted into my ear.

"You're mine."

Chapter One Hundred Thirty-Eight

KAI

After taking Imani down from the rope suspended in my room, I laid her on the bed and undid her legs. She curled up next to me, pulling the blankets over her naked body and staring at the plain wall opposite my bed.

"Is Landon staying here?" Imani asked, spotting Landon's stuff on the couch.

"For a bit," I said.

She furrowed her brows, hurt flashing onto her face for a moment, and then she turned onto her belly, elbows posted on the pillow, and stared down at me. The light bounced off her brown eyes, making them glow in the dim room.

"Will you tell me what's going on?" she asked, her lips curled into a frown. "Why do I need to learn how to shoot a gun again? Everyone, even my mom, has been acting different lately, and I'm nervous."

But Imani knew exactly why she was here. She wanted to learn as much as I wanted to teach her. Still, I didn't want to tell her that her life was in danger. I couldn't protect Dad or Mom. I could protect Imani. I *wanted* to protect Imani.

So, could I tell her about what Akio had said to me yesterday? Could I tell her that his parents were after her? Could I tell her that she might needed to defend herself at some point?

No.

"You know things are getting more dangerous," I said, gently caressing her hip bone. "I want you to be able to defend yourself if anything or anyone tries to hurt you. I can't let anything happen to you."

She swallowed hard. "You know something, don't you?"

After glancing from eye to eye, I clenched my jaw and looked away, unable to lie while looking her in the eye, unlike João. "Tonight, at Poison's place, we have a meeting with Nicole, head cheerleader and head *bitch*. Meet me back here after. I want to teach you to shoot."

"Okay," she said after a few moments, as if she believed me without question. "But ... if you're going to teach me how to shoot a gun, then I get to ask you something, and you have to answer me honestly."

"What's that?" I asked.

"What's going on with you and Allie?" she asked, eyes suddenly wavering and voice breaking. "I see the way you look at her. I don't know what ... I don't know what it means. But I need to know, Kai. I need you to tell me."

I stared at her, desperately wanting to tell her. Because I did. I wanted to tell her everything that I'd been holding back. I wanted to tell her about my father's motorcycle *accident* and my mother's death a short time after. It hadn't been an accident, and she knew that. But she didn't know the extent of it.

She didn't know who Allie really was to me. Neither did Allie.

After swallowing hard, I brushed my knuckles against her cheek and pushed some thick, curly hair behind her ear. "I want to tell you," I said, knowing that this might break her. Hell, knowing that it *would*. "I really, really do."

I stayed quiet for a long time, my breathing hitching. I couldn't say it. I wanted to tell her so badly, but I couldn't. I physically couldn't.

"But you're not gonna tell me, are you?" Imani asked.

I didn't wanna tell her no, but that was what I had to tell her.

"I can't tell you. Not right now. But I can tell you that I don't like her the way I like you. I don't think about her the way I think about you. She doesn't mean to me what you mean to me, Imani. You're the best fucking thing to happen to Poison."

Imani sat up beside me and suddenly pushed my hand away.

Instead of lying with me like I wanted her to, she stood up from the bed with a small blanket covering her tight body and refused to make eye contact with me. "I have to go," she said. "I have to get back to class."

I knew that if I had told her, she would've stayed with me. Imani would've fucking stayed.

"Imani, please, wait." I jumped up from the bed and followed after her, rushing through my small downstairs before she ran up the stairs. "Please, you have to believe me. I really want to tell you."

"If you wanted to tell me, then you would tell me. I want to know what she means to you." Imani turned around to face me with tears in her eyes. "João won't tell me that he loves me. I know you won't tell me whatever I mean to you. I just ... I feel so helpless." She sobbed. "Because I love you guys."

Almost as if she hadn't known what she was saying, she slapped her hand over her mouth and widened her eyes. Then, after another moment, she shook her head and dropped her hand. "It doesn't matter. You already know that. I fucking love you guys, okay? All I want is for you to be happy. And maybe ... maybe I want you to love me too."

"Imani," I whispered, my heart racing.

I'd been so alone. So fucking alone for the past few years. I didn't have any family. João and Landon were the only two people I really spoke to anymore. And now ... now, Imani was telling me this.

"Please, stop," I begged.

But Imani didn't stop. She found her clothes, then pulled them on, and then she grabbed her things and ran out the door.

I didn't blame her. I should've fucking told her.

Chapter One Hundred Thirty-Nine

IMANI

After I found my way back to school, it was lunchtime. I texted Mom that I was okay, even when my morning teachers had reported me as missing, and then I stared at the cafeteria doors and took a deep breath. My stomach turned.

Kai walked into the building through the doors to my right, taking one long look at me. I gulped and hurried into the cafeteria, heading straight for Landon, who stood in the cafeteria line for food from the lunch ladies.

"Hey," I said, gently knocking my shoulder against his. "You're staying with Kai?"

"Who told you that?" Landon asked, grabbing some milk.

"Kai did," I said, rocking back on my heels. "Why didn't you want to stay with me?"

He placed a tattooed hand against the side of my head and pulled me closer, placing a kiss on my forehead. "Because your mom wouldn't like it. I stay out late with the guys, have a gun, and come home with blood on my knuckles. She's warming up to me, and I don't want to ruin that."

While I wanted to protest, I knew that he was right. My mom was warming up to him. And Landon never really had a good family life. My mom was the only person to really care about him, so he couldn't stay at our house. Because Landon Caddell was bad news. Landon Caddell was a part of Poison. And Landon Caddell killed.

"Why don't you come over and sit with us?" Landon asked.

I glanced over at Kai and João, sitting at Poison's infamous lunch table. But I shook my head. "I can't."

Memories of what had happened earlier at Kai's house flooded through my mind. If I sat next to him, I didn't know what I would do. I'd be a hot mess.

And João ... we hadn't spoken a word to each other since the mall. Since our kiss.

"I'm going to sit with Allie today. I think she needs it. And ... I feel like I haven't talked to her in so long, like really had a good girl talk with her."

"João said you should come sit with us, but ..." Landon looked over at the guys, then down at me, a smirk on his face. "When he gets angry, don't complain to me about it. He's a fucking asshole."

"João told you to tell me to sit with you guys?" I asked, completely and utterly shocked.

"Yep."

After that kiss, I'd been worried all night. Worried that I had done something wrong. Worried that I would lose them. Worried that I cared too much about them, more than they cared about me. João never showed his feelings like that and really didn't invite me to sit at the lunch table with them.

I didn't want to get hurt. Neither did João. But that was all he seemed to do was hurt people.

"Well ... that's a first," I said.

"I'm gonna go eat. See ya," Landon said, walking off to Poison's table.

I turned on my heel and walked toward Allie's table, but before I could get there, Maddie Weber from Mr. Barnes's Biology class cut me off and smiled sweetly at me.

"Hey," Maddie said, pushing some red hair over her shoulder. "Where'd you go during Mr. Barnes's class?"

"Oh," I said, taken off guard. My cheeks flushed as I thought back to earlier at Kai's house. "Nowhere really. I just got some sudden cramps." *In my vagina, from Kai.* "But I'm feeling better now."

"Good. We got partnered up for a Bio project," she said. With her hands clasped against her backpack straps, she flicked her finger over a couple gaming and anime pins nervously. "I'm pretty busy for the rest of this week, and I was wondering if you wanted to get a head start on it tonight. If not, I can make time but—"

"That's fine," I said, glancing over at the Poison boys watching me intently from their designated table. "As long as you don't mind, uh, working over at Landon's place tonight. I promise that they're not going to hurt you."

As soon as the words left my mouth, I felt so freaking stupid. It had all come out wrong. I didn't want to scare her away, but I needed to be over Landon's tonight. João might've been an ass this weekend, but I refused to let them make any more bad decisions without me.

They wanted me to be a part of Poison. *I* wanted to be a part of Poison. And Poison made decisions together. João had told me that they wouldn't get in trouble for anything that they had done and recorded, but I needed to make sure myself.

If I lost them—any one of them, even João—I would hate myself because I couldn't stop it. I didn't know what it was, but thinking about being without them all ... I couldn't do it. After the mall the other day and after João kissed me, he had left without saying even a couple more words and with so many ... fears.

What would Mom do when she found out that I wasn't only dating Landon? That I had feelings for João and Kai too? What would she think when she found out that all the Poison boys were mine?

Maddie teetered back and forth for a couple moments, chewing on the inside of her lip and looking over at Poison.

Knowing that I had probably freaked her out, I grasped her hands and smiled reassuringly. "I promise, they won't."

After a couple tense moments, Maddie nodded. "Okay. Text me the address tonight."

Before she could walk away, her brother, Oliver, and Alec Wolfe— her secret lover maybe—and a couple other guys from the hockey team came up to us. Oliver and she exchanged a couple tense words, and Alec gave her a sneaky look that nobody, except me and her, caught.

"You're Imani, right?" one of the guys said, his hockey gear slung over his shoulder.

"Um," I said, trying to remember his name. "Yes, I am."

"I've seen you around Redwood and—"

João slammed his fist into the side of his face, sending the guy to the ground.

My eyes widened, heart pounding inside my chest. "João?!" I shouted, crouching down beside the guy to make sure he was okay. "What the hell are you even—"

Before I could even finish my sentence, João snatched my elbow and pulled me to my feet, thrusting me behind him. "Don't talk to her again," João said between gritted teeth, his knuckles covered with blood. "She's ours."

With that, he pulled me straight past the teachers, who didn't say a freaking word to him after what he had done, then out the cafeteria door.

I pulled myself out of his grip and smacked him hard on the chest. "What the fuck?! You're annoying as hell!" I whisper-yelled.

"And you're a part of Poison now," he said, lips curled into a small smirk. "You're ours. Nobody gets to talk to you, to touch you, or to take from us. We run the school. This town. And now, you, Imani Abara. But you should have already known that."

"You don't run me," I said between gritted teeth. Anger pooled within me, and I had the urge to thrust my hands against his chest and shove him away. I didn't understand how one little comment from him could make me feel this way.

We both hated each other but loved each other. In some fucked up way.

"You don't think we do?" He turned his lips up into a wicked grin and brushed his bloody knuckles across my cheek. "You're wrong. Poison always makes decisions together. And we decided a long time ago, before you joined, that you were ours to do whatever the fuck we wanted."

Chapter One Hundred Forty

KAI

"Who's the chick?" Landon asked, staring at Maddie, who Imani had basically brought over to his place after school.

Imani ushered Maddie into the basement and toward the stained couch, near Jace and Allie. They all had gotten here about five minutes ago and were waiting for Nicole to show because she apparently had *information* about her father and other Redwood rich that we could use against them.

"We didn't invite her."

Imani crossed her arms. "Well, I did."

"It's okay. I can go," Maddie whispered, glancing nervously at us. "I wanted to thank you for what you did to Principal Vaughn. He—"

"What'd we do?" I asked from the other couch, drawing my finger against the muzzle of my gun and looking from her to Imani, desperately trying to figure out a way to get her alone. I needed to talk to her, but she had easily avoided a conversation by bringing Maddie.

Maddie stopped short, cheeks flaming, and shrugged. "Um ..."

"Don't answer them," Imani said.

"I thought you hated us?" João said to Imani after inhaling smoke from his bong. He placed it down on the cement floor and blew the smoke from his nose, eyes closing briefly. "Why are you here?"

After sitting next to Allie, Imani crossed one leg over the other and rested her head against her shoulder. "Because I'm not letting you guys make any more dumb decisions without my consent."

"What? You think you own us now?" João said to her, leaning forward with his forearms on his knees. He laughed lifelessly at her. "We make decisions around here. You take no part in it, not even if you fucking beg to."

"No," Imani said strongly. "I get a say in it. You've made it clear that you want me to be a part of your little gang. And if I am, that means I get to voice my opinion on what you should and shouldn't be doing. You guys think you know the Redwood rich like the backs of your hands, but you don't know everything. I have connections to people too."

After they quarreled back and forth for another five minutes, Nicole came clanking down the stairs in a pair of red heels and a small black dress. The entire room did a collective eye roll, and Allie scooted closer to Jace protectively.

"Hey, guys," Nicole said when she stepped into the room. Everyone, except Maddie, glared at her, not really wanting her here, but she was the only one who probably had solid information on her father. She looked at Maddie and scrunched her nose. "Weird that you're here, but okay."

She kicked off her heels and sat on the sofa next to Jace.

Allie pulled him closer to her, so they weren't even touching, and clenched her jaw. "You said you had information. Tell us or get out."

Nicole widened her eyes at Allie, but none of us had time for Nicole's bullshit. She was known to talk in circles and to talk forever, making up lies and gossip that the entire school would end up believing somehow. I just wanted to spend my time tonight talking to Imani and teaching her how to shoot a gun.

Jace placed a hand on Allie's knee and squeezed gently. "We'll leave soon, baby. Settle down."

Nicole straightened herself out and cleared her throat. "About my father ..." She looked from João to Landon to me. "This can't ... nobody can know that this information came from me. Please, if you can make it look like you got it some other way, please, do it. I don't want my father to be angry with me. I want him put away."

My eyes widened slightly. Put away? As in ... thrown in jail? As far as I knew, Nicole never seemed like she hated her father. She had always gushed about how much money he would spend on her. She acted as if she hadn't moved from the bad part of Redwood to the rich when we were in middle school and as if she had grown up rich her entire life.

"He's using the cheer team to do his dirty work."

Landon rolled his eyes. "God, why is it always the cheer team in the drama?"

Nicole pressed her lips together, and I actually saw tears in her eyes. "I'm being serious. He found out that Principal Vaughn was taping people in the locker rooms. It started with the cheer squad. He let it slide as long as he was able to take some of the film of the girls. He's been using it against us and blackmailing us into getting information about people in Redwood for him, threatening to leak the tapes and ruin our lives if we don't." She turned to Jace. "That's why I slept with Carter. I never loved you. I just ... my father wanted me to get information out of you. I knew it was wrong. I fucking knew it."

"What?" Jace asked, staring over at her. "He's doing that?"

She wiped tears from her cheeks with a shaky hand. "That's not all. He's roped some of the girls into a sex ring, and he was helping pimp them out at one point. He's doing it all for the money. He's so ... so greedy. He doesn't care."

If what she was saying was true, then Dad was right. He was fucking right.

"I-I-I'm one of those girls," she said, a complete and utter mess of tears and snot. "He used me, forced me to have sex with men sixty years older than me. Just to get a quick few bucks. I'm sorry for everything I've done. I'm so sorry."

Everyone stared at Nicole with wide eyes as she bawled into Jace's chest. Jace awkwardly patted her shoulder but inched closer to Allie, as if he was uncomfortable.

"Prove it," Landon said, waving her off and lighting up a cigarette. "Why should we believe you? All you have done is lie for and protect your father for the past few years. Why tell us now?"

Nicole sat back up and wiped her eyes. "Because ... because I know that you can do something about it now. I know that you can put him away for years, if you … if you want to. And I'm begging you to do something. If you don't, I'll be stuck here for the rest of my life."

Staring back and forth between Nicole and Poison, Allie furrowed her brows.

After a few moments, Nicole stood and shook her head. "You don't believe me, do you?"

João looked at me, and I shrugged. "I didn't find any of that footage when we went through the principal's computer, but he could've stashed it elsewhere. I don't know. She could be lying, or she could be telling us the truth about her father. We know he's a prick."

After a few moments, João nodded to the door. "Get out."

Allie's eyes widened. "You're going to make her leave? After what she told you?"

"She can't prove this. We have nothing to go off of and nothing to hurt her father with," João said, glancing back at her. "You bring me all the shit you can find to prove to me that you're not lying, and we'll help you out. If you can't, then you're stuck."

Nicole shook her head, fear evident on her face. "But I-I—what am I supposed to get? How am I supposed to give it to you? What kind of evidence do you need? He doesn't let me into his office, and he somehow always knows if I try to sneak in there or not. I can't get you anything." She rubbed the back of her neck and stared at the ground with wide eyes. "Please, you have to believe me."

João sighed heavily through his mouth and stood, grabbing her by the arm and dragging her to the door. "I told you that I want you out," he said through clenched teeth. "Come back when you have something that we can use."

Nicole looked back at us, staring at Jace and then at Allie. "You have to believe me. Please, Allie, please. You're the only one who does. I can see it. Don't let them—"

João shoved her out and slammed the door in her face.

"Jace," Allie whispered, curling closer to him. "Do you think she'll be okay?"

Jace grimaced at the door. "I don't know, Allie. I don't like her. She always lies about everything. And you can't believe a liar, not even when they're telling the truth."

I stared at Allie, then at Imani, who was glaring at my proximity to

Allie. She clenched her jaw, then hurried toward the exit of the room toward a side room off the basement.

"I need to get something to drink," Imani said. "That was a lot."

Hating—loathing—the hurt in her eyes, I followed after her and captured her wrist as we left the room. She wasn't leaving the room to get anything to drink. She was leaving because she thought that I liked Allie.

When the door closed, Imani shook her head. "You like her," Imani said, agony in every word. "You like my best friend."

"I don't like Allie," I said, all those painful memories coming back and haunting me.

She stared at me with tears in her eyes.

"You're not going to ask me anything else?" I asked, expecting her to at least try to pry some more. That was what she had been doing for weeks about my relationship with Allie, but all she'd gotten was nothing.

"No," she said, ripping herself away from me. "It's not like you'd actually tell me anyway."

"Imani," I whispered, grasping her hand again.

She turned toward me. "What, Kai?! What do you want from me? To fuck?" She shoved me back and shook her head. "Is that all you want from—"

"Allie is my sister."

Chapter One Hundred Forty-One

IMANI

"Allie is your sister," I whispered, completely taken aback.

My heart pounded inside my chest. The mere thought was so outlandish that I almost didn't believe it. It didn't make any sense to me. How could he and Allie be siblings? They didn't look anything alike.

He nodded and nervously chewed on the inside of his cheek. "Yes, she's my sister."

I inhaled sharply and shuffled my feet. If what he was saying was true, then Allie's dad or mom would have cheated. How could I tell something like that to Allie? Would she even believe me? But I guessed it wasn't my place to tell her after all.

"Please, don't tell her," Kai pleaded.

He paced around the room as if he was nervous, and it was the first time I'd ever seen him like this. Kai was never nervous. He was quiet, reserved, and deadly. Never nervous.

"I ... I just want to be able to tell her myself." He paused. "When I'm ready."

"I ... I don't know what to say."

He walked up to me and grabbed my hands in his larger ones, squeezing them tightly. "You don't have to say anything. I just don't wanna lose you. That's why I told you. I haven't told anyone, except the guys, and honestly, I didn't think I ever would. I'm so nervous about this."

Still though, how could this be? How could Allie be Kai's sister? Allie's mom and dad had loved each other. They had freaking loved each other more than anyone ever. Part of me wanted to believe that this was all a lie because Allie would be heartbroken. But ... I didn't know.

"Do you believe me?" Kai asked. "I need you to believe me. I can bring you home and show you evidence. I have pictures and our father's gun, all the little knick knacks that he gave us both to play with."

While I wanted to see the evidence and the pictures, I couldn't go anywhere right now. Nicole had just broken the worst news to us. Not only that, but Maddie was waiting for me. We had a project to do right now.

"I ... I can't right now, Kai. How about later?"

He paused for a moment. "Sure, later. I'll prove it to you that Allie is family, that I don't like her the way I like you, that I don't feel the same way about her that I feel about you. I just wanna protect her. Redwood is shit. What Principal Vaughn did to her on school grounds was fucking terrible."

"I know," I whispered, curling my fingers into his chest muscle. "It was terrible."

After a few moments, I walked back out into the basement, where everyone was chatting tensely, and grabbed Maddie's hands.

"Where is that drink you needed so badly?" João taunted.

I turned on my heel with gritted teeth and glared at him. He always had something to say, and it was never fucking nice. I was so tired of fighting endlessly with that boy while juggling to keep Landon and Kai okay.

"That's none of your business," I said.

Ignoring his other remarks, I pulled Maddie toward the secluded table in the back of the room and deposited my backpack on the chair beside us. Pulling out my books for Biology, I started on the project with her. Every so often, I would look over at the guys, specifically Kai and Allie and how they interacted with each other.

And while I wanted to be jealous and I wanted to hurt, I knew that this was a good thing. Not only did I not feel jealous anymore, but now, I felt joy, joy that my best friend had a brother and that my best friend now had somebody else in her life who could love her as much as I did.

She deserved it. She'd been so alone these past few years after her father died.

And Kai ... as far as I knew, he didn't have anyone else either. The only people he had were himself, Poison, and me. His father and his mother were both gone. Allie was the only other family member who was still alive.

That made me happy for both of them.

Chapter One Hundred Forty-Two

LANDON

After Kai and Imani walked back into the room twenty minutes ago, I had sat tensely in the basement and gritted my teeth. I hadn't been able to stop since Maddie and Imani had started working on their project in the back of the room because Imani kept looking over at Kai and Kai kept looking over at Imani.

It was back and forth, back and forth, and I didn't know if I could handle any more.

I needed to know what they were to each other. I didn't want to sit back and let this happen. If they were friends, I wanted to know if they were friends. If they just had sex, I wanted to know that they just had sex. If they loved each other ...

I took a deep breath.

If they loved each other, I needed to know.

Both Imani and Kai deserved to be happy. But so did I. And I didn't want to fall back into that hole of worrying endlessly about what she was doing behind my back because she hadn't done anything that I didn't know about. I assumed the worst. That wasn't fair to her.

Deep down, I knew that Kai and João both meant more to her now than they ever had meant to Imani. João would never admit it, but Kai was close to telling her that he loved her. I could see it in his eyes. He had never looked so content.

Still, the insecurity built up inside.

"See you at school," Imani said from the doorway, waving Maddie and Allie off from the basement door.

It was just Kai, João, and Imani left with me here, and I needed to talk to her so badly.

After everyone was gone, Imani shut the door. I stood as Kai did, and I knew that he was about to walk over to Imani and sweep her away back to his place, but I needed to talk to her first. I needed to know. I needed to tell her how I was feeling because that was what my therapist had told me to do.

That was what Imani wanted me to do.

"Hey, can I talk to you for a couple seconds?" I said, nerves bubbling up inside me.

I hadn't felt this nervous around her in a long time now. I didn't know what she was going to say. Nobody cared about me the way she did. Nobody ever asked me to tell them my feelings. When I had been growing up, Mom and Dad hadn't given a shit about me.

Part of me—that terrible part of me—made me wonder if Imani would care.

I knew that she would. But still, it was so hard to unlearn all those little behaviors and thoughts, all those feelings that my parents had beaten into me physically and mentally over the years. Whoever the fuck got through their trauma and made it out alive on the other side was strong as fuck.

"Yeah!" She smiled at me, her cheeks rounding and her eyes wide. "Wanna go upstairs?"

After taking her hands, I pulled her up the basement steps and around the corner into my parents' house.

She turned on the light and looked back at me. "What do you want to talk about?"

I took a deep breath and looked into her eyes. My stomach turned, my throat closing up. "I ..."

I was suddenly lost for words, or maybe that wasn't it. Maybe I was too nervous to ask her what they meant to her. I knew that I wouldn't like the answer either way, but what if she thought less of me? Dad had always told me never to share my feelings. He'd taught me that it was weak for a man to show any emotion. I was trying so hard to unlearn everything that they had shoved down my throat.

Imani stepped closer to me, stood on her tiptoes, and pushed some hair off my forehead. "What is it?"

After swallowing my pride, I took her hand and squeezed them hard. "What do Kai and João mean to you?"

Her eyes widened, face flushing. "I ..." Suddenly, she pulled her hand away from me and started pacing the room. "Landon ... I love you so much. Like, I love you so *fucking* much." She licked her lips and looked at me with tears in her eyes now. "I promised myself that I would love you and only you, but I'm afraid ... I'm going to lose you when I tell you that ..." She ran her hands through her hair and pushed away some tears. "But I also think I'm falling for Kai and João too."

The last part of her sentence was only a mere whisper.

I had known that it was coming. All these weeks of lying in my bed and staring up at the ceiling, wondering if she really did like them or not, I'd prepared myself for her answer and even her reaction.

"I don't want you to feel crushed or feel like I don't love you. Because I do. You're the first guy that I've ever felt this strongly for before. You're the first guy that I've ever loved. I hadn't told anybody that before I told you. Please," she whispered, suddenly clutching on to me tighter than ever. "Please, I can't lose you."

"Imani ..." I said.

I'd prepared for this, yet I still didn't know what to say.

"I am so confused. I don't know what to do. I don't wanna be without you. I don't wanna lose any of you, but I also don't want to choose. I can't choose." She cried. "I'm sorry, Landon. I'm so sorry."

Anguish spread across her face. I could feel how much she was hurting.

"It's okay," I said, brushing some curly black hair off her face. "I know what they mean to you. Deep down, I've always known. But I told you that Poison is forever. I dedicated my life to these guys and to destroying this town. You're not going to tear us apart with your decision."

"So, does that mean ... that you ... that you're going to leave me?"

"That I'm gonna leave you?" I asked, completely taken aback. "There is no fucking way that I would ever leave you, no matter what.

Poison isn't the only one to change my life. You showed me what it means to love someone and to be loved.

"I'm not leaving you, nor am I leaving Poison. I ..." I started, nerves still piling up in my stomach. I fucking hated talking about my feelings. I hated that I needed reassurance over and over again that she wouldn't leave me. It made me feel so shitty, especially to her because she had done nothing wrong. Nothing fucking wrong. She wasn't like Mom and Dad, yet still, it was so hard to unlearn all those toxic fucking feelings that had literally become part of me.

"I just need some more open communication," I finally managed to say.

"I want to love you, and I want you to love me too, Imani," I said desperately. "Please."

Her lips curled into a smile. "Of course, Landon."

I widened my eyes and pulled her closer to me, placing a kiss on her forehead and finally feeling the stress roll off my shoulders. Nobody, not even the other two guys, would come between us. I would love Imani until my very last breath.

<h1>Chapter One Hundred Forty-Three</h1>

KAI

To my surprise, Imani and Landon came back into the basement, looking happier than ever. I thought for sure, by the way Landon had kept glaring at me, that he was going to be pissed off at Imani for getting closer to me and João.

"I'm gonna go over to Kai's place for a little bit," Imani said to Landon, standing on her tiptoes and placing a kiss on his lips.

"You're welcome to come, Landon," I said.

Again, surprisingly, he shook his head and nodded to João and Ana in the basement. João glared at me, then at Imani, who was inching closer to me by the second. "I'm going to clean up here a little bit with them, and then I'll be over a bit later."

"All right," I said, taking Imani's hand in mine and pulling her toward the basement door.

I was nervous but excited to show her the pictures of Allie and me. I hadn't shown the pictures to anyone, except the guys, only a couple of times. But I really, really wanted to show Imani. Not only did I want her to believe me, but I also finally wanted to feel happy. I wanted to tell someone else who Allie really was to me and who I really was to Allie.

After we drove to my house, I opened the door and let Imani head down the stairs before me. Last time we had been here, this morning,

I'd tied her up and fucked her senseless in my bedroom. But tonight, I was going to show her another side of me and then teach her how to shoot a gun.

Because she fucking sucked at it.

"I'm actually so excited," Imani said. "You really care about Allie, and I believe you. I saw the way you looked at her tonight and realized that it's not the way you look at me. Allie needs someone in her life right now. Her mom is ... not in a good place, it seems, especially with Allie's new stepdad."

"I know," I said. "I'm trying to figure it out. I want to protect Allie, but I don't want her to know yet. I'm nervous that she's going to ... freak out. Because she looked up to her dad. She wants to believe that he did nothing wrong. He was just trying to save Redwood too."

Once we walked down the stairs, I guided her toward my bedroom. Locked away in one of my many drawers was a box. A box of things I'd collected of Dad and Allie over the years. After taking a deep breath, I pulled out the box and sat on the side of the bed next to Imani, nervous to open it up.

When I finally did, all the memories of being young and carefree came rushing back—running through the grass in the backyard, grinning from ear to ear like Redwood wasn't all that bad after all.

Lying on top of all the other items was a picture. I took it in my hands and brushed my fingers over the faces in the image, and then I handed the picture to Imani.

"My dad took a couple photos of us when we were babies." I scratched the back of my head. "He had gotten my mom pregnant before he met Allie's mom. They were both really young. High school age, I think, but then he went to the Army."

I took a long, deep breath. My stomach was tight, feelings of growing up so lonely spreading throughout my body.

Our father had chosen Allie's family over ours most of the time. He still came to visit, and we hung out a lot, at least once every week. But he lived with Allie.

All I wanted was to be with them. All my fucking life, I wanted to see my sister and for us to be happy together. We had lived right down the road from her, but it hadn't been the same.

"Allie doesn't know it, but she's gotten me through these past few years. After our dad died, my mom overdosed on drugs. I was so fucking alone, Imani. Allie was the only thing that I had. I've been holding on to the hope that one day, I would be able to tell Allie who she really is to me." Tears pricked the corners of my eyes. "I felt so alone for so long. I wanted to tell her … I *wanna* tell her so badly. I'm so nervous, so fucking nervous."

Imani moved closer to me and enveloped me with a hug, squeezing me tightly and resting her head on my chest. "I know; it's so hard," she whispered, "just hearing you say it."

"Do you think … do you think she'll hate me after that? After I tell her what her parents did?"

So many questions rushed through my mind. What if I told Allie and she didn't believe me, or what if I told her and she hated me because of it? She didn't know who her father really was. She didn't know that he had a son her age too. What the fuck *could* I tell her? I didn't want to lose her. I didn't have her now, but still … at least I got to see her.

All those terrible memories of my parents' death years ago rushed through my head. I wanted my mom and dad back. For one fucking day, I wanted a family. That was all I ever fucking wanted.

A fucking tear slid down my cheek, and Imani pushed it away. My emotions were so raw. Why had Dad done that to me? Why had he chosen Allie? I just wanted him. I wanted him back whether he chose me or not. As long as I got to see him again, I fucking wished he was still alive.

"I don't want to screw up," I said to Imani.

She took my face in her hands and gently caressed my cheeks with her thumbs. "You're not going to screw up. Allie needs someone as much as you need someone, but neither of you will ever admit it."

Wanting to hold someone, I wrapped my arms around her shoulders and pulled her flush against my chest. "She's the only family I have left. I can't lose her. God, I don't want to lose her." There was nothing but anguish in my trembling voice.

Imani pulled me to the bed and pushed me down, and then she curled up next to me and laid her head on my chest again, holding me so tightly. So fucking tightly. Just like Mom used to. Fuck, I fucking missed Mom.

Chapter One Hundred Forty-Four

IMANI

During Kai's breakdown, so many tears had formed in my eyes, but I refused to let them fall. I couldn't let them fall. Kai was so raw and emotional right now. He had been there for me, so I wanted to be there for him. This was my time to console him, not his to console me.

After an hour of lying with him, his body finally relaxed underneath mine, his fingers digging into my backside. "We should go practice shooting your gun. You need to learn," he hummed. "Come on. Let's get up."

"Are you okay?" I asked, watching him move around the room and turn on the light.

"Yeah, I'm fine," he said quietly, hurt still lingering in his voice.

I didn't want to push it, so I let it go for now. I stood up behind him and followed him throughout the small house until we reached the underground shooting range and his weapons room. He gave me a gun that fit in my hand perfectly, the grip solid and comfortable against my palm.

I nervously walked over to one of the lanes and stood in front of the target where I had stood another night with Poison. Except this time, it was only Kai here with me. He stood back at first, watching me carefully and readjusting me whenever I needed it.

Once I faced the target, I lifted my arms and aimed.

My heart was racing against my chest. I never liked doing this. Even last time, I had been so nervous. But I knew that Kai wouldn't let me get out of it. I knew that he was forcing me to do this for some reason. And I was sure that I didn't want to know what that reason really was.

But I already did.

After taking a deep breath, I aimed and pulled the trigger one time. The bullet whizzed through the air and pierced the corner of the target. I swallowed hard, my hand starting to tremble slightly, and looked over at Kai.

"Keep your hips steady," he said, taking a step toward me.

It was like he was stalking his prey, moving toward me so quietly and so slowly, and it made my heart race even more. I didn't think I would ever be able to keep my hand or hips stable, to think clearly when he was around.

I looked forward and stared at the target again, feeling his body heat from behind me. Like last time, Kai's hands came around my hips, his thumbs slightly digging into my ass and his fingers strumming against the tops of my thighs. I cursed at myself for how my body reacted to him. It always reacted to him the same way, like he was about to tie me up again and have his way with me.

"Steady," he whispered into my ear, his voice gruff. "Deep breaths. And then"—he drifted one hand up my body to the gun and straightened my trembling hands—"shoot."

Almost as if on command, I shot the gun. Another bullet whizzed through the air, this time hitting closer to the center of the target.

"You're getting better," he said, giving me a breathtaking smile. "You might not think it, but last time, you barely hit the target on your first few shots."

So, throughout the night, I continued to fire bullet after bullet after bullet at a target, never hitting the center, but getting damn close. Kai was teaching me how to shoot without reacting, without my hands trembling or my heart racing.

He wanted me to be able to do this without thinking. If my life was in danger, I needed to be able to defend myself.

"Why?" I finally asked him, setting the gun down on a stand

behind me. "You know the reason why you're making me do this, don't you?"

Instead of telling me, Kai handed me the gun back and nodded to the target. "Continue practicing. You're getting better."

"It's Akio's family, isn't it?" I whispered, knowing that it had to be them. Nobody else that I knew of wanted my family dead. "They beat up my mom and dad a while ago, and my parents act like it was nothing. But I know my mom is terrified of them. Are they planning something?"

Kai ran his tongue over his teeth and didn't answer.

And that was the only thing I needed, the only thing I fucking needed to understand that this was because of Akio's family. Kai wanted me to learn how to protect myself because he was afraid that he would lose me, too, like he had lost his father.

Chapter One Hundred Forty-Five

JOÃO

'd screwed the fuck up this weekend.

After that stupid fucking kiss with Imani at the mall, I'd left her there. I didn't know what to say to her. I didn't know what to do. So, I'd just left her.

I hadn't fucking found a way to tell her yet either. To tell her that I loved her.

Once I parked my car in front of my house, I stared emptily through the windshield, my hand tightening around the steering wheel. Ana sat in the backseat, kicking my chair with her strong-ass legs.

"João, I have to go to the potty. Please, can we go inside?" she asked. "It's cold out here, and Mama has the lights on. She must be inside, waiting for us."

"Go on in," I said, exhaling harshly. "I'm gonna stay out here for a couple minutes."

I needed to fucking think. I needed to think about *everything*. Landon and Kai were both getting closer to Imani, and I had even been getting closer to her at one point. Then, I fucked everything up big time.

I wanted to be with her too, but I didn't know how to say it. I didn't want her to leave me.

Ana unstrapped herself from the backseat and jumped out of the car, wobbling back and forth all the way to the front door. She knocked on it with a tiny fist and stood on her tiptoes to look in through the door window.

"Mama!" she called. "Mama, open the door. I have to use the potty!"

Mom was probably too fucked up on drugs to move right now.

Ana jumped up and down on her toes and pulled her coat together. I glided a hand over my face and took another deep exhale. I didn't know what to fucking do. Between Mom and Imani and watching Ana all the time, I was fucking overwhelmed. I couldn't do anything with Poison. I needed to find someone to watch Ana, needed to get Mom off the fucking drugs, and needed to tell Imani how I really felt about her.

"Mama!" Ana yelled again. She furrowed her brows, then looked back at me. "Mama is inside, sleeping. Can you please help me, João? I have to use the bathroom really bad. I'm going to pee my pants."

After shutting off the car, I zipped up my coat and got out into the cold. I walked over to the front door and pressed my key into it, turning the knob and stepping into the bright room. Ana ran over to the bathroom and slammed the door shut. I placed my keys on the table and took off my coat, glancing over at Mom, who was asleep on the couch, like she usually was nowadays.

I was surprised that there weren't pill bottles next to her.

The toilet flushed in the next room over, and then Ana came bouncing out of the bathroom.

She walked over to Mom and rested her head on the pillow beside her, gently stroking Mom's face. "Mama, wake up. We're home."

I collapsed on a kitchen chair and decided to fuck around on my phone until Ana finally fell asleep. I looked at Imani's contact and wanted so badly to text her, but what the fuck would I say? *Hey, what's up?* That was fucking stupid. Why the fuck was I so bad at this?

"Mama! Wake up!" Ana sat out on her knees now on the couch beside Mom and gently pushed on Mom's shoulders. "Mama, wake up, please. I want to tell you about my day at school. It was so much fun!"

My gaze shifted from my phone to the relatively clear table in front of me. There was a yellow envelope addressed to Mom from an unknown address. I thrust my hand into the open envelope and pulled out an empty container or package of some sort that was unmarked. My stomach tightened.

Ana looked over at me through wide eyes. "Mama isn't waking up. Do you know why? Do you think she's tired?"

I glanced around the room to see that it wasn't messy, like it had been since Mom had gotten addicted to drugs again. In fact, everything looked like she had just cleaned it; everything seemed a bit too in place. It felt surreal.

"João!" Ana shouted.

I looked over to her, then at the coffee table beside Mom. The wooden table was clear of all plates, all food, and all mail. Instead, it had one thing on it. One fucking thing.

A note.

My heart dropped, and I hurried over to Ana. I pulled her off the couch and sat her beside me, then collapsed next to Mom. I placed two fingers on her pulse, desperately trying to find it. Just really trying to find something. Her face was so cold, so fucking ... gray.

No, no. Fuck no.

"Hey, look," Ana said from behind me. "Mommy wrote us a note. I think that it says..." She paused. "That she loves us. And that she is sorry. Why is Mommy—"

I snatched the note from her hand, tears pouring out of my eyes. She was dead. She was fucking dead.

Chapter One Hundred Forty-Six

IMANI

An hour after I got home from Kai's, I lay in my bed, freshly showered, with my face washed for the first time in what seemed like forever and my hair wrapped up. I pulled the blankets over my body and wished that Landon were here with me tonight, but he'd stayed with Kai.

My phone buzzed on the bedside table, but I ignored it for the first ring. I needed to sleep. I had to wake up for school in only a couple hours, and I couldn't skip another day *or* another class. Kai had already pulled me out of Biology.

As the phone continued to buzz, I glanced over at it to see João's number. I clenched my jaw and snatched the phone from the table, squeezing it until my hand turned a shade lighter. Why did he have to call at the most inconvenient times? He probably wanted me to come over to be his little booty call tonight or something.

He sure as hell wasn't going to confess his feelings after what he did at the mall this weekend.

I thought he'd get my drift after the third unanswered ring, but the phone continued to buzz. My finger hovered over the Decline Call button, but something in the pit of my stomach told me to answer the damn phone.

Something didn't feel right.

Cursing myself, I clicked the Answer button and held the phone to my ear. "It's two in the morning, João. What do you want?"

"Hi, Imani," Ana said, her voice sounding so small and fragile over the phone.

"Hi, Ana," I said, guilt washing over me. "What's up? Why are you calling me so late?"

"Um ..." She paused for a long moment, and I heard something muffled in the back.

"Ana ..." I sat up from my bed, brows furrowed in worry and heart beating a little faster. So many questions raced through my head. Why is she calling me so late on João's phone? Where is he? And who is talking muffled in the background? "What's going on?"

"Can you come over?" Ana asked. "João is crying, and Mama isn't waking up."

My eyes widened slightly, and I jumped out of bed, then raced toward my bedroom door, grabbing my car keys and shoes on the way out. "What do you mean, your mom isn't waking up? Please, put João on the phone."

"Okay ... João, can you—"

The muffled chatter turned into heartbreaking sobs, and João was crying out for his mother. Tears welled up in my eyes, my chest tightening as I feared the worst. I slammed my bedroom door closed, rested my phone between my ear and my shoulder, and banged on my parents' bedroom door.

"Mom!" I shouted, barely able to hold myself together.

João's sobs were shrill and filled with sorrow and pain, all his emotions that he'd held in over the past few years, everything that he'd bottled up and held back from me. It killed me inside, knowing that whatever was happening had broken him so deeply that he couldn't hold it in any longer.

Mom opened her bedroom door and wiped her tired eyes. "What is it, Imani? I have to get up for work in an hour. I have an early sur—"

"I have to go to João's," I said, then quickly ran down the stairs. I would suffer the consequences with her tomorrow, but at least I'd let her know where I was going. After shooting with Kai tonight, I felt like I had to tell her.

We both knew that Akio's family was out to get me.

Once I slid into the car, I turned it on and hit the gas pedal, backing out of the driveway as quickly as I could. My tires squealed against the snowy street, the snow gently floating down from the skies.

My hands trembled as thoughts of what could've happened to João's mother racing through my head. What if she had overdosed again? What if someone from Akio's family had killed her? What if … what if one of those men who had raped her did something terrible to her?

I grabbed my phone as I pulled up to a red light, my knee bouncing, and quickly dialed Landon's number. I was the farthest from João's house. From here, it would take me at least fifteen minutes, even with speeding.

Landon answered on the second ring. "Imani, are you—"

"Get to João's house," I said, my voice cracking. "Something happened. I don't know anything right now, but Ana called me from João's phone. João was …" Tears started streaming down my face as I remembered how broken he had sounded. "He was sobbing." I pushed some tears off my cheeks, so I could see where I was going, and I hit the accelerator. "Please, hurry."

"We're on our way," Landon said.

My stomach was in knots. I didn't know if Ana and João were still in danger or if they were in danger at all, but I had the gun Kai had given me in the glove box. Still, I wanted everyone to be prepared for whatever it was too.

"Tell Kai to bring his gun," I said, voice trailing off. "I don't know what's going to be there."

"All right," Landon said. "See you soon."

After getting off the phone with Landon, I took the back roads to João's house because I knew that I'd miss all the red lights and I could whiz through most of the Stop signs around here. Besides, most of the cops weren't out this far into the slums.

When I reached João's house, Kai and Landon stood outside in the cold with Ana, who was barely sleeping in Kai's arms. I parked the car and hurried out, slamming my door and running toward them. Kai's face was completely void of any emotion, the mere look terrifying, while Landon's face was whiter than I had ever seen it.

"No," I whispered, not needing to hear them say anything. "Where is he? Where's João?"

"In the house."

I sprinted to the front door and yanked it open, rushing into the room filled with shrill sobs. Shivers ran down my spine, tears pricking the corners of my eyes again. I needed to be strong, if not for myself, then for João.

João hovered over his mother, who lay on the couch, his arms wrapped tightly around her shoulders to pull her closely to his chest. His body heaved back and forth, his cries becoming louder. "Mama! Mama!"

"João," I said, hurrying over and stopping behind him.

He clutched on to her desperately, fingers digging into her shoulders and tears streaming down his cheeks. "Mama! Come back. Come fucking back to me, to Ana. She needs you. I can't do this by myself. I can't—" His voice broke, body trembling harder. "I can't do this without you!"

I crouched down behind him, wrapping my arms around his torso to try to keep him steady. I couldn't tear him away from his mother, couldn't stop the tears from streaming down *my own* face. Instead, I pressed my lips together and looked away, pressing my head against his shoulder and trying hard not to let out a sob.

She was gone.

She was fucking gone.

"João," I managed to say, holding on to him tighter with every second that passed.

His grip began slipping from his mother's corpse, his body struggling, twitching, trembling in my hold. When she slipped from him completely and fell back against the couch cushions, João collapsed back on his ass and back against me, completely torn with trembling lips and bloodshot eyes.

I wrapped my arms around his shoulders, gently stroking his hair in one hand and rocking us back and forth. "I'm sorry," I whispered into his ear, letting him tremble even harder. "I'm so sorry, João."

Chapter One Hundred Forty-Seven

JOÃO

"We have to call the police," Imani said, resting her head against mine. "She needs to be taken out of here, so Ana can ... so she can sleep here for the night, and her house doesn't reek of ..." She trailed off and pressed her lips to my forehead again.

At some point, I had stopped my body from trembling, but I could feel the sadness lingering inside of me, ready to burst at any moment. All I could do was stare at Mom, lying dead on the couch with a suicide note beside her.

I brushed some brown hair off her forehead and tucked it behind her ear. Her skin felt so cold, and she felt so ... so gone, like she had killed herself early this morning while Ana and I were at school.

"We can't call the police," Landon said from the doorway. "They won't do anything about it, especially not after what we did to Principal Vaughn. They'll laugh in his face and dump her body in the trash."

"We have to do something," Imani said.

My lips trembled, my jaw twitching. "Call Rick Santos."

"Who's Rick Santos?" Imani asked, holding me tighter.

"We can't," Landon said, glancing at me briefly. "Jace killed him."

"What?!" she said from behind me. "Jace killed someone?!"

"Fuck," I grunted and ran my fingers across Mom's cheeks.

It would have been shitty to let him lay Mom to rest anyway. He wasn't a good man, but with the right amount of money, he would've done what I wanted, if he were still alive.

Still, Imani was right. Mom's body would decay here if we didn't move her soon.

"I'll figure it out." Landon dialed a number on his phone and walked outside into the frigid winter air.

Unable to take my fucking eyes off Mom, I stared at her for as long as I fucking could because I knew that this would be the last time I would ever see her. Ana would never see her again. The last image she had gotten of Mom would be of her sleeping and not waking up.

Dark circles lay underneath her eyes, and her lips were white and chapped. She should've gone for a haircut this month to snip her bangs back like she used to do when I was a kid. She always had such a youthful expression and complexion, but right now, she looked so ... old.

"What can I do for you?" Imani stroked her fingers across my shoulders. "Tell me."

But I didn't say anything to her. I couldn't. If I did, I would start sobbing again.

Instead, I rested my forehead against Mom's arm and squeezed my eyes closed, remembering what life had been like before Dad fucking ruined it all. She would take me to the playground every afternoon and ride down the slides with me, buy me strawberry ice cream and take me on long walks by the Overlook when Dad went on business trips.

"I want you back," I whispered, chest tightening once more and my voice cracking. Sorrow spread throughout my body quickly, the tears reforming in my eyes. "I just want you fucking back, Mama."

Sometime while I was knee deep in my memories, the front door opened. The two guys who had thrown Vaughn's head onto the football field for us and then disposed of his body walked in. I didn't trust many thugs in Redwood, but they had gotten the job done for us many times before. They would help us now.

Still ...

I didn't want them to take her away. I wasn't ready.

One walked over to the couch and grabbed Mom in his arms,

pulling her off the couch and away from me—from her son, from one of her children who only wanted her to be back, wanted this all to be a sick fucking joke.

"Don't take her away!" I screamed, chest tight. "Please, don't take my mom away."

Landon nodded to the guys, then the door. The thug walked away from me and toward him with her corpse in his arms, her arms and legs dangling in the air. I shot up from Imani's hold and followed after them, grabbing her.

I couldn't control myself.

"She's the only other person that Ana has," I said, my voice barely above a whisper.

I wanted to hold on to Mom's corpse for-fucking-ever. I didn't want them to take her away or for her to leave. I'd been so hard on her lately, wanting her to clean up her act, but I didn't want her fucking gone. I couldn't have her fucking gone.

"Please," I begged, holding on to her shoulders for as long as I could.

Imani pulled on my torso from behind, her smaller arms wrapping around me tightly to hold me back into the house as this thug did his job to lay Mom to rest somewhere. Imani's body was trembling behind me, but she held herself strong and refused to let me pull her through the doorway.

"Don't let Ana see her," I pleaded, spotting Ana lying in Kai's arms inside Imani's heated car, her head on his shoulder and her fingers playing with the ends of his hair. "Please, I don't want her to see Mom like this."

The man stopped at the front door, then went around the back of the house instead of walking by Ana to his car. They pulled their van around back and deposited Mom in the backseat, her body looking so fragile and frail. I stared at her with tears in my eyes and hurt in my heart.

My entire world was shattering. This couldn't be real.

This was selfish of her, so fucking selfish. Life was hard for everyone. But instead of trying to get clean, she had quit on everyone who loved her, on everyone who looked up to her, on everyone who knew that she could get better.

She had given up on Ana.

She had given up on *me*.

I had been with her every fucking step of the way since Dad had left and Ana had gotten sick. I had done so much to help her get clean and to help her stay clean. Blood of the Redwood rich covered my hands for her.

And she had decided that she didn't want to help care for Ana anymore.

Chapter One Hundred Forty-Eight

LANDON

"Where are we bringing Ana?" Kai asked me, standing outside Imani's car.

Ana sat in the backseat, yawning and barely able to keep her eyes open as she brushed a Barbie doll's hair with a small pink brush. She kept nodding off, and I wished she would fall asleep by now because I didn't know what to do with her or what to say to her.

"Your place?" I said, shrugging one shoulder.

"We can't bring her to my place," Kai said. "I barely have room as it is and don't have any shit that she's going to want. You know the moment we get back into that car, she's going to be wide awake and asking to make brigadeiros. She always does when she's nervous."

Glancing back at João's house, I grimaced. He and Imani hadn't come back out since they had taken his mother away. I didn't blame him either. Besides Ana, his mother was the only person he had left. If Imani wasn't here, he would've fucking broken even worse.

"Let's take her to Mrs. Abara's house," I said, unsure if we really should or not.

We weren't on the best terms, but she was growing closer to me and starting to warm up to us. We kept Imani safe, especially around Akio and his parents. The least she could do was let us crash for the night, right?

"You think she'll appreciate being woken up at this time?" Kai asked, brows drawn together. "It's almost six in the morning. She's either sleeping or probably at work already. School should be starting soon for all of us."

"Well, screw it," I said, walking toward the front door. "We don't have anywhere else to go. It's already been a long night. We're not going to that shithole, and Ana is staying home today. She can't go to day care after that."

Kai ran a hand over his face and slid into the driver's seat of Imani's car. It wasn't like we'd be getting back on his bike or walking to her house in this frigid fucking air. It was barely even December yet, and Redwood was cold as fuck.

When I opened the front door, Imani sat on the floor with her back against the couch and João sleeping in her arms. His body twitched, his cheeks stained with tears. She looked up at me through tired eyes and frowned.

"How are you holding up?" I asked her.

She closed her teary eyes and shook her head. "I just want to keep crying."

"I know."

"I don't understand how someone could do that," she croaked, lips trembling.

"Neither can I," I said, my gaze dropping to João. "If you weren't here, João would be so much worse off. You're ..." I couldn't believe that I was saying this because only a couple hours ago, I had gotten pissed off that Kai had Imani's attention. "You're holding us together. All of us."

Imani gave a hoarse laugh. "I don't know about that. I can barely hold myself together."

My bottom lip curled up slightly, as I wanted to show her that no matter what she thought, she was really the one who had helped us through so much shit these past few months. I knew that João wouldn't be able to get through this without her.

"He needs you right now," I said. "Stay with him."

"You're not going to be upset if I do?"

"No," I said honestly.

"Thank you," she whispered, gently stroking his hair.

"We're taking Ana back to your house in your car. Is that okay?"

She nodded to her purse on the kitchen table. "Yeah, my house key is in my wallet. You'll have to turn off the security system with a code when you get into the house. My code is five-six-seven-four. Don't forget because my dad will still probably be sleeping."

"And your mom?"

Imani looked out the window at the early morning sunlight shining in. "She's probably at work, but she might still be home. She's been trying to call me all night. I kinda left in a rush and haven't been able to call her back. If you see her, tell her that I'm okay."

"I will." I walked over to her and kissed her. "I love you."

"I love you too, Landon," she said, watching me walk out of the house and shut the door.

I didn't want to leave because I knew that they were both hurting on the inside. But Kai and I had to take care of Ana, and Kai wasn't getting into Mrs. Abara's house alone. She had only warmed up to me so far.

After sliding into the passenger seat, I looked back at Ana, who kicked her legs back and forth the way she always did when something was bothering her. Like Kai had said she would be, she was wide awake now.

"Where are we going?" she asked.

"To Imani's house."

She stayed quiet for a long time. "What happened to Mama?"

My entire body tensed, and I sat back in my seat and glanced over at Kai. I didn't know what to say to children, especially after something like that happened, and Kai had always been more comfortable with her anyway.

"She's ..." He looked over at me, pulling off João's street.

"She must've been really tired," Ana said with a yawn.

This wasn't our place to tell her that her mother had died. Hell, how the fuck did you tell a child that? Would she understand what happened? That her mother hadn't wanted to live anymore, so she had ended her life?

Fuck, this was hard for *me* to think about, and she wasn't even related to me.

"Yeah," I said because Kai looked lost for words too. "We're all tired tonight, Ana."

"Do you think Imani's mom has some brigadeiros? I want to make some to give to Mama when she wakes up." Ana smiled out the foggy window, eyes lighting up at the mere thought. "They always make her happy."

It only made me feel worse.

I didn't know what the fuck we were going to do.

"She might have some ingredients," Kai said, hand tightening around the steering wheel. "But how about we get some sleep first? It's really late at night. Everyone is either sleeping still or just waking up for school and work."

"What time do I go to school?" she asked.

"You're staying home," I said.

Throughout the entire car ride, Ana continued to ask questions that neither of us could answer honestly. When Kai finally pulled up to Imani's house, I hurried out of the car to open the front door. Imani's father walked into the foyer with his phone pressed to his ear.

"Hold on, sweetheart," he said into the phone, watching us carefully.

I pressed Imani's code into the keypad and looked over my shoulder at Kai, who had Ana in his arms, then back at her father. "Imani said that it was okay to come here. I'll tell you everything that you want to know, but she's safe. We need a place to crash for the night."

"It's six in the morning," her father said, then looked at Ana and let out a long sigh, nodding to the stairs. "Go ahead. Her room is upstairs to the left and down the hallway. You can't miss—"

"We know where her room is," Kai said, walking with Ana up the stairs.

Mr. Abara raised an eyebrow and placed his phone against his ear again. "Imani is safe."

"Is that Landon?" I heard Mrs. Abara say through the phone.

"Yes, sweetheart."

"Let me talk to him."

He handed the phone to me.

"Hi, Mrs. Abara."

"What happened, Landon?" she asked, worry laced in her voice.

Hospital noises echoed in the background. "Is everything okay? Imani ran out in a hurry hours ago. She looked like she was a mess."

"Imani's okay, but ..."

"But what?"

"But João's mother is dead."

Chapter One Hundred Forty-Nine

JOÃO

I tossed and turned all night, my body restless and my mind jolting me awake with nightmares of finding Mom dead over and over again. The mind was the cruelest fucking part of the body sometimes, making me think about shit that I wanted to bury.

When I finally opened my puffy eyes, sunlight blared through the window. I lay on the ground in my living room and in the arms of Imani. She had her head back against the couch, her lips parted slightly, her fingers in my hair, and her breathing even. She should've fucking been at school.

But she was here with me.

She had stayed the night, had come when Ana called, and hell, picked up the phone when my number flashed on her screen, even when she was pissed at me. I wouldn't have blamed her if she hadn't shown up. I had been an asshole to her lately.

Part of me didn't think I deserved her love.

I stared up at her and drew my fingers gently across her high cheekbones, the curve of her nose, and down her jaw. Then, I just fucking cried. I couldn't hold it back any longer. So many emotions were rushing through my head.

Mom had killed herself. I now had to take care of Ana by myself. And all I wanted was to tell Imani that I loved her before it was too late and she left me too. I could barely get through last night with her by my side.

If she hadn't been here …

Closing my eyes, I blinked back some tears and clenched my jaw. I didn't know if *I* would've survived last night without her. Still, I couldn't fathom what had been going through Mom's head yesterday when she took those pills—whatever the fuck they were.

How could she leave us? How could she have been so selfish?

What the hell was I supposed to tell Ana?

Ana.

I shot up in Imani's arms and looked around the room, trying to figure out where the hell she had gone off to last night. I had been such a mess that I could barely think straight, and now, she was gone and I—

"Lie back down with me," Imani whispered, her eyes opened slightly and her arms wrapping back around my shoulders. "Ana is at my house with Landon and Kai. She's safe. Landon called this morning when he got there."

Relief washed over me, yet so much guilt ran through my body as well. I'd pushed Mom to do this. I hadn't let her see Ana while she was getting high, and now, Ana wouldn't ever see her again. I'd punished Ana for Mom's wrongdoings.

"How are you feeling?"

"This is my fault," I whispered.

Almost immediately, Imani scrambled around me to sit beside me instead of behind me. She grabbed my face in her soft hands, forcing me to look at her, then shook her head. "This isn't your fault. You couldn't have stopped this."

"All I wanted was for her to get clean," I said, hurt spreading throughout my body.

"You tried your hardest," Imani said. "This was her decision."

I placed my hands over my face and hung my head low. "I tried so fucking hard."

Imani crawled into my lap, straddling my waist, and tugged my hands away from my face, so she could see how fucking broken I was, how many tears streamed down my cheeks, how much this destroyed my soul.

"You couldn't have done anything," Imani whispered, brushing my tears away with her thumbs. "You tried to get her clean. You supported your family the best way you could, being only a teenager still. You're not even out of high school yet, João."

My hands came around her waist, and I clutched her so tightly. I didn't want her to disappear from me too. I needed her more than I had been leading on, more than anyone even thought, even myself.

I couldn't lose her.

Fingers digging into her frame, I inhaled sharply and shook my head. "What am I going to tell Ana? How do I tell her that her mother didn't love her enough to ... to stay alive? To watch her grow up, to watch her survive?"

Imani stayed quiet for a long time. "I can't fathom how you're feeling," she whispered. "But I know that your mother loved you both so fucking much, João. She sold her body every single night to give you both the best life she could. She loved you and Ana."

But it felt like she hadn't. If she had, why would she have done this to us?

"Promise me that you won't ever leave me," I said, struggling to keep eye contact with her because I hated showing my feelings, but I wanted her to know that I was serious this time. "Promise me, Imani." I grasped her tighter. "I can't lose you. I can't fucking lose you."

"I'm not going to leave you," she whispered, dragging her fingers through my hair again.

"Promise me."

"I promise that I won't ever leave you," she said.

My heart swelled, my chest tightening. I stared into her glossy brown eyes and couldn't believe that after everything I had done to her, after everything that had happened, she was still here with me. She hadn't left.

"I love you," I whispered, my voice trembling. "I love you so fucking much, Imani Abara."

Chapter One Hundred Fifty

IMANI

"I love you so fucking much, Imani Abara."

The words replayed over and over in my head as I stared at João, who poured his entire soul out to me. My heart was beating so quickly that I thought it would burst out of my freaking chest. I rested my hands on his muscular shoulders.

Was he saying this because he was hurt? Or did he really mean it?

He was hurting so badly right now, and I didn't want him to hurt more. I *refused* to let him hurt more. It was so painful to see someone whose strength I admired—even if I had never said it aloud before—look so defeated and destroyed emotionally.

I wasn't going to fight with him. I wasn't going to bitch him out for hurting me.

"I love you too," I whispered. I tucked some dark hair behind his ear and curled my lips into a smile. "You don't know how much that means to me to hear you say that, especially now. I know that you're hurting."

João gripped my waist so tightly that I was sure he'd leave bruises, but I'd rather have bruises than watch him fall apart. "I wanted to tell you sooner. I didn't want it to come to something like this. But I didn't know how to say it."

"It's okay."

"It's fucking not, Imani. It took my mom killing herself for me to realize that I can't fucking lose you. I wouldn't be okay. I won't ever be okay from this shit, but …" He ran a hand through his hair. "I can't lose anyone else I care about."

While my mind was reeling with so many different thoughts and feelings, warmth spread throughout my chest, down my torso, and to each of my limbs, overwhelming me completely. It felt so wrong to talk about this after his mom had died, but this was João.

He was never good with his feelings.

"I'm sorry about everything," I said after a long period of silence. "I'm sorry that I couldn't do more, but I promise that I will help you take care of Ana, and so will Landon and Kai. We're in this forever, João. She won't suffer because of this."

João gave me a small smile, the first spark of lightness in his eyes. "Poison forever."

"Poison forever," I repeated.

After a few moments, João rested his head back against the couch and closed his eyes. The stress that had disappeared a few short minutes ago was suddenly back and looked so much worse.

"You know …" I ran my fingers through his unkempt hair and toyed with the ends. "We could fix up Landon's house, put more security cameras around the property, get better locks, and replace the windows, so you and Ana have somewhere to stay that isn't here …"

I looked around the small house and frowned. I didn't know if I was overstepping; this place might've held so many good memories for him, but I knew that I wouldn't be able to sleep in the house that my mother had killed herself in.

"It's big enough to have a room for each of you guys, even Kai," I said. "I did some snooping and found out that the house is paid off, so you won't have to worry about that or any rent. I'm sure Landon wouldn't mind, and I can get my mom to help us out. As much as you don't think she likes you, she's willing to help you."

"I don't want your mom's money," he said tensely. "Then, I'd have to owe her. That's how it works in Redwood, whether you like it or not, Imani."

"You'll pay her back by protecting me, her daughter," I said. "She's in deep with Akio's family. She will do anything to protect me, including helping you out of a tough situation because Poison is defending her daughter."

João shook his head, but something shifted in his eyes. "I'm not making any promises, so don't go home and tell your mom shit. But I'll think about it. Ana needs a place to sleep, and I don't think I'll be able to get a good night's sleep here ever again."

I grabbed his hands and smiled at him. "You're going to get through this."

"God, I fucking hope so," he said, looking over my shoulder at the note on the coffee table.

Ever since Landon had left with Kai and Ana earlier, I hadn't stopped looking over at it either. Even during the few hours of sleep that I had gotten, I'd kept waking up, and it was the first thing that I saw. I knew that it was a suicide note, a last good-bye.

Maybe it would give João some closure.

Or at least the answer to his question, *Did my mom ever love me?*

"You should read it," I said, giving him my best reassuring smile. "It doesn't have to be right now, but it might, you know, give you some closure or something. I don't know, but it might ..." I didn't know where I was going with this.

I just had a feeling that it'd help João, like I'd had a feeling that I should answer João's phone call early this morning. I couldn't really explain it, especially not to João, who was neither religious nor spiritual.

João grabbed the note from the coffee table, keeping it folded closed and turning it over and over in his hands. He drew his fingers across the folds, every once in a while flipping the corner up, as if he was going to open it.

But he never did.

Instead, he tucked it away in his jeans that he had fallen asleep in last night and looked at the ground between his legs. "Maybe one day, when I'm not angry at her, I'll open it up and get that closure, but not now."

Chapter One Hundred Fifty-One

JOÃO

"What am I supposed to say to her?" I said, rubbing my dry hands together and staring into Imani's house through the windows beside her front door. From a distance, I caught sight of Ana running into the kitchen with a small apron on. My chest tightened at the mere thought of telling her anything.

"I don't know," Imani whispered, her fingers gently scratching my back through my coat.

After standing in the bitter cold for another moment, I opened the front door and walked into the house behind Imani. The guys sat in the foyer, chatting tensely with each other about something. When I walked in, they stood and grimaced. Neither of them had said much since they had left my house.

"You okay?" Kai asked even though I probably looked like shit.

"Is Ana in the kitchen alone?" I asked, ignoring his question because we all knew that I wasn't all right, and I didn't know if I would ever be all right again. This was bound to fuck me up for the next few weeks, months, maybe even years.

"No, she's with Mrs. Abara," Landon said.

I grimaced and walked toward the kitchen, smelling the rich scent of brigadeiros drifting through the house. In the kitchen, Ana stood on a chair with a small white apron on and a chef's hat, stirring a big pot of chocolate.

"João!" she said, grinning. "We're making brigadeiros!"

"Are they coming out good?" I asked, giving her my best smile.

"Yeah!" She handed the spoon to Imani's mother, who gave me a half-smile, and then she jumped down from the chair and barreled toward the refrigerator. She pulled open the door, revealing over two plates full of chocolate sprinkle–coated chocolate balls. "Wanna have one?"

My eyes widened slightly. "How many have you made, Ana? You're not going to eat these all."

"We've been making them all morning," Imani's mother said.

While I didn't like Imani's mother—because I saw right through that nice-woman facade that she put up—I appreciated that she had allowed Ana to stay with them this morning and had been keeping Ana busy. I sure as hell couldn't even think straight last night, never mind take care of someone else.

So, I swallowed my fucking pride and said, "Thank you."

Ana loved baking these things. It took her mind off the world around her.

"Do you think Mama will want some?" Ana asked.

Everyone in the room stiffened.

I stared down at my feet, my jaw twitching slightly, then nodded toward the other room. "We need to talk, Ana. Let the guys take over in the kitchen for a couple minutes, okay?"

"Okay," Ana said, closing the fridge. She turned to Landon. "Make them how I showed you. Don't mess anything up this time."

I took her hand and walked with her out to the porch. I sat on Imani's mother's front steps in the freezing fucking cold and pulled Ana onto my lap. At least it wasn't snowing outside right now. I held her tightly to me, my body straining so that I wouldn't let out another sob in front of her. All morning, the pain had come in waves.

"Are we going to see Mama today?" she asked, turning her head around to look at me.

"Mom's going to be gone for a while," I whispered, desperate to stay strong.

Ana furrowed her dark brows and turned around in my hold, her arms around my shoulders and her small lips pulled into a frown. "But I didn't get to say bye to her. Where did she go? Is she working?"

With my lips parted, I bit back more pain. "No, she's not working," I said, my voice choppy and almost on the verge of cracking, almost on the fucking verge of breaking into a cry, a whimper, something for Mom.

"Then, where is she?"

No matter what I told Ana, she wouldn't understand. I wanted to be honest with Ana about where Mom was and about how she would never get to see her again, but I couldn't say anything. I couldn't tell my little sister that. I wanted to protect her from everything.

"She's gone," I said, swallowing hard. "Mama is gone."

It wasn't a lie, but it wasn't the truth either. It was all I could muster.

Ana pushed some hair off my forehead with her smaller, warmer hands. "Don't cry, João. Mama will be back. She always comes back to us." She rested her forehead against mine. "I *know* she will. She loves us."

My entire body trembled, but I forced myself not to let out a cry. I wanted to read Mom's suicide note. I wanted to see why she had really done this to us, why she had really left. But at the same time, I didn't want to read that thing because how could she be so selfish to leave Ana? I could understand why she'd want to leave me, but Ana? She was so innocent and still a child.

Five minutes later, when I finally calmed down, I looked back up into her wide brown eyes and tucked some hair behind her ear. "We're going to stay at Landon's from now on, okay? At least for a little while. It'll be us and Poison."

"And Imani." Ana took my shoulders in her hands again. "Please, João! And Imani."

The corner of my lips curled up slightly. "And Imani."

She giggled, and the sound was the only thing keeping me fucking sane right now. She threw her arms around my shoulders and her legs around my waist, holding on to me so tightly. "Can I go get all my toys from our house?"

"We've already got them all in my car," I said, nodding to the truck.

Ana grinned ear to ear, and I felt so guilty. "Yay!" she cheered.

I should've told her what had really happened to Mom, but I couldn't think about it. One day, I would have to come clean and tell her that Mom loved her but that she wasn't ever coming back to us. She was gone from this world forever.

"Why don't you go say good-bye to everyone?" I said, picking her up and setting her on her feet beside me. I looked through the glass windows beside the front door and spotted the guys talking with Imani and her mother in the foyer. "We're going to go get settled in because you gotta go to school tomorrow."

After yanking open the door, Ana ran into the house with her pigtails bouncing and her mouth pulled into a full-on grin. I frowned at her departing figure and squeezed my eyes closed, blinking back the tears. She had no fucking idea what really was going on, and I hated it.

But part of me was jealous of my little sister because she didn't have to feel this pain.

To her, everything was fine.

To me, my entire world had already fallen apart.

Chapter One Hundred Fifty-Two

"What do we need from here?" I asked, shaking some snow off my coat and walking into the Home Depot. I pulled up the Notes app on my iPhone and added a shopping list. "I'm making a list, so we don't forget anything."

As Kai started listing things off to buy in order to make Landon's house livable for two more people, I added them to the list and followed Landon down a couple aisles with a cart. The wheels on the damn thing squealed loudly, drawing attention to us, but I refused to give a fuck. So much had happened these past few hours.

Landon and Kai threw in blinds, lights, security cameras, sensors, and more as we walked through the store. I aimlessly pushed the cart and thought about how hurt João must be right now. My mind felt so numb from thinking about him.

I wished that I could take away his pain.

All of it.

I wanted to help him in some other way, but I didn't know how. He was so broken and shattered that I almost didn't think anyone would be able to fix him. Maybe he could talk to Landon's therapist or something—but that would be huge for him to even consider something like that.

When we reached the section for front door locks, I left the cart where it was and told the guys that I wanted to pick up some cleaning supplies before we left. I never cleaned. Mom had always hired someone to do it for us. But I'd noticed how dirty Landon's parents' bedroom floor was. And that basement—God, that basement reeked of weed.

Staring up at the aisle of cleaning supplies, I grabbed some air fresheners, a mop, and some other supplies that I hoped would help fix up the place. I wanted Ana and João to feel as comfortable as they did at their own house.

"Imani," someone called from behind me.

I glanced over my shoulder to see Akio's father pushing a cart down the aisle. My mouth dried, my chest tightening. Something didn't feel right about this. In fact, after I had gathered that information from Kai earlier that Akio's family wanted to hurt mine, something felt terribly wrong.

"What are you doing here?" he asked, stopping right in front of me.

While I hated his wife more than I hated him, he ran the Redwood mob right alongside her. He probably did as much dirty work as he could, especially with him working as a doctor with Mom at the hospital. I didn't put it past him to take people off life support or inject some kind of medication into their bodies to kill them, if his wife wanted them dead.

"Shopping," I said to keep the conversation short.

"I needed to pick up some supplies," he said with a long pause, looking down into his cart once, which was enough for me to look too.

Duct tape, a tarp, rope, and a saw lay within the large cart—stuff that he could've retrieved in a smaller basket.

But it seemed as if he wanted me to see it, as if he wanted it to stand out.

"You should pick up some Band-Aids too," I said, refusing to let him see me nervous. My gun might've been in the car, but Kai was somewhere in the store, picking out a couple new locks. He and Landon would protect me, if needed.

"Oh, and why's that?" he said, amused.

"So it's not obvious the next time you beat up your son."

And with that, I twirled around and hurried down the aisle. I didn't know if I had fucked up or if I had maybe knocked some sense into him not to beat up Akio. It was probably not the latter, but I couldn't stop myself.

My legs moved quickly. I wanted to put as much distance between us as possible.

Just as I turned the corner, I bumped into Kai. He grabbed my elbow to steady me before I stumbled back, and he looked at my bewildered expression.

"What's going on?"

"I just wanted to find some cleaning supplies for Landon's place, and I ..." I glanced over my shoulder to see that Akio's father was gone. He had disappeared so quickly that I thought I'd imagined him altogether, but I knew that I hadn't. "Akio's father was here."

Kai tensed. "Akio's father?"

"Yes," I whispered. "He had some *supplies* in his cart and very obviously wanted me to see them."

After grabbing my hand tightly, Kai pulled me through the next aisle to Landon, who stared at the locks, trying to decide which ones were best for his home. When we reached him, Kai released my hand and reached behind him into his waistband.

"Watch Imani," he said to Landon.

Landon pulled me closer and grasped my hand, squeezing tightly. My heart pounded inside my chest as I watched Kai disappear out of the aisle. Then, I turned to the locks Landon had been looking at and could only think the worst.

What was Kai going to do to him if he found him? Kill him? Then, the entire Redwood mob would be after us along with the police force and everyone else who did shady business around Redwood.

"Are you okay?" Landon asked, gently rubbing circles on the back of my hand with his thumb. "I know you didn't know João's mother as well as you know João, but I can tell that it is still bothering you, that it has since you walked into their house earlier."

My lips trembled slightly, but I held back the tears. I would cry later when I returned back home for the night. Mom had told me that she wanted to talk about it and had even taken the night off for me. While I might've hated her at one point, I really needed someone outside of Poison right now because this shit was so heavy.

"João told me that he loves me," I whispered, holding tighter on to

Landon's hand. I didn't want him to think I loved him any less because I didn't. I loved him so fucking much, but João needed me—needed all of us—so much right now.

Landon tensed for a moment but didn't freak out like I'd thought he would, nor did he look back at the locks and pretend like I hadn't really said what I had said.

Instead, he looked down at me and actually smiled. "I'm not sure he's said that to anyone other than his mother and sister."

"One night, when this is all over, we all need to sit down and talk about what ..." I gulped and gently grasped his face. "About what we all are. I have so many questions and don't want to hurt anyone, especially you."

After taking my hands, he smiled genuinely and leaned down to kiss me. "I know."

A few moments later, Kai stormed down the aisle toward us with his teeth gritted. There was a fiery rage within his eyes, the quiet and collected Kai gone and replaced with the one who didn't flinch when killing a man.

"Pick whichever lock you want," Kai said. "And let's get out of here. Akio's father completely disappeared. His cart was sitting in one of the back aisles, and something just doesn't feel right. We need to get back home."

Chapter One Hundred Fifty-Three

IMANI

Friday morning, I sat in the cafeteria, across from Allie, and picked at my food. I *had* decided to come to school today because I needed to get my mind off things and see Allie. If I had stayed at home for another hour, I would have cried and cried and cried. I didn't know why this was affecting me so much, but maybe it was because this was the first real death of someone relatively close to me that I had witnessed.

It was obvious that Redwood didn't care about people. Hell, João didn't even trust the police enough to have them take away his mother in an ambulance. He trusted his goons more than people who had vowed to protect the citizens of this town.

Maddie walked into the cafeteria right before Alec Wolfe, the guy I believed she was dating. As of right now, it hadn't been confirmed, but Maddie kept staring at him in the halls whenever she got the chance.

"Do you think they're dating or ... fucking?" Allie said, following my gaze.

"They're definitely fucking, but ... I don't know about dating," I said, chewing on the inside of my lip and thinking back to João again. I had come to school in hopes of getting my mind off this all, but I couldn't.

I glanced over at head cheerleader Nicole, who walked into the room behind Alec. She was dressed in her tight, tiny cheer uniform with a smile that looked so fake. It was funny that after one talk with her, everything seemed so different.

"Do you think Nicole is telling the truth about her being abused by her father?" I asked Allie.

She looked over at the cheer table. Nicole sat at the end of the table, picking at some mashed potatoes on her tray. While I always thought that she was the head bitch of the cheer team, her friends seemed to ignore her.

Shrugging her shoulders, she turned back to her food and frowned. "I don't know."

I munched on a carrot and opened my Biology textbook. "My dad wanted me to tell you that he got you an interview for next Monday after school. And when he says 'interview' "—I did air quotes around the word—"he means that you already have the internship at his company. You just have to go talk one of the HR guys."

It wasn't spectacular news, but it was better than talking or thinking about João's mom.

Allie stared behind me, her gaze far away and her face expressionless. It was how I felt deep inside. Part of me wished that I could've stayed home today with João and Landon as they fixed up Landon's house, but I couldn't miss another day.

As my mind wandered, my gaze did too, and now, Maddie was outside in the hallway, chatting tensely with Alec.

"Earth to Allie!" I said, waving a hand in front of her face and wanting to talk. When she glanced at me, I nodded to the hallway. "Do you think that they're banging extra hard, seeing as Alec is Maddie's brother's best friend? You know how we *love* all that taboo shit." I winked.

She snorted and grinned. "I don't know, but he's like a walking hockey god. I sure hope she's getting it good."

"Who's a walking hockey god?" Jace said, walking toward us, arching a brow, and plopping his ass next to her.

"Alec," I said, sipping on my chocolate milk. "Captain of Redwood's hockey team."

Jace leaned closer to Allie. "You think he's hot?"

Allie gnawed on the inside of her cheek and gave her best awkward laugh. "Um, yes? But don't worry about Alec. I only date guys who are one thousand percent more asshole-y than he is," she said, nudging Jace.

Jace arched his brow and grasped her jaw. "Well, this asshole"—he pointed to himself—"expects you to be at Senior Night tomorrow. And you'd better not be late," Jace mumbled against her lips. "Or I'll excuse myself from the field to come find your ass."

"Well ..." I said, scrunching my nose at Allie and standing from the table. "I'll leave you two to get handsy together. I have to get to class. Talk later, Als."

After packing up my things, I walked out of the cafeteria and down the hallway to my locker. Akio stood next to it, rubbing his hands together and frowning at me when I arrived. I opened my lock and pushed in my lunch box. "What's up?"

"Nothing," he said, but he looked beyond stressed lately.

"Has anything happened with your parents lately?" I asked, wanting more information.

After meeting his father at the store yesterday, something didn't feel right. I didn't know if he had been there to intimidate me or what, but it was really throwing me off amid all this other stuff happening.

He went to open his mouth, then snapped it shut. Pain crossed over his face, and I could tell that he was still hurt from the other day when his parents must've kicked the shit out of him for talking to me. This must've been risky for him, but still, he was willing to risk another beating.

"What is it?"

"What happened the other night?" he asked me. "My parents were gone and didn't come home until early morning. When we had break-fast, they were oddly quiet and mentioned Poison the few times they spoke. Do you know anything?"

I looked back at Kai, who lingered in the hallway a few feet away, his jaw clenched. "I shouldn't tell you. It's really not my place, but someone close to them committed suicide."

"Was it violent?"

Furrowing my brows, I stared at him in confusion. "What do you mean? It was a suicide."

"Was there blood? Did he or she use a gun or a knife, any kind of weapon?"

"No, pills," I said.

Akio grimaced and ran a hand over his face. "Thank fucking God."

"Why?"

"I thought my mother had killed someone. She had blood on her blouse during breakfast. When you and Poison didn't show up for school yesterday, I thought it was you." He paced the hallway, running a hand through his hair and shaking his head. "I thought they had fucking killed you."

"I'm still here," I said. "But I need a favor. Poison's not in a good place right now, and they were planning on finding some medicine for João's sister during this chaos after the principal died, but I'm not sure that's possible now. Is there any way that you can ... find some for us? I can pay you."

Akio stopped pacing and stared at me for a few moments, his face blank. "I can see what I can do, but I can't make any promises. Just, promise me, you'll stay away from all this drama. Things are only heating up in Redwood. I can feel it. Something bad is coming."

Chapter One Hundred Fifty-Four

KAI

"What did Akio say to you earlier?" I asked Imani an hour after school ended, spotting Akio walking to his car with his hands clasped around his backpack straps and his glasses sitting low on his nose. He was going home late. "Anything about what his father wanted?"

When we had been out yesterday, getting shit for Landon's place, and Imani told me that she spotted Akio's father in one of the many aisles, I had searched every last inch of that store for him but couldn't find him anywhere.

He wasn't there to shop, like he had said. He was there for her. He'd wanted something.

"Nothing much. Just that his mother came home with blood on her the other morning. He thought that she had ..." She trailed off, her cheeks paling. "That she had killed me, especially after we didn't show up for school yesterday."

I gritted my teeth. His mother was the one who deserved to die. His mother had made Dad's death seem like a motorcycle accident, like a drunk driver had killed him, and nothing more. But Dad had been investigating them and the rest of the police force, like we were. And I wouldn't let them touch Imani.

After scanning the parking lot to make sure nobody was watching

596

us, I opened Imani's car door for her and ushered her into the car. "Drive to Landon's and nowhere else. I'll meet you there in a few. I need to talk to Akio first."

"Don't hurt him," she pleaded. "He didn't do anything."

As much as I hated the kid, I wasn't going to kill him. Yet.

"I won't," I said, shutting her door once she sat.

Once I watched her drive off into the direction of Landon's place, I glanced over my shoulder to catch Akio standing at his car, almost as if he was waiting for me, so I walked over to him. "Did you find any information on your parents?"

"No," he said, stuffing his hands into his pockets. "Nothing yet."

"Your father showed up while we were out shopping yesterday."

"He did?"

I grabbed him by his collar and slammed him against the car door. "Don't fuck with me."

"I'm not," Akio said, holding his hands up. "I swear, I didn't know. I don't know anything about what they do. I've been trying to find something without them being suspicious. I've never wanted to be part of the family."

"You promised me that you'd get information."

"I will," he said, pushing on my hands. "I promise, I will."

"What do you know about Nicole?" I asked, wanting to see if his family knew anything about what she had admitted to us the other night about her father.

"What do you mean?" he asked, confusion clouding his face.

"Nicole. The girl you have a crush on, head of the cheerleading squad—that Nicole?" I said. When he still didn't say anything, I continued, "Your parents work closely with the police, don't they? Nicole told Poison a couple days ago that they're using her."

"What?" he asked, his voice barely above a whisper. "What do you mean, they're using her? For what? Information?"

"Information and," I said, watching him carefully, "sex."

Sex? he mouthed.

"She told us that her father is forcing her to sleep with everyone in town so he can get info on them to use for blackmail. Doesn't that sound like something your parents would be a part of?"

Akio's innocent expression turned into one of fury and viciousness within a moment. His upper lip curled, his brown eyes suddenly becoming darker and more sinister, and his hands were clenched tightly by his sides.

"You didn't know?" I asked.

"You're lying," he said.

"Ask her yourself."

"I can't ask her," he said between gritted teeth. "She doesn't even know who I am."

"Then, ask your parents about it."

While I wanted to get him angry—because fuck him; he was getting too close to my girl—I also wanted to use him to get closer to his family. He might not want to get involved, but he was knee fucking deep in this shit.

His family were monsters.

"I have to go," he said, yanking open his car door and collapsing into the driver's seat.

When he slammed the door and started the car, I shoved my hands into my pockets and walked to my motorcycle. Maybe that would get him motivated to stop his parents too.

He sped out of the parking lot and down the road. I slid onto the back of my bike and pulled on my helmet, wanting to follow him but deciding that it would be best to head to Landon's place instead. We still needed to install the new locks and security cameras.

Just as I started my bike, Akio came speeding back into the parking lot. He pulled up next to me, rolled down his window, and threw me a package. "I forgot to give this to you. Imani asked me to find João's sister some medication. Don't lose it. It's the last few bottles that our pharmacy had in stock."

And with that, he took off again, out of the parking lot and in the direction of his home.

I stared down at the medication in my hands. A small smile tugged at the corner of my lips, but I pushed it away and shoved the package inside my backpack. Then, I kicked up the kickstand and drove off school grounds toward Landon's house.

I cut through a couple main streets, passing some cars going a bit too slow, rounded the corner that led to the Overlook, then headed down some back streets toward the slums. Less traffic than usual was out today, and I was fucking thankful. It was too damn cold for this shit.

On the street before Landon's, I spotted Imani's car parked on the side of the road with a dark black SUV with flashing red and blue lights parked behind her. My stomach tightened, and I pulled up next to Imani and shut off the bike.

The guy in the car eyed me, his gaze hard. I stared back at him and shook my head. To anyone else, this would've looked like a cop making a traffic stop. But this wasn't a cop, not even an undercover one.

After Dad had died, I had memorized every single face that belonged to a Redwood police officer. I had made regular surveillance stops by the police station to check which cars were pulling in and out daily. This wasn't one of them. I was certain.

Chapter One Hundred Fifty-Five

KAI

Imani rolled down her window.

"I told you to go right to Landon's," I said, getting off my bike and standing by her door.

"I was heading there, but"—she hiked her thumb back—"I kinda got stopped."

"Does he have your license?"

"Yes."

"Shit," I said underneath my breath.

"Why? What's wrong?"

I didn't want to worry her, but this wasn't good. Not at fucking all.

When the *cop* stepped out of his car, dressed like a fool in a Redwood Police uniform, I reached behind me for my gun in case things headed south from here.

He walked up to us and handed Imani her license. "Everything looks good. Make sure you're going the speed limit next time."

"She was speeding?" I asked, pushing him. "By how much?"

"Seven miles over the speed limit."

"So, thirty-two miles per hour?"

The *cop* rocked back on his heels. "Yep."

"It's thirty-five on this road. She's going under. What're you stopping—"

"Kai," Imani scolded, telling me with her eyes that she wanted to get out of here.

Knowing that he was caught, he gave me a half-smirk and pulled a small wrapped package out of his back pocket and handed it to me. "You got me. I stopped her because I needed to deliver a package to Imani Abara."

"From who?" I asked.

The guy shook his head and thrust the package toward Imani. "I'm the deliveryman. I don't ask questions."

Before Imani could grab it, I took it from him. Whatever it was, I planned to find out before she did. I didn't want her opening any sort of package from a fake police officer who had pulled her over and didn't even know the fucking speed limit on this road.

Once the *officer* walked back to his car, I watched him drive off and then slapped the side of Imani's door. "Drive to Landon's. Don't stop for anything. I'm going to follow you." I hurried back to my bike, threw the package inside my backpack with Ana's medication, then followed her down the road to Landon's.

When we pulled up, I immediately took her hand and escorted her to the front door, where Landon was attaching a new lock. I didn't even stop for Imani to kiss Landon, just kept pulling her into the house, where I knew she would be safe.

Ana sat on João's lap on the couch in the main living room. Since this morning, they had swept the floors, ditched all of Landon's father's beer bottles, wiped down the walls, and redecorated the place.

"João, Landon," I said, letting Imani's hand go and ushering her to the couch with Ana to keep her busy. We had work to do. We at least had to figure out what the fuck this package was. "Other room. Now."

João set Ana on Imani's lap, his lips pulled into a frown. Once Landon finished with the lock on the front door, he pulled it shut and followed us into the other room. I threw the package of medication to João and told him to keep it safe, then pulled out the small envelope.

"What's that?" Landon asked.

"Imani got pulled over by someone pretending to be a cop. He gave her this."

The guys tensed as I set it down on the kitchen counter. It was taped up extremely well and reeked of something. I wasn't sure what it could even be, as the package was so small that it could fit in the palm of my hand.

"What do you think it is?" Landon asked.

"Just open the fucking thing," João said.

I grabbed a knife from the counter and ripped apart some of the tape. As soon as the tape was torn, the vile scent filled the room and made me gag. It smelled like decaying animals or some shit. I grimaced and continued opening the package, freezing when I saw it.

Short and slender.

Pale and bloody.

One single finger.

Chapter One Hundred Fifty-Six

IMANI

Ana fell asleep on the couch in record time, curled up into my lap. Staying up late the other night must've really been hitting her hard today, or maybe she unconsciously knew that something terrible had happened. Kids could always tell when something was wrong.

Once I knew she wouldn't wake up, I placed her head down on a pillow and walked over to the room that the guys had disappeared into a few moments ago. I opened the door and crept in, spotting Kai holding something.

"What the hell is that?!" I whisper-yelled, staring at the boys with wide eyes.

Kai held the package that the *officer* had given me in one hand and a finger in the other. A drop of dried blood ran vertically down the length of the finger, the stench almost unbearable. It looked like it must've been rotting for a couple days now.

"Whose finger is that?!" I asked, closing the door behind me so Ana wouldn't wake up.

While I would've thought that Poison had cut the finger off someone, I knew that this had come in that package, which meant that this was meant for me. Akio's family had been bothering me lately, especially his father.

They wanted to show me what would happen.

"We don't know," Landon said. "It could be anyone's."

I reached for the small yellow package that the finger had come in, opened it up, and turned it upside down, not daring to reach inside of it. I didn't know what kind of diseases might've been trapped up there, waiting for me. Akio's parents were psychos.

A slip of paper floated down to the ground and landed at my feet. I swallowed hard, unsure if I even wanted to pick it up, and then—to show Poison that I wasn't afraid, to show that I was now one of them —I reached down and grabbed it.

It was crumpled and looked as if it had gotten wet with water or bodily liquid or something but had recently dried. I flipped the paper upside down and stared in horror at the note on the opposite side.

"*Your family is next*," I read, my mouth drying. "*We'll do worse.*"

My fingers trembled, the paper slipping from my hands. I stared at the ground and shook my head, trying to moisten my dry lips. This couldn't be happening. This ... this was my worst fear. I might've hated Mom and Dad at times, but I didn't want to lose them. Nor did I want to lose my guys.

If Akio's family was coming for my family, they were coming for Poison and me too.

I refused to let them ... to let them kill any of us. I wanted to be able to protect us all. I wanted everyone to survive. We wouldn't be another Redwood statistic that got lost in the sea of unexplainable events that unfolded here.

"I want to practice," I said, glancing up at Kai. "Please."

While Landon stared at me in confusion, Kai knew exactly what I was talking about, and he nodded. João stared at the finger in Kai's hand, then grabbed it. And Landon took the paper from the ground.

"What do you mean, you want to practice?" Landon asked.

"Shooting a gun," Kai said, staring at me for confirmation. "When we figure out whose finger this is, I'll bring you back to my place and let you practice some more."

"I need to," I whispered, swallowing hard. "I don't want my family to die."

"I know."

Tears welled up in my eyes at the mere thought of it. These past few days had been so emotional, and I wasn't sure how much longer I would be able to keep myself together. After João's mother's suicide, our worlds had seemed to turn upside down.

Deciding that I needed to call my parents to make sure they were okay, I pulled out my phone and paced the room. The phone rang and rang. Every second that went by felt like a fucking eternity. And when Mom's voice mail message played, my heart dropped.

Without leaving a message, I turned off the call and dialed Dad's number. It rang once. Then twice. Then, finally, he picked up the damn phone.

"Sweetheart, what's up? Where are you? Your mother has been worried."

"I'm with Poison," I said, hearing people chat in the background. "Where are you?"

"We're out at dinner with Akio's family."

My face paled, and my mouth went dry. "What?" I asked, my voice barely even a whisper.

"Are you there?" he asked after a few moments.

"Dad," I said, straightening my back. "Put Mom on the phone. Now."

"Hold on," he said, fumbling around on the other end.

"Hello?" Mom said. "Sweetheart, are you there?"

"Mom," I said.

I was thankful that I could hear her voice but terrified that this would be the last time that I did. What if Akio's parents did something to them? What did they even want? My parents had done nothing. Poison had been the one to expose the principal.

So many thoughts raced through my head. I couldn't keep them straight.

"I can't talk for long," she said. "What do you need?"

"Please, be careful," I pleaded. "Don't drink anything. Don't eat any food they've tampered with. They want to ..." I could barely get the words past my lips. It hurt too much. "They want to kill you."

Mom didn't say anything for a long time, and then she must've put her hand against the phone because the next words were muffled. It sounded like she was talking to Dad. "Imani says that the roads are really icy right now and that we should head back soon."

Walking toward Landon with my phone still pressed to my ear, I rested the top of my forehead against his sternum and tapped my foot on the ground, wanting them out of there now. "Mom?" I called.

"We'll be careful on our way home, sweetheart," she said to not give anything away.

"Okay," I whispered, not wanting to hang up, but not wanting to alert Akio's parents.

They probably already knew. Hell, they had probably sent the damn package. They had known when I was leaving school tonight and where the hell I was heading to. They must've been following me. Maybe tracking my every move.

"I have to go now, sweetheart," Mom said. "Talk to you later."

Then, the line went dead.

My stomach twisted, and I shoved my phone into my back pocket. Nerves shot up and down my arms, nightmares and thoughts haunting my fucking mind. I hoped that they'd actually come home tonight in one piece. I hoped that—

"No," João said suddenly, still examining the finger. He spit on his thumb and dragged it across the splotchy red blood that covered the length of the flesh. When the blood disappeared, a tattoo with a date appeared underneath it. João froze, jaw tight and eyes full of rage. "Fuck no!"

"What is it?" I asked, eyes wide.

João snatched the package from Kai and stormed out of the room. "This is my mother's finger."

Chapter One Hundred Fifty-Seven

JOÃO

With my foot on the accelerator, I sped right through a motherfucking Stop sign to those goons' home. I had fucking trusted them to keep my mother safe and bury her because Redwood would fail me yet again with that, but they obviously couldn't do shit without me directing their every fucking move.

Which meant that I would have to kill them.

They had let my mother get into the wrong hands. Hell, I wouldn't be surprised if Akio's family had offered them a bunch of dirty money to hand over my mother to them, so they could fuck with us, to fuck with me.

Kai sat in the passenger seat, directing me toward their home. I tightened my hand on the steering wheel, pulled up to the side of the road, nearly hitting three cars, and slammed on my brakes. I swore to fucking God, I couldn't wait to get my hands on them.

The lights were off in the house, but I didn't give a fuck. I stormed up to the front door, banged three times without answer, then barged right into the home. It reeked of beer and three-day-old pizza that hadn't been refrigerated.

Behind me, Kai shut the door and turned on the lights. With food, alcohol, and shit fucking everywhere, it looked like these guys hadn't been home in a couple days. If they had skipped town, I would track them the fuck down tonight.

After searching every inch of this small place and not finding anything, I hurled my fist through the nearest wall. The drywall broke to pieces, bloodying my knuckles. But I didn't give a shit. I hit the wall again and again because how fucking dare Akio's parents!

Mom was already dead. Why tarnish her more?

I couldn't stop myself from slamming my fist into the wall. I refused to stop.

Kai grabbed my shoulders and threw me backward into their kitchen table. "Get a grip, João. They're not here, and you're not going to fix anything by tearing their house to pieces. We need to find your mother."

I glared at him, loving the feeling of the pain shooting from my knuckles to up my arm. I felt like I fucking deserved it because I had fucked up so much in life. I had kept Ana away from our mother, then lied to her that Mom was coming back. I hadn't stopped Mom from slipping into drugs. And I had almost lost Imani because I had been so fucking rude to her.

"I want the pain," I said through gritted teeth, trying to get around him to slam my fist into the wall again. "I want all the fucking pain."

But Kai caught me yet again and pushed me out the front door and back toward my car. After he forced me into the passenger seat, he grabbed the keys from me and started the car himself. I glared out the window and punched the dashboard as he drove toward my house.

I hated my life here. I hated Redwood so much.

I ... I ... I missed Mom.

I fucking missed her.

When Kai pulled up to my place, I glared through the windshield at the house. "Why the fuck are we here?"

"We have to start somewhere," Kai said.

So, I got out of the car with him and dragged my fucking feet all the way to the front door. I pulled out my keys and thrust it into the lock, but the door creaked open without me having to even turn the key.

As soon as I opened the fucking door, I saw Mom. She hung from the ceiling by a thick, coarse rope, her feet inches off the ground and her body lifeless. So many emotions flooded through me. I almost couldn't keep myself together. It was like finding her dead all over again.

I hurried over to her and took her in my arms. After pulling Mom down from the rope, I laid her down on the couch and grabbed a shovel from the front door that we used for the snow. Tonight, I would bury her myself. We couldn't trust anyone other than ourselves now.

"Well," Kai said, standing at the back door with his arms crossed over his chest, "I found the two goons."

They both lay at the back door with their throats cut and all their fingers cut off too. They were scattered around the back lawn in the sanguine-colored snow, sticking up like flowers would in the summer. Akio's family fucking disgusted me.

Once I stepped over the two guys, I walked into my backyard. It might've been small, but Mom had loved gardening in the summer. So, I found where her favorite flowers bloomed in the spring and started to dig a hole six feet deep.

The dirt was frozen solid, but I slammed the shovel into the ground three times and broke it slightly. I used all of my strength in each slam, the frigid air burning my cheeks and numbing my fingers. But I continued for hours.

Sweat covered my back. I pulled off my jacket and wiped a bead from my forehead, then threw some dirt behind me. I stepped into the three-foot hole and shoveled more and more and more, the dirt piling up behind me and the sweat pouring off me now.

It was almost immediately freezing in the cold wind, but I didn't care.

"João," Kai called after he took care of the goons' bodies.

I ignored him and continued digging for another hour—or however the fuck it took to hit six feet deep. Then, I threw the shovel on the ground and pulled myself out of the hole, walking back to the house.

Kai stood quietly in the living room, watching over my mother's body. I knelt by her side and kissed her forehead, pushing some hair off her pale face and holding her close one last time for good.

"I miss you already," I whispered. "But I'll do anything to keep Ana safe. I know that's what you would've wanted."

After picking her up, I walked into my backyard and gently placed her down into the hole. Once I placed her cut-off finger down in her makeshift grave too, I grabbed my shovel. I refused to let any tears fall as I stared down at her from above, her pale face and tiny frame.

With my throat dry and my chest tight, I let the first shovel full of dirt spread over her body. I continued to fill the hole with dirt, holding back the tears, until only her face was left visible to me. As I picked up another batch of dirt, a tear streamed down my cheek.

"I love you, Mama. I love you so much."

Then, I covered her face and never saw her again.

Chapter One Hundred Fifty-Eight

Once we finished burying João's mother, João wanted to find Akio for information. He didn't have anything—or at least, I didn't think he did—but there was no use in *not* trying to get something out of him.

"Akio's not going to fucking be here," João said, glaring out the foggy windshield with blood covering his hands. He tightened his fists around the steering wheel and parked the car in front of a run-down house in the slums. "His family conducts business on the other side of town."

"I put a tracker on his phone," I said, looking at the one-story home with its windows smashed and the siding falling off the house. I had placed the tracker recently because I didn't trust him around Imani. "He's here."

After shoving my phone into my pocket, I opened the door and walked around the back to find a sheet-covered car parked behind a dumpster that smelled like it hadn't been cleaned in years. I pulled up the blanket to find Akio's expensive car sitting around in the middle of the slums.

"I told you," I said, glancing back at João.

He lit a cigarette the way he always did when he was anxious, then held it between his bloody fingers and crossed his arms. "Let's get this fucking over with. I'm ready to kill his ass."

I walked toward the back door and picked the lock. "We're not going to kill him."

Hearing those words come out of *my own* mouth sounded so ... foreign. So unreal. I had wanted to kill Akio for so long. I wanted to be the one to take away something precious from his mother and father. But the more I learned about him, the more I realized that his parents couldn't care less about their only son. If he died, he died. They wouldn't hurt the way that I had when they killed my father. Hell, they'd probably be happy.

After opening the door, I followed João into the single-room home to find Akio fucking furious. Akio slammed his heel into a Redwood police officer's face, knocking two teeth right out of his mouth and making blood spurt everywhere. His clothes were covered in splattered blood, his hands with dirt, and his eyes more rageful than I had ever seen them.

João parted his lips in surprise, the cigarette falling out of his mouth and onto the wooden floorboards. He looked over at me, then back at Akio, who didn't stop smashing that man's face into the ground. Akio must've found out that what I had told him about Nicole—the girl he had a little crush on—was true.

The police really must've been pimping her out.

"You fucking believe this?" João said, stomping out his cigarette with the tip of his sneaker and pointing to Akio.

Truthfully, I *couldn't* believe this. Under his dark-framed glasses and that innocent boy facade, Akio had a dark side that he had just seemed to release to the world. I hadn't even thought an innocent kid like him could even think about death, never mind wrap it up and give it to someone with his fists.

But I remembered the first time I had killed someone.

I had been so blinded, so hurt, so irate that I couldn't stop slamming my fists into his face as he struggled underneath me. I'd refused to stop until his body went limp and his face fell pale. It was the most terrifying yet freeing feeling in the world.

This would be the first man that Akio had ever killed, and I refused to stop him.

"All right, I'm fucking done waiting," João growled, stepping forward and pulling out a gun.

After placing a hand on his chest, I held him back and stared at Akio, who landed a final punch right to this man's chin. He had hit the officer so hard and for so many times that I couldn't even recognize him.

When the guy stopped moving, Akio scrambled to his feet and stared down at him with his chest rising and falling quickly and his cheeks flushed. A couple moments passed, and his eyes widened, realization flooding through them. He stumbled back toward us, shaking his head, as if he couldn't believe what he had done.

"Good job," I said.

Akio jumped, reached for his gun in his back pocket, and turned around quickly. Surprise was written all over his face, his cheeks pale and fear heavy in his eyes. When he saw it was me and João, his hands shook.

João grabbed the barrel of the gun and pointed the muzzle toward the ground, so it wasn't aimed directly at us. Akio dropped the gun completely, ran a hand through his hair, and began pacing the room.

"I just killed a man," he said. "I couldn't stop myself."

"Why'd you kill him?" João asked, crouching beside him. "We could've used him."

"He did it to protect his girl," I said, watching Akio. "That's why you did it, isn't it?"

Akio stopped with his back turned and tense. He rested his hands on the doorframe and gripped it so hard that he almost pulled the damn thing off the wall. "I didn't have proof, but I found him with Nicole, and I lost my shit."

João pulled up a chair from a table—which was the only other piece of furniture in the room—grabbed Akio by the shoulders, and shoved him down into it roughly. Then, he gripped a fistful of his dark hair, pulled it back, and shoved the muzzle of his gun underneath his chin.

"I don't give a fuck what you did. What do you know about my mother?"

Akio froze, then shook his head. "I-I don't know what you're talking about."

"She committed suicide. I had two guys I trusted take her out of my house and place her somewhere safe. Today, my mother's finger was delivered to Imani, and I found those men dead. What the fuck do you know?!"

"All I know is, my parents came home with blood on them yesterday morning," Akio said, holding his hands up into the air. "I-I don't know anything else. Ask Kai. I haven't even had enough time to make it home. I-I left school—"

"Shut the fuck up," João said, hitting him in the temple with the side of his gun. "I don't want excuses. I need fucking answers. Where the hell are your parents? I'm done playing around with Redwood. I'm going to take care of them and every other problem here."

Akio's face paled.

"If what you know about Nicole is true and your parents are part of this," I interjected, trying to reason with Akio, "you're going to want them dead. And besides, they've threatened to kill Imani and her family." I pulled out the note that had come along with the finger this afternoon and placed it into his hand. "They'll kill you, too, once they find out what you've done to one of their trustworthy men. And you fucking know that too. They don't give a fuck about what happens to you."

"Okay," Akio said, nodding. "The next time I see them, I will—"

"I want them now!" João growled.

"I don't know where they are now!" Akio said. "They went out to dinner with Imani's family hours ago, and then they told me they were going on a *vacation*, which means that they're going into hiding. They don't give me any information about anything."

"Where'd they go out to dinner?" I asked so we at least had a starting place.

"Ocean View."

Chapter One Hundred Fifty-Nine

IMANI

"I'm so nervous," I whispered in the kitchen, glancing over at Ana sleeping in the living room, then toward the front door. "João and Kai still aren't back yet. It's been hours, Landon. Do you think they found his mother?"

"I don't know," Landon said from behind me. He gently rubbed my shoulders, fingers kneading into my tense muscles, and kissed on my neck, his slight stubble sending shivers down my spine. "You need to relax."

"Landon, this is not the time for this," I said. "Ana's here."

"She's sleeping," Landon mumbled against my throat, lips dragging against my flesh and making me warm in all the places it shouldn't. He pressed himself against my ass from behind, grinding against me. "And in the other room."

"How can you be hard at a time like this?"

"I'm fucked up, baby."

He dipped his hand between my legs and gently rubbed my clit. I felt like I hadn't been touched in so long that I couldn't stop the moan that escaped my lips.

"And it seems like you are too."

"Landon," I whispered.

"I'll be quick," Landon murmured into my ear. "Please."

"Not while Ana is here."

"Let me at least touch you then," he said, "and make you feel good. I know how hard this has been for you. You need to relax."

And while I wanted to push him away, I couldn't quite get myself to do it. My body relaxed in his arms as he gently pressed me against the kitchen counter and rubbed my aching clit. I dug my fingers into the countertop and curled my toes, spreading my legs apart a couple inches farther.

"I can't wait to get you alone again," Landon whispered, grasping my jaw with his free hand and pushing his thumb between my lips. "I want to eat this tight, wet pussy until you're fucking begging me to be inside you."

My pussy tightened around him, and I squeezed my eyes closed. "Landon ..."

"God, I want to pound into you all night long while you try to keep yourself quiet because your mother is in the next room."

I wrapped my smaller hand around his wrist tightly, the pressure rising quickly in my core. It was so intense, the feeling almost overwhelming. If he tipped me over the edge, I thought I would—

"Come for me," he said, sucking on my neck and grinding his dick against my ass.

After slapping a hand over my mouth, I threw my head back and moaned into it, pleasure rushing through me. Landon continued to rub my clit until I came down from the high and completely relaxed in his arms.

My phone buzzed on the counter, and I hazily opened my eyes to glance over at it.

Mom: We're back home. Where are you?

I placed a hand against my racing heart and sighed softly to myself, thanking whoever the hell was out there that they were safe and hadn't been killed by Akio's family. I didn't know what they were up to. Was it a scare tactic or something more?

Me: At Landon's. The guys will take me home a bit later. Something happened, and we're waiting for Kai and João to come back. I'll keep you updated when I leave. Is everything okay?

While Mom might've been annoying as hell with keeping tabs on me, this time, I appreciated it. After what had happened with João's mother, I couldn't stop thinking about what it would be like to lose Mom and never talk to her again. The more I thought about it, the more I realized that I never wanted that to happen.

Mom: Your father is feeling a bit sick, but I gave him some medication. I will keep an eye on him to make sure they didn't spike his drink or anything. What happened there? You're safe, right?

Me: I'll explain later. Keep your doors locked.

As I was about to shove my phone into my back pocket, someone wiggled the front door knob. My heart dropped, my eyes widening. João and Kai would've come in or knocked. They both had a key.

"What was that?" I whispered, staring at the locked door.

Landon opened a drawer and pulled out two loaded guns. "I don't know, but I'm not taking any chances."

After he picked up Ana, I followed him to the back room. The door began rattling harder and harder by the second, and all I could think of was the worst. When Landon deposited Ana on a bed, I crawled up with her and held her close. Landon handed me one of the guns.

"Landon," I whisper-yelled. "What do you expect me to do with this?!"

"If something happens to me and they get through that door—"

"Don't say stuff like that," I said, brows drawn together. "Please, I can't lose you."

He placed his hands on my shoulders and stared me right in the eyes. "If something happens to me and they get through that door," he said, pointing behind him, "you protect yourself and Ana by shooting them right in the fucking head. Do you understand me? You're Poison."

"Poison," I whispered.

I might've been Poison, but I was also scared shitless.

When Landon left the room, my heart raced about a thousand miles a fucking minute. Ana still slept next to me, her head in the crook of my shoulder. I wrapped my right arm around her smaller body and rested my hand on her forehead, gently stroking it to calm myself down.

If anything happened, I would have to ... to kill someone to protect her.

I couldn't freak the hell out. I needed to stay calm. I needed to think straight.

From a distance, I heard the front door shake again. I held up my gun, aiming at the bedroom door, ready to fire if anyone came in to hurt us. My hand trembled uncontrollably, and my mouth was so dry.

Akio's parents were after us. If they showed up at Landon's house, they wouldn't think twice about killing him dead. After everything that had happened within these past few days, I was terrified that they'd kill *all* of us.

Chapter One Hundred Sixty

LANDON

Standing at the front door, I closed my eyes for a brief moment and took a deep breath, promising myself that I would do anything to protect Imani and Ana even if that meant risking my own life. Poison might've been known for killing people, but we protected those we cared about, too. That was what I would do now.

When the doorknob rattled again, I pulled open the door and aimed my gun at ... my parents. Dad stumbled back a few feet until he reached Mom's side. She stood next to him with a thin spring jacket curled around her body, shivering.

"Landon," she said softly. "It's been so long."

Dad walked closer to me. "Son, how are you doing?"

"What the fuck are you doing?!" I shouted at them.

Dad opened his big mouth to say something, but Mom beat him to it. "We're back. We realized our mistakes and wanted to tell you that we're sorry. We want to be with you again. We've been trying to contact you for weeks now."

It sounded so real, but it was a fucking lie. Now that I had been without them for so fucking long, I could see right through her.

"Get out of here!" I said, refusing to move from the front door.

Once they knew that I wasn't fucking moving for them, Mom's friendly smile turned into a menacing scowl. She was never happy.

Never fucking happy. I hoped that wherever they had run off to, it was shittier than the Redwood slums.

"This is my home," Mom said. "And you will not take it away from me."

"This isn't your home," I said between gritted teeth. "I paid the mortgage payments for the last three years with Poison's money. I cleaned the house up after you left. And my friends—my *family*—live here now. You've done nothing but destroy this house and use me for years, all because I wanted to protect you from that monster." I pointed to Dad and stepped closer to her to show her that I was through with it. "It took me all this time to realize that *you're* a monster, too."

Mom went to slap me, but I stepped away from her and took the safety off my gun. Mom and Dad might've been family by blood, but Imani, Ana, and Poison were the only real family I had.

I would do anything to protect them from people who threatened us.

Anything.

"I'm your mother, Landon. You don't scare me," she said, baring her teeth.

"I don't give a fuck who you are to me. I'm done with you and him." My hand tightened around the grip of the gun, the rage boiling inside me. They thought that I would let them come back after everything they had done to me, after all the pain they had caused. "You guys fucked me up! Dad shot me, and then you guys fucking ran away. You taunted me, calling me over and over and never leaving a fucking message."

"He's just a scared little boy," Dad said to Mom, resting a hand on her shoulder. "Put the fucking gun down, Landon, before you shoot someone."

"Just like you fucking did to me?" I asked, shaking my head in disgust. "And this shit isn't about me being afraid of you. This is me protecting my family."

Mom scoffed. "You think that girl you have is going to stay with you forever? You think you can be loved for all your faults, Landon? Because she'll be gone the moment she graduates from high school. She'll—"

Knowing that she was going to derail me again if she kept talking, I pressed the muzzle right against the bottom of her chin to shut her and Dad up. I forced her to look up at me, to see that I was dead fucking serious. "If I ever see you again, I will kill you, and I won't hesitate."

I wasn't only living for myself anymore. I wasn't going to take this abuse.

Imani had shown me that I deserved better.

"You're full of shit," Dad said, grabbing the front door handle and flinging the door open. "I'll do what I—"

I aimed the gun at him, pulled the trigger, and ended his life.

Nobody threatened my family.

Chapter One Hundred Sixty-One

LANDON

I'd thought that I would feel bad for killing my father.

But I didn't feel a single ounce of pain as he took his last breath, as Mom hurried over to him with tears in her eyes, as he died from a single bullet through his skull. No matter what Mom tried to pin on me, I had done the right thing. I had protected my real family.

If Dad had gotten into the house, he would have shot Imani. I wouldn't put it past him. He had fucking shot me weeks ago, then skipped town like it was nobody's business. He would have killed the only fucking woman I ever cared about without a second thought.

"You just killed your father!" Mom screamed.

And while she might've outed me to the entire neighborhood, the people around here feared Poison, and they hated my father almost as much as I did. They wouldn't say shit to the police about me.

That didn't mean Mom wouldn't.

"I'm going to get you arrested!" she said, getting all up into my face. "I'm going to make sure tonight is the last night you enjoy with that bitch who you claim loves you and your stupid friends who have done nothing but destroy your life."

"*You* destroyed my life!" I shouted back.

I had wanted to tell her and Dad that for so fucking long that it felt good, getting it off my chest. I wanted to show them that I wasn't the problem child and that they were just shitty people who didn't know how to parent a child.

"I don't give a fuck, Landon," she said, glaring at me. "You've been nothing but a pain and a bother since I pushed you out. I wish that I had given you up the moment you let out your first cry."

My hand tightened around the gun, her words still cutting me deeply. I should've learned that everything she said was to hurt me, but I couldn't help the agonizing feelings rushing through my body. She wished that I was never fucking born, that I never existed.

She hated me that much.

I wanted her out of my life. I didn't want to see her again. I wished she had stayed gone—far, far away from here—and had never come back into my life. It wasn't like she cared that much, anyway.

But if I let her go, she would really run to the police and tell them what I had done. She would turn in her own son for killing the man who had abused her for the past eighteen fucking years. She didn't give a fuck about anyone other than herself.

Still ... I didn't want to kill her. I would feel bad for killing her—and not because I still had feelings for her. But because Kai had lost both his parents and João had just experienced his mother dying. How could I kill both of mine? How could I be the one to end *both* their lives? A tremendous amount of guilt weighed heavily on my shoulders.

"Landon," Imani said, opening the front door and widening her brown eyes. Cheeks flushed, she stared in horror at me, then at my father, who lay at my feet. "What's going on? What-what happened?"

"Get back inside, Imani," I said, clenching my jaw.

"You took my son away from me," Mom said between gritted teeth, lunging toward Imani with spite in her step and anguish in her eyes. Mom only wanted the fucking world to rot because that was how she lived. "You stupid, little—"

Imani held up her gun, pointing it straight at Mom, who stopped dead in her tracks. Imani glanced over at me for a quick moment, eyes wavering. "Landon, what's going on? Why is she here?" She glanced down at my father and inhaled sharply again. "Tell me, Landon. Please."

"Kill me," Mom said to Imani, suddenly regaining her confidence and stepping forward until Imani pressed the muzzle of her gun against the center of Mom's chest. Imani's hands shook uncontrollably. "Or move out of the way because this is my house."

Knowing that I had to do this or else Mom would continue to harass us, I stepped forward and placed the tip of my gun against the back of Mom's neck, right against her spine. "Imani might not kill you, but I will."

She showed no ounce of terror. "Do it then, Landon."

She honestly didn't think I would do it, or maybe she wanted to be done with her shitty life. Maybe she wanted to join Dad in purgatory, where they'd both rot for eternity because they weren't going to any good place. That was for sure.

"Step out of the way, Imani," I said, not wanting her in the direct line of a bullet.

Imani glanced over at me, brows furrowed, as if to ask me if I was serious. When I made no indication that I was moving from this spot or dropping my gun, Imani stepped off to the side and watched us in fear.

"Kill m—"

I pulled the trigger.

The bullet went straight through Mom's head, and she dropped to the ground at our feet.

Imani jumped back in surprise, her brown eyes nearly popping out of her head, and she swallowed hard. She looked from my mother, to the gun in my hands, to me, then burst into tears. Instead of running away like she would've weeks ago, Imani ran toward me and wrapped her arms around my shoulders.

"Thank goodness that you're safe," she said into my ear. "I thought it was Akio's family."

"I ... I just killed in front of you, and you're okay with that?" I asked, needing to make sure.

She might've seen people die before—we'd done some pretty fucked up shit with her around—but she'd never seen *me* kill anyone before. At least, not that I could recall.

But who the fuck knew? My head wasn't in the right place right now. I was plagued with guilt for killing both my parents even though they'd deserved it. My parents might've been assholes, but at least they had both still been alive.

Now, nobody in Poison had anyone. Nobody except Imani.

"You were protecting me," she said, stroking my face with her soft hand. "And you said it yourself ... I'm Poison now. I would never be afraid of you, Landon, because I know that you would never hurt me. We're in this together, to the very end."

"Until the very end," I whispered.

Chapter One Hundred Sixty-Two

IMANI

"We tried to find Akio's parents last night," João said, lingering beside my locker the next morning with a lit cigarette hanging out of his mouth. His knuckles were bruised, the skin split open. "But we fucking couldn't. We searched all over town. When I see them, I'm going to fucking kill them."

"Did you at least find your mom?" Landon asked, grabbing two of my textbooks from me.

Kai eyed João, then looked back at us. He didn't have to say anything for me to know that they had found her somewhere, but João wasn't going to tell us that. At least not now, and I wasn't sure if I even *wanted* to know.

Landon leaned back against the locker beside me and stared down the hallway. People in Redwood were whispering a lot more than usual today, and I wasn't sure if it was because of us or something else.

"Nobody bothered you guys last night?" Kai asked, changing the subject.

I froze, unsure about what to say. It wasn't really my place to tell.

"I killed my parents last night," Landon said, brushing it off as if it were nothing, then nodding down the hall, where Akio walked through the crowd of people toward us. "Why don't you ask Akio where his parents—"

"You killed your fucking parents?" João asked, cutting off Landon. "How are you so nonchalant about that? I thought that they were fucking gone?"

"I don't want to talk about it," Landon said as Akio approached.

Kai eyed Landon for another moment, then looked at Akio almost ... normally, as if he hadn't wanted to kill Akio for the past few years. What had happened with them? And *when*?

"You got info?" Kai asked.

"I tried calling them this morning," Akio said, scratching the back of his neck with bruised fingers. "And nothing."

I grabbed his hands, which earned me a growl from *each* of my guys, but I ignored them. Bruised and bloody knuckles might've been Poison's thing, but Akio *never* hurt anyone or anything.

"What happened to your hands, Akio? Who did this to you?"

Akio glanced down at his hands, then quickly pulled them away from me and shoved them into his pockets. He gave me a sheepish, boyish smile that I saw right through. If I didn't know him that well, I wouldn't have thought anything was wrong.

"Nothing," he said. "Don't worry about it."

Suddenly, as more people flooded into the hallway, the chatter in the halls became louder. I glanced around, unsure about what was happening with everyone this morning. Sure, it might've been Senior Night tonight for the football team, but this sounded like drama.

The crowd of students parted for Alec, captain of the hockey team and Maddie Weber's secret fling. He hurried through the hallway toward an upset Maddie, who had tears pricking the corners of her eyes.

She ran toward him and slammed her hands against his chest. "How dare you!" She shoved him. "I told you that I wanted to keep us a secret." Another shove. "And instead, you tell everyone that I'm a desperate slut who you bagged?!"

Alec stumbled back. "Maddie, stop it. You have it all wrong."

"No!" she shouted. "You're a piece of shit. I should've never trusted you."

"I swear, I didn't do it."

"All the videos are from your social media accounts!"

"I was hacked, Maddie. I swear."

As they argued back and forth, I pulled out my phone and opened Instagram. There were videos and images of Maddie and Alec having sex on school grounds, posted from, of course, Alec Wolfe's account.

Shit had been brewing in Redwood.

"You have to believe me," Alec said desperately, stepping closer to Maddie.

But she stepped back with hurt and betrayal sewn into her expression. Even from across the hallway, I could feel her pain. She looked so lost, so upset, and so alone despite having Vera and Piper as friends. They couldn't help her. Those videos and images were out in the world.

Everyone in the halls watched them argue and confront each other, and then the crowd parted again as Maddie's brother stormed down the hallway toward them. Before Alec could finish a sentence, Oliver slammed his fist into the side of Alec's face. Once, then twice.

"Get out of the way, Maddie," Vera said, pulling Maddie back. "You're going to get hurt."

"What the fuck are you doing to my sister?" Oliver seethed at Alec, hurling another fist at him. It collided with his cheek. "This is for putting your hands on her." Another fist to the eye socket this time. "And this is for that fucking post."

Fists began flying from both of the friends and teammates.

"We have to stop this," I said, hurrying toward the fight.

Maddie seemed so upset, and I hated it. I didn't want her to watch them fight and couldn't bear to see her look this upset because her boyfriend and brother were tearing each other apart.

João grabbed my wrist and yanked me back. "You're not going in there. Let them fight."

"Please," I pleaded.

João shoved me against the locker to hold me in place. "No."

A couple moments later, four guys from the hockey team pushed through the crowd and pulled Oliver and Alec away from each other, holding them back.

"How could you do this?" Oliver asked, finally calming down slightly and looking at Maddie for an answer, upper lip curled in disgust.

"I ... we ..." Maddie nervously licked her lips. "It happened, Oliver. I don't know what you want me to say."

"Why didn't you tell me that this was happening? He is my best fucking friend!"

Alec growled, "Don't shout at her."

"Why don't you shut the fuck up, Wolfe? I'm talking to my sister."

"You're talking down to my girl," Alec said. "I'm not fucking cool with that."

"You don't need to be cool with it. She's not yours."

"The fuck she isn't."

My head snapped side to side, watching the guys argue.

Oliver turned back to Maddie. "Guys like him will do nothing but hurt you. He sleeps around. Remember what happened with your last boyfriend?"

"I can date anyone I want to, Oliver," Maddie said. "As much as you think you do, you don't own me."

"If I don't look out for you, who will?"

"What don't you understand about this?! I don't want you to look out for me! I can make my own decisions. Stop acting like our parents because you aren't! If I want to date Alec, then I can date him!"

"Don't come crying to me when he breaks your heart," he said, storming off.

The crowd erupted into murmurs again, and then Alec grabbed Maddie's hand and looked around. "I don't care who is angry about it. Maddie Weber is mine. And if you have a problem with that, you will deal with me. And when I fucking find out which one of you hacked my accounts, I'll personally fuck you up."

"God-fucking-damn," João said, pulling the cigarette from his mouth and blowing out some smoke. "I fucking hate Redwood."

Once the dean of students came to settle everything down, Maddie hurried out of the hallway, Vera following after her. She showed nothing but hurt and anguish, her brows drawn together, her lips in a frown. I might've only talked to her a handful of times, but she was so distraught. I wanted to show her that while most people in Redwood sucked, not everyone did.

Chapter One Hundred Sixty-Three

KAI

At lunchtime, I waited at the entrance to the cafeteria for Imani because I wanted to sneak her into the library to talk. After watching João bury his mom last night, I hadn't been able to stop thinking about my parents. And neither João nor Landon was good at talking about shit.

As a herd of wild students pushed to get into the cafeteria first, I spotted Imani at the rear of the crowd, pulling off her reading glasses and shoving them into her case.

She looked over at me and smiled. "What are you—"

Before she could finish her sentence, I took her hand and whisked her away toward the library. "I want to eat lunch with you alone today," I said, not mentioning my parents yet. I didn't know *what* I would even say to her about it anyway, but I... I really needed to talk. "Come on."

"You never want to eat lunch with me alone," Imani said, hurrying after me. "Is everything okay?"

When we reached the library, I released her hand. The librarian looked over at us and gave me a weird look, but then she returned to reading her smutty porno book that she hid underneath a thick-ass copy of *Moby Dick*.

I brought Imani all the way to the back of the library, where there were some desks that overlooked the front of Redwood Academy.

Mom was heavy on my mind, and I knew that Imani would gladly talk with me about it. I just didn't know what to say to her. João's mother might've committed suicide by using some drug, and mine had died from a drug overdose after Dad's passing, but I ... I couldn't stop thinking about what life would've been like with her.

All those memories flooded back into my head and plagued my fucking mind.

It had been Akio's parents' fault that my mother had fallen into despair without my father, and then they'd had the fucking audacity to disgrace João's mother's corpse. They couldn't let her stay dead in peace, but they'd had to hijack her body and cut off her finger to taunt us with it.

"Kai?" Imani said, waving a hand in front of my face, then pulling out her lunch box. "You okay?"

"My mom overdosed on drugs after my father died," I said abruptly, forcing the words past my lips.

I had already told her once, but I had more to say about it. I didn't like talking about them—I fucking hated it, honestly—but I wanted to tell Imani. She had won Landon's heart and torn down João's walls. I had been sorta feeling left out lately.

But I could never allow myself to open up to Imani as much as the way the other guys did.

Not until Akio's parents were taken care of. Not until they were dead.

I refused to give myself to someone else, love them with my whole heart, only to have it ripped out of my fucking chest and smashed to pieces by the barrel of Akio's family's gun. I had been holding back so much rage and sorrow inside my body for them. I couldn't let them do the same with Imani, and if they tried, I couldn't be too attached until I knew they would never get to have her, until I knew that I could love her without constantly looking over our shoulders to make sure she was going to be okay from the trauma and drama that came with Redwood.

"It was cocaine," I said because I was so shit at talking. I'd rather bottle this up, but that hadn't gone over so well with João. "I found it on her when I came home that night. She was already long gone, not that long after my father died."

After she had died, I hadn't embraced the pain. I fucking became it.

I'd wanted the world to burn because my insides were on fire, sizzling, melting to a fucking crisp. And nobody had helped me because I didn't have anyone. Allie had her mother. I had ... my-fucking-self and Poison.

"I've killed so many people since then," I whispered. "So fucking many of them. I want to rid myself of this pain and make this place more livable and survivable for the kids in the slums like me."

"How do you feel after"—Imani swallowed hard—"killing?"

"I'm fucking numb to it now," I said. "It gives me a rush, and then it's fucking gone."

Imani furrowed her brows. "Well, this was not the reason I thought you wanted to eat lunch with me today, but I'm glad that you did. You're quiet, Kai Koh, but you always surprise me."

"That's not the only reason that I wanted to talk to you. You shouldn't go to Senior Night tonight," I said to Imani. "You nor Allie."

They both loved attending the football games, but with Akio's family threatening her and her family, it wasn't a good idea. All I wanted to do was hide her in my home and hope that Akio's family didn't know where the fuck I was located. I refused to let them take someone else from me, especially her.

"I know that we shouldn't," Imani said. "But this is Jace's last night playing football on the Redwood Academy field. Allie isn't going to stay home, and I'm definitely not going to let her go alone, especially not after what Nicole admitted happened to her with the police. Who knows what those filthy Redwood cops might try to do with her?"

Imani wasn't *not* going to go, and I didn't think there was a way to convince her otherwise. She'd been to almost every football game since freshman year with Allie. This was the last game ever.

"Be safe," I said. "Don't do anything stupid. Take your gun with you."

"I will, *Mom*," she joked with me. When I didn't laugh—because this shit was serious—she dropped her smile and sighed softly. "I know to be safe. I was planning on bringing my gun, anyway. I'm not going to let anyone hurt Allie. She's just as important to me as she is to you."

After a few moments, she bit into her apple and leaned closer, lowering her voice. "When are you going to tell her that she's your sister?" Imani asked, brushing some hair off my forehead, her finger curling around the back of my ear. "It's getting so hard for me *not* to tell her. She's going through a rough time right now with her mom and stepfather. It would be nice for her to have someone else in her life."

While I knew that it would—hell, because I wanted someone else too—I still wasn't ready. I wanted Allie to join us in taking down all the corrupt shitheads in Redwood. I wanted her to follow Dad's dream of exposing everyone for who they really were.

But she wasn't ready to know the truth about Redwood or about me being her brother.

Chapter One Hundred Sixty-Four

IMANI

In the student parking lot, I shut off my car and glanced over at Allie in the passenger seat. She stared out the windshield at all the cops and security walking around the field and the school grounds for Senior Night tonight. It was the last home game of the year.

While Kai was right about staying home tonight, I couldn't let Allie go to the football game alone. Akio's family *had* to have known that Kai and Allie were related, which meant that they would target her too.

After checking my jacket to make sure—again—that I had my gun, I stepped out of the car and zipped up my coat. The wind seared my cheeks, and I hoped that tonight would go smoothly. I didn't want any interruptions and wanted to enjoy this last game.

We walked side by side to the entrance of the stadium, where two cops stood with metal detectors. My face paled, my stomach tightening. Fuck, they would find me out. They would swipe that damn thing across my body and ... and ... take me in.

"Allie," I said, stopping in the middle of the sidewalk. "I ..."

I didn't want to go in without the gun. That would be stupid of me. Hell, it *was* stupid of me to be here. But I sure as hell wasn't willing to go put the piece of metal down in my car and risk our damn lives even more.

Knowing that I was stuck, I watched cops swipe the metal detector over some guys that I swore I had seen with Poison before. The cops let them in without problem, easily let them slide, which meant that the metal detectors didn't really work, or the cops really didn't care because those two goons *had* to have guns or weapons on them.

Allie pulled me along and toward the doors. I gulped, the nerves bubbling up in my stomach, and stopped in front of the cops with Allie by my side.

"Arms up, girls," one policeman said, lip curled into a smirk. "We need to check you."

They scanned Allie first, and the machine didn't beep at all, but those bastards told Allie to pull everything out of her back pockets as they stared at her hips. Allie handed her wallet to me as I nervously crossed my arms and tapped my shoe.

"She's fine," I snapped. "She doesn't have anything."

The officer swiped his detector against her backside again and paused. "Anything else back there?" he asked, crouched down behind her with his head parallel to her ass.

As soon as that man crouched behind her, I wanted to sock him in the head. Allie had nothing on her, but this guy wanted to touch Allie. I could tell by the look in his eyes that he didn't care about breaking the law.

Allie reached into her back pockets again to feel around, then pulled her hand back out and shook her head. "There's nothing," she said, glancing back down at him and catching the *fucking bulge* in his pants.

"We're going to have to search you," he said.

My chest tightened, and I wanted to stand up for her, but I had a fucking gun in my jacket. If they found that, I would go right to fucking jail.

"No, you're not searching me," Allie said.

"If you want to make this difficult," the officer said, "you can leave."

But she wouldn't leave. This was Jace's last football game.

"Just let me pass," Allie said. "I don't have anything."

"Says everyone who's guilty."

"Please," she whispered.

"I'm so, so, so late!" Nicole said, suddenly hurrying in behind us in a scandalous cheerleading uniform that barely covered her ass. She pushed Allie to the side, whispering for us to hurry past the officers, and held her hands up. "Please, let me through."

The officer whisked his metal detector over the back of her body, then the front, stopping when he reached her breasts. "What do you have under your shirt?" he asked her, shamelessly staring at her chest.

She gave him a sweet smile, but it didn't reach her dull eyes. "Do you want to check?"

"I'll have to take you somewhere private to be certain. We aren't taking any chances tonight, especially after what happened at the last game," the officer said, but that was a lie. He wanted to touch her, to feel her up, to break the fucking law and fuck a minor tonight.

"All right," she said, glancing at us, then at the field, as if to tell us to get out of here.

I grabbed Allie's reluctant hand and pulled her up to the bleachers. "Come on."

While I sorta felt bad for Nicole—after she told Poison that her father had been pimping her out to the police force and the Redwood rich—I didn't want the cops to touch or search either of us anymore. We would be fucked.

When Nicole and the police officer disappeared into a small building, Allie clenched her jaw. Kai Koh walked in the front entrance a few moments later, not harassed by the police at all. Hell, he hadn't even gotten fucking scanned for guns and weapons—a test that he'd definitely fail.

"I hate them," Allie said from my side. She balled her hands into fists, watching as the police stopped girl after girl to *check* them for weapons of any kind. "So much."

I looked over at Allie for a moment, and Kai completely disappeared in the crowd. It was only a couple moments later when I found him standing at the far side of the stadium, leaning against the chain-linked fence and smoking a cigarette while staring at me. I had known that telling him I was attending Senior Night with Allie was a bit too easy. Of course, he'd follow me.

But I didn't mind like I used to. Instead, I smiled gently at him and tapped my jacket where I held my gun. Before I had gotten ready with

Allie, I had gone over to his place to practice shooting a bit. I still wasn't the best, but I felt confident that if I aimed a gun at someone, I would be able to shoot them.

A couple moments later, Akio arrived into the stadium and walked over to Kai. They chatted tensely for a couple moments, and then Akio hurried off toward the bleachers, but he never made it onto them. Instead, he stormed up to the police officer who Nicole had disappeared into the building with and followed him out of the stadium and to his police car.

Right before I lost sight of both of them, I saw Akio slam his fist into the side of the officer's face and throw him into the backseat of the police car. Then, Akio got into the driver's seat and sped away.

My eyes widened slightly as I looked back in Kai's direction. He disappeared from the chain-linked fence, but I knew that he was still here, somewhere, lurking around and watching both me and Allie, his sister.

He wasn't taking any chances, but I wondered what the hell Kai had told Akio. Were they suddenly friends now? Were they working together? What the hell had gotten into good-boy Akio, who had gotten scared after shooting someone to protect me?

Chapter One Hundred Sixty-Five

IMANI

After the football game, I leaned back in the driver's seat, blew out a deep breath, and pulled out the gun from my jacket pocket. I hadn't needed to take it out once, but more and more, cops had kept showing up during the night that I was feeling a bit too ... anxious.

Allie stared at the gun in horror and leaned as far away from me as she could. "Imani! What are you doing with a gun?!"

"Using it to protect us," I said, not able to keep it in anymore.

Allie was in as much danger as I was, and it wasn't like her ultra-rich stepfather was going to protect her. Hell, I doubted Jace Harbor even knew how to hold a gun correctly.

"A gun?!" she asked, eyes wide.

"Yes, a gun. Now, will you stop screaming?! I need you to put it in the glove box. I've had it on me all night, and I really need a break from it," I said, acting as if it were an annoying child or something, but I'd never held one on my body for that long.

Once Allie opened the glove box and stuffed the gun inside it, I started the car and blasted the heat to warm up my frozen fingers and toes. I spotted Kai on his bike a few parking spaces back with a black helmet covering his face.

We were safe for now. He would follow us for the rest of the night.

"I don't want to go home yet tonight," Allie said. "Jace is probably going to hang out with Jamal for a bit after the game, and I told him that I would be spending some time with you and *not* going back home to my mom and stepdad. So ... can we do something?"

I backed out of my parking space, making sure not to hit any students—though I wouldn't mind running over a few of them after what they had done to Maddie earlier—and drove out of the parking lot toward the Overlook, just for a quick ride.

"We shouldn't stay out long," I said.

"We could go look for Maddie," Allie suggested. "She lives on the good side of town, I think, so it should be pretty safe there, and she seemed so upset earlier."

"I know," I whispered, still in disbelief about what had happened with her during school.

Those images and videos still hadn't been taken down and were circulating Redwood Academy's social media.

I didn't know what I would do if all my video chats with Landon circulated Redwood.

Spotting Kai's bike lingering behind me on the road, I nodded. At least, if another *police officer* tried to pull me over, Kai would be here. João and Landon must've been out with Ana tonight and planning their next Redwood rich deaths.

"I added her on social media when I worked with her on that Bio project," I said to Allie, pulling up to a Stop sign and handing her my phone. "Last time I checked, she had her location shared on her phone. Why don't you check that?"

Allie paused for a moment. "She's at the Overlook."

"At the Overlook?" I asked, continuing to drive there. "Why would she be there?"

Once Allie shrugged, she put the phone down and pulled her glasses off to defog them. "Maybe she needed some time to think. I sure as hell did after pictures of Jace and I were posted literally everywhere. Hers are so much worse, though."

After turning into the Overlook, I spotted Alec and Maddie chatting tensely on the side of the road. Her body was trembling in the frigid air, and tears were running down her cheeks. I just wanted to jump out of the damn car to hug her.

When I pulled up closer, they got into their car. I flashed my high beams at them, then pulled up beside the car. Allie rolled down her window, and we both looked out toward them. It was rude to stare, but I wanted to make sure she was okay.

A couple moments later, she rolled down her window. "Imani? Allie?"

"Sorry for interrupting," I shouted. "Are you okay?"

Maddie stayed quiet for a long time, and then Alec said, "You gonna answer them?"

"Thank you," Maddie finally whispered, voice hoarse. "I'm good."

"Redwood is shit," I said, eyeing Alec. "If you ever need anything, we're here."

"Actually," Maddie said with a smile, "there is something you can help with. We need a favor from Kai."

* * *

Twenty minutes later, I stood in front of Poison in Landon's basement with Maddie and Alec behind me. Maddie uncomfortably stood with her arms wrapped around her body.

I crossed my arms, tapped my boot on the concrete floor, and gritted my teeth at João. "It's one simple favor, João. Come on."

"If you want us to hack into your accounts and delete all that shit from the internet," João said to Maddie and Alec, and he lit a cigarette and gently pushed on Alec's chest, "then it's going to cost you."

I rolled my eyes. "Please, can you do this one thing for me? You know how shitty Maddie and Alec have had it today. All Maddie wants is to have her life back."

João raised a brow and glared harder at me. His mere stare didn't affect me the way it used to. A few weeks ago, he would've scared me shitless. Now, I matched his glare with one of my own and refused to back down.

"Please," I pleaded when I knew he wouldn't give in.

"No," João said.

"It's fine," Kai said from the couch, scrolling on his computer. "I'm already in." He looked up at me. "But only this once."

Grinning wickedly at João, I nodded and walked to the couch beside Kai. I patted beside me for Maddie to sit, but she didn't move. Alec didn't either. Instead, they both stood awkwardly in the middle of the basement as Ana watched cartoons on the small television screen in the corner with Allie.

"Do you know who did it?" I asked Maddie and Alec.

"No," Maddie said, finally relaxing when João stopped glaring at me and disappeared up the stairs with Landon. Maddie grabbed Alec's hand and walked over to me, leaning against the opposite wall and glancing around. "We have no idea."

I jumped up and hiked my thumb back to the stairs, where the other two members of Poison had disappeared. "Well, if you find them, let me know. I'll get those two on them to kick their ass. Nobody should go through what you did. Students at Redwood are nasty."

"Thank you," she said. "This means so much to me."

"Anytime, girl."

"Got it," Kai finally said, looking up at Alec. "I've changed your password for all your social media accounts and took down what I could of the videos left up online of you and Maddie in the locker room. Make sure that you change your passwords once more to something that you will remember, but don't make them all the same thing. That's how you get hacked and locked out of your accounts."

After Alec thanked Kai and changed his passwords, he pulled Kai over to the side and talked quietly to him about something that neither Maddie nor I could quite hear. I pulled Maddie down onto the couch next to me.

"I know this next week at school is probably going to be hell for you," she said. "You, Vera, and Piper are welcome to sit with me and Allie at lunch. If you sit with us, people will know to back off you."

"I'll have to take you up on that," Maddie said. "Vera would like that, too, but Piper is a bit more ... well, she doesn't like *that* many people, so I'm not sure if she'd join."

"That's fine!" I said, leaning closer to her. "And Allie and I are having a girls' day tomorrow. We would love it if you and Vera could come!"

Maddie's eyes got wide. "Really?!"

"Yes!"

When Alec walked back over to Maddie, he took her hand and pulled her off the couch.

"Well then, I'll see you and Allie tomorrow!"

Chapter One Hundred Sixty-Six

JOÃO

Imani and Kai were downstairs, entertaining those assholes from Redwood—or maybe they had left already. I didn't know. I just wanted them out of here. I hated doing any sort of business around Ana, especially after what happened to Mom.

I sat on the couch with Ana curled up into the crook of my arm. She shifted in my arms for the fifteenth time in the past twenty minutes and didn't giggle at the cartoons like she usually did. She didn't even want to watch any Disney princess movies tonight.

After she moved, I readjusted Mom's suicide note in my pocket. I hadn't opened it yet. Didn't know if I would anytime soon, but I knew that I had to tell Ana sooner rather than later about Mom. If I kept it from her for much longer, she might think that I'd hidden other things from her too.

Ana crawled over my lap to grab the remote and turned off the TV, making the room dark. The only light was from the moon flooding in through the windows. Ana shifted in my lap and frowned up at me, tears wavering in her eyes.

"What's wrong?" I asked.

"Where's Mama?" she asked.

I tensed and said, "She's at home," because she was buried in our backyard.

"Something is wrong with her," Ana said, chin quivering. "Something isn't right. We always see her. At least every couple days. But Mama hasn't even tried to find us. What happened to Mama?"

My throat tightened. I couldn't keep this a secret from her for the rest of her life. If I continued to lie to her the way I was, then she would grow up to hate me, and she was the only family that I had left.

After placing Ana down on the couch, I walked over to turn the light on. Secrets might've been easier in the dark, but the truth needed to be told in the light, so Ana would know that I was serious about everything I was about to say to her.

I sat down on the couch beside her and pulled her onto my lap. "Do you remember when Mama used to bring us to the playground?" I asked softly, rocking Ana back and forth and reminiscing on all our memories.

Ana's lips curled up slightly. "Yeah, she would go on the slides with me, and you'd push me super high in the air on the swings. I felt like I was flying! I miss those times, João. I want to go back."

"I'll take you there one day," I said. "We can go with Imani."

"Really?" Ana asked, eyes widening. "You will let Imani come?"

"Of course I will."

I glanced into the other room, catching Imani grabbing some water from the kitchen sink as she let those kids from Redwood Academy out of Landon's house. She looked over at me and smiled softly, her gaze falling to Ana.

While I didn't want kids now—especially not in this town—I wouldn't mind putting them in Imani one day. She was so fucking good with Ana and had helped me grow closer to her too.

I smiled back at her, and then Ana grabbed my face to force me to look at her.

"Are you and Imani *dating*, dating, like, for real now?"

"Dating João?" Imani said, peeking her head into the room and scrunching her nose playfully. "Ew, boys are gross."

Ana giggled for the first time tonight, and then she turned back to me and pointed at Imani. "But I know that you like her. She's so pretty and perfect for you, João. You have *so* much in common, like you both love *me*!"

After ruffling her hair, I glanced once more over at Imani, who opened the basement door. She threw me a wink before descending the stairs, and I couldn't help the grin that broke out on my face. She might've been the most annoying girl I'd ever come across, but God, was she fucking amazing.

"What about Mama? Will she come, too?" Ana asked.

I stared down at her, sudden tears in my eyes. "No, Mama won't be there."

Ana shifted in my arms and pushed some tears off my cheeks. "Why are you crying?"

"Because, Ana, Mama is gone for good." My voice faltered for a moment, but I had to stay strong. I couldn't break down in tears in front of my sister. I was *her* only family left too. "Mama passed away."

"Passed away? What does that mean?"

"It means that Mama is ..."

Fuck. I couldn't do this.

"João?" Ana asked with worry. "Please, what does that mean?"

"It means that Mama is dead."

Ana's eyes widened, tears immediately filling them. "Mama is dead?" she asked, chin quivering and tears rushing down her cheeks. She buried her face into the crook of my neck and cried, "Mama is dead!"

"I'm sorry, Ana," I whispered, holding her tight and desperately trying to hold myself together. "I'm so sorry. I didn't want to tell you, but I don't want to lie to you anymore. She loved you so fucking much."

Ana's small body shook uncontrollably in my arms. "Mama is dead!"

I didn't know if I should've told her or not, but I hadn't wanted to keep lying to her. I couldn't. I wanted her to trust me with everything that she could possibly need. She already had a father who had let her get fucking HIV and a mother who had killed herself because she couldn't handle this life anymore.

Ana needed to trust me, or maybe I needed to trust her. Maybe I was the one who needed someone. Maybe I was the one who needed to be honest with someone for the first time in my fucking life.

I wasn't okay.

I didn't know if I would ever be okay.

"Mama!" Ana cried, holding on to me tightly and trembling in my arms. "I want Mama!"

I bit back my sobs. "I know that I'll never replace her, but I will protect you through everything, Ana. You won't have to worry about anything ever again. I promise you that. I will never leave you."

Chapter One Hundred Sixty-Seven

KAI

I sat in Landon's basement and scrolled tiredly through the security cameras posted all around Redwood, searching for a trace of Akio's family. Akio had said that they went into hiding, and it seemed like he was telling the truth because I hadn't seen them at all on here.

My phone buzzed in my pocket, jolting me awake.

Landon: Text me the address. I need to get rid of their bodies.

Imani sat at the table, finishing up some homework, and glanced over at me with her phone in her hand. "Where'd Landon go?" she asked. "I've been texting him since Maddie left, but he hasn't answered."

"Off disposing of his parents' bodies," I said, texting him the address of where I had burned the principal and the places where I'd buried his remains where nobody would ever find them. It wasn't like anyone cared about the people we killed and buried. I'd bet that most people wanted them dead, anyway.

"You say it like it's nothing," she said.

"It isn't," I said. "They deserved to die. They'd done nothing but abuse Landon for as long as I could fucking remember. I always told him that his mother wasn't any good, but he loved her almost as much as he loves you."

While she stayed quiet for a long time, she pressed her lips together and looked at me with those big fucking eyes. "Love," she whispered.

She fucking loved him, too, and I wanted her to say that to me as well one day, but I didn't know if it would ever be soon.

A long pause fell over us.

"Have you ever loved someone?" she suddenly asked.

After staring at her for a couple moments, I forced myself to tear my gaze away. "No."

Lie.

Straight-up fucking lie.

"Never?" she asked, leaning onto the table and staring directly at me. Her stare was smoldering and hot, burning me from the inside out. "Not even ..." She swallowed hard and paused for another moment. "Not even now?"

I glanced back at my computers and the security cameras and clenched my jaw. "No."

Once Imani turned back to her books, I looked up at her. She didn't even look like she was reading the pages, just staring down at them with hurt in her dark brown eyes. I wanted to tell her the truth, but I couldn't. Not until Akio's parents were taken care of.

Still, I was done looking at these fucking cameras for tonight, and I wanted her attention. Landon and João took up so much of her time that I barely got to spend any with her. And, fuck, I didn't want her to drift away from me. She was the best fucking thing that had happened to Poison.

"You want to learn how to fight some more, for times similar to today, where you can't bring a gun into places?" I asked, pulling out my keychain and handing her a kubotan. It was a long metal stick that could do some damage if applied to the right pressure points in the body.

Though it would never compare to a gun, it was something.

Imani glanced up from her books and closed them. "Sure."

So, for the next hour and a half, I showed Imani a handful of useful techniques she could use to protect herself from someone when she might not have a weapon on her. It was bad to rely on a single weapon, especially with Akio's family being after her.

"What happened to Akio?" Imani asked, glancing at me sometime later.

"Nothing."

"You said something to him during the game tonight, and then I watched him knock out a police officer, throw him into the back of his vehicle, then literally steal the police car and drive off of Redwood property."

"He's doing it for his girl," I said.

"For Nicole?"

"You know that he likes her?"

"Yeah, he mentioned it a while ago, but I didn't think he was *that* serious." Imani paused and chewed on the inside of her cheek. "Do you think he has … killed anyone yet? He could barely shoot a gun a couple weeks ago, and now, he's kidnapping the cops?!"

"They deserve it."

"Yeah, I know, but this is Akio, for crying out loud," Imani said, shaking her head.

"It's no different than me doing something for you," I said.

"So …" She paused, a small smile making its way onto her face. "Does that make me your girl?"

My entire body tensed, and I found myself unable to look away from her. She was grinning a bit too widely, and I liked the thought of her being mine way too much for me to lie to her again tonight.

"If I had to kidnap a cop and kill him for you, I would, Imani."

She moved closer to me, brushing her fingers against my forearm and making the hairs on my skin stand right up. "That didn't answer my question. I want to hear you say it."

I swallowed hard, her presence becoming the only fucking thing in the entire room that I could focus on, and tugged on one of her curls. My heart pounded inside my chest. This feeling was so foreign.

"You're my girl." The words came out so much softer than I'd intended them to, but that didn't stop Imani from stretching her smile ear to ear and beaming at me.

She didn't say anything in response. Hell, she didn't need to. Her smile told me fucking everything.

When a silence fell over us—because I didn't know what the fuck I was supposed to say after that—Imani leaned closer. "How are you feeling? Is there … is there anything I could do to help you along with your … parents? I've been thinking about it all day since you told me about it in the library."

"No," I said.

"But I want to—"

"I told you because I needed to talk to someone, Imani," I said, brushing some of her curls off her forehead. "You don't have to try to fix everyone, though … you did a pretty good job with Landon and João."

"I didn't fix anyone, and I don't want to fix you," she said. "I want to make sure you're okay."

But maybe I wanted her to fix me because a normal eighteen-year-old kid shouldn't enjoy killing the people who had hurt his family and his girl. He might've wanted revenge, but he wouldn't get off on it the way that I did.

Imani was the only person that I felt this way for, and I couldn't help myself every time I was close to her. I'd vowed to stay away from her for as long as I could, until Akio's parents were gone for good, but that was proving more and more difficult.

I feared that I wouldn't be able to protect Imani from them.

I feared that the same thing that had happened to my parents would happen to her, too.

I feared that they would take her away from me.

Chapter One Hundred Sixty-Eight

IMANI

After Landon came home and Kai finished teaching me how to defend myself for the night, João put Ana to bed and came down to the basement to relax. He lay back on the couch and grabbed a bong from Landon, inhaling a cloud of smoke.

I watched from the opposite couch as he pulled back and coughed, then handed it to Kai. Landon sat beside me, his feet kicked up onto the coffee table and a cigarette between his fingers. He glanced over at me as Kai placed the damn smoke stick on the table.

"Don't you dare," Landon said when I eyed it.

"I'm not going to do anything," I said, arching a brow at him. "Don't worry."

João leaned back his head and stared at me through hazy red eyes. "Why don't you take off your clothes?"

My eyes widened. "Ana is right upstairs."

"She's sleeping."

I narrowed my eyes at him, waiting for him to become uninterested and grab the bong again, but he continued to stare at me, refusing to back down.

"Take off your clothes, come over here, and"—he patted his knee—"ride this dick."

Heat swarmed around in my core. I pressed my thighs together and stood, pulling my shirt over my head and shimmying out of my bottoms. "If Ana wakes up, promise me that one of you will go up to tend to her."

"Don't worry about Ana," João said again, unbuckling his pants. "We've both had a long fucking day. I need something to relax, and I want your warm pussy wrapped around my cock, stroking it until it's quivering on me."

I unclipped my bra and let it slide down my arms, then pushed down my panties and stepped out of them. Wetness pooled between my thighs, and I walked over to him to straddle his lap. He set his hands on my hips and turned me around, so my back was against his chest and my body was facing Landon.

João spread my legs, placing my feet on the opposite sides of his thighs so Landon and Kai could see my glistening pussy, and then he pressed himself against my entrance. My pussy tightened, readying for him to slide himself into me.

We all needed to relax.

When he pushed himself inside of me, I squirmed in his arms, the pleasure shooting through my body. Fuck. Fuck. Fuck. Fuck. Fuck. I loved the way he felt inside of me. I loved the way that they *all* felt inside me.

"Eyes over here, Imani," Landon said, standing and walking over.

I gazed over at him, my pussy tightening even more on João and making him grunt into my ear, his voice filled with pleasure. Landon placed his hand on his thigh. I glanced down at his jeans, seeing the imprint of his cock against it and remembering the first time I'd *ever* seen it in real life. It'd looked so big on camera, but even bigger in reality.

"Spread her legs, João. Her pussy is desperate for another cock," he said.

João curled his arms under my legs and spread them wider so everyone could see his cock ram into me. From my left, Kai grasped one of my breasts in his hand and tugged on my nipple. I threw my head back, brows furrowed, and moaned loudly.

João groaned under me, thrusting his cock harder into me. Landon stepped out of his pants and rubbed the head of his huge cock against my glistening pussy lips, using it to play with my clit. When he slapped his head against me, I screamed out and clenched.

Landon moved it lower down my slit and pressed himself against João's dick and against my entrance. Inch by inch, he slid it into my filled hole until he was as deep as João, and then he grunted. Standing over me with his muscles flexing and the light shining from above him, he grabbed my ankles from João and spread my legs even wider to open me up.

"Jerk Kai off," João growled into my ear. "Then, let him fuck your filthy little mouth."

I placed my hand on Kai's bulge next to me, then skillfully undid the button on his cargo pants with one hand. After pulling out his cock, I spit on my hand, wrapped it around his base, and stroked it up and down.

Every time, I stroked him faster and faster. He grew harder in my hand until his cock was raging hard, the veins in it pronounced and his shaft glistening with my spit.

I leaned over and placed my mouth on his. "Please, fuck my mouth," I mumbled against his lips.

Kai pressed his lips against mine, sucking my bottom lip between his teeth for a brief moment, and then he kicked off his pants and laced his hand through my hair. I leaned down as best as I could as the others fucked my pussy.

After I opened my mouth wide, Kai thrust himself into me, bobbing my head up and down on his length. Spit and drool rolled down my chin, and my eyes filled with tears. But the pleasure felt too good. I loved being full of cock.

Way back then, they had been right. I was Poison's slut.

And I wouldn't change it for the world.

My pussy tightened around João and Landon, shaping to their sizes for each pump.

Landon groaned, eyes closing. "God, you feel so fucking good." He grasped my thighs, holding them apart as they began to tremble, and pumped into me slower. One of his hands slid down my thigh, and he harshly rubbed my clit.

The pressure already started to build in my throat and pussy, and I curled my toes, letting them use me. I loved it so fucking much. His fingers moved quicker around my swollen clit, my juices getting on them. João grasped my breasts from behind and squeezed both of my nipples between his fingers.

My body jerked up into the air, and I screamed out as the pleasure pumped out of me. My legs shook in Landon's hands, yet he didn't stop thrusting into me. Instead, he pumped harder and faster, giving me everything.

Kai shoved his cock deep into my mouth, thrusting faster until he suddenly came.

"Are you going to come?" João asked. "Your pussy just got so fucking wet."

I furrowed my brows and nodded, spit dripping down my chin. João stilled under me, then pulled out of me, his cum dripping out of my pussy, as Landon gave it three more hard strokes, giving me all of him.

Chapter One Hundred Sixty-Nine

IMANI

The next morning, I sat at the kitchen island and drank coffee with Mom as we waited for the girls to come over for a girls' day. She scrolled through a Redwood news article on her phone and looked over at me.

"Did anything happen last night at the game?" she asked. "There was a police officer who was kidnapped and had his car stolen. They tracked it to an abandoned house out in the woods but couldn't find the officer anywhere."

My entire body tensed, my stomach tightening. Mom probably thought that this was Poison's doing. Hell, everyone would probably blame them for this anyway, but this had nothing to do with them. This was all Akio.

"I didn't hear anything about it," I said, sipping my coffee.

Mom side-eyed me and raised a brow, *knowing* that I knew something. Thankfully, she didn't push it, and I was damn grateful. I didn't really want to get into it. She knew that Akio wasn't like his parents, and if she found out that he had done this, then she might have a hard time trusting him too.

"How's Dad?" I asked.

"He's still feeling a bit under the weather, but he's better than he was," Mom said. "He must've eaten something upsetting the other night."

The doorbell chimed, and I jumped out of my seat to get out of this conversation. I wanted to talk to Mom, but something didn't feel right at the moment. What if Akio's family had bugged the house and were listening to *everything* we were saying?

After placing my coffee cup in the sink, I walked to the front door and pulled it open to see Allie standing on the porch with Nicole.

She smiled at me, then stepped into the house and pulled Nicole in with her. "Morning, Mrs. Abara!"

"Morning, Allie," Mom called back.

I closed the door behind them and eyed Nicole as we walked up the stairs to my bedroom to prepare for the other girls. We all needed some time to relax after what had been happening with each of us at Redwood. We were all dealing with our own shit.

But I hadn't invited Nicole.

Shit might've happened to her, but she had hurt Allie so badly, so many times. I didn't like the bitch one bit and didn't want her here with Allie. While I might've felt bad for her, I ... ugh, I didn't want her to take a stab at Allie again.

So, as Nicole entered my bedroom, I pulled Allie to the side. "What the hell is she doing here?" I asked. "I thought we hated her?"

Allie shrugged her shoulders. "She doesn't have any friends."

"She has the entire cheer squad."

Frowning, she grasped my hands. "Just for today. If it doesn't go well and she doesn't fit in with us, then we don't have to hang out with her like this anymore. I promise. I ... please. I need to do this one thing for her."

After staring at her for a couple more moments, I sighed. "Only because you're my best friend. If you weren't, I would've thrown her out the second that she stepped onto my driveway." I pointed a finger at her. "But don't make me regret this."

She wrapped her arm around me and rested her head against my shoulder. "Thank you."

The doorbell chimed again, and Mom answered the door. A couple moments later, two sets of footsteps ascended the stairs. Maddie and Vera appeared in the hallway and smiled.

"I hope you don't mind us coming. I really needed to get out of the house, and Vera needs to take a break from writing those smutty stories of hers."

With long, silky hair and bright brown eyes, Vera blushed and glared playfully at Maddie. "Can you not?" she said to Maddie, narrowing her eyes and pushing up her glasses. "I don't need the entire world knowing."

I rocked back on my heels and stared at Vera. "You babysit Ana sometimes for João with your boyfriend, don't you? What is his name again? Blake? Blaise? Is that his name?"

"I do not hang out with Blaise," she said, her thick Latina accent coming through.

Because I loved the drama, I smirked and ushered them down the hall to my bedroom. "Sure you don't. I bet you don't even like him either, like Maddie doesn't like her brother's best friend." I wiggled my brows at Allie. "And Allie over there *hates* her stepbrother."

Allie rolled her eyes playfully at me. I grinned at her wickedly, then peered over at Nicole, my smiling dropping a bit.

I didn't want her to be here, but the least I could do was try to make her feel invited. So, I asked, "Do you *hate* anyone, Nicole?"

Nicole placed down her bags of makeup and sat on the bed, looking between me and Allie. Her lip curled into a half-smile, the expression on her face seeming like nobody had asked her something like that before.

"Maybe ..." She glanced down at her freshly manicured nails and smiled wider. "I have my sights on one boy, but he'll never date me. He's way too smart, and he makes me feel like such a fool sometimes." After a moment of silence, she unzipped her makeup bag. "So, makeovers?"

Chapter One Hundred Seventy

LANDON

"You want a smoke?" I asked Jace Harbor, who was visiting us while the girls had a day to themselves.

Three hours ago, he had come over to talk about his father and what he wanted done to him along with the rest of Redwood.

I pulled out a cigarette from the pack and handed one to João, then took one for myself and pushed it between my lips, lighting it up when Jace refused. "So, are we really going to believe Nicole?" I asked.

Kai looked up from scrolling on his computer. "I believe her because of how Akio reacted to that police officer taking her into the building during the game last night, but we need solid evidence to prove it to the rest of Redwood."

João puffed on his cigarette. "She texted me this morning, told me that she'll get us something solid by lunchtime on Monday."

After pulling the cigarette from my mouth, I leaned back on the couch and stared up at the ceiling. Someone knocked on the basement door, and we all glanced over at it. We weren't supposed to have any visitors.

"You invite someone?" João asked, cigarette hanging out of his mouth.

After Jace shook his head, João set the cigarette down in the ashtray and walked over to the door, reaching into his back waistband for his gun. He opened the door a few inches and grumbled something to himself. "What are you doing here?"

"João, don't be annoying," Imani called from outside. "Let us in."

A few moments later, the door opened wider, and the girls walked into the room.

"Jace, your girl's here," João called.

Jace shot up from the couch, grabbed his coat and keys, and hurried over to the door. "I'll see you guys later. Text me when you come up with a plan. I'm down to meet whenever, now that football is over for the season."

Standing at the door, both Imani and Allie had their hair and makeup done.

"Thought I'd find you here," Allie said to Jace. "We just dropped Nicole off at her house."

"Baby," Jace cooed at her, burying his face against the crook of her neck. "You look so good. You haven't done your makeup, put perfume on, or straightened your hair like this for, what, two years now?"

She giggled and playfully pushed Jace's chest. "Jace, stop it."

"Gross," Imani said playfully, scrunching her nose and walking over to me.

"Why are you here?" Allie asked Jace.

"I came here to convince Poison that Nicole was telling the truth," Jace said to her, gently stroking her face. He glanced back over his shoulder at us, then back at her. "After what you told me this morning, I thought it was necessary."

A smile stretched across her face. "You really did?"

He nodded and grabbed her hand. "Now, come on. I want to bring you out. Once they have a plan, they'll text me. We're going to bring him down, one way or another. The police chief and these other fuckers in Redwood aren't going to get away with what they've done."

Once they left, Imani sat down on my lap and rested her head on my shoulder. "Nicole came to hang out with us today, and it was surprisingly ... nice. She isn't as mean as I thought she was, and she actually seems like she was telling the truth about her father."

Kai arched a brow, giving João and me a look. "Told you guys."

"We still need something fucking solid. If she can get us texts, videos, anything, we can destroy him. Otherwise, nobody is going to believe us over the fucking cops, no matter how corrupt they are," João said.

Kai's phone buzzed on the table. He picked it up, face hardening. "Fuck."

"What is it?" Imani asked.

"Akio is standing at the front door," Kai said, pulling up the security cameras.

I placed Imani on the couch beside me and walked up the stairs to the basement door, then pulled it open. Instead of waiting for me to ask him to come in, he stormed right into the house and hurried down the stairs to find Kai.

"I have news about my family. Something that you all are going to want to know about."

Chapter One Hundred Seventy-One

KAI

Akio stuffed his hands into his pockets and paced around the room, worried etched onto every inch of his face. Blood was splattered all over his shirt, which no doubt belonged to the police officer he had kidnapped earlier.

"I hate this town," Akio said, shaking his head and looking at the ground.

"What did you do?" Imani asked. "What happened?"

"My parents have been in on this," he said to me, shaking his head. "They've been in on this whole thing that has happened to Nicole, every single fucking thing that goes on in Redwood. I should've done more. I should've stopped this earlier."

"Slow down," I said, pulling out a pack of cigarettes from my back pocket and handing him one. He swatted it away and continued to pace the room, his strides becoming even faster. "What the fuck happened? Did they contact you?"

"No," Akio growled. "He told me everything."

"Who?" Landon asked.

Akio looked up at me. Without him saying a word, I already knew who he meant. He had kidnapped that officer after I told him that Nicole had disappeared into the building with him. Akio had already broken and already killed a man. I had watched it with my own eyes.

He had stopped caring about being a good boy and staying out of his parents' business.

He was far too deep in their shit, and he was the only person who could help us.

"He told me fucking everything," Akio said to me, gritting his teeth and tightening his fists. "And I want to kill them all. It isn't fair what they have done to her. Nobody should have to go through what she has."

"If that's all the shit you got," João started, taking the pack of cigarettes from me, "get out. We're busy with other shit. Don't come back until you have information on your parents' whereabouts. We have no use for you."

But João was wrong.

If we pushed Akio away, he would go off the fucking rails, just like I had when I had nobody. He needed someone to help him hone his anger and direct it to the people who had hurt him the worst—his own two parents.

Akio might've acted like he had the perfect life, but nobody had a good life as a Mafia leader's son. His parents abused him to further their life and status in this town. They acted all holy and mighty.

It was all bullshit.

"Join us," I said, never once thinking that I would say those words.

"Kai," João growled, sending me a death glare.

"He's not joining Poison," Landon said.

I shook my head and stepped closer to Akio. "You're not joining Poison, but you should work with us. You have information. You want this shit to end. Don't let your parents run or ruin your life and your relationship with your girl," I said, glancing over my shoulder at Imani. "They don't deserve to take something important away from you."

I didn't know how to say it, but I was trying to relay to Imani that I wouldn't let them take her away from me either, that I liked her more than I had let on, that when she had asked me if I loved someone and I said no, I had straight-up fucking lied.

"You want me to help you guys?" Akio asked, staring from me to Landon to eventually João, who looked beyond pissed off.

He didn't like new people working with us, especially the son of the two people who had disgraced his mother's dead body.

But as much as it hurt to say, we needed him. He had proven to be useful so far.

"Not as a member of Poison," I reiterated. "But we could use the help."

Akio stared at the ground for a few long moments, then looked up at Imani. They shared a certain kind of look that I couldn't quite decipher. And while old me would've thought that he still liked her, I knew that wasn't true.

He was the one who had told her to stay away from us weeks ago.

Now, we were asking him to join us and to take down Redwood.

"If my parents find out ..." He trailed off.

"Screw your parents," Imani said, brows furrowed. "They've done nothing but hurt you. Do you remember that they kicked your ass because of something that *I* did? Do you remember that they have done nothing but stress you the fuck out and do shady shit around town?"

After swallowing hard, Akio finally looked me in the eye. "Fine."

"Fine?"

"I'll do it. I'll work with you guys. I want them gone. All of them."

My lips curled into a smirk, and I glanced over at Imani, who was also smiling. He might've been the guy we beat up to get what we wanted and needed for Ana and for information, but now, he was working with us.

We had the same goal.

João growled and rolled his eyes, heading back to spend time with Ana. Landon disappeared into the back room with him. But I stayed with Imani and Akio, and Imani moved closer to him.

"You know ..." Imani said, grinning from ear to ear at Akio, slyness in her eyes. "I hung out with Nicole today for a girls' day. Allie brought her over to my house, and we talked about the boys we like."

"What'd she say?" Akio asked, moving closer to us.

"That she had this crush on this kid."

Suddenly, Akio's relatively soft expression hardened. "Who?"

Imani grinned even more wickedly. "I don't know."

"Imani," Akio growled. "Who?"

She pinched his flushed cheek. "Look at you, getting all possessive. I didn't think Kai was telling me the truth when he said that you kidnapped that police officer for Nicole. You really like her, huh?"

Akio cut his glare to me. "You told her?"

"She saw you take the police car," I said to him. "What'd you do to him? Draw some blood?"

Instead of answering me, Akio pulled his keys from his pocket and walked back toward the front door. "I'll see you in school on Monday," Akio mumbled, then walked out of Landon's house. No doubt on his way to go find Nicole.

Chapter One Hundred Seventy-Two

IMANI

"Where were you guys?" I asked, arching a brow at Allie and picking at my turkey sandwich that Dad had made me this morning. In the Redwood Academy cafeteria, I glanced over at Poison and hiked my thumb toward them. "I had to spend the majority of lunch with these assholes."

"That must've been *terrible*," Allie said sarcastically to me, cracking a smile. "Especially when Landon can't stop touching you under the table."

I sneered and pushed Landon's hand away from me, scolding him to stop it because people could definitely see. It didn't matter how hard they tried to hide it; the Poison boys weren't the best at keeping things secret at Redwood either, especially when it came to touching me. We had barely escaped the principal's office without anyone knowing they had fucked me.

"He's not touching me," I said.

"I'm claiming her," Landon clarified.

Allie smirked at me. "And you think we"—she gestured to herself and Jace—"are messed up. You can't even decide if you want them or not." She leaned closer to Jace. "At least I know what I want."

Jace unwrapped a sandwich. "To be fucked in the library."

I laughed as Allie cut her eyes to Jace and slapped his chest.

"Thanks for the help."

"Anyway," Jace said, looking at João, "we need to move things along. My father is about to snap." Jace placed a hand on Allie's thigh and squeezed. "And when I say move them along, I mean, by the end of this week. We can't wait much longer. Redwood needs to burn."

Nicole walked into the cafeteria, glancing from the cheerleader table to ours and gnawing on her cheek. Allie gave her a smile and waved her over, patting the seat beside her.

Though she looked nervously between Poison, Jace, and me, she sat on the bench. "Hey."

"What are you doing here?" Jamal, one of Jace's friends, asked, taking a seat across from her.

She pressed her red lips together. "I'm sitting with my ... my friends." After whispering the word, as if she didn't know if we considered her a friend yet, she pulled her backpack onto her lap and rummaged inside of it. "I have a video that might help prove myself to you."

"You don't have to," Allie said, leaning closer to her. "They believe you."

Nicole looked between the Poison boys and shook her head, giving them a flash drive, anyway. "I spent all night trying to find it on my father's computer. I'm not going to let all my hard work go to waste. I ... I need a place to crash for a couple nights. As soon as my dad gets home from work tonight, he's going to know that I went in there."

When nobody offered Nicole to stay at their place—I would've, but I had enough problems with Akio's family—Jamal cleared his throat. "You can stay at my place, but what's on the video? Why do you need it?"

"It's ... a video of my father and me," Nicole whispered. "If you can't find anything incriminating on my father, use this. I want this to be over as quickly as possible. I don't want any of you guys getting hurt anymore."

Kai pulled out his computer and stuffed the flash drive into the USB port, eyes widening. Almost immediately, he snapped the computer closed and looked around the cafeteria to make sure that nobody had seen. "Fuck, this is worse than I thought."

Nicole pressed her lips together and looked down at the table.

"Please, use that. I don't want any of the other girls to have a video of them leaked or ... or something worse. If you can incriminate him with this, then do what you need to."

Kai leaned closer. "Nicole, this is a video of your father mol—"

"I know it is," she snapped. "It fucking happened to me. I don't need to relive it. Just do what you have to do with it and fucking destroy that fucking bastard, so he doesn't hurt anyone else like he has me."

Everyone at the table went silent, and Allie gently rubbed Nicole's shoulder. I didn't want to even see what was on that flash drive. By the mere way Kai—*Kai!*—had paled when he saw it, I knew that it'd sicken me right down to the very core.

Allie rested her head on her shoulder. "Thank you, Nicole. You don't know how much we needed this right now," she whispered because it was true. Without this video and without evidence, we wouldn't be able to get anywhere. "Jace and I are in your debt."

She gave Allie her best smile. "No, you're not. I did this so nobody else will get hurt or used by the Redwood Police or disgusting old teachers who have nothing else to do than jerk off to underage students."

"Sorry that we're late to the party!" Maddie said, approaching our table with Vera in tow. "Did we miss anything good?"

"Nope," I said, cutting my eyes to the rest of the table.

We hadn't had many friends before, and I didn't want to get them involved in our messy drama. We had other things to deal with and to worry about.

So, I pushed over to make room for them. "We were just waiting for you girls."

The girls fell into an easy conversation with Allie as Jace started talking business with Poison about what they were going to do with the video and when they were going to put the Redwood rich through hell.

A few moments later, Nicole glanced up from her lunch and toward the cafeteria doors. She shifted in her seat, pupils dilating as she spotted Akio standing there with his hands around his backpack straps and his reading glasses covered in splotches of snow.

He looked mad, pissed even.

Innocent ol' Akio.

"I'll catch you guys later," Nicole said, standing up and heading toward the door.

As she passed him, she glanced at him quickly, then hurried down the hall with him following behind her. While Akio looked like he wanted to say something to Nicole, I couldn't picture him ever having the courage to do that.

But who knew? Maybe he had some fight in him after our conversation yesterday.

<h1 style="text-align:center">Chapter One Hundred Seventy-Three</h1>

JOÃO

That afternoon, I grabbed Ana's hand and walked through Redwood Grocery. After I told her that Mom died, she hadn't been that cheery, happy girl that she usually was. She had been walking around Landon's place like a zombie, just going through the motions.

While I didn't blame her—because what person could really come to fucking terms that their family wasn't alive?—I didn't want her to feel like shit anymore, so I decided that I'd make brigadeiros with her tonight and ask Imani to come over.

"Do you want chocolate or rainbow sprinkles?" I asked, staring at the selection in the baking aisle. They had sprinkles for every fucking occasion here, it seemed, because these rich people had celebrations for everything. "They have blue too, if you want."

Ana stood quietly by my side, not saying a word.

I placed the sprinkles down and crouched to her level. "Come on, Ana," I said, poking her stomach and hoping to get a smile out of her. "I texted Imani to see if she wants to make some with us. Don't you want to make them? They're our favorite."

"It's not the same," Ana whispered, staring at the ground.

My lips curled into a frown, and I gently grasped her small chin and lifted her face, so she was looking right at me. Tears lay heavily in her eyes, her small lips in a frown.

"I know it's not the same. I know it will never be the same."

"I miss her," she said. "So much."

"Me too."

"You do?" she asked.

"Yes. I think about her all the time."

"But you don't cry."

All I wanted was to be Ana's strong big brother, the type of guy she looked up to when she needed to talk to someone or tell secrets to, the guy who would kick anyone's ass who hurt her. I didn't want her to see me sad.

But that was what I was.

"I cry sometimes," I whispered, brushing some hair out of her face. "I cried when I found out. Imani held me all night, like I hold you when you cry. I do get sad, Ana. She was our mom who'd been with us forever. That's why I want to make brigadeiros with you because that's something you guys loved doing together."

"Yeah," Ana said softly, "we did."

"So, are you going to make some with me, or do I have to do it myself?"

After a couple moments, Ana smiled, her eyes lighting back up, and nodded eagerly at me. She grabbed my hand and turned toward the sprinkles. "I think I want the blue ones. Blue was Mama's favorite color. She would be so happy."

"Blue it is." I grabbed the blue sprinkles from the aisle and tossed it into our basket. "Now, we have to find some condensed milk and cocoa powder."

"I know where it is!" Ana said, running ahead and toward the next aisle.

When she left my sight, I quickly followed after her because we weren't the most popular people in Redwood right now. Who the fuck knew who was here and wanted to hurt us in some way? Akio's parents could be hiding around the corner.

Ana stood halfway down the next aisle, staring up at the condensed milk. She stood on her tiptoes, trying to grab a can from a higher shelf. I let out a deep breath when I saw her and walked toward her.

A young woman smiled at her and grabbed the condensed milk for her, and then she crouched down to her level and handed it to her. "Here you go," she said with a grin. "You gotta grow a little bit taller to reach all the way up there."

Once she took the can, Ana gave the woman an uncomfortable smile. "Thank you."

I eyed the woman and stood behind Ana, placing my hand on her shoulder to let this woman know that Ana wasn't to be messed with. The woman looked like she had innocent intentions, but so did the rest of the Redwood rich on the outside.

"You know," the woman continued talking to Ana, "I heard you talking to your brother about your mom, and I wanted to tell you that I'm so sorry. A little girl like you should never have to grow up without a mother. It's too bad, what happened to her."

Gritting my teeth, I yanked Ana away from the woman and started back down the aisle to find the cocoa powder. Who the fuck had that much audacity to say that to a little girl? Who the hell was she anyway?

Like a fucking snake, the woman followed us. "It's a shame, what she did to herself."

After holding Ana close, I turned around and snapped at her, "Shut the fuck up and mind your own fucking business. You don't know shit about what happened, and you sure as fuck aren't going to talk about this shit while my sister is listening."

The woman stared at me in shock for a few moments, then curled her lips into an evil-as-fuck, menacing smirk. She moved closer to me and laid her hand on my shoulder. "I'm here to let you know that The Family is always watching, João."

"Get the fuck out of here," I growled, shoving her off me.

I scooped up Ana in my arms and hurried down the aisle, grabbing cocoa powder on the way out and heading right for the self-checkout. We were getting out of here as soon as fucking possible because when Akio's family finally came out of hiding, I didn't want Ana anywhere near trouble.

"João," Ana said, wrapping her arms around my shoulders and holding me close. "Who was that?"

"Nobody."

"What did Mama do?"

"Nothing, Ana," I said, slipping my chip into the card reader to pay. "They're trying to mess with us. They're bad people who hurt Mama and us. We need to get you back home, where you are safe."

Who knew if these people would follow me or if they had bugged our place or some shit? I needed to find out how they were tracking and watching our every move before we gave them exactly what they wanted—information on their downfall.

Chapter One Hundred Seventy-Four

IMANI

"Give me the keys to your car," João said, hurrying into Landon's basement with Ana on his hip. He set her down, handed her a brown paper bag from Redwood Grocery, and then reached out his hand for the keys to all our cars. "Everyone. Now."

I pulled my keys out of my purse and handed them to him. "Why?"

After Kai handed him keys to his bike, João hurried back up the stairs. "Because I had a little run-in with people from Akio's family while I was at the grocery store with Ana. They have info on us, and I think they bugged our cars or some shit."

When João disappeared out the door, Ana walked over to me and handed me the bag. "Can you help me start making brigadeiros? João said he'd make them with me and that you would help."

"Sure!" I said, taking her hand and heading up to the kitchen with Landon and Kai behind me.

Kai disappeared out the door where João had gone as Landon started the stove.

I pulled out the ingredients. "Blue sprinkles?!"

Ana grinned. "Yeah, it was Mama's favorite color!"

"She would've loved them," I said, glancing over at Landon, who watched us.

Once I pulled out a cooking pan to make the brigadeiros, I dumped the ingredients inside and gave Ana a large wooden spoon, so she could mix. She wrapped her entire palm around the spoon and grinned widely as she stirred.

A few moments later, João walked back into the room with three crushed trackers and microphones in his hand. He threw them onto the ground and stomped on them once more for good measure, then threw them into the trash. "I fucking hate them."

"João!" Ana said. "Are you going to make them with us?"

By the looks of it, João was too pissed to make some brigadeiros with his sister. But to my surprise, he took a deep breath, pulled off his coat, and walked to the stovetop next to Ana. "Sure, Ana."

My eyes widened slightly, but I found myself smiling like a dumbass at him. He might've been annoying as hell to be around, but we all kinda, sorta fit together very well. We worked in some fucked up way.

I didn't know what we all really were—that was something that we'd have to talk about once this was all over—but I loved where our relationship was going and what we had become. If only Kai would open up to me more.

Kai walked into the house and shut the door behind him, shaking off the snow from his black hoodie and sitting at the kitchen table. This place was actually really nice to hang out in and live in when there weren't beer bottles scattered around the room.

After he pulled out his laptop, he opened the cameras around Redwood and started researching the woman that João must've met at the grocery store. He grimaced and shook his head. "Her name is Vikky Ito, Akio's second cousin."

"Vikky," João huffed over the stove, "fucking Ito. I'm going to kill her."

Ana grabbed João's face and directed him back to the brigadeiros. "If you stop stirring, they're going to come out bad. Pay attention."

Someone knocked on the back door twice.

João protectively laid a hand on Ana's shoulder and looked over at it. "Who the fuck is that? We didn't invite anyone over, did we?" With his free hand, he reached into his waistband for his gun. "It'd better not be those asses."

"It's just Nicole," Kai said, walking toward the door to answer it. "I asked her to come over to talk about the video and what she wants us to do about it. Akio mentioned that his family knew more than what they were letting on, and I want us to be a step ahead of them."

Once João went back to making brigadeiros, Kai opened the door.

Nicole walked into the room, brushing off some snow from her faux fur coat, and gave us a small smile. "Sorry if I startled you guys. I wanted to come over a bit earlier."

"It's okay," I said to her.

While I might've still hated her for what she had done to Allie and Jace, after seeing that video today at lunch of her basically getting raped by her own father, I could only feel sympathy for her. She had been through so freaking much.

She sat at the kitchen table and sniffed the air. "Something smells good."

"We're making brigadeiros!" Ana chimed. "Do you want one when they're done?"

"Sure," Nicole said, then turned back to Kai. "So, what'd you want to talk about?"

"You probably don't want us to share that video," Kai started. "But people won't believe us without it, without even a couple seconds of it. We need to use it if you want to take down the Redwood Police and everyone else who's used you."

Nicole sat at the kitchen table tensely and stayed quiet. She fiddled with her fingers and gnawed on the inside of her cheek. "I ... I don't know. I don't want anyone to ever see that. You know how people in Redwood really are. What if they don't believe me? What if ... all they do is put me down because my father used me? That's how the cheer team acts to me now."

"You have people who will support you," I said, giving her my best half-smile. "Allie and I will be here if you need anyone to talk to or lean on. I know that we all haven't had the best relationship with you before, but ... we're here now."

"Really?" Nicole asked, tears wavering in her eyes.

"Yeah."

She let a tear slip down her cheek. "That means so much to me."

Kai and Landon glanced over at me as Nicole wiped away another tear. God, they were useless when a girl was crying. They didn't know the first thing to say or how to act around her, so Kai cleared his throat and continued.

"Anyway," Kai interrupted, "we need to use it, but I wanted your permission."

Still, Nicole seemed hesitant.

"Everyone knows the police are shit, but when they see *this*," João started, still mixing the ingredients over the stovetop with Ana, "they'll think twice about trusting them for anything. This town will be ruined for good."

Nicole swallowed hard. "Promise?"

"Yeah, pinkie promise or whatever shit you want," João said.

I rolled my eyes and sat at the opposite end of the table. "They're going to use it to help you, Nicole. They're not going to try to fuck with you, and if they do"—I shot them daggers with my eyes—"I'll kill them."

"Okay," Nicole finally said. "You can use it, but I ... I need protection. A lot of it. My father will try to find me and kill me if he finds out that I was part of this. Sleeping over Jamal's place won't do anything."

"We'll get you protection," Kai said. "Don't worry about that."

Chapter One Hundred Seventy-Five

KAI

Later that night, Imani wanted to practice her shooting, so we all went to my place to let her practice in the shooting range. Even Ana came with João and a huge plate of brigadeiros, to watch the security camera footage of Redwood.

Imani stood at the target, steadied her hips, and aimed her gun at the center. When she pulled the trigger, she stumbled back slightly, but the recoil wasn't as bad as it had been that first night I brought her here.

"You're getting better," I said, walking to her.

I placed one hand on her hip, the other on her wrist to help her aim a bit more accurately. She was inches off from the center, inches away from being able to kill someone, if she needed.

"You think?" she asked, a smile on her lips.

"Yes, the only question is ..." I paused and glanced down at her. "Are you actually going to be able to shoot to kill someone in real life? There is a difference between a target and a live human being standing in front of you."

Imani glanced down and nodded. "I know, but if it is to protect the people I care about, then I have to do it."

"Then, shoot again," I said.

Imani squared her hips, aimed once more, then pulled the trigger. The bullet whizzed through the air and pierced right through the

677

center of the target, a clean, straight shot. She placed the gun down and threw her arms around me. "Finally!"

"Good job," I said, unable to hold back a smile.

Because, fuck, hers was beautiful. She was getting so strong, becoming even sexier to me, if that was even possible. Sweet Imani was turning into a woman who could protect herself without the help of anyone else.

After a couple moments, Imani's smile dropped. She parted her lips, then pressed them back together, looking unsure. Then, she finally came out with it.

"I know something is holding you back," she said, "but I wanted to let you know that you make me feel so safe and strong, and I ... I *appreciate* it so much more than you will ever know. I've never felt this confident before I met you guys."

It looked like she wanted to say more.

Fuck, I *wanted* her to say more.

But my fucking phone had to ruin it all, buzzing in my pocket and cutting through the silence. Imani cracked another smile, then turned back toward the shooting range to practice some more.

I stared at her smaller frame for a few long moments, wishing that I could tell her that I loved and cared about her the same way she cared about me. I wanted her to tell me that she loved me too, not just appreciated me.

Another buzz.

After sighing, I pulled out my phone to read a group chat between Poison and Jace.

Jace Harbor: We still on?

João: Pierce Road. Five minutes. Alone.

At lunch earlier, Jace fucking Harbor had asked us to teach him how to shoot a gun. He wanted to be able to protect Allie against his short-tempered killer father, if he ever needed to. So, I had invited him over to my place tonight. I wanted to protect Allie, too, but for different reasons.

"Landon!" I called.

A moment later, Landon appeared at the door.

"Watch Imani. I have something I need to take care of." I walked out into the main room with all my monitors.

Ana sat on João's lap and stared up at all the monitors displaying security camera footage from around Redwood. We were still looking nonstop for Akio's family. They hadn't shown their faces once. Neither had Vikky Ito.

I leaned against the wall and stared at the cameras, nodding to João. "Jace will be here soon. If I don't go out there, he's going to be driving all around these streets to try to find my place."

After jogging up the stairs, I tugged on a black hoodie and walked out into the frigid fucking cold. A white puff of air drifted out from my mouth. I pulled my hood up and stuffed my hands into my pockets.

Down the street, Jace Harbor pulled up to the curb in his Maserati. When he got out of his car and looked over at me, I nodded to my place and walked back into the house because it was too fucking cold.

Jace jogged up to my side door, checked behind him to ensure nobody had followed him, then slipped into the house. He followed me down the stairs and into the main room with all my monitors.

"Hi!" Ana said to him, waving her small hand.

"Hey," he said, looking around. "This is your place, Kai?"

"Don't touch anything," I said, dead-bolting the basement door behind him.

I led him into the back room, where we had our weapons stash. He stepped into the room and widened his eyes even further, taking in all the weapons, like Imani had only a few short weeks ago.

"Which one you want?" João asked, leaning against the doorframe to block Ana from seeing inside the room and gesturing to the guns.

Jace pulled a gun out of his waistband. "I have this."

I didn't know where the fuck he had gotten it from—maybe his father—but I took it from him so he wasn't aimlessly pointing it at me, then whistled. I looked it up and down. "This is pretty nice, but"—I drew my fingers down the barrel and tossed it down—"it's broken. Won't shoot cleanly or accurately. Pick something else out. There are tons of them here."

Staring around the room, Jace studied each gun carefully. I didn't even think he knew what he was looking at, but he surely took his time choosing the right weapon for himself. After glancing around at a couple more, he walked over to one and brushed his fingers against it. "How about this one?"

I looked over my shoulder and tensed. "Anything, except that one. That one was my—" I paused and looked down for a moment. Jace didn't know that Allie and I were half-siblings, and I wanted to keep it that way. "That one was Allie's father's from when he was in the military. You're going to want something lighter and newer."

"Why do you have his gun?" he asked.

"His business is his business," João said, nodding to the other guns. "Pick a gun and get out of here. We have shit that we need to figure out and to plan for Nicole's father. We can't spend all day holding your fucking hand as you pick your poison."

After sighing through his nose, Jace picked up a handgun. "How about this one?"

"That's fine." I tossed him some ammo and nodded to another room. "Practice in there and don't come back out until you hit the center of the target. You'll get one, maybe two shots in real life before your father reacts. You can't miss."

Chapter One Hundred Seventy-Six

JOÃO

At lunch the next day, I slid into an empty seat across from Jace and Allie. With the information on her father that Nicole had brought us the other day and that video she had given us yesterday, we didn't have any more fucking time to waste.

Sending out the video would hopefully bring Akio's fucking family out of hiding. They were working with the police, and all their shit was going to be out in the open. They would have no other choice than to come find us.

And when they did—I gritted my teeth and lit a cigarette in the middle of the cafeteria—I would fucking kill those bastards for what they had done to Mom, Kai's family, and everyone fucking else that they hurt.

"Tomorrow," I said to Jace, tugging the cigarette out of my mouth and referring to when we'd release the information. After he had practiced shooting that gun last night, he had been fucking begging me to let him know when we'd do it. "We talked to Nicole about what's going on. If everything goes smoothly, I'd suggest not returning to school tomorrow. This town will go fucking insane when they learn about it."

Allie blew out a deep breath and slouched in her seat as half the student body stared at us. Redwood was always filled with rumors and drama, and today, someone in the student body thought it'd be funny to spread another rumor about Allie—that she was pregnant, which just so happened did wonders for our plans.

I didn't know where the fuck it had come from or if it was true. But I didn't give a fuck.

After taking another puff on the cigarette, I spotted Imani walking into the cafeteria and leaned closer to Allie. "And your pregnancy rumors are a perfect distraction for the student body right now, so bravo to you on that. You and Carter the quarterback having a baby together ..." I blew a cloud of smoke out of my nose. "Never would've guessed."

Allie kicked me hard in the motherfucking shin, and I grunted.

Imani sat at the table beside me, tugged the cigarette out of my mouth, and stomped on it. "Why is it that every time I see you, you're always smoking? Stop that. It's bad for your health. You're going to get lung cancer and die." She frowned sarcastically. "On second thought ... why don't you smoke all of them at once to speed it up a little bit?"

Stifling a laugh, Allie smiled at us and rested her head on Jace's shoulder, stuffing some more of her sandwich into her mouth for those *pregnancy cravings.* I turned back to Imani and eyed her as she pushed some curls over her shoulder and pulled out some brigadeiros, handing me one.

"Ana helped me pack my lunch last night," she said.

My lips curled into a small smile, and I ... I wondered how the fuck I had gotten so lucky for someone like her to love me. Don't get me fucking wrong; I was still going to set this town on fucking fire.

The only thing that was different now was that Imani would be there with me.

A few moments later, Carter the quarterback sauntered into the cafeteria, pulling the stares away from us. And to ignite Allie's pregnancy rumors even more, he walked right up to our table and sat in the empty seat next to her. "What's up, babe?"

This would be interesting.

I didn't have to do shit to keep the heat off Poison today. Carter's stupid ass was doing it for me. We'd slide right under the students' and teachers' radars for the day. Hell, nobody would bat an eye tomorrow when none of us showed up either.

Jace gritted his teeth and wrapped a possessive arm around Allie's waist. But Carter decided to take things up a fucking notch as the rest of the student body gawked at us, and he laid an arm around Allie's shoulders.

Stuffing the brigadeiro into my mouth, I leaned back and watched the refreshing Redwood drama unfold.

Jace stood up and grabbed Carter by the collar. "Get your fucking hands off my girl," Jace said through clenched teeth.

"I can do what I want with her. She's carrying my baby," Carter said.

A chuckle escaped my lips as the two started throwing punches and kicks like shitheads who didn't know the first thing about fighting. God, this was too good, like a front row seat at the fucking theater, and hell, I didn't even enjoy drama that much.

Imani elbowed me hard in the side and narrowed her eyes, as if to say to shut my fucking mouth. Allie leaned her elbows on the table, placed her face in her hands, and blew out a deep breath.

"Allie," Imani said, staring worriedly at the scene behind her, "you should stop Jace."

Allie looked over her shoulder at Jace, who straddled Carter's waist in the middle of the cafeteria and rained down a series of punches on that pretty boy's face. But instead of helping her boyfriend beat up the quarterback, Allie smiled and turned back around to continue eating her lunch.

A crowd gathered around us, whispering and recording the fight— well, more like the smackdown on Carter—on their phones. Allie sank deeper in her seat like nothing was happening. Imani looked at me to break it up.

But I wasn't going to do shit.

Carter deserved to have a couple of black eyes.

"Break it up!" someone shouted over the crowd.

The students parted ways for Jace's football coach—who I guessed was now subbing as the principal until they found someone more suitable.

He grabbed Jace and yanked him off Carter, shoving him toward the office. "Get in my office. You know better, Harbor."

After Jace stormed out, Allie handed Jace's coach his backpack and smirked at the puddle of blood under Carter. That man fucking deserved everything Jace had given him. He had been nothing but a prick to everyone since freshman year.

I fucking hoped that this was enough to keep prying eyes and ears off Poison for tonight.

Chapter One Hundred Seventy-Seven

IMANI

Later that day, Landon and I took Ana to Redwood Grocery to stock up on some supplies. This entire town would be going to shit by tomorrow morning, and I wanted us all to be prepared. Who knew what the fuck would happen?

Ana stood at the end of the cart, being pushed by Landon down the aisle. I smiled at the exchange and thought about how good each member of Poison was with kids. They might've been the bad boys who blew up this town, but they had soft spots.

I hooked my arm around Landon and rested my head on his shoulder. "What do you want to do when we graduate?"

We hadn't talked about what would come after graduation and when we finally got the chance to leave Redwood for good. Would the guys stay here to help raise Ana? Would they want to move elsewhere? Would they go somewhere with me?

"I haven't really thought that far ahead," Landon admitted, scratching the back of his head and glancing down at Ana as she skipped down the aisle. "It's hard to think about shit like the future when you're a poor kid just trying to survive."

I had been thinking about college since middle school. It was hard to grasp not thinking about it at all, but Landon and I were so different. I'd had the luxury of living a comfortable life, sheltered from the truth. He hadn't.

"My grades are shit, so I can't get into any colleges, anyway. I didn't even apply."

"You don't have to go to college to be successful," I said. "There's trade school."

Landon shrugged his shoulders. "None of that shit really interests me."

I glanced up at his neck that was covered in tattoos. "What about a tattoo artist?"

Just before Landon was about to shoot that idea down too, he paused and glanced over at me. "A tattoo artist?" he asked in awe, as if he had thought about it before but wasn't sure about it. "Maybe."

"Would you ever give me one?" I asked playfully, grinning up at him as Ana ran down the aisle toward the toilet paper. I leaned closer to him. "I want one right across my ass that says, *Property of Poison.*"

Landon chuckled. "I'm sure João would love that."

"Come on. For real though," I said, lightly pushing him. "Have you ever given someone a tattoo before? You have a ton of them all over your body."

He pulled up his sleeve to show me a tattoo on his left forearm of a skull surrounded by a bunch of roses. "I tattooed this on me about six months ago."

My eyes widened. "You did this yourself?! It's so intricate."

"Yeah," Landon said, cheeks flushing slightly. "I didn't do the skull, but the roses around it. It was a few months after we started talking online. You mentioned how you liked the skull tattoo, and I liked your screen name—Rosy. So, I, uh, put a couple roses around it."

Warmth spread throughout my chest. I stared up at him in awe and pulled him closer to me, unable to stop the grin from stretching across my face. God, this man surprised me more and more every single day of my life.

"You did the roses for me?" I whispered against his lips.

"Maybe," Landon said, cheeks bright red now.

"I think you should do it," I said, following Ana. "Or at least give it a try."

"You think?" Landon said, still hesitant.

And part of me hurt because I knew the reason why. He never really had anyone believe in him before. His parents had done nothing but hurt him and made him feel like he wasn't good enough for this life.

I wanted to make sure he did whatever made him happy.

"Yes!" I said. "Please, try it. You'll be so good."

"Maybe I will," Landon said, grabbing some toilet paper from Ana.

My phone buzzed in my pocket, and I pulled it out.

Mom: Where are you?

I gently patted Landon's arm. "I have to call my mom, but we're not finished with this convo."

"Don't give away too much," Landon said, taking Ana's hand and leading us down the aisle toward the packages of bottle water. "We don't know if Akio's parents are listening in on our phone conversations either. After those trackers that they put in our cars, who the fuck knows?"

Nodding, I dialed Mom's number. I wasn't going to give anything away, but I wanted her to be prepared for tomorrow. I would bring her some supplies later tonight when I went home, but still ... I didn't know if it would be enough.

A war could break out in Redwood as soon as the video was released.

A war that could last a long freaking time.

Mom answered on the third ring. "Imani?"

"Hey, Mom," I said, nerves bubbling in the pit of my stomach. "What's up?"

"Nothing much, sweetie. I just got home from the hospital. We've been swamped lately, so I think I'm going to take a bubble bath tonight. I brought you some roses to put in the vase in your room."

"Cool. Uh, do we have bottled water at home?" I asked innocently enough.

"I don't think so," Mom said. "Do you need some?"

"Yeah, and maybe some toilet paper and essentials too." I grabbed a couple packages of water and put them into our cart, then followed Landon down the aisle. "I'm picking some up, too, but I thought we should have a bit more."

Mom paused for a long moment. "Yeah, I'll go get some now. Is everything okay?"

"Yes," I lied, hoping that she'd see right through it. "Everything is fine."

"Okay."

"All right, well, I'll talk to you later."

She paused again. "Okay, sweetie."

"Hey, Mom," I said, heart racing. "I love you."

"I love you too," she said, and I could hear the happiness in her voice. If I were at home talking to her, she'd probably be grinning from ear to ear. We might not have always gotten along, but these past few weeks had been progress.

I hadn't told Mom that I loved her and actually meant it for a long time now.

"Okay, I gotta go," I said. "See you soon."

When she hung up, I held the phone to my ear for a few empty moments. I didn't know why I did it, but it felt wrong not to. We were so close to this entire town blowing up, and I didn't want my parents to be in the middle of it.

But they already were.

We all already were.

Chapter One Hundred Seventy-Eight

JOÃO

Kai: BIG PROBLEM.

Kai: Nicole's father found the missing footage. We need to move things along and release the video tonight. I don't want them raiding the house, especially with Ana and Imani out. I'm picking Allie up from her internship. Tell Jace.

After school, I sat in my car and scanned the area in front of my old house. I had wanted to come here to see Mom, but it looked like I didn't have any fucking time today. Landon and Imani had taken Ana to the store to pick up some supplies. I'd asked her if she wanted me to go too, and she'd straight-up said fucking no. She knew that she could smooth Imani and Landon over into buying her more ingredients to make brigadeiros.

So, since I was *rudely* not invited, I drove around Redwood, looking for Jace Harbor until I found his car sitting in the parking lot to Mustang Ranch, a burger joint that had just switched ownership and gone to shit.

I parked beside him, walked into the restaurant, and ignored the hostess smiling *pleasantly* at me. After finding Jace in the back, I grabbed a glass of water from a random waitress hurrying through the tables of people and took a sip.

"I looked all fucking around Redwood for you," I said through gritted teeth, sliding in on the other side of the booth. "Check your fucking phone next time. Allie could've been calling you."

"Allie's at her internship," Jace said, biting into the burger and staring emptily at me. "What do you want?"

"Who made up the rumor about Carter getting Allie pregnant?"

"It's not a rumor," Jace said, lying through his fucking teeth.

"It was your father, huh?" I took one of his fries. "Fucking bastard."

"What's it to you?" Jace asked.

"Nothing."

"Then, why're you here?"

I shrugged one shoulder and looked around. "We have to release the video tonight. Kai is picking Allie up from her internship, so nothing happens to her when it is released. We don't know how people are going to react."

Placing his burger down, Jace sat up straight and leaned forward. "Why? I thought the plan was to release it tomorrow during school? What happened? Who found out about it?"

"Nicole's father found the missing footage. He knows that Nicole took it. She's with Jamal now, so she should be fine until the video releases at least. She called me earlier, a snotting mess, and told him to do it as soon as possible."

Jace swallowed hard and cursed under his breath, running a hand through his hair.

I leaned closer. "We're going to fucking destroy all the billionaires in Redwood, all of the fucking assholes here. Don't fucking worry about it."

"That's not a nice word," a young girl with brown hair said, walking past our table with a big glass of root beer that she was spilling everywhere. She couldn't have been older than four years old. "Not all rich people are bad."

"Who the fuck is this?" I asked Jace, brows furrowed.

Jace shrugged a shoulder and looked back at her, her eyes big and brown.

She smiled and tilted her head, sipping the drink that she could barely hold straight. "Me and my mommy got saved by a rich person. She said that they were so nice."

"Olivia," a woman a few booths down called, her back turned toward us.

"That's me," the girl said, grinning even wider at us. She held out her hand as if she wanted him to shake it, her soda beginning to spill off the side of her glass. "What's your name?"

Jace grabbed the glass to hold it upright, so she wouldn't spill it anymore, and took her hand hesitantly. "Jace," he said to her and actually smiled back.

She turned to me and held out her hand, waving it as if she was waiting for me to shake it, too. But I stared at her and curled my lip into an ugly grimace.

She placed one hand on her hip, giving me attitude. "I'm waiting."

"Shouldn't she be afraid of me?" I said.

Usually, the only kid who would even approach me was Ana. And, hell, I wasn't shaking anybody's hand, no matter how innocent they looked. For all I knew, this woman who wouldn't look back at us was part of Akio's fucked up family.

Olivia pulled her hand back and wrapped it around her soda, taking another sip. "I'm not afraid of you just because you have tattoos and look like a monster. My mommy has tattoos, too, and hers are soooo much cooler than yours. They're white."

"White tattoos?" I asked.

"Yeah!" Olivia said. "All over her body, even her head!" She pointed to a scar on my forearm. "They look like that."

"Olivia!" her mother scolded, still turned away. "Come back here."

Olivia departed back to her booth. And almost immediately, her mother picked her up and placed her on her hip, placing her soda on the table and walking with her out of the restaurant.

Olivia waved. "Bye, Jace!"

Jace's lips curled into a small smile, and he waved back to her.

I arched a brow at him and nodded over my shoulder. "Who was the kid? She seemed to like you."

"She would've liked you too, if you'd told her your name."

"I don't fucking give my name out to strangers."

"She was a kid."

"I don't give a fuck if a dog rolled up in the restaurant and asked for my name."

Jace rolled his eyes and called for the waitress, wanting a box and the check.

The waitress brought over a box without the check and smiled at us. "That woman with the cute little girl paid for your food," she said to him. "I guess there's always some good in Redwood after all."

But there was no good in Redwood. That woman wanted something.

KAI

Allie interned under Imani's father at his biotech company. I paced back and forth in the lobby, impatiently waiting for the receptionist to find Allie and let her out early. We didn't have much more time before everything went to shit.

As soon as she walked out of the hallway, Allie spotted me and shrugged on her coat. "Kai?" she asked, brows furrowed and eyes wide as saucers. "What are you doing here? Jace is supposed to pick me up in, like, a half hour."

I thanked the receptionist, grabbed Allie's wrist, and pulled her out into the frigid December air. "We have to go. I already texted João, who's with Jace. He knows that I'm picking you up."

Her eyes widened as she stumbled after me in the snow, the slush, and the ice. When we reached my bike, I tossed her my helmet.

She stared at me like I was absolutely insane. "What's going on, and why are you driving a motorcycle in the middle of winter?"

"It's the only thing I have." I kicked one leg over the bike and sat. "And I'll explain later."

"If you want me to leave with you, you'll tell me now," she said, scrambling through her purse to find her phone. "What is going on? What's wrong? Something has to be because Jace told me not to go with anyone else."

Needing to get out of here now, I placed the helmet on her head and strapped it on. "We have to release the information about Nicole now instead of when we planned to tomorrow. Her dad found out. And when it's released, you need to be safe. This town will fucking blow up over the police force pimping out underage girls."

Through the helmet, Allie stared at me in shock, and then she got onto the back of the bike and wrapped her arms around my waist to hold on tightly. "If Imani finds out that I rode on the back of your bike, she's going to freak out. She likes you a helluva lot."

And while that might've been true a couple weeks ago, Imani knew what Allie meant to me. And tonight ... I would have to tell Allie what she meant to me too. It was now or never, and I didn't have the heart to wait anymore.

Anything could happen at any point, especially with the rumor of Allie being pregnant floating around Redwood. Akio's family—or Jace's father—might try to hurt her or some shit. I needed her to trust me enough so that I could protect her.

* * *

Twenty minutes later, I pulled up to my run-down house in the middle of the slums. Once Allie texted Jace so he knew where she was, she handed me my helmet. I guided her to the side door and down a set of creaky-ass stairs to the basement.

Allie watched as I typed a code into my lock, clicking the heavy metal door open and gesturing for her to walk inside. Hesitantly, she stepped into the room and stared in awe at all the computers, monitors, and screens.

After I typed another code into my security system, I placed my jacket and the helmet down on a table, flicking on the lights and making the room come alive. Monitors turned on, lights flashed, computers pulled up programs with security footage and social media accounts.

"Make yourself at home," I said, sliding onto a seat in front of the main computer with my stomach in knots. "We need to release the video as soon as possible, before Nicole's father finds her at Jamal's place."

I didn't give a fuck about releasing this video, but the nerves of telling Allie that she was my sister were eating me away on the inside. How the hell would she react? How would she ... take it? I'd watched and protected her from afar for so long. I didn't want her to hate me or Dad. He had done so much for her too.

Allie sat beside me and looked over my shoulder, watching me type a string of letters and numbers into a program, the screens around us changing colors and pulling up websites like Facebook, Twitter, Instagram, and even the Redwood news stations.

"Nicole is safe, though?" she asked, brows drawn together in worry.

"For now," I said, grimacing. "Landon is with Imani, and João is with Jace. Don't worry."

"Why'd you come to get me?" she asked.

I froze, my heartbeat in my ears. What could I say to that? Should I tell her now? I didn't want her to run out of here in tears once I told her. She had always looked up to our father, and ... we never really talked that much. I didn't want to lose the little interaction that we had.

After taking a deep breath, I continued typing. "Jace would kill me if we left you at your internship when this all went down."

Not entirely a lie, but it wasn't the complete truth either.

I needed to protect her.

"Jace wouldn't kill you," she said, crossing her arms and staring at the side of my face like she knew something. "You know how to use a gun. You've been in way more street fights than he has. There's something else. Why can't you tell me?"

I paused for a moment and looked over. "Why can't I be nice?" I asked, my voice quieter than it had ever been.

João might've been cold to anyone who wasn't his family, but at least he knew how to interact with Ana. I didn't know the first thing about having a sister and what that kind of relationship was. But, fuck, I craved someone. I wanted a family.

"Being nice would've been texting me and telling me to leave my internship, not picking me up from it in the frigid snow when all you have is a motorcycle," she said to me, arching a brow. "Poison isn't just nice to random people like me."

"You're not a random person, Allie," I said, sucking in a sharp breath and glancing back at my computer screen. "Wait," I said, fingers moving even faster across the keyboard. I paused for a moment and looked up at the screens, and then I pressed the Enter key and sent the video out to the world from anonymous accounts that couldn't be traced back to me easily.

Our phones buzzed almost immediately, social media lighting up with videos, retweets, and chaos about the police force, the video being shared almost a thousand times within the first few minutes.

I sat back and stared over at Allie, who was scrolling through her phone. God, why was this so hard? I felt like I was about the throw up my fucking lunch, just looking at her. What if she ... what if she didn't accept me?

When Allie glanced up at me, I scratched the back of my head and looked away. "So, how's your internship?"

"That didn't answer my question," she said.

"It will." I stood and nodded to another locked room, my stomach in knots. "Come with me."

Part of me wanted her to forget her question. The other part wanted her to finally see me as her brother.

Hopping up, she followed me into a room filled with guns from ceiling to floor, wall to wall. I locked the door behind us and leaned over a table in the center of the room.

"How's your internship?" I asked her again.

"It's good," she said, staring wide-eyed at all the guns and walking around the room in amazement.

"What department are you in?" I asked.

"None yet. I have to choose by tomorrow. Why?"

I paused, silently debating on whether or not I had the fucking confidence to tell her today. Not only that, but I also wanted to ask her to join us in taking Redwood down. She hated this place as much as we all did.

"Because this is the start of the chaos in Redwood. The rich will try to silence the poor, like they've done for fucking decades. They'll kill them with no repercussions, and I want to give us a fighting fucking chance," I said.

"And you're suggesting ..."

"Work with me," I said, fingers paling on the table and heart racing even faster. "You're the smartest person to come out of Redwood in years, and Mr. Abara's company is making tech that is only seen in cyberpunk fiction, tech that will change the world of war and of life forever."

Her eyes widened. "You want me to ... to steal their ideas and make it for you?"

"It's fucking crazy, I know. I didn't even want to get you involved in it in the first place, but we're not prepared for what's to come. You know that the rich will slaughter the poor, will walk all over us, and put the blame on *us*. They'll split the town up, so kids in the slums won't get a proper education anymore. They'll leave us homeless. You saw it when you lived here. I know you did."

"Kai ..." she whispered. "You're asking me to make you weapons for a gang."

"Not for me," I said. "To level the playing field."

She paced around the room and shook her head. I knew that she wouldn't agree without knowing the entire truth. I needed to tell her as much as it hurt me inside to know that she might not want anything to do with me after this.

I grabbed her hands. "Dad wanted this."

"Dad?" she asked, brows furrowed. "My dad or yours?"

"*Our* dad."

Allie's face went completely blank. The moments passed so slowly, so *agonizingly* slowly. Then, she finally ... laughed. "What the fuck, Kai? What are you even saying? My dad ... wasn't ..."

"Yes, he was," I said before she could finish her thought, nerves bubbling in my stomach. "He didn't want you to know that he had another family, that he had gotten another woman pregnant before he met your mother. He didn't want you to see him in a bad light."

She shook her head, voice quiet. "You're not serious, are you?"

"I'm not lying. I have a DNA test to prove it." I walked around her to grab Dad's handgun and placed it in her hands. "That's why I have this. That's *why I'm telling you this* and pleading with you to help me. A rich motherfucker killed our father and got away with it. They do this shit all the time and never get punished for it. It's time that stops. It's time we fight back."

"Kai," she whispered, the gun trembling in her hands. "That's why you ... you've been so protective of me?"

"You're the only family I have left," I whispered. "My mother overdosed three months after Dad died. The rich rip families apart and leave us with nothing. *Nothing*, Allie. And your mother ... is in the same boat as Jace's mother, isn't she? She might die too, and if she does, you know that nobody will give a fuck."

Tears welled up in her eyes. "Kai, I don't ... I don't believe this."

"If you don't want to help us, that's fine," I said, glancing down at my feet and feeling happy that I had gotten it off my chest.

Maybe she'd finally let it sink in and hate me later for it, but she wasn't running away and crying now; she wasn't leaving me like the rest of my family had.

"Just think about it, okay?"

Allie stared at me, her eyes wavering. "Okay."

KAI

Allie stared at me for what seemed like hours until she finally threw her arms around me and hugged me tight. I stayed frozen to the spot, not expecting that she'd react like *this*, then forced myself to snap out of it and hug her back.

My eyes became hot and watery, the thought of finally having family making me warm. It had been years since that day that Mom had died, years since I had found Dad's body at the crime scene of a motorcycle *accident*.

"Allie!" someone shouted from another room, and then the door was ripped open.

Jace Harbor barreled into the room, tore me off Allie, and took her in his arms. She widened her eyes and hurried back over to me.

"What the fuck, Allie?" he asked her through gritted teeth.

"He's my brother, Jace," she snapped, then turned back to him, regret written across her face. "Sorry, I didn't mean to snap at you. I just ... he's my brother." She looked over her shoulder at me and gently grabbed Jace's hands. "My dad had another kid, I guess ... I still can't wrap my head around it."

Jace glanced over at me. "You're Allie's brother?"

I gave a half-smile and looked at Allie. "You know, I always hated that Dad lived with you and not my mom and me, but after he died ...

I, uh … I realized that we were both the same—both lost a parent, both grew up on the bad side of town, both had mothers who kinda spaced out after he died."

Allie smiled at me. "I'm still mad that nobody told me sooner, but I'm glad you did. I feel like I don't have anyone anymore."

"Yo, enough with this lovey-dovey shit. Where the *fuck* is Landon?" João asked, stepping into the room behind Jace and Allie and lighting up a cigarette.

I shrugged and placed our father's gun back on the shelf. "Probably fucking Imani somewhere. I don't fucking know. I've been here, making sure the video is out and going viral. He hasn't called."

"It's fucking crazy out there already, dude." João paced around the room and shook his head. "If they don't get back here in the next five minutes, I'm going out there to find them."

"Does the one guy who hated Imani the most now care about her?" I asked, lips curling into a smirk. "Cute."

João growled and cut his eyes to me. "Don't push it."

I walked back into the other room and gazed at all the monitors of local news channels and social media articles. It was blowing up about the police force already, and the hashtag *#SaveNicole* was trending across the entire state, not even the town anymore.

Pacing around the room, João ran a hand across his face.

Jace leaned closer to Allie, resting his head on her shoulder. "I'm glad you're okay. I don't know what I'd do without you, Allie." He kissed her temple, watching as she looked over at him with big eyes. "What's wrong?"

"I'm worried about Nicole," she said, gnawing on the inside of her cheek. "What if her father finds her at Jamal's and … and does something worse than rape her? What if he kills her, Jace, and we never find her body? She disappears out of nowhere?"

"If anything, her father will come here before he checks Jamal's house," I said, switching over one of the monitors to a security camera that I had installed right outside Jamal's house. "And I got it covered."

Allie blew out a deep breath and relaxed back against the couch. This was all going to be over soon. I wouldn't have to worry about Allie, Imani, or Akio's family killing us all. After all this chaos, there would be nothing but peace, and we could finish our senior year without the constant threat of murder.

"All right, I'm fuckin—" João started.

The door opened, and Landon walked in with Imani and Ana, who looked up and smiled at him.

"I hate you, you know that?" Imani said to him, then stopped and turned to us. "Why is everyone staring at us? What's wrong?"

After Landon shut the door behind them, João clenched his jaw and glared at him. "Answer your fucking phone next time and get back here sooner. It's fucking crazy outside. Imani and Ana shouldn't be out there."

Allie moved closer to Jace and giggled. "They're so in love with her. I never thought I would say this, but it's actually cute." She reached for Imani's hand and pulled Imani down next to her. "I'm so glad you got back safely."

"You too, girl. I already texted Maddie and Vera. They're safe with Maddie's brother and some of the guys on the hockey team." Imani glanced between Allie and Jace, brows furrowed. "Have you spoken to Nicole? How is she? I saw that video ... and ..." Imani choked up. "And I feel so bad about this entire thing."

"You saw the video?" I asked, clenching my jaw and then turning to Landon. "I told you not to show her."

Imani hopped up. "It's not his fault. I snuck a peek at it while using the bathroom."

Allie glanced between us all, then tugged on Jace's hand to pull him up to his feet. "We should go back home. I don't want Harlan alone with Mom."

"You should wait a little bit," I said, desperate to keep her safe, too. "If Nicole's father finds any of us out there, he'll do God knows what to find Nicole. Wait a couple hours until he has other shit around Redwood that he has to deal with—angry rioters, murders, fires. You can't go now."

And so we waited for Redwood to burn to the motherfucking ground.

Chapter One Hundred Eighty-One

JOÃO

Everyone else slept at Kai's house.

But tonight, I couldn't seem to shut my fucking eyes. With my hand stuffed into my sweatpants pocket, I laid in bed, stared up at the bland ceiling, and rubbed my fingers against Mom's suicide note. As ironic as it was, the note was the only thing keeping me sane right now.

Ana lay next to Imani on Kai's bed, her head in the crook of her shoulder and her eyes closed for once. Lately, she'd had a hard time sleeping, but not tonight. She had fallen asleep like she hadn't slept in ages.

If only I could've.

But after seeing that woman with her daughter at the restaurant today, all I could seem to think about was Mom and Ana. I wanted her back so badly and would do anything—fucking anything—to have her again, so Ana could have a normal life.

After cursing, I shuffled out of bed and walked to the front door. I punched in the fucking security code and walked outside into the frigid fucking air. Shockingly, tonight, the slums of Redwood weren't as loud as they usually were. We were used to this shit and this drama.

None of us were surprised that the Redwood rich were corrupt.

Once I sat on the front steps, I pulled out everything inside my pocket and tossed them onto the concrete next to me. I took a cigarette out of the pack and lit it up, drawing in the smoke and letting it fucking ruin me.

I stared at the suicide note for seconds, minutes, hours. There were creases that I'd made all over it, small tears at the side, and dark cursive handwriting that bled through the thin sheet.

I couldn't read it. Not now. I had too much other shit on my mind. I had to protect Ana and Imani, and I couldn't do that if I was a sopping fucking mess because of Mom, because *Mom* had decided to end her life and leave me with all these responsibilities. I couldn't fucking do it.

But I needed to. I needed to do it so badly.

"Fuck it," I muttered, grabbing the note and unfolding it.

When I saw Mom's handwriting in Portuguese and tears staining the ink on the page, I drew the cigarette out of my mouth and placed a hand over my face instead to hold back my sobs because it had been so long since I'd heard her voice in my head, since I had seen a part of her again.

Dear beloved children,

Always remember that Mama loves you both so much. I am sorry that I have worked so much these past few years after your father left. I am sorry that I couldn't get you both off the bus every single day and have you both come home to a warm meal. But most of all, I am so sorry that we can't make more brigadeiros ever again as a family.

João, I've tried so hard to get clean for you and for Ana, but I know that I will never be able to live without that high. I've tried twice and have failed both times.

Tonight, I cleaned the house for you for the last time. It took more in me than it did to scrounge for money to buy drugs from men you'd kill if you met them.

Please, don't be angry with me. I've done everything that I could to be your mother. But I don't think I am cut out for such a job. I don't deserve such a job, as a moment can't go by without me thinking about a way to get high.

I'm sorry if you feel alone. I'm sorry if you can't forgive me.

Please take care of your sister. Please let her know that I tried my hardest, but my hardest wasn't good enough. Nobody's hardest is ever good enough in the Redwood slums.

Again, I'm sorry, and I love you.

Love,

Mama

A sob loud enough to wake the neighborhood escaped my fucking mouth. I doubled over on the front steps, one hand covering my face and the other grabbing the note tightly in my grasp. This was the last piece of Mom that I had left, and I never wanted to let it go.

I didn't know how long I sat on those front steps and cried, but it was a long fucking time.

When I gathered myself together enough, I walked back inside, crawled up into the bed next to Imani, and wrapped my arms around her waist, resting my head against her shoulder and breathing in her vanilla scent. My body trembled back and forth, the thought of being without Mom forever actually sinking into me.

Never again would I see her fucking smile.

Imani shifted in my arms, her curls brushing against my face. "João?"

"Go back to sleep," I whispered, desperate for my voice not to fucking shatter.

"What's wrong?" she asked, glancing over at me with worry in her eyes.

I stared at her for what seemed like an eternity, not wanting to tell her that I would never be over my mother killing herself. I would never be able to heal from that pain, knowing that my mother had had such a shit time in Redwood and had done *everything* she could and still could not survive down here alone.

I had tried hard to make this life livable for her, but I'd failed. I'd fucking failed.

Instead of saying anything, I pulled the note from my pocket and held it up in a shaky hand. Imani's eyes widened, and she suddenly shuffled up to the headboard and pulled me closer, her arms wrapped tightly around my body.

"Oh, João," she whispered.

While I had vowed to be the strong man that nobody had to care for all those years ago, somehow, I crumpled in Imani's arms. I hugged her closer to me and found myself sobbing in her embrace, my entire body trembling hard.

"I miss her so much," I said quietly so Ana wouldn't wake up.

"I know," Imani whispered, dragging her fingers through my hair. "She was your mother, João. Of course you're going to miss her. I know you like to put up a front around Ana, but she sees it too. You're allowed to cry. It's okay."

I crawled up closer to her and hugged her tightly. "I love you so fucking much. I can't afford to lose you, too."

Chapter One Hundred Eighty-Two

KAI

When I woke up the next morning, Allie and Jace were gone. I shifted in my seat in front of the monitors and rubbed my tired eyes. Allie had left me a note with a smiley face, telling me that she'd think about my proposal and thanking me for letting them crash here last night.

My heart warmed, but my only fear was that they wouldn't make it home safely this morning. I hadn't been out in Redwood yet today, and I didn't know how crazy it had gotten, especially on the rich side of town.

After glancing into my bedroom to see Imani asleep on my bed with João and Ana and Landon passed out in a chair on the other side of the room, I grabbed a fresh set of clothes from my closet and looked at the bed once more.

While she had been sleeping when I walked in, Imani now had her eyes open slightly, as if she had just woken up and was watching me intently. She shifted onto her side, João's arm falling off her stomach, and she tucked her hand underneath the pillow.

"Morning," she whispered, voice soft.

Fuck, I wanted her to wake up next to *me* like that one of these days. I couldn't fucking wait until Akio's parents were taken care of, so

"

I could give her all of me. It was getting hard to hold back because the more I saw her, the deeper and deeper I fell.

"Morning."

She reached over João's body, grabbed my forearm, and pulled me toward her, placing her soft lips right onto mine. When she pulled away, she fell back onto the pillows and beamed at me. "Do you remember the first time we were here, alone?"

I glanced over at Ana to make sure she was still sleeping, then scooped Imani into my arms to pick her up out of the bed. After setting her onto her feet, I rested my forehead against hers and sucked her bottom lip between my teeth. "Of course I do."

"Tie me up again sometime," she whispered, dragging her fingers down my abdomen and curling them inside my waistband. "With everything going on, I've been aching for it again. It's been too long."

"You think it's been long *for you*?" I chuckled.

She had no fucking idea how many times I'd jerked off to the thought of having her like that again, having her arms pulled into the air, her naked body restrained and ready for whatever I wanted to do to it, her being completely submissive to me.

"Get a fucking room," João growled from the bed, pushing himself up to lean against the headboard and scowling at us in complete disgust.

No matter how rude João was to Imani, she gave him a small smile, her eyes lighting up. She looked at me the same way, but it still felt different between her and me. We had chemistry, but I hadn't told her that I loved her yet.

But I wanted to tell her so badly.

So fucking badly.

"Morning," Landon said, standing next to her, shirtless. He leaned down and placed a kiss on her lips, like she had kissed me earlier. Except she kissed him for a bit longer, with a bit more passion, with more ... love.

Fuck.

I swallowed hard and rubbed a hand over my face, letting Imani's hand slip from my hand and mumbling that I would go check on the monitors in the other room. She looked upset as I left her with João and Landon, but I couldn't watch.

It had taken everything inside me to tell Allie what she meant to me yesterday. And I knew that Imani would tell me that she loved me back. I just ... I ... I didn't want Akio's parents to take her away from me. I couldn't let them get in the way this time.

After slouching down in my chair, I aimlessly scrolled through the monitors around Redwood. Shit was still wild as hell, and I hoped that Allie had gotten home safely. I didn't want to lose her either after last night.

The bedroom door opened. From the corner of my eye, I watched Imani pad out of the room and walk toward me. I clenched my jaw and focused my gaze on the screens, but all I could really focus on was her coming toward me.

Before I could stop her, she sat on my lap bridal-style and wrapped her arms around my shoulders. "What's going on? Why'd you leave like that? I wanted to talk to you about last night and how it went with Allie."

"It went fine," I said, cutting it short. But then I glanced over at her and felt so much guilt. I wrapped my arms around her body, slowly coming undone, the way I always did around her, and sighed. "It went better than I'd thought it would," I whispered. "Thank you for pushing me to tell her or else I wouldn't have."

Imani grinned at me, not saying a word. I stared into her huge brown eyes and wondered where we all would've been without her. She had come into our world and changed our fucking lives, especially mine.

Before her, I had felt nothing. I had been so numb.

Now, fucking God, I felt a world of emotions come crashing down upon me.

She pushed some hair out of my face, a smile coming onto her lips. "Kai, I l—"

Imani's phone buzzed between us, and she sucked in a sharp breath and stopped talking completely. I knew what she wanted to tell me. It was the same thing that I had wanted to tell her for so long. And she was about to say it.

Imani sighed and pulled out her phone, as both of us could sense that the moment was ruined. "It's Allie," she whispered, climbing out of my lap. "I need to take this. I didn't even realize that she'd left."

After she placed the phone to her ear, she paced around the room, her neutral expression turning into one of confusion, then fear. "What?" she whispered. "Allie, slow down. Allie, please. I—" She stopped walking and looked at me with tears in her eyes. "We'll be there soon. We're coming."

"What happened?"

Once Imani shut off the phone, she placed her hand over her mouth and let out a sob. "Allie's stepfather shot Allie's mother. She's in the hospital. We need to go now."

Chapter One Hundred Eighty-Three

IMANI

I sat in the corner of the hospital lobby with Poison and Ana, who had become fussy in the past ten minutes. While I knew João wanted to take her home, he hadn't moved from his spot next to me.

Tears welled up in my eyes at the thought of Allie losing her mother.

She looked so heartbroken, lying in Jace's lap and sobbing for the past few hours. She hadn't stopped once and had barely looked up from the floor when we walked into the room. But I refused to go anywhere. My best friend was hurting. Badly.

Jace glanced over at me, frowning, and hugged Allie closer. He wanted to know when my mother would come out with any news about Allie's mother, as she was the only damn person in this hospital who would give us any information.

But I sure as hell didn't know.

We hadn't had much time to speak since I had made it to the hospital, but she'd come out every hour or so to give us an update. And everything up until now had been something short, nothing promising.

I feared the worst for Allie and her mom.

Kai rubbed his hands together across from me and clenched his jaw. By the mere look on his face, I could tell that he was just as nervous about this outcome as Allie was. Allie's mother might not be his own, but he still wanted Allie to have a family. He knew what life was like without any parents.

Landon squeezed my hand and leaned down toward me. "Are you okay?"

Chewing on the inside of my cheek, I shook my head. "No."

Truthfully, I was scared shitless that Mom would walk through those doors at any minute and tell us that Allie's mother had passed away. My friends had gone through so much drama and pain these past few months. We needed good news.

Something to give us hope.

A back door opened, and two doctors, along with Mom, walked through them, scanning the emergency room for us. Allie snapped her head in their direction, hopped up, and rushed over, wiping the tears from her cheeks.

"When can I see her? Is she okay? How bad is it?" she asked desperately.

I hurried over to them and grabbed Allie's hand to let her know that I would be here for her through anything. Mom placed a hand on Allie's shoulder and showed no emotion on her face. None. No smile. No frown. No sense of relief or despair.

Instead, Mom glanced nervously at me. And I fucking knew something was very wrong.

"Allie, your mother lost a lot of blood," Mom started. "*A lot.*"

Before she could continue, Allie took a step back and shook her head, agony on every inch of her face. "Please, don't continue," she whispered, her knees giving out and her voice becoming distant, as if she wasn't here anymore.

I caught her and held her steady. "Be strong, Allie. It's what your mom would've wanted."

It took her a few moments, but Allie bit back a sob and stood up on trembling legs. She grabbed Jace's hand as hard as she could. "If you're going to tell me that Mom died, I can't ... I can't hear it." Her lips trembled. "Please, spare me the pain and heartbreak, Mrs. Abara, please."

Mom swallowed hard and took Allie into her arms, rocking her back and forth. Resting her cheek on Allie's head, Mom said, "Your mother has fallen into a coma and is in the ICU. We don't know when *or if* she'll awaken."

"So, she's alive?" Jace asked, eyes wide.

"You can see her now," Mom said, looking up at Jace. "Please, come with Allie."

Scooping Allie's hand in his, Jace followed Mom and pulled Allie down the hallway toward the ICU. Wanting to go with them, I followed them into the elevator, went up three floors, and paused behind Allie when we reached a frighteningly quiet foyer.

Mom led us down a hallway to a lonely room in the back. She let Allie and Jace in first, then captured my wrist before I made it into the room. "Please, come home tonight, Imani. We need to talk."

I glanced up at her and nodded. "I will." And because too many mothers had been dying or close to death lately in Redwood, I pulled Mom in for a hug. "Sometimes, you get on my nerves, but I love you so much, Mom. I don't know what I would do without you."

Chapter One Hundred Eighty-Four

KAI

After we left the hospital, Imani came back to my place with us. All night, I watched her chat with João and Landon and play with Ana from afar. And all fucking night, I tried to gather up the courage to finally tell her.

At ten p.m., João took Ana into the bedroom to put her to bed, Landon was half-asleep in my chair, and Imani stood up and walked toward me with her purse hanging off her shoulder.

"My phone's dying," she said.

"I have a charger."

She frowned. "And I should get home to talk to my mom."

"You're not going alone."

"The chaos has died down enough," she said to me, walking up the stairs to the door. When we walked out, she glanced at my bike. "It's just a drive across the neighborhood, and I don't want you driving on that thing in the ice. It's too dangerous. Please, stay here with them."

I stared at her pleading expression and nodded. She didn't have to know that I'd follow her home. I always followed her home to make sure that she got in safely. And I wasn't about to let her leave my place while Akio's family was still lurking out there.

They might crash their car into hers, killing her, and make it *look* like an accident.

713

Not again.

"Thank you," she whispered, pulling me closer.

As she wrapped her arms around me, I hugged her back like I had with Allie the other night. It felt so ... different, but still like I had family. Imani might've been in my life for only a couple months, but I felt like I could tell her fucking anything now.

Her warmth spread around me, taking me in. All I'd wanted to do all night was hold her tightly. My heart swelled with happiness at the thought of finally being able to be with someone who made me feel ... good.

But when she dropped her arms, I felt so fucking cold.

"I'll text you when I get in safely. Don't worry about me," she said, walking to her car.

I crossed my arms and chewed on the inside of my cheek. My heart pounded inside my chest, and I could do nothing but watch her leave me. The second she pulled out onto the road, I'd hop on my bike and follow her, but I ... I didn't want her to go.

Not without me telling her the truth.

"Wait," I called.

Imani stopped at the side of her car and glanced over her shoulder. "Wha—"

I jogged over to her, grabbed her face in my rough hands, and kissed her hard on the mouth. She froze for a moment, then placed her hands over mine and smiled into our kiss. Resting her forehead against me, she moved her lips on mine.

"I love you," I whispered as soon as she pulled away. "I love you so much."

"Kai," she whispered. "I thought you wanted to wait."

"I can't anymore." I seized her waist and pulled her closer to me, wanting to touch every single inch of her. "I can't wait until we take care of Akio's parents. I want you to know how I feel about you now."

Time seemed to stop as I waited and waited and waited for her to say it back.

Finally, she curled her soft lips into a smile and pushed some hair behind my ear. "I love you, too."

Heat shot through my body, my lips curling into a smile. I wrapped her up into my arms, picked her up off the ground, and pulled her into the air, unable to stop the fucking happiness that I felt. It wasn't like anything I ever felt before.

She giggled into the crook of my neck and wrapped her arms tightly around my shoulders. "You don't know how long I've been waiting for you to say that. I've been wanting to tell you forever."

After a few moments, I placed her down.

"I really would like to stay with you all tonight," Imani said, glancing over my shoulder and toward the door. "But I need to go see my mom. I need to talk to her and make sure that nobody hurt or threatened her during work."

"I know," I whispered. "I'm going to follow you to make sure you get in safely."

She playfully rolled her brown eyes. "Fine."

Once she pecked me on the lips, she slid into her car and started it. I slipped onto the back of my bike and followed after the light hum of her car. She drove slowly down the roads, braking over the ice all the way to her community.

When she finally pulled into her driveway, I let out a small sigh and waved her off. She was home safely, and I could fucking sleep tonight without the thought of Akio's family staging a fucking car accident and killing her.

Fifteen minutes later, I made it back home, dusted the snow off my baggie sweatshirt, and punched the security code into my house. Laughter spilled out from Ana below—João obviously couldn't get her to sleep. I smiled and thought about how ... everything was falling into place.

We were all working in some odd way.

The moment that I collapsed onto the couch to relax, my phone buzzed in my pocket. My lips curled into a smile, as I thought that it was from Imani. I felt like I was on top of the fucking world tonight. Nothing could dampen my mood because I had just scored my fucking dream girl.

Akio: You need to get to Imani's house ASAP.

Akio: NOW.

Akio: I can't stop my mother.

My heart dropped, and I shot up from my seat. The guys glanced over at me.

"We have to go," I said through gritted teeth. "Now."

"What happened?" Landon asked.

"It's Imani."

Landon stood up quickly as João grabbed Ana's hand. I balled my hands into fists, knowing that if we didn't get there soon, whatever Akio's parents were planning wasn't going to be good.

They must've been waiting there for her. I should've fucking waited until she got in. I should've brought her to the door and stayed with her for tonight. I shouldn't have left her to die in their hands.

I dialed her number on her phone that had died, hoping that it'd somehow magically get some fucking juice in it. When it went immediately to voice mail, I hurled the phone against the ground and let it smash against the concrete.

"We need to go fucking now," I growled.

Just after I had told her I loved her, fucking minutes after, this fucking happened.

They were going to take her away from me, like they had taken Dad away from me.

Instead of waiting for the guys to get situated, I sprinted to my bike and sped down the road to head for Imani's house. My gun was in the waistband of my pants, my hands tight around the bars.

"I'm fucking coming for you, Imani."

Chapter One Hundred Eighty-Five

IMANI

After being with the boys all day and all night, I needed to get home to make sure that Mom was okay. It had been over twenty-four hours since I had really talked to her, and Redwood had been going insane from what I had seen all over social media and the news.

Kai had left about fifteen minutes ago. I sat in the car in my driveway, enjoying a few moments to myself. Today had been so fucking stressful with Allie's mother almost dying in the hospital and the outrage that happened outside.

Once I calmed myself down and prepared myself to talk with Mom, I exited the car, tugged my key out of my purse, and unlocked the door.

"Mom!" I shouted, walking into the house and dumping my bag on the foyer's couch.

The house was silent for a few moments, and then Mom finally answered.

"In here, sweetheart!" she shouted from the living room.

Texting Landon that I made it to my house safely with Kai, I glanced down at my phone and walked into the quiet room. Surprisingly, everything in my neighborhood wasn't as bad as everyone had made it out to be. Maybe it was because our neighborhood was guarded.

It didn't make a diff—

For a brief moment, I glanced up from my phone and let out a piercing scream.

Mom and Dad sat in the middle of the living room floor, on their knees, with Akio and Akio's parents holding up guns to their heads. My mouth dried, and my eyes filled with tears almost immediately.

"Wh-what is happening?" I whispered.

Only then did I realize that we weren't alone. Men were posted at almost every corner. All held guns. All pointed them in our direction, focusing them on me and my family.

I glanced over at Akio, who refused to look me in the eyes.

This was ... this had been ... a setup? Had they been waiting for me? What the fuck was going on? What did they want? For me to rat out Poison? Give them their location? No fucking way would I let them hurt any of my guys or Ana.

And what the fuck was Akio doing here? He *hated* his parents. He had fucking told Poison that he'd work with them in taking down the Redwood Mafia. How could he betray me and us after everything that had happened, especially with Nicole? How could he live with himself?

"Cooperate with us, Imani," Akio's mother said. "And I'll only kill your parents."

"Kill them?" I whispered.

"Kill them."

Hot, rage-filled tears welled up in my eyes. I didn't know whether to feel hurt, betrayed, or terrified about what was happening tonight.

But I refused to be civil with them. They had been threatening my family for weeks on end now, had been using us to gain resources from Dad's work and more money, and ... they had made this place a shithole.

No more backing down. No more being intimidated.

Tonight, I wouldn't cooperate with them. Tonight, I would rather die.

And by the looks of it ... tonight, I *would* die.

"What do you want?" I asked through gritted teeth.

I tried to look intimidating, to show that she wasn't affecting me the way she was, but the tears wavering in my eyes gave me away. And sure, it might've looked weak, but it wasn't. Tonight, I refused to give them any information, and I would die alongside my parents.

"Join me."

"I'm not giving you—" I paused when her words finally stuck and stared at her. "What?"

"Join me," she said, lowering her gun and stepping forward. "I want you to work with me, Imani. Your mother and father have betrayed me these past few years. They're backstabbing assholes who can't follow orders. But you ..."

She stalked around me like I was some prey and pushed some hair back behind my shoulder with the barrel of her gun. My entire body tensed, as I hadn't been ready for such a question, nor was I ready to have a gun brush against me as gently as she was doing.

"You interrupted Poison's agenda. You've pushed them to do more than they thought capable. They are nothing but loyal to you, as you are loyal to them. You're stronger than you think. And ..." She walked all the way around me and stopped right behind me, her lips dangerously close to my ear. "And you've done some work on my son too."

My eyes widened, and I glanced over at Akio. "What do you mean?"

"I mean that my son would've never held a gun and shot at someone before you. I've tried hard so many times. I've tried to inspire him relentlessly to join us. And tonight, he told me that he would."

Dazed, I teetered from foot to foot.

My stomach tightened, and I had the urge to puke up my fucking breakfast, lunch, and dinner. This couldn't be the truth. Akio couldn't have been lying to me this entire time. He couldn't have been putting up a front. He cared about Nicole, who was being *abused* by his family. They were working with the police force to pimp out girls, to pimp out Nicole. He wouldn't join them.

Unless ... he was afraid of them.

I glanced over at him, *knowing* that he wouldn't hurt me or my parents. He had done everything in his power to help Ana and steal medication, even when he didn't have to. He knew why she needed it and still helped Poison.

Akio's mother placed her gun into my hand and wrapped my fingers around the grip. "Kill your mother."

Shakily, I grabbed the gun from her and aimed it at my mother. From her knees, Mom stared up at me and let her tears fall down her blood-stained cheeks.

I didn't know what to do. One way, we all died. The other way, only my parents did. Mom would want me to stay alive, to survive the wrath of the Redwood rich and to become someone better than her.

But I ...

I tightened my hand around the grip, trembling even harder.

But I couldn't do it.

"I can't," I whispered, lowering the gun. "I won't."

Akio's mother grabbed the barrel in her fist and aimed it right at Mom's forehead. "Do it."

"No."

"Do it, or"—she held out her free hand and took a gun from her husband—"I'll kill you."

"Imani," Mom whispered, tears streaming down her cheeks. "Just do it, please. I don't want you to die at her hands. Kill me and your father. I've been nothing but a pain for you all these years. Get your revenge."

"I can't."

"She's done nothing but trap you in this house and hold you back, Imani," Akio's mother said firmly. "You've thrived with those boys and become something admirable to our family. We've been watching you every step of your journey. We've watched you become a killer."

"A killer?" Mom whispered. "Imani, have you killed someone?"

"No," I whispered, shaking my head.

While I hadn't taken someone's life, I'd broken the shell of the perfect girl Mom always wanted me to be and become a monster with Poison. I hadn't done anything that I regretted *yet*, but I knew that I was capable of much more.

"Kill your mother and prove yourself to me."

Something inside me snapped. How could this woman even *think* that I wanted to prove something to her? How could she fucking think that I would ever trust her or be loyal to her like I was to Poison? I would never.

"Let go of the gun," I said, my frown turning into a scowl. "And let me do it myself."

She curled her lips into a devilish smirk and released the gun, turning her body to face my mother. This woman had taken so much from my family and constantly threatened them. There was no way that I would kill my mother for her.

So, I peeked quickly at Akio and then turned the gun on his mother. Before I could realize what I was doing, my body reacted. I shot the gun once. Then twice. Then unloaded all the bullets into Akio's mother.

Killing her.

Chapter One Hundred Eighty-Six

IMANI

Bullets started blazing from every which direction, whizzing by me. As the gun fell from my hand, I collapsed onto the ground and covered my head, hoping that none would pierce through me or kill me.

In the midst of the gunfire and smoke, Akio stood over his father and slammed his fist into his father's face over and over and over again until he sent him to the ground and his father's head bounced against it.

When he stood back up, he glanced over at me. "Get out of here, Imani," he shouted, raising his gun to the air, shooting it once. The bullet went right through the ceiling and silenced the rest of his parents' guards. "I'll take care of this."

My eyes widened as he commanded the attention of the men like he had done it before, though I knew that he never had. This wasn't the Akio that I knew from school. This was the Akio who had been broken one too many times and refused to let anyone hurt him again.

"Now, Imani," Akio growled.

I picked up a gun, held it tightly to my chest, then dragged Mom's beaten body across our hardwood floor and toward the front door. Dad crawled out behind us, a bullet hole through his shoulder and blood everywhere.

After glancing into the room one last time and watching Akio finally stand up to his parents' men, I slammed the door closed and collapsed outside it in the frigid air. My chest rose and fell. There was blood all over me from Akio's mother.

When I glanced down at the blood on my trembling hands, reality finally set in. I had killed someone. I had just fucking killed someone. I had taken the life out of someone's body and removed them from this world with the click of a fucking gun.

Loud, shouting voices came from within the house, then another few clicks of guns. I stared at my parents who lay helplessly on our front lawn and clutched the gun tightly in my hands. I didn't know if I was stupid for wanting to go back inside to help Akio, but part of me told me that he was in trouble.

I needed to do something. I couldn't sit around and wait as he died in there.

Someone slammed into the front door, making it shake.

I gripped the gun tighter and gritted my teeth, tears wavering in my eyes as I stared at my parents. "Please, don't hate me for this. I love you guys so fucking much."

"Imani," Mom said, clutching on to Dad, "what are you—"

Standing from my spot, I grabbed the doorknob and cursed to myself. I was being stupid and irrational, but these guys had done so much worse to my friends and my family these past few weeks. I didn't want to let them kill Akio, too.

I wasn't a killer, but I did protect the people I cared about.

So, I shoved the door open and knocked one of the guards back onto his ass. He didn't have a gun in his hand, but I didn't care. I shot him in the knee and set him back, clutching his wound.

Mom screamed at me to come back, but Akio's mother was right. I couldn't let Mom hold me back anymore from anything. I was stronger than even I realized and was loyal to the people who cared and protected me.

Now, it was my turn to protect them.

And the only way to do that was to kill every last member of the Redwood Mafia here.

Pushing my way through the others, I kicked and fought and killed every one of them that got in my way. When I made it inside, I caught

Akio holding a gun in a shaky hand and pinned against a wall by a huge dude who must've been seven feet tall and three times his size. His forearm was pressed against Akio's neck, cutting off his only way of breathing.

Akio positioned the gun at the man's gut and shot it twice, but all the gun did was click. No bullets came out. No wounds were open. No blood was splattered. Akio was out of ammo and out of time.

After he dropped the gun, Akio grasped on to the man's forearm and desperately tried to peel himself away. But the guy was too strong, and Akio got nowhere. As Akio made eye contact with me, his eyes widened, and he shook his head.

He didn't want me here. He wanted to do this himself.

But friends didn't leave friends behind.

I had one bullet left inside my gun. One.

Akio's face turned a shade of blue, his fingers slipping off the man's forearm, as if he didn't have enough energy to keep pushing forward and to kill him.

I aimed it at the guard's head and pulled the trigger.

Blood splattered everywhere. Flesh flew in every which direction. The man stumbled back, and then his body smacked against the ground, a puddle of blood forming underneath him. Akio doubled over, spitting and choking on the air.

My chest rose and fell, adrenaline pumping through my system. I glanced around the living room to see eight members of the Redwood Mafia lying on the floor, their blood coating the floorboards and staining the couches.

A couple seconds later, the front door burst open. I quickly grabbed a loaded gun from one of the corpses and aimed it at the doorway, waiting for someone to walk into the room from the foyer. Landon, João, and Kai hurried through the doorway and stopped when they saw me.

Each stared from me to Akio to the men scattered around the room. I stared at them with tears filling my eyes, realizing what I had done, and dropped the gun from my shaky hand.

We had killed them all here.

Every last one of them.

This was over.

"Imani," Landon whispered.

I ran forward and threw my arms around all of them, pulling them into a tight hug. "You don't know how glad I am to see you guys."

Chapter One Hundred Eighty-Seven

IMANI

"**Y**ou sure about this, *killer*?" Kai said, standing across from me with his arms crossed.

It had been two weeks since my *killing spree*, and things had somewhat returned to normal. Allie's mother was recovering in the hospital, though she hadn't woken up yet. And my parents had taken a much-needed vacation down to Jamaica.

I sat, reclined in a large, cushioned black chair with my shirt pulled up past my ribs and my fingers intertwined with Landon's, squeezing tightly. Donovan, our tattoo artist, cleaned a spot on my ribs, where I'd finally be tatted.

It wasn't something that I'd always dreamed of, but it was a sign of teenage rebellion.

And ever since I had met these three boys, I had done nothing but rebel. Besides, I *was* a member of Poison now, and being a member of the most ruthless gang in town meant that I had to play the part. I had already killed someone, who had threatened my mother, but nobody had to know that.

"You ready?" Donovan asked. "This is one of the more sensitive parts of the body."

"Just do it already," João snapped, smoking a cigarette and eyeing how close Donovan was to me.

Looked like *someone* was a bit jealous of another man touching me. Joke was on him—his best friends did more than just touch me every night.

"Yeah, I'm ready," I said, squeezing Landon's hand tighter.

A light hum echoed from the tattoo gun. I squeezed my eyes closed and braced for intense pain. As soon as the needle hit my flesh, I let out a whimper that I had been holding in since I had made it here.

I opened my eyes and glanced down at Donovan. All night, I had been bracing myself for the pain, but I'd kinda, sorta expected it to be worse than this. Don't get me wrong; this still felt terrible. But ... it wasn't *all* that bad.

So, I lay back in the chair as he wiped the blood and ink off my skin for over the next hour. When he finally finished, Landon tugged me off the chair and pulled me toward a mirror, so I could see the tattoo that we *all* had on our ribs to symbolize us, Poison.

A grayscale poison bottle tattoo with a skull in the center and four roses behind it.

"All right, you guys," I said, tapping my toe on the tiled floor and smirking at my guys through the mirror's reflection, "time to admit it. Out of all of us, *I'm* the deadliest member of Poison."

Kai stifled a laugh as João straight-up chuckled in my face.

"You have that all backward," João said.

"I do not," I defended, pulling down my shirt and feeling freedom. Absolute freedom.

"My turn!" Ana squealed, climbing up into the big black chair and pulling up her shirt to show her ribs. "I want a tattoo, too!"

Before Donovan could move, João grabbed his shoulder. "You put a real tattoo on my sister, and I will kill you."

Donovan chuckled and leaned toward Ana. "Why don't you hold your brother's hand and squeeze your eyes closed? This might hurt a lot. Gotta be prepared."

When Ana closed her eyes and grabbed on to João's hand, Donovan pulled out a box of temporary tattoos he had in a cupboard. He wiped off Ana's skin with an alcohol wipe and placed the tattoo on her body.

Ana winced and scrunched her nose. "Ow!"

"Is that too much for you?" Donovan asked. "I can stop."

"No!" Ana said, nervously shuffling her feet. "I want one!"

"All right, here we go." Donovan placed a wet rag over the temporary tattoo to make it stick. After a few moments, he pulled it away and peeled the white sheet of paper off her skin. "There you go! All done."

Ana opened her eyes and jumped out of the seat, running toward the mirror. "That was so easy! I don't know why all you guys acted so hurt. Even *I* could do it! And it is so cute!"

"What's your tattoo, Ana?" I asked, crouching down next to her.

Landon and I had ordered a bunch of temporary tattoos to bring with us today to the shop because, somehow, I knew that Ana would be wanting one. She wouldn't want to feel left out. And while she didn't get the same tattoo as the rest of us, hers was pretty fire.

"It's a brigadeiro!" she squealed.

"A brigadeiro?! Whoa!" Kai said, scooping her up into his arms, throwing her over his shoulder.

The guys had told me that last time they brought her to the tattoo parlor, she didn't want to leave.

After João thanked Donovan and walked to the exit with Landon, I lingered behind for a couple moments as Donovan cleaned up the area.

"Hey, um ... are you, uh ..." I glanced behind me at the guys who stood at the door with Ana, focusing my gaze on Landon. "Are you taking interns? I know a guy who *might* be interested in learning how to tattoo."

Donovan smiled at me and glanced over my shoulder. "Landon?"

"How'd you know?"

"He was asking me about it yesterday."

"He was?"

"Yeah, said he might be interested. He's going to swing by next Tuesday after school."

Warmth spread throughout my chest. Landon might not have had a plan for the future when we got together ages ago, but I was happy that I could push him to find a place in this crazy little world of ours.

Now, I just had to figure out where the other guys would fit into our new Redwood.

Once I thanked him, I hurried out the door to João's car and slipped into the backseat with Ana. Since we had shit that we needed to do today other than tattoos, I had found a babysitter for Ana.

A couple moments later, they pulled up to Vera's house, and I jumped out of the car, grabbed Ana from the back, and walked to the front door. Vera answered the door with Blaise Harleen behind her.

"Thank you for watching Ana today," I said to Vera.

Vera placed her hands over Ana's ears and moved closer, glancing at João. "He's always so hard to deal with, but Maddie and I will always watch her when we can. It's the least we can do after what happened to their mother."

My lips curled into a small smile, and I crouched down to Ana's level to tell her to be good. Once I made it back to the car, João had kicked Landon out of the passenger seat, so I could sit up front with him.

We might've been far from destroying Redwood completely, but we were closer than we had been two weeks ago. We were the gang who ran Redwood now. We got to decide how shit went down.

"Only thing left to do," João said, turning on the car and gripping the steering wheel. "Find the person who infected Ana and beat the shit out of him." João looked over at me. "You ready?"

I pulled my gun out of my waistband and gripped the handle. "I'm ready."

We were the new rulers of Redwood. And we were going to change this place for good.

Preorder The Bad Boy, the next book in the series, today.

Also by Emilia Rose

Scan the QR code with your phone to view all of Emilia's books!

Also by Emilia Rose

Contemporary Romance

Stepbrother

Poison

The Bad Boy

Detention

Excite Me

Paranormal Romance

Submitting to the Alpha

Come Here, Kitten

Alpha Maddox

My Werewolf Professor

The Twins

Four Masked Wolves

Monster Lover

Erotica

Climax: Erotic One-Shot Collection

About the Author

Emilia Rose is a USA Today best-selling author of steamy romance. Highly inspired by her study abroad trip to Greece in 2019, Emilia loves to include Greek and Roman mythology in her writing.

She graduated from the University of Pittsburgh with a degree in psychology and a minor in creative writing in 2020 and now writes novels as her day job.

With over 18 million combined book views online and a growing presence on reading apps, she hopes to inspire other young novelists with her tales of growth and imagination, so they go on to write the stories that need to be told.

Join Emilia's newsletter for exclusive giveaways, early chapter releases, and more!